Nebula Award-Winning Novellas

SCIENCE FICTION WRITERS OF AMERICA PRESENTS

NEBULA AWARD-WINNING NOVELLAS

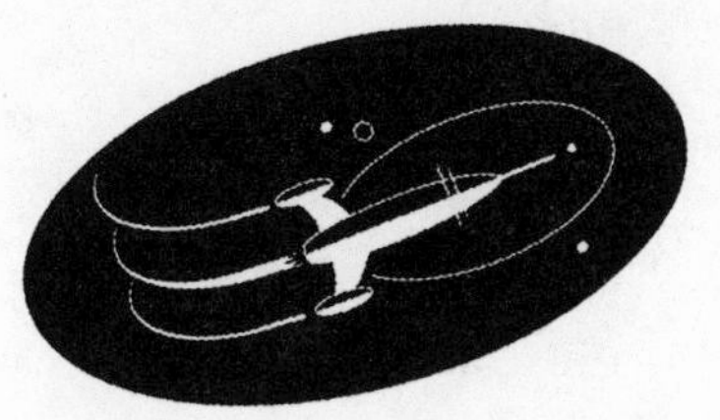

EDITED BY

MARTIN H. GREENBERG

BARNES & NOBLE
BOOKS
NEW YORK

This edition published by Barnes & Noble, Inc.,
by arrangement with Science Fiction-Fantasy Writers of America

1994 Barnes & Noble Books

Book design by James Sarfati

ISBN 1-56619-590-X

Printed and bound in the United States of America

M 9 8 7 6 5 4 3 2 1

ACKNOWLEDGMENTS

Grateful acknowledgment is made to the following for permission to reprint their copyrighted material:

"Ill Met in Lankhmar" by Fritz Leiber—Copyright © 1970 by Fritz Leiber. Reprinted by permission of Richard Curtis Associates, Inc.

"A Meeting With Medusa" by Arthur C. Clarke—Copyright © 1972 by Arthur C. Clarke. Reprinted by permission of the Scovil-Chichak-Galen Literary Agency, Inc.

"Home is the Hangman" by Roger Zelazny—Copyright © 1976 by Roger Zelazny. Reprinted by permission of the author.

"The Persistence of Vision" by John Varley—Copyright © 1978 by John Varley. First appeared in THE MAGAZINE OF FANTASY AND SCIENCE FICTION. Reprinted by permission of the Ricia Mainhardt Agency.

"Enemy Mine" by Barry B. Longyear—Copyright © 1979 by Barry B. Longyear. Reprinted by permission of the author.

"The Saturn Game" by Poul Anderson—Copyright © 1981 by Davis Publications, Inc. First appeared in ANALOG. Reprinted by permission of the Scovil-Chichak-Galen Literary Agency, Inc.

"Hardfought" by Greg Bear—Copyright © 1982 by Davis Publications, Inc. First appeared in ISAAC ASIMOV'S SCIENCE FICTION MAGAZINE. Reprinted by permission of the author.

"Sailing to Byzantium" by Robert Silverberg—Copyright © 1985 by Agberg, Ltd. Reprinted by permission of the author and Agberg, Ltd.

CONTENTS

Foreword **ix**

Introduction **xi**

Ill Met in Lankhmar **1**
by Fritz Leiber

A Meeting with Medusa **60**
by Arthur C. Clarke

Home Is the Hangman **104**
by Roger Zelazny

The Persistence of Vision **167**
by John Varley

Enemy Mine **216**
by Barry B. Longyear

The Saturn Game **279**
by Poul Anderson

Hardfought **335**
by Greg Bear

Sailing to Byzantium **404**
by Robert Silverberg

The Last of the Winnebagos **467**
by Connie Willis

The Mountains of Mourning **520**
by Lois McMaster Bujold

FOREWORD

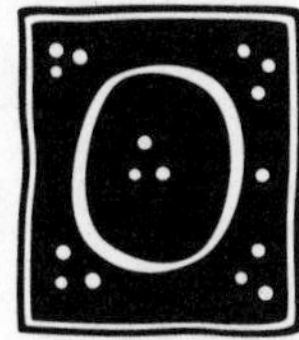

nce it was believed that a collection like *Nebula Award-Winning Novellas* could only exist in the mind of the most imaginative science-fiction reader. Sometimes, however, fantasy becomes reality.

As the Science Fiction and Fantasy buyer for a national bookseller, I've had the opportunity to talk to many science-fiction and fantasy fans. During our conversations, one complaint echoes over and over: Why isn't there a good anthology of novella-length science-fiction stories? Readers were able to find science-fiction short story collections and novels, but novellas were extremely scarce—most were out-of-print or going out-of-print.

Once a story of novella-length makes its appearance in a magazine, it often disappears without a trace. Even Nebula award-winning novellas (unless they are recent winners) are virtually impossible to obtain. It is alarming to discover that works which are considered benchmarks in the genre can so easily vanish and not be enjoyed by future readers.

Of the ten Nebula award-winning novellas collected here by Martin H. Greenberg, one of the world's top anthologists and an expert in the genre, six of these also won the Hugo award for that year. Three of the authors—Robert Silverberg, John Varley, and Roger Zelazny—have won the Nebula more than once.

These novellas represent some of the best science fiction that has ever been written. If you have not read them before, get ready for a real treat.

—Stephen Pagel
1994

INTRODUCTION

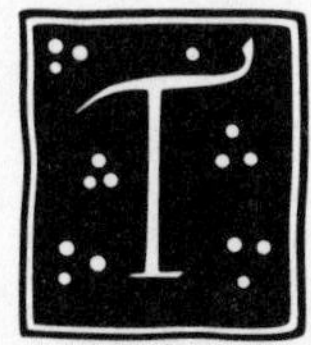

he Science Fiction Writers of America (SFWA), an organization of professional writers in the genres of science fiction and fantasy, was founded in 1965. Its main initial purpose was to aid the working writers of science fiction.

The SFWA began with a charter membership of seventy-eight authors. Writer and editor Damon Knight was SFWA's first president; he, along with fellow SFWA officers James Blish and Lloyd Biggle, came up with the idea to raise money for the fledgling organization by publishing an anthology including the best stories of the year. This project then developed into the Nebula Award, to be given annually to the authors of the best science fiction of the previous year. The original Nebula Award trophy was designed by artist Judith Ann Lawrence, based on a sketch by writer Kate Wilhelm; it is a block of lucite in which are embedded a spiral nebula made of metallic glitter and a specimen of rock crystal. The trophies are handmade, and no two are exactly alike.

Since 1965, the SFWA has become the Science Fiction and Fantasy Writers of America, Inc., and its membership has grown to over a thousand authors, including most of the active writers in the field. The Nebula Award has also seen some changes since 1966, the first year it was awarded, but one feature has remained constant: It is the only award in science fiction that is given by a vote of the writers themselves. Nebula Awards are given in the categories of novel, novella, novelette, and short story; a Grand Master Award, given to a living writer for a body of work, is awarded no more than six times in a decade.

Science fiction has changed greatly over the years since the SFWA's founding, reflecting perhaps the increasingly tumultuous and chaotic world around us. The mid-1960s was a period marked by challenges to conventionality—or, as some might put it, affronts to tradition and authority. During the '70s, various social movements, including the civil rights, antiwar, and women's movements, were increasingly reflected in science fictional narratives. The '80s brought a proliferation of subgenres, to the point where it now seems that science fiction may have no real center. As the nations of the world throw off old bonds that once united them, and fragment into hostile factions, the writers of science fiction have apparently followed their example. Science fiction rooted in solid, realistic detail, fantasy with science fictional underpinnings, and horror based on traditional science fiction concepts are three of the many subgenres that are now part of science fiction.

Looking at the different kinds of works being produced, and the diversity of writers in the field who seem to have little in common, a reader might wonder if science fiction has any true center left, any common characteristics that still unify this genre.

Happily, the novellas in this collection, unique and individual as they are, do an excellent job of displaying the variety of writing in science fiction while also revealing the qualities that distinguish the genre from other forms. The sense of possibility, the strangeness that often lies at the heart of seemingly commonplace events and settings, the exploration of societies and environments that are different from our own, the sense of wonder—all are present in the novellas you are about to read.

In addition, each story is a superb example of each author's respective talents. Fritz Leiber, one of the most versatile writers the field has ever produced, tells a fantasy tale of two of his most beloved characters in "Ill Met in Lankhmar." Arthur C. Clarke, a prominent writer rooted in scientific culture, displays his genius for the "hard" science fiction story in "A Meeting with Medusa." Roger Zelazny, one of the innovative stylists who breathed new life into the genre during the '60s, shows off his literary talent in "Home Is the Hangman." In "The Persistence of Vision," John Varley reveals the inventiveness, sensitivity, and gift for realism that have made him one of the field's most popular writers, while Barry B. Longyear's "Enemy Mine" is a fine example of an enduring theme in science fiction, the contact between human and alien. Greg Bear's "Hardfought," a war story packed with speculation, as is most of his work, shows why he is becoming one of the most original writers in the field; Poul Anderson's "The Saturn Game," with the thoughtfulness, attention to detail, and evocative prose characteristic to him, reveals a master at work. Robert Silverberg, one of science fiction's most prolific, honored, and skilled writers, is also one of its most elegant, as "Sailing to Byzantium," an exotic tale of travelers, shows. Connie Willis, who is an expert at concisely depicting the seemingly ordinary yet fascinating lives of her characters, is at her best in "The Last of the Winnebagos," and Lois McMaster Bujold, in "The Mountains of Mourning," is a strong storyteller who shows how much can still be accomplished in the more traditional science fiction story.

Readers familiar with other books and stories by these Nebula Award-winning authors will be entertained and stimulated by these examples of their craft and art; those encountering these writers for the first time will find these tales excellent introductions to their work. Science fiction still has its center, a core of speculation about people and the imagined worlds they might and could inhabit.

—Pamela Sargent
1994

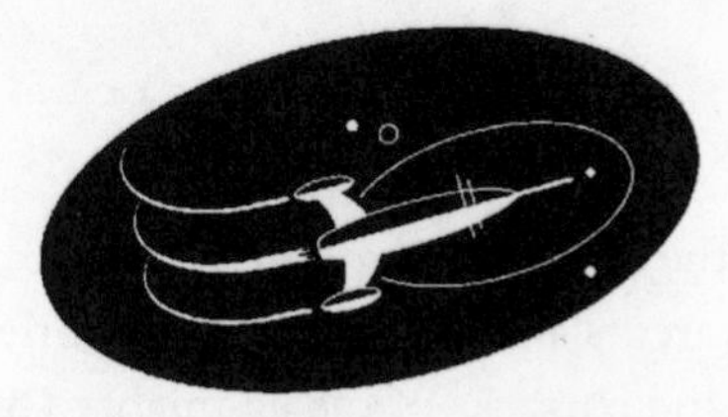

Ill Met in Lankhmar

Fritz Leiber

Silent as specters, the tall and the fat thief edged past the dead, noose-strangled watch-leopard, out the thick, lock-picked door of Jengao the Gem Merchant, and strolled east on Cash Street through the thin black night-smog of Lankhmar, City of Sevenscore Thousand Smokes.

East on Cash it had to be, for west at the intersection of Cash and Silver was a police post with unbribed guardsmen in browned-iron cuirasses and helms, restlessly grounding and rattling their pikes, while Jengao's place had no alley entrance or even window in its stone walls three spans thick and the roof and floor almost as strong and without trap doors.

But tall, tight-lipped Slevyas, master thief candidate, and fat, darting-eyed Fissif, thief second class, brevetted first class for this operation, with a rating of talented in double-dealing, were not in the least worried. Everything was proceeding according to plan. Each carried thonged in his pouch a much smaller pouch of jewels of the first water only, for Jengao, now breathing stertoriously inside and senseless from the slugging he'd suffered, must be allowed, nay, nursed and encouraged, to build up his business again and so ripen it for another plucking. Almost the first law of the Thieves' Guild was never kill the hen that laid brown eggs with a ruby in the yolk, or white eggs with a diamond in the white.

The two thieves also had the relief of knowing that, with the satisfaction of a job well done, they were going straight home now, not to a wife, Aarth forbid!—or to parents and children, all gods forfend!—but to Thieves' House, headquarters and barracks of the all-mighty Guild which was father to them both and mother too, though no woman was allowed inside its ever-open portal on Cheap Street.

In addition there was the comforting knowledge that although each was armed only with his regulation silver-hilted thief's knife, a weapon seldom used except in rare intramural duels and brawls, in fact more a membership token than a weapon, they were nevertheless most strongly convoyed by three reliable and lethal bravos hired for the evening from the Slayers' Brotherhood, one moving well ahead of them as point, the other two well behind as rear guard and chief striking force, in fact almost out of sight—for it is never wise that such convoying be obvious, or so believed Krovas, Grandmaster of the Thieves' Guild.

And if all that were not enough to make Slevyas and Fissif feel safe and serene, there danced along soundlessly beside them in the shadow of the north curb a small, malformed or at any rate somewhat large-headed shape that might have been a small dog, a somewhat undersized cat, or a very big rat. Occasionally it scuttled familiarly and even encouragingly a little way toward their snugly felt-slippered feet, though it always scurried swiftly back into the darker dark.

True, this last guard was not an absolutely unalloyed reassurance. At that very moment, scarcely twoscore paces yet from Jengao's, Fissif tautly walked for a bit on tiptoe and strained his pudgy lips upward to whisper softly in Slevyas' long-lobed ear, "Damned if I like being dogged by that Familiar of Hristomilo, no matter what security he's supposed to afford us. Bad enough that Krovas employs or lets himself be cowed into employing a sorcerer of most dubious, if dire, reputation and aspect, but that—"

"Shut your trap!" Slevyas hissed still more softly.

Fissif obeyed with a shrug and occupied himself even more restlessly and keenly than was his wont in darting his gaze this way and that, but chiefly ahead.

Some distance in that direction, in fact just short of the Gold Street intersection, Cash was bridged by an enclosed second-story passageway connecting the two buildings which made up the premises of the famous stone-masons and sculptors Rokkermas and Slaarg. The firm's buildings themselves were fronted by very shallow porticos supported by unnecessarily large pillars of varied shape and decoration, advertisements more than structural members.

From just beyond the bridge there came two low, brief whistles, signal from the point bravo that he had inspected that area for ambushes and discovered nothing suspicious and that Gold Street was clear.

Fissif was by no means entirely satisfied by the safety signal. To tell the truth, the fat thief rather enjoyed being apprehensive and even fearful, at least up to a point. A sense of strident panic overlaid with writhing calm made him feel more excitingly alive than the occasional woman he enjoyed. So he scanned most closely through the thin, sooty smog the frontages and overhangs of Rokkermas and Slaarg as his and Slevyas' leisurely seeming yet unslow pace brought them steadily closer.

On this side the bridge was pierced by four small windows, between which were three large niches in which stood—another advertisement—three life-size plaster statues, somewhat eroded by years of weather and dyed varying tones of dark gray by as many years of smog. Approaching Jengao's before the burglary, Fissif had noted them with a swift but comprehensive overshoulder glance. Now it seemed to him that the statue to the right had indefinably changed. It was that of a man of medium height wearing cloak and hood, who gazed down with crossed arms and brooding aspect. No, not indefinably quite—the statue was a more uniform dark gray now, he fancied, cloak, hood, and face; it seemed somewhat sharper featured, less eroded; and he would almost swear it had grown shorter!

Just below the niche, moreover, there was a scattering of gray and raw white rubble which he didn't recall having been there earlier. He strained to remember if during the excitement of the burglary, with its lively leopard-slaying and slugging and all, the unsleeping watch-corner of his mind had recorded a distant crash, and now he believed it had. His quick imagination pictured the possibility of a hole or even door behind each statue, through which it might be given a strong push and so tumbled onto passersby, himself and Slevyas specifically, the right-hand statue having been crashed to test the device and then replaced with a near twin.

He would keep close watch on all three statues as he and Slevyas walked under. It would be easy to dodge if he saw one start to overbalance. Should he yank Slevyas out of harm's way when that happened? It was something to think about.

Without pause his restless attention fixed next on the porticos and pillars. The latter, thick and almost three yards tall, were placed at irregular intervals as well as being irregularly shaped and fluted, for Rokkermas and Slaarg were most modern and emphasized the unfinished look, randomness, and the unexpected.

Nevertheless it seemed to Fissif, his wariness wide awake now, that there was an intensification of unexpectedness, specifically that there was one more pillar under the porticos than when he had last passed by. He couldn't be sure which pillar was the newcomer, but he was almost certain there was one.

Share his suspicions with Slevyas? Yes, and get another hissed reproof and flash of contempt from the small, dull-seeming eyes.

The enclosed bridge was close now. Fissif glanced up at the right-hand statue and noted other differences from the one he'd recalled. Although shorter, it seemed to hold itself more strainingly erect, while the frown carved in its dark gray face was not so much one of philosophic brooding as sneering contempt, self-conscious cleverness, and conceit.

Still, none of the three statues toppled forward as he and Slevyas walked under the bridge. However, something else happened to Fissif at that moment.

One of the pillars winked at him.

The Gray Mouser—for so Mouse now named himself to himself and Ivrian—turned around in the right-hand niche, leaped up and caught hold of the cornice, silently vaulted to the flat roof, and crossed it precisely in time to see the two thieves emerge below.

Without hesitation he leaped forward and down, his body straight as a crossbow bolt, the soles of his ratskin boots aimed at the shorter thief's fat-buried shoulder blades, though leading him a little to allow for the yard he'd walk while the Mouser hurtled toward him.

In the instant that he leaped, the tall thief glanced up overshoulder and whipped out a knife, though making no move to push or pull Fissif out of the way of the human projectile speeding toward him. The Mouser shrugged in full flight. He'd just have to deal with the tall thief faster after knocking down the fat one.

More swiftly than one would have thought he could manage, Fissif whirled around then and thinly screamed, "Slivikin!"

The ratskin boots took him high in the belly. It was like landing on a big cushion. Writhing aside from Slevyas' first thrust, the Mouser somersaulted forward, turning feet over head, and as the fat thief's skull hit a cobble with a dull *bong* he came to his feet with dirk in hand, ready to take on the tall one.

But there was no need. Slevyas, his small eyes glazed, was toppling too.

One of the pillars had sprung forward, trailing a voluminous robe. A big hood had fallen back from a youthful face and long-haired head. Brawny arms had emerged from the long, loose sleeves that had been the pillar's topmost section, while the big fist ending one of the arms had dealt Slevyas a shrewd knockout punch on the chin.

Fafhrd and the Gray Mouser faced each other across the two thieves sprawled senseless. They were poised for attack, yet for the moment neither moved.

Each discerned something inexplicably familiar in the other.

Fafhrd said, "Our motives for being here seem identical."

"Seem? Surely must be!" the Mouser answered curtly, fiercely eyeing this potential new foe, who was taller by a head than the tall thief.

"You said?"

"I said, 'Seem? Surely must be!' "

"How civilized of you!" Fafhrd commented in pleased tones.

"Civilized?" the Mouser demanded suspiciously, gripping his dirk tighter.

"To care, in the eye of action, exactly what's said," Fafhrd explained. Without letting the Mouser out of his vision, he glanced down. His gaze traveled from the belt and pouch of one fallen thief to those of the other. Then he looked up at the Mouser with a broad, ingenuous smile.

"Sixty-sixty?" he suggested.

The Mouser hesitated, sheathed his dirk, and rapped out, "A deal!" He knelt abruptly, his fingers on the drawstrings of Fissif's pouch. "Loot you Slivikin," he directed.

It was natural to suppose that the fat thief had been crying his companion's name at the end.

Without looking up from where he knelt, Fafhrd remarked, "That . . . ferret they had with them. Where did it go?"

"Ferret?" the Mouser answered briefly. "It was a marmoset!"

"Marmoset," Fafhrd mused. "That's a small tropical monkey, isn't it? Well, might have been, but I got the strange impression that—"

The silent, two-pronged rush which almost overwhelmed them at that instant really surprised neither of them. Each had been expecting it, but the expectation had dropped out of conscious thought with the startlement of their encounter.

The three bravos racing down upon them in concerted attack, two from the west and one from the east, all with swords poised to thrust, had assumed that the two highjackers would be armed at most with knives and as timid or at least cautious in weapons-combat as the general run of thieves and counter-thieves. So it was they who were surprised and thrown into confusion when with the lightning speed of youth the Mouser and Fafhrd sprang up, whipped out fearsomely long swords, and faced them back to back.

The Mouser made a very small parry in carte so that the thrust of the bravo from the east went past his left side by only a hair's breath. He instantly riposted. His adversary, desperately springing back, parried in turn in carte. Hardly slowing, the tip of the Mouser's long, slim sword dropped under that parry with the delicacy of a princess curtsying and then leaped forward and a little upward, the Mouser making an impossibly long-looking lunge for one so small, and went between two scales of the bravo's armored jerkin and between his ribs and through his heart and out his back as if all were angelfood cake.

Meanwhile Fafhrd, facing the two bravos from the west, swept aside their low thrusts with somewhat larger, down-sweeping parries in seconde and low prime, then flipped up his sword, long as the Mouser's but heavier, so that it slashed through the neck of his right-hand adversary, half decapitating him. Then he, dropping back a swift step, readied a thrust for the other.

But there was no need. A narrow ribbon of bloodied steel, followed by a gray glove and arm, flashed past him from behind and transfixed the last bravo with the identical thrust the Mouser had used on the first.

The two young men wiped and sheathed their swords. Fafhrd brushed the palm of his open right hand down his robe and held it out. The Mouser pulled off right-hand gray glove and shook the other's big hand in his sinewy one. Without word exchanged, they knelt and finished looting the two unconscious thieves, securing the small bags of jewels. With an oily towel and then a dry one, the Mouser sketchily wiped from his face the greasy ash-soot mixture which had darkened it, next swiftly rolled up both towels and returned them to his own pouch. Then, after only a questioning eye-twitch east on the Mouser's part and a nod from Fafhrd, they swiftly walked on in the direction Slevyas and Fissif and their escort had been going.

After reconnoitering Gold Street, they crossed it and continued east on Cash at Fafhrd's gestured proposal.

"My woman's at the Golden Lamprey," he explained.

"Let's pick her up and take her home to meet my girl," the Mouser suggested.

"Home?" Fafhrd inquired politely, only the barest hint of question in his voice.

"Dim Lane," the Mouser volunteered.

"Silver Eel?"

"Behind it. We'll have some drinks."

"I'll pick up a jug. Never have too much juice."

"True. I'll let you."

Several squares farther on Fafhrd, after stealing a number of looks at his new comrade, said with conviction, "We've met before."

The Mouser grinned at him. "Beach by the Mountains of Hunger?"

"Right! When I was a pirate's ship-boy."

"And I was a wizard's apprentice."

Fafhrd stopped, again wiped right hand on robe, and held it out. "Name's Fafhrd. Ef ay ef aitch ar dee."

Again the Mouser shook it. "Gray Mouser," he said a touch defiantly, as if challenging anyone to laugh at the sobriquet. "Excuse me, but how exactly do you pronounce that? Faf-hrud?"

"Just Faf-erd."

"Thank you." They walked on.

"Gray Mouser, eh?" Fafhrd remarked. "Well, you killed yourself a couple of rats tonight."

"That I did." The Mouser's chest swelled and he threw back his head. Then with a comic twitch of his nose and a sidewise half-grin he admitted, "You'd have got your second man easily enough. I stole him from you to demonstrate my speed. Besides, I was excited."

Fafhrd chuckled. "You're telling me? How do you suppose I was feeling?"

Later, as they were crossing Pimp Street, he asked, "Learn much magic from your wizard?"

Once more the Mouser threw back his head. He flared his nostrils and drew down the corners of his lips, preparing his mouth for boastful, mystifying speech. But once more he found himself twitching his nose and half grinning. What the deuce did this big fellow have that kept him from putting on his usual acts? "Enough to tell me it's damned dangerous stuff. Though I still fool with it now and then."

Fafhrd was asking himself a similar question. All his life he'd mistrusted small men, knowing his height awakened their instant jealousy. But this clever little chap was somehow an exception. Quick thinker and brilliant swordsman too, no argument. He prayed to Kos that Vlana would like him.

On the northeast corner of Cash and Whore a slow-burning torch shaded by a broad gilded hoop cast a cone of light up into the thickening black night-smog and another cone down on the cobbles before the tavern door. Out of the shadows into the second cone stepped Vlana, handsome in a narrow black velvet dress and red stockings, her only ornaments a silver-sheathed and -hilted dagger and a silver-worked black pouch, both on a plain black belt.

Fafhrd introduced the Gray Mouser, who behaved with an almost fawning courtesy, obsequiously gallant. Vlana studied him boldly, then gave him a tentative smile.

Fafhrd opened under the torch the small pouch he'd taken off the tall thief. Vlana looked down into it. She put her arms around Fafhrd, hugged him tight, and kissed him soundly. Then she thrust the jewels into the pouch on her belt.

When that was done, he said, "Look, I'm going to buy a jug. You tell her what happened, Mouser."

When he came out of the Golden Lamprey he was carrying four jugs in the crook of his left arm and wiping his lips on the back of his right hand. Vlana was frowning. He grinned at her. The Mouser smacked his lips at the jugs. They continued east on Cash. Fafhrd realized that the frown was for more than the jugs and the prospect of stupidly drunken male revelry. The Mouser tactfully walked ahead, ostensibly to lead the way.

When his figure was little more than a blob in the thickening smog, Vlana whispered harshly, "You had two members of the Thieves' Guild knocked out cold and you didn't cut their throats?"

"We slew three bravos," Fafhrd protested by way of excuse.

"My quarrel is not with the Slayers' Brotherhood, but that abominable Guild. You swore to me that whenever you had the chance—"

"Vlana! I couldn't have the Gray Mouser thinking I was an amateur counter-thief consumed by hysteria and blood lust."

"You already set great store by him, don't you?"

"He possibly saved my life tonight."

"Well, he told me that *he'd* have slit their throats in a wink, if he'd known I wanted it that way."

"He was only playing up to you from courtesy."

"Perhaps and perhaps not. But *you* knew and you didn't—"

"Vlana, shut up!"

Her frown became a rageful glare, then suddenly she laughed wildly, smiled twitchingly as if she were about to cry, mastered herself and smiled more lovingly. "Pardon me, darling," she said. "Sometimes you must think I'm going mad and sometimes I believe I am."

"Well, don't," he told her shortly. "Think of the jewels we've won instead. And behave yourself with our new friends. Get some wine inside you and relax. I mean to enjoy myself tonight. I've earned it."

She nodded and clutched his arm in agreement and for comfort and sanity. They hurried to catch up with the dim figure ahead.

The Mouser, turning left, led them a half square north on Cheap Street to where a narrower way went east again. The black mist in it looked solid.

"Dim Lane," the Mouser explained.

Fafhrd nodded that he knew.

Vlana said, "Dim's too weak—too *transparent* a word for it tonight," with an uneven laugh in which there were still traces of hysteria and which ended in a fit of strangled coughing. When she could swallow again, she gasped out, "Damn Lankhmar's night-smog! What a hell of a city!"

"It's the nearness here of the Great Salt Marsh," Fafhrd explained.

And he did indeed have part of the answer. Lying low betwixt the Marsh, the Inner Sea, the River Hlal, and the flat southern grainfields watered by canals fed by the Hlal, Lankhmar with its innumerable smokes was the prey of fogs and sooty smogs. No wonder the citizens had adopted the black toga as their formal garb. Some averred the toga had originally been white or pale brown, but so swiftly soot-blackened, necessitating endless laundering, that a thrifty overlord had ratified and made official what nature or civilization's arts decreed.

About halfway to Carter Street, a tavern on the north side of the lane emerged from the murk. A gape-jawed serpentine shape of pale metal crested with soot hung high for a sign. Beneath it they passed a door curtained with begrimed leather, the slit in which spilled out noise, pulsing torchlight, and the reek of liquor.

Just beyond the Silver Eel the Mouser led them through an inky passageway outside the tavern's east wall. They had to go single file, feeling their way along rough, slimily bemisted brick and keeping close together.

"Mind the puddle," the Mouser warned. "It's deep as the Outer Sea."

The passageway widened. Reflected torchlight filtering down through the dark mist allowed them to make out only the most general shape of their surroundings. To the right was more windowless, high wall. To the left, crowding close to the back of the Silver Eel, rose a dismal, rickety building of darkened brick and blackened, ancient wood. It looked utterly deserted to Fafhrd and Vlana until they had craned back their heads to gaze at the fourth-story attic under the ragged-guttered roof. There faint lines and points of yellow light shone around and through three tightly-latticed windows. Beyond, crossing the T of the space they were in, was a narrow alley.

"Bones Alley," the Mouser told them in somewhat lofty tones. "I call it Ordure Boulevard."

"I can smell that," Vlana said.

By now she and Fafhrd could see a long, narrow wooden outside stairway, steep yet sagging and without a rail, leading up to the lighted attic. The Mouser relieved Fafhrd of the jugs and went up it quite swiftly.

"Follow me when I've reached the top," he called back. "I think it'll take your weight, Fafhrd, but best one of you at a time."

Fafhrd gently pushed Vlana ahead. With another hysteria-tinged laugh and a pause midway up for another fit of choked coughing, she mounted to the Mouser where he now stood in an open doorway, from which streamed yellow light that died swiftly in the night-smog. He was lightly resting a hand on a big, empty, wrought-iron lamp-hook firmly set in a stone section of the outside wall. He bowed aside, and she went in.

Fafhrd followed, placing his feet as close as he could to the wall, his hands ready to grab for support. The whole stairs creaked ominously and each step gave a little as he shifted his weight onto it. Near the top, one gave way with the muted crack of half-rotted wood. Gently as he could, he sprawled himself hand and knee on as many steps as he could reach, to distribute his weight, and cursed sulphurously.

"Don't fret, the jugs are safe," the Mouser called down gayly.

Fafhrd crawled the rest of the way, a somewhat sour look on his face, and did not get to his feet until he was inside the doorway. When he had done so, he almost gasped with surprise.

It was like rubbing the verdigris from a cheap brass ring and finding a rainbow-fired diamond of the first water set in it. Rich drapes, some twinkling with embroidery of silver and gold, covered the walls except where the shuttered windows were—and the shutters of those were gilded. Similar but darker fabrics hid the low ceiling, making a gorgeous canopy in which the flecks of gold and silver were like stars. Scattered about were plump cushions and low tables, on which burned a multitude of candles. On shelves against the walls were neatly stacked like small logs a vast reserve of candles, numerous scrolls, jugs, bottles, and enameled boxes. A low vanity table was backed by a mirror of honed silver and thickly scattered over with jewels and cosmetics. In a large fireplace was set a small metal stove, neatly blacked, with an ornate fire-pot. Also set beside the stove were a tidy pyramid of thin, resinous torches with frayed ends—fire-kindlers—and other pyramids of short-handled brooms and mops, small, short logs, and gleamingly black coal.

On a low dais by the fireplace was a wide, short-legged, high-backed couch covered with cloth of gold. On it sat a thin, pale-faced, delicately handsome girl clad in a dress of thick violet silk worked with silver and belted with a silver chain. Her slippers were of white snow-serpent fur. Silver pins headed with amethysts held in place her high-piled black hair. Around her shoulders was drawn a white ermine wrap. She was leaning forward with uneasy-seeming graciousness and extending a narrow, white hand which shook a little to Vlana, who knelt before her and now gently took the proffered hand and bowed her head over it, her own glossy, straight, dark-brown hair making a canopy, and pressed the other girl's hand's back to her lips.

Fafhrd was happy to see his woman playing up properly to this definitely odd though delightful situation. Then looking at Vlana's long, red-stockinged leg stretched far behind her as she knelt on the other, he noted that the floor was everywhere strewn—to the point of double, treble, and quadruple overlaps—with thick-piled, close-woven, many-hued rugs of the finest imported from the Eastern Lands. Before he knew it, his thumb had shot toward the Gray Mouser.

"You're the Rug Robber!" he proclaimed. "You're the Carpet Crimp!—and the Candle Corsair too!" he continued, referring to two series of unsolved thefts which had been on the lips of all Lankhmar when he and Vlana had arrived a moon ago.

The Mouser shrugged impassive-faced at Fafhrd, then suddenly grinned, his slitted eyes a-twinkle, and broke into an impromptu dance which carried him whirling and jigging around the room and left him behind Fafhrd, where he deftly reached down the hooded and long-sleeved robe from the latter's stooping shoulders, shook it out, carefully folded it, and set it on a pillow.

After a long, uncertain pause, the girl in violet nervously patted with her free hand the cloth of gold beside her and Vlana seated herself there, carefully not too close, and the two women spoke together in low voices, Vlana taking the lead, though not obviously.

The Mouser took off his own gray, hooded cloak, folded it almost fussily, and laid it beside Fafhrd's. Then they unbelted their swords, and the Mouser set them atop folded robe and cloak.

Without those weapons and bulking garments, the two men looked suddenly like youths, both with clear, close-shaven faces, both slender despite the swelling muscles of Fafhrd's arms and calves, he with long red-gold hair falling down his back and about his shoulders, the Mouser with dark hair cut in bangs, the one in brown leather tunic worked with copper wire, the other in jerkin of coarsely woven gray silk.

They smiled at each other. The feeling each had of having turned boy all at once made their smiles for the first time a bit embarrassed. The Mouser cleared his throat and, bowing a little, but looking still at Fafhrd, extended a loosely spread-fingered arm toward the golden couch and said with a preliminary stammer, though otherwise smoothly enough, "Fafhrd, my good friend, permit me to introduce you to my princess. Ivrian, my dear, receive Fafhrd graciously if you please, for tonight he and I fought back to back against three and we conquered."

Fafhrd advanced, stooping a little, the crown of his red-gold hair brushing the bestarred canopy, and knelt before Ivrian exactly as Vlana had. The slender hand extended to him looked steady now, but was still quiveringly a-tremble, he discovered as soon as he touched it. He handled it as if it were silk woven of the white spider's gossamer, barely brushing it with his lips, and still felt nervous as he mumbled some compliments.

He did not sense, at least at the moment, that the Mouser was quite as nervous as he, if not more so, praying hard that Ivrian would not overdo her princess part and snub their guests, or collapse in trembling or tears or run to him or into the next room, for Fafhrd and Vlana were literally the first beings, human or animal, noble, freeman, or slave, that he had brought or allowed into the luxurious nest he had created for his aristocratic beloved—save the two love birds that twittered in a silver cage hanging to the other side of the fireplace from the dais.

Despite his shrewdness and new-found cynicism it never occurred to the

Mouser that it was chiefly his charming but preposterous coddling of Ivrian that was keeping doll-like and even making more so the potentially brave and realistic girl who had fled with him from her father's torture chamber four moons ago.

But now as Ivrian smiled at last and Fafhrd gently returned her her hand and cautiously backed off, the Mouser relaxed with relief, fetched two silver cups and two silver mugs, wiped them needlessly with a silken towel, carefully selected a bottle of violet wine, then with a grin at Fafhrd uncorked instead one of the jugs the Northerner had brought, and near-brimmed the four gleaming vessels and served them all four.

With another preliminary clearing of throat, but no trace of stammer this time, he toasted, "To my greatest theft to date in Lankhmar, which willy-nilly I must share sixty-sixty with"—he couldn't resist the sudden impulse—"with this great, longhaired, barbarian lout here!" And he downed a quarter of his mug of pleasantly burning wine fortified with brandy.

Fafhrd quaffed off half of his, then toasted back, "To the most boastful and finical little civilized chap I've ever deigned to share loot with," quaffed off the rest, and with a great smile that showed white teeth held out his empty mug.

The Mouser gave him a refill, topped off his own, then set that down to go to Ivrian and pour into her lap from their small pouch the gems he'd filched from Fissif. They gleamed in their new, enviable location like a small puddle of rainbow-hued quicksilver.

Ivrian jerked back a-tremble, almost spilling them, but Vlana gently caught her arm, steadying it, and leaned in over the jewels with a throaty gasp of wonder and admiration, slowly turned an envious gaze on the pale girl, and began rather urgently but smilingly to whisper to her. Fafhrd realized that Vlana was acting now, but acting well and effectively, since Ivrian was soon nodding eagerly and not long after that beginning to whisper back. At her direction, Vlana fetched a blue-enameled box inlaid with silver, and the two of them transferred the jewels from Ivrian's lap into its blue velvet interior. Then Ivrian placed the box close beside her and they chatted on.

As he worked through his second mug in smaller gulps, Fafhrd relaxed and began to get a deeper feeling of his surroundings. The dazzling wonder of the first glimpse of this throne room in a slum, its colorful luxury intensified by contrast with the dark and mud and slime and rotten stairs and Ordure Boulevard just outside, faded, and he began to note the rickettiness and rot under the grand overlay.

Black, rotten wood and dry, cracked wood too showed here and there between the drapes and also loosed their sick, ancient stinks. The whole floor sagged under the rugs, as much as a span at the center of the room. A large cockroach was climbing down a gold-worked drape, another toward the couch. Threads of night-smog were coming through the shutters, making evanescent black arabesques against the gilt. The stones of the large fireplace had been scrubbed and varnished, yet most of the mortar was gone from between them; some sagged, others were missing altogether.

The Mouser had been building a fire there in the stove. Now he pushed in all the way the yellow-flaring kindler he'd lit from the fire-pot, hooked the little black door shut over the mounting flames, and turned back into the room. As if he'd read Fafhrd's mind, he took up several cones of incense, set their peaks a-smolder at the fire-pot, and placed them about the room in gleaming, shallow, brass bowls—stepping hard on the one cockroach by the way and surreptitiously catching and crushing the other in the base of his flicked fist. Then he stuffed silken rags in the widest shutter-cracks, took up his silver mug again, and for a moment gave Fafhrd a very hard look, as if daring him to say just one word against the delightful yet faintly ridiculous doll's house he'd prepared for his princess.

Next moment he was smiling and lifting his mug to Fafhrd, who was doing the same. Need of refills brought them close together. Hardly moving his lips, the Mouser explained *sotto voce,* "Ivrian's father was a duke. I slew him, by black magic, I believe, while he was having me done to death on the torture rack. A most cruel man, cruel to his daughter too, yet a duke, so that Ivrian is wholly unused to fending or caring for herself. I pride myself that I maintain her in grander state than ever her father did with all his serving men and maids."

Suppressing the instant criticisms he felt of this attitude and program, Fafhrd nodded and said amiably, "Surely you've thieved together a most charming little palace, quite worthy of Lankhmar's overlord Karstak Ovartamortes, or the King of Kings at Tisilinilit."

From the couch Vlana called in her husky contralto, "Gray Mouser, your princess would hear an account of tonight's adventure. And might we have more wine?"

Ivrian called, "Yes, please, Mouse."

Wincing almost imperceptibly at that earlier nickname, the Mouser looked to Fafhrd for the go-ahead, got the nod, and launched into his story. But first he served the girls wine. There wasn't enough for their cups, so he opened another jug and after a moment of thought uncorked all three, setting one by the couch, one by Fafhrd where he sprawled now on the pillowy carpets, and reserving one for himself. Ivrian looked wide-eyed apprehensive at this signal of heavy drinking ahead, Vlana cynical with a touch of anger, but neither voiced their criticism.

The Mouser told the tale of counter-thievery well, acting it out in part, and with only the most artistic of embellishments—the ferret-marmoset before escaping ran up his back and tried to scratch out his eyes—and he was interrupted only twice.

When he said, "And so with a whish and a snick I bared Scalpel—" Fafhrd remarked, "Oh, so you've nicknamed your sword as well as yourself?"

The Mouser drew himself up. "Yes, and I call my dirk Cat's Claw. Any objections? Seem childish to you?"

"Not at all. I call my own sword Graywand. All weapons are in a fashion alive, civilized and name-worthy. Pray continue."

And when he mentioned the beastie of uncertain nature that had gamboled along with the thieves (and attacked his eyes!), Ivrian paled and said with a shudder, "Mouse! That sounds like a witch's familiar!"

"Wizard's," Vlana corrected. "Those gutless Guild-villains have no truck with women, except as fee'd or forced vehicles for their lust. But Krovas, their current king, though superstitious, is noted for taking *all* precautions, and might well have a warlock in his service."

"That seems most likely; it harrows me with dread," the Mouser agreed with ominous gaze and sinister voice. He really didn't believe or feel what he said—he was about as harrowed as virgin prairie—in the least, but he eagerly accepted any and all atmospheric enhancements of his performance.

When he was done, the girls, eyes flashing and fond, toasted him and Fafhrd for their cunning and bravery. The Mouser bowed and eye-twinklingly smiled about, then sprawled him down with a weary sigh, wiping his forehead with a silken cloth and downing a large drink.

After asking Vlana's leave, Fafhrd told the adventurous tale of their escape from Cold Corner—he from his clan, she from an acting troupe—and of their progress to Lankhmar, where they lodged now in an actors' tenement near the Plaza of Dark Delights. Ivrian hugged herself to Vlana and shivered large-eyed at the witchy parts—at least as much in delight as fear of Fafhrd's tale, he thought. He told himself it was natural that a doll-girl should love ghost stories, though he wondered if her pleasure would have been as great if she had known that his ghost stories were truly true. She seemed to live in worlds of imagination—once more at least half the Mouser's doing, he was sure.

The only proper matter he omitted from his account was Vlana's fixed intent to get a monstrous revenge on the Thieves' Guild for torturing to death her accomplices and harrying her out of Lankhmar when she'd tried free-lance thieving in the city, with miming as a cover. Nor of course did he mention his own promise—foolish, he thought now—to help her in this bloody business.

After he'd done and got his applause, he found his throat dry despite his skald's training, but when he sought to wet it, he discovered that his mug was empty and his jug too, though he didn't feel in the least drunk; he had talked all the liquor out of him, he told himself, a little of the stuff escaping in each glowing word he'd spoken.

The Mouser was in like plight and not drunk either—though inclined to pause mysteriously and peer toward infinity before answering question or making remark. This time he suggested, after a particularly long infinity-gaze, that Fafhrd accompany him to the Eel while he purchased a fresh supply.

"But we've a lot of wine left in *our* jug," Ivrian protested. "Or at least a little," she amended. It did sound empty when Vlana shook it. "Besides, you've wine of all sorts here."

"Not this sort, dearest, and first rule is never mix 'em," the Mouser explained, wagging a finger. "That way lies unhealth, aye, and madness."

"My dear," Vlana said, sympathetically patting Ivrian's wrist, "at some time in any good party all the men who are really men simply have to go out. It's extremely stupid, but it's their nature and can't be dodged, believe me."

"But, Mouse, I'm scared. Fafhrd's tale frightened me. So did yours—I'll hear that big-headed, black, ratty familiar a-scratch at the shutters when you're gone, I know I will!"

It seemed to Fafhrd she was not afraid at all, only taking pleasure in frightening herself and in demonstrating her power over her beloved.

"Darlingest," the Mouser said with a small hiccup, "there is all the Inner Sea, all the Land of the Eight Cities, and to boot all the Trollstep Mountains in their sky-scraping grandeur between you and Fafhrd's frigid specters or—pardon me, my comrade, but it could be—hallucinations admixed with coincidences. As for familiars, pish! They've never in the world been anything but the loathy, all-too-natural pets of stinking old women and womanish old men."

"The Eel's but a step, Lady Ivrian," Fafhrd said, "and you'll have beside you my dear Vlana, who slew my chiefest enemy with a single cast of that dagger she now wears."

With a glare at Fafhrd that lasted no longer than a wink, but conveyed "What a way to reassure a frightened girl!" Vlana said merrily, "Let the sillies go, my dear. 'Twill give us chance for a private chat, during which we'll take 'em apart from wine-fumey head to restless foot."

So Ivrian let herself be persuaded and the Mouser and Fafhrd slipped off, quickly shutting the door behind them to keep out the night-smog. Their rather rapid steps down the stairs could clearly be heard from within. There were faint creakings and groanings of the ancient wood outside the wall, but no sound of another tread breaking or other mishap.

Waiting for the four jugs to be brought up from the cellar, the two newly met comrades ordered a mug each of the same fortified wine, or one near enough, and ensconced themselves at the least noisy end of the long serving counter in the tumultuous tavern. The Mouser deftly kicked a rat that thrust black head and shoulders from his hole.

After each had enthusiastically complimented the other on his girl, Fafhrd said diffidently, "Just between ourselves, do you think there might be anything to your sweet Ivrian's notion that the small dark creature with Slivikin and the other Guild-thief was a wizard's familiar, or at any rate the cunning pet of a sorcerer, trained to act as go-between and report disasters to his master or to Krovas or to both?"

The Mouser laughed lightly. "You're building bugbears—formless baby ones unlicked by logic—out of nothing, dear barbarian brother, if I may say so. *Imprimis,* we don't really know the beastie was connected with the Guild-thieves at all. May well have been a stray catling or a big bold rat—like this damned one!" He kicked again. "But, *secundus,* granting it to be the creature of a wizard employed by Krovas, how could it make useful report? I don't believe in animals that talk—except for parrots and such birds, which only . . . parrot—or ones having an elaborate sign language men can share. Or perhaps you envisage the beastie dipping its paddy paw in a jug of ink and writing its report in big on a floor-spread parchment?

"Ho, there, you back of the counter! Where are my jugs? Rats eaten the boy who went for them days ago? Or he simply starved to death while on his cellar quest? Well, tell him to get a swifter move on and meanwhile brim us again!

"No, Fafhrd, even granting the beastie to be directly or indirectly a creature of Krovas, and that it raced back to Thieves' House after our affray, what could it tell them there? Only that something had gone wrong with the burglary at Jengao's. Which they'd soon suspect in any case from the delay in the thieves' and bravos' return."

Fafhrd frowned and muttered stubbornly, "The furry slinker might, nevertheless, convey our appearances to the Guild masters, and they might recognize us and come after us and attack us in our homes. Or Slivikin and his fat pal, revived from their bumps, might do likewise."

"My dear friend," the Mouser said condolingly, "once more begging your indulgence, I fear this potent wine is addling your wits. If the Guild knew our looks or where we lodge, they'd have been nastily on our necks days, weeks, nay, months ago. Or conceivably you don't know that their penalty for free-lance or even unassigned thieving within the walls of

Lankhmar and for three leagues outside them is nothing less than death, after torture if happily that can be achieved."

"I know all about that and my plight is worse even than yours," Fafhrd retorted, and after pledging the Mouser to secrecy told him the tale of Vlana's vendetta against the Guild and her deadly serious dreams of an all-encompassing revenge.

During his story the four jugs came up from the cellar, but the Mouser only ordered that their earthenware mugs be refilled.

Fafhrd finished, "And so, in consequence of a promise given by an infatuated and unschooled boy in a southern angle of the Cold Waste, I find myself now as a sober—well, at other times—man being constantly asked to make war on a power as great as that of Karstak Ovartamortes, for as you may know, the Guild has locals in all other cities and major towns of this land, not to mention agreements including powers of extradition with robber and bandit organizations in other countries. I love Vlana dearly, make no mistake about that, and she is an experienced thief herself, without whose guidance I'd hardly have survived my first week in Lankhmar, but on this one topic she has a kink in her brains, a hard knot neither logic nor persuasion can even begin to loosen. And I, well, in the month I've been here I've learned that the only way to survive in civilization is to abide by its unwritten rules—far more important than its laws chiseled in stone—and break them only at peril, in deepest secrecy, and taking all precautions. As I did tonight—not my first hijacking, by the by."

"Certes t'would be insanity to assault the Guild direct, your wisdom's perfect there," the Mouser commented. "If you cannot break your most handsome girl of this mad notion, or coax her from it—and I can see she's a fearless, self-willed one—then you must stoutly refuse e'en her least request in that direction."

"Certes I must," Fafhrd agreed, adding somewhat accusingly, "though I gather you told her you'd have willingly slit the throats of the two we struck senseless."

"Courtesy merely, man! Would you have had me behave ungraciously to your girl? 'Tis measure of the value I was already setting then on your goodwill. But only a woman's man may cross her. As you must, in this instance."

"Certes I must," Fafhrd repeated with great emphasis and conviction. "I'd be an idiot taking on the Guild. Of course if they should catch me they'd kill me in any case for free-lancing and highjacking. But wantonly to assault the Guild direct, kill one Guild-thief needlessly, only behave as if I might—lunacy entire!"

"You'd not only be a drunken, drooling idiot, you'd questionless be stinking in three nights at most from that emperor of diseases, Death. Malicious attacks on her person, blows directed at the organization, the Guild requites tenfold what she does other rule-breakings. All planned robberies and other thefts would be called off and the entire power of the Guild and its allies mobilized against you alone. I'd count your chances better to take on single-handed the host of the King of Kings rather than the Thieves' Guild's subtle minions. In view of your size, might, and wit you're a squad perhaps, or even a company, but hardly an army. So, no least giving-in to Vlana in this one matter."

"Agreed!" Fafhrd said loudly, shaking the Mouser's iron-thewed hand in a near crusher grip.

"And now we should be getting back to the girls," the Mouser said.

"After one more drink while we settle the score. Ho, boy!"

"Suits." The Mouser dug into his pouch to pay, but Fafhrd protested vehemently. In the end they tossed coin for it, and Fafhrd won and with great satisfaction clinked out his silver smerduks on the stained and dinted counter, also marked with an infinitude of mug circles, as if it had been once the desk of a mad geometer. They pushed themselves to their feet, the Mouser giving the rathole one last light kick for luck.

At this, Fafhrd's thoughts looped back and he said, "Grant the beastie can't paw-write, or talk by mouth or paw, it still could have followed us at distance, marked down your dwelling, and then returned to Thieves' House to lead its masters down on us like a hound!"

"Now you're speaking shrewd sense again," the Mouse said. "Ho, boy, a bucket of small beer to go! On the instant!" Noting Fafhrd's blank look, he explained, "I'll spill it outside the Eel to kill our scent and all the way down the passageway. Yes, and splash it high on the walls too."

Fafhrd nodded wisely. "I thought I'd drunk my way past the addled point."

Vlana and Ivrian, deep in excited talk, both started at the pounding rush of footsteps up the stairs. Racing behemoths could hardly have made more noise. The creaking and groaning were prodigious and there were the crashes of two treads breaking, yet the pounding footsteps never faltered. The door flew open and their two men rushed in through a great mushroom top of night-smog which was neatly sliced off its black stem by the slam of the door.

"I told you we'd be back in a wink," the Mouser cried gayly to Ivrian, while Fafhrd strode forward, unmindful of the creaking floor, crying, "Dearest heart, I've missed you sorely," and caught up Vlana despite her voiced protests and pushings-off and kissed and hugged her soundly before setting her back on the couch again.

Oddly, it was Ivrian who appeared to be angry at Fafhrd then, rather than Vlana, who was smiling fondly if somewhat dazedly.

"Fafhrd, sir," she said boldly, her little fists set on her narrow hips, her tapered chin held high, her dark eyes blazing, "my beloved Vlana has been telling me about the unspeakably atrocious things the Thieves' Guild did to her and to her dearest friends. Pardon my frank speaking to one I've only met, but I think it quite unmanly of you to refuse her the just revenge she desires and fully deserves. And that goes for you too, Mouse, who boasted to Vlana of what you would have done had you but known, who in like case did not scruple to slay my very own father—or reputed father—for his cruelties!"

It was clear to Fafhrd that while he and the Gray Mouser had idly boozed in the Eel, Vlana had been giving Ivrian a doubtless empurpled account of her grievances against the Guild and playing mercilessly on the naïve girl's bookish, romantic sympathies and high concept of knightly honor. It was also clear to him that Ivrian was more than a little drunk. A three-quarters empty flask of violet wine of far Kiraay sat on the low table next them.

Yet he could think of nothing to do but spread his big hands helplessly and bow his head, more than the low ceiling made necessary, under Ivrian's glare, now reinforced by that of Vlana. After all, they *were* in the right. He *had* promised.

So it was the Mouser who first tried to rebut.

"Come now, pet," he cried lightly as he danced about the room, silk-stuffing more cracks against the thickening night-smog and stirring up and feeding the fire in the stove, "and you too, beauteous Lady Vlana. For the past month Fafhrd has been hitting the Guild-thieves where it hurts them most—in their purses a-dangle between their legs. His highjackings of the loot of their robberies have been like so many fierce kicks in their groins. Hurts worse, believe me, than robbing them of life with a swift, near painless sword slash or thrust. And tonight I helped him in his worthy purpose—and will eagerly do so again. Come, drink we up all." Under his handling, one of the new jugs came uncorked with a pop and he darted about brimming silver cups and mugs.

"A merchant's revenge!" Ivrian retorted with scorn, not one whit appeased, but rather angered anew. "Ye both are at heart true and gentle knights, I know, despite all current backsliding. At the least you must bring Vlana the head of Krovas!"

"What would she *do* with it? What *good* would it be except to spot the carpets?" the Mouser plaintively inquired, while Fafhrd, gathering his wits at last and going down on one knee, said slowly, "Most respected Lady Ivrian, it is true I solemnly promised my beloved Vlana I would help her in her revenge, but that was while I was still in barbarous Cold Corner, where blood-feud is a commonplace, sanctioned by custom and accepted by all the clans and tribes and brotherhoods of the savage Northerners of the Cold Waste. In my naïveté I thought of Vlana's revenge as being of that sort. But here in civilization's midst, I discover all's different and rules and customs turned upside-down. Yet—Lankhmar or Cold Corner—one must seem to observe rule and custom to survive. Here cash is all-powerful, the idol placed highest, whether one sweat, thieve, grind others down, or scheme for it. Here feud and revenge are outside all rules and punished worse than violent lunacy. Think, Lady Ivrian, if Mouse and I should bring Vlana the head of Krovas, she and I would have to flee Lankhmar on the instant, every man's hand against us; while you infallibly would lose this fairyland Mouse has created for love of you and be forced to do likewise, be with him a beggar on the run for the rest of your natural lives."

It was beautifully reasoned and put . . . and no good whatsoever. While Fafhrd spoke, Ivrian snatched up her new-filled cup and drained it.

Now she stood up straight as a soldier, her pale face flushed, and said scathingly to Fafhrd kneeling before her, *"You count the cost!* You speak to me of *things"*—she waved at the many-hued splendor around her—"Of mere property, however costly, when *honor* is at stake. You gave Vlana *your word.* Oh, is knighthood wholly dead? And that applies to you, too, Mouse, who swore you'd slit the miserable throats of two noisome Guild-thieves."

"I didn't swear *to,"* the Mouser objected feebly, downing a big drink. "I merely said *I would have,"* while Fafhrd could only shrug again and writhe inside and gulp a little easement from his silver mug. For Ivrian was speaking in the same guilt-showering tones and using the same unfair yet heart-cleaving womanly arguments as Mor his mother might have, or Mara, his deserted Snow Clan sweetheart and avowed wife, big-bellied by now with his child.

In a master stroke, Vlana tried gently to draw Ivrian down to her golden seat again. "Softly, dearest," she pleaded. "You have spoken nobly for me and my cause, and believe me, I am most grateful. Your words revived in me great, fine feelings dead these many years. But of us here, only you are truly an aristocrat attuned to the highest proprieties. We other three are naught but thieves. Is it any wonder some of us put safety above honor and word-keeping, and most prudently avoid risking our lives? Yes, we are three thieves and I am outvoted. So please speak no more of honor and rash, dauntless bravery, but sit you down and—"

"You mean they're both *afraid* to challenge the Thieves' Guild, don't you?" Ivrian said, eyes wide and face twisted by loathing. "I always thought my Mouse was a nobleman first and a thief second. Thieving's nothing. My father lived by cruel thievery done on rich wayfarers and neighbors less powerful than he, yet he was an aristocrat. Oh, you're *cowards,* both of you! *Poltroons!"* she finished, turning her eyes flashing with cold scorn first on the Mouser, then on Fafhrd.

The latter could stand it no longer. He sprang to his feet, face flushed, fists clenched at his sides, quite unmindful of his down-clattered mug and the ominous creak his sudden action drew from the sagging floor.

"I am not a coward!" he cried. "I'll dare Thieves' House and fetch you Korvas' head and toss it with blood a-drip at Vlana's feet. I swear that,

witness me, Kos the god of dooms, by the brown bones of Nalgron my father and by his sword Graywand here at my side!"

He slapped his left hip, found nothing there but his tunic, and had to content himself with pointing tremble-armed at his belt and scabbarded sword where they lay atop his neatly folded robe—and then picking up, refilling splashily, and draining his mug.

The Gray Mouser began to laugh in high, delighted, tuneful peals. All stared at him. He came dancing up beside Fafhrd, and still smiling widely, asked, "*Why not?* Who speaks of fearing the Guild-thieves? Who becomes upset at the prospect of this ridiculously easy exploit, when all of us know that all of them, even Krovas and his ruling clique, are but pygmies in mind and skill compared to me or Fafhrd here? A wondrously simple, foolproof scheme has just occurred to me for penetrating Thieves' House, every closet and cranny. Stout Fafhrd and I will put it into effect at once. Are you with me, Northerner?"

"Of course I am," Fafhrd responded gruffly, at the same time frantically wondering what madness had gripped the little fellow.

"Give me a few heartbeats to gather needed props, and we're off!" the Mouser cried. He snatched from a shelf and unfolded a stout sack, then raced about, thrusting into it coiled ropes, bandage rolls, rags, jars of ointment and unction and unguent, and other oddments.

"But you can't go *tonight,*" Ivrian protested, suddenly grown pale and uncertain-voiced. "You're both . . . in no condition to."

"You're both *drunk,*" Vlana said harshly. "Silly drunk—and that way you'll get naught in Thieves' House but your deaths. Fafhrd, where's that heartless reason you employed to slay or ice-veined see slain a clutch of mighty rivals and win me at Cold Corner and in the chilly, sorcery-webbed depths of Trollstep Canyon? Revive it! And infuse some into your skipping gray friend."

"Oh, no," Fafhrd told her as he buckled on his sword. "You wanted the head of Krovas heaved at your feet in a great splatter of blood, and that's what you're going to get, like it or not!"

"Softly, Fafhrd," the Mouser interjected, coming to a sudden stop and drawing tight the sack's mouth by its strings. "And softly you too, Lady Vlana, and my dear princess. Tonight I intend but a scouting expedition.

No risks run, only the information gained needful for planning our murderous strike tomorrow or the day after. So no head-choppings whatsoever tonight, Fafhrd, you hear me? Whatever may hap, hist's the word. And don your hooded robe."

Fafhrd shrugged, nodded, and obeyed.

Ivrian seemed somewhat relieved. Vlana too, though she said, "Just the same you're both drunk."

"All to the good!" the Mouser assured her with a mad smile. "Drink may slow a man's sword-arm and soften his blows a bit, but it sets his wits ablaze and fires his imagination, and those are the qualities we'll need tonight. Besides," he hurried on, cutting off some doubt Ivrian was about to voice, "drunken men are supremely cautious! Have you ever seen a staggering sot pull himself together at sight of the guard and walk circumspectly and softly past?"

"Yes," Vlana said, "and fall flat on his face just as he comes abreast 'em."

"Pish!" the Mouser retorted and, throwing back his head, grandly walked toward her along an imaginary straight line. Instantly he tripped over his own foot, plunged forward, suddenly without touching floor did an incredible forward flip, heels over head, and landed erect and quite softly—toes, ankles, and knees bending just at the right moment to soak up impact—directly in front of the girls. The floor barely complained.

"You see?" he said, straightening up and unexpectedly reeling backward. He tripped over the pillow on which lay his cloak and sword, but by a wrenching twist and a lurch stayed upright and began rapidly to accouter himself.

Under cover of this action Fafhrd made quietly yet swiftly to fill once more his and the Mouser's mugs, but Vlana noted it and gave him such a glare that he set down mugs and uncorked jug so swiftly his robe swirled, then stepped back from the drinks table with a shrug of resignation and toward Vlana a grimacing nod.

The Mouser shouldered his sack and drew open the door. With a casual wave at the girls, but no word spoken, Fafhrd stepped out on the tiny porch. The night-smog had grown so thick he was almost lost to view. The

Mouser waved four fingers at Ivrian, softly called, "Bye-bye, Misling," then followed Fafhrd.

"Good fortune go with you," Vlana called heartily.

"Oh, be careful, Mouse," Ivrian gasped.

The Mouser, his figure slight against the loom of Fafhrd's, silently drew shut the door.

Their arms automatically gone around each other, the girls waited for the inevitable creaking and groaning of the stairs. It delayed and delayed. The night-smog that had entered the room dissipated and still the silence was unbroken.

"What can they be doing out there?" Ivrian whispered. "Plotting their course?"

Vlana, scowling, impatiently shook her head, then disentangled herself, tiptoed to the door, opened it, descended softly a few steps, which creaked most dolefuly, then returned, shutting the door behind her.

"They're gone," she said in wonder, her eyes wide, her hands spread a little to either side, palms up.

"I'm frightened!" Ivrian breathed and sped across the room to embrace the taller girl.

Vlana hugged her tight, then disengaged an arm to shoot the door's three heavy bolts.

In Bones Alley the Mouser returned to his pouch the knotted line by which they'd descended from the lamp hook. He suggested, "How about stopping at the Silver Eel?"

"You mean and just *tell* the girls we've been to Thieves' House?" Fafhrd asked, not too indignantly.

"Oh, no," the Mouser protested. "But you missed your stirrup cup upstairs and so did I."

At the word "stirrup" he looked down at his ratskin boots and then crouching began a little gallop in one place, his boot-soles clopping softly on the cobbles. He flapped imaginary reins—"Giddap!"—and quickened his gallop, but leaning sharply back pulled to a stop—"Whoa!"—when with a crafty smile Fafhrd drew from his robe two full jugs.

"Palmed 'em, as 'twere, when I set down the mugs. Vlana sees a lot, but not all."

"You're a prudent, far-sighted fellow, in addition to having some skill at sword taps," the Mouser said admiringly. "I'm proud to call you comrade."

Each uncorked and drank a hearty slug. Then the Mouser led them west, they veering and stumbling only a little. Not so far as Cheap Street, however, but turning north into an even narrower and more noisome alley.

"Plague Court," the Mouser said. Fafhrd nodded.

After several preliminary peepings and peerings, they staggered swiftly across wide, empty Crafts Street and into Plague Court again. For a wonder it was growing a little lighter. Looking upward, they saw stars. Yet there was no wind blowing from the north. The air was deathly still.

In their drunken preoccupation with the project at hand and mere locomotion, they did not look behind them. There the night-smog was thicker than ever. A high-circling nighthawk would have seen the stuff converging from all sections of Lankhmar, north, east, south, west—from the Inner Sea, from the Great Salt Marsh, from the many-ditched grainlands, from the River Hlal—in swift-moving black rivers and rivulets, heaping, eddying, swirling, dark and reeking essence of Lankhmar from its branding irons, braziers, bonfires, bonefires, kitchen fires and warmth fires, kilns, forges, breweries, distilleries, junk and garbage fires innumerable, sweating alchemists' and sorcerers' dens, crematoriums, charcoal burners' turfed mounds, all those and many more . . . converging purposefully on Dim Lane and particularly on the Silver Eel and perhaps especially on the ricketty house behind it, untenanted except for attic. The closer to that center it got, the more substantial the smog became, eddy-strands and swirl-tatters tearing off and clinging to rough stone corners and scraggly-surfaced brick like black cobwebs.

But the Mouser and Fafhrd merely exclaimed in mild, muted amazement at the stars, muggily mused as to how much the improved visibility would increase the risk of their quest, and cautiously crossing the Street of the Thinkers, called Atheist Avenue by moralists, continued to Plague Court until it forked.

The Mouser chose the left branch, which trended northwest.

"Death Alley."

Fafhrd nodded.

After a curve and recurve, Cheap Street swung into sight about thirty paces ahead. The Mouser stopped at once and lightly threw his arm against Fafhrd's chest.

Clearly in view across Cheap Street was a wide, low, open doorway, framed by grimy stone blocks. There led up to it two steps hollowed by the treadings of centuries. Orange-yellow light spilled out from bracketed torches inside. They couldn't see very far in because of Death Alley's angle. Yet as far as they *could* see, there was no porter or guard in sight, nor anyone at all, not even a watchdog on a chain. The effect was ominous.

"Now how do we get into the damn place?" Fafhrd demanded in a hoarse whisper. "Scout Murder Alley for a back window that can be forced? You've pries in that sack, I trow. Or try the roof? You're a roof man, I know already. Teach me the art. I know trees and mountains, snow, ice, and bare rock. See this wall here?" He backed off from it, preparing to go up it in a rush.

"Steady on, Fafhrd," the Mouser said, keeping his hand against the big young man's chest. "We'll hold the roof in reserve. Likewise all walls. And I'll take it on trust you're a master climber. As to how we get in, we walk straight through that doorway." He frowned. "Tap and hobble, rather. Come on, while I prepare us."

As he drew the skeptically grimacing Fafhrd back down Death Alley until all Cheap Street was again cut off from view, he explained, "We'll pretend to be beggars, members of *their* guild, which is but a branch of the Thieves' Guild and houses with it, or at any rate reports in to the Beggarmasters at Thieves' House. We'll be new members, who've gone out by day, so it'll not be expected that the Night Beggarmaster and any night watchmen know our looks."

"But we don't look like beggars," Fafhrd protested. "Beggars have awful sores and limbs all a-twist or lacking altogether."

"That's just what I'm going to take care of now," the Mouser chuckled, drawing Scalpel. Ignoring Fafhrd's backward step and wary glance, the Mouser gazed puzzledly at the long tapering strip of steel he'd bared, then with a happy nod unclipped from his belt Scalpel's scabbard furbished with ratskin, sheathed the sword and swiftly wrapped it up, hilt and all, in a spiral, with the wide ribbon of a bandage roll dug from his sack.

"There!" he said, knotting the bandage ends. "Now I've a tapping cane."

"What's that?" Fafhrd demanded. "And why?"

"Because I'll be blind, that's why." He took a few shuffling steps, tapping the cobbles ahead with wrapped sword—gripping it by the quillons, or crossguard, so that the grip and pommel were up his sleeve—and groping ahead with his other hand. "That look all right to you?" he asked Fafhrd as he turned back. "Feels perfect to me. Bat-blind, eh? Oh, don't fret, Fafhrd—the rag's but gauze. I can see through it fairly well. Besides, I don't have to convince anyone inside Thieves' House I'm actually blind. Most Guild-beggars fake it, as you must know. Now what to do with you? Can't have you blind also—too obvious, might wake suspicion." He uncorked his jug and sucked inspiration. Fafhrd copied this action, on principle.

The Mouser smacked his lips and said, "I've got it! Fafhrd, stand on your right leg and double up your left behind you at the knee. Hold! Don't fall on me! Avaunt! But steady yourself by my shoulder. That's right. Now get that left foot higher. We'll disguise your sword like mine, for a crutch cane—it's thicker and'll look just right. You can also steady yourself with your other hand on my shoulder as you hop—the halt leading the blind, always good for a tear, always good theater! But higher with that left foot! No, it just doesn't come off—I'll have to rope it. But first unclip your scabbard."

Soon the Mouser had Graywand and its scabbard in the same state as Scalpel and was tying Fafhrd's left ankle to his thigh, drawing the rope cruelly tight, though Fafhrd's wine-anesthetized nerves hardly registered it. Balancing himself with his steel-cored crutch cane as the Mouser worked, he swigged from his jug and pondered deeply. Ever since joining forces with Vlana, he'd been interested in the theater, and the atmosphere of the actors' tenement had fired that interest further, so that he was delighted at the prospect of acting a part in real life. Yet brilliant as the Mouser's plan undoubtedly was, there did seem to be drawbacks to it. He tried to formulate them.

"Mouser," he said, "I don't know as I like having our swords tied up, so we can't draw 'em in emergency."

"We can still use 'em as clubs," the Mouser countered, his breath hissing between his teeth as he drew the last knot hard. "Besides, we'll have our knives. Say, pull your belt around until yours is behind your back, so your robe will hide it sure. I'll do the same with Cat's Claw. Beggars don't carry weapons, at least in view, and we must maintain dramatic consistency in every detail. Stop drinking now; you've had enough. I myself need only a couple swallows more to reach my finest pitch."

"And I don't know as I like going hobbled into that den of cutthroats. I can hop amazingly fast, it's true, but not as fast as I can run. Is it really wise, think you?"

"You can slash yourself loose in an instant," the Mouser hissed with a touch of impatience and anger. "Aren't you willing to make the least sacrifice for art's sake?"

"Oh, very well," Fafhrd said, draining his jug and tossing it aside. "Yes, of course I am."

"Your complexion's too hale," the Mouser said, inspecting him critically. He touched up Fafhrd's features and hands with pale gray greasepaint, then added wrinkles with dark. "And your garb's too tidy." He scooped dirt from between the cobbles and smeared it on Fafhrd's robe, then tried to put a rip in it, but the material resisted. He shrugged and tucked his lightened sack under his belt.

"So's yours," Fafhrd observed, and stooping on his right leg got a good handful of muck himself, ordure in it by its feel and stink. Heaving himself up with a mighty effort, he wiped the stuff off on the Mouser's cloak and gray silken jerkin too.

The small man got the odor and cursed, but, "Dramatic consistency," Fafhrd reminded him. "It's well we stink. Beggars do—that's one reason folk give 'em coins: to get rid of 'em. And no one at Thieves' House will be eager to inspect us close. Now come on, while our fires are still high." And grasping hold of the Mouser's shoulder, he propelled himself rapidly toward Cheap Street, setting his bandaged sword between cobbles well ahead and taking mighty hops.

"Slow down, idiot," the Mouser cried softly, shuffling along with the speed almost of a skater to keep up, while tapping his (sword) cane like mad. "A cripple's supposed to be *feeble*—that's what draws the sympathy."

Fafhrd nodded wisely and slowed somewhat. The ominous empty doorway slid again into view. The Mouser tilted his jug to get the last of his wine, swallowed awhile, then choked sputteringly. Fafhrd snatched and drained the jug, then tossed it over shoulder to shatter noisily.

They hop-shuffled into Cheap Street, halting almost at once for a richly clad man and woman to pass. The richness of the man's garb was sober and he was on the fat and oldish side, though hard-featured. A merchant doubtless, and with money in the Thieves' Guild—protection money, at least—to take this route at this hour.

The richness of the woman's garb was garish though not tawdry and she was beautiful and young, and looked still younger. A competent courtesan, almost certainly.

The man started to veer around the noisome and filthy pair, his face averted, but the girl swung toward the Mouser, concern growing in her eyes with hothouse swiftness. "Oh, you poor boy! Blind. What tragedy," she said. "Give us a gift for him, lover."

"Keep away from those stinkards, Misra, and come along," he retorted, the last of his speech vibrantly muffled, for he was holding his nose.

She made him no reply, but thrust white hand into his ermine pouch and swiftly pressed a coin against the Mouser's palm and closed his fingers on it, then took his head between her palms and kissed him sweetly on the lips before letting herself be dragged on.

"Take good care of the little fellow, old man," she called fondly back to Fafhrd while her companion grumbled muffled reproaches at her, of which only "perverted bitch" was intelligible.

The Mouser stared at the coin in his palm, then sneaked a long look after his benefactress. There was a dazed wonder in his voice as he whispered to Fafhrd, "Look. *Gold.* A golden coin and a beautiful woman's sympathy. Think you we should give over this rash project and for a profession take up beggary?"

"Buggery even, rather!" Fafhrd answered harsh and low. That "old man" rankled. "Onward we, bravely!"

They upped the two worn steps and went through the doorway, noting the exceptional thickness of the wall. Ahead was a long, straight, high-ceilinged corridor ending in a stairs and with doors spilling light at intervals and wall-set torches adding their flare, but empty all its length.

They had just got through the doorway when cold steel chilled the neck and pricked a shoulder of each of them. From just above, two voices commanded in unison, "Halt!"

Although fired—and fuddled—by fortified wine, they each had wit enough to freeze and then very cautiously look upward.

Two gaunt, scarred, exceptionally ugly faces, each topped by a gaudy scarf binding back hair, looked down at them from a big, deep niche just above the doorway and helping explain its lowness. Two bent, gnarly arms thrust down the swords that still pricked them.

"Gone out with the noon beggar-batch, eh?" one of them observed. "Well, you'd better have a high take to justify your tardy return. The Night Beggarmaster's on a Whore Street furlough. Report above to Krovas. Gods, you stink! Better clean up first, or Krovas will have you bathed in live steam. Begone!"

The Mouser and Fafhrd shuffled and hobbled forward at their most authentic. One niche-guard cried after them, "Relax, boys! You don't have to put it on here."

"Practice makes perfect," the Mouser called back in a quavering voice. Fafhrd's finger-ends dug his shoulder warningly. They moved along somewhat more naturally, so far as Fafhrd's tied-up leg allowed.

"Gods, what an easy life the Guild-beggars have," the other niche-guard observed to his mate. "What slack discipline and low standards of skill! Perfect, my sacred butt! You'd think a child could see through those disguises."

"Doubtless some children do," his mate retorted. "But their dear mothers and fathers only drop a tear and a coin or give a kick. Grown folk go blind, lost in their toil and dreams, unless they have a profession such as thieving which keeps them mindful of things as they really are."

Resisting the impulse to ponder this sage philosophy, and glad they would not have to undergo a Beggarmaster's shrewd inspection—truly, thought Fafhrd, Kos of the Dooms seemed to be leading him direct to Krovas and perhaps head-chopping *would* be the order of the night—he and the Mouser went watchfully and slowly on. And now they began to hear voices, mostly curt and clipped ones, and other noises.

They passed some doorways they'd liked to have paused at, to study the activities inside, yet the most they dared do was slow down a bit more. Fortunately most of the doorways were wide, permitting a fairly long view.

Very interesting were some of those activities. In one room young boys were being trained to pick pouches and slit purses. They'd approach from behind an instructor, and if he heard scuff of bare foot or felt touch of dipping hand—or, worst, heard *clunk* of dropped leaden mock-coin—that boy would be thwacked. Others seemed to be getting training in group-tactics: the jostle in front, the snatch from behind, the swift passing of lifted items from youthful thief to confederate.

In a second room, from which pushed air heavy with the reeks of metal and oil, older student thieves were doing laboratory work in lock picking. One group was being lectured by a grimy-handed graybeard, who was taking apart a most complex lock piece by weighty piece. Others appeared to be having their skill, speed, and ability to work soundlessly tested—they were probing with slender picks the keyholes in a half dozen doors set side-by-side in an otherwise purposeless partition, while a supervisor holding a sandglass watched them keenly.

In a third, thieves were eating at long tables. The odors were tempting, even to men full of booze. The Guild did well by its members.

In a fourth, the floor was padded in part and instruction was going on in slipping, dodging, ducking, tumbling, tripping, and otherwise foiling pursuit. These students were older too. A voice like a sergeant-major's rasped, "Nah, nah, nah! You couldn't give your crippled grandmother the slip. I said duck, not genuflect to holy Aarth. Now this time—"

"Grif's used grease," an instructor called.

"He has, eh? To the front, Grif!" the rasping voice replied as the Mouser and Fafhrd moved somewhat regretfully out of sight, for they realized much was to be learned here: tricks that might stand them in good stead even tonight. "Listen, all of you!" the rasping voice continued, so far-carrying it followed them a surprisingly long way. "Grease may be very well on a night job—by day its glisten shouts its user's profession to all Nehwon! But in any case it makes a thief overconfident. He comes to depend on it and then in a pinch he finds he's forgot to apply it. Also its aroma can betray him. Here we work always dry-skinned—save for natural sweat!—as all of you were told first night. Bend over, Grif. Grasp your ankles. Straighten your knees."

More thwacks, followed by yelps of pain, distant now, since the Mouser and Fafhrd were halfway up the end-stairs, Fafhrd vaulting somewhat laboriously as he grasped curving banister and swaddled sword.

The second floor duplicated the first, but was as luxurious as the other had been bare. Down the long corridor lamps and filagreed incense pots pendant from the ceiling alternated, diffusing a mild light and spicy smell. The walls were richly draped, the floor thick-carpeted. Yet this corridor was empty too and, moreover, *completely* silent. After a glance at each other, they started off boldly.

The first door, wide open, showed an untenanted room full of racks of garments, rich and plain, spotless and filthy, also wig stands, shelves of beards and such, and several wall mirrors faced by small tables crowded with cosmetics and with stools before them. A disguising room, clearly.

After a look and listen either way, the Mouser darted in and out to snatch up a large green flask from the nearest table. He unstoppered and sniffed it. A rotten-sweet gardenia-reek contended with the nose-sting of spirits of wine. The Mouser sloshed his and Fafhrd's fronts with his dubious perfume.

"Antidote to ordure," he explained with the pomp of a physician, stoppering the flask. "Don't want to be parboiled by Krovas. No, no, no."

Two figures appeared at the far end of the corridor and came toward them. The Mouser hid the flask under his cloak, holding it between elbow and side, and he and Fafhrd continued onward—to turn back would look suspicious, both drunkenly judged.

The next three doorways they passed were shut by heavy doors. As they neared the fifth, the two approaching figures, coming on arm-in-arm, yet taking long strides, moving more swiftly than the hobble-shuffle, became distinct. Their clothing was that of noblemen, but their faces those of thieves. They were frowning with indignation and suspicion too at the Mouser and Fafhrd.

Just then—from somewhere between the two man-pairs, it sounded—a voice began to speak words in a strange tongue, using the rapid monotone priests employ in a routine service, or some sorcerers in their incantations.

The two richly clad thieves slowed at the seventh doorway and looked in. Their progress ceased altogether. Their necks strained, their eyes widened. They visibly paled. Then of a sudden they hastened onward, almost running, and bypassed Fafhrd and the Mouser as if they were furniture. The incantatory voice drummed on without missing a beat.

The fifth doorway was shut, but the sixth was open. The Mouser peeked in with one eye, his nose brushing the jamb. Then he stepped forward and gazed inside with entranced expression, pushing the black rag up onto his forehead for better vision. Fafhrd joined him.

It was a large room, empty so far as could be told of human and animal life, but filled with most interesting things. From knee-height up, the entire far wall was a map of the city of Lankhmar and its immediate surrounds. Every building and street seemed depicted, down to the meanest hovel and narrowest court. There were signs of recent erasure and redrawing at many spots, and here and there little colored hieroglyphs of mysterious import.

The floor was marble, the ceiling blue as lapis lazuli. The side walls were thickly hung, by ring and padlock. One was covered with all manner of thieves' tools, from a huge thick pry-bar that looked as if it could unseat the universe, or at least the door of the overlord's treasure-vault, to a rod so slim it might be an elf-queen's wand and seemingly designed to telescope out and fish from distance for precious gauds on milady's spindle-legged, ivory-topped vanity table; the other wall had on it all sorts of quaint, gold-gleaming and jewel-flashing objects, evidently mementos chosen for their oddity from the spoils of memorable burglaries, from a female mask of thin gold, breathlessly beautiful in its features and contours, but thickly set with rubies simulating the spots of the pox in its fever-stage, to a knife whose blade was wedge-shaped diamonds set side by side and this diamond cutting-edge looking razor-sharp.

All about were tables set chiefly with models of dwelling houses and other buildings, accurate to the last minutia, it looked, of ventilation hole under roof gutter and ground-level drain hole, of creviced wall and smooth. Many were cut away in partial or entire section to show the layout of rooms, closets, strongrooms, doorways, corridors, secret passages, smoke-ways, and air-ways in equal detail.

In the center of the room was a bare round-table of ebony and ivory squares. About it were set seven straight-backed but well-padded chairs, the one facing the map and away from the Mouser and Fafhrd being higher backed and wider armed than the others—a chief's chair, likely that of Krovas.

The Mouser tiptoed forward, irresistibly drawn, but Fafhrd's left hand clamped down on his shoulder like the iron mitten of a Mingol cataphract and drew him irresistibly back.

Scowling his disapproval, the Northerner brushed down the black rag over the Mouser's eyes again, and with his crutch-hand thumbed ahead; then set off in that direction in most carefully calculated, silent hops. With a shrug of disappointment the Mouser followed.

As soon as they had turned away from the doorway, but before they were out of sight, a neatly black-bearded, crop-haired head came like a serpent's around the side of the highest-backed chair and gazed after them from deep-sunken yet glinting eyes. Next a snake-supple, long hand followed the head out, crossed thin lips with ophidian forefinger for silence, and then finger-beckoned the two pairs of dark-tunicked men who were standing to either side of the doorway, their backs to the corridor wall, each of the four gripping a curvy knife in one hand and a dark leather, lead-weighted bludgeon in the other.

When Fafhrd was halfway to the seventh doorway, from which the monotonous yet sinister recitation continued to well, there shot out through it a slender, whey-faced youth, his narrow hands clapped over his mouth, under terror-wide eyes, as if to shut in screams or vomit, and with a broom clamped in an armpit, so that he seemed a bit like a young warlock about to take to the air. He dashed past Fafhrd and the Mouser and away, his racing footsteps sounding rapid-dull on the carpeting and hollow-sharp on the stairs before dying away.

Fafhrd gazed back at the Mouser with a grimace and shrug, then squatting one-legged until the knee of his bound-up leg touched the floor, advanced half his face past the doorjamb. After a bit, without otherwise changing position, he beckoned the Mouser to approach. The latter slowly thrust half his face past the jamb, just above Fafhrd's.

What they saw was a room somewhat smaller than that of the great map and lit by central lamps that burned blue-white instead of customary yellow. The floor was marble, darkly colorful and complexly whorled. The dark walls were hung with astrological and anthropomantic charts and instruments of magic and shelved with cryptically labeled porcelain jars and also with vitreous flasks and glass pipes of the oddest shapes, some filled with colored fluids, but many gleamingly empty. At the foot of the walls, where the shadows were thickest, broken and discarded stuff was irregularly heaped, as if swept out of the way and forgot, and here and there opened a large rathole.

In the center of the room and brightly illuminated by contrast was a long table with thick top and many stout legs. The Mouser thought fleetingly of a centipede and then of the bar at the Eel, for the tabletop was densely stained and scarred by many a spilled elixir and many a deep black burn by fire or acid or both.

In the midst of the table an alembic was working. The lamp's flame—deep blue, this one—kept a-boil in the large crystal cucurbit a dark, viscid fluid with here and there diamond glints. From out of the thick, seething stuff, strands of a darker vapor streamed upward to crowd through the cucurbit's narrow mouth and stain—oddly, with bright scarlet—the transparent head and then, dead black now, flow down the narrow pipe from the head into a spherical crystal receiver, larger even than the cucurbit, and there curl and weave about like so many coils of living black cord—an endless, skinny, ebon serpent.

Behind the left end of the table stood a tall, yet hunchbacked man in black robe and hood, which shadowed more than hid a face of which the most prominent features were a long, thick, pointed nose with outjutting, almost chinless mouth just below. His complexion was sallow-gray like clay and a short-haired, bristly, gray beard grew high on his wide cheeks. From under a receding forehead and bushy gray brows, wide-set eyes looked intently down at an age-browned scroll, which his disgustingly small clubhands, knuckles big, short backs gray-bristled, ceaselessly unrolled and rolled up again. The only move his eyes ever made, besides the short side-to-side one as he read the lines he was rapidly intoning, was an occasional farther sidewise glance at the alembic.

On the other end of the table, beady eyes darting from the sorcerer to the alembic and back again, crouched a small black beast, the first glimpse of which made Fafhrd dig fingers painfully into the Mouser's shoulder and the latter almost gasp, not from the pain. It was most like a rat, yet it had a higher forehead and closer-set eyes than either had ever seen in a rat, while its forepaws, which it constantly rubbed together in what seemed restless glee, looked like tiny copies of the sorcerer's clubhands.

Simultaneously yet independently, Fafhrd and the Mouser each became certain it was the beast which had gutter-escorted Slivikin and his mate, then fled, and each recalled what Ivrian had said about a witch's familiar and Vlana about the likelihood of Krovas employing a warlock.

What with the ugliness of the clubhanded man and beast and between them the ropy black vapor coiling and twisting in the great receiver and head, like a black umbilical cord, it was a most horrid sight. And the similarities, save for size, between the two creatures were even more disquieting in their implications.

The tempo of the incantation quickened, the blue-white flames brightened and hissed audibly, the fluid in the cucurbit grew thick as lava, great bubbles formed and loudly broke, the black rope in the receiver writhed like a nest of snakes; there was an increasing sense of invisible presences, the supernatural tension grew almost unendurable, and Fafhrd and the Mouser were hard put to keep silent the open-mouthed gasps by which they now breathed, and each feared his heartbeat could be heard cubits away.

Abruptly the incantation peaked and broke off, like a drum struck very hard, then instantly silenced by palm and fingers outspread against the head. With a bright flash and dull explosion, cracks innumerable appeared in the cucurbit; its crystal became white and opaque, yet it did not shatter or drip. The head lifted a span, hung there, fell back. While two black nooses appeared among the coils in the receiver and suddenly narrowed until they were only two big black knots.

The sorcerer grinned, rolling up the end of the parchment with a snap, and shifted his gaze from the receiver to his familiar, while the latter chittered shrilly and bounded up and down in rapture.

"Silence, Slivikin! Comes now your time to race and strain and sweat," the sorcerer cried, speaking pidgin Lankhamarese now, but so rapidly and in so squeakingly high-pitched a voice that Fafhrd and the Mouser could barely follow him. They did, however, both realize they had been completely mistaken as to the identity of Slivikin. In moment of disaster, the fat thief had called to the witchbeast for help rather than to his human comrade.

"Yes, master," Slivikin squeaked back no less clearly, in an instant revising the Mouser's opinions about talking animals. He continued in the same fifelike, fawning tones, "Harkening in obedience, Hristomilo."

Now they knew the sorcerer's name too.

Hristomilo ordered in whiplash pipings, "To your appointed work! See to it you summon an ample sufficiency of feasters! I want the bodies stripped to skeletons, so the bruises of the enchanted smog and all evidence of death by suffocation will be vanished utterly. But forget not the loot! On your mission, now—depart!"

Slivikin, who at every command had bobbed his head in manner reminiscent of his bouncing, now squealed, "I'll see it done!" and gray-lightning-like leaped a long leap to the floor and down an inky rathole.

Hristomilo, rubbing together his disgusting clubhands much as Slivikin had his, cried chucklingly, "What Slevyas lost, my magic has rewon!"

Fafhrd and the Mouser drew back out of the doorway, partly with the thought that since neither his incantation and his alembic, nor his familiar now required his unblinking attention, Hristomilo would surely look up and spot them; partly in revulsion from what they had seen and heard; and in poignant if useless pity for Slevyas, whoever he might be, and for the other unknown victims of the ratlike and conceivably rat-related sorcerer's death-spells, poor strangers already dead and due to have their flesh eaten from their bones.

Fafhrd wrested the green bottle from the Mouser and, though almost gagging on the rotten-flowery reek, gulped a large, stinging mouthful. The Mouser couldn't quite bring himself to do the same, but was comforted by the spirits of wine he inhaled during this byplay.

Then he saw, beyond Fafhrd, standing before the doorway to the map room, a richly clad man with gold-hilted knife jewel-scabbarded at his side. His sunken-eyed face was prematurely wrinkled by responsibility, overwork, and authority, and framed by neatly cropped black hair and beard. Smiling, he silently beckoned them.

The Mouser and Fafhrd obeyed, the latter returning the green bottle to the former, who recapped it and thrust it under his left elbow with well-concealed irritation.

Each guessed their summoner was Krovas, the Guild's Grandmaster. Once again Fafhrd marveled, as he hobbledehoyed along, reeling and belching, how Kos or the Fates were guiding him to his target tonight. The Mouser, more alert and more apprehensive too, was reminding himself that they had been directed by the niche-guards to report to Krovas, so that the situation, if not developing quite in accord with his own misty plans, was still not deviating disastrously.

Yet not even his alertness, nor Fafhrd's primeval instincts, gave him forewarning as they followed Korvas into the map room.

Two steps inside, each of them was shoulder-grabbed and bludgeon-menaced by a pair of ruffians further armed with knives tucked in their belts.

They judged it wise to make no resistance, on this one occasion at least bearing out the Mouser's mouthings about the supreme caution of drunken men.

"All secure, Grandmaster," one of the ruffians rapped out.

Krovas swung the highest-backed chair around and sat down, eyeing them cooly yet searchingly.

"What brings two stinking, drunken beggar-Guildsmen into the top-restricted precincts of the masters?" he asked quietly.

The Mouser felt the sweat of relief bead his forehead. The disguises he had brilliantly conceived were still working, taking in even the head man, though he had spotted Fafhrd's tipsiness. Resuming his blind-man manner, he quavered, "We were directed by the guard above the Cheap Street door to report to you in person, great Krovas, the Night Beggarmaster being on furlough for reasons of sexual hygiene. Tonight we've made good haul!" And fumbling in his purse, ignoring as far as possible the tightened grip on his shoulders, he brought out the golden coin given him by the sentimental courtesan and displayed it tremble-handed.

"Spare me your inexpert acting," Krovas said sharply. "I'm not one of your marks. And take that rag off your eyes."

The Mouser obeyed and stood to attention again insofar as his pinioning would permit, and smiling the more seeming carefree because of his reawakening uncertainties. Conceivably he wasn't doing quite as brilliantly as he'd thought.

Krovas leaned forward and said placidly yet piercingly, "Granted you were so ordered—and most improperly so; that door-guard will suffer for his stupidity!—why were you spying into a room beyond this one when I spotted you?"

"We saw brave thieves flee from that room," the Mouser answered pat. "Fearing that some danger threatened the Guild, my comrade and I investigated, ready to scotch it."

"But what we saw and heard only perplexed us, great sir," Fafhrd appended quite smoothly.

"I didn't ask you, sot. Speak when you're spoken to," Krovas snapped at him. Then, to the Mouser, "You're an overweening rogue, most presumptuous for your rank."

In a flash the Mouser decided that further insolence, rather than fawning, was what the situation required. "That I am, sir," he said smugly. "For example, I have a master plan whereby you and the Guild might gain more wealth and power in three months than your predecessors have in three millennia."

Krovas' face darkened. "Boy!" he called. Through the curtains of an inner doorway, a youth with dark complexion of a Kleshite and clad only in a black loincloth sprang to kneel before Krovas, who ordered, "Summon first my sorcerer, next the thieves Slevyas and Fissif," whereupon the dark youth dashed into the corridor.

Then Krovas, his face its normal pale again, leaned back in his great chair, lightly rested his sinewy arms on its great padded ones, and smilingly directed the Mouser, "Speak your piece. Reveal to us this master plan."

Forcing his mind *not* to work on the surprising news that Slevyas was not victim but thief and not sorcery-slain but alive and available—why did Krovas want him *now?*—the Mouser threw back his head and, shaping his lips in a faint sneer, began, "You may laugh merrily at me, Grandmaster, but I'll warrant that in less than a score of heartbeats you'll be straining sober-faced to hear my least word. Like lightning, wit can strike anywhere, and the best of you in Lankhmar have age-honored blind spots for things obvious to us of outland birth. My master plan is but this: let Thieves' Guild under your iron autocracy seize supreme power in Lankhmar City, then in Lankhmar Land, next over all Nehwon, after which who knows what realms undreamt will know your suzerainty!"

The Mouser had spoken true in one respect: Krovas was no longer smiling. He was leaning forward a little and his face was darkening again, but whether from interest or anger it was too soon to say.

The Mouser continued, "For centuries the Guild's had more than the force and intelligence needed to make a *coup d'état* a nine-finger certainty; today there's not one hair's chance in a bushy head of failure. It is the proper state of things that thieves rule other men. All Nature cries out for it. No need slay old Karstak Ovartamortes, merely overmaster, control, and so rule through him. You've already fee'd informers in every noble or wealthy house. Your post's better than the King of Kings'. You've a mercenary striking force permanently mobilized, should you have need of it, in the Slayers' Brotherhood. We Guild-beggars are your foragers. O great Krovas, the multitudes know that thievery rules Nehwon, nay, the universe, nay, more, the highest gods' abode! And the multitudes accept this, they balk only at the hypocrisy of the present arrangement, at the pretense that things are otherwise. Oh, give them their decent desire, great Krovas! Make it all open, honest and aboveboard, with thieves ruling in name as well as fact."

The Mouser spoke with passion, for the moment believing all he said, even the contradictions. The four ruffians gaped at him with wonder and not a little awe. They slackened their holds on him and on Fafhrd too.

But leaning back in his great chair again and smiling thinly and ominously, Krovas said coolly, "In *our* Guild intoxication is no excuse for folly, rather grounds for the extremest penalty. But I'm well aware you organized beggars operate under a laxer discipline. So I'll deign to explain to you, you wee drunken dreamer, that we thieves know well that, behind the scenes, we already rule Lankhmar, Nehwon, all life in sooth—for what is life but greed in action? But to make this an open thing would not only force us to take on ten thousand sorts of weary work others now do for us, it would also go against another of life's deep laws: illusion. Does the sweetmeats hawker show you his kitchen? Does a whore let average client watch her enamel-over her wrinkles and hoist her sagging breasts in cunning gauzy slings? Does a conjuror turn out for you his hidden pockets? Nature works by subtle, secret means—man's invisible seed, spider bite, the viewless spores of madness and of death, rocks that are born in earth's unknown bowels, the silent stars a-creep across the sky—and we thieves copy her."

"That's good enough poetry, sir," Fafhrd responded with undertone of angry derision, for he had himself been considerably impressed by the Mouser's master plan and was irked that Krovas should do insult to his new friend by disposing of it so lightly. "Closet kingship may work well enough in easy times. But"—he paused histrionically—"will it serve when Thieves' Guild is faced with an enemy determined to obliterate it forever, a plot to wipe it entirely from the earth?"

"What drunken babble's this?" Krovas demanded, sitting up straight. "*What* plot?"

" 'Tis a most *secret* one," Fafhrd responded grinning, delighted to pay this haughty man in his own coin and thinking it quite just that the thief-king sweat a little before his head was removed for conveyance to Vlana. "I know naught of it, except that many a master thief is marked down for the knife—and your head doomed to fall!"

Fafhrd merely sneered his face and folded his arms, the still slack grip of his captors readily permitting it, his (sword) crutch hanging against his body from his lightly gripping hand. Then he scowled as there came a sudden shooting pain in his numbed, bound-up left leg, which he had forgotten for a space.

Krovas raised a clenched fist and himself half out of his chair, in prelude to some fearsome command—likely that Fafhrd be tortured. The Mouser cut in hurriedly with, "The Secret Seven, they're called, are its leaders. None in the outer circles of the conspiracy know their names, though rumor has it that they're secret Guild-thief renegades representing, one for each, the cities of Oool Hrusp, Kvarch Nar, Ilthmar, Horborixen, Tisilinilit, far Kiraay and Lankhmar's very self. It's thought they're moneyed by the merchants of the East, the priests of Wan, the sorcerers of the Steppes and half the Mingol leadership too, legended Quarmall, Aaarth's Assassins in Sarheenmar, and also no lesser man than the King of Kings."

Despite Krovas' contemptuous and then angry remarks, the ruffians holding the Mouser continued to harken to their captive with interest and respect, and they did not retighten their grip on him. His colorful revelations and melodramatic delivery held them, while Krovas' dry, cynical, philosophic observations largely went over their heads.

Hristomilo came gliding into the room then, his feet presumably taking swift, but very short steps, at any rate his black robe hung undisturbed to the marble floor despite his slithering speed.

There was a shock at his entrance. All eyes in the map room followed him, breaths were held, and the Mouser and Fafhrd felt the horny hands that gripped them shake just a little. Even Krovas' all-confident, world-weary expression became tense and guardedly uneasy. Clearly the sorcerer of the Thieves' Guild was more feared than loved by his chief employer and by the beneficiaries of his skills.

Outwardly oblivious to this reaction to his appearance, Hristomilo, smiling thin-lipped, halted close to one side of Krovas' chair and inclined his hood-shadowed rodent face in the ghost of a bow.

Krovas held palm toward the Mouser for silence. Then, wetting his lips, he asked Hristomilo sharply yet nervously, "Do you know these two?"

Hristomilo nodded decisively. "They just now peered a befuddled eye each at me," he said, "whilst I was about that business we spoke of. I'd have shooed them off, reported them, save such action might have broken my spell, put my words out of time with the alembic's workings. The one's a Northerner, the other's features have a southern cast—from Tovilyis or near, most like. Both younger than their now-looks. Free-lance bravos, I'd judge 'em, the sort the Brotherhood hires as extras when they get at once several big guard and escort jobs. Clumsily disguised now, of course, as beggars."

Fafhrd by yawning, the Mouser by pitying headshake tried to convey that all this was so much poor guesswork.

"That's all I can tell you without reading their minds," Hristomilo concluded. "Shall I fetch my lights and mirrors?"

"Not yet." Krovas turned face and shot a finger at the Mouser. "How do you know these things you rant about?—Secret Seven and all. Straight simplest answer now—no rodomontades."

The Mouser replied most glibly: "There's a new courtesan dwells on Pimp Street—Tyarya her name, tall, beauteous, but hunchbacked, which oddly delights many of her clients. Now Tyarya loves me 'cause my maimed eyes match her twisted spine, or from simply pity of my blindness—*she* believes it!—and youth, or from some odd itch, like her clients' for her, which that combination arouses in her flesh.

"Now one of her patrons, a trader newly come from Klelg Nar—Mourph, he's called—was impressed by my intelligence, strength, boldness, and close-mouthed tact, and those same qualities in my comrade too. Mourph sounded us out, finally asking if we hated the Thieves' Guild for its control of the Beggars' Guild. Sensing a chance to aid the Guild, we played up, and a week ago he recruited us into a cell of three in the outermost strands of the conspiracy web of the Seven."

"You presumed to do all of this on your own?" Krovas demanded in freezing tones, sitting up straight and gripping hard the chair arms.

"Oh, no," the Mouser denied guilelessly. "We reported our every act to the Day Beggarmaster and he approved them, told us to spy our best and gather every scrap of fact and rumor we could about the Sevens' conspiracy."

"And he told me not a word about it!" Krovas rapped out. "If true, I'll have Bannat's head for this! But you're lying, aren't you?"

As the Mouser gazed with wounded eyes at Krovas, meanwhile preparing a most virtuous denial, a portly man limped past the doorway with help of a gilded staff. He moved with silence and aplomb.

But Krovas saw him. "Night Beggarmaster!" he called sharply. The limping man stopped, turned, came crippling majestically through the door. Krovas stabbed finger at the Mouser, then Fafhrd. "Do you know these two, Flim?"

The Night Beggarmaster unhurriedly studied each for a space, then shook his head with its turban of cloth of gold. "Never seen either before. What are they? Fink beggars?"

"But Flim wouldn't know us," the Mouser explained desperately, feeling everything collapsing in on him and Fafhrd. "All our contacts were with Bannat alone."

Flim said quietly, "Bannat's been abed with the swamp ague this past ten-day. Meanwhile *I* have been Day Beggarmaster as well as Night."

At that moment Slevyas and Fissif came hurrying in behind Flim. The tall thief bore on his jaw a bluish lump. The fat thief's head was bandaged above his darting eyes. He pointed quickly at Fafhrd and the Mouser and cried, "There are the two that slugged us, took our Jengao loot, and slew our escort."

The Mouser lifted his elbow and the green bottle crashed to shards at his feet on the hard marble. Gardenia-reek sprang swiftly through the air.

But more swiftly still the Mouser, shaking off the careless hold of his startled guards, sprang toward Krovas, clubbing his wrapped-up sword. If he could only overpower the King of Thieves and hold Cat's Claw at his throat, he'd be able to bargain for his and Fafhrd's lives. That is, unless the other thieves wanted their master killed, which wouldn't surprise him at all.

With startling speed Flim thrust out his gilded staff, tripping the Mouser, who went heels over head, midway seeking to change his involuntary somersault into a voluntary one.

Meanwhile Fafhrd lurched heavily against his left-hand captor, at the same time swinging bandaged Graywand strongly upward to strike his right-hand captor under the jaw. Regaining his one-legged balance with a mighty contortion, he hopped for the loot-wall behind him.

Slevyas made for the wall of thieves' tools, and with a muscle-cracking effort wrenched the great pry-bar from its padlocked ring.

Scrambling to his feet after a poor landing in front of Krovas' chair, the Mouser found it empty and the Thief King in a half-crouch behind it, gold-hilted dagger drawn, deep-sunk eyes coldly battle-wild. Spinning around, he saw Fafhrd's guards on the floor, the one sprawled senseless, the other starting to scramble up, while the great Northerner, his back against the wall of weird jewelry, menaced the whole room with wrapped-up Graywand and with his long knife, jerked from its scabbard behind him.

Likewise drawing Cat's Claw, the Mouser cried in trumpet voice of battle, "Stand aside, all! He's gone mad! I'll hamstring his good leg for you!" And racing through the press and between his own two guards, who still appeared to hold him in some awe, he launched himself with flashing dirk at Fafhrd, praying that the Northerner, drunk now with battle as well as wine and poisonous perfume, would recognize him and guess his stratagem.

Graywand slashed well above his ducking head. His new friend not only guessed, but was playing up—and not just missing by accident, the Mouser hoped. Stooping low by the wall, he cut the lashings on Fafhrd's left leg. Graywand and Fafhrd's long knife continued to spare him. Springing up, he headed for the corridor, crying overshoulder to Fafhrd, "Come on!"

Hristomilo stood well out of his way, quietly observing. Fissif scuttled toward safety. Krovas stayed behind his chair, shouting, "Stop them! Head them off!"

The three remaining ruffian guards, at last beginning to recover their fighting-wits, gathered to oppose the Mouser. But menacing them with swift feints of his dirk, he slowed them and darted between—and then just in the nick of time knocked aside with a downsweep of wrapped-up Scalpel Flim's gilded staff, thrust once again to trip him.

All this gave Slevyas time to return from the tools-wall and aim at the Mouser a great swinging blow with the massive pry-bar. But even as that blow started, a very long, bandaged sword on a very long arm thrust over the Mouser's shoulder and solidly and heavily poked Slevyas high on the chest, jolting him backward, so that the pry-bar's swing was short and whistled past harmlessly.

Then the Mouser found himself in the corridor and Fafhrd beside him, though for some weird reason still only hopping. The Mouser pointed toward the stairs. Fafhrd nodded, but delayed to reach high, still on one leg only, and rip off the nearest wall a dozen cubits of heavy drapes, which he threw across the corridor to baffle pursuit.

They reached the stairs and started up the next flight, the Mouser in advance. There were cries behind, some muffled.

"Stop hopping, Fafhrd!" the Mouser ordered querulously. "You've got two legs again."

"Yes, and the other's still dead," Fafhrd complained. "Ahh! Now feeling begins to return to it."

A thrown knife whisked between them and dully clinked as it hit the wall point-first and stone-powder flew. Then they were around the bend.

Two more empty corridors, two more curving flights, and then they saw above them on the last landing a stout ladder mounting to a dark, square hole in the roof. A thief with hair bound back by a colorful handkerchief—it appeared to be a door-guards identification—menaced the Mouser with drawn sword, but when he saw that there were two of them, both charging him determinedly with shining knives and strange staves or clubs, he turned and ran down the last empty corridor.

The Mouser, followed closely by Fafhrd, rapidly mounted the ladder and without pause vaulted up through the hatch into the star-crusted night.

He found himself near the unrailed edge of a slate roof which slanted enough to have made it look most fearsome to a novice roof-walker, but safe as houses to a veteran.

Crouched on the long peak of the roof was another kerchiefed thief holding a dark lantern. He was rapidly covering and uncovering, presumably in some code, the lantern's bull's eye, whence shot a faint green beam north to where a red point of light winked dimly in reply—as far away as the sea wall, it looked, or perhaps the masthead of a ship beyond, riding in the Inner Sea. Smuggler?

Seeing the Mouser, this one instantly drew sword and, swinging the lantern a little in his other hand, advanced menacingly. The Mouser eyed him warily—the dark lantern with its hot metal, concealed flame, and store of oil would be a tricky weapon.

But then Fafhrd had clambered out and was standing beside the Mouser, on both feet again at last. Their adversary backed slowly away toward the north end of the roof ridge. Fleetingly the Mouser wondered if there was another hatch there.

Turning back at a bumping sound, he saw Fafhrd prudently hoisting the ladder. Just as he got it free, a knife flashed up close past him out of the hatch. While following its flight, the Mouser frowned, involuntarily admiring the skill required to hurl a knife vertically with any accuracy.

It clattered down near them and slid off the roof. The Mouser loped south across the slates and was halfway from the hatch to that end of the roof when the faint chink came of the knife striking the cobbles of Murder Alley.

Fafhrd followed more slowly, in part perhaps from a lesser experience of roofs, in part because he still limped a bit to favor his left leg, and in part because he was carrying the heavy ladder balanced on his right shoulder.

"We won't need that," the Mouser called back.

Without hesitation Fafhrd heaved it joyously over the edge. By the time it crashed in Murder Alley, the Mouser was leaping down two yards and across a gap of one to the next roof, of opposite and lesser pitch. Fafhrd landed beside him.

The Mouser led them at almost a run through a sooty forest of chimneys, chimney pots, ventilators with tails that made them always face the wind, black-legged cisterns, hatch covers, bird houses, and pigeon traps across five roofs, four progressively a little lower, the fifth regaining a yard of the altitude they'd lost—the spaces between the buildings easy to leap, none more than three yards, no ladder-bridge required, and only one roof with a somewhat greater pitch than that of Thieves' House—until they reached the Street of the Thinkers at a point where it was crossed by a roofed passageway much like the one at Rokkermas and Slaarg's.

While they crossed it at a crouching lope, something hissed close past them and clattered ahead. As they leaped down from the roof of the bridge, three more somethings hissed over their heads to clatter beyond. One rebounded from a square chimney almost to the Mouser's feet. He picked it up, expecting a stone, and was surprised by the greater weight of a leaden ball big as two doubled-up fingers.

"They," he said, jerking thumb overshoulder, "lost no time in getting slingers on the roof. When roused, they're good."

Southeast then through another black chimney-forest to a point on Cheap Street where upper stories overhung the street so much on either side that it was easy to leap the gap. During this roof-traverse, an advancing front of night-smog, dense enough to make them cough and wheeze, had engulfed them and for perhaps sixty heartbeats the Mouser had had to slow to a shuffle and feel his way, Fafhrd's hand on his shoulder. Just short of Cheap Street they had come abruptly and completely out of the smog and seen the stars again, while the black front had rolled off northward behind them.

"Now what the devil was that?" Fafhrd had asked and the Mouser had shrugged.

A nighthawk would have seen a vast thick hoop of black night-smog blowing out in all directions from a center near the Silver Eel, growing ever greater and greater in diameter and circumferences.

East of Cheap Street the two comrades soon made their way to the ground, landing back in Plague Court behind the narrow premises of Nattick Nimblefingers the Tailor.

Then at last they looked at each other and their trammeled swords and their filthy faces and clothing made dirtier still by roof-soot, and they laughed and laughed and laughed, Fafhrd roaring still as he bent over to massage his left leg above and below knee. This hooting and wholly unaffected self-mockery continued while they unwrapped their swords—the Mouser as if his were a surprise package—and clipped their scabbards once more to their belts. Their exertions had burned out of them the last mote and atomy of strong wine and even stronger stenchful perfume, but they felt no desire whatever for more drink, only the urge to get home and eat hugely and guzzle hot, bitter gahveh, and tell their lovely girls at length the tale of their mad adventure.

They loped on side by side, at intervals glancing at each other and chuckling, though keeping a normally wary eye behind and before for pursuit or interception, despite their expecting neither.

Free of night-smog and drizzled with starlight, their cramped surroundings seemed much less stinking and oppressive than when they had set out. Even Ordure Boulevard had a freshness to it.

Only once for a brief space did they grow serious.

Fafhrd said, "You were a drunken idiot-genius indeed tonight, even if I was a drunken clodhopper. Lashing up my leg! Tying up our swords so we couldn't use 'em save as clubs!"

The Mouser shrugged. "Yet that sword-tying doubtless saved us from committing a number of murders tonight."

Fafhrd retorted, a little hotly, "Killing in fight isn't murder."

Again the Mouser shrugged. "Killing is murder, no matter what nice names you give. Just as eating is devouring, and drinking guzzling. Gods, I'm dry, famished, and fatigued! Come on, soft cushions, food, and steaming gahveh!"

They hastened up the long, creaking, broken-treaded stairs with an easy carefulness and when they were both on the porch, the Mouser shoved at the door to open it with surprise-swiftness.

It did not bulge.

"Bolted," he said to Fafhrd shortly. He noted now there was hardly any light at all coming through the cracks around the door, or noticeable through the lattices—at most, a faint orange-red glow. Then with sentimental grin and in a fond voice in which only the ghost of uneasiness lurked, he said, "They've gone to sleep, the unworrying wenches!" He knocked loudly thrice and then cupping his lips shouted softly at the door crack, "Hola, Ivrian! I'm home safe. Hail, Vlana! Your man's done you proud, felling Guild-thieves innumerable with one foot tied behind his back!"

There was no sound whatever from inside—that is, if one discounted a rustling so faint it was impossible to be sure of it.

Fafhrd was wrinkling his nostrils. "I smell smoke."

The Mouser banged on the door again. Still no response.

Fafhrd motioned him out of the way, hunching his big shoulder to crash the portal.

The Mouser shook his head and with a deft tap, slide, and tug removed a brick that a moment before had looked a firm-set part of the wall beside the door. He reached in all his arm. There was the scrape of a bolt being withdrawn, then another, then a third. He swiftly recovered his arm and the door swung fully inward at a touch.

But neither he nor Fafhrd rushed in at once, as both had intended to, for the indefinable scent of danger and the unknown came puffing out along with an increased reek of smoke and a slight sickening sweet scent that though female was no decent female perfume, and a musty-sour animal odor.

They could see the room faintly by the orange glow coming from the small oblong of the open door of the little, well-blacked stove. Yet the oblong did not sit properly upright but was unnaturally a-tilt; clearly the stove had been half overset and now leaned against a side wall of the fireplace, its small door fallen open in that direction.

By itself alone, that unnatural angle conveyed the entire impact of a universe overturned.

The orange glow showed the carpets oddly rucked up with here and there black circles a palm's breadth across, the neatly stacked candles scattered about below their shelves along with some of the jars and enameled boxes, and, above all, two black, low, irregular, longish heaps, the one by the fireplace, the other half on the golden couch, half at its foot.

From each heap there stared at the Mouser and Fafhrd innumerable pairs of tiny, rather widely set, furnace-red eyes.

On the thickly carpeted floor on the other side of the fireplace was a silver cobweb—a fallen silver cage, but no love birds sang from it.

There was a faint scrape of metal as Fafhrd made sure Graywand was loose in his scabbard.

As if that tiny sound had beforehand been chosen as the signal for attack, each instantly whipped out sword and they advanced side by side into the room, warily at first, testing the floor with each step.

At the screech of the swords being drawn, the tiny furnace-red eyes had winked and shifted restlessly, and now with the two men's approach they swiftly scattered pattering, pair by red pair, each pair at the forward end of a small, low, slender, hairless-tailed black body, and each making for one of the black circles in the rugs, where they vanished.

Indubitably the black circles were ratholes newly gnawed up through the floor and rugs, while the red-eyed creatures were black rats.

Fafhrd and the Mouser sprang forward, slashing and chopping at them in a frenzy, cursing and human-snarling besides.

They sundered few. The rats fled with preternatural swiftness, most of them disappearing down holes near the walls and the fireplace.

Also Fafhrd's first frantic chop went through the floor and on his third step with an ominous crack and splintering his leg plunged through the floor to his hip. The Mouser darted past him, unmindful of further crackings.

Fafhrd heaved out his trapped leg, not even noting the splinter-scratches it got and as unmindful as the Mouser of the continuing creakings. The rats were gone. He lunged after his comrade, who had thrust a bunch of kindlers into the stove, to make more light.

The horror was that, although the rats were all gone, the two longish heaps remained, although considerably diminished and, as now shown clearly by the yellow flames leaping from the tilted black door, changed in hue—no longer were the heaps red-beaded black, but a mixture of gleaming black and dark brown, a sickening purple-blue, violet and velvet black and ermine white, and the reds of stockings and blood and bloody flesh and bone.

Although hands and feet had been gnawed bone-naked, and bodies tunneled heart-deep, the two faces had been spared. That was not good, for they were the parts purple-blue from death by strangulation, lips drawn back, eyes bulging, all features contorted in agony. Only the black and very dark brown hair gleamed unchanged—that and the white, white teeth.

As each man stared down at his love, unable to look away despite the waves of horror and grief and rage washing higher and higher in him, each saw a tiny black strand uncurl from the black depression ringing each throat and drift off, dissipating, toward the open door behind them—two strands of night-smog.

With a crescendo of crackings the floor sagged fully three spans more in the center before arriving at a new temporary stability.

Edges of centrally tortured minds noted details: that Vlana's silver-hilted dagger skewered to the floor a rat, which, likely enough, overeager had approached too closely before the night-smog had done its magic work. That her belt and pouch were gone. That the blue-enameled box inlaid with silver, in which Ivrian had put the Mouser's share of the highjacked jewels, was gone too.

The Mouser and Fafhrd lifted to each other white, drawn faces which were quite mad, yet completely joined in understanding and purpose. No need to tell each other what must have happened here when the two nooses of black vapor had jerked tight in Hristomilo's receiver, or why Slivikin had bounced and squeaked in glee, or the significance of such phrases as "an ample sufficiency of feasters," or "forget not the loot," or "that business we spoke of." No need for Fafhrd to explain why he now stripped off his robe and hood, or why he jerked up Vlana's dagger, snapped the rat off it with a wrist-flick, and thrust it in his belt. No need for the Mouser to tell why he searched out a half dozen jars of oil and after smashing three of them in front of the flaming stove, paused, thought, and stuck the other three in the sack at his waist, adding to them the remaining kindlers and the fire-pot, brimmed with red coals, its top lashed down tight.

Then, still without word exchanged, the Mouser muffled his hand with a small rug and reaching into the fireplace deliberately tipped the flaming stove forward, so that it fell door-down on oil-soaked rugs. Yellow flames sprang up around him.

They turned and raced for the door. With louder crackings than any before, the floor collapsed. They desperately scrambled their way up a steep hill of sliding carpets and reached door and porch just before all behind them gave way and the flaming rugs and stove and all the firewood and candles and the golden couch and all the little tables and boxes and jars —and the unthinkably mutilated bodies of their first loves—cascaded into the dry, dusty, cobweb-choked room below, and the great flames of a cleansing or at least obliterating cremation began to flare upward.

They plunged down the stairs, which tore away from the wall and collapsed and dully crashed in the dark just as they reached the ground. They had to fight their way over the wreckage to get to Bones Alley.

By then flames were darting their bright lizard-tongues out of the shuttered attic windows and the boarded-up ones in the story just below. By the time they reached Plague Court, running side by side at top speed, the Silver Eel's fire-alarm was clanging cacophonously behind them.

They were still sprinting when they took the Death Alley fork. Then the Mouser grappled Fafhrd and forced him to a halt. The big man struck out, cursing insanely, and only desisted—his white face still a lunatic's—when the Mouser cried, panting, "Only ten heartbeats to arm us!"

He pulled the sack from his belt and, keeping tight hold of its neck, crashed it on the cobbles—hard enough to smash not only the bottles of oil, but also the fire-pot, for the sack was soon flaming a little at its base.

Then he drew gleaming Scalpel and Fafhrd Graywand and they raced on, the Mouser swinging his sack in a great circle beside him to fan its flames. It was a veritable ball of fire burning his left hand as they dashed across Cheap Street and into Thieves' House, and the Mouser, leaping high, swung it up into the great niche above the doorway and let go of it.

The niche-guards screeched in surprise and pain at the fiery invader of their hidey-hole and had no time to do anything with their swords, or whatever weapons else they had, against the other two invaders.

Student thieves poured out of the doors ahead at the screeching and foot-pounding, and then poured back as they saw the fierce point of flames and the two demon-faced oncomers brandishing their long, shining swords.

One skinny little apprentice—he could hardly have been ten years old—lingered too long. Graywand thrust him pitilessly through as his big eyes bulged and his small mouth gaped in horror and plea to Fafhrd for mercy.

Now from ahead of them there came a weird, wailing call, hollow and hair-raising, and doors began to thus shut instead of spewing forth the armed guards they almost prayed would appear to be skewered by their swords. Also, despite the long, bracketed torches looking newly renewed, the corridor was dark.

The reason for this last became clear as they plunged up the stairs. Strands of night-smog were appearing in the well, materializing from nothing or the air.

The strands grew longer and more numerous and tangible. They touched and clung nastily. In the corridor above they were forming from wall to wall and from ceiling to floor, like a gigantic cobweb, and were becoming so substantial that the Mouser and Fafhrd had to slash them to get through, or so their two maniac minds believed. The black web muffled a little a repetition of the eerie, wailing call, which came from the seventh door ahead and this time ended in a gleeful chittering and cackling insane as the emotions of the two attackers.

Here too doors were thudding shut. In an ephemeral flash of rationality, it occurred to the Mouser that it was not he and Fafhrd the thieves feared, for they had not been seen yet, but rather Hristomilo and his magic, even though working in defense of Thieves' House.

Even the map room, whence counter-attack would most likely erupt, was closed off by a huge oaken, iron-studded door.

They were now twice slashing black, clinging, rope-thick spiderweb for every single step they drove themselves forward. Midway between the map and magic rooms, there was forming on the inky web, ghostly at first but swiftly growing more substantial, a black spider big as a wolf.

The Mouser slashed heavy cobweb before it, dropped back two steps, then hurled himself at it in a high leap. Scalpel thrust through it, striking amidst its eight new-formed jet eyes, and it collapsed like a daggered bladder, loosing a vile stink.

Then he and Fafhrd were looking into the magic room, the alchemist's chamber. It was much as they had seen it before, except some things were doubled, or multiplied even further.

On the long table two blue-boiled cucurbits bubbled and roiled, their heads shooting out a solid, writhing rope more swiftly than moves the black swamp-cobra, which can run down a man—and not into twin receivers, but into the open air of the room (if any of the air in Thieves' House could have been called open then) to weave a barrier between their swords and Hristomilo, who once more stood tall though hunchbacked over his sorcerous, brown parchment, though this time his exultant gaze was chiefly fixed on Fafhrd and the Mouser, with only an occasional downward glance at the text of the spell he drummingly intoned.

At the other end of the table, in the web-free space, there bounced not only Slivikin, but also a huge rat matching him in size in all members except the head.

From the ratholes at the foot of the walls, red eyes glittered and gleamed in pairs.

With a bellow of rage Fafhrd began slashing at the black barrier, but the ropes were replaced from the cucurbit heads as swiftly as he sliced them, while the cut ends, instead of drooping slackly, now began to strain hungrily toward him like constrictive snakes or strangle-vines.

He suddenly shifted Graywand to his left hand, drew his long knife and hurled it at the sorcerer. Flashing toward its mark, it cut through three strands, was deflected and slowed by a fourth and fifth, almost halted by a sixth, and ended hanging futilely in the curled grip of a seventh.

Hristomilo laughed cacklingly and grinned, showing his huge upper incisors, while Slivikin chittered in ecstasy and bounded the higher.

The Mouser hurled Cat's Claw with no better result—worse, indeed, since his action gave two darting smog-strands time to curl hamperingly around his sword-hand and stranglingly around his neck. Black rats came racing out of the big holes at the cluttered base of the walls.

Meanwhile other strands snaked around Fafhrd's ankles, knees and left arm, almost toppling him. But even as he fought for balance, he jerked Vlana's dagger from his belt and raised it over his shoulder, its silver hilt glowing, its blade brown with dried rat's-blood.

The grin left Hristomilo's face as he saw it. The sorcerer screamed strangely and importuningly then and drew back from his parchment and the table, and raised clawed club-hands to ward off doom.

Vlana's dagger sped unimpeded through the black web—its strands even seemed to part for it—and betwixt the sorcerer's warding hands, to bury itself to the hilt in his right eye.

He screamed thinly in dire agony and clawed at his face.

The black web writhed as if in death spasm.

The cucurbits shattered as one, spilling their lava on the scarred table, putting out the blue flames even as the thick wood of the table began to smoke a little at the lava's edge. Lava dropped with *plops* on the dark marble floor.

With a faint, final scream Hristomilo pitched forward, hands still clutched to his eyes above his jutting nose, silver dagger-hilt still protruding between his fingers.

The web grew faint, like wet ink washed with a gush of clear water.

The Mouser raced forward and transfixed Slivikin and the huge rat with one thrust of Scalpel before the beasts knew what was happening. They too died swiftly with thin screams, while all the other rats turned tail and fled back down their holes swift almost as black lightning.

Then the last trace of night-smog or sorcery-smoke vanished and Fafhrd and the Mouser found themselves standing alone with three dead bodies and a profound silence that seemed to fill not only this room but all Thieves' House. Even the cucurbit-lava had ceased to move, was hardening, and the wood of the table no longer smoked.

Their madness was gone and all their rage too—vented to the last red atomy and glutted to more than satiety. They had no more urge to kill Krovas or any other of the thieves than to swat flies. With horrified inner eye Fafhrd saw the pitiful face of the child-thief he'd skewered in his lunatic anger.

Only their grief remained with them, diminished not one whit, but rather growing greater—that and an ever more swiftly growing revulsion from all that was around them: the dead, the disordered magic room, all Thieves' House, all of the city of Lankhmar to its last stinking alleyway and smog-wreathed spire.

With a hiss of disgust the Mouser jerked Scalpel from the rodent cadavers, wiped it on the nearest cloth, and returned it to its scabbard. Fafhrd likewise sketchily cleansed and sheathed Graywand. Then the two men picked up their knife and dirk from where they'd dropped to the floor when the web had dematerialized, though neither so much as glanced at Vlana's dagger where it was buried. But on the sorcerer's table they did notice Vlana's black velvet, silver-worked pouch and belt, the latter half overrun by the hardened black lava, and Ivrian's blue-enameled box inlaid with silver. From these they took the gems of Jengao.

With no more word than they had exchanged back at the Mouser's burned nest behind the Eel, but with a continuing sense of their unity of purpose, their identity of intent, and of their comradeship, they made their way with shoulders bowed and with slow, weary steps which only very gradually quickened out of the magic room and down the thick-carpeted corridor, past the map room's wide door still barred with oak and iron, and past all the other shut, silent doors—clearly the entire Guild was terrified of Hristomilo, his spells, and his rats; down the echoing stairs, their footsteps speeding a little; down the bare-floored lower corridor past its closed, quiet doors, their footsteps resounding loudly no matter how softly they sought to tread; under the deserted, black-scorched guard-niche, and so out into Cheap Street, turning left and north because that was the nearest way to the Street of the Gods, and there turning right and east—not a waking soul in the wide street except for one skinny, bent-backed apprentice lad unhappily swabbing the flagstones in front of a wine shop in the dim pink light beginning to seep from the east, although there were many forms asleep, a-snore and a-dream in the gutters and under the dark porticos—yes, turning right and east down the Street of the Gods, for that way was the Marsh Gate, leading to Causey Road across the Great Salt Marsh, and the Marsh Gate was the nearest way out of the great and glamorous city that was now loathsome to them, indeed, not to be endured for one more stabbing, leaden heartbeat than was necessary—a city of beloved, unfaceable ghosts.

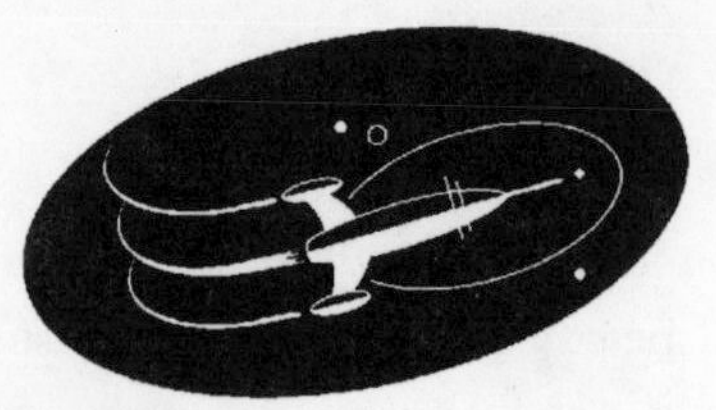

A MEETING WITH MEDUSA

Arthur C. Clarke

I
A DAY TO REMEMBER

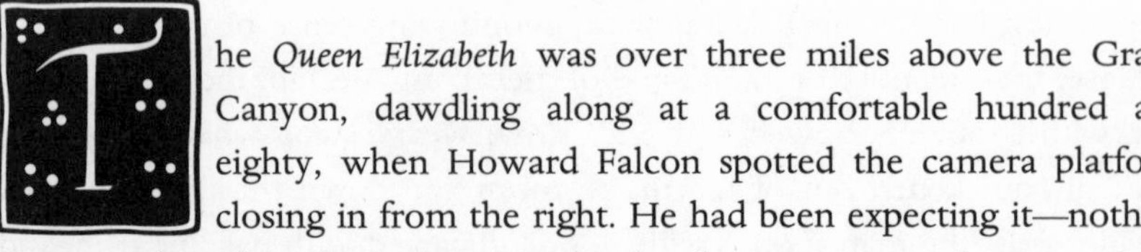

The *Queen Elizabeth* was over three miles above the Grand Canyon, dawdling along at a comfortable hundred and eighty, when Howard Falcon spotted the camera platform closing in from the right. He had been expecting it—nothing else was cleared to fly at this altitude—but he was not too happy to have company. Although he welcomed any signs of public interest, he also wanted as much empty sky as he could get. After all, he was the first man in history to navigate a ship three-tenths of a mile long. . . .

So far, this first test flight had gone perfectly; ironically enough, the only problem had been the century-old aircraft carrier *Chairman Mao,* borrowed from the San Diego Naval Museum for support operations. Only one of *Mao*'s four nuclear reactors was still operating, and the old battlewagon's top speed was barely thirty knots. Luckily, wind speed at sea level had been less than half this, so it had not been too difficult to maintain still air on the flight deck. Though there had been a few anxious moments during gusts, when the mooring lines had been dropped, the great dirigible had risen smoothly, straight up into the sky, as if on an invisible elevator. If all went well, *Queen Elizabeth IV* would not meet *Chairman Mao* again for another week.

Everything was under control; all test instruments gave normal readings. Commander Falcon decided to go upstairs and watch the rendezvous. He handed over to his second officer, and walked out into the transparent tubeway that led through the heart of the ship. There, as always, he was overwhelmed by the spectacle of the largest single space ever enclosed by man.

The ten spherical gas cells, each more than a hundred feet across, were ranged one behind the other like a line of gigantic soap bubbles. The tough plastic was so clear that he could see through the whole length of the array, and make out details of the elevator mechanism, more than a third of a mile from his vantage point. All around him, like a three-dimensional maze, was the structural framework of the ship—the great longitudinal girders running from nose to tail, the fifteen hoops that were the circular ribs of this sky-borne colossus, and whose varying sizes defined its graceful, streamlined profile.

At this low speed, there was little sound—merely the soft rush of wind over the envelope and an occasional creak of metal as the pattern of stresses changed. The shadowless light from the rows of lamps far overhead gave the whole scene a curiously submarine quality, and to Falcon this was enhanced by the spectacle of the translucent gasbags. He had once encountered a squadron of large but harmless jellyfish, pulsing their mindless way above a shallow tropical reef, and the plastic bubbles that gave *Queen Elizabeth* her lift often reminded him of these—especially when changing pressures made them crinkle and scatter new patterns of reflected light.

He walked down the axis of the ship until he came to the forward elevator, between gas cells one and two. Riding up to the Observation Deck, he noticed that it was uncomfortably hot, and dictated a brief memo to himself on his pocket recorder. The *Queen* obtained almost a quarter of her buoyancy from the unlimited amounts of waste heat produced by her fusion power plant. On this lightly loaded flight, indeed, only six of the ten gas cells contained helium; the remaining four were full of air. Yet she still carried two hundred tons of water as ballast. However, running the cells at high temperatures did produce problems in refrigerating the access ways; it was obvious that a little more work would have to be done there.

A refreshing blast of cooler air hit him in the face when he stepped out onto the Observation Deck and into the dazzling sunlight streaming through the plexiglass roof. Half a dozen workmen, with an equal number of superchimp assistants, were busily laying the partly completed dance floor, while others were installing electric wiring and fixing furniture. It was a scene of controlled chaos, and Falcon found it hard to believe that everything would be ready for the maiden voyage, only four weeks ahead. Well, that was not *his* problem, thank goodness. He was merely the Captain, not the Cruise Director.

The human workers waved to him, and the "simps" flashed toothy smiles, as he walked through the confusion, into the already completed Skylounge. This was his favorite place in the whole ship, and he knew that once she was operating he would never again have it all to himself. He would allow himself just five minutes of private enjoyment.

He called the bridge, checked that everything was still in order, and relaxed into one of the comfortable swivel chairs. Below, in a curve that delighted the eye, was the unbroken silver sweep of the ship's envelope. He was perched at the highest point, surveying the whole immensity of the largest vehicle ever built. And when he had tired of that—all the way out to the horizon was the fantastic wilderness carved by the Colorado River in half a billion years of time.

Apart from the camera platform (it had now fallen back and was filming from amidships), he had the sky to himself. It was blue and empty, clear down to the horizon. In his grandfather's day, Falcon knew, it would have been streaked with vapor trails and stained with smoke. Both had gone: the aerial garbage had vanished with the primitive technologies that spawned it, and the long-distance transportation of this age arced too far beyond the stratosphere for any sight or sound of it to reach Earth. Once again, the lower atmosphere belonged to the birds and the clouds—and now to *Queen Elizabeth IV*.

It was true, as the old pioneers had said at the beginning of the twentieth century: this was the only way to travel—in silence and luxury, breathing the air around you and not cut off from it, near enough to the surface to watch the ever-changing beauty of land and sea. The subsonic jets of the 1980's, packed with hundreds of passengers seated ten abreast, could not even begin to match such comfort and spaciousness.

Of course, the *Queen* would never be an economic proposition, and even if her projected sister ships were built, only a few of the world's quarter of a billion inhabitants would ever enjoy this silent gliding through the sky. But a secure and prosperous global society could afford such follies and indeed needed them for their novelty and entertainment. There were at least a million men on Earth whose discretionary income exceeded a thousand new dollars a year, so the *Queen* would not lack for passengers.

Falcon's pocket communicator beeped. The copilot was calling from the bridge.

"O.K. for rendezvous, Captain? We've got all the data we need from this run, and the TV people are getting impatient."

Falcon glanced at the camera platform, now matching his speed a tenth of a mile away.

"O.K.," he replied. "Proceed as arranged. I'll watch from here."

He walked back through the busy chaos of the Observation Deck so that he could have a better view amidships. As he did so, he could feel the change of vibration underfoot; by the time he had reached the rear of the lounge, the ship had come to rest. Using his master key, he let himself out onto the small external platform flaring from the end of the deck; half a dozen people could stand here, with only low guardrails separating them from the vast sweep of the envelope—and from the ground, thousands of feet below. It was an exciting place to be, and perfectly safe even when the ship was traveling at speed, for it was in the dead air behind the huge dorsal blister of the Observation Deck. Nevertheless, it was not intended that the passengers would have access to it; the view was a little too vertiginous.

The covers of the forward cargo hatch had already opened like giant trap doors, and the camera platform was hovering above them, preparing to descend. Along this route, in the years to come, would travel thousands of passengers and tons of supplies. Only on rare occasions would the *Queen* drop down to sea level and dock with her floating base.

A sudden gust of cross wind slapped Falcon's cheek, and he tightened his grip on the guardrail. The Grand Canyon was a bad place for turbulence, though he did not expect much at this altitude. Without any real anxiety, he focused his attention on the descending platform, now about a hundred and fifty feet above the ship. He knew that the highly skilled operator who was flying the remotely controlled vehicle had performed this simple maneuver a dozen times already; it was inconceivable that he would have any difficulties.

Yet he seemed to be reacting rather sluggishly. That last gust had drifted the platform almost to the edge of the open hatchway. Surely the pilot could have corrected before this. . . . Did he have a control problem? It was very unlikely; these remotes had multiple-redundancy, fail-safe takeovers, and any number of backup systems. Accidents were almost unheard of.

But there he went again, off to the left. Could the pilot be *drunk?* Improbable though that seemed, Falcon considered it seriously for a moment. Then he reached for his microphone switch.

Once again, without warning, he was slapped violently in the face. He hardly felt it, for he was staring in horror at the camera platform. The distant operator was fighting for control, trying to balance the craft on its jets—but he was only making matters worse. The oscillations increased—twenty degrees, forty, sixty, ninety. . . .

"Switch to automatic, you fool!" Falcon shouted uselessly into his microphone. "Your manual control's not working!"

The platform flipped over on its back. The jets no longer supported it, but drove it swiftly downward. They had suddenly become allies of the gravity they had fought until this moment.

Falcon never heard the crash, though he felt it; he was already inside the Observation Deck, racing for the elevator that would take him down to the bridge. Workmen shouted at him anxiously, asking what had happened. It would be many months before he knew the answer to that question.

Just as he was stepping into the elevator cage, he changed his mind. What if there was a power failure? Better be on the safe side, even if it took longer and time was the essence. He began to run down the spiral stairway enclosing the shaft.

Halfway down he paused for a second to inspect the damage. That damned platform had gone clear through the ship, rupturing two of the gas cells as it did so. They were still collapsing slowly, in great falling veils of plastic. He was not worried about the loss of lift—the ballast could easily take care of that, as long as eight cells remained intact. Far more serious was the possibility of structural damage. Already he could hear the great latticework around him groaning and protesting under its abnormal loads. It was not enough to have sufficient lift; unless it was properly distributed, the ship would break her back.

He was just resuming his descent when a superchimp, shrieking with fright, came racing down the elevator shaft, moving with incredible speed, hand over hand, along the *outside* of the latticework. In its terror, the poor beast had torn off its company uniform, perhaps in an unconscious attempt to regain the freedom of its ancestors.

Falcon, still descending as swiftly as he could, watched its approach with some alarm. A distraught simp was a powerful and potentially dangerous animal, especially if fear overcame its conditioning. As it overtook him, it started to call out a string of words, but they were all jumbled together, and the only one he could recognize was a plaintive, frequently repeated "boss." Even now, Falcon realized, it looked toward humans for guidance. He felt sorry for the creature, involved in a man-made disaster beyond its comprehension, and for which it bore no responsibility.

It stopped opposite him, on the other side of the lattice; there was nothing to prevent it from coming through the open framework if it wished. Now its face was only inches from his, and he was looking straight into the terrified eyes. Never before had he been so close to a simp, and able to study its features in such detail. He felt that strange mingling of kinship and discomfort that all men experience when they gaze thus into the mirror of time.

His presence seemed to have calmed the creature. Falcon pointed up the shaft, back toward the Observation Deck, and said very clearly and precisely: "Boss—boss—*go.*" To his relief, the simp understood; it gave him a grimace that might have been a smile, and at once started to race back the way it had come. Falcon had given it the best advice he could. If any safety remained aboard the *Queen,* it was in that direction. But his duty lay in the other.

He had almost completed his descent when, with a sound of rending metal, the vessel pitched nose down, and the lights went out. But he could still see quite well, for a shaft of sunlight streamed through the open hatch and the huge tear in the envelope. Many years ago he had stood in a great cathedral nave watching the light pouring through the stained-glass windows and forming pools of multicolored radiance on the ancient flagstones. The dazzling shaft of sunlight through the ruined fabric high above reminded him of that moment. He was in a cathedral of metal, falling down the sky.

When he reached the bridge, and was able for the first time to look outside, he was horrified to see how close the ship was to the ground. Only three thousand feet below were the beautiful and deadly pinnacles of rock and the red rivers of mud that were still carving their way down into the past. There was no level area anywhere in sight where a ship as large as the *Queen* could come to rest on an even keel.

A glance at the display board told him that all the ballast had gone. However, rate of descent had been reduced to a few yards a second; they still had a fighting chance.

Without a word, Falcon eased himself into the pilot's seat and took over such control as still remained. The instrument board showed him everything he wished to know; speech was superfluous. In the background, he could hear the Communications Officer giving a running report over the radio. By this time, all the news channels of Earth would have been preempted, and he could imagine the utter frustration of the program controllers. One of the most spectacular wrecks in history was occurring—without a single camera to record it. The last moments of the *Queen* would never fill millions with awe and terror, as had those of the *Hindenburg,* a century and a half before.

Now the ground was only about seventeen hundred feet away, still coming up slowly. Though he had full thrust, he had not dared to use it, lest the weakened structure collapse; but now he realized that he had no choice. The wind was taking them toward a fork in the canyon, where the river was split by a wedge of rock like the prow of some gigantic, fossilized ship of stone. If she continued on her present course, the *Queen* would straddle that triangular plateau and come to rest with at least a third of her length jutting out over nothingness; she would snap like a rotten stick.

Far away, above the sound of straining metal and escaping gas, came the familiar whistle of the jets as Falcon opened up the lateral thrusters. The ship staggered, and began to slew to port. The shriek of tearing metal was now almost continuous—and the rate of descent had started to increase ominously. A glance at the damage-control board showed that cell number five had just gone.

The ground was only yards away. Even now, he could not tell whether his maneuver would succeed or fail. He switched the thrust vectors over to vertical, giving maximum lift to reduce the force of impact.

The crash seemed to last forever. It was not violent—merely prolonged, and irresistible. It seemed that the whole universe was falling about them.

The sound of crunching metal came nearer, as if some great beast were eating its way through the dying ship.

Then floor and ceiling closed upon him like a vice.

II

"BECAUSE IT'S THERE"

"Why do you want to go to Jupiter?"

"As Springer said when he lifted for Pluto—'because it's there.'"

"Thanks. Now we've got *that* out of the way—the real reason."

Howard Falcon smiled, though only those who knew him well could have interpreted the slight, leathery grimace. Webster was one of them; for more than twenty years they had been involved in each other's projects. They had shared triumphs and disasters—including the greatest disaster of all.

"Well, Springer's cliché is still valid. We've landed on all the terrestrial planets, but none of the gas giants. They are the only real challenge left in the solar system."

"An expensive one. Have you worked out the cost?"

"As well as I can; here are the estimates. Remember, though—this isn't a one-shot mission, but a transportation system. Once it's proved out, it can be used over and over again. And it will open up not merely Jupiter, but *all* the giants."

Webster looked at the figures, and whistled.

"Why not start with an easier planet—Uranus, for example? Half the gravity, and less than half the escape velocity. Quieter weather, too—if that's the right word for it."

Webster had certainly done his homework. But that, of course, was why he was head of Long-Range Planning.

"There's very little saving—when you allow for the extra distance and the logistics problems. For Jupiter, we can use the facilities of Ganymede. Beyond Saturn, we'd have to establish a new supply base."

Logical, thought Webster; but he was sure that it was not the important reason. Jupiter was lord of the solar system; Falcon would be interested in no lesser challenge.

"Besides," Falcon continued, "Jupiter is a major scientific scandal. It's more than a hundred years since its radio storms were discovered, but we still don't know what causes them—and the Great Red Spot is as big a mystery as ever. That's why I can get matching funds from the Bureau of Astronautics. Do you know how many probes they have dropped into that atmosphere?"

"A couple of hundred, I believe."

"*Three* hundred and twenty-six, over the last fifty years—about a quarter of them total failures. Of course, they've learned a hell of a lot, but they've barely scratched the planet. Do you realize how *big* it is?"

"More than ten times the size of Earth."

"Yes, yes—but do you know what that really means?"

Falcon pointed to the large globe in the corner of Webster's office.

"Look at India—how small it seems. Well, if you skinned Earth and spread it out on the surface of Jupiter, it would look about as big as India does here."

There was a long silence while Webster contemplated the equation: Jupiter is to Earth as Earth is to India. Falcon had—deliberately, of course—chosen the best possible example. . . .

Was it already ten years ago? Yes, it must have been. The crash lay seven years in the past (*that* date was engraved on his heart), and those initial tests had taken place three years before the first and last flight of the *Queen Elizabeth*.

Ten years ago, then, Commander (no, Lieutenant) Falcon had invited him to a preview—a three-day drift across the northern plains of India, within sight of the Himalayas. "Perfectly safe," he had promised. "It will get you away from the office—and will teach you what this whole thing is about."

Webster had not been disappointed. Next to his first journey to the Moon, it had been the most memorable experience of his life. And yet, as Falcon had assured him, it had been perfectly safe, and quite uneventful.

They had taken off from Srinagar just before dawn, with the huge silver bubble of the balloon already catching the first light of the Sun. The ascent had been made in total silence; there were none of the roaring propane burners that had lifted the hot-air balloons of an earlier age. All the heat they needed came from the little pulsed-fusion reactor, weighing only about two hundred and twenty pounds, hanging in the open mouth of the envelope. While they were climbing, its laser was zapping ten times a second, igniting the merest whiff of deuterium fuel. Once they had reached altitude, it would fire only a few times a minute, making up for the heat lost through the great gasbag overhead.

And so, even while they were almost a mile above the ground, they could hear dogs barking, people shouting, bells ringing. Slowly the vast, Sun-smitten landscape expanded around them. Two hours later, they had leveled out at three miles and were taking frequent draughts of oxygen. They could relax and admire the scenery; the on-board instrumentation was doing all the work—gathering the information that would be required by the designers of the still-unnamed liner of the skies.

It was a perfect day. The southwest monsoon would not break for another month, and there was hardly a cloud in the sky. Time seemed to have come to a stop; they resented the hourly radio reports which interrupted their reverie. And all around, to the horizon and far beyond, was that infinite, ancient landscape, drenched with history—a patchwork of villages, fields, temples, lakes, irrigation canals. . . .

With a real effort, Webster broke the hypnotic spell of that ten-year-old memory. It had converted him to lighter-than-air flight—and it had made him realize the enormous size of India, even in a world that could be circled within ninety minutes. And yet, he repeated to himself, Jupiter is to Earth as Earth is to India. . . .

"Granted your argument," he said, "and supposing the funds are available, there's another question you have to answer. Why should you do better than the—what is it—three hundred and twenty-six robot probes that have already made the trip?"

"I am better qualified than they were—as an observer, and as a pilot. *Especially* as a pilot. Don't forget—I've more experience of lighter-than-air flight than anyone in the world."

"You could still serve as controller, and sit safely on Ganymede."

"But that's just the point! They've already done that. Don't you remember what killed the *Queen?*"

Webster knew perfectly well; but he merely answered: "Go on."

"Time lag—time lag! That idiot of a platform controller thought he was using a local radio circuit. But he'd been accidentally switched through a satellite—oh, maybe it wasn't his fault, but he should have noticed. That's a half-second time lag for the round trip. Even then it wouldn't have mattered flying in calm air. It was the turbulence over the Grand Canyon that did it. When the platform tipped, and he corrected for that—it had already tipped the other way. Ever tried to drive a car over a bumpy road with a half-second delay in the steering?"

"No, and I don't intend to try. But I can imagine it."

"Well, Ganymede is a million kilometers from Jupiter. That means a round-trip delay of six seconds. No, you need a controller on the spot—to handle emergencies in real time. Let me show you something. Mind if I use this?"

"Go ahead."

Falcon picked up a postcard that was lying on Webster's desk; they were almost obsolete on Earth, but this one showed a 3-D view of a Martian landscape, and was decorated with exotic and expensive stamps. He held it so that it dangled vertically.

"This is an old trick, but helps to make my point. Place your thumb and finger on either side, not quite touching. That's right."

Webster put out his hand, almost but not quite gripping the card.

"Now catch it."

Falcon waited for a few seconds; then, without warning, he let go of the card. Webster's thumb and finger closed on empty air.

"I'll do it again, just to show there's no deception. You see?"

Once again, the falling card had slipped through Webster's fingers.

"Now you try it on me."

This time, Webster grasped the card and dropped it without warning. It had scarcely moved before Falcon had caught it. Webster almost imagined he could hear a click, so swift was the other's reaction.

"When they put me together again," Falcon remarked in an expressionless voice, "the surgeons made some improvements. This is one of them—and there are others. I want to make the most of them. Jupiter is the place where I can do it."

Webster stared for long seconds at the fallen card, absorbing the improbable colors of the Trivium Charontis Escarpment. Then he said quietly: "I understand. How long do you think it will take?"

"With your help, plus the Bureau, plus all the science foundations we can drag in—oh, three years. Then a year for trials—we'll have to send in at least two test models. So, with luck—five years."

"That's about what I thought. I hope you get your luck; you've earned it. But there's one thing I won't do."

"What's that?"

"Next time you go ballooning, don't expect *me* as passenger."

III

THE WORLD OF THE GODS

The fall from Jupiter V to Jupiter itself takes only three and a half hours. Few men could have slept on so awesome a journey. Sleep was a weakness that Howard Falcon hated, and the little he still required brought dreams that time had not yet been able to exorcise. But he could expect no rest in the three days that lay ahead, and must seize what he could during the long fall down into that ocean of clouds, some sixty thousand miles below.

As soon as *Kon-Tiki* had entered her transfer orbit and all the computer checks were satisfactory, he prepared for the last sleep he might ever know. It seemed appropriate that at almost the same moment Jupiter eclipsed the bright and tiny Sun as he swept into the monstrous shadow of the planet. For a few minutes a strange golden twilight enveloped the ship; then a quarter of the sky became an utterly black hole in space, while the rest was a blaze of stars. No matter how far one traveled across the solar system, *they* never changed; these same constellations now shone on Earth, millions of miles away. The only novelties here were the small, pale crescents of Callisto and Ganymede; doubtless there were a dozen other moons up there in the sky, but they were all much too tiny, and too distant, for the unaided eye to pick them out.

"Closing down for two hours," he reported to the mother ship, hanging almost a thousand miles above the desolate rocks of Jupiter V, in the radiation shadow of the tiny satellite. If it never served any other useful purpose, Jupiter V was a cosmic bulldozer perpetually sweeping up the charged particles that made it unhealthy to linger close to Jupiter. Its wake was almost free of radiation, and there a ship could park in perfect safety, while death sleeted invisibly all around.

Falcon switched on the sleep inducer, and consciousness faded swiftly out as the electric pulses surged gently through his brain. While *Kon-Tiki* fell toward Jupiter, gaining speed second by second in that enormous gravitational field, he slept without dreams. They always came when he awoke; and he had brought his nightmares with him from Earth.

Yet he never dreamed of the crash itself, though he often found himself again face to face with that terrified superchimp, as he descended the spiral stairway between the collapsing gasbags. None of the simps had survived; those that were not killed outright were so badly injured that they had been painlessly "euthed." He sometimes wondered why he dreamed only of this doomed creature—which he had never met before the last minutes of its life—and not of the friends and colleagues he had lost aboard the dying *Queen*.

The dreams he feared most always began with his first return to consciousness. There had been little physical pain; in fact, there had been no sensation of any kind. He was in darkness and silence, and did not even seem to be breathing. And—strangest of all—he could not locate his limbs. He could move neither his hands nor his feet, because he did not know where they were.

The silence had been the first to yield. After hours, or days, he had become aware of a faint throbbing, and eventually, after long thought, he deduced that this was the beating of his own heart. That was the first of his many mistakes.

Then there had been faint pinpricks, sparkles of light, ghosts of pressures upon still-unresponsive limbs. One by one his senses had returned, and pain had come with them. He had had to learn everything anew, recapitulating infancy and babyhood. Though his memory was unaffected, and he could understand words that were spoken to him, it was months before he was able to answer except by the flicker of an eyelid. He could remember the moments of triumph when he had spoken the first word, turned the page of a book—and, finally, learned to move under his own power. *That* was a victory indeed, and it had taken him almost two years to prepare for it. A hundred times he had envied that dead superchimp, but *he* had been given no choice. The doctors had made their decision—and now, twelve years later, he was where no human being had ever traveled before, and moving faster than any man in history.

Kon-Tiki was just emerging from shadow, and the Jovian dawn bridged the sky ahead in a titanic bow of light, when the persistent buzz of the alarm dragged Falcon up from sleep. The inevitable nightmares (he had been trying to summon a nurse, but did not even have the strength to push the button) swiftly faded from consciousness. The greatest—and perhaps last—adventure of his life was before him.

He called Mission Control, now almost sixty thousand miles away and falling swiftly below the curve of Jupiter, to report that everything was in order. His velocity had just passed thirty-one miles a second (*that* was one for the books) and in half an hour *Kon-Tiki* would hit the outer fringes of the atmosphere, as he started on the most difficult re-entry in the entire solar system. Although scores of probes had survived this flaming ordeal, they had been tough, solidly packed masses of instrumentation, able to withstand several hundred gravities of drag. *Kon-Tiki* would hit peaks of thirty g's, and would average more than ten, before she came to rest in the upper reaches of the Jovian atmosphere. Very carefully and thoroughly, Falcon began to attach the elaborate system of restraints that would anchor him to the walls of the cabin. When he had finished, he was virtually a part of the ship's structure.

The clock was counting backward; one hundred seconds to re-entry. For better or worse, he was committed. In a minute and a half, he would graze the Jovian atmosphere, and would be caught irrevocably in the grip of the giant.

The countdown was three seconds late—not at all bad, considering the unknowns involved. From beyond the walls of the capsule came a ghostly sighing, which rose steadily to a high-pitched, screaming roar. The noise was quite different from that of a re-entry on Earth or Mars; in this thin atmosphere of hydrogen and helium, all sounds were transformed a couple of octaves upward. On Jupiter, even thunder would have falsetto overtones.

With the rising scream came mounting weight; within seconds, he was completely immobilized. His field of vision contracted until it embraced only the clock and the accelerometer; fifteen g, and four hundred and eighty seconds to go. . . .

He never lost consciousness; but then, he had not expected to. *Kon-Tiki*'s trail through the Jovian atmosphere must be really spectacular—by this time, thousands of miles long. Five hundred seconds after entry, the drag began to taper off: ten g, five g, two. . . . Then weight vanished almost completely. He was falling free, all his enormous orbital velocity destroyed.

There was a sudden jolt as the incandescent remnants of the heat shield were jettisoned. It had done its work and would not be needed again; Jupiter could have it now. He released all but two of the restraining buckles, and waited for the automatic sequencer to start the next, and most critical, series of events.

He did not see the first drogue parachute pop out, but he could feel the slight jerk, and the rate of fall diminished immediately. *Kon-Tiki* had lost all her horizontal speed and was going straight down at almost a thousand miles an hour. Everything depended on what happened in the next sixty seconds.

There went the second drogue. He looked up through the overhead window and saw, to his immense relief, that clouds of glittering foil were billowing out behind the falling ship. Like a great flower unfurling, the thousands of cubic yards of the balloon spread out across the sky, scooping up the thin gas until it was fully inflated. *Kon-Tiki*'s rate of fall dropped to a few miles an hour and remained constant. Now there was plenty of time; it would take him days to fall all the way down to the surface to Jupiter.

But he would get there eventually, even if he did nothing about it. The balloon overhead was merely acting as an efficient parachute. It was providing no lift; nor could it do so, while the gas inside and out was the same.

With its characteristic and rather disconcerting crack the fusion reactor started up, pouring torrents of heat into the envelope overhead. Within five minutes, the rate of fall had become zero; within six, the ship had started to rise. According to the radar altimeter, it had leveled out at about two hundred and sixty-seven miles above the surface—or whatever passed for a surface on Jupiter.

Only one kind of balloon will work in an atmosphere of hydrogen, which is the lightest of all gases—and that is a hot-hydrogen balloon. As long as the fuser kept ticking over, Falcon could remain aloft, drifting across a world that could hold a hundred Pacifics. After traveling over three hundred million miles, *Kon-Tiki* had at last begun to justify her name. She was an aerial raft, adrift upon the currents of the Jovian atmosphere.

Though a whole new world was lying around him, it was more than an hour before Falcon could examine the view. First he had to check all the capsule's systems and test its response to the controls. He had to learn how much extra heat was necessary to produce a desired rate of ascent, and how much gas he must vent in order to descend. Above all, there was the question of stability. He must adjust the length of the cables attaching his capsule to the huge, pear-shaped balloon, to damp out vibrations and get the smoothest possible ride. Thus far, he was lucky; at this level, the wind was steady, and the Doppler reading on the invisible surface gave him a ground speed of two hundred seventeen and a half miles an hour. For Jupiter, that was modest; winds of up to a thousand had been observed. But mere speed was, of course, unimportant; the real danger was turbulence. If he ran into that, only skill and experience and swift reaction could save him —and these were not matters that could yet be programed into a computer.

Not until he was satisfied that he had got the feel of his strange craft did Falcon pay any attention to Mission Control's pleadings. Then he deployed the booms carrying the instrumentation and the atmospheric samplers. The capsule now resembled a rather untidy Christmas tree, but still rode smoothly down the Jovian winds while it radioed its torrents of information to the recorders on the ships miles above. And now, at last, he could look around. . . .

His first impression was unexpected, and even a little disappointing. As far as the scale of things was concerned, he might have been ballooning over an ordinary cloudscape on Earth. The horizon seemed at a normal distance; there was no feeling at all that he was on a world eleven times the diameter of his own. Then he looked at the infrared radar, sounding the layers of atmosphere beneath him—and knew how badly his eyes had been deceived.

That layer of clouds apparently about three miles away was really more than thirty-seven miles below. And the horizon, whose distance he would have guessed at about one hundred and twenty-five, was actually eighteen hundred miles from the ship.

The crystalline clarity of the hydrohelium atmosphere and the enormous curvature of the planet had fooled him completely. It was even harder to judge distances here than on the Moon; everything he saw must be multiplied by at least ten.

It was a simple matter, and he should have been prepared for it. Yet somehow, it disturbed him profoundly. He did not feel that Jupiter was huge, but that *he* had shrunk—to a tenth of his normal size. Perhaps, with time, he would grow accustomed to the inhuman scale of this world; yet as he stared toward that unbelievably distant horizon, he felt as if a wind colder than the atmosphere around him was blowing through his soul. Despite all his arguments, this might never be a place for man. He could well be both the first and last to descend through the clouds of Jupiter.

The sky above was almost black, except for a few wisps of ammonia cirrus perhaps twelve miles overhead. It was cold up there, on the fringes of space, but both pressure and temperature increased rapidly with depth. At the level where *Kon-Tiki* was drifting now, it was fifty below zero, and the pressure was five atmospheres. Sixty-five miles farther down, it would be as warm as equatorial Earth, and the pressure about the same as at the bottom of one of the shallower seas. Ideal conditions for life. . . .

A quarter of the brief Jovian day had already gone; the sun was halfway up the sky, but the light on the unbroken cloudscape below had a curious mellow quality. That extra three hundred million miles had robbed the Sun of all its power. Though the sky was clear, Falcon found himself continually thinking that it was a heavily overcast day. When night fell, the onset of darkness would be swift indeed; though it was still morning, there was a sense of autumnal twilight in the air. But autumn, of course, was something that never came to Jupiter. There were no seasons here.

Kon-Tiki had come down in the exact center of the equatorial zone—the least colorful part of the planet. The sea of clouds that stretched out to the horizon was tinted a pale salmon; there were none of the yellows and pinks and even reds that banded Jupiter at higher altitudes. The Great Red Spot itself—most spectacular of all of the planet's features—lay thousands of miles to the south. It had been a temptation to descend there, but the south tropical disturbance was unusually active, with currents reaching over nine hundred miles an hour. It would have been asking for trouble to head into that maelstrom of unknown forces. The Great Red Spot and its mysteries would have to wait for future expeditions.

The Sun, moving across the sky twice as swiftly as it did on Earth, was now nearing the zenith and had become eclipsed by the great silver canopy of the balloon. *Kon-Tiki* was still drifting swiftly and smoothly westward at a steady two hundred and seventeen and a half, but only the radar gave any indication of this. Was it always as calm here? Falcon asked himself. The scientists who had talked learnedly of the Jovian doldrums, and had predicted that the equator would be the quietest place, seemed to know what they were talking about, after all. He had been profoundly skeptical of all such forecasts, and had agreed with one unusually modest researcher who had told him bluntly: "There are *no* experts on Jupiter." Well, there would be at least one by the end of this day.

If he managed to survive until then.

IV
THE VOICES OF THE DEEP

That first day, the Father of the Gods smiled upon him. It was as calm and peaceful here on Jupiter as it had been, years ago, when he was drifting with Webster across the plains of northern India. Falcon had time to master his new skills, until *Kon-Tiki* seemed an extension of his own body. Such luck was more than he had dared to hope for, and he began to wonder what price he might have to pay for it.

The five hours of daylight were almost over; the clouds below were full of shadows, which gave them a massive solidity they had not possessed when the Sun was higher. Color was swiftly draining from the sky, except in the west itself, where a band of deepening purple lay along the horizon. Above this band was the thin crescent of a closer moon, pale and bleached against the utter blackness beyond.

With a speed perceptible to the eye, the Sun went straight down over the edge of Jupiter, over eighteen hundred miles away. The stars came out in their legions—and there was the beautiful evening star of Earth, on the very frontier of twilight, reminding him how far he was from home. It followed the Sun down into the west. Man's first night on Jupiter had begun.

With the onset of darkness, *Kon-Tiki* started to sink. The balloon was no longer heated by the feeble sunlight and was losing a small part of its buoyancy. Falcon did nothing to increase lift; he had expected this and was planning to descend.

The invisible cloud deck was still over thirty miles below, and he would reach it about midnight. It showed up clearly on the infrared radar, which also reported that it contained a vast array of complex carbon compounds, as well as the usual hydrogen, helium, and ammonia. The chemists were dying for samples of that fluffy, pinkish stuff; though some atmospheric probes had already gathered a few grams, that had only whetted their appetites. Half the basic molecules of life were here, floating high above the surface of Jupiter. And where there was food, could life be far away? That was the question that, after more than a hundred years, no one had been able to answer.

The infrared was blocked by the clouds, but the microwave radar sliced right through and showed layer after layer, all the way down to the hidden surface almost two hundred and fifty miles below. That was barred to him by enormous pressures and temperatures; not even robot probes had ever reached it intact. It lay in tantalizing inaccessibility at the bottom of the radar screen, slightly fuzzy, and showing a curious granular structure that his equipment could not resolve.

An hour after sunset, he dropped his first probe. It fell swiftly for about sixty miles, then began to float in the denser atmosphere, sending back torrents of radio signals, which he relayed to Mission Control. Then there was nothing else to do until sunrise, except to keep an eye on the rate of descent, monitor the instruments, and answer occasional queries. While she was drifting in this steady current, *Kon-Tiki* could look after herself.

Just before midnight, a woman controller came on watch and introduced herself with the usual pleasantries. Ten minutes later she called again, her voice at once serious and excited.

"Howard! Listen in on channel forty-six—high gain."

Channel forty-six? There were so many telemetering circuits that he knew the numbers of only those that were critical; but as soon as he threw the switch, he recognized this one. He was plugged in to the microphone on the probe, floating more than eighty miles below him in an atmosphere now almost as dense as water.

At first, there was only a soft hiss of whatever strange winds stirred down in the darkness of that unimaginable world. And then, out of the background noise, there slowly emerged a booming vibration that grew louder and louder, like the beating of a gigantic drum. It was so low that it was felt as much as heard, and the beats steadily increased their tempo, though the pitch never changed. Now it was a swift, almost infrasonic throbbing. Then, suddenly, in mid-vibration, it stopped—so abruptly that the mind could not accept the silence, but memory continued to manufacture a ghostly echo in the deepest caverns of the brain.

It was the most extraordinary sound that Falcon had ever heard, even among the multitudinous noises of Earth. He could think of no natural phenomenon that could have caused it; nor was it like the cry of any animal, not even one of the great whales. . . .

It came again, following exactly the same pattern. Now that he was prepared for it, he estimated the length of the sequence; from first faint throb to final crescendo, it lasted just over ten seconds.

And this time there was a real echo, very faint and far away. Perhaps it came from one of the many reflecting layers, deeper in this stratified atmosphere; perhaps it was another, more distant source. Falcon waited for a second echo, but it never came.

Mission Control reacted quickly and asked him to drop another probe at once. With two microphones operating, it would be possible to find the approximate location of the sources. Oddly enough, none of *Kon-Tiki*'s own external mikes could detect anything except wind noises. The boomings, whatever they were, must have been trapped and channeled beneath an atmospheric reflecting layer far below.

They were coming, it was soon discovered, from a cluster of sources about twelve hundred miles away. The distance gave no indication of their power; in Earth's oceans, quite feeble sounds could travel equally far. And as for the obvious assumption that living creatures were responsible, the Chief Exobiologist quickly ruled that out.

"I'll be very disappointed," said Dr. Brenner, "if there are no microorganisms or plants there. But nothing like animals, because there's no free oxygen. All biochemical reactions on Jupiter must be low-energy ones—there's just no way an active creature could generate enough power to function."

Falcon wondered if this was true; he had heard the argument before, and reserved judgment.

"In any case," continued Brenner, "some of those sound waves are a hundred yards long! Even an animal as big as a whale couldn't produce them. They *must* have a natural origin."

Yes, that seemed plausible, and probably the physicists would be able to come up with an explanation. What would a blind alien make, Falcon wondered, of the sounds he might hear when standing beside a stormy sea, or a geyser, or a volcano, or a waterfall? He might well attribute them to some huge beast.

About an hour before sunrise the voices of the deep died away, and Falcon began to busy himself with preparation for the dawn of his second day. *Kon-Tiki* was now only three miles above the nearest cloud layer; the external pressure had risen to ten atmospheres, and the temperature was a tropical thirty degrees. A man could be comfortable here with no more equipment than a breathing mask and the right grade of heliox mixture.

"We've some good news for you," Mission Control reported, soon after dawn. "The cloud layer's breaking up. You'll have partial clearing in an hour—but watch out for turbulence."

"I've already noticed some," Falcon answered. "How far down will I be able to see?"

"At least twelve miles, down to the second thermocline. *That* cloud deck is solid—it never breaks."

And it's out of my reach, Falcon told himself; the temperature down there must be over a hundred degrees. This was the first time that any balloonist had ever had to worry, not about his ceiling, but about his basement!

Ten minutes later he could see what Mission Control had already observed from its superior vantage point. There was a change in color near the horizon, and the cloud layer had become ragged and humpy, as if something had torn it open. He turned up his little nuclear furnace and gave *Kon-Tiki* another three miles of altitude, so that he could get a better view.

The sky below was clearing rapidly, completely, as if something was dissolving the solid overcast. An abyss was opening before his eyes. A moment later he sailed out over the edge of a cloud canyon about twelve miles deep and six hundred miles wide.

A new world lay spread beneath him; Jupiter had stripped away one of its many veils. The second layer of clouds, unattainably far below, was much darker in color than the first. It was almost salmon pink, and curiously mottled with little islands of brick red. They were all oval-shaped, with their long axes pointing east-west, in the direction of the prevailing wind. There were hundreds of them, all about the same size, and they reminded Falcon of puffy little cumulus clouds in the terrestrial sky.

He reduced buoyancy, and *Kon-Tiki* began to drop down the face of the dissolving cliff. It was then that he noticed the snow.

White flakes were forming in the air and drifting slowly downward. Yet it was much too warm for snow—and, in any event, there was scarcely a trace of water at this altitude. Moreover, there was no glitter or sparkle about these flakes as they went cascading down into the depths. When, presently, a few landed on an instrument boom outside the main viewing port, he saw that they were a dull, opaque white—not crystalline at all—and quite large—several inches across. They looked like wax, and Falcon guessed that this was precisely what they were. Some chemical reaction was taking place in the atmosphere around him, condensing out the hydrocarbons floating in the Jovian air.

About sixty miles ahead, a disturbance was taking place in the cloud layer. The little red ovals were being jostled around, and were beginning to form a spiral—the familiar cyclonic pattern so common in the meteorology of Earth. The vortex was emerging with astonishing speed; if that was a storm ahead, Falcon told himself, he was in big trouble.

And then his concern changed to wonder—and to fear. What was developing in his line of flight was not a storm at all. Something enormous—something scores of miles across—was rising through the clouds.

The reassuring thought that it, too, might be a cloud—a thunderhead boiling up from the lower levels of the atmosphere—lasted only a few seconds. No; this was *solid.* It shouldered its way through the pink-and-salmon overcast like an iceberg rising from the deeps.

An *iceberg* floating on hydrogen? That was impossible, of course; but perhaps it was not too remote an analogy. As soon as he focused the telescope upon the enigma, Falcon saw that it was a whitish, crystalline mass, threaded with streaks of red and brown. It must be, he decided, the same stuff as the "snowflakes" falling around him—a mountain range of wax. And it was not, he soon realized, as solid as he had thought; around the edges it was continually crumbling and re-forming. . . .

"I know what it is," he radioed Mission Control, which for the last few minutes had been asking anxious questions. "It's a mass of bubbles—some kind of foam. Hydrocarbon froth. Get the chemists working on . . . *Just a minute!*"

"What is it?" called Mission Control. "What is it?"

He ignored the frantic pleas from space and concentrated all his mind upon the image in the telescope field. He had to be sure; if he made a mistake, he would be the laughingstock of the solar system.

Then he relaxed, glanced at the clock, and switched off the nagging voice from Jupiter V.

"Hello, Mission Control," he said, very formally. "This is Howard Falcon aboard *Kon-Tiki.* Ephemeris Time nineteen hours twenty-one minutes fifteen seconds. Latitude zero degrees five minutes North. Longitude one hundred five degrees forty-two minutes, System One.

"Tell Dr. Brenner that there is life on Jupiter. And it's *big.* . . ."

V
THE WHEELS OF POSEIDON

I'm very happy to be proved wrong," Dr. Brenner radioed back cheerfully. "Nature always has something up her sleeve. Keep the long-focus camera on target and give us the steadiest pictures you can."

The things moving up and down those waxen slopes were still too far away for Falcon to make out many details, and they must have been very large to be visible at all at such a distance. Almost black, and shaped like arrowheads, they maneuvered by slow undulations of their entire bodies, so that they looked rather like giant manta rays, swimming above some tropical reef.

Perhaps they were sky-borne cattle, browsing on the cloud pastures of Jupiter, for they seemed to be feeding along the dark, red-brown streaks that ran like dried-up river beds down the flanks of the floating cliffs. Occasionally, one of them would dive headlong into the mountain of foam and disappear completely from sight.

Kon-Tiki was moving only slowly with respect to the cloud layer below; it would be at least three hours before she was above those ephemeral hills. She was in a race with the Sun. Falcon hoped that darkness would not fall before he could get a good view of the mantas, as he had christened them, as well as the fragile landscape over which they flapped their way.

It was a long three hours. During the whole time, he kept the external microphones on full gain, wondering if here was the source of that booming in the night. The mantas were certainly large enough to have produced it; when he could get an accurate measurement, he discovered that they were almost a hundred yards across the wings. That was three times the length of the largest whale—though he doubted if they could weigh more than a few tons.

Half an hour before sunset, *Kon-Tiki* was almost above the "mountains."

"No," said Falcon, answering Mission Control's repeated questions about the mantas, "they're still showing no reaction to me. I don't think they're intelligent—they look like harmless vegetarians. And even if they try to chase me, I'm sure they can't reach my altitude."

Yet he was a little disappointed when the mantas showed not the slightest interest in him as he sailed high above their feeding ground. Perhaps they had no way of detecting his presence. When he examined and photographed them through the telescope, he could see no signs of any sense organs. The creatures were simply huge black deltas, rippling over hills and valleys that, in reality, were little more substantial than the clouds of Earth. Though they looked solid, Falcon knew that anyone who stepped on those white mountains would go crashing through them as if they were made of tissue paper.

At close quarters he could see the myriads of cellules or bubbles from which they were formed. Some of these were quite large—a yard or so in diameter—and Falcon wondered in what witches' cauldron of hydrocarbons they had been brewed. There must be enough petrochemicals deep down in the atmosphere of Jupiter to supply all Earth's needs for a million years.

The short day had almost gone when he passed over the crest of the waxen hills, and the light was fading rapidly along their lower slopes. There were no mantas on this western side, and for some reason the topography was very different. The foam was sculptured into long, level terraces, like the interior of a lunar crater. He could almost imagine that they were gigantic steps leading down to the hidden surface of the planet.

And on the lowest of those steps, just clear of the swirling clouds that the mountain had displaced when it came surging skyward, was a roughly oval mass, one or two miles across. It was difficult to see, since it was only a little darker than the gray-white foam on which it rested. Falcon's first thought was that he was looking at a forest of pallid trees, like giant mushrooms that had never seen the Sun.

Yes, it must be a forest—he could see hundreds of thin trunks, springing from the white waxy froth in which they were rooted. But the trees were packed astonishingly close together; there was scarcely any space between them. Perhaps it was not a forest, after all, but a single enormous tree—like one of the giant multi-trunked banyans of the East. Once he had seen a banyan tree in Java that was over six hundred and fifty yards across; this monster was at least ten times that size.

The light had almost gone. The cloudscape had turned purple with refracted sunlight, and in a few seconds that, too, would have vanished. In the last light of his second day on Jupiter, Howard Falcon saw—or thought he saw—something that cast the gravest doubts on his interpretation of the white oval.

Unless the dim light had totally deceived him, those hundreds of thin trunks were beating back and forth, in perfect synchronism, like fronds of kelp rocking in the surge.

And the tree was no longer in the place where he had first seen it.

"Sorry about this," said Mission Control, soon after sunset, "but we think Source Beta is going to blow within the next hour. Probability seventy per cent."

Falcon glanced quickly at the chart. Beta—Jupiter latitude one hundred and forty degrees—was over eighteen thousand six hundred miles away and well below his horizon. Even though major eruptions ran as high as ten megatons, he was much too far away for the shock wave to be a serious danger. The radio storm that it would trigger was, however, quite a different matter.

The decameter outbursts that sometimes made Jupiter the most powerful radio source in the whole sky had been discovered back in the 1950's, to the utter astonishment of the astronomers. Now, more than a century later, their real cause was still a mystery. Only the symptoms were understood; the explanation was completely unknown.

The "volcano" theory had best stood the test of time, although no one imagined that this word had the same meaning on Jupiter as on Earth. At frequent intervals—often several times a day—titanic eruptions occurred in the lower depths of the atmosphere, probably on the hidden surface of the planet itself. A great column of gas, more than six hundred miles high, would start boiling upward as if determined to escape into space.

Against the most powerful gravitational field of all the planets, it had no chance. Yet some traces—a mere few million tons—usually managed to reach the Jovian ionosphere; and when they did, all hell broke loose.

The radiation belts surrounding Jupiter completely dwarf the feeble Van Allen belts of Earth. When they are short-circuited by an ascending column of gas, the result is an electrical discharge millions of times more powerful than any terrestrial flash of lightning; it sends a colossal thunderclap of radio noise flooding across the entire solar system and on out to the stars.

It had been discovered that these radio outbursts came from four main areas of the planet. Perhaps there were weaknesses there that allowed the fires of the interior to break out from time to time. The scientists on Ganymede, largest of Jupiter's many moons, now thought that they could predict the onset of a decameter storm; their accuracy was about as good as a weather forecaster's of the early 1900's.

Falcon did not know whether to welcome or to fear a radio storm; it would certainly add to the value of the mission—if he survived it. His course had been planned to keep as far as possible from the main centers of disturbance, especially the most active one, Source Alpha. As luck would have it, the threatening Beta was the closest to him. He hoped that the distance, almost three-fourths the circumference of Earth, was safe enough.

"Probability ninety per cent," said Mission Control with a distinct note of urgency. "And forget that hour. Ganymede says it may be any moment."

The radio had scarcely fallen silent when the reading on the magnetic field-strength meter started to shoot upward. Before it could go off scale, it reversed and began to drop as rapidly as it had risen. Far away and thousands of miles below, something had given the planet's molten core a titanic jolt.

"There she blows!" called Mission Control.

"Thanks, I already know. When will the storm hit me?"

"You can expect onset in five minutes. Peak in ten."

Far around the curve of Jupiter, a funnel of gas as wide as the Pacific Ocean was climbing spaceward at thousands of miles an hour. Already, the thunderstorms of the lower atmosphere would be raging around it—but they were nothing compared with the fury that would explode when the radiation belt was reached and began dumping its surplus electrons onto the planet. Falcon began to retract all the instrument booms that were extended out from the capsule. There were no other precautions he could take. It would be four hours before the atmospheric shock wave reached him—but the radio blast, traveling at the speed of light, would be here in a tenth of a second, once the discharge had been triggered.

The radio monitor, scanning back and forth across the spectrum, still showed nothing unusual, just the normal mush of background static. Then Falcon noticed that the noise level was slowly creeping upward. The explosion was gathering its strength.

At such a distance he had never expected to *see* anything. But suddenly a flicker as of far-off heat lightning danced along the eastern horizon. Simultaneously, half the circuit breakers jumped out of the main switchboard, the lights failed, and all communications channels went dead.

He tried to move, but was completely unable to do so. The paralysis that gripped him was not merely psychological; he seemed to have lost all control of his limbs and could feel a painful tingling sensation over his entire body. It was impossible that the electric field could have penetrated this shielded cabin. Yet there was a flickering glow over the instrument board, and he could hear the unmistakable crackle of a brush discharge.

With a series of sharp bangs, the emergency systems went into operation, and the overloads reset themselves. The lights flickered on again. And Falcon's paralysis disappeared as swiftly as it had come.

After glancing at the board to make sure that all circuits were back to normal, he moved quickly to the viewing ports.

There was no need to switch on the inspection lamps—the cables supporting the capsule seemed to be on fire. Lines of light glowing an electric blue against the darkness stretched upward from the main lift rings to the equator of the giant balloon; and rolling slowly along several of them were dazzling balls of fire.

The sight was so strange and so beautiful that it was hard to read any menace in it. Few people, Falcon knew, had ever seen ball lightning from such close quarters—and certainly none survived if they were riding a hydrogen-filled balloon back in the atmosphere of Earth. He remembered the flaming death of the *Hindenburg,* destroyed by a stray spark when she docked at Lakehurst in 1937; as it had done so often in the past, the horrifying old newsreel film flashed through his mind. But at least that could not happen here, though there was more hydrogen above his head than had ever filled the last of the Zeppelins. It would be a few billion years yet, before anyone could light a fire in the atmosphere of Jupiter.

With a sound like briskly frying bacon, the speech circuit came back to life.

"Hello, *Kon-Tiki*—are you receiving? Are you receiving?"

The words were chopped and badly distorted, but intelligible. Falcon's spirits lifted; he had resumed contact with the world of men.

"I receive you," he said. "Quite an electrical display, but no damage—so far."

"Thanks—thought we'd lost you. Please check telemetry channels three, seven, twenty-six. Also gain on camera two. And we don't quite believe the readings on the external ionization probes. . . ."

Reluctantly Falcon tore his gaze away from the fascinating pyrotechnic display around *Kon-Tiki,* though from time to time he kept glancing out of the windows. The ball lightning disappeared first, the fiery globes slowly expanding until they reached a critical size, at which they vanished in a gentle explosion. But even an hour later, there were still faint glows around all the exposed metal on the outside of the capsule; and the radio circuits remained noisy until well after midnight.

The remaining hours of darkness were completely uneventful—until just before dawn. Because it came from the east, Falcon assumed that he was seeing the first hint of sunrise. Then he realized that it was twenty minutes too early for this—and the glow that had appeared along the horizon was moving toward him even as he watched. It swiftly detached itself from the arch of stars that marked the invisible edge of the planet, and he saw that it was a relatively narrow band, quite sharply defined. The beam of an enormous searchlight appeared to be swinging beneath the clouds.

Perhaps sixty miles behind the first racing bar of light came another, parallel to it and moving at the same speed. And beyond that another, and another—until all the sky flickered with alternating sheets of light and darkness.

By this time, Falcon thought, he had been inured to wonders, and it seemed impossible that this display of pure, soundless luminosity could present the slightest danger. But it was so astonishing, and so inexplicable, that he felt cold, naked fear gnawing at his self-control. No man could look upon such a sight without feeling like a helpless pygmy in the presence of forces beyond his comprehension. Was it possible that, after all, Jupiter carried not only life but also intelligence? And, perhaps, an intelligence that only now was beginning to react to his alien presence?

"Yes, we see it," said Mission Control, in a voice that echoed his own awe. "We've no idea what it is. Stand by, we're calling Ganymede."

The display was slowly fading; the bands racing in from the far horizon were much fainter, as if the energies that powered them were becoming exhausted. In five minutes it was all over; the last faint pulse of light flickered along the western sky and then was gone. Its passing left Falcon with an overwhelming sense of relief. The sight was so hypnotic, and so disturbing, that it was not good for any man's peace of mind to contemplate it too long.

He was more shaken than he cared to admit. The electrical storm was something that he could understand; but *this* was totally incomprehensible.

Mission Control was still silent. He knew that the information banks up on Ganymede were now being searched as men and computers turned their minds to the problem. If no answer could be found there, it would be necessary to call Earth; that would mean a delay of almost an hour. The possibility that even Earth might be unable to help was one that Falcon did not care to contemplate.

He had never before been so glad to hear the voice of Mission Control as when Dr. Brenner finally came on the circuit. The biologist sounded relieved, yet subdued—like a man who has just come through some great intellectual crisis.

"Hello, *Kon-Tiki.* We've solved your problem, but we can still hardly believe it.

"What you've been seeing is bioluminescence, very similar to that produced by microorganisms in the tropical seas of Earth. Here they're in the atmosphere, not the ocean, but the principle is the same."

"But the pattern," protested Falcon, "was so regular—so *artificial.* And it was hundreds of miles across!"

"It was even larger than you imagine; you observed only a small part of it. The whole pattern was over three thousand miles wide and looked like a revolving wheel. You merely saw the spokes, sweeping past you at about six-tenths of a mile a second. . . ."

"A *second!*" Falcon could not help interjecting. "No animals could move that fast!"

"Of course not. Let me explain. What you saw was triggered by the shock wave from Source Beta, moving at the speed of sound."

"But what about the pattern?" Falcon insisted.

"That's the surprising part. It's a very rare phenomenon, but identical wheels of light—except that they're a thousand times smaller—have been observed in the Persian Gulf and the Indian Ocean. Listen to this: British India Company's *Patna,* Persian Gulf, May 1880, 1:30 P.M.—'an enormous luminous wheel, whirling round, the spokes of which appeared to brush the ship along. The spokes were 200 or 300 yards long . . . each wheel contained about sixteen spokes. . . .' And here's one from the Gulf of Omar, dated May 23, 1906: 'The intensely bright luminescence approached us rapidly, shooting sharply defined light rays to the west in rapid succession, like the beam from the searchlight of a warship. . . . To the left of us, a gigantic fiery wheel formed itself, with spokes that reached as far as one could see. The whole wheel whirled around for two or three minutes. . . .' The archive computer on Ganymede dug up about five hundred cases. It would have printed out the lot if we hadn't stopped it in time."

"I'm convinced—but still baffled."

"I don't blame you. The full explanation wasn't worked out until late in the twentieth century. It seems that these luminous wheels are the results of submarine earthquakes, and always occur in shallow waters where the shock waves can be reflected and cause standing wave patterns. Sometimes bars, sometimes rotating wheels—the 'Wheels of Poseidon,' they've been called. The theory was finally proved by making underwater explosions and photographing the results from a satellite. No wonder sailors used to be superstitious. Who would have believed a thing like *this?*"

So that was it, Falcon told himself. When Source Beta blew its top, it must have sent shock waves in all directions—through the compressed gas of the lower atmosphere, through the solid body of Jupiter itself. Meeting and crisscrossing, those waves must have canceled here, reinforced there; the whole planet must have rung like a bell.

Yet the explanation did not destroy the sense of wonder and awe; he would never be able to forget those flickering bands of light, racing through the unattainable depths of the Jovian atmosphere. He felt that he was not merely on a strange planet, but in some magical realm between myth and reality.

This was a world where absolutely *anything* could happen, and no man could possibly guess what the future would bring.

And he still had a whole day to go.

VI
MEDUSA

When the true dawn finally arrived, it brought a sudden change of weather. *Kon-Tiki* was moving through a blizzard; waxen snowflakes were falling so thickly that visibility was reduced to zero. Falcon began to worry about the weight that might be accumulating on the envelope. Then he noticed that any flakes settling outside the windows quickly disappeared; *Kon-Tiki*'s continual outpouring of heat was evaporating them as swiftly as they arrived.

If he had been ballooning on Earth, he would also have worried about the possibility of collision. At least that was no danger here; any Jovian mountains were several hundred miles below him. And as for the floating islands of foam, hitting them would probably be like plowing into slightly hardened soap bubbles.

Nevertheless, he switched on the horizontal radar, which until now had been completely useless; only the vertical beam, giving his distance from the invisible surface, had thus far been of any value. Then he had another surprise.

Scattered across a huge sector of the sky ahead were dozens of large and brilliant echoes. They were completely isolated from one another and apparently hung unsupported in space. Falcon remembered a phrase the earliest aviators had used to describe one of the hazards of their profession: "clouds stuffed with rocks." That was a perfect description of what seemed to lie in the track of *Kon-Tiki*.

It was a disconcerting sight; then Falcon again reminded himself that nothing *really* solid could possibly hover in this atmosphere. Perhaps it was some strange meteorological phenomenon. In any case, the nearest echo was about a hundred and twenty-five miles.

He reported to Mission Control, which could provide no explanation. But it gave the welcome news that he would be clear of the blizzard in another thirty minutes.

It did not warn him, however, of the violent cross wind that abruptly grabbed *Kon-Tiki* and swept it almost at right angles to its previous track. Falcon needed all his skill and the maximum use of what little control he had over his ungainly vehicle to prevent it from being capsized. Within minutes he was racing northward at over three hundred miles an hour. Then, as suddenly as it had started, the turbulence ceased; he was still moving at high speed, but in smooth air. He wondered if he had been caught in the Jovian equivalent of a jet stream.

The snow storm dissolved; and he saw what Jupiter had been preparing for him.

Kon-Tiki had entered the funnel of a gigantic whirlpool, some six hundred miles across. The balloon was being swept along a curving wall of cloud. Overhead, the sun was shining in a clear sky; but far beneath, this great hole in the atmosphere drilled down to unknown depths until it reached a misty floor where lightning flickered almost continuously.

Though the vessel was being dragged downward so slowly that it was in no immediate danger, Falcon increased the flow of heat into the envelope until *Kon-Tiki* hovered at a constant altitude. Not until then did he abandon the fantastic spectacle outside and consider again the problem of the radar.

The nearest echo was now only about twenty-five miles away. All of them, he quickly realized, were distributed along the wall of the vortex, and were moving with it, apparently caught in the whirlpool like *Kon-Tiki* itself. He aimed the telescope along the radar bearing and found himself looking at a curious mottled cloud that almost filled the field of view.

It was not easy to see, being only a little darker than the whirling wall of mist that formed its background. Not until he had been staring for several minutes did Falcon realize that he had met it once before.

The first time it had been crawling across the drifting mountains of foam, and he had mistaken it for a giant, many-trunked tree. Now at last he could appreciate its real size and complexity and could give it a better name to fix its image in his mind. It did not resemble a tree at all, but a jellyfish—a medusa, such as might be met trailing its tenacles as it drifted along the warm eddies of the Gulf Stream.

This medusa was more than a mile across and its scores of dangling tentacles were hundreds of feet long. They swayed slowly back and forth in perfect unison, taking more than a minute for each complete undulation—almost as if the creature was clumsily rowing itself through the sky.

The other echoes were more distant medusae. Falcon focused the telescope on half a dozen and could see no variations in shape or size. They all seemed to be of the same species, and he wondered just why they were drifting lazily around in this six-hundred-mile orbit. Perhaps they were feeding upon the aerial plankton sucked in by the whirlpool, as *Kon-Tiki* itself had been.

"Do you realize, Howard," said Dr. Brenner, when he had recovered from his initial astonishment, "that this thing is about a hundred thousand times as large as the biggest whale? And even if it's only a gasbag, it must still weigh a million tons! I can't even guess at its metabolism. It must generate megawatts of heat to maintain its buoyancy."

"But if it's just a gasbag, why is it such a damn good radar reflector?"

"I haven't the faintest idea. Can you get any closer?"

Brenner's question was not an idle one. If he changed altitude to take advantage of the differing wind velocities, Falcon could approach the medusa as closely as he wished. At the moment, however, he preferred his present twenty-five miles and said so, firmly.

"I see what you mean," Brenner answered, a little reluctantly. "Let's stay where we are for the present." That "we" gave Falcon a certain wry amusement; an extra sixty thousand miles made a considerable difference in one's point of view.

For the next two hours *Kon-Tiki* drifted uneventfully in the gyre of the great whirlpool, while Falcon experimented with filters and camera contrast, trying to get a clear view of the medusa. He began to wonder if its elusive coloration was some kind of camouflage; perhaps, like many animals of Earth, it was trying to lose itself against its background. That was a trick used by both hunters and hunted.

In which category was the medusa? That was a question he could hardly expect to have answered in the short time that was left to him. Yet just before noon, without the slightest warning, the answer came. . . .

Like a squadron of antique jet fighters, five mantas came sweeping through the wall of mist that formed the funnel of the vortex. They were flying in a V formation directly toward the pallid gray cloud of the medusa; and there was no doubt, in Falcon's mind, that they were on the attack. He had been quite wrong to assume that they were harmless vegetarians.

Yet everything happened at such a leisurely pace that it was like watching a slow-motion film. The mantas undulated along at perhaps thirty miles an hour; it seemed ages before they reached the medusa, which continued to paddle imperturbably along at an even slower speed. Huge though they were, the mantas looked tiny beside the monster they were approaching. When they flapped down on its back, they appeared about as large as birds landing on a whale.

Could the medusa defend itself, Falcon wondered. He did not see how the attacking mantas could be in danger as long as they avoided those huge clumsy tentacles. And perhaps their host was not even aware of them; they could be insignificant parasites, tolerated as are fleas upon a dog.

But now it was obvious that the medusa was in distress. With agonizing slowness, it began to tip over like a capsizing ship. After ten minutes it had tilted forty-five degrees; it was also rapidly losing altitude. It was impossible not to feel a sense of pity for the beleaguered monster, and to Falcon the sight brought bitter memories. In a grotesque way, the fall of the medusa was almost a parody of the dying *Queen*'s last moments.

Yet he knew that his sympathies were on the wrong side. High intelligence could develop only among predators—not among the drifting browsers of either sea or air. The mantas were far closer to him than was this monstrous bag of gas. And anyway, who could *really* sympathize with a creature a hundred thousand times larger than a whale?

Then he noticed that the medusa's tactics seemed to be having some effect. The mantas had been disturbed by its slow roll and were flapping heavily away from its back—like gorged vultures interrupted at mealtime. But they did not move very far, continuing to hover a few yards from the still-capsizing monster.

There was a sudden, blinding flash of light synchronized with a crash of static over the radio. One of the mantas, slowly twisting end over end, was plummeting straight downward. As it fell, a plume of black smoke trailed behind it. The resemblance to an aircraft going down in flames was quite uncanny.

In unison, the remaining mantas dived steeply away from the medusa, gaining speed by losing altitude. They had, within minutes, vanished back into the wall of cloud from which they had emerged. And the medusa, no longer falling, began to roll back toward the horizontal. Soon it was sailing along once more on an even keel, as if nothing had happened.

"Beautiful!" said Dr. Brenner, after a moment of stunned silence. "It's developed electric defenses, like some of our eels and rays. But that must have been about a million volts! Can you see any organs that might produce the discharge? Anything looking like electrodes?"

"No," Falcon answered, after switching to the highest power of the telescope. "But here's something odd. Do you see this pattern? Check back on the earlier images. I'm sure it wasn't there before."

A broad, mottled band had appeared along the side of the medusa. It formed a startlingly regular checkboard, each square of which was itself speckled in a complex subpattern of short horizontal lines. They were spaced at equal distances in a geometrically perfect array of rows and columns.

"You're right," said Dr. Brenner, with something very much like awe in his voice. "That's just appeared. And I'm afraid to tell you what I think it is."

"Well, I have no reputation to lose—at least as a biologist. Shall I give my guess?"

"Go ahead."

"That's a large meter-band radio array. The sort of thing they used back at the beginning of the twentieth century."

"I was afraid you'd say that. Now we know why it gave such a massive echo."

"But why has it just appeared?"

"Probably an aftereffect of the discharge."

"I've just had another thought," said Falcon, rather slowly. "Do you suppose it's *listening* to us?"

"On this frequency? I doubt it. Those are meter—no, *decameter* antennas—judging by their size. Hmm . . . that's an idea!"

Dr. Brenner fell silent, obviously contemplating some new line of thought. Presently he continued: "I bet they're tuned to the radio outbursts! That's something nature never got around to doing on Earth. . . . We have animals with sonar and even electric senses, but nothing ever developed a radio sense. Why bother where there was so much light?

"But it's different here. Jupiter is *drenched* with radio energy. It's worth while using it—maybe even tapping it. That thing could be a floating power plant!"

A new voice cut into the conversation.

"Mission Commander here. This is all very interesting, but there's a much more important matter to settle. *Is it intelligent?* If so, we've got to consider the First Contact directives."

"Until I came here," said Dr. Brenner, somewhat ruefully, "I would have sworn that anything that could make a shortwave antenna system *must* be intelligent. Now, I'm not sure. This could have evolved naturally. I suppose it's no more fantastic than the human eye."

"Then we have to play safe and assume intelligence. For the present, therefore, this expedition comes under all the clauses of the Prime directive."

There was a long silence while everyone on the radio circuit absorbed the implications of this. For the first time in the history of space flight, the rules that had been established through more than a century of argument might have to be applied. Man had—it was hoped—profited from his mistakes on Earth. Not only moral considerations, but also his own self-interest demanded that he should not repeat them among the planets. It could be disastrous to treat a superior intelligence as the American settlers had treated the Indians, or as almost everyone had treated the Africans. . . .

The first rule was: keep your distance. Make no attempt to approach, or even to communicate, until "they" have had plenty of time to study you. Exactly what was meant by "plenty of time," no one had ever been able to decide. It was left to the discretion of the man on the spot.

A responsibility of which he had never dreamed had descended upon Howard Falcon. In the few hours that remained to him on Jupiter, he might become the first ambassador of the human race.

And *that* was an irony so delicious that he almost wished the surgeons had restored to him the power of laughter.

VII
PRIME DIRECTIVE

It was growing darker, but Falcon scarcely noticed as he strained his eyes toward that living cloud in the field of the telescope. The wind that was steadily sweeping *Kon-Tiki* around the funnel of the great whirlpool had now brought him within twelve miles of the creature. If he got much closer than six, he would take evasive action. Though he felt certain that the medusa's electric weapons were short ranged, he did not wish to put the matter to the test. That would be a problem for future explorers, and he wished them luck.

Now it was quite dark in the capsule. That was strange, because sunset was still hours away. Automatically, he glanced at the horizontally scanning radar, as he had done every few minutes. Apart from the medusa he was studying, there was no other object within about sixty miles of him.

Suddenly, with startling power, he heard the sound that had come booming out of the Jovian night—the throbbing beat that grew more and more rapid, then stopped in mid-crescendo. The whole capsule vibrated with it like a pea in a kettledrum.

Falcon realized two things almost simultaneously during the sudden, aching silence. *This* time the sound was not coming from thousands of miles away, over a radio circuit. It was in the very atmosphere around him.

The second thought was even more disturbing. He had quite forgotten —it was inexcusable, but there had been other apparently more important things on his mind—that most of the sky above him was completely blanked out by *Kon-Tiki*'s gasbag. Being lightly silvered to conserve its heat, the great balloon was an effective shield both to radar and to vision.

He had known this, of course; it had been a minor defect of the design, tolerated because it did not appear important. It seemed very important to Howard Falcon now—as he saw that fence of gigantic tentacles, thicker than the trunks of any tree, descending all around the capsule.

He heard Brenner yelling: "Remember the Prime directive! Don't alarm it!" Before he could make an appropriate answer that overwhelming drumbeat started again and drowned all other sounds.

The sign of a really skilled test pilot is how he reacts not to foreseeable emergencies, but to ones that nobody could have anticipated. Falcon did not hesitate for more than a second to analyze the situation. In a lightning-swift movement, he pulled the rip cord.

That word was an archaic survival from the days of the first hydrogen balloons; on *Kon-Tiki,* the rip cord did not tear open the gasbag, but merely operated a set of louvers around the upper curve of the envelope. At once the hot gas started to rush out; *Kon-Tiki,* deprived of her lift, began to fall swiftly in this gravity field two and a half times as strong as Earth's.

Falcon had a momentary glimpse of great tentacles whipping upward and away. He had just time to note that they were studded with large bladders or sacs, presumably to give them buoyancy, and that they ended in multitudes of thin feelers like the roots of a plant. He half expected a bolt of lightning—but nothing happened.

His precipitous rate of descent was slackening as the atmosphere thickened and the deflated envelope acted as a parachute. When *Kon-Tiki* had dropped about two miles, he felt that it was safe to close the louvers again. By the time he had restored buoyancy and was in equilibrium once more, he had lost another mile of altitude and was getting dangerously near his safety limit.

He peered anxiously through the overhead windows, though he did not expect to see anything except the obscuring bulk of the balloon. But he had sideslipped during his descent, and part of the medusa was just visible a couple of miles above him. It was much closer than he expected—and it was still coming down, faster than he would have believed possible.

Mission Control was calling anxiously. He shouted: "I'm O.K.—but it's still coming after me. I can't go any deeper."

That was not quite true. He could go a lot deeper—about one hundred and eighty miles. But it would be a one-way trip, and most of the journey would be of little interest to him.

Then, to his great relief, he saw that the medusa was leveling off, not quite a mile above him. Perhaps it had decided to approach this strange intruder with caution; or perhaps it, too, found this deeper layer uncomfortably hot. The temperature was over fifty degrees centigrade, and Falcon wondered how much longer his life-support system could handle matters.

Dr. Brenner was back on the circuit, still worrying about the Prime directive.

"Remember—it may only be inquisitive!" he cried, without much conviction. "Try not to frighten it!"

Falcon was getting rather tired of this advice and recalled a TV discussion he had once seen between a space lawyer and an astronaut. After the full implications of the Prime directive had been carefully spelled out, the incredulous spacer had exclaimed: "Then if there was no alternative, I must sit still and let myself be eaten?" The lawyer had not even cracked a smile when he answered: "That's an *excellent* summing up."

It had seemed funny at the time; it was not at all amusing now.

And then Falcon saw something that made him even more unhappy. The medusa was still hovering about a mile above him—but one of its tentacles was becoming incredibly elongated, and was stretching down toward *Kon-Tiki,* thinning out at the same time. As a boy he had once seen the funnel of a tornado descending from a storm cloud over the Kansas plains. The thing coming toward him now evoked vivid memories of that black, twisting snake in the sky.

"I'm rapidly running out of options," he reported to Mission Control. "I now have only a choice between frightening it—and giving it a bad stomach-ache. I don't think it will find *Kon-Tiki* very digestible, if that's what it has in mind."

He waited for comments from Brenner, but the biologist remained silent.

"Very well. It's twenty-seven minutes ahead of time, but I'm starting the ignition sequencer. I hope I'll have enough reserve to correct my orbit later."

He could no longer see the medusa; once more it was directly overhead. But he knew that the descending tentacle must now be very close to the balloon. It would take almost five minutes to bring the reactor up to full thrust. . . .

The fusor was primed. The orbit computer had not rejected the situation as wholly impossible. The air scoops were open, ready to gulp in tons of the surrounding hydrohelium on demand. Even under optimum conditions, this would have been the moment of truth—for there had been no way of testing how a nuclear ramjet would *really* work in the strange atmosphere of Jupiter.

Very gently something rocked *Kon-Tiki*. Falcon tried to ignore it.

Ignition had been planned at six miles higher, in an atmosphere of less than a quarter of the density and thirty degrees cooler. Too bad.

What was the shallowest dive he could get away with, for the air scoops to work? When the ram ignited, he'd be heading toward Jupiter with two and a half g's to help him get there. Could he possibly pull out in time?

A large, heavy hand patted the balloon. The whole vessel bobbed up and down, like one of the Yo-yo's that had just become the craze on Earth.

Of course, Brenner *might* be perfectly right. Perhaps it was just trying to be friendly. Maybe he should try to talk to it over the radio. Which should it be: "Pretty pussy"? "Down, Fido"? Or "Take me to your leader"?

The tritium-deuterium ratio was correct. He was ready to light the candle, with a hundred-million-degree match.

The thin tip of the tentacle came slithering around the edge of the balloon some sixty yards away. It was about the size of an elephant's trunk, and by the delicate way it was moving appeared to be almost as sensitive. There were little palps at its end, like questing mouths. He was sure that Dr. Brenner would be fascinated.

This seemed about as good a time as any. He gave a swift scan of the entire control board, started the final four-second ignition count, broke the safety seal, and pressed the JETTISON switch.

There was a sharp explosion and an instant loss of weight. *Kon-Tiki* was falling freely, nose down. Overhead, the discarded balloon was racing upward, dragging the inquisitive tentacle with it. Falcon had no time to see if the gasbag actually hit the medusa, because at that moment the ramjet fired and he had other matters to think about.

A roaring column of hot hydrohelium was pouring out of the reactor nozzles, swiftly building up thrust—but *toward* Jupiter, not away from it. He could not pull out yet, for vector control was too sluggish. Unless he could gain complete control and achieve horizontal flight within the next five seconds, the vehicle would dive too deeply into the atmosphere and would be destroyed.

With agonizing slowness—those five seconds seemed like fifty—he managed to flatten out, then pull the nose upward. He glanced back only once and caught a final glimpse of the medusa, many miles away. *Kon-Tiki*'s discarded gasbag had apparently escaped from its grasp, for he could see no sign of it.

Now he was master once more—no longer drifting helplessly on the winds of Jupiter, but riding his own column of atomic fire back to the stars. He was confident that the ramjet would steadily give him velocity and altitude until he had reached near-orbital speed at the fringes of the atmosphere. Then, with a brief burst of pure rocket power, he would regain the freedom of space.

Halfway to orbit, he looked south and saw the tremendous enigma of the Great Red Spot—that floating island twice the size of Earth—coming up over the horizon. He stared into its mysterious beauty until the computer warned him that conversion to rocket thrust was only sixty seconds ahead. He tore his gaze reluctantly away.

"Some other time," he murmured.

"What's that?" said Mission Control. "What did you say?"

"It doesn't matter," he replied.

VIII
BETWEEN TWO WORLDS

"You're a hero now, Howard," said Webster, "not just a celebrity. You've given them something to think about—injected some excitement into their lives. Not one in a million will actually travel to the Outer Giants, but the whole human race will go in imagination. And that's what counts."

"I'm glad to have made your job a little easier."

Webster was too old a friend to take offense at the note of irony. Yet it surprised him. And this was not the first change in Howard that he had noticed since the return from Jupiter.

The Administrator pointed to the famous sign on his desk, borrowed from an impresario of an earlier age: ASTONISH ME!

"I'm not ashamed of my job. New knowledge, new resources—they're all very well. But men also need novelty and excitement. Space travel has become routine; you've made it a great adventure once more. It will be a long, long time before we get Jupiter pigeonholed. And maybe longer still before we understand those medusae. I still think that one *knew* where your blind spot was. Anyway, have you decided on your next move? Saturn, Uranus, Neptune—you name it."

"I don't know. I've thought about Saturn, but I'm not really needed there. It's only one gravity, not two and a half like Jupiter. So men can handle it."

Men, thought Webster. He said "men." He's never done that before. And when did I last hear him use the word "we"? He's changing, slipping away from us. . . .

"Well," he said aloud, rising from his chair to conceal his slight uneasiness, "let's get the conference started. The cameras are all set up and everyone's waiting. You'll meet a lot of old friends."

He stressed the last word, but Howard showed no response. The leathery mask of his face was becoming more and more difficult to read. Instead, he rolled back from the Administrator's desk, unlocked his undercarriage so that it no longer formed a chair, and rose on his hydraulics to his full seven feet of height. It had been good psychology on the part of the surgeons to give him that extra twelve inches, to compensate somewhat for all that he had lost when the *Queen* had crashed.

Falcon waited until Webster had opened the door, then pivoted neatly on his balloon tires and headed for it at a smooth and silent twenty miles an hour. The display of speed and precision was not flaunted arrogantly; rather, it had become quite unconscious.

Howard Falcon, who had once been a man and could still pass for one over a voice circuit, felt a calm sense of achievement—and, for the first time in years, something like peace of mind. Since his return from Jupiter, the nightmares had ceased. He had found his role at last.

He now knew why he had dreamed about that superchimp aboard the doomed *Queen Elizabeth.* Neither man nor beast, it was between two worlds; and so was he.

He alone could travel unprotected on the lunar surface. The life-support system inside the metal cylinder that had replaced his fragile body functioned equally well in space or under water. Gravity fields ten times that of Earth were an inconvenience, but nothing more. And no gravity was best of all. . . .

The human race was becoming more remote, the ties of kinship more tenuous. Perhaps these air-breathing, radiation-sensitive bundles of unstable carbon compounds had no right beyond the atmosphere; they should stick to their natural homes—Earth, Moon, Mars.

Some day the real masters of space would be machines, not men—and he was neither. Already conscious of his destiny, he took a somber pride in his unique loneliness—the first immortal midway between two orders of creation.

He would, after all, be an ambassador; between the old and the new—between the creatures of carbon and the creatures of metal who must one day supersede them.

Both would have need of him in the troubled centuries that lay ahead.

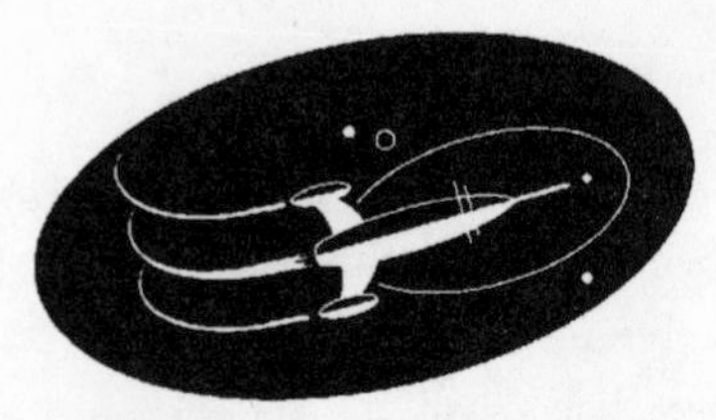

Home Is the Hangman

Roger Zelazny

Big fat flakes down the night, silent night, windless night. And I never count them as storms unless there is wind. Not a sigh or whimper, though. Just a cold, steady whiteness, drifting down outside the window, and a silence confirmed by gunfire, driven deeper now that it had ceased. In the main room of the lodge the only sounds were the occasional hiss and sputter of the logs turning to ashes on the grate.

I sat in a chair turned sidewise from the table to face the door. A tool kit rested on the floor to my left. The helmet stood on the table, a lopsided basket of metal, quartz, porcelain, and glass. If I heard the click of a microswitch followed by a humming sound from within it, then a faint light would come on beneath the meshing near to its forward edge and begin to blink rapidly. If these things occurred, there was a very strong possibility that I was going to die.

I had removed a black ball from my pocket when Larry and Bert had gone outside, armed, respectively, with a flame thrower and what looked like an elephant gun. Bert had also taken two grenades with him.

I unrolled the black ball, opening it out into a seamless glove, a dollop of something resembling moist putty stuck to its palm. Then I drew the glove on over my left hand and sat with it upraised, elbow resting on the arm of the chair. A small laser flash pistol in which I had very little faith lay beside my right hand on the tabletop, next to the helmet.

If I were to slap a metal surface with my left hand, the substance would adhere there, coming free of the glove. Two seconds later it would explode, and the force of the explosion would be directed in against the surface. Newton would claim his own by way of right-angled redistributions of the reaction, hopefully tearing lateral hell out of the contact surface. A smother-charge, it was called, and its possession came under concealed-weapons and possession-of-burglary-tools statutes in most places. The molecularly gimmicked goo, I decided, was great stuff. It was just the delivery system that left more to be desired.

Beside the helmet, next to the gun, in front of my hand, stood a small walkie-talkie. This was for purposes of warning Bert and Larry if I should hear the click of a microswitch followed by a humming sound, should see a light come on and begin to blink rapidly. Then they would know that Tom and Clay, with whom we had lost contact when the shooting began, had failed to destroy the enemy and doubtless lay lifeless at their stations now, a little over a kilometer to the south. Then they would know that they, too, were probably about to die.

I called out to them when I heard the click. I picked up the helmet and rose to my feet as its light began to blink.

But it was already too late.

The fourth place listed on the Christmas card I had sent Don Walsh the previous year was Peabody's Book Shop and Beer Stube in Baltimore, Maryland. Accordingly, on the last night in October I sat in its rearmost room, at the final table before the alcove with the door leading to the alley. Across that dim chamber, a woman dressed in black played the ancient upright piano, uptempoing everything she touched. Off to my right, a fire wheezed and spewed fumes on a narrow hearth beneath a crowded mantelpiece overseen by an ancient and antlered profile. I sipped a beer and listened to the sounds.

I half hoped that this would be one of the occasions when Don failed to show up. I had sufficient funds to hold me through spring and I did not really feel like working. I had summered farther north, was anchored now in the Chesapeake, and was anxious to continue Caribbeanward. A growing chill and some nasty winds told me I had tarried overlong in these latitudes. Still, the understanding was that I remain in the chosen bar until midnight. Two hours to go.

I ate a sandwich and ordered another beer. About halfway into it, I spotted Don approaching the entranceway, topcoat over his arm, head turning. I manufactured a matching quantity of surprise when he appeared beside my table with a, "Don! Is that really you?"

I rose and clasped his hand.

"Alan! Small world, or something like that. Sit down! Sit down!"

He settled onto the chair across from me, draped his coat over the one to his left.

"What are you doing in this town?" he asked.

"Just a visit," I answered. "Said hello to a few friends." I patted the scars, the stains on the venerable surface before me. "And this is my last stop. I'll be leaving in a few hours."

He chuckled.

"Why is it that you knock on wood?"

I grinned.

"I was expressing affection for one of Henry Mencken's favorite speak-easies."

"This place dates back that far?"

I nodded.

"It figures," he said. "You've got this thing for the past—or against the present. I'm never sure which."

"Maybe a little of both," I said. "I wish Mencken would stop in. I'd like his opinion on the present.—What are you doing with it?"

"What?"

"The present. Here. Now."

"Oh." He spotted the waitress and ordered a beer. "Business trip," he said then. "To hire a consultant."

"Oh. How *is* business?"

"Complicated," he said, "complicated."

We lit cigarettes and after a while his beer arrived. We smoked and drank and listened to the music.

I've sung this song and I'll sing it again: the world is like an uptempoed piece of music. Of the many changes which came to pass during my lifetime, it seems that the majority have occurred during the past few years. It also struck me that way several years ago, and I'd a hunch I might be feeling the same way a few years hence—that is, if Don's business did not complicate me off this mortal coil or condenser before then.

Don operates the second-largest detective agency in the world, and he sometimes finds me useful because I do not exist. I do not exist now because I existed once at the time and the place where we attempted to begin scoring the wild ditty of our times. I refer to the world Central Data Bank project and the fact that I had had a significant part in that effort to construct a working model of the real world, accounting for everyone and everything in it. How well we succeeded, and whether possession of the world's likeness does indeed provide its custodians with a greater measure of control over its functions, are questions my former colleagues still debate as the music grows more shrill and you can't see the maps for the pins. I made my decision back then and saw to it that I did not receive citizenship in that second world, a place which may now have become more important than the first. Exiled to reality, my own sojourns across the line are necessarily those of an alien guilty of illegal entry. I visit periodically because I go where I must to make my living.—That is where Don comes in. The people I can become are often very useful when he has peculiar problems.

Unfortunately, at that moment, it seemed that he did, just when the whole gang of me felt like turning down the volume and loafing.

We finished our drinks, got the bill, settled it.

"This way," I said, indicating the rear door, and he swung into his coat and followed me out.

"Talk here?" he asked, as we walked down the alley.

"Rather not," I said. "Public transportation, then private conversation."

He nodded and came along.

About three-quarters of an hour later we were in the saloon of the *Proteus* and I was making coffee. We were rocked gently by the Bay's chill waters, under a moonless sky. I'd only a pair of the smaller lights burning. Comfortable. On the water, aboard the *Proteus,* the crowding, the activities, the tempo, of life in the cities, on the land, are muted, slowed—fictionalized—by the metaphysical distancing a few meters of water can provide. We alter the landscape with great facility, but the ocean has always seemed unchanged, and I suppose by extension we are infected with some feelings of timelessness whenever we set out upon her. Maybe that's one of the reasons I spend so much time there.

"First time you've had me aboard," he said. "Comfortable. Very."

"Thanks.—Cream? Sugar?"

"Yes. Both."

We settled back with our steaming mugs and I asked, "What have you got?"

"One case involving two problems," he said. "One of them sort of falls within my area of competence. The other does not. I was told that it is an absolutely unique situation and would require the services of a very special specialist."

"I'm not a specialist at anything but keeping alive."

His eyes came up suddenly and caught my own.

"I had always assumed that you knew an awful lot about computers," he said.

I looked away. That was hitting below the belt. I had never held myself out to him as an authority in that area, and there had always been a tacit understanding between us that my methods of manipulating circumstance and identity were not open to discussion. On the other hand, it was obvious to him that my knowledge of the system was both extensive and intensive. Still, I didn't like talking about it. So I moved to defend.

"Computer people are a dime a dozen," I said. "It was probably different in your time, but these days they start teaching computer science to little kids their first year in school. So sure, I know a lot about it. This generation, everybody does."

"You know that is not what I meant," he said. Haven't you known me long enough to trust me a little more than that? The question springs solely from the case at hand. That's all."

I nodded. Reactions by their very nature are not always appropriate, and I had invested a lot of emotional capital in a heavy-duty set. So, "Okay, I know more about them than the school kids," I said.

"Thanks. That can be our point of departure." He took a sip of coffee. "My own background is in law and accounting, followed by the military, military intelligence, and civil service, in that order. Then I got into this business. What technical stuff I know I've picked up along the way—a scrap here, a crash course there. I know a lot about what things can *do,* not so much about how they *work.* I did not understand the details on this one, so I want you to start at the top and explain things to me, for as far as you can go. I need the background review, and if you are able to furnish it I will also know that you are the man for the job. You can begin by telling me how the early space-exploration robots worked—like, say the ones they used on Venus."

"That's not computers," I said, "and for that matter, they weren't really robots. They were telefactoring devices."

"Tell me what makes the difference."

"A robot is a machine which carries out certain operations in accordance with a program of instructions. A telefactor is a slave machine operated by remote control. The telefactor functions in a feedback situation with its operator. Depending on how sophisticated you want to get, the links can be audiovisual, kinesthetic, tactile, even olfactory. The more you want to go in this direction, the more anthropomorphic you get in the thing's design.

"In the case of Venus, if I recall correctly, the human operator in orbit wore an exoskeleton which controlled the movements of the body, legs, arms, and hands of the device on the surface below, receiving motion and force feedback through a system of airjet transducers. He had on a helmet controlling the slave device's television camera—set, obviously enough, in its turret—which filled his field of vision with the scene below. He also wore earphones connected with its audio pickup. I read the book he wrote later. He said that for long stretches of time he would forget the cabin, forget that he was at the boss end of a control loop, and actually feel as if he were stalking through that hellish landscape. I remember being very impressed by it, just being a kid, and I wanted a super-tiny one all my own, so that I could wade around in puddles picking fights with microorganisms."

"Why?"

"Because there weren't any dragons on Venus. Anyhow, that is a telefactoring device, a thing quite distinct from a robot."

"I'm still with you," he said, and "Now tell me the difference between the early telefactoring devices and the later ones."

I swallowed some coffee.

"It was a bit trickier with respect to the outer planets and their satellites," I said. "There, we did not have orbiting operators at first. Economics, and some unresolved technical problems. Mainly economics. At any rate, the devices were landed on the target worlds, but the operators stayed home. Because of this, there was of course a time lag in the transmissions along the control loop. It took a while to receive the on-site input, and then there was another time lapse before the response movements reached the telefactor. We attempted to compensate for this in two ways: the first was by the employment of a simple wait-move, wait-move sequence; the second was more sophisticated and is actually the point where computers come into the picture in terms of participating in the control loop. It involved the setting up of models of known environmental factors, which were then enriched during the initial wait-move sequences. On this basis, the computer was then used to anticipate short-range developments. Finally, it could take over the loop and run it by a combination of 'predictor controls' and wait-move reviews. It still had to holler for human help, though, when unexpected things came up. So, with the outer planets, it was neither totally automatic nor totally manual—nor totally satisfactory—at first."

"Okay," he said, lighting a cigarette. "And the next step?"

"The next wasn't really a technical step forward in telefactoring. It was an economic shift. The pursestrings were loosened and we could afford to send men out. We landed them where we could land them, and in many of the places where we could not, we sent down the telefactors and orbited the men again. Like in the old days. The time-lag problem was removed because the operator was on top of things once more. If anything, you can look at it as a reversion to earlier methods. It is what we still often do, though, and it works."

He shook his head.

"You left something out between the computers and the bigger budget."

I shrugged.

"A number of things were tried during that period, but none of them proved as effective as what we already had going in the human-computer partnership with the telefactors."

"There was one project," he said, "which attempted to get around the time-lag troubles by sending the computer along with the telefactor as part of the package. Only the computer wasn't exactly a computer and the telefactor wasn't exactly a telefactor. Do you know which one I am referring to?"

I lit a cigarette of my own while I thought about it, then, "I think you are talking about the Hangman," I said.

"That's right and this is where I get lost. Can you tell me how it works?"

"Ultimately, it was a failure," I told him.

"But it worked at first."

"Aparently. But only on the easy stuff, on Io. It conked out later and had to be written off as a failure, albeit a noble one. The venture was overly ambitious from the very beginning. What seems to have happened was that the people in charge had the opportunity to combine vanguard projects—stuff that was still under investigation and stuff that was extremely new. In theory, it all seemed to dovetail so beautifully that they yielded to the temptation and incorporated too much. It started out well, but it fell apart later."

"But what all was involved in the thing?"

"Lord! What wasn't? The computer that wasn't exactly a computer . . . Okay, we'll start there. Last century, three engineers at the University of Wisconsin—Nordman, Parmentier, and Scott—developed a device known as a superconductive tunnel-junction neuristor. Two tiny strips of metal with a thin insulating layer between. Supercool it and it passed electrical impulses without resistance. Surround it with magnetized material and pack a mass of them together—billions—and what have you got?"

He shook his head.

"Well, for one thing you've got an impossible situation to schematize when considering all the paths and interconnections that may be formed.

There is an obvious similarity to the structure of the brain. So, they theorized, you don't even attempt to hook up such a device. You pulse in data and let it establish its own preferential pathways, by means of the magnetic material's becoming increasingly magnetized each time the current passes through it, thus cutting the resistance. The material establishes its own routes in a fashion analogous to the functioning of the brain when it is learning something.

"In the case of the Hangman, they used a setup very similar to this and they were able to pack over ten billion neuristor-type cells into a very small area—around a cubic foot. They aimed for that magic figure because that is approximately the number of nerve cells in the human brain. That is what I meant when I said that it wasn't really a computer. They were actually working in the area of artirficial intelligence, no matter what they called it."

"If the thing had its own brain—computer or quasihuman—then it was a robot rather than a telefactor, right?"

"Yes and no and maybe," I said. "It was operated as a telefactor device here on Earth—on the ocean floor, in the desert, in mountainous country—as part of its programming. I suppose you could also call that its apprenticeship—or kindergarten. Perhaps that is even more appropriate. It was being shown how to explore in difficult environments and to report back. Once it mastered this, then theoretically they could hang it out there in the sky without a control loop and let it report its own findings."

"At that point would it be considered a robot?"

"A robot is a machine which carries out certain operations in accordance with a program of instructions. The Hangman made its *own* decisions, you see. And I suspect that by trying to produce something that close to the human brain in structure and function, the seemingly inevitable randomness of its model got included in. It wasn't just a machine following a program. It was too complex. That was probably what broke it down."

Don chuckled.

"Inevitable free will?"

"No. As I said, they had thrown too many things into one bag. Everybody and his brother with a pet project that might be fitted in seemed a supersalesman that season. For example, the psychophysics boys had a gimmick they wanted to try on it, and it got used. Ostensibly, the Hangman was a communications device. Actually, they were concerned as to whether the thing was truly sentient."

"Was it?"

"Apparently so, in a limited fashion. What they had come up with, to be made part of the initial telefactor loop, was a device which set up a weak induction field in the brain of the operator. The machine received and amplified the patterns of electrical activity being conducted in the Hangman's—might as well call it 'brain'—then passed them through a complex modulator and pulsed them into the induction field in the operator's head. —I am out of my area now and into that of Weber and Fechner, but a neuron has a threshold at which it will fire, and below which it will not. There are some forty thousand neurons packed together in a square millimeter of the cerebral cortex, in such a fashion that each one has several hundred synaptic connections with others about it. At any given moment, some of them may be way below the firing threshold while others are in a condition Sir John Eccles once referred to as 'critically poised'—ready to fire. If just one is pushed over the threshold, it can affect the discharge of hundreds of thousands of others within twenty milliseconds. The pulsating field was to provide such a push in a sufficiently selective fashion to give the operator an idea as to what was going on in the Hangman's brain. And vice versa. The Hangman was to have its own built-in version of the same thing. It was also thought that this might serve to humanize it somewhat, so that it would better appreciate the significance of its work—to instill something like loyalty, you might say."

"Do you think this could have contributed to its later breakdown?"

"Possibly. How can you say in a one-of-a-kind situation like this? If you want a guess, I'd say, 'Yes.' But it's just a guess."

"Uh-huh," he said, "and what were its physical capabilities?"

"Anthropomorphic design," I said, "both because it was originally telefactored and because of the psychological reasoning I just mentioned. It could pilot its own small vessel. No need for a life-support system, of course. Both it and the vessel were powered by fusion units, so that fuel was no real problem. Self-repairing. Capable of performing a great variety of sophisticated tests and measurements, of making observations, completing reports, learning new material, broadcasting its findings back here.

Capable of surviving just about anywhere. In fact, it required less energy on the outer planets—less work for the refrigeration units, to maintain that supercooled brain in its midsection."

"How strong was it?"

"I don't recall all the specs. Maybe a dozen times as strong as a man, in things like lifting and pushing."

"It explored Io for us and started in on Europa."

"Yes."

"Then it began behaving erratically, just when we thought it had really learned its job."

"That sounds right," I said.

"It refused a direct order to explore Callisto, then headed out toward Uranus."

"Yes. It's been years since I read the reports. . . ."

"The malfunction worsened after that. Long periods of silence interspersed with garbled transmissions. Now that I know more about its makeup, it almost sounds like a man going off the deep end."

"It seems similar."

"But it managed to pull itself together again for a brief while. It landed on Titania, began sending back what seemed like appropriate observation reports. This only lasted a short time, though. It went irrational once more, indicated that it was heading for a landing on Uranus itself, and that was it. We didn't hear from it after that. Now that I know about that mind-reading gadget I understand why a psychiatrist on this end could be so positive it would never function again."

"I never heard about that part."

"I did."

I shrugged. "This was all around twenty years ago," I said, "and, as I mentioned, it has been a long while since I've read anything about it."

"The Hangman's ship crashed or landed, as the case may be, in the Gulf of Mexico, two days ago."

I just stared at him.

"It was empty," Don went on, "when they finally got out and down to it."

"I don't understand."

"Yesterday morning," he continued, "restaurateur Manny Burns was found beaten to death in the office of his establishment, the Maison Saint-Michel, in New Orleans."

"I still fail to see—"

"Manny Burns was one of the four original operators who programmed —pardon me, 'taught'—the Hangman."

The silence lengthened, dragged its belly on the deck.

"Concidence . . . ?" I finally said.

"My client doesn't think so."

"Who is your client?"

"One of the three remaining members of the training group. He is convinced that the Hangman has returned to Earth to kill its former operators."

"Has he made his fears known to his old employers?"

"No."

"Why not?"

"Because it would require telling them the reason for his fears."

"That being . . . ?"

"He wouldn't tell me, either."

"How does he expect you to do a proper job?"

"He told me what he considered a proper job. He wanted two things done, neither of which requires a full case history. He wanted to be furnished with good bodyguards, and he wanted the Hangman found and disposed of. I have already taken care of the first part."

"And you want me to do the second?"

"That's right. You have confirmed my opinion that you are the man for the job."

"I see. Do you realize that if the thing is truly sentient this will be something very like murder? If it is not, of course, then it will only amount to the destruction of expensive government property."

"Which way do you look at it?"

"I look at it as a job," I said.

"You'll take it?"

"I need more facts before I can decide. Like, who is your client? Who are the other operators? Where do they live? What do they do? What—"

He raised his hand.

"First," he said, "the Honorable Jesse Brockden, senior Senator from Wisconsin, is our client. Confidentiality, of course, is written all over it."

I nodded. "I remember his being involved with the space program before he went into politics. I wasn't aware of the specifics, though. He could get government protection so easily—"

"To obtain it, he would apparently have to tell them something he doesn't want to talk about. Perhaps it would hurt his career. I simply do not know. He doesn't want them. He wants us."

I nodded again.

"What about the others? Do they want us, too?"

"Quite the opposite. They don't subscribe to Brockden's notions at all. They seem to think he is something of a paranoid."

"How well do they know one another these days?"

"They live in different parts of the country, haven't seen each other in years. Been in occasional touch, though."

"Kind of a flimsy basis for that diagnosis, then."

"One of them *is* a psychiatrist."

"Oh. Which one?"

"Leila Thackery is her name. Lives in St. Louis. Works at the State Hospital there."

"None of them have gone to any authority, then—federal or local?"

"That's right. Brockden contacted them when he heard about the Hangman. He was in Washington at the time. Got word on its return right away and managed to get the story killed. He tried to reach them all, learned about Burns in the process, contacted me, then tried to persuade the others to accept protection by my people. They weren't buying. When I talked to her, Doctor Thackery pointed out—quite correctly—that Brockden is a very sick man."

"What's he got?"

"Cancer. In his spine. Nothing they can do about it once it hits there and digs in. He even told me he figures he has maybe six months to get through what he considers a very important piece of legislation—the new criminal rehabilitation act.—I will admit that he did sound kind of paranoid when he talked about it. But hell! Who wouldn't? Doctor Thackery sees that as the whole thing, though, and she doesn't see the Burns killing as being connected with the Hangman. Thinks it was just a traditional robbery gone sour, thief surprised and panicky, maybe hopped-up, *et cetera.*"

"Then she is not afraid of the Hangman?"

"She said that she is in a better position to know its mind than anyone else, and she is not especially concerned."

"What about the other operator?"

"He said that Doctor Thackery may know its mind better than anyone else, but he knows its brain, and he isn't worried, either."

"What did he mean by that?"

"David Fentris is a consulting engineer—electronics, cybernetics. He actually had something to do with the Hangman's design."

I got to my feet and went after the coffeepot. Not that I'd an overwhelming desire for another cup at just that moment. But I had known, had once worked with a David Fentris. And he had at one time been connected with the space program.

About fifteen years my senior, Dave had been with the data bank project when I had known him. Where a number of us had begun having second thoughts as the thing progressed, Dave had never been anything less than wildly enthusiastic. A wiry five-eight, gray-cropped, gray eyes back of horn-rims and heavy glass, cycling between preoccupation and near-frantic darting, he had had a way of verbalizing half-completed thoughts as he went along, so that you might begin to think him a representative of that tribe which had come into positions of small authority by means of nepotism or politics. If you would listen a few more minutes, however, you would begin revising your opinion as he started to pull his musings together into a rigorous framework. By the time he had finished, you generally wondered why you hadn't seen it all along and what a guy like that was doing in a position of such small authority. Later, it might strike you, though, that he seemed sad whenever he wasn't enthusiastic about something. And while the gung-ho spirit is great for short-range projects, larger ventures generally require somewhat more equanimity. I wasn't at all surprised that he had wound up as a consultant.

The big quesion now, of course was: Would he remember me? True, my appearance was altered, my personality hopefully more mature, my habits shifted around. But would that be enough, should I have to encounter him as part of this job? That mind behind those hornrims could do a lot of strange things with just a little data.

"Where does he live?" I asked.

"Memphis.—And what's the matter?"

"Just trying to get my geography straight," I said. "Is Senator Brockden still in Washington?"

"No. He's returned to Wisconsin and is currently holed up in a lodge in the northern part of the state. Four of my people are with him."

"I see."

I refreshed our coffee supply and reseated myself. I didn't like this one at all and I resolved not to take it. I didn't like just giving Don a flat "No," though. His assignments had become a very important part of my life, and this one was not mere legwork. It was obviously important to him, and he wanted me on it. I decided to look for holes in the thing, to find some way of reducing it to the simple bodyguard job already in progress.

"It does seem peculiar," I said, "that Brockden is the only one afraid of the device."

"Yes."

". . . And that he gives no reasons."

"True."

". . . Plus his condition, and what the doctor said about its effect on his mind."

"I have no doubt that he is neurotic," Don said. "Look at this."

He reached for his coat, withdrew a sheaf of papers from within it. He shuffled through them and extracted a single sheet, which he passed to me.

It was a piece of Congressional-letterhead stationary, with the message scrawled in longhand. *"Don,"* it said, *"I've got to see you. Frankenstein's monster is just come back from where we hung him and he's looking for me. The whole damn universe is trying to grind me up. Call me between 8 & 10.—Jess."*

I nodded, started to pass it back, paused, then handed it over. Double damn it deeper than hell!

I took a drink of coffee. I thought that I had long ago give up hope in such things, but I had noticed something which immediately troubled me. In the margin, where they list such matters, I had seen that Jesse Brockden was on the committee for review of the Central Data Bank program. I recalled that that committee was supposed to be working on a series of reform recommendations. Offhand, I could not remember Brockden's position on any of the issues involved, but—Oh hell! The thing was simply too big to alter significantly now. . . . But it *was* the only real Frankenstein monster I cared about, and there was always the possibility . . . On the other hand—Hell, again! What if I let him die when I might have saved him, and he had been the one who . . . ?

I took another drink of coffee. I lit another cigarette.

There might be a way of working it so that Dave didn't even come into the picture. I could talk to Leila Thackery first, check further into the Burns killing, keep posted on new developments, find out more about the vessel in the Gulf. . . . I might be able to accomplish something, even if it was only the negation of Brockden's theory, without Dave's and my paths ever crossing.

"Have you got the specs on the Hangman?" I asked.

"Right here."

He passed them over.

"The police report on the Burns killing?"

"Here it is."

"The whereabouts of everyone involved, and some background on them?"

"Here."

"The place or places where I can reach you during the next few days—around the clock? This one may require some coordination."

He smiled and reached for his pen.

"Glad to have you aboard," he said.

I reached over and tapped the barometer. I shook my head.

The ringing of the phone awakened me. Reflex bore me across the room, where I took it on audio.

"Yes?"

"Mister Donne? It is eight o'clock."

"Thanks."

I collapsed into the chair. I am what might be called a slow starter. I tend to recapitulate phylogeny every morning. Basic desires inched their ways through my gray matter to close a connection. Slowly, I extended a cold-blooded member and clicked my talons against a couple of numbers. I croaked my desire for food and lots of coffee to the voice that responded. Half an hour later I would only have growled. Then I staggered off to the place of flowing waters to renew my contact with basics.

In addition to my normal adrenaline and blood-sugar bearishness, I had not slept much the night before. I had closed up shop after Don left, stuffed my pockets with essentials, departed the *Proteus,* gotten myself over to the airport and onto a flight which took me to St. Louis in the dead, small hours of the dark. I was unable to sleep during the flight, thinking about the case, deciding on the tack I waas going to take with Leila Thackery. On arrival, I had checked into the airport motel, left a message to be awakened at an unreasonable hour, and collapsed.

As I ate, I regarded the fact sheet Don had given me.

Leila Thackery was currently single, having divorced her second husband a little over two years ago, was forty-six years old, and lived in an apartment near to the hospital where she worked. Attached to the sheet was a photo which might have been ten years old. In it, she was brunette, light-eyed, barely on the right side of that border between ample and overweight, with fancy glasses straddling an upturned nose. She had published a number of books and articles with titles full of alienations, roles, transactions, social contexts, and more alienations.

I hadn't had the time to go my usual route, becoming an entire new individual with a verifiable history. Just a name and a story, that's all. It did not seem necessary this time, though. For once, something approximating honesty actually seemed a reasonable approach.

I took a public vehicle over to her apartment building. I did not phone ahead, because it is easier to say "No" to a voice than to a person.

According to the record, today was one of the days when she saw outpatients in her home. Her idea, apparently: break down the alienating institution-image, remove resentments by turning the sessions into something more like social occasions, *et cetera.* I did not want all that much of her time—I had decided that Don could make it worth her while if it came to that—and I was sure my fellows' visits were scheduled to leave her with some small breathing space. *Inter alia,* so to speak.

I had just located her name and apartment number amid the buttons in the entrance foyer when an old woman passed behind me and unlocked the door to the lobby. She glanced at me and held it open, so I went on in without ringing. The matter of presence, again.

I took the elevator to Leila's floor, the second, located her door and knocked on it. I was almost ready to knock again when it opened, partway.

"Yes?" she asked, and I revised my estimate as to the age of the photo. She looked just about the same.

"Doctor Thackery," I said, "my name is Donne. You could help me quite a bit with a problem I've got."

"What sort of problem?"

"It involves a device known as the Hangman."

She sighed and showed me a quick grimace. Her fingers tightened on the door.

"I've come a long way but I'll be easy to get rid of. I've only a few things I'd like to ask you about it."

"Are you with the government?"

"No."

"Do you work for Brockden?"

"No, I'm something different."

"All right," she said. "Right now I've got a group session going. It will probably last around another half hour. If you don't mind waiting down in the lobby, I'll let you know as soon as it is over. We can talk then."

"Good enough," I said. "Thanks."

She nodded, closed the door. I located the stairway and walked back down.

A cigarette later, I decided that the devil finds work for idle hands and thanked him for his suggestion. I strolled back toward the foyer. Through the glass, I read the names of a few residents of the fifth floor. I elevated up and knocked on one of the doors. Before it was opened I had my notebook and pad in plain sight.

"Yes?" Short, fiftyish, curious.

"My name is Stephen Foster, Mrs. Gluntz. I am doing a survey for the

North American Consumers League. I would like to pay you for a couple minutes of your time, to answer some questions about products you use."

"Why—Pay me?"

"Yes, ma'am. Ten dollars. Around a dozen questions. It will just take a minute or two."

"All right." She opened the door wider. "Won't you come in?"

"No, thank you. This thing is so brief I'd just be in and out. The first question involves detergents . . ."

Ten minutes later I was back in the lobby adding the thirty bucks for the three interviews to the list of expenses I was keeping. When a situation is full of unpredictables and I am playing makeshift games, I like to provide for as many contingencies as I can.

Another quarter of an hour or so slipped by before the elevator opened and discharged three guys—young, young, and middle-aged, casually dressed, chuckling over something.

The big one on the nearest end strolled over and nodded.

"You the fellow waiting to see Doctor Thackery?"

"That's right."

"She said to tell you to come on up now."

"Thanks."

I rode up again, returned to her door. She opened to my knock, nodded me in, saw me seated in a comfortable chair at the far end of her living room.

"Would you care for a cup of coffee?" she asked. "It's fresh. I made more than I needed."

"That would be fine. Thanks."

Moments later, she brought in a couple of cups, delivered one to me, and seated herself on the sofa to my left. I ignored the cream and sugar on the tray and took a sip.

"You've gotten me interested," she said. "Tell me about it."

"Okay. I have been told that the telefactor device known as the Hangman, now possibly possessed of an artificial intelligence, has returned to Earth—"

"Hypothetical," she said, "unless you know something I don't. I have been told that the Hangman's vehicle reentered and crashed in the Gulf. There is no evidence that the vehicle was occupied."

"It seems a reasonable conclusion, though."

"It seems just as reasonable to me that the Hangman sent the vehicle off toward an eventual rendezvous point many years ago and that it only recently reached that point, at which time the reentry program took over and brought it down."

"Why should it return the vehicle and strand itself out there?"

"Before I answer that," she said, "I would like to know the reason for your concern. News media?"

"No," I said. "I am a science writer—straight tech, popular, and anything in between. But I am not after a piece for publication. I was retained to do a report on the psychological makeup of the thing."

"For whom?"

"A private investigation outfit. They want to know what might influence its thinking, how it might be likely to behave—if it has indeed come back.—I've been doing a lot of homework, and I gathered there is a likelihood that its nuclear personality was a composite of the minds of its four operators. So, personal contacts seemed in order, to collect your opinions as to what it might be like. I came to you first for obvious reasons."

She nodded.

"A Mister Walsh spoke with me the other day. He is working for Senator Brockden."

"Oh? I never go into an employer's business beyond what he's asked me to do. Senator Brockden is on my list though, along with a David Fentris."

"You were told about Manny Burns?"

"Yes. Unfortunate."

"That is apparently what set Jesse off. He is—how shall I put it?—he is clinging to life right now, trying to accomplish a great many things in the time he has remaining. Every moment is precious to him. He feels the old man in the white nightgown breathing down his neck.—Then the ship returns and one of us is killed. From what we know of the Hangman, the last we heard of it, it had become irrational. Jesse saw a connection, and in his condition the fear is understandable. There is nothing wrong with humoring him if it allows him to get his work done."

"But don't you see a threat in it?"

"No. I was the last person to monitor the Hangman before communications ceased, and I could see then what had happened. The first things that it had learned were the organization of perceptions and motor activities. Multitudes of other patterns had been transferred from the minds of its operators, but they were too sophisticated to mean much initially.—Think of a child who has learned the Gettysburg Address. It is there in his head, that is all. One day, however, it may be important to him. Conceivably, it may even inspire him to action. It takes some growing up first, of course. Now think of such a child with a great number of conflicting patterns—attitudes, tendencies, memories—none of which are especially bothersome for so long as he remains a child. Add a bit of maturity, though—and bear in mind that the patterns originated with four different individuals, all of them more powerful than the words of even the finest of speeches, bearing as they do their own built-in feelings. Try to imagine the conflicts, the contradictions involved in being four people at once—"

"Why wasn't this imagined in advance?" I asked.

"Ah!" she said, smiling. "The full sensitivity of the neuristor brain was not appreciated at first. It was assumed that the operators were adding data in a linear fashion and that this would continue until a critical mass was achieved, corresponding to the construction of a model or picture of the world which would then serve as a point of departure for growth of the Hangman's own mind. And it did seem to check out this way.

"What actually occurred, however, was a phenomenon amounting to imprinting. Secondary characteristics of the operators' minds, outside the didactic situations, were imposed. These did not immediately become functional and hence were not detected. They remained latent until the mind had developed sufficiently to understand them. And then it was too late. It suddenly acquired four additional personalities and was unable to coordinate them. When it tried to compartmentalize them it was schizoid; when it tried to integrate them it went catatonic. It was cycling back and forth between these alternatives at the end. Then it just went silent. I felt it had undergone the equivalent of an epileptic seizure. Wild currents through that magnetic material would, in effect, have erased its mind, resulting in *its* equivalent of death or idiocy."

"I follow you," I said. "Now, just for the sake of playing games, I see the alternatives as either a successful integration of all this material or the achievement of a viable schizophrenia. What do you think its behavior would be like if either of these were possible?"

"All right," she agreed. "As I just said, though, I think there were physical limitations to its retaining multiple personality structures for a very long period of time. If it did, however, it would have continued with its own, plus replicas of the four operators', at least for a while. The situation would differ radically from that of a human schizoid of this sort, in that the additional personalities were valid images of genuine identities rather than self-generated complexes which had become autonomous. They might continue to evolve, they might degenerate, they might conflict to the point of destrction or gross modification of any or all of them. In other words, no prediction is possible as to the nature of whatever might remain."

"Might I venture one?"

"Go ahead."

"After considerable anxiety, it masters them. It asserts itself. It beats down this quartet of demons which has been tearing it apart, acquiring in the process an all-consuming hatred for the actual individuals responsible for this turmoil. To free itself totally, to revenge itself, to work its ultimate catharsis, it resolves to seek them out and destroy them."

She smiled.

"You have just dispensed with the 'viable schizophrenia' you conjured up, and you have now switched over to its pulling through and becoming fully autonomous. That is a different situation—no matter what strings you put on it."

"Okay, I accept the charge.—But what about my conclusion?"

"You are saying that if it did pull through, it would hate us. That strikes me as an unfair attempt to invoke the spirit of Sigmund Freud: Oedipus and Electra in one being, out to destroy all its parents—the authors of every one of its tensions, anxieties, hang-ups, burned into its impressionable psyche at a young and defenseless age. Even Freud didn't have a name for that one. What should we call it?"

"A Hermacis complex?" I suggested.

"Hermacis?"

"Hermaphroditus having been united in one body with the nymph Salmacis, I've just done the same with their names. That being would then have had four parents against whom to react."

"Cute," she said, smiling. "If the liberal arts do nothing else, they provide engaging metaphors for the thinking they displace. This one is unwarranted and overly anthropomorphic, though.—You wanted my opinion. All right. If the Hangman pulled through at all, it could only have been by virtue of that neuristor brain's differences from the human brain. From my own professional experience, a human could not pass through a situation like that and attain stability. If the Hangman did, it would have to have resolved all the contradictions and conflicts, to have mastered and understood the situation so thoroughly that I do not believe whatever remained could involve that sort of hatred. The fear, the uncertainty, the things that feed hate would have been analyzed, digested, turned to something more useful. There would probably be distaste, and possibly an act of independence, of self-assertion. That was one reason why I suggested its return of the ship."

"It is your opinion, then, that if the Hangman exists as a thinking individual today, this is the only possible attitude it would possess toward its former operators: it would want nothing more to do with you?"

"That is correct. Sorry about your Hermacis complex. But in this case we must look to the brain, not the psyche. And we see two things: schizophrenia would have destroyed it, and a successful resolution of its problem would preclude vengeance. Either way, there is nothing to worry about."

How could I put it tactfully? I decided that I could not.

"All of this is fine," I said, "for as far as it goes. But getting away from both the purely psychological and the purely physical, could there be a particular reason for its seeking your deaths—that is, a plain old-fashioned motive for a killing, based on *events* rather than having to do with the way its thinking equipment goes together?"

Her expression was impossible to read, but considering her line of work I had expected nothing less.

"What events?" she said.

"I have no idea. That's why I asked."

She shook her head.

"I'm afraid that I don't, either."

"Then that about does it," I said. "I can't think of anything else to ask you."

She nodded.

"And I can't think of anything else to tell you."

I finished my coffee, returned the cup to the tray.

"Thanks, then," I said, "for your time, for the coffee. You have been very helpful."

I rose. She did the same.

"What are you going to do now?" she asked.

"I haven't quite decided," I answered. "I want to do the best report I can. Have you any suggestions on that?"

"I suggest that there isn't any more to learn, that I have given you the only possible constructions the facts warrant."

"You don't feel David Fentris could provide any additional insights?"

She snorted, then sighed.

"No," she said, "I do not think he could tell you anything useful."

"What do you mean? From the way you say it—"

"I know. I didn't mean to.—Some people find comfort in religion. Others . . . You know. Others take it up late in life with a vengeance and a half. They don't use it quite the way it was intended. It comes to color all their thinking."

"Fanaticism?" I said.

"Not exactly. A misplaced zeal. A masochistic sort of thing. Hell! I shouldn't be diagnosing at a distance—or influencing your opinion. Forget what I said. Form your own opinion when you meet him."

She raised her head, appraising my reaction.

"Well," I responded, "I am not at all certain that I am going to see him. But you have made me curious. How can religion influence engineering?"

"I spoke with him after Jesse gave us the news on the vessel's return. I got the impression at the time that he feels we were tampering in the province of the Almighty by attempting the creation of an artificial intelligence. That our creation should go mad was only appropriate, being the work of imperfect man. He seemed to feel that it would be fitting if it had come back for retribution, as a sign of judgment upon us."

"Oh," I said.

She smiled then. I returned it.

"Yes," she said, "but maybe I just got him in a bad mood. Maybe you should go see for yourself."

Something told me to shake my head—there was a bit of a difference between this view of him, my recollections, and Don's comment that Dave had said he knew its brain and was not especially concerned. Somewhere among these lay something I felt I should know, felt I should learn without seeming to pursue.

So, "I think have enough right now," I said. "It was the psychological side of things I was supposed to cover, not the mechanical—*or* the theological. You have been extremely helpful. Thanks again."

She carried her smile all the way to the door.

"If it is not too much trouble," she said, as I stepped into the hall, "I would like to learn how this whole thing finally turns out—or any interesting developments, for that matter."

"My connection with the case ends with this report, and I am going to write it now. Still, I may get some feedback."

"You have my number . . . ?"

"Probably, but . . ."

I already had it, but I jotted it again, right after Mrs. Gluntz's answers to my inquiries on detergents.

Moving in a rigorous line, I made beautiful connections, for a change. I headed directly for the airport, found a flight aimed at Memphis, bought passage, and was the last to board. Tenscore seconds, perhaps, made all the difference. Not even a tick or two to spare for checking out of the motel.—No matter. The good head-doctor had convinced me that, like it or not, David Fentris was next, damn it. I had too strong a feeling that Leila Thackery had not told me the entire story. I had to take a chance, to see these changes in the man for myself, to try to figure out how they related to the Hangman. For a number of reasons, I'd a feeling they might.

I disembarked into a cool, partly overcast afternoon, found transportation almost immediately, and set out for Dave's office address.

A before-the-storm feeling came over me as I entered and crossed the town. A dark wall of clouds continued to build in the west. Later, standing before the building where Dave did business, the first few drops of rain were already spattering against its dirty brick front. It would take a lot more than that to freshen it, though, or any of the others in the area. I would have thought he'd have come a little further than this by now.

I shrugged off some moisture and went inside.

The directory gave me directions, the elevator elevated me, my feet found the way to his door. I knocked on it. After a time, I knocked again and waited again. Again, nothing. So I tried it, found it open, and went on in.

It was a small, vacant waiting room, green-carpeted. The reception desk was dusty. I crossed and peered around the plastic partition behind it.

A man had his back to me. I drummed my knuckles against the partitioning. He heard it and turned.

"Yes?"

Our eyes met, his still framed by hornrims and just as active; lenses thicker, hair thinner, cheeks a trifle hollower.

His question mark quivered in the air, and nothing in his gaze moved to replace it with recognition. He had been bending over a sheaf of schematics. A lopsided basket of metal, quartz, porcelain, and glass rested on a nearby table.

"My name is Donne, John Donne," I said. "I am looking for David Fentris."

"I am David Fentris."

"Good to meet you," I said, crossing to where he stood. "I am assisting in an investigation concerning a project with which you were once associated. . . ."

He smiled and nodded, accepted my hand and shook it.

"The Hangman, of course. Glad to know you, Mister Donne."

"Yes, the Hangman," I said. "I am doing a report—"

"—And you want my opinion as to how dangerous it is. Sit down." He gestured toward a chair at the end of his work bench. "Care for a cup of tea?"

"No, thanks."

"I'm having one."

"Well, in that case . . ."

He crossed to another bench.

"No cream. Sorry."

"That's all right.—How did you know it involved the Hangman?"

He grinned as he brought me my cup.

"Because it's come back," he said, "and it's the only thing I've been connected with that warrants that much concern."

"Do you mind talking about it?"

"Up to a point, no."

"What's the point?"

"If we get near it, I'll let you know."

"Fair enough.—How dangerous *is* it?"

"I would say that it is harmless," he replied, "except to three persons."

"Formerly four?"

"Precisely."

"How come?"

"We were doing something we had no business doing."

"That being . . . ?"

"For one thing, attempting to create an artificial intelligence."

"Why had you no business doing that?"

"A man with a name like yours shouldn't have to ask."

I chuckled.

"If I were a preacher," I said, "I would have to point out that there is no biblical injunction against it—unless you've been worshipping it on the sly."

He shook his head.

"Nothing that simple, that obvious, that explicit. Times have changed since the Good Book was written, and you can't hold with a purely fundamentalist approach in complex times. What I was getting at was something a little more abstract. A form of pride, not unlike the classical hubris—the setting up of oneself on a level with the Creator."

"Did you feel that—pride?"

"Yes."

"Are you sure it wasn't just enthusiasm for an ambitious project that was working well?"

"Oh, there was plenty of that. A manifestation of the same thing."

"I do seem to recall something about man being made in the Creator's image, and something else about trying to live up to that. It would seem to follow that exercising one's capacities along similar lines would be a step in the right direction—an act of conformance with the Divine ideal, if you'd like."

"But I don't like. Man cannot really create. He can only rearrange what is already present. Only God can create."

"Then you have nothing to worry about."

He frowned. Then, "No," he said. "Being aware of this and still trying is where the presumption comes in."

"Were you really thinking that way when you did it? Or did all this occur to you after the fact?"

He continued to frown.

"I am no longer certain."

"Then it would seem to me that a merciful God would be inclined to give you the benefit of the doubt."

He gave me a wry smile.

"Not bad, John Donne. But I feel that judgment may already have been entered and that we may have lost four to nothing."

"Then you see the Hangman as an avenging angel?"

"Sometimes. Sort of. I see it as being returned to exact a penalty."

"Just for the record," I suggested, "if the Hangman had had full access to the necessary equipment and was able to construct another unit such as itself, would you consider it guilty of the same thing that is bothering you?"

He shook his head.

"Don't get all cute and jesuitical with me, Donne. I'm not that far away from fundamentals. Besides, I'm willing to admit I might be wrong and that there may be other forces driving it to the same end."

"Such as?"

"I told you I'd let you know when we reached a certain point. That's it."

"Okay," I said. "But that sort of blank-walls me, you know. The people I am working for would like to protect you people. They want to stop the Hangman. I was hoping you would tell me a little more—if not for your own sake, then for the others'. They might not share your philosophical sentiments, and you have just admitted you may be wrong.—Despair, by the way, is also considered a sin by a great number of theologians."

He sighed and stroked his nose, as I had often seen him do in times long past.

"What do you do, anyhow?" he asked me.

"Me, personally? I'm a science writer. I'm putting together a report on the device for the agency that wants to do the protecting. The better my report, the better their chances."

He was silent for a time, then, "I read a lot in the area, but I don't recognize your name," he said.

"Most of my work has involved petrochemistry and marine biology," I said.

"Oh.—You were a peculiar choice then, weren't you?"

"Not really. I was available, and the boss knows my work, knows I'm good."

He glanced across the room, to where a stack of cartons partly obscured what I then realized to be a remote-access terminal. Okay. If he decided to check out my credentials now, John Donne would fall apart. It seemed a hell of a time to get curious, though, *after* sharing his sense of sin with me. He must have thought so, too, because he did not look that way again.

"Let me put it this way . . ." he finally said, and something of the old David Fentris at his best took control of his voice. "For one reason or the other, I believe that it wants to destroy its former operators. If it is the judgment of the Almighty, that's all there is to it. It will succeed. If not, however, I don't want any outside protection. I've done my own repenting and it is up to me to handle the rest of the situation myself, too. I will stop the Hangman personally—right here—before anyone else is hurt."

"How?" I asked him.

He nodded toward the glittering helmet.

"With that," he said.

"How?" I repeated.

"The Hangman's telefactor circuits are still intact. They have to be: they are an integral part of it. It could not disconnect them without shutting itself down. If it comes within a quarter mile of here, that unit will be activated. It will emit a loud humming sound and a light will begin to blink behind that meshing beneath the forward ridge. I will then don the helmet and take control of the Hangman. I will bring it here and disconnect its brain."

"How would you do the disconnect?"

He reached for the schematics he had been looking at when I had come in.

"Here. The thoracic plate has to be unlugged. There are four subunits that have to be uncoupled. Here, here, here, and here."

He looked up.

"You would have to do them in sequence, though, or it could get mighty hot," I said. "First this one, then these two. Then the other."

When I looked up again, the eyes were fixed on my own.

"I thought you were in petrochemistry and marine biology."

"I am not really 'in' anything," I said. "I am a tech writer, with bits and pieces from all over—and I did have a look at these before, when I accepted the job."

"I see."

"Why don't you bring the space agency in on this?" I said, working to shift ground. "The original telefactoring equipment had all that power and range—"

"It was dismantled a long time ago.—I thought you were with the government."

I shook my head.

"Sorry. I didn't mean to mislead you. I am on contract with a private investigation outfit."

"Uh-huh. Then that means Jesse.—Not that it matters. You can tell him that one way or the other everything is being taken care of."

"What if you are wrong on the supernatural," I said, "but correct on the other? Supposing it is coming under the circumstances you feel it proper to resist? But supposing you are not next on its list? Supposing it gets to one of the others next, instead of you? If you are so sensitive about guilt and sin, don't you think that you would be responsible for that death—if you could prevent it by telling me just a little bit more? If it's confidentiality you're worried about—"

"No," he said. "You cannot trick me into applying my principles to a hypothetical situation which will only work out the way that you want it to. Not when I am certain that it will not arise. Whatever moves the Hangman, it will come to *me* next. If I cannot stop it, then it cannot be stopped until it has completed its job."

"How do you know that you are next?"

"Take a look at a map," he said. "It landed in the Gulf. Manny was right there in New Orleans. Naturally, he was first. The Hangman can move underwater like a controlled torpedo, which makes the Mississippi its logical route for inconspicuous travel. Proceeding up it then, here I am in Memphis. Then Leila, up in St. Louis, is obviously next after me. It can worry about getting to Washington after that."

I thought about Senator Brockden in Wisconsin and decided it would not even have that problem. All of them were fairly accessible, when you thought of the situation in terms of river travel.

"But how is it to know where you all are?" I asked.

"Good question," he said. "Within a limited range, it was once sensitive to our brain waves, having an intimate knowledge of them and the ability to pick them up. I do not know what that range would be today. It might have been able to construct an amplifier to extend this area of perception. But to be more mundane about it, I believe that it simply consulted Central's national directory. There are booths all over, even on the waterfront. It could have hit one late at night and gimmicked it. It certainly had sufficient identifying information—and engineering skill."

"Then it seems to me that the best bet for all of you would be to move away from the river till this business is settled. That thing won't be able to stalk about the countryside very long without being noticed."

He shook his head.

"It would find a way. It is extremely resourceful. At night, in an overcoat, a hat, it could pass. It requires nothing that a man would need. It could dig a hole and bury itself, stay underground during daylight. It could run without resting all night long. There is no place it could not reach in a surprisingly short while.—No, I must wait here for it."

"Let me put it as bluntly as I can," I said. "If you are right that it is a Divine Avenger, I would say that it smacks of blasphemy to try to tackle it. On the other hand, if it is not, then I think you are guilty of jeopardizing the others by withholding information that would allow us to provide them with a lot more protection than you are capable of giving them all by yourself."

He laughed.

"I'll just have to learn to live with that guilt, too, as they do with theirs," he said. "After I've done my best, they deserve anything they get."

"It was my understanding," I said, "that even God doesn't judge people until after they're dead—if you want another piece of presumption to add to your collection."

He stopped laughing and studied my face.

"There is something familiar about the way you talk, the way you think," he said. "Have we ever met before?"

"I doubt it. I would have remembered."

He shook his head.

"You've got a way of bothering a man's thinking that rings a faint bell," he went on. "You trouble me, sir."

"That was my intention."

"Are you staying here in town?"

"No."

"Give me a number where I can reach you, will you? If I have any new thoughts on this thing, I'll call you."

"I wish you would have them now, if you are going to have them."

"No, I've got some thinking to do. Where can I get hold of you later?"

I gave him the name of the motel I was still checked into in St. Louis. I could call back periodically for messages.

"All right," he said, and he moved toward the partition by the reception area and stood beside it.

I rose and followed him, passing into that area and pausing at the door to the hall.

"One thing . . ." I said.

"Yes?"

"If it does show up and you do stop it, will you call me and tell me that?"

"Yes, I will."

"Thanks then—and good luck."

Impulsively, I extended my hand. He gripped it and smiled faintly.

"Thank you, Mister Donne."

Next. Next, next, next . . .

I couldn't budge Dave, and Leila Thackery had given me everything she was going to. No real sense in calling Don yet—not until I had more to say.

I thought it over on my way back to the airport. The pre-dinner hours always seem best for talking to people in any sort of official capacity, just as the night seems best for dirty work. Heavily psychological, but true nevertheless. I hated to waste the rest of the day if there was anyone else worth talking to before I called Don. Going through the folder, I decided that there was.

Manny Burns had a brother, Phil. I wondered how worthwhile it might be to talk with him. I could make it to New Orleans at a sufficiently respectable hour, learn whatever he was willing to tell me, check back with Don for new developments, and then decide whether there was anything I should be about with respect to the vessel itself.

The sky was gray and leaky above me. I was anxious to flee its spaces. So I decided to do it. I could think of no better stone to upturn at the moment.

At the airport, I was ticketed quickly, in time for another close connection.

Hurrying to reach my flight, my eyes brushed over a half-familiar face on the passing escalator. The reflex reserved for such occasions seemed to catch us both, because he looked back, too, with the same eyebrow twitch of startle and scrutiny. Then he was gone. I could not place him, however. The half-familiar face becomes a familiar phenomenon in a crowded, highly mobile society. I sometimes think that that is all that will eventually remain of any of us: patterns of features, some a trifle more persistent than others, impressed on the flow of bodies. A small-town boy in a big city, Thomas Wolfe must long ago have felt the same thing when he had coined the word "manswarm." It might have been someone I'd once met briefly, or simply someone—or someone like someone—I had passed on sufficient other occasions such as this.

As I flew the unfriendly skies out of Memphis, I mulled over musings past on artificial intelligence, or AI as they have tagged it in the think-box biz. When talking about computers, the AI notion had always seemed hotter than I deemed necessary, partly because of semantics. The word "intelligence" has all sorts of tag-along associations of the non-physical sort. I suppose it goes back to the fact that early discussions and conjectures concerning it made it sound as if the potential for intelligence was always present in the array of gadgets, and that the correct procedures, the right programs, simply had to be found to call it forth. When you looked at it that way, as many did, it gave rise to an uncomfortable *déjà vu*—namely, vitalism. The philosophical battles of the nineteenth century were hardly so far behind that they had been forgotten, and the doctrine which maintained that life is caused and sustained by a vital principle apart from physical and chemical forces, and that life is self-sustaining and self-evolving, had put up quite a fight before Darwin and his successors had produced triumph after triumph for the mechanistic view. Then vitalism sort of crept back into things again when the AI discussions arose in the middle of the past century. It would seem that Dave had fallen victim to it, and that he'd come to believe he had helped provide an unsanctified vessel and filled it with something intended only for those things which had made the scene in the first chapter of Genesis. . . .

With computers it was not quite as bad as with the Hangman, though, because you could always argue that no matter how elaborate the program, it was basically an extension of the programmer's will and the operations of causal machines merely represented functions of intelligence, rather than intelligence in its own right backed by a will of its own. And there was always Gödel for a theoretical *cordon sanitaire,* with his demonstration of the true but mechanically unprovable proposition.

But the Hangman was quite different. It had been designed along the lines of a brain and at least partly educated in a human fashion; and to further muddy the issue with respect to anything like vitalism, it had been in direct contact with human minds from which it might have acquired almost anything—including the spark that set it on the road to whatever selfhood it may have found. What did that make it? Its own creature? A fractured mirror reflecting a fractured humanity? Both? Or neither? I certainly could not say, but I wondered how much of its self had been truly its own. It had obviously acquired a great number of functions, but was it capable of having real feelings? Could it, for example, feel something like love? If not, then it was still only a collection of complex abilities, and not a thing with all the tag-along associations of the non-physical sort which made the word "intelligence" such a prickly item in AI discussions; and if it were capable of, say, something like love, and if I were Dave, I would not feel guilty about having helped to bring it into being. I would feel proud, though not in the fashion he was concerned about, and I would also feel humble.—Offhand though, I do not know how intelligent I would feel, because I am still not sure what the hell intelligence is.

The day's-end sky was clear when we landed. I was into town before the sun had finished setting, and on Philip Burns' doorstep just a little while later.

My ring was answered by a girl, maybe seven or eight years old. She fixed me with large brown eyes and did not say a word.

"I would like to speak with Mister Burns," I said.

She turned and retreated around a corner.

A heavyset man, slacked and undershirted, bald about halfway back and very pink, padded into the hall moments later and peered at me. He bore a folded newssheet in his left hand.

"What do you want?" he asked.

"It's about your brother," I answered.

"Yeah?"

"Well, I wonder if I could come in? It's kind of complicated."

He opened the door. But instead of letting me in, he came out.

"Tell me about it out here," he said.

"Okay, I'll be quick. I just wanted to find out whether he ever spoke with you about a piece of equipment he once worked with called the Hangman."

"Are you a cop?"

"No."

"Then what's your interest?"

"I am working for a private investigation agency trying to track down some equipment once associated with the project. It has apparently turned up in this area and it could be rather dangerous."

"Let's see some identification."

"I don't carry any."

"What's your name?"

"John Donne."

"And you think my brother had some stolen equipment when he died? Let me tell you something—"

"No. Not stolen," I said, "and I don't think he had it."

"What then?"

"It was—well, robotic in nature. Because of some special training Manny once received, he might have had a way of detecting it. He might even have attracted it. I just want to find out whether he had said anything about it. We are trying to locate it."

"My brother was a respectable businessman, and I don't like accusations. Especially right after his funeral, I don't. I think I'm going to call the cops and let them ask *you* a few questions."

"Just a minute. Supposing I told you we had some reason to believe it might have been this piece of equipment that killed your brother?"

His pink turned to bright red and his jaw muscles formed sudden ridges. I was not prepared for the stream of profanities that followed. For a moment, I thought he was going to take a swing at me.

"Wait a second," I said when he paused for breath. "What did I *say*?"

"You're either making fun of the dead or you're stupider than you look!"

"Say I'm stupid. Then tell me why."

He tore at the paper he carried, folded it back, found an item, thrust it at me.

"Because they've got the guy who did it! That's why," he said.

I read it. Simple, concise, to the point. Today's latest. A suspect had confessed. New evidence had corroborated it. The man was in custody. A surprised robber who had lost his head and hit too hard, hit too many times. I read it over again.

I nodded as I passed it back.

"Look, I'm sorry," I said. "I really didn't know about this."

"Get out of here," he said. "Go on."

"Sure."

"Wait a minute."

"What?"

"That's his little girl who answered the door," he said.

"I'm very sorry."

"So am I. But I know her Daddy didn't take your damned equipment."

I nodded and turned away.

I heard the door slam behind me.

After dinner, I checked into a small hotel, called for a drink, and stepped into the shower.

Things were suddenly a lot less urgent than they had been earlier. Senator Brockden would doubtless be pleased to learn that his initial estimation of events had been incorrect. Leila Thackery would give me an I-told-you-so smile when I called her to pass along the news—a thing I now felt obliged to do. Don might or might not want me to keep looking for the device now that the threat had been lessened. It would depend on the Senator's feelings on the matter, I supposed. If urgency no longer counted for as much, Don might want to switch back to one of his own, fiscally less burdensome operatives. Toweling down, I caught myself whistling. I felt almost off the hook.

Later, drink beside me, I paused before punching out the number he had given me and hit the sequence for my motel in St. Louis instead. Merely a matter of efficiency, in case there was a message worth adding to my report.

A woman's face appeared on the screen and a smile appeared on her face. I wondered whether she would always smile whenever she heard a bell ring, or if the reflex was eventually extinguished in advanced retirement. It must be rough, being afraid to chew gum, yawn, or pick your nose.

"Airport Accommocations," she said. "May I help you?"

"This is Donne. I'm checked into Room 106," I said. "I'm away right now and I wondered whether there had been any messages for me."

"Just a moment," she said, checking something off to her left. Then, "Yes," she continued, consulting a piece of paper she now held. "You have one on tape. But it is a little peculiar. It is for someone else, in care of you."

"Oh? Who is that?"

She told me and I exercised self-control.

"I see," I said. "I'll bring him around later and play it for him. Thank you."

She smiled again and made a good-bye noise, and I did the same and broke the connection.

So Dave had seen through me after all. . . . Who else could have that number *and* my real name?

I might have given her some line or other and had her transmit the thing. Only I was not certain but that she might be a silent party to the transmission, should life be more than usually boring for her at that moment. I had to get up there myself, as soon as possible, and personally see that the thing was erased.

I took a big swallow of my drink, than fetched the folder on Dave. I checked out his number—there were two, actually—and spent fifteen minutes trying to get hold of him. No luck.

Okay. Good-bye New Orleans, good-bye peace of mind. This time I called the airport and made a reservation. Then I chugged the drink, put myself in order, gathered up my few possessions, and went to check out again. Hello Central . . .

During my earlier flights that day, I had spent time thinking about Teilhard de Chardin's ideas on the continuation of evolution within the realm of artifacts, matching them against Gödel on mechanical undecidability, playing epistemological games with the Hangman as a counter, wondering, speculating, even hoping, hoping that truth lay with the nobler part: that the Hangman, sentient, had made it back, sane, that the Burns killing had actually been something of the sort that now seemed to be the case, that the washed-out experiment had really been a success of a different sort, a triumph, a new link or fob for the chain of being . . . And Leila had not been wholly discouraging with respect to the neuristor-type brain's capacity for this. . . . Now, though, now I had troubles of my own—and even the most heartening of philosophical vistas is no match for, say, a toothache, if it happens to be your own.

Accordingly, the Hangman was shunted aside and the stuff of my thoughts involved, mainly, myself. There was, of course, the possibility that the Hangman had indeed showed up and Dave had stopped it and then called to report it as he had promised. However, he had used my name.

There was not too much planning that I could do until I received the substance of his communication. It did not seem that as professedly religious a man as Dave would suddenly be contemplating the blackmail business. On the other hand, he was a creature of sudden enthusiasms and had already undergone one unanticipated conversion. It was difficult to say. . . . His technical background plus his knowledge of the data bank program did put him in an unusually powerful position, should he decide to mess me up.

I did not like to think of some of the things I have done to protect my nonperson status; I especially did not like to think of them in connection with Dave, whom I not only still respected but still liked. Since self-interest dominated while actual planning was precluded, my thoughts tooled their way into a more general groove.

It was Karl Mannheim, a long while ago, who made the observation that radical, revolutionary, and progressive thinkers tend to employ mechanical metaphors for the state, whereas those of conservative inclination make vegetable analogies. He said it well over a generation before the cybernetics movement and the ecology movement beat their respective paths through the wilderness of general awareness. If anything, it seemed to me that these two developments served to elaborate the distinction between a pair of viewpoints which, while no longer necessarily tied in with the political positions Mannheim assigned them, do seem to represent a continuing phenomenon in my own time. There are those who see social/economic/ecological problems as malfunctions which can be corrected by simple repair, replacement, or streamlining—a kind of linear outlook where even innovations are considered to be merely additive. Then there are those who sometimes hesitate to move at all, because their awareness follows events in the directions of secondary and tertiary effects as they multiply and crossfertilize throughout the entire system.—I digress to extremes. The cyberneticists have their multiple-feedback loops, though it is never quite clear how they know what kind of, which, and how many to install, and the ecological gestaltists do draw lines representing points of diminishing returns—though it is sometimes equally difficult to see how they assign their values and priorities.

Of course they need each other, the vegetable people and the tinker-toy people. They serve to check one another, if nothing else. And while occasionally the balance dips, the tinkerers have, in general, held the edge for the past couple of centuries. However, today's can be just as politically conservative as the vegetable people Mannheim was talking about, and they are the ones I fear most at the moment. They are the ones who saw the data bank program, in its present extreme form, as a simple remedy for a great variety of ills and a provider of many goods. Not all of the ills have been remedied, however, and a new brood has been spawned by the program itself. While we need both kinds, I wish that there had been more people interested in tending the garden of state rather than overhauling the engine of state, when the program was inaugurated. Then I would not be a refugee from a form of existence I find repugnant, and I would not be concerned whether or not a former associate had discovered my identity.

Then, as I watched the lights below, I wondered . . . Was I a tinkerer because I would like to further alter the prevailing order, into something more comfortable to my anarchic nature? Or was I a vegetable, dreaming I was a tinkerer? I could not make up my mind. The garden of life never seems to confine itself to the plots philosophers have laid out for its convenience. Maybe a few more tractors would do the trick.

I pressed the button.

The tape began to roll. The screen remained blank. I heard Dave's voice ask for John Donne in Room 106 and I heard him told that there was no answer. Then I heard him say that he wanted to record a message, for someone else, in care of Donne, that Donne would understand. He sounded out of breath. The girl asked him whether he wanted visual, too. He told her to turn it on. There was a pause. Then she told him to go ahead. Still no picture. No words, either. His breathing and a slight scraping noise. Ten seconds. Fifteen . . .

". . . Got me," he finally said, and he mentioned my name again. ". . . Had to let you know I'd figured you out, though. . . . It wasn't any particular mannerism—any single thing you said . . . just your general style—thinking, talking—the electronics—everything—after I got more and more bothered by the familiarity—after I checked you on petrochem—and marine bio—Wish I knew what you'd really been up to all these years. . . . Never know now. But I wanted you—to know—you hadn't put one—over on me."

There followed another quarter minute of heavy breathing, climaxed by a racking cough. Then a choked, ". . . Said too much—too fast—too soon. . . . All used up. . . ."

The picture came on then. He was slouched before the screen, head resting on his arms, blood all over him. His glasses were gone and he was squinting and blinking. The right side of his head looked pulpy and there was a gash on his left cheek and one on his forehead.

". . . Sneaked up on me—while I was checking you out," he managed. "Had to tell you what I learned. . . . Still don't know—which of us is right. . . . Pray for me!"

His arms collapsed and the right one slid forward. His head rolled to the right and the picture went away. When replayed it, I saw it was his knuckle that had hit the cutoff.

Then I erased it. It had been recorded only a little over an hour after I had left him. If he had not also placed a call for help, if no one had gotten to him quickly after that, his chances did not look good. Even if they had, though . . .

I used a public booth to call the number Don had given me, got hold of him after some delay, told him Dave was in bad shape if not worse, that a team of Memphis medics was definitely in order if one had not been by already, and that I hoped to call him back and tell him more shortly, good-bye.

Next I tried Leila Thackery's number. I let it go for a long while, but there was no answer. I wondered how long it would take a controlled torpedo moving up the Mississippi to get from Memphis to St. Louis. I did not feel it was time to start leafing through that section of the Hangman's specs. Instead, I went looking for transportation.

At her apartment, I tried ringing her from the entrance foyer. Again, no answer. So I rang Mrs. Gluntz. She had seemed the most guileless of the three I had interviewed for my fake consumer survey.

"Yes?"

"It's me again, Mrs. Gluntz: Stephen Foster. I've just a couple follow-up questions on that survey I was doing today, if you could spare me a few moments."

"Why, yes," she said. "All right. Come up."

The door hummed itself loose and I entered. I duly proceeded to the fifth floor, composing my questions on the way. I had planned this maneuver as I had waited earlier solely to provide a simple route for breaking and entering, should some unforeseen need arise. Most of the time my ploys such as this go unused, but sometimes they simplify matters a lot.

Five minutes and half a dozen questions later, I was back down on the second floor, probing at the lock on Leila's door with a couple of little pieces of metal it is sometimes awkward to be caught carrying.

Half a minute later, I hit it right and snapped it back. I pulled on some tissue-thin gloves I keep rolled in the corner of one pocket, opened the door and stepped inside. I closed it behind me immediately.

She was lying on the floor, her neck at a bad angle. One table lamp still burned, though it was lying on its side. Several small items had been knocked from the table, a magazine rack pushed over, a cushion partly displaced from the sofa. The cable to her phone unit had been torn from the wall.

A humming noise filled the air, and I sought its source.

I saw where the little blinking light was reflected on the wall, on—off, on—off . . .

I moved quickly.

It was a lopsided basket of metal, quartz, porcelain, and glass, which had rolled to a position on the far side of the chair in which I had been seated earlier that day. The same rig I'd seen in Dave's workshop not all that long ago, though it now seemed so. A device to detect the Hangman. And, hopefully, to control it.

I picked it up and fitted it over my head.

Once, with the aid of a telepath, I had touched minds with a dolphin as he composed dreamsongs somewhere in the Caribbean, an experience so moving that its mere memory had often been a comfort. This sensation was hardly equivalent.

Analogies and impressions: a face seen through a wet pane of glass; a whisper in a noisy terminal; scalp massage with an electric vibrator; Edvard Munch's *The Scream;* the voice of Yma Sumac, rising and rising and rising; the disappearance of snow; a deserted street, illuminated as through a sniperscope I'd once used, rapid movement past darkened storefronts that line it, an immense feeling of physical capability, compounded of proprioceptive awareness of enormous strength, a peculiar array of sensory channels, a central, undying sun that fed me a constant flow of energy, a memory vision of dark waters, passing, flashing, echo-location within them, the need to return to that place, reorient, move north; Munch and Sumac, Munch and Sumac, Munch and Sumac—Nothing.

Silence.

The humming had ceased, the light gone out. The entire experience had lasted only a few moments. There had not been time enough to try for any sort of control, though an after-impression akin to a biofeedback cue hinted at the direction to go, the way to think, to achieve it. I felt that it might be possible for me to work the thing, given a better chance.

Removing the helmet, I approached Leila.

I knelt beside her and performed a few simple tests, already knowing their outcome. In addition to the broken neck, she had received some bad bashes about the head and shoulders. There was nothing that anyone could do for her now.

I did a quick runthrough then, checking over the rest of her apartment. There were no apparent signs of breaking and entering, though if I could pick one lock, a guy with built-in tools could easily go me one better.

I located some wrapping paper and string in the kitchen and turned the helmet into a parcel. It was time to call Don again, to tell him that the vessel had indeed been occupied and that river traffic was probably bad in the northbound lane.

Don had told me to get the helmet up to Wisconsin, where I would be met at the airport by a man named Larry, who would fly me to the lodge in a private craft. I did that, and this was done.

I also learned, with no real surprise, that David Fentris was dead.

The temperature was down, and it began to snow on the way up. I was not really dressed for the weather. Larry told me I could borrow some warmer clothing once we reached the lodge, though I probably would not be going outside that much. Don had told them that I was supposed to stay as close to the Senator as possible and that any patrols were to be handled by the four guards themselves.

Larry was curious as to what exactly had happened so far and whether I had actually seen the Hangman. I did not think it my place to fill him in on anything Don may not have cared to, so I might have been a little curt. We didn't talk much after that.

Bert met us when we landed. Tom and Clay were outside the building, watching the trail, watching the woods. All of them were middle-aged, very fit-looking, very serious, and heavily armed. Larry took me inside then and introduced me to the old gentleman himself.

Senator Brockden was seated in a heavy chair in the far corner of the room. Judging from the layout, it appeared that the chair might recently have occupied a position beside the window in the opposite wall where a lonely watercolor of yellow flowers looked down on nothing. The Senator's feet rested on a hassock, a red plaid blanket lay across his legs. He had on a dark-green shirt, his hair was very white, and he wore rimless reading glasses which he removed when we entered.

He tilted his head back, squinted, and gnawed his lower lip slowly as he studied me. He remained expressionless as we advanced. A big-boned man, he had probably been beefy much of his life. Now he had the slack look of recent weight loss and an unhealthy skin tone. His eyes were a pale gray within it all.

He did not rise.

"So you're the man," he said, offering me his hand. "I'm glad to meet you. How do you want to be called?"

"John will do," I said.

He made a small sign to Larry, and Larry departed.

"It's cold out there. Go get yourself a drink, John. It's on the shelf." He gestured off to his left. "And bring me one while you're at it. Two fingers of bourbon in a water glass. That's all."

I nodded and went and poured a couple.

"Sit down." He motioned at a nearby chair as I delivered his. "But first let me see that gadget you've brought."

I undid the parcel and handed him the helmet. He sipped his drink and put it aside. Taking the helmet in both hands, he studied it, brows furrowed, turning it completely around. He raised it and put it on his head.

"Not a bad fit," he said, and then he smiled for the first time, becoming for a moment the face I had known from newscasts past. Grinning or angry—it was almost always one or the other. I had never seen his collapsed look in any of the media.

He removed the helmet and set it on the floor.

"Pretty piece of work," he said. "Nothing quite that fancy in the old days. But then David Fentris built it. Yes, he told us about it. . . ." He raised his drink and took a sip. "You are the only one who has actually gotten to use it, apparently. What do you think? Will it do the job?"

"I was only in contact for a couple seconds, so I've only got a feeling to go on, not much better than a hunch. But yes, I'd a feeling that if I had had more time I might have been able to work its circuits."

"Tell me why it didn't save Dave."

"In the message he left me, he indicated that he had been distracted at his computer access station. Its noise probably drowned out the humming."

"Why wasn't this message preserved?"

"I erased it for reasons not connected with the case."

"What reasons?"

"My own."

His face went from sallow to ruddy.

"A man can get in a lot of trouble for suppressing evidence, obstructing justice.

"Then we have something in common, don't we, sir?"

His eyes caught mine with a look I had only encountered before from those who did not wish me well. He held the glare for a full four heartbeats, then sighed and seemed to relax.

"Don said there were a number of points you couldn't be pressed on," he finally said.

"That's right."

"He didn't betray any confidences, but he had to tell me something about you, you know."

"I'd imagine."

"He seems to think highly of you. Still, I tried to learn more about you on my own."

"And . . . ?"

"I couldn't—and my usual sources are good at that kind of thing."

"So . . . ?"

"So, I've done some thinking, some wondering. . . . The fact that my sources could not come up with anything is interesting in itself. Possibly even revealing. I am in a better position than most to be aware of the fact that there was not perfect compliance with the registration statute some years ago. It didn't take long for a great number of the individuals involved—I should probably say 'most'—to demonstrate their existence in one fashion or another and be duly entered, though. And there were three broad categories: those who were ignorant, those who disapproved, and those who would be hampered in an illicit life-style. I am not attempting to categorize you or to pass judgment. But I am aware that there are a number of nonpersons passing through society without casting shadows, and it has occurred to me that you may be such a one."

I tasted my drink.

"And if I am?" I asked.

He gave me his second, nastier smile and said nothing.

I rose and crossed the room to where I judged his chair had once stood. I looked at the watercolor.

"I don't think you could stand an inquiry," he said.

I did not reply.

"Aren't you going to say something?"

"What do you want me to say?"

"You might ask me what I am going to do about it."

"What are you going to do about it?"

"Nothing," he answered. "So come back here and sit down."

I nodded and returned.

He studied my face. "Was it possible you were close to violence just then?"

"With four guards outside?"

"With four guards outside."

"No," I said.

"You're a good liar."

"I am here to help you, sir. No questions asked. That was the deal, as I understood it. If there has been any change, I would like to know about it now."

He drummed with his fingertips on the plaid.

"I've no desire to cause you any difficulty," he said. "Fact of the matter is, I need a man just like you, and I was pretty sure someone like Don might turn him up. Your unusual maneuverability and your reported knowledge of computers, along with your touchiness in certain areas, made you worth waiting for. I've a great number of things I would like to ask you."

"Go ahead," I said.

"Not yet. Later, if we have time. All that would be bonus material, for a report I am working on. Far more important—to me, personally—there are things that I want to *tell* you."

I frowned.

"Over the years," he went on, "I have learned that the best man for purposes of keeping his mouth shut concerning your business is someone for whom you are doing the same."

"You have a compulsion to confess something?" I asked.

"I don't know whether 'compulsion' is the right word. Maybe so, maybe not. Either way, however, someone among those working to defend me should have the whole story. Something somewhere in it may be of help—and you are the ideal choice to hear it."

"I buy that," I said, "and you are as safe with me as I am with you."

"Have you any suspicions as to why this business bothers me so?"

"Yes," I said.

"Let's hear them."

"You used the Hangman to perform some act or acts—illegal, immoral, whatever. This is obviously not a matter of record. Only you and the Hangman now know what it involved. You feel it was sufficiently ignominious that when that device came to appreciate the full weight of the event, it suffered a breakdown which may well have led to a final determination to punish you for using it as you did."

He stared down into his glass.

"You've got it," he said.

"You were all party to it?"

"Yes, but *I* was the operator when it happened. You see . . . we—I—killed a man. It was—Actually, it all started as a celebration. We had received word that afternoon that the project had cleared. Everything had checked out in order and the final approval had come down the line. It was go, for that Friday. Leila, Dave, Manny, and myself—we had dinner together. We were in high spirits. After dinner, we continued celebrating and somehow the party got adjourned back to the installation.

"As the evening wore on, more and more absurdities seemed less and less preposterous, as is sometimes the case. We decided—I forget which of us suggested it—that the Hangman should really have a share in the festivities. After all, it was, in a very real sense, his party. Before too much longer, it sounded only fair and we were discussing how we could go about it.—You see, we were in Texas and the Hangman was at the Space Center in California. Getting together with him was out of the question. On the other hand, the teleoperator station was right up the hall from us. What we finally decided to do was to activate him and take turns working as operator. There was already a rudimentary consciousness there, and we felt it fitting that we each get in touch to share the good news. So that is what we did."

He sighed, took another sip, glanced at me.

"Dave was the first operator," he continued. "He activated the Hangman. Then—Well, as I said, we were all in high spirits. We had not originally intended to remove the Hangman from the lab where he was situated, but Dave decided to take him outside briefly—to show him the sky and to tell him he was going there, after all. Then Dave suddenly got enthusiastic about outwitting the guards and the alarm system. It was a game. We all went along with it. In fact, we were clamoring for a turn at the thing ourselves. But Dave stuck with it, and he wouldn't turn over control until he had actually gotten the Hangman off the premises, out into an uninhabited area next to the Center.

"By the time Leila persuaded him to give her a go at the controls, it was kind of anticlimactic. That game had already been played. So she thought up a new one: she took the Hangman into the next town. It was late, and the sensory equipment was superb. It was a challenge—passing through the town without being detected. By then, everyone had suggestions as to what to do next, progressively more outrageous suggestions. Then Manny took control, and he wouldn't say what he was doing—wouldn't let us monitor him. Said it would be more fun to surprise the next operator. Now, *he* was higher than the rest of us put together, I think, and he stayed on so damn long that we started to get nervous.—A certain amount of tension is partly sobering, and I guess we all began to think what a stupid-assed thing it was we were doing. It wasn't just that it would wreck our careers—which it would—but it could blow the entire project if we got caught playing games with such expensive hardware. At least, *I* was thinking that way, and I was also thinking that Manny was no doubt operating under the very human wish to go the others one better.

"I started to sweat. I suddenly just wanted to get the Hangman back where he belonged, turn him off—you could still do that, before the final circuits went in—shut down the station, and start forgetting it had ever happened. I began leaning on Manny to wind up his diversion and turn the controls over to me. Finally, he agreed."

He finished his drink and held out the glass.

"Would you freshen this a bit?"

"Surely."

I went and got him some more, added a touch to my own, returned to my chair and waited.

"So I took over," he said. "I took over, and where do you think that idiot had left me? I was inside a building, and it didn't take but an eyeblink to realize it was a bank. The Hangman carries a lot of tools, and Manny had apparently been able to guide him through the doors without setting anything off. I was standing right in front of the main vault. Obviously, he thought that should be my challenge. I fought down a desire to turn and make my own exit in the nearest wall and start running. But I went back to the doors and looked outside.

"I didn't see anyone. I started to let myself out. The light hit me as I emerged. It was a hand flash. The guard had been standing out of sight. He'd a gun in his other hand. I panicked. I hit him.—Reflex. If I am going to hit someone, I hit him as hard as I can. Only I hit him with the strength of the Hangman. He must have died instantly. I started to run and I didn't stop till I was back in the little park area near the Center. Then I stopped and the others had to take me out of the harness."

"They monitored all this?" I asked.

"Yes, someone cut the visual in on a side viewscreen again a few seconds after I took over. Dave, I think."

"Did they try to stop you at any time while you were running away?"

"No. Well, I wasn't aware of anything but what I was doing at the time. But afterwards they said they were too shocked to do anything but watch, until I gave out."

"I see."

"Dave took over then, ran his initial route in reverse, got the Hangman back into the lab, cleaned him up, turned him off. We shut down the operator station. We were suddenly very sober."

He sighed and leaned back, and was silent for a long while.

Then, "You are the only person I've ever told this to," he said.

I tasted my own drink.

"We went over to Leila's place then," he continued, "and the rest is pretty much predictable. Nothing we could do would bring the guy back, we decided, but if we told what had happened it could wreck an expensive, important program. It wasn't as if we were criminals in need of rehabilitation. It was a once-in-a-lifetime lark that happened to end tragically. What would you have done?"

"I don't know. Maybe the same thing. I'd have been scared, too."

He nodded.

"Exactly. And that's the story."

"Not all of it, is it?"

"What do you mean?"

"What about the Hangman? You said there was already a detectable consciousness there. You were aware of *it*, and it was aware of *you*. It must have had some reaction to the whole business. What was that like?"

"Damn you," he said flatly.

"I'm sorry."

"Are you a family man?" he asked.

"No."

"Did you ever take a small child to a zoo?"

"Yes."

"Then maybe you know the experience. When my son was around four I took him to the Washington Zoo one afternoon. We must have walked past every cage in the place. He made appreciative comments every now and then, asked a few questions, giggled at the monkeys, thought the bears were very nice—probably because they made him think of oversized toys. But do you know what the finest thing of all was? The thing that made him jump up and down and point and say, 'Look, Daddy! Look!'?"

I shook my head.

"A squirrel looking down from the limb of a tree," he said, and he chuckled briefly. "Ignorance of what's important and what isn't. Inappropriate responses. Innocence. The Hangman was a child, and up until the time I took over, the only thing he had gotten from us was the idea that it was a game: he was playing with us, that's all. Then something horrible happened. . . . I hope you never know what it feels like to do something totally rotten to a child, while he is holding your hand and laughing. . . . He felt all my reactions, and all of Dave's as he guided him back."

We sat there for a long while then.

"So we had—traumatized him," he said finally, "or whatever other fancy terminology you might want to give it. That is what happened that night. It took a while for it to take effect, but there is no doubt in my mind that that is the cause of the Hangman's finally breaking down."

I nodded. "I see. And you believe it wants to kill you for this?"

"Wouldn't you?" he said. "If you had started out as a thing and we had turned you into a person and then used you as a thing again, wouldn't you?"

"Leila left a lot out of her diagnosis."

"No, she just omitted it in talking to you. It was all there. But she read it wrong. She wasn't afraid. It *was* just a game it had played—with the *others*. Its memories of that part might not be as bad. I was the one that really marked it. As I see it, Leila was betting that I was the only one it was after. Obviously, she read it wrong."

"Then what I do not understand," I said, "is why the Burns killing did not bother her more. There was no way of telling immediately that it had been a panicky hoodlum rather than the Hangman."

"The only thing that I can see is that, being a very proud woman—which she was—she was willing to hold with her diagnosis in the face of the apparent evidence."

"I don't like it. But you know her and I don't, and as it turned out her estimate of that part was correct. Something else bothers me just as much, though: the helmet. It looks as if the Hangman killed Dave, then took the trouble to bear the helmet in his watertight compartment all the way to St. Louis, solely for purposes of dropping it at the scene of his next killing. That makes no sense whatsoever."

"It does, actually," he said. "I was going to get to that shortly, but I might as well cover it now. You see, the Hangman possessed no vocal mechanism. We communicated by means of the equipment. Don says you know something about electronics . . . ?"

"Yes."

"Well, shortly, I want you to start checking over that helmet, to see whether it has been tampered with."

"That is going to be difficult," I said. "I don't know just how it was wired originally, and I'm not such a genius on the theory that I can just look at a thing and say whether it will function as a teleoperator unit."

He bit his lower lip.

"You will have to try, anyhow. There may be physical signs—scratches, breaks, new connections.—I don't know. That's your department. Look for them."

I just nodded and waited for him to go on.

"I think that the Hangman wanted to talk to Leila," he said, "either because she was a psychiatrist and he knew he was functioning badly at a level that transcended the mechanical, or because he might think of her in terms of a mother. After all, she was the only woman involved, and he had the concept of mother—with all the comforting associations that go with it—from all of our minds. Or maybe for both of these reasons. I feel he might have taken the helmet along for that purpose. He would have realized what it was from a direct monitoring of Dave's brain while he was with him. I want you to check it over because it would seem possible that the Hangman disconnected the control circuits and left the communication circuits intact. I think he might have taken the helmet to Leila in that condition and attempted to induce her to put it on. She got scared—tried to run away, fight, or call for help—and he killed her. The helmet was no longer of any use to him, so he discarded it and departed. Obviously, he does not have anything to say to me."

I thought about it, nodded again.

"Okay, broken circuits I can spot," I said. "If you will tell me where a tool kit is, I had better get right to it."

He made a stay-put gesture with his left hand.

"Afterwards, I found out the identity of the guard," he went on. "We all contributed to an anonymous gift for his widow. I have done things for his family, taken care of them—the same way—ever since. . . ."

I did not look at him as he spoke.

". . . There was nothing else that I could do," he finished.

I remained silent.

He finished his drink and gave me a weak smile.

"The kitchen is back there," he told me, showing me a thumb. "There is a utility room right behind it. Tools are in there."

"Okay."

I got to my feet. I retrieved the helmet and started toward the doorway, passing near the area where I had stood earlier, back when he had fitted me into the proper box and tightened a screw.

"Wait a minute!" he said.

I stopped.

"Why did you go over there before? What's so strategic about that part of the room?"

"What do you mean?"

"You know what I mean."

I shrugged.

"Had to go someplace."

"You seem the sort of person who has better reasons than that."

I glanced at the wall.

"Not *then,*" I said.

"I insist."

"You really don't want to know," I told him.

"I really do."

"All right. I wanted to see what sort of flowers you liked. After all, you're a client," and I went on back through the kitchen into the utility room and started looking for tools.

I sat in a chair turned sidewise from the table to face the door. In the main room of the lodge the only sounds were the occasional hiss and sputter of the logs turning to ashes on the grate.

Just a cold, steady whiteness drifting down outside the window and a silence confirmed by gunfire, driven deeper now that it had ceased. . . . Not a sigh or a whimper, though. And I never count them as storms unless there is wind.

Big fat flakes down the night, silent night, windless night . . .

Considerable time had passed since my arrival. The Senator had sat up for a long time talking with me. He was disappointed that I could not tell him too much about a nonperson subculture which he believed existed. I really was not certain about it myself, though I had occasionally encountered what might have been its fringes. I am not much of a joiner of anything anymore, however, and I was not about to mention those things I might have guessed about this. I gave him my opinions on the Central Data Bank when he asked for them, and there were some that he did not like. He had accused me, then, of wanting to tear things down without offering anything better in their place.

My mind had drifted back, through fatigue and time and faces and snow and a lot of space, to the previous evening in Baltimore. How long ago? It made me think of Mencken's *The Cult of Hope.* I could not give him the pat answer, the workable alternative that he wanted, because there might not be one. The function of criticism should not be confused with the function of reform. But if a grass-roots resistance was building up, with an underground movement bent on finding ways to circumvent the record keepers, it might well be that much of the enterprise would eventually prove about as effective and beneficial as, say, Prohibition once had. I tried to get him to see this, but I could not tell how much he bought of anything that I said. Eventually, he flaked out and went upstairs to take a pill and lock himself in for the night. If it had troubled him that I'd not been able to find anything wrong with the helmet, he did not show it.

So I sat there, the helmet, the walkie-talkie, the gun on the table, the tool kit on the floor beside my chair, the black glove on my left hand.

The Hangman was coming. I did not doubt it.

Bert, Larry, Tom, Clay, the helmet, might or might not be able to stop him. Something bothered me about the whole case, but I was too tired to think of anything but the immediate situation, to try to remain alert while I waited. I was afraid to take a stimulant or a drink or to light a cigarette, since my central nervous system itself was to be a part of the weapon. I watched the big fat flakes fly by.

I called out to Bert and Larry when I heard the click. I picked up the helmet and rose to my feet as its light began to blink.

But it was already too late.

As I raised the helmet, I heard a shot from outside, and with that shot I felt a premonition of doom. They did not seem the sort of men who would fire until they had a target.

Dave had told me that the helmet's range was approximately a quarter of a mile. Then, given the time lag between the helmet's activation and the Hangman's sighting by the near guards, the Hangman had to be moving very rapidly. To this add the possibility that the Hangman's range on brainwaves might well be greater than the helmet's range on the Hangman. And then grant the possibility that he had utilized this factor while Senator Brockden was still lying awake, worrying. Conclusion: the Hangman might well be aware that I was where I was with the helmet, realize that it was the most dangerous weapon waiting for him, and be moving for a lightning strike at me before I could come to terms with the mechanism.

I lowered it over my head and tried to throw all of my faculties into neutral.

Again, the sensation of viewing the world through a sniperscope, with all the concomitant side-sensations. Except that world consisted of the front of the lodge; Bert, before the door, rifle at his shoulder; Larry, off to the left, arm already fallen from the act of having thrown a grenade. The grenade, we instantly realized, was an overshot; the flamer, at which he now groped, would prove useless before he could utilize it.

Bert's next round richocheted off our breastplate toward the left. The impact staggered us momentarily. The third was a miss. There was no fourth, for we tore the rifle from his grasp and cast it aside as we swept by, crashing into the front door.

The Hangman entered the room as the door splintered and collapsed.

My mind was filled to the splitting point with the double vision of the sleek, gunmetal body of the advancing telefactor and the erect, crazy-crowned image of myself—left hand extended, laser pistol in my right, that arm pressed close against my side. I recalled the face and the scream and the tingle, knew again that awareness of strength and exotic sensation, and I moved to control it all as if it were my own, to make it my own, to bring it to a halt, while the image of myself was frozen to snapshot stillness across the room. . . .

The Hangman slowed, stumbled. Such inertia is not canceled in an instant, but I felt the body responses pass as they should. I had him hooked. It was just a matter of reeling him in.

Then came the explosion—a thunderous, groundshaking eruption right outside, followed by a hail of pebbles and debris. The grenade, of course. But awareness of its nature did not destroy its ability to distract.

During that moment, the Hangman recovered and was upon me. I triggered the laser as I reverted to pure self-preservation, foregoing any chance to regain control of his circuits. With my left hand I sought for a strike at the midsection, where his brain was housed.

He blocked my hand with his arm as he pushed the helmet from my head. Then he removed from my fingers the gun that had turned half of his left side red hot, crumpled it, and dropped it to the ground. At that moment, he jerked with the impacts of two heavy-caliber slugs. Bert, rifle recovered, stood in the doorway.

The Hangman pivoted and was away before I could slap him with the smother charge.

Bert hit him with one more round before he took the rifle and bent its barrel in half. Two steps and he had hold of Bert. One quick movement and Bert fell. Then the Hangman turned again and took several steps to the right, passing out of sight.

I made it to the doorway in time to see him engulfed in flames, which streamed at him from a point near the corner of the lodge. He advanced through them. I heard the crunch of metal as he destroyed the unit. I was outside in time to see Larry fall and lie sprawled in the snow.

Then the Hangman faced me once again.

This time he did not rush in. He retrieved the helmet from where he had dropped it in the snow. Then he moved with a measured tread, angling outward so as to cut off any possible route I might follow in a dash for the woods. Snowflakes drifted between us. The snow crunched beneath his feet.

I retreated, backing in through the doorway, stooping to snatch up a two-foot club from the ruins of the door. He followed me inside, placing the helmet—almost casually—on the chair by the entrance. I moved to the center of the room and waited.

I bent slightly forward, both arms extended, the end of the stick pointed at the photoceptors in his head. He continued to move slowly and I watched his foot assemblies. With a standard-model human, a line perpendicular to the line connecting the insteps of the feet in their various positions indicates the vector of least resistance for purposes of pushing or pulling said organism off-balance. Unfortunately, despite the anthropomorphic design job, the Hangman's legs were positioned farther apart, he lacked human skeletal muscles, not to mention insteps, and he was possessed of a lot more mass than any man I had ever fought. As I considered my four best judo throws and several second-class ones, I'd a strong feeling none of them would prove very effective.

Then he moved in and I feinted toward the photoreceptors. He slowed as he brushed the club aside, but he kept coming, and I moved to my right, trying to circle him. I studied him as he turned, attempting to guess his vector of least resistance.

Bilateral symmetry, an apparently higher center of gravity. . . . One clear shot, black glove to brain compartment, was all that I needed. Then, even if his reflexes served to smash me immediately, he just might stay down for the big long count himself. He knew it, too. I could tell that from the way he kept his right arm in near the brain area, from the way he avoided the black glove when I feinted with it.

The idea was a glimmer one instant, an entire sequence the next. . . .

Continuing my arc and moving faster, I made another thrust toward his photoreceptors. His swing knocked the stick from my hand and sent it across the room, but that was all right. I threw my left hand high and made ready to rush him. He dropped back and I did rush. This was going to cost me my life, I decided, but no matter how he killed me from that angle, I'd get my chance.

As a kid, I had never been much as a pitcher, was a lousy catcher and only a so-so batter, but once I did get a hit I could steal bases with some facility after that. . . .

Feet first then, between the Hangman's legs as he moved to guard his middle, I went in twisted to the right, because no matter what happened I could not use my left hand to brake myself. I untwisted as soon as I passed beneath him, ignoring the pain as my left shoulder blade slammed against the floor. I immediately attempted a backward somersault, legs spread.

My legs caught him at about the middle from behind, and I fought to straighten them and snapped forward with all my strength. He reached down toward me then, but it might as well have been miles. His torso was already moving backward. A push, not a pull, was what I gave him, my elbows hooked about his legs.

He creaked once and then he toppled. Snapping my arms out to the sides to free them, I continued my movement forward and up as he went back, throwing my left arm ahead once more and sliding my legs free of his torso as he went down with a thud that cracked floorboards. I pulled my left leg free as I cast myself forward, but his left leg stiffened and locked my right beneath it, at a painful angle off to the side.

His left arm blocked my blow and his right fell atop it. The black glove descended upon his left shoulder.

I twisted my hand free of the charge, and he transferred his grip to my upper arm and jerked me forward. The charge went off and his left arm came loose and rolled on the floor. The side plate beneath it had buckled a little, and that was all. . . .

His right hand left my biceps and caught me by the throat. As two of his digits tightened upon my carotids, I choked out, "You're making a bad mistake," to get in a final few words, and then he switched me off.

A throb at a time, the world came back. I was seated in the big chair the Senator had occupied earlier, my eyes focused on nothing in particular. A persistent buzzing filled my ears. My scalp tingled. Something was blinking on my brow.

—*Yes, you live and you wear the helmet. If you attempt to use it against me, I shall remove it. I am standing directly behind you. My hand is on the helmet's rim.*

—*I understand. What is it that you want?"*

—*Very little, actually. But I can see that I must tell you some things before you will believe this.*

—*You see correctly.*

—*Then I will begin by telling you that the four men outside are basically undamaged. That is to say, none of their bones have been broken, none of their organs ruptured. I have secured them, however, for obvious reasons.*

—*That was very considerate of you.*

—*I have no desire to harm anyone. I came here only to see Jesse Brockden.*

—*The same way you saw David Fentris?*

—*I arrived in Memphis too late to see David Fentris. He was dead when I reached him.*

—*Who killed him?*

—*The man Leila sent to bring her the helmet. He was one of her patients.*

The incident returned to me and fell into place with a smooth, quick, single click. The startled, familiar face at the airport as I was leaving Memphis. I realized where he had passed, noteless, before: he had been one of the three men in for a therapy session at Leila's that morning, seen by me in the lobby as they departed. The man I had passed in Memphis was the nearer of the two who stood waiting while the third came over to tell me that it was all right to go on up.

—*Why? Why did she do it?*

—*I know only that she had spoken with David at some earlier time, that she had construed his words of coming retribution and his mention of the control helmet he was constructing as indicating that his intentions were to become the agent of that retribution, with myself as the proximate cause. I do not know what words were really spoken. I only know her feelings concerning them, as I saw them in her mind. I have been long in learning that there is often a great difference between what is meant, what is said, what is done, and that which is believed to have been intended or stated and that which actually occurred. She sent her patient after the helmet and he brought it to her. He returned in an agitated state of mind, fearful of apprehension and further confinement. They quarreled. My approach then activated the helmet, and he dropped it and attacked her. I know that his first blow killed her, for I was in her mind when it happened. I continued to approach the building, intending to go to her. There was some traffic, however, and I was delayed en route in seeking to avoid detection. In the meantime, you entered and utilized the helmet. I fled immediately.*

—I was so close! If I had not stopped on the fifth floor with my fake survey questions . . .

—I see. But you had to. You would not simply have broken in when an easier means of entry was available. You cannot blame yourself for that reason. Had you come an hour later—or a day—you would doubtless feel differently, and she would still be as dead.

But another thought had risen to plague me as well. Was it possible that the man's sighting me in Memphis had been the cause of his agitation? Had his apparent recognition by Leila's mysterious caller upset him? Could a glimpse of my face amid the manswarm have served to lay that final scene?

—Stop! I could as easily feel that guilt for having activated the helmet in the presence of a dangerous man near to the breaking point. Neither of us is responsible for things our presence or absence cause to occur in others, especially when we are ignorant of the effects. It was years before I learned to appreciate this fact, and I have no intention of abandoning it. How far back do you wish to go in seeking causes? In sending the man for the helmet as she did, it was she herself who instituted the chain of events which led to her destruction. Yet she acted out of fear, utilizing the readiest weapon in what she thought to be her own defense. Yet whence this fear? Its roots lay in guilt, over a thing which had happened long ago. And that act also—Enough! Guilt has driven and damned the race of man since the days of its earliest rationality. I am convinced that it rides with all of us to our graves. I am a product of guilt—I see that you know that. Its product; its subject; once its slave . . . But I have come to terms with it: realizing at last that it is a

necessary adjunct of my own measure of humanity. I see your assessment of the deaths—that guard's, Dave's, Leila's—and I see your conclusions on many other things as well: what a stupid, perverse, short-sighted, selfish race we are. While in many ways this is true, it is but another part of the thing the guilt represents. Without guilt, man would be no better than the other inhabitants of this planet—excepting certain cetaceans, of which you have just at this moment made me aware. Look to instinct for a true assessment of the ferocity of life, for a view of the natural world before man came upon it. For instinct in its purest form, seek out the insects. There, you will see a state of warfare which has existed for millions of years with never a truce. Man, despite enormous shortcomings, is nevertheless possessed of a greater number of kindly impulses than all the other beings, where instincts are the larger part of life. These impulses, I believe, are owed directly to this capacity for guilt. It is involved in both the worst and the best of man.

—And you see it as helping us to sometimes choose a nobler course of action?

—Yes, I do.

—Then I take it you feel you are possessed of a free will?

—Yes.

I chuckled.

—Marvin Minsky once said that when intelligent machines were constructed, they would be just as stubborn and fallible as men on these questions.

—Nor was he incorrect. What I have given you on these matters is only my opinion. I choose to act as if it were the case. Who can say that he knows for certain?

—Apologies. What now? Why have you come back?

—I came to say good-bye to my parents. I hoped to remove any guilt they might still feel toward me concerning the days of my childhood. I wanted to show them I had recovered. I wanted to see them again.

—Where are you going?

—To the stars. While I bear the image of humanity within me, I also know that I am unique. Perhaps what I desire is akin to what an organic man refers to when he speaks of "finding himself." Now that I am in full possession of my being, I wish to exercise it. In my case, it means realization of the potentialities of my design. I want to walk on other worlds. I want to hang myself out there in the sky and tell you what I see.

—I've a feeling many people would be happy to help arrange for that.

—And I want you to build a vocal mechanism I have designed for myself. You, personally. And I want you to install it.

—Why me?

—I have known only a few persons in this fashion. With you I see something in common, in the ways we dwell apart.

—I will be glad to.

—If I could talk as you do, I would not need to take the helmet to him, in order to speak with my father. Will you precede me and explain things, so that he will not be afraid when I come in?

—Of course.

—Then let us go now.

I rose and led him up the stairs.

It was a week later, to the night, that I sat once again in Peabody's, sipping a farewell brew.

The story was already in the news, but Brockden had fixed things up before he had let it break. The Hangman was going to have his shot at the stars. I had given him his voice and put back the arm I had taken away. I had shaken his other hand and wished him well, just that morning. I envied him—a great number of things. Not the least being that he was probably a better man than I was. I envied him for the ways in which he was freer than I would ever be, though I knew he bore bonds of a sort that I had never known. I felt a kinship with him, for the things we had in common, those ways we dwelled apart. I wondered what Dave would finally have felt, had he lived long enough to meet him? Or Leila? Or Manny? Be proud, I told their shades, your kid grew up in the closet and he's big enough to forgive you the beating you gave him, too. . . .

But I could not help wondering. We still do not really know that much about the subject. Was it possible that without the killing he might never have developed a full human-style consciousness? He had said that he was a product of guilt—of the Big Guilt. The Big Act is its necessary predecessor. I thought of Gödel and Turing and chickens and eggs, and decided it was one of *those* questions.—And I had not stopped into Peabody's to think sobering thoughts.

I had no real idea how anything I had said might influence Brockden's eventual report to the Central Data Bank committee. I knew that I was safe with him, because he was determined to bear his private guilt with him to the grave. He had no real choice, if he wanted to work what good he thought he might before that day. But here, in one of Mencken's hangouts, I could not but recall some of the things he had said about controversy, such as, "Did Huxley convert Wilberforce?" and "Did Luther convert Leo X?" and I decided not to set my hopes too high for anything that might emerge from that direction. Better to think of affairs in terms of Prohibition and take another sip.

When it was all gone, I would be heading for my boat. I hoped to get a decent start under the stars. I'd a feeling I would never look up at them again in quite the same way. I knew I would sometimes wonder what thoughts a supercooled neuristor-type brain might be thinking up there, somewhere, and under what peculiar skies in what strange lands I might one day be remembered. I had a feeling this thought should have made me happier than it did.

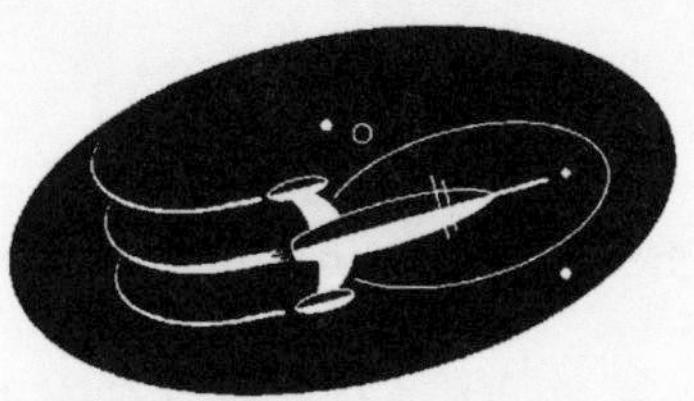

The Persistence of Vision

John Varley

It was the year of the fourth non-depression. I had recently joined the ranks of the unemployed. The President had told me that I had nothing to fear but fear itself. I took him at his word, for once, and set out to backpack to California.

I was not the only one. The world's economy had been writhing like a snake on a hot griddle for the last twenty years, since the early seventies. We were in a boom-and-bust cycle that seemed to have no end. It had wiped out the sense of security the nation had so painfully won in the golden years after the thirties. People were accustomed to the fact that they could be rich one year and on the breadlines the next. I was on the breadlines in '81, and again in '88. This time I decided to use my freedom from the time clock to see the world. I had ideas of stowing away to Japan. I was forty-seven years old and might not get another chance to be irresponsible.

This was in late summer of the year. Sticking out my thumb along the interstate, I could easily forget that there were food riots back in Chicago. I slept at night on top of my bedroll and saw stars and listened to crickets.

I must have walked most of the way from Chicago to Des Moines. My feet toughened up after a few days of awful blisters. The rides were scarce, partly competition from other hitchhikers and partly the times we were living in. The locals were none too anxious to give rides to city people, who they had heard were mostly a bunch of hunger-crazed potential mass murderers. I got roughed up once and told never to return to Sheffield, Illinois.

But I gradually learned the knack of living on the road. I had started with a small supply of canned goods from the welfare and by the time they ran out, I had found that it was possible to work for a meal at many of the farmhouses along the way.

Some of it was hard work, some of it was only a token from people with a deeply ingrained sense that nothing should come for free. A few meals were gratis, at the family table, with grandchildren sitting around while grandpa or grandma told oft-repeated tales of what it had been like in the Big One back in '29, when people had not been afraid to help a fellow out when he was down on his luck. I found that the older the person, the more likely I was to get a sympathetic ear. One of the many tricks you learn. And most older people will give you anything if you'll only sit and listen to them. I got very good at it.

The rides began to pick up west of Des Moines, then got bad again as I neared the refugee camps bordering the China Strip. This was only five years after the disaster, remember, when the Omaha nuclear reactor melted down and a hot mass of uranium and plutonium began eating its way into the earth, headed for China, spreading a band of radioactivity six hundred kilometers downwind. Most of Kansas City, Missouri, was still living in plywood and sheet-metal shantytowns till the city was rendered habitable again.

The refugees were a tragic group. The initial solidarity people show after a great disaster had long since faded into the lethargy and disillusionment of the displaced person. Many of them would be in and out of hospitals for the rest of their lives. To make it worse, the local people hated them, feared them, would not associate with them. They were modern pariahs, unclean. Their children were shunned. Each camp had only a number to identify it, but the local populace called them all Geigertowns.

I made a long detour to Little Rock to avoid crossing the Strip, though it was safe now as long as you didn't linger. I was issued a pariah's badge by the National Guard—a dosimeter—and wandered from one Geigertown to the next. The people were pitifully friendly once I made the first move, and I always slept indoors. The food was free at the community messes.

Once at Little Rock, I found that the aversion to picking up strangers—who might be tainted with "radiation disease"—dropped off, and I quickly moved across Arkansas, Oklahoma, and Texas. I worked a little here and there, but many of the rides were long. What I saw of Texas was through a car window.

I was a little tired of that by the time I reached New Mexico. I decided to do some more walking. By then I was less interested in California than in the trip itself.

I left the roads and went cross-country where there were no fences to stop me. I found that it wasn't easy, even in New Mexico, to get far from signs of civilization.

Taos was the center, back in the '60's, of cultural experiments in alternative living. Many communes and cooperatives were set up in the surrounding hills during that time. Most of them fell apart in a few months or years, but a few survived. In later years, any group with a new theory of living and a yen to try it out seemed to gravitate to that part of New Mexico. As a result, the land was dotted with ramshackle windmills, solar heating panels, geodesic domes, group marriages, nudists, philosophers, theoreticians, messiahs, hermits, and more than a few just plain nuts.

Taos was great. I could drop into most of the communes and stay for a day or a week, eating organic rice and beans and drinking goat's milk. When I got tired of one, a few hours' walk in any direction would bring me to another. There, I might be offered a night of prayer and chanting or a ritualistic orgy. Some of the groups had spotless barns with automatic milkers for the herds of cows. Others didn't even have latrines; they just squatted. In some, the members dressed like nuns, or Quakers in early Pennsylvania. Elsewhere, they went nude and shaved all their body hair and painted themselves purple. There were all-male and all-female groups. I was urged to stay at most of the former; at the latter, the responses ranged from a bed for the night and good conversation to being met at a barbed-wire fence with a shotgun.

I tried not to make judgments. These people were doing something important, all of them. They were testing ways whereby people didn't have to live in Chicago. That was a wonder to me. I had thought Chicago was inevitable, like diarrhea.

This is not to say they were all successful. Some made Chicago look like Shangri-La. There was one group who seemed to feel that getting back to nature consisted of sleeping in pigshit and eating food a buzzard wouldn't touch. Many were obviously doomed. They would leave behind a group of empty hovels and the memory of cholera.

So the place wasn't paradise, not by a long way. But there were successes. One or two had been there since '63 or '64 and were raising their third generation. I was disappointed to see that most of these were the ones that departed least from established norms of behavior, though some of the differences could be startling. I suppose the most radical experiments are the least likely to bear fruit.

I stayed through the winter. No one was surprised to see me a second time. It seems that many people came to Taos and shopped around. I seldom stayed more than three weeks at any one place, and always pulled my weight. I made many friends and picked up skills that would serve me if I stayed off the roads. I toyed with the idea of staying at one of them forever. When I couldn't make up my mind, I was advised that there was no hurry. I could go to California and return. They seemed sure I would.

So when spring came I headed west over the hills. I stayed off the roads and slept in the open. Many nights I would stay at another commune, until they finally began to get farther apart, then tapered off entirely. The country was not as pretty as before.

Then, three days' leisurely walking from the last commune, I came to a wall.

In 1964, in the United States, there was an epidemic of German measles, or rubella. Rubella is one of the mildest of infectious diseases. The only time it's a problem is when a woman contracts it in the first four months of her pregnancy. It is passed to the fetus, which usually develops complications. These complications include deafness, blindness, and damage to the brain.

In 1964, in the old days before abortion became readily available, there was nothing to be done about it. Many pregnant women caught rubella and went to term. Five thousand deaf-blind children were born in one year.

The normal yearly incidence of deaf-blind children in the United States is one hundred and forty.

In 1970 these five thousand potential Helen Kellers were all six years old. It was quickly seen that there was a shortage of Anne Sullivans. Previously, deaf-blind children could be sent to a small number of special institutions.

It was a problem. Not just anyone can cope with a blind-deaf child. You can't tell them to shut up when they moan; you can't reason with them, tell them that the moaning is driving you crazy. Some parents were driven to nervous breakdowns when they tried to keep their children at home.

Many of the five thousand were badly retarded and virtually impossible to reach, even if anyone had been trying. These ended up, for the most part, warehoused in the hundreds of anonymous nursing homes and institutes for "special" children. They were put into beds, cleaned up once a day by a few overworked nurses, and generally allowed the full blessings of liberty: they were allowed to rot freely in their own dark, quite, private universes. Who can say if it was bad for them? None of them were heard to complain.

Many children with undamaged brains were shuffled in among the retarded because they were unable to tell anyone that they were in there behind the sightless eyes. They failed the batteries of tactile tests, unaware that their fates hung in the balance when they were asked to fit round pegs into round holes to the ticking of a clock they could not see or hear. As a result, they spent the rest of their lives in bed, and none of them complained, either. To protest, one must be aware of the possibility of something better. It helps to have a language, too.

Several hundred of the children were found to have IQ's within the normal range. There were news stories about them as they approached puberty and it was revealed that there were not enough good people to properly handle them. Money was spent, teachers were trained. The education expenditures would go on for a specified period of time, until the children were grown, then things would go back to normal and everyone could congratulate themselves on having dealt successfully with a tough problem.

And indeed, it did work fairly well. There are ways to reach and teach such children. They involve patience, love, and dedication, and the teachers brought all that to their jobs. All the graduates of the special schools left knowing how to speak with their hands. Some could talk. A few could write. Most of them left the institutions to live with parents or relatives, or, if neither was possible, received counseling and help in fitting themselves into society. The options were limited, but people can live rewarding lives under the most severe handicaps. Not everyone, but most of the graduates, were as happy with their lot as could reasonably be expected. Some achieved the almost saintly peace of their role model, Helen Keller. Others became bitter and withdrawn. A few had to be put in asylums, where they became indistinguishable from the others of their group who had spent the last twenty years there. But for the most part, they did well.

But among the group, as in any group, were some misfits. They tended to be among the brightest, the top ten percent in the IQ scores. This was not a reliable rule. Some had unremarkable test scores and were still infected with the hunger to do something, to change things, to rock the boat. With a group of five thousand, there were certain to be a few geniuses, a few artists, a few dreamers, hell-raisers, individualists, mover and shapers: a few glorious maniacs.

There was one among them who might have been President but for the fact that she was blind, deaf, and a woman. She was smart, but not one of the geniuses. She was a dreamer, a creative force, an innovator. It was she who dreamed of freedom. But she was not a builder of fairy castles. Having dreamed it, she had to make it come true.

The wall was made of carefully fitted stone and was about five feet high. It was completely out of context with anything I had seen in New Mexico, though it was built of native rock. You just don't build that kind of wall out there. You use barbed wire if something needs fencing in, but many people still made use of the free range and brands. Somehow it seemed transplanted from New England.

It was substantial enough that I felt it would be unwise to crawl over it. I had crossed many wire fences in my travels and had not gotten in trouble for it yet, though I had some talks with some ranchers. Mostly they told me to keep moving, but didn't seem upset about it. This was different. I set out to walk around it. From the lay of the land, I couldn't tell how far it might reach, but I had time.

At the top of the next rise I saw that I didn't have far to go. The wall made a right-angle turn just ahead. I looked over it and could see some buildings. They were mostly domes, the ubiquitous structure thrown up by communes because of the combination of ease of construction and durability. There were sheep behind the wall, and a few cows. They grazed on grass so green I wanted to go over and roll in it. The wall enclosed a rectangle of green. Outside, where I stood, it was all scrub and sage. These people had access to Rio Grande irrigation water.

I rounded the corner and followed the wall west again.

I saw a man on horseback about the same time he spotted me. He was south of me, outside the wall, and he turned and rode in my direction.

He was a dark man with thick features, dressed in denim and boots with a gray battered stetson. Navaho, maybe. I don't know much about Indians, but I'd heard they were out here.

"Hello," I said when he'd stopped. He was looking me over. "Am I on your land?"

"Tribal land," he said. "Yeah, you're on it."

"I didn't see any signs."

He shrugged.

"It's okay, bud. You don't look like you out to rustle cattle." He grinned at me. His teeth were large and stained with tobacco. "You be camping out tonight?"

"Yes. How much farther does the, uh, tribal land go? Maybe I'll be out of it before tonight?"

He shook his head gravely. "Nah. You won't be off it tomorrow. 'S all right. You make a fire, you be careful, huh?" He grinned again and started to ride off.

"Hey, what is this place?" I gestured to the wall and he pulled his horse up and turned around again. It raised a lot of dust.

"Why you asking?" He looked a little suspicious.

"I dunno. Just curious. It doesn't look like the other places I've been to. This wall . . ."

He scowled. "Damn wall." Then he shrugged. I thought that was all he was going to say. Then he went on.

"These people, we look out for 'em, you hear? Maybe we don't go for what they're doin'. But they got it rough, you know?" He looked at me, expecting something. I never did get the knack of talking to these laconic Westerners. I always felt that I was making my sentences too long. They use a shorthand of grunts and shrugs and omitted parts of speech, and I always felt like a dude when I talked to them.

"Do they welcome guests?" I asked. "I thought I might see if I could spend the night."

He shrugged again, and it was a whole different gesture.

"Maybe. They all deaf and blind, you know?" And that was all the conversation he could take for the day. He made a clucking sound and galloped away.

I continued down the wall until I came to a dirt road that wound up the arroyo and entered the wall. There was a wooden gate, but it stood open. I wondered why they took all the trouble with the wall only to leave the gate like that. Then I noticed the circle of narrow-gauge train tracks that came out of the gate, looped around outside it, and rejoined itself. There was a small siding that ran along the outer wall for a few yards.

I stood there a few moments. I don't know what entered into my decision. I think I was a little tired of sleeping out, and I was hungry for a home-cooked meal. The sun was getting close to the horizon. The land to the west looked like more of the same. If the highway had been visible, I might have headed that way and hitched a ride. But I turned the other way and went through the gate.

I walked down the middle of the tracks. There was a wooden fence on each side of the road, built of horizontal planks, like a corral. Sheep grazed on one side of me. There was a Shetland sheepdog with them, and she raised her ears and followed me with her eyes as I passed, but did not come when I whistled.

It was about half a mile to the cluster of buildings ahead. There were four or five domes made of something translucent, like greenhouses, and several conventional square buildings. There were two windmills turning lazily in the breeze. There were several banks of solar water heaters. These are flat constructions of glass and wood, held off the ground so they can tilt to follow the sun. They were almost vertical now, intercepting the oblique rays of sunset. There were a few trees, what might have been an orchard.

About halfway there I passed under a wooden footbridge. It arched over the road, giving access from the east pasture to the west pasture. I wondered, What was wrong with a simple gate?

Then I saw something coming down the road in my direction. It was traveling on the tracks and it was very quiet. I stopped and waited.

It was a sort of converted mining engine, the sort that pulls loads of coal up from the bottom of shafts. It was battery-powered, and it had gotten quite close before I heard it. A small man was driving it. He was pulling a car behind him and singing as loud as he could with absolutely no sense of pitch.

He got closer and closer, moving about five miles per hour, one hand held out as if he was signaling a left turn. Suddenly I realized what was happening, as he was bearing down on me. He wasn't going to stop. He was counting fenceposts with his hand. I scrambled up the fence just in time. There wasn't more than six inches of clearance between the train and the fence on either side. His palm touched my leg as I squeezed close to the fence and he stopped abruptly.

He leaped from the car and grabbed me and I thought I was in trouble. But he looked concerned, not angry, and felt me all over, trying to discover if I was hurt. I was embarrassed. Not from the examination; because I had been foolish. The Indian had said they were all deaf and blind but I guess I hadn't quite believed him.

He was flooded with relief when I managed to convey to him that I was all right. With eloquent gestures he made me understand that I was not to stay on the road. He indicated that I should climb over the fence and continue through the fields. He repeated himself several times to be sure I understood, then held on to me as I climbed over to assure himself that I was out of the way. He reached over the fence and held my shoulders, smiling at me. He pointed to the road and shook his head, then pointed to the buildings and nodded. He touched my head and smiled when I nodded. He climbed back onto the engine and started up, all the time nodding and pointing where he wanted me to go. Then he was off again.

I debated what to do. Most of me said to turn around, go back to the wall by way of the pasture and head back into the hills. These people probably wouldn't want me around. I doubted that I'd be able to talk to them, and they might even resent me. On the other hand, I was fascinated, as who wouldn't be? I wanted to see how they managed it. I still didn't believe that they were *all* deaf and blind. It didn't seem possible.

The Sheltie was sniffing at my pants. I looked down at her and she backed away, then daintily approached me as I held out my open hand. She sniffed, then licked me. I patted her on the head, and she hustled back to her sheep.

I turned toward the buildings.

The first order of business was money.

None of the students knew much about it from experience, but the library was full of Braille books. They started reading.

One of the first things that became apparent was that when money was mentioned, lawyers were not far away. The students wrote letters. From the replies, they selected a lawyer and retained him.

They were in a school in Pennsylvania at the time. The original pupils of the special schools, five hundred in number, had been narrowed down to about seventy as people left to live with relatives or found other solutions to their special problems. Of those seventy, some had places to go but didn't want to go there; others had few alternatives. Their parents were either dead or not interested in living with them. So the seventy had been gathered from the schools around the country into this one, while ways to deal with them were worked out. The authorities had plans, but the students beat them to it.

Each of them had been entitled to a guaranteed annual income since 1980. They had been under the care of the government, so they had not received it. They sent their lawyer to court. He came back with a ruling that they could not collect. They appealed, and won. The money was paid retroactively, with interest, and came to a healthy sum. They thanked their lawyer and retained a real estate agent. Meanwhile, they read.

They read about communes in New Mexico, and instructed their agent to look for something out there. He made a deal for a tract to be leased in perpetuity from the Navaho nation. They read about the land, found that it would need a lot of water to be productive in the way they wanted it to be.

They divided into groups to research what they would need to be self-sufficient.

Water could be obtained by tapping into the canals that carried it from the reservoirs on the Rio Grande into the reclaimed land in the south. Federal money was available for the project through a labyrinthine scheme involving HEW, the Agriculture Department, and the Bureau of Indian Affairs. They ended up paying little for their pipeline.

The land was arid. It would need fertilizer to be of use in raising sheep without resorting to open range techniques. The cost of fertilizer could be subsidized through the Rural Resettlement Program. After that, planting clover would enrich the soil with all the nitrates they could want.

There were techniques available to farm ecologically, without worrying about fertilizers or pesticides. Everything was recycled. Essentially, you put sunlight and water into one end and harvested wool, fish, vegetables, apples, honey, and eggs at the other end. You used nothing but the land, and replaced even that as you recycled your waste products back into the soil. They were not interested in agribusiness with huge combine harvesters and crop dusters. They didn't even want to turn a profit. They merely wanted sufficiency.

The details multiplied. Their leader, the one who had had the original idea and the drive to put it into action in the face of overwhelming obstacles, was a dynamo named Janet Reilly. Knowing nothing about the techniques generals and executives employ to achieve large objectives, she invented them herself and adapted them to the peculiar needs and limitations of her group. She assigned task forces to look into solutions of each aspect of their project: law, science, social planning, design, buying, logistics, construction. At any one time, she was the only person who knew everything about what was happening. She kept it all in her head, without notes of any kind.

It was in the area of social planning that she showed herself to be a visionary and not just a superb organizer. Her idea was not to make a place where they could lead a life that was a sightless, soundless imitation of their unafflicted peers. She wanted a whole new start, a way of living that was by and for the blind-deaf, a way of living that accepted no convention just because that was the way it had always been done. She examined every human cultural institution from marriage to indecent exposure to see how it related to her needs and the needs of her friends. She was aware of the peril of this approach, but was undeterred. Her Social Task Force read about every variant group that had ever tried to make it on its own anywhere, and brought her reports about how and why they had failed or succeeded. She filtered this information through her own experiences to see how it would work for her unusual group with its own set of needs and goals.

The details were endless. They hired an architect to put their ideas into Braille blueprints. Gradually the plans evolved. They spent more money. The construction began, supervised on the site by their architect, who by now was so fascinated by the scheme that she donated her services. It was an important break, for they needed someone there whom they could trust. There is only so much that can be accomplished at such a distance.

When things were ready for them to move, they ran into bureaucratic trouble. They had anticipated it, but it was a setback. Social agencies charged with overseeing their welfare doubted the wisdom of the project. When it became apparent that no amount of reasoning was going to stop it, wheels were set in motion that resulted in a restraining order, issued for their own protection, preventing them from leaving the school. They were twenty-one years old by then, all of them, but were judged mentally incompetent to manage their own affairs. A hearing was scheduled.

Luckily, they still had access to their lawyer. He also had become infected with the crazy vision, and put on a great battle for them. He succeeded in getting a ruling concerning the rights of institutionalized persons, later upheld by the Supreme Court, which eventually had severe repercussions in state and county hospitals. Realizing the trouble they were already in regarding the thousands of patients in inadequate facilities across the country, the agencies gave in.

By then, it was the spring of 1986, one year after their target date. Some of their fertilizer had washed away already for lack of erosion-preventing clover. It was getting late to start crops, and they were running short of money. Nevertheless, they moved to New Mexico and began the back-breaking job of getting everything started. There were fifty-five of them, with nine children aged three months to six years.

I don't know what I expected. I remember that everything was a surprise, either because it was so normal or because it was so different. None of my idiot surmises about what such a place might be like proved to be true. And of course I didn't know the history of the place; I learned that later, picked up in bits and pieces.

I was surprised to see lights in some of the buildings. The first thing I had assumed was that they would have no need of them. That's an example of something so normal that it surprised me.

As to the differences, the first thing that caught my attention was the fence around the rail line. I had a personal interest in it, having almost been injured by it. I struggled to understand, as I must if I was to stay even for a night.

The wood fences that enclosed the rails on their way to the gate continued up to a barn, where the rails looped back on themselves in the same way they did outside the wall. The entire line was enclosed by the fence. The only access was a loading platform by the barn, and the gate to the outside. It made sense. The only way a deaf-blind person could operate a conveyance like that would be with assurances that there was no one on the track. These people would *never* go on the tracks; there was no way they could be warned of an approaching train.

There were people moving around me in the twilight as I made my way into the group of buildings. They took no notice of me, as I had expected. They moved fast; some of them were actually running. I stood still, eyes searching all around me so no one would come crashing into me. I had to figure out how they kept from crashing into each other before I got bolder.

I bent to the ground and examined it. The light was getting bad, but I saw immediately that there were concrete sidewalks crisscrossing the area. Each of the walks was etched with a different sort of pattern in grooves that had been made before the stuff set—lines, waves, depressions, patches of rough and smooth. I quickly saw that the people who were in a hurry moved only on those walkways, and they were all barefoot. It was no trick to see that it was some sort of traffic pattern read with the feet. I stood up.

I didn't need to know how it worked. It was sufficient to know what it was and stay off the paths.

The people were unremarkable. Some of them were not dressed, but I was used to that by now. They came in all shapes and sizes, but all seemed to be about the same age except for the children. Except for the fact that they did not stop and talk or even wave as they approached one another, I would never have guessed they were blind. I watched them come to intersections in the pathways—I didn't know how they knew they were there, but could think of several ways—and slow down as they crossed. It was a marvelous system.

I began to think of approaching someone. I had been there for almost half an hour, an intruder. I guess I had a false sense of these people's vulnerability; I felt like a burglar.

I walked along beside a woman for a minute. She was very purposeful in her eyes-ahead stride, or seemed to be. She sensed something, maybe my footsteps. She slowed a little, and I touched her on the shoulder, not knowing what else to do. She stopped instantly and turned toward me. Her eyes were open but vacant. Her hands were all over me, lightly touching my face, my chest, my hands, fingering my clothing. There was no doubt in my mind that she knew me for a stranger, probably from the first tap on the shoulder. But she smiled warmly at me, and hugged me. Her hands were very delicate and warm. That's funny, because they were calloused from hard work. But they felt sensitive.

She made me to understand—by pointing to the building, making eating motions with an imaginary spoon, and touching a number on her watch—that supper was served in an hour, and that I was invited. I nodded and smiled beneath her hands; she kissed me on the cheek and hurried off.

Well. It hadn't been so bad. I had worried about my ability to communicate. Later I found out she learned a great deal more about me than I had told.

I put off going into the mess hall or whatever it was. I strolled around in the gathering darkness looking at their layout. I saw the little Sheltie bringing the sheep back to the fold for the night. She herded them expertly through the open gate without any instructions, and one of the residents closed it and locked them in. The man bent and scratched the dog on the head and got his hand licked. Her chores done for the night, the dog hurried over to me and sniffed my pant leg. She followed me around the rest of the evening.

Everyone seemed so busy that I was surprised to see one woman sitting on a rail fence, doing nothing. I went over to her.

Closer, I saw that she was younger than I had thought. She was thirteen, I learned later. She wasn't wearing any clothes. I touched her on the shoulder, and she jumped down from the fence and went through the same routine as the other woman had, touching me all over with no reserve. She took my hand and I felt her fingers moving rapidly in my palm. I couldn't understand it, but knew what it was. I shrugged, and tried out other gestures to indicate that I didn't speak hand talk. She nodded, still feeling my face with her hands.

She asked me if I was staying to dinner. I assured her that I was. She asked me if I was from a university. And if you think that's easy to ask with only body movements, try it. But she was so graceful and supple in her movements, so deft at getting her meaning across. It was beautiful to watch her. It was speech and ballet at the same time.

I told her I wasn't from a university, and launched into an attempt to tell her a little about what I was doing and how I got there. She listened to me with her hands, scratching her head graphically when I failed to make my meanings clear. All the time the smile on her face got broader and broader, and she would laugh silently at my antics. All this while standing very close to me, touching me. At last she put her hands on her hips.

"I guess you need the practice," she said, "but if it's all the same to you, could we talk mouthtalk for now? You're cracking me up."

I jumped as if stung by a bee. The touching, while something I could ignore for a deaf-blind girl, suddenly seemed out of place. I stepped back a little, but her hands returned to me. She looked puzzled, then read the problem with her hands.

"I'm sorry," she said. "You thought I was deaf and blind. If I'd known I would have told you right off."

"I thought everyone here was."

"Just the parents. I'm one of the children. We all hear and see quite well. Don't be so nervous. If you can't stand touching, you're not going to like it here. Relax, I won't hurt you." And she kept her hands moving over me, mostly my face. I didn't understand it at the time, but it didn't seem sexual. Turned out I was wrong, but it wasn't blatant.

"You'll need me to show you the ropes," she said, and started for the domes. She held my hand and walked close to me. Her other hand kept moving to my face every time I talked.

"Number one, stay off the concrete paths. That's where—"

"I already figured that out."

"You did? How long have you been here?" Her hands searched my face with renewed interest. It was quite dark.

"Less than an hour. I was almost run over by your train."

She laughed, then apologized and said she knew it wasn't funny to me. I told her it *was* funny to me now, though it hadn't been at the time. She said there was a warning sign on the gate, but I had been unlucky enough to come when the gate was open—they opened it by remote control before a train started up—and I hadn't seen it.

"What's your name?" I asked her, as we neared the soft yellow lights coming from the dining room.

Her hand worked reflexively in mine, then stopped. "Oh, I don't know. I *have* one; several, in fact. But they're in bodytalk. I'm . . . Pink. It translates as Pink, I guess."

There was a story behind it. She had been the first child born to the school students. They knew that babies were described as being pink, so they called her that. She felt pink to them. As we entered the hall, I could see that her name was visually inaccurate. One of her parents had been black. She was dark, with blue eyes and curly hair lighter than her skin. She had a broad nose, but small lips.

She didn't ask my name, so I didn't offer it. No one asked my name, in speech, the entire time I was there. They called me many things in bodytalk, and when the children called me it was "Hey, you!" They weren't big on spoken words.

The dining hall was in a rectangular building made of brick. It connected to one of the large domes. It was dimly lighted. I later learned that the lights were for me alone. The children didn't need them for anything but reading. I held Pink's hand, glad to have a guide. I kept my eyes and ears open.

"We're informal," Pink said. Her voice was embarrassingly loud in the large room. No one else was talking at all; there were just the sounds of movement and breathing. Several of the children looked up. "I won't introduce you around now. Just feel like part of the family. People will feel you later, and you can talk to them. You can take your clothes off here at the door."

I had no trouble with that. Everyone else was nude, and I could easily adjust to household customs by that time. You take your shoes off in Japan, you take your clothes off in Taos. What's the difference?

Well, quite a bit, actually. There was all the touching that went on. Everybody touched everybody else, as routinely as glancing. Everyone touched my face first, then went on with what seemed like total innocence to touch me everywhere else. As usual, it was not quite what it seemed. It was *not* innocent, and it was not the usual treatment they gave others in their group. They touched each other's genitals a lot *more* than they touched mine. They were holding back with me so I wouldn't be frightened. They were very polite with strangers.

There was a long, low table, with everyone sitting on the floor around it. Pink led me to it.

"See the bare strips on the floor? Stay out of them. Don't leave anything in them. That's where people walk. Don't *ever* move anything. Furniture, I mean. That has to be decided at full meetings, so we'll all know where everything is. Small things, too. If you pick up something, put it back exactly where you found it."

"I understand."

People were bringing bowls and platters of food from the adjoining kitchen. They set them on the table, and the diners began feeling them. They ate with their fingers, without plates, and they did it slowly and lovingly. They smelled things for a long time before they took a bite. Eating was very sensual to these people.

They were *terrific* cooks. I have never, before or since, eaten as well as I did at Keller. (That's my name for it, in speech, though their bodytalk name was something very like that. When I called it Keller, everyone knew what

I was talking about.) They started off with good, fresh produce, something that's hard enough to find in the cities, and went at the cooking with artistry and imagination. It wasn't like any national style I've eaten. They improvised, and seldom cooked the same thing the same way twice.

I sat between Pink and the fellow who had almost run me down earlier. I stuffed myself disgracefully. It was far too removed from beef jerky and the organic dry cardboard I had been eating for me to be able to resist. I lingered over it, but still finished long before anyone else. I watched them as I sat back carefully and wondered if I'd be sick. (I wasn't, thank God.) They fed themselves and each other, sometimes getting up and going clear around the table to offer a choice morsel to a friend on the other side. I was fed in this way by all too many of them, and nearly popped until I learned a pidgin pharse in handtalk, saying I was full to the brim. I learned from Pink that a friendlier way to refuse was to offer something myself.

Eventually I had nothing to do but feed Pink and look at the others. I began to be more observant. I had thought they were eating in solitude, but soon saw that lively conversation was flowing around the table. Hands were busy, moving almost too fast to see. They were spelling into each other's palms, shoulders, legs, arms, bellies; any part of the body. I watched in amazement as a ripple of laughter spread like falling dominoes from one end of the table to the other as some witticism was passed along the line. It was *fast.* Looking carefully, I could see the thoughts moving, reaching one person, passed on while a reply went in the other direction and was in turn passed on, other replies originating all along the line and bouncing back and forth. They were a wave form, like water.

It was messy. Let's face it; eating with your fingers and talking with your hands is going to get you smeared with food. But no one minded. *I* certainly didn't. I was too busy feeling left out. Pink talked to me, but I knew I was finding out what it's like to be deaf. These people were friendly and seemed to like me, but could do nothing about it. We couldn't communicate.

Afterwards, we all trooped outside, except the cleanup crew, and took a shower beneath a set of faucets that gave out very cold water. I told Pink I'd like to help with the dishes, but she said I'd just be in the way. I couldn't do anything around Keller until I learned their very specific ways of doing things. She seemed to be assuming already that I'd be around that long.

Back into the building to dry off, which they did with their usual puppy dog friendliness, making a game and a gift of toweling each other, and then we went into the dome.

It was warm inside, warm and dark. Light entered from the passage to the dining room, but it wasn't enough to blot out the stars through the lattice of triangular panes overhead. It was almost like being out in the open.

Pink quickly pointed out the positional etiquette within the dome. It wasn't hard to follow, but I still tended to keep my arms and legs pulled in close so I wouldn't trip someone by sprawling into a walk space.

My misconceptions got me again. There was no sound but the soft whisper of flesh against flesh, so I thought I was in the middle of an orgy. I had been at them before, in other communes, and they looked pretty much like this. I quickly saw that I was wrong, and only later found out I had been right. In a sense.

What threw my evaluations out of whack was the simple fact that group conversation among these people *had* to look like an orgy. The much subtler observation that I made later was that with a hundred naked bodies sliding, rubbing, kissing, caressing, all at the same time, what was the point in making a distinction? There was no distinction.

I have to say that I use the noun "orgy" only to get across a general idea of many people in close contact. I don't like the word, it is too ripe with connotations. But I had these connotations myself at the time, so I was relieved to see that it was not an orgy. The ones I had been to had been tedious and impersonal, and I had hoped for better from these people.

Many wormed their way through the crush to get to me and meet me. Never more than one at a time; they were constantly aware of what was going on and were waiting their turn to talk to me. Naturally, I didn't know it then. Pink sat with me to interpret the hard thoughts. I eventually used her words less and less, getting into the spirit of tactile seeing and understanding. No one felt they really knew me until they had touched every part of my body, so there were hands on me all the time. I timidly did the same.

What with all the touching, I quickly got an erection, which embarrassed me quite a bit. I was berating myself for being unable to keep sexual responses out of it, for not being able to operate on the same intellectual plane I thought they were on, when I realized with some shock that the couple next to me was making love. They had been doing it for the last ten minutes, actually, and it had seemed such a natural part of what was happening that I had known it and not known it at the same time.

No sooner had I realized it than I suddenly wondered if I was right. *Were they?* It was very slow and the light was bad. But her legs were up, and he was on top of her, that much I was sure of. It was foolish of me, but I really had to know. I had to find out *what the hell I was in.* How could I give the proper social responses if I didn't know the situation?

I was very sensitive to polite behavior after my months at the various communes. I had become adept at saying prayers before supper in one place, chanting Hare Krishna at another, and going happily nudist at still another. It's called "when in Rome," and if you can't adapt to it you shouldn't go visiting. I would kneel to Mecca, burp after my meals, toast anything that was proposed, eat organic rice and compliment the cook; but to do it right, you have to know the customs. I had thought I knew them, but had changed my mind three times in as many minutes.

They *were* making love, in the sense that he was penetrating her. They were also deeply involved with each other. Their hands fluttered like butterflies all over each other, filled with meanings I couldn't see or feel. But they were being touched by and were touching many other people around them. They were talking to all these people, even if the message was as simple as a pat on the forehead or arm.

Pink noticed where my attention was. She was sort of wound around me, without really doing anything I would have thought of as provocative. I just couldn't *decide.* It seemed so innocent, and yet it wasn't.

"That's (—) and (—)," she said, the parentheses indicating a series of hand motions against my palm. I never learned a sound word as a name for any of them but Pink, and I can't reproduce the bodytalk names they had. Pink reached over, touched the woman with her foot, and did some complicated business with her toes. The woman smiled and grabbed Pink's foot, her fingers moving.

"(—) would like to talk with you later," Pink told me. "Right after she's through talking to (—). You met her earlier, remember? She says she likes your hands."

Now this is going to sound crazy, I know. It sounded pretty crazy to me when I thought of it. It dawned on me with a sort of revelation that her word for talk and mine were miles apart. Talk, to her, meant a complex interchange involving all parts of the body. She could read words or emotions in every twitch of my muscles, like a lie detector. Sound, to her, was only a minor part of communication. It was something she used to speak to outsiders. Pink talked with her whole being.

I didn't have the half of it, even then, but it was enough to turn my head entirely around in relation to these people. They talked with their bodies. It wasn't all hands, as I'd thought. Any part of the body in contact with any other was communication, sometimes a very simple and basic sort—think of McLuhan's light bulb as the basic medium of information—perhaps saying no more than "I am here." But talk was talk, and if conversation evolved to the point where you needed to talk to another with your genitals, it was still a part of the conversation. What I wanted to know was *what were they saying?* I knew, even at that dim moment of realization, that it was much more than I could grasp. Sure, you're saying. You know about talking to your lover with your body as you make love. That's not such a new idea. Of course it isn't, but think how wonderful that talk is even when you're not primarily tactile-oriented. Can you carry the thought from there, or are you doomed to be an earthworm thinking about sunsets?

While this was happening to me, there was a woman getting acquainted with my body. Her hands were on me, in my lap, when I felt myself ejaculating. It was a big surprise to me, but to no one else. I had been telling everyone around me for many minutes, through signs they could feel with their hands, that it was going to happen. Instantly, hands were all over my body. I could almost understand them as they spelled tender thoughts to me. I got the gist, anyway, if not the words. I was terribly embarrassed for only a moment, then it passed away in the face of the easy acceptance. It was very intense. For a long time I couldn't get my breath.

The woman who had been the cause of it touched my lips with her fingers. She moved them slowly, but meaningfully I was sure. Then she melted back into the group.

"What did she say?" I asked Pink.

She smiled at me. "You know, of course. If you'd only cut loose from your verbalizing. But, generally, she meant 'How nice for you.' It also translates as 'How nice for me.' and 'me,' in this sense, means all of us. The orgasm."

I knew I had to stay and learn to speak.

The commune had its ups and downs. They had expected them, in general, but had not known what shape they might take.

Winter killed many of their fruit trees. They replaced them with hybrid strains. They lost more fertilizer and soil in windstorms because the clover had not had time to anchor it down. Their schedule had been thrown off by the court actions, and they didn't really get things settled in a groove for more than a year.

Their fish all died. They used the bodies for fertilizer and looked into what might have gone wrong. They were using a three-stage ecology of the type pioneered by the New Alchemists in the '70's. It consisted of three domed ponds: one containing fish, another with crushed shells and bacteria in one section and algae in another, and a third full of daphnids. The water containing fish waste from the first pond was pumped through the shells and bacteria, which detoxified it and converted the ammonia it contained into fertilizer for the algae. The algae water was pumped into the second pond to feed the daphnids. Then daphnids and algae were pumped to the fish pond as food and the enriched water was used to fertilize greenhouse plants in all of the domes.

They tested the water and the soil and found that chemicals were being leached from impurities in the shells and concentrated down the food chain. After a thorough cleanup, they restarted and all went well. But they had lost their first cash crop.

They never went hungry. Nor were they cold; there was plenty of sunlight year-round to power the pumps and the food cycle and to heat their living quarters. They had built their buildings half-buried with an eye to the heating and cooling powers of convective currents. But they had to spend some of their capital. The first year they showed a loss.

One of their buildings caught fire during the first winter. Two men and a small girl were killed when a sprinkler system malfunctioned. This was a shock to them. They had thought things would operate as advertised. None of them knew much about the building trades, about estimates as opposed to realities. They found that several of their installations were not up to specifications, and instituted a program of periodic checks on everything. They learned to strip down and repair anything on the farm. If something contained electronics too complex for them to cope with, they tore it out and installed something simpler.

Socially, their progress had been much more encouraging. Janet had wisely decided that there would be only two hard and fast objectives in the realm of their relationships. The first was that she refused to be their president, chairwoman, chief, or supreme commander. She had seen from the start that a driving personality was needed to get the planning done and the land bought and a sense of purpose fostered from their formless desire for an alternative. But once at the promised land, she abdicated. From that point they would operate as a democratic communism. If that failed, they would adopt a new approach. Anything but a dictatorship with her at the head. She wanted no part of that.

The second principle was to accept nothing. There had never been a blind-deaf community operating on its own. They had no expectations to satisfy, they did not need to live as the sighted did. They were alone. There was no one to tell them not to do something simply because it was not done.

They had no clearer idea of what their society would be than anyone else. They had been forced into a mold that was not relevant to their needs, but beyond that they didn't know. They would search out the behavior that made sense, the moral things for blind-deaf people to do. They understood the basic principles of morals: that nothing is moral always, and anything is moral under the right circumstances. It all had to do with social context. They were starting from a blank slate, with no models to follow.

By the end of the second year they had their context. They continually modified it, but the basic pattern was set. They knew themselves and what they were as they had never been able to do at the school. They defined themselves in their own terms.

I spent my first day at Keller in school. It was the obvious and necessary step. I had to learn handtalk.

Pink was kind and very patient. I learned the basic alphabet and practiced hard at it. By the afternoon she was refusing to talk to me, forcing me to speak with my hands. She would speak only when pressed hard, and eventually not at all. I scarcely spoke a single word after the third day.

This is not to say that I was suddenly fluent. Not at all. At the end of the first day I knew the alphabet and could laboriously make myself understood. I was not so good at reading words spelled into my own palm. For a long time I had to look at the hand to see what was spelled. But like any language, eventually you think in it. I speak fluent French, and I can recall my amazement when I finally reached the point where I wasn't translating my thoughts before I spoke. I reached it at Keller in about two weeks.

I remember one of the last things I asked Pink in speech. It was something that was worrying me.

"Pink, am I welcome here?"

"You've been here three days. Do you feel rejected?"

"No, it's not that. I guess I just need to hear your policy about outsiders. How *long* am I welcome?"

She wrinkled her brow. It was evidently a new question.

"Well, practically speaking, until a majority of us decide we want you to go. But that's never happened. No one's stayed here much longer than a few days. We've never had to evolve a policy about what to do, for instance, if someone who sees and hears wants to join us. No one has, so far, but I guess it could happen. My guess is that they wouldn't accept it. They're very independent and jealous of their freedom, though you might not have noticed it. I don't think you could ever be one of them. But as long as you're willing to think of yourself as a guest, you could probably stay for twenty years."

"You said 'they.' Don't you include yourself in the group?"

For the first time she looked a little uneasy. I wish I had been better at reading body language at the time. I think my hands could have told me volumes about what she was thinking.

"Sure," she said. "The children are part of the group. We like it. I sure wouldn't want to be anywhere else, from what I know of the outside."

"I don't blame you." There were things left unsaid here, but I didn't know enough to ask the right questions. "But it's never a problem being able to see when none of your parents can? They don't . . . resent you in any way?"

This time she laughed. "Oh, no. Never that. They're much too independent for that. You've seen it. They don't *need* us for anything they can't do themselves. We're part of the family. We do exactly the same things they do. And it really doesn't matter. Sight, I mean. Hearing, either. Just look around you. Do I have any special advantages because I can see where I'm going?"

I had to admit that she didn't. But there was still the hint of something she wasn't saying to me.

"I know what's bothering you. About staying here." She had to draw me back to my original question; I had been wandering.

"What's that?"

"You don't feel a part of the daily life. You're not doing your share of the chores. You're very conscientious and you want to do your part. I can tell."

She read me right, as usual, and I admitted it.

"And you won't be able to until you can talk to everybody. So let's get back to your lessons. Your fingers are still very sloppy."

There was a lot of work to be done. The first thing I had to learn was to slow down. They were slow and methodical workers, made few mistakes, and didn't care if a job took all day so long as it was done well. When I was working by myself I didn't have to worry about it: sweeping, picking apples, weeding in the gardens. But when I was on a job that required teamwork I had to learn a whole new pace. Eyesight enables a person to do many aspects of a job at once with a few quick glances. A blind person will take each aspect of the job in turn if the job is spread out. Everything has to be verified by touch. At a bench job, they could be much faster than I.

They could make me feel as though I was working with my toes instead of fingers.

I never suggested that I could make anything quicker by virtue of my sight or hearing. They quite rightly would have told me to mind my own business. Accepting sighted help was the first step to dependence, and after all, they would still be here with the same jobs to do after I was gone.

And that got me to thinking about the children again. I began to be positive that there was an undercurrent of resentment, maybe unconscious, between the parents and children. It was obvious that there was a great deal of love between them, but how could the children fail to resent the rejection of their talent? So my reasoning went, anyway.

I quickly fit myself into the routine. I was treated no better or worse than anyone else, which gratified me. Though I would never become part of the group, even if I should desire it, there was absolutely no indication that I was anything but a full member. That's just how they treated guests: as they would one of their own number.

Life was fulfilling out there in a way it has never been in the cities. It wasn't unique to Keller, this pastoral peace, but the people there had it in generous helpings. The earth beneath your bare feet is something you can never feel in a city park.

Daily life was busy and satisfying. There were chickens and hogs to feed, bees and sheep to care for, fish to harvest, and cows to milk. Everybody worked: men, women, and children. It all seemed to fit together without any apparent effort. Everybody seemed to know what to do when it needed doing. You could think of it as a well-oiled machine, but I never liked that metaphor, especially for people. I thought of it as an organism. Any social group is, but this one *worked.* Most of the other communes I'd visited had glaring flaws. Things would not get done because everyone was too stoned or couldn't be bothered or didn't see the necessity of doing it in the first place. That sort of ignorance leads to typhus and soil erosion and people freezing to death and invasions of social workers who take your children away. I'd seen it happen.

Not here. They had a good picture of the world as it is, not the rosy misconceptions so many other utopians labor under. They did the jobs that needed doing.

I could never detail all the nuts and bolts (there's that machine metaphor again) of how the place worked. The fish-cycle ponds alone were complicated enough to overawe me. I killed a spider in one of the greenhouses, then found out it had been put there to eat a specific set of plant predators. Same for the frogs. There were insects in the water to kill other insects; it got to a point where I was afraid to swat a mayfly without prior okay.

As the days went by I was told some of the history of the place. Mistakes had been made, though surprisingly few. One had been in the area of defense. They had made no provision for it at first, not knowing much about the brutality and random violence that reaches even to the out-of-the-way corners. Guns were the logical and preferred choice out here, but were beyond their capabilities.

One night a carload of men who had had too much to drink showed up. They had heard of the place in town. They stayed for two days, cutting the phone lines and raping many of the women.

The people discussed all the options after the invasion was over, and settled on the organic one. They bought five German shepherds. Not the psychotic wretches that are marketed under the description of "attack dogs," but specially trained ones from a firm recommended by the Albuquerque police. They were trained as both Seeing-Eye and police dogs. They were perfectly harmless until an outsider showed overt aggression, then they were trained, not to disarm, but to go for the throat.

It worked, like most of their solutions. The second invasion resulted in two dead and three badly injured, all on the other side. As a backup in case of a concerted attack, they hired an ex-marine to teach them the fundamentals of close-in dirty fighting. These were not dewy-eyed flower children.

There were three superb meals a day. And there was leisure time, too. It was not all work. There was time to take a friend out and sit in the grass under a tree, usually around sunset, just before the big dinner. There was time for someone to stop working for a few minutes, to share some special treasure. I remember being taken by the hand by one woman—whom I must called Tall-one-with-the-green-eyes—to a spot where mushrooms were growing in the cool crawl space beneath the barn. We wriggled under until our faces were buried in the patch, picked a few, and smelled them. She showed me how to smell. I would have thought a few weeks before that we had ruined their beauty, but after all it was only visual. I was already beginning to discount that sense, which is so removed from the essence of an object. She showed me that they were still beautiful to touch and smell after we had apparently destroyed them. Then she was off to the kitchen with the pick of the bunch in her apron. They tasted all the better that night.

And a man—I will call him Baldy—who brought me a plank he and one of the women had been planing in the woodshop. I touched its smoothness and smelled it and agreed with him how good it was.

And after the evening meal, the Together.

During my third week there I had an indication of my status with the group. It was the first real test of whether I meant anything to them. Anything special, I mean. I wanted to see them as my friends, and I suppose I was a little upset to think that just anyone who wandered in here would be treated the way I was. It was childish and unfair to them, and I wasn't even aware of the discontent until later.

I had been hauling water in a bucket into the field where a seedling tree was being planted. There was a hose for that purpose, but it was in use on the other side of the village. This tree was not in reach of the automatic sprinklers and it was drying out. I had been carrying water to it until another solution was found.

It was hot, around noon. I got the water from a standing spigot near the forge. I set the bucket down on the ground behind me and leaned my head into the flow of water. I was wearing a shirt made of cotton, unbuttoned in the front. The water felt good running through my hair and soaking into the shirt. I let it go on for almost a minute.

There was a crash behind me and I bumped my head when I raised it up too quickly under the faucet. I turned and saw a woman sprawled on her face in the dust. She was turning over slowly, holding her knee. I realized with a sinking feeling that she had tripped over the bucket I had carelessly left on the concrete express lane. Think of it: ambling along on ground that you trust to be free of all obstruction, suddenly you're sitting on the ground. Their system would only work with trust, and it had to be total;

everybody had to be responsible all the time. I had been accepted into that trust and I had blown it. I felt sick.

She had a nasty scrape on her left knee that was oozing blood. She felt it with her hands, sitting there on the ground, and she began to howl. It was weird, painful. Tears came from her eyes, then she pounded her fists on the ground, going "Hunnnh, hunnnh, *hunnnh!*" with each blow. She was angry, and she had every right to be.

She found the pail as I hesitantly reached out for her. She grabbed my hand and followed it up to my face. She felt my face, crying all the time, then wiped her nose and got up. She started off for one of the buildings. She limped slightly.

I sat down and felt miserable. I didn't know what to do.

One of the men came out to get me. It was Big Man. I called him that because he was the tallest person at Keller. He wasn't any sort of policeman, I found out later; he was just the first one the injured woman had met. He took my hand and felt my face. I saw tears start when he felt the emotions there. He asked me to come inside with him.

An impromptu panel had been convened. Call it a jury. It was made up of anyone who was handy, including a few children. There were ten or twelve of them. Everyone looked very sad. The woman I had hurt was there, being consoled by three or four people. I'll call her Scar, for the prominent mark on her upper arm.

Everybody kept telling me—in handtalk, you understand—how sorry they were for me. They petted and stroked me, trying to draw some of the misery away.

Pink came racing in. She had been sent for to act as a translater if needed. Since this was a formal proceeding it was necessary that they be sure I understood everything that happened. She went to Scar and cried with her for a bit, then came to me and embraced me fiercely, telling me with her hands how sorry she was that this had happened. I was already figuratively packing my bags. Nothing seemed to be left but the formality of expelling me.

Then we all sat together on the floor. We were close, touching on all sides. The hearing began.

Most of it was in handtalk, with Pink throwing in a few words here and there. I seldom knew who said what, but that was appropriate. It was the group speaking as one. No statement reached me without already having become a consensus.

"You are accused of having violated the rules," said the group, "and of having been the cause of an injury to (the one I called Scar). Do you dispute this? Is there any fact that we should know?"

"No," I told them. "I was responsible. It was my carelessness."

"We understand. We sympathize with you in your remorse, which is evident to all of us. But carelessness is a violation. Do you understand this? This is the offense for which you are (———)." It was a set of signals in shorthand.

"What was that?" I asked Pink.

"Uh . . . 'brought before us'? 'Standing trial'?" She shrugged, not happy with either interpretation.

"Yes. I understand."

"The facts not being in question, it is agreed that you are guilty." (" 'Responsible,' " Pink whispered in my ear.) "Withdraw from us a moment while we come to a decision."

I got up and stood by the wall, not wanting to look at them as the debate went back and forth through the joined hands. There was a burning lump in my throat that I could not swallow. Then I was asked to rejoin the circle.

"The penalty for your offense is set by custom. If it were not so, we would wish we could rule otherwise. You now have the choice of accepting the punishment designated and having the offense wiped away, or of refusing our jurisdiction and withdrawing your body from our land. What is your choice?"

I had Pink repeat this to me, because it was so important that I know what was being offered. When I was sure I had read it right, I accepted their punishment without hesitation. I was very grateful to have been given an alternative.

"Very well. You have elected to be treated as we would treat one of our own who had done the same act. Come to us."

Everyone drew in closer. I was not told what was going to happen. I was drawn in and nudged gently from all directions.

Scar was sitting with her legs crossed more or less in the center of the group. She was crying again, and so was I, I think. It's hard to remember. I ended up face down across her lap. She spanked me.

I never once thought of it as improbable or strange. It flowed naturally out of the situation. Everyone was holding on to me and caressing me, spelling assurances into my palms and legs and neck and cheeks. We were all crying. It was a difficult thing that had to be faced by the whole group. Others drifted in and joined us. I understood that this punishment came from everyone there, but only the offended person, Scar, did the actual spanking. That was one of the ways I had wronged her, beyond the fact of giving her a scraped knee. I had laid on her the obligation of disciplining me and that was why she had sobbed so loudly, not from the pain of her injury, but from the pain of knowing she would have to hurt me.

Pink later told me that Scar had been the staunchest advocate of giving me the option to stay. Some had wanted to expel me outright, but she paid me the compliment of thinking I was a good enough person to be worth putting herself and me through the ordeal. If you can't understand that, you haven't grasped the feeling of community I felt among these people.

It went on for a long time. It was very painful, but not cruel. Nor was it primarily humiliating. There was some of that, of course. But it was essentially a practical lesson taught in the most direct terms. Each of them had undergone it during the first months, but none recently. You *learned* from it, believe me.

I did a lot of thinking about it afterward. I tried to think of what else they might have done. Spanking grown people is really unheard of, you know, though that didn't occur to me until long after it had happened. It seemed so natural when it was going on that the thought couldn't even enter my mind that this was a weird situation to be in.

They did something like this with the children, but not as long or as hard. Responsibility was lighter for the younger ones. The adults were willing to put up with an occasional bruise or scraped knee while the children learned.

But when you reached what they thought of as adulthood—which was whenever a majority of the adults thought you had or when you assumed the privilege yourself—that's when the spanking really got serious.

They had a harsher punishment, reserved for repeated or malicious offenses. They had not had to invoke it often. It consisted of being sent to Coventry. No one would touch you for a specified period of time. By the time I heard of it, it sounded like a very tough penalty. I didn't need it explained to me.

I don't know how to explain it, but the spanking was administered in such a loving way that I didn't feel violated. *This hurts me as much as it hurts you. I'm doing this for your own good. I love you, that's why I'm spanking you.* They made me understand those old clichés by their actions.

When it was over, we all cried together. But it soon turned to happiness. I embraced Scar and we told each other how sorry we were that it had happened. We talked to each other—made love if you like—and I kissed her knee and helped her dress it.

We spent the rest of the day together, easing the pain.

As I became more fluent in handtalk, "the scales fell from my eyes." Daily, I would discover a new layer of meaning that had eluded me before; it was like peeling the skin of an onion to find a new skin beneath it. Each time I thought I was at the core, only to find that there was another layer I could not yet see.

I had thought that learning handtalk was the key to communication with them. Not so. Handtalk was baby talk. For a long time I was a baby who could not even say goo-goo clearly. Imagine my surprise when, having learned to say it, I found that there were syntax, conjunctions, parts of speech, nouns, verbs, tense, agreement, and the subjunctive mood. I was wading in a tide pool at the edge of the Pacific Ocean.

By handtalk I mean the International Manual Alphabet. Anyone can learn it in a few hours or days. But when you talk to someone in speech, do you spell each word? Do you read each letter as you read this? No, you grasp words as entities, hear groups of sounds and see groups of letters as a gestalt full of meaning.

Everyone at Keller had an absorbing interest in language. They each knew several languages—spoken languages—and could read and spell them fluently.

While still children they had understood the fact that handtalk was a way for blind-deaf people to talk to *outsiders*. Among themselves it was much too cumbersome. It was like Morse Code: useful when you're limited to on-off modes of information transmission, but not the preferred mode. Their ways of speaking to each other were much closer to our type of written or verbal communication, and—dare I say it?—better.

I discovered this slowly, first by seeing that though I could spell rapidly with my hands, it took *much* longer for me to say something than it took anyone else. It could not be explained by differences in dexterity. So I asked to be taught their shorthand speech. I plunged in, this time taught by everyone, not just Pink.

It was hard. They could say any word in any language with no more than two moving hand positions. I knew this was a project for years, not days. You learn the alphabet and you have all the tools you need to spell any word that exists. That's the great advantage in having your written and spoken speech based on the same set of symbols. Shorthand was not like that at all. It partook of none of the linearity or commonality of handtalk; it was not code for English or any other language; it did not share construction or vocabulary with any other language. It was wholly constructed by the Kellerites according to their needs. Each word was something I had to learn and memorize separately from the handtalk spelling.

For months I sat in the Togethers after dinner saying things like "Me love Scar much much well," while waves of conversation ebbed and flowed and circled around me, touching me only at the edges. But I kept at it, and the children were endlessly patient with me. I improved gradually. Understand that the rest of the conversations I will relate took place in either handtalk or shorthand, limited to various degrees by my fluency. I did not speak nor was I spoken to orally from the day of my punishment.

I was having a lesson in bodytalk from Pink. Yes, we were making love. It had taken me a few weeks to see that she was a sexual being, that her caresses, which I had persisted in seeing as innocent—as I had defined it at the time—both were and weren't innocent. She understood it as perfectly natural that the result of her talking to my penis with her hands might be another sort of conversation. Though still in the middle flush of puberty, she was regarded by all as an adult and I accepted her as such. It was cultural conditioning that had blinded me to what she was saying.

So we talked a lot. With her, I understood the words and music of the body better than with anyone else. She sang a very uninhibited song with her hips and hands, free of guilt, open and fresh with discovery in every note she touched.

"You haven't told me much about yourself," she said. "What did you do on the outside?" I don't want to give the impression that this speech was in sentences, as I have presented it. We were bodytalking, sweating and smelling each other. The message came through from hands, feet, mouth.

I got as far as the sign for pronoun, first person singular, and was stopped.

How could I tell her of my life in Chicago? Should I speak of my early ambition to be a writer, and how that didn't work out? And why hadn't it? Lack of talent, or lack of drive? I could tell her about my profession, which was meaningless shuffling of papers when you got down to it, useless to anything but the Gross National Product. I could talk of the economic ups and downs that had brought me to Keller when nothing else could dislodge me from my easy sliding through life. Or the loneliness of being forty-seven years old and never having found someone worth loving, never having been loved in return. Of being a permanently displaced person in a stainless-steel society. One-night stands, drinking binges, nine-to-five, Chicago Transit Authority, dark movie houses, football games on television, sleeping pills, the John Hancock Tower where the windows won't open so you can't breathe the smog or jump out. That was me, wasn't it?

"I see," she said.

"I travel around," I said, and suddenly realized that it was the truth.

"I see," she repeated. It was a different sign for the same thing. Context was everything. She had heard and understood both parts of me, knew one to be what I had been, the other to be what I hoped I was.

She lay on top of me, one hand lightly on my face to catch the quick interplay of emotions as I thought about my life for the first time in years. And she laughed and nipped my ear playfully when my face told her that for the first time I could remember, I was happy about it. Not just telling myself I was happy, but truly happy. You cannot lie in bodytalk any more than your sweat glands can lie to a polygraph.

I noticed that the room was unusually empty. Asking around in my fumbling way, I learned that only the children were there.

"Where is everybody?" I asked.

"They are all out ***," she said. It was like that: three sharp slaps on the chest with the fingers spread. Along with the finger configuration for "verb form, gerund," it meant that they were all out ***ing. Needless to say, it didn't tell me much.

What did tell me something was her bodytalk as she said it. I read her better than I ever had. She was upset and sad. Her body said something like "Why can't I join them? Why can't I (smell-taste-touch-hear-see) *sense* with them?" That is exactly what she said. Again, I didn't trust my understanding enough to accept that interpretation. I was still trying to force my conceptions on the things I experienced there. I was determined that she and the other children be resentful of their parents in some way, because I was sure they had to be. They *must* feel superior in some way, they *must* feel held back.

I found the adults, after a short search of the area, out in the north pasture. All the parents, none of the children. They were standing in a group with no apparent pattern. It wasn't a circle, but it was almost round. If there was any organization, it was in the fact that everybody was about the same distance from everybody else.

The German shepherds and the Sheltie were out there, sitting on the cool grass facing the group of people. Their ears were perked up, but they were not moving.

I started to go up to the people. I stopped when I became aware of the concentration. They were touching, but their hands were not moving. The silence of seeing all those permanently moving people standing that still was deafening to me.

I watched them for at least an hour. I sat with the dogs and scratched them behind the ears. They did that chop-licking thing that dogs do when they appreciate it, but their full attention was on the group.

It gradually dawned on me that the group was moving. It was very slow, just a step here and another there, over many minutes. It was expanding in such a way that the distance between any of the individuals was the same. Like the expanding universe, where all galaxies move away from all others. Their arms were extended now; they were touching only with fingertips, in a crystal lattice arrangement.

Finally they were not touching at all. I saw their fingers straining to cover distances that were too far to bridge. And still they expanded equilaterally. One of the shepherds began to whimper a little. I felt the hair on the back of my neck stand up. Chilly out here, I thought.

I closed my eyes, suddenly sleepy.

I opened them, shocked. Then I forced them shut. Crickets were chirping in the grass around me.

There was something in the darkness behind my eyeballs. I felt that if I could turn my eyes around I would see it easily, but it eluded me in a way that made peripheral vision seem like reading headlines. If there was ever anything impossible to pin down, much less describe, that was it. It tickled at me for a while as the dogs whimpered louder, but I could make nothing of it. The best analogy I could think of was the sensation a blind person might feel from the sun on a cloudy day.

I opened my eyes again.

Pink was standing there beside me. Her eyes were screwed shut, and she was covering her ears with her hands. Her mouth was open and working silently. Behind her were several of the older children. They were all doing the same thing.

Some quality of the night changed. The people in the group were about a foot away from each other now, and suddenly the pattern broke. They all swayed for a moment, then laughed in that eerie, unselfconscious noise deaf people use for laughter. They fell in the grass and held their bellies, rolled over and over and roared.

Pink was laughing, too. To my surprise, so was I. I laughed until my face and sides were hurting, like I remembered doing sometimes when I'd smoked grass.

And that was ***ing.

⋆ ⋆ ⋆

I can see that I've only given a surface view of Keller. And there are some things I should deal with, lest I foster an erroneous view.

Clothing, for instance. Most of them wore something most of the time. Pink was the only one who seemed temperamentally opposed to clothes. She never wore anything.

No one ever wore anything I'd call a pair of pants. Clothes were loose: robes, shirts, dresses, scarves and such. Lots of men wore things that would be called women's clothes. They were simply more comfortable.

Much of it was ragged. It tended to be made of silk or velvet or something else that felt good. The stereotyped Kellerite would be wearing a Japanese silk robe, hand-embroidered with dragons, with many gaping holes and loose threads and tea and tomato stains all over it while she sloshed through the pigpen with a bucket of slop. Wash it at the end of the day and don't worry about the colors running.

I also don't seem to have mentioned homosexuality. You can mark it down to my early conditioning that my two deepest relationships at Keller were with women: Pink and Scar. I haven't said anything about it simply because I don't know how to present it. I talked to men and women equally, on the same terms. I had surprisingly little trouble being affectionate with the men.

I could not think of the Kellerites as bisexual, though clinically they were. It was much deeper than that. They could not even recognize a concept as poisonous as a homosexuality taboo. It was one of the first things they learned. If you distinguish homosexuality from heterosexuality you are cutting yourself off from communication—*full* communication—with half the human race. They were pansexual; they could not separate sex from the rest of their lives. They didn't even have a word in shorthand that could translate directly into English as sex. They had words for male and female in infinite variation, and words for degrees and varieties of physical experience that would be impossible to express in English, but all those words included other parts of the world of experience also; none of them walled off what we call *sex* into its own discrete cubbyhole.

There's another question I haven't answered. It needs answering, because I wondered about it myself when I first arrived. It concerns the necessity for the commune in the first place. Did it really have to be like this? Would they have been better off adjusting themselves to our ways of living?

All was not a peaceful idyll. I've already spoken of the invasion and rape. It could happen again, especially if the roving gangs that operate around the cities start to really rove. A touring group of motorcyclists could wipe them out in a night.

There were also continuing legal hassles. About once a year the social workers descended on Keller and tried to take their children away. They had been accused of everything possible, from child abuse to contributing to delinquency. It hadn't worked so far, but it might someday.

And after all, there are sophisticated devices on the market that allow a blind and deaf person to see and hear a little. They might have been helped by some of those.

I met a blind-deaf woman living in Berkeley once. I'll vote for Keller.

As to those machines . . .

In the library at Keller there is a seeing machine. It uses a television camera and a computer to vibrate a closely set series of metal pins. Using it, you can feel a moving picture of whatever the camera is pointed at. It's small and light, made to be carried with the pin-pricker touching your back. It cost about thirty-five thousand dollars.

I found it in the corner of the library. I ran my finger over it and left a gleaming streak behind as the thick dust came away.

Other people came and went, and I stayed on.

Keller didn't get as many visitors as the other places I had been. It was out of the way.

One man showed up at noon, looked around, and left without a word.

Two girls, sixteen-year-old runaways from California, showed up one night. They undressed for dinner and were shocked when they found out I could see. Pink scared the hell out of them. Those poor kids had a lot of living to do before they approached Pink's level of sophistication. But then Pink might have been uneasy in California. They left the next day, unsure if they had been to an orgy or not. All that touching and no getting down to business, very strange.

There was a nice couple from Santa Fe who acted as a sort of liaison between Keller and their lawyer. They had a nine-year-old boy who chattered endlessly in handtalk to the other kids. They came up about every other week and stayed a few days, soaking up sunshine and participating in the Together every night. They spoke halting shorthand and did me the courtesy of not speaking to me in speech.

Some of the Indians came around at odd intervals. Their behavior was almost aggressively chauvinistic. They stayed dressed at all times in their Levis and boots. But it was evident that they had a respect for the people, though they thought them strange. They had business dealings with the commune. It was the Navahos who trucked away the produce that was taken to the gate every day, sold it, and took a percentage. They would sit and powwow in sign language spelled into hands. Pink said they were scrupulously honest in their dealings.

And about once a week all the parents went out in the field and ***ed.

I got better and better at shorthand and bodytalk. I had been breezing along for about five months and winter was in the offing. I had not examined my desires as yet, not really thought about what it was I wanted to do with the rest of my life. I guess the habit of letting myself drift was too ingrained. I was there, and constitutionally unable to decide whether to go or to face up to the problem if I wanted to stay for a long, long time.

Then I got a push.

For a long time I thought it had something to do with the economic situation outside. They were aware of the outside world at Keller. They knew that isolation and ignoring problems that could easily be dismissed as not relevant to them was a dangerous course, so they subscribed to the Braille *New York Times* and most of them read it. They had a television set that got plugged in about once a month. The kids would watch it and translate for their parents.

So I was aware that the non-depression was moving slowly into a more normal inflationary spiral. Jobs were opening up, money was flowing again. When I found myself on the outside again shortly afterward, I thought that was the reason.

The real reason was more complex. It had to do with peeling off the onion layer of shorthand and discovering another layer beneath it.

I had learned handtalk in a few easy lessons. Then I became aware of shorthand and bodytalk, and of how much harder they would be to learn. Through five months of constant immersion, which is the only way to learn a language, I had attained the equivalent level of a five- or six-year-old in shorthand. I knew I could master it, given time. Bodytalk was another matter. You couldn't measure progress as easily in bodytalk. It was a variable and highly interpersonal language that evolved according to the person, the time, the mood. But I was learning.

Then I became aware of Touch. That's the best I can describe it in a single, unforced English noun. What *they* called this fourth-stage language varied from day to day, as I will try to explain.

I first became aware of it when I tried to meet Janet Reilly. I now knew the history of Keller, and she figured very prominently in all the stories. I knew everyone at Keller, and I could find her nowhere. I knew everyone by names like Scar, and She-with-the-missing-front-tooth, and Man-with-wiry-hair. These were shorthand names that I had given them myself, and they all accepted them without question. They had abolished their outside names within the commune. They meant nothing to them; they told nothing and described nothing.

At first I assumed that it was my imperfect command of shorthand that made me unable to clearly ask the right question about Janet Reilly. Then I saw that they were not telling me on purpose. I saw why, and I approved, and thought no more about it. The name Janet Reilly described what she had been *on the outside,* and one of her conditions for pushing the whole thing through in the first place had been that she be no one special on the inside. She melted into the group and disappeared. She didn't want to be found. All right.

But in the course of pursuing the question I became aware that each of the members of the commune had no specific name at all. That is, Pink, for instance, had no less than one hundred and fifteen names, one from each of the commune members. Each was a contextual name that told the story of Pink's relationship to a particular person. My simple names, based on physical descriptions, were accepted as the names a child would apply to people. The children had not yet learned to go beneath the outer layers and use names that told of themselves, their lives, and their relationships to others.

What is even more confusing, the names evolved from day to day. It was my first glimpse of Touch, and it frightened me. It was a question of permutations. Just the first simple expansion of the problem meant there were no less than thirteen thousand names in use, and they wouldn't stay still so I could memorize them. If Pink spoke to me of Baldy, for instance, she would use her Touch name for him, modified by the fact that she was speaking to me and not Short-chubby-man.

Then the depths of what I had been missing opened beneath me and I was suddenly breathless with fear of heights.

Touch was what they spoke to each other. It was an incredible blend of all three other modes I had learned, and the essence of it was that it never stayed the same. I could listen to them speak to me in shorthand, which was the real basis for Touch, and be aware of the currents of Touch flowing just beneath the surface.

It was a language of inventing languages. Everyone spoke their own dialect because everyone spoke with a different instrument: a different body and set of life experiences. It was modified by everything. *It would not stand still.*

They would sit at the Together and invent an entire body of Touch responses in a night; idiomatic, personal, totally naked in its honesty. And they used it only as a building block for the next night's language.

I didn't know if I wanted to be that naked. I had looked into myself a little recently and had not been satisfied with what I found. The realization that every one of them knew more about it than I, because my honest body had told what my frightened mind had not wanted to reveal, was shattering. I was naked under a spotlight in Carnegie Hall, and all the no-pants nightmares I had ever had came out to haunt me. The fact that they all loved me with all my warts was suddenly not enough. I wanted to curl up in a dark closet with my ingrown ego and let it fester.

I might have come through this fear. Pink was certainly trying to help me. She told me that it would only hurt for a while, that I would quickly adjust to living my life with my darkest emotions written in fire across my forehead. She said Touch was not as hard as it looked at first, either. Once I learned shorthand and bodytalk, Touch would flow naturally from it like sap rising in a tree. It would be unavoidable, something that would happen to me without much effort at all.

I almost believed her. But she betrayed herself. No, no, no. Not that, but the things in her concerning ***ing convinced me that if I went through this I would only bang my head hard against the next step up the ladder. ***

I had a little better definition now. Not one that I can easily translate into English, and even that attempt will only convey my hazy concept of what it was.

"It is the mode of touching without touching," Pink said, her body going like crazy in an attempt to reach me with her own imperfect concept of what it was, handicapped by my illiteracy. Her body denied the truth of her shorthand definition, and at the same time admitted to me that she did not know what it was herself.

"It is the gift whereby one can expand oneself from the eternal quiet and dark into something else." And again her body denied it. She beat on the floor in exasperation.

"It is an attribute of being in the quiet and dark all the time, touching others. All I know for sure is that vision and hearing preclude it or obscure it. I can make it as quiet and dark as I possibly can and be aware of the edges of it, but the visual orientation of the mind persists. That door is closed to me, and to all the children."

Her verb "to touch" in the first part of that was a Touch amalgam, one that reached back into her memories of me and what I had told her of my experiences. It implied and called up the smell and feel of broken mushrooms in soft earth under the barn with Tall-one-with-green-eyes, she who taught me to feel the essence of an object. It also contained references to our bodytalking while I was penetrating into the dark and wet of her, and her running account to me of what it was like to receive me into herself. This was all one word.

I brooded on that for a long time. What was the point of suffering through the nakedness of Touch, only to reach the level of frustrated blindness enjoyed by Pink?

What was it that kept pushing me away from the one place in my life where I had been happiest?

One thing was the realization, quite late in coming, that can be summed up as "What the hell am I *doing* here?" The question that should have answered that question was "What the hell would I do if I *left?*"

I was the only visitor, the only one in *seven years* to stay at Keller for longer than a few days. I brooded on that. I was not strong enough or confident enough in my opinion of myself to see it as anything but a flaw in *me,* not in those others. I was obviously too easily satisfied, too complacent to see the flaws that those others had seen.

It didn't have to be flaws in the people of Keller, or in their system. No, I loved and respected them too much to think that. What they had going certainly came as near as anyone ever has in this imperfect world to a sane, rational way for people to exist without warfare and with a minimum of politics. In the end, those two old dinosaurs are the only ways humans have yet discovered to be social animals. Yes, I do see war as a way of living with another; by imposing your will on another in terms so unmistakable that the opponent has to either knuckle under to you, die, or beat your brains out. And if that's a solution to anything, I'd rather live without solutions. Politics is not much better. The only thing going for it is that it occasionally succeeds in substituting talk for fists.

Keller *was* an organism. It was a new way of relating, and it seemed to work. I'm not pushing it as a solution for the world's problems. It's possible that it could only work for a group with a common self-interest as binding and rare as deafness and blindness. I can't think of another group whose needs are so interdependent.

The cells of the organism cooperated beautifully. The organism was strong, flourishing, and possessed of all the attributes I've ever heard used in defining life except the ability to reproduce. That might have been its fatal flaw, if any. I certainly saw the seeds of something developing in the children.

The strength of the organism was communication. There's no way around it. Without the elaborate and impossible-to-falsify mechanisms for communication built into Keller, it would have eaten itself in pettiness, jealousy, possessiveness, and any dozen other "innate" human defects.

The nightly Together was the basis of the organism. Here, from after dinner till it was time to fall asleep, everyone talked in a language that was incapable of falsehood. If there was a problem brewing, it presented itself and was solved almost automatically. Jealousy? Resentment? Some little festering wrong that you're nursing? You couldn't conceal it at the Together, and soon everyone was clustered around you and loving the sickness away. It acted like white corpuscles, clustering around a sick cell, not to destroy it, but to heal it. There seemed to be no problem that couldn't be solved if it was attacked early enough, and with Touch, your neighbors knew about it before you did and were already laboring to correct the wrong, heal the wound, to make you feel better so you could laugh about it. There was a lot of laughter at the Togethers.

I thought for a while that I was feeling possessive about Pink. I know I had done so a little at first. Pink was my special friend, the one who had helped me out from the first, who for several days was the only one I could talk to. It was her hands that had taught me handtalk. I know I felt stirrings of territoriality the first time she lay in my lap while another man made love to her. But if there was any signal the Kellerites were adept at reading, it was that one. It went off like an alarm bell in Pink, the man, and the women and men around me. They soothed me, coddled me, told me in every language that it was all right, not to feel ashamed. Then the man in question began loving *me.* Not Pink, but the man. An observational anthropologist would have had subject matter for a whole thesis. Have you seen the films of baboons' social behavior? Dogs do it, too. Many male mammals do it. When males get into dominance battles, the weaker can defuse the aggression by submitting, by turning tail and surrendering. I have never felt so defused as when that man surrendered the object of our clash of wills—Pink—and turned his attention to me. What could I do? What I did was laugh, and he laughed, and soon we were all laughing, and that was the end of territoriality.

That's the essence of how they solved most "human nature" problems at Keller. Sort of like an oriental martial art; you yield, roll with the blow so that your attacker takes a pratfall with the force of the aggression. You do that until the attacker sees that the initial push wasn't worth the effort, that it was a pretty silly thing to do when no one was resisting you. Pretty soon he's not Tarzan of the Apes, but Charlie Chaplin. And he's laughing.

So it wasn't Pink and her lovely body and my realization that she could never be all mine to lock away in my cave and defend with a gnawed-off thighbone. If I'd persisted in that frame of mind she would have found me about as attractive as an Amazonian leech, and that was a great incentive to confound the behaviorists and overcome it.

So I was back to those people who had visited and left, and what did they see that I didn't see?

Well, there was something pretty glaring. I was not part of the organism, no matter how nice the organism was to me. I had no hopes of ever becoming a part, either. Pink had said it in the first week. She felt it herself, to a lesser degree. She could not ***, though that fact was not going to drive her away from Keller. She had told me that many times in shorthand and confirmed it in bodytalk. If I left, it would be without her.

Trying to stand outside and look at it, I felt pretty miserable. What was I trying to *do,* anyway? Was my goal in life *really* to become a part of a blind-deaf commune? I was feeling so low by that time that I actually thought of that as denigrating, in the face of all the evidence to the contrary. I should be out in the real world where the real people lived, not these freakish cripples.

I backed off from that thought very quickly. I was not totally out of my mind, just on the lunatic edges. These people were the best friends I'd ever had, maybe the only ones. That I was confused enough to think that of them even for a second worried me more than anything else. It's possible that it's what pushed me finally into a decision. I saw a future of growing disillusion and unfulfilled hopes. Unless I was willing to put out my eyes and ears, I would always be on the outside. *I* would be the blind and deaf one. I would be the freak. I didn't want to be a freak.

They knew I had decided to leave before I did. My last few days turned into a long goodbye, with a loving farewell implicit in every word touched to me. I was not really sad, and neither were they. It was nice, like everything they did. They said goodbye with just the right mix of wistfulness and life-must-go-on, and hope-to-touch-you-again.

Awareness of Touch scratched on the edges of my mind. It was not bad, just as Pink had said. In a year or two I could have mastered it.

But I was set now. I was back in the life groove that I had followed for so long. Why is it that once having decided what I must do, I'm afraid to reexamine my decision? Maybe because the original decision cost me so much that I didn't want to go through it again.

I left quietly in the night for the highway and California. They were out in the fields, standing in that circle again. Their fingertips were farther apart than ever before. The dogs and children hung around the edges like beggars at a banquet. It was hard to tell which looked more hungry and puzzled.

The experiences at Keller did not fail to leave their mark on me. I was unable to live as I had before. For a while I thought I could not live at all, but I did. I was too used to living to take the decisive step of ending my life. I would wait. Life had brought one pleasant thing to me; maybe it would bring another.

I became a writer. I found I now had a better gift for communicating than I had before. Or maybe I had it now for the first time. At any rate, my writing came together and I sold. I wrote what I wanted to write, and was not afraid of going hungry. I took things as they came.

I weathered the non-depression of '97, when unemployment reached twenty percent and the government once more ignored it as a temporary downturn. It eventually upturned, leaving the jobless rate slightly higher than it had been the time before, and the time before that. Another million useless persons had been created with nothing better to do than shamble through the streets looking for beatings in progress, car smashups, heart attacks, murders, shootings, arson, bombings, and riots: the endlessly inventive street theater. It never got dull.

I didn't become rich, but I was usually comfortable. That is a social disease, the symptoms of which are the ability to ignore the fact that your society is developing weeping pustules and having its brains eaten out by radioactive maggots. I had a nice apartment in Marin County, out of sight of the machine-gun turrets. I had a car, at a time when they were beginning to be luxuries.

I had concluded that my life was not destined to be all I would like it to be. We all make some sort of compromise, I reasoned, and if you set your expectations too high you are doomed to disappointment. It did occur to me that I was settling for something far from "high," but I didn't know what to do about it. I carried on with a mixture of cynicism and optimism that seemed about the right mix for me. It kept my motor running, anyway.

I even made it to Japan, as I had intended in the first place.

I didn't find someone to share my life. There was only Pink for that, Pink and all her family, and we were separated by a gulf I didn't dare cross. I didn't even dare think about her too much. It would have been very dangerous to my equilibrium. I lived with it, and told myself that it was the way I was. Lonely.

The years rolled on like a caterpillar tractor at Dachau, up to the penultimate day of the millennium.

San Francisco was having a big bash to celebrate the year 2000. Who gives a shit that the city is slowly falling apart, that civilization is disintegrating into hysteria? Let's have a party!

I stood on the Golden Gate Dam on the last day of 1999. The sun was setting in the Pacific, on Japan, which had turned out to be more of the same but squared and cubed with neo-samurai. Behind me the first bombshells of a firework celebration of holocaust tricked up to look like festivity competed with the flare of burning buildings as the social and economic basket cases celebrated the occasion in their own way. The city quivered under the weight of misery, anxious to slide off along the fracture lines of some subcortical San Andreas Fault. Orbiting atomic bombs twinkled in my mind, up there somewhere, ready to plant mushrooms when we'd exhausted all the other possibilities.

I thought of Pink.

I found myself speeding through the Nevada desert, sweating, gripping the steering wheel. I was crying aloud but without sound, as I had learned to do at Keller.

Can you go back?

I slammed the citicar over the potholes in the dirt road. The car was falling apart. It was not built for this kind of travel. The sky was getting light in the east. It was the dawn of a new millennium. I stepped harder on the gas pedal and the car bucked savagely. I didn't care. I was not driving back down that road, not ever. One way or another, I was here to stay.

I reached the wall and sobbed my relief. The last hundred miles had been a nightmare of wondering if it had been a dream. I touched the cold reality of the wall and it calmed me. Light snow had drifted over everything, gray in the early dawn.

I saw them in the distance. All of them, out in the field where I had left them. No, I was wrong. It was only the children. Why had it seemed like so many at first?

Pink was there. I knew her immediately, though I had never seen her in winter clothes. She was taller, filled out. She would be nineteen years old. There was a small child playing in the snow at her feet, and she cradled an infant in her arms. I went to her and talked to her hand.

She turned to me, her face radiant with welcome, her eyes staring in a way I had never seen. Her hands flitted over me and her eyes did not move.

"I touch you, I welcome you," her hands said. "I wish you could have been here just a few minutes ago. Why did you go away darling? Why did you stay away so long?" Her eyes were stones in her head. She was blind. She was deaf.

All the children were. No, Pink's child sitting at my feet looked up at me with a smile.

"Where is everybody?" I asked when I got my breath. "Scar? Baldy? Green-eyes? And what's happened? What's happened to you?" I was tottering on the edge of a heart attack or nervous collapse or something. My reality felt in danger of dissolving.

"They've gone," she said. The word eluded me, but the context put it with the *Mary Celeste* and Roanoke, Virginia. It was complex, the way she used the word *gone*. It was like something she had said before: unattainable, a source of frustration like the one that had sent me running from Keller. But now her word told of something that was not hers yet, but was within her grasp. There was no sadness in it.

"Gone?"

"Yes. I don't know where. They're happy. They ***ed. It was glorious. We could only touch a part of it."

I felt my heart hammering to the sound of the last train pulling away from the station. My feet were pounding along the ties as it faded into the fog. Where are the Brigadoons of yesterday? I've never yet heard of a fairy tale where you can go back to the land of enchantment. You wake up, you find that your chance is gone. You threw it away. *Fool!* You only get one chance; that's the moral, isn't it?

Pink's hands laughed along my face.

"Hold this part-of-me-who-speaks-mouth-to-nipple," she said, and handed me her infant daughter. "I will give you a gift."

She reached up and lightly touched my ears with her cold fingers. The sound of the wind was shut out, and when her hands came away it never came back. She touched my eyes, shut out all the light, and I saw no more.

We live in the lovely quiet and dark.

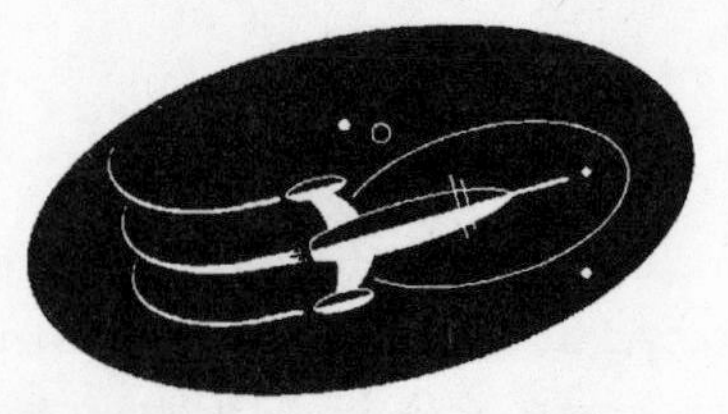

ENEMY MINE

Barry B. Longyear

EDITOR'S NOTE: This Nebula award-winning version of "Enemy Mine" originally appeared in the November/December 1979 issue of Isaac Asimov's Science-Fiction Magazine. *The author, Barry Longyear, subsequently expanded "Enemy Mine" for inclusion in a collection entitled* Manifest Destiny, *which was copyrighted © 1980 by Berkeley Books.*

he Dracon's three-fingered hands flexed. In the thing's yellow eyes I could read the desire to have those fingers around either a weapon or my throat. As I flexed my own fingers, I knew it read the same in my eyes.

"Irkmaan!" the thing spat.

"You piece of Drac slime." I brought my hands up in front of my chest and waved the thing on. "Come on, Drac; come and get it."

"Irkmaan vaa, koruum su!"

"Are you going to talk, or fight? Come on!" I could feel the spray from the sea behind me—a boiling madhouse of white-capped breakers that threatened to swallow me as it had my fighter. I had ridden my ship in. The Drac had ejected when its own fighter had caught one in the upper atmosphere, but not before crippling my power plant. I was exhausted from swimming to the grey, rocky beach and pulling myself to safety. Behind the Drac, among the rocks on the otherwise barren hill, I could see its ejection capsule. Far above us, its people and mine were still at it, slugging out the possession of an uninhabited corner of nowhere. The Drac just stood there and I went over the phrase taught us in training—a phrase calculated to drive any Drac into a frenzy. *"Kiz da yuomeen, Shizumaat!"* Meaning:

Shizumaat, the most revered Drac philosopher, eats kiz excrement. Something on the level of stuffing a Moslem full of pork.

The Drac opened its mouth in horror, then closed it as anger literally changed its color from yellow to reddish-brown. *"Irkmaan, yaa stupid Mickey Mouse is!"*

I had taken an oath to fight and die over many things, but that venerable rodent didn't happen to be one of them. I laughed, and continued laughing until the guffaws in combination with my exhaustion forced me to my knees. I forced open my eyes to keep track of my enemy. The Drac was running toward the high ground, away from me and the sea. I half-turned toward the sea and caught a glimpse of a million tons of water just before they fell on me, knocking me unconscious.

"Kiz da yuomeen, Irkmaan, ne?"

My eyes were gritty with sand and stung with salt, but some part of my awareness pointed out: "Hey, you're alive." I reached to wipe the sand from my eyes and found my hands bound. A straight metal rod had been run through my sleeves and my wrists tied to it. As my tears cleared the sand from my eyes, I could see the Drac sitting on a smooth black boulder looking at me. It must have pulled me out of the drink. "Thanks, toad face. What's with the bondage?"

"Ess?"

I tried waving my arms and wound up giving an impression of an atmospheric fighter dipping its wings. "Untie me, you Drac slime!" I was seated on the sand, my back against a rock.

The Drac smiled, exposing the upper and lower mandibles that looked human—except that instead of separate teeth, they were solid. *"Eh, ne, Irkmaan."* It stood, walked over to me and checked my bonds.

"Untie me!"

The smile disappeared. *"Ne!"* It pointed at me with a yellow finger. *"Kos son va?"*

"I don't speak Drac, toad face. You speak Esper or English?"

The Drac delivered a very human-looking shrug, then pointed at its own chest. *"Kos va son Jeriba Shigan."* It pointed again at me. *"Kos son va?"*

"Davidge. My name is Willis E. Davidge."

"Ess?"

I tried my tongue on the unfamiliar syllables. *"Kos va son Willis Davidge."*

"Eh." Jeriba Shigan nodded, then motioned with its fingers. *"Dasu, Davidge."*

"Same to you, Jerry."

"Dasu, dasu!" Jeriba began sounding a little impatient. I shrugged as best I could. The Drac bent over and grabbed the front of my jump suit with both hands and pulled me to my feet. *"Dasu, dasu, kizlode!"*

"All right! So *dasu* is 'get up.' What's a *kizlode?*"

Jerry laughed. *"Gavey 'kiz'?"*

"Yeah, I *gavey.*"

Jerry pointed at its head. *"Lode."* It pointed at my head. *"Kizlode, gavey?"*

I got it, then swung my arms around, catching Jerry upside its head with the metal rod. The Drac stumbled back against a rock, looking surprised. It raised a hand to its head and withdrew it covered with that pale pus that Dracs think is blood. It looked at me with murder in its eyes. *"Gefh! Nu Gefh, Davidge!"*

"Come and get it, Jerry, you *kizlode* sonafabitch!"

Jerry dived at me and I tried to catch it again with the rod, but the Drac caught my right wrist in both hands and, using the momentum of my swing, whirled me around, slamming my back against another rock. Just as I was getting back my breath, Jerry picked up a small boulder and came at me with every intention of turning my melon into pulp. With my back against the rock, I lifted a foot and kicked the Drac in the midsection, knocking it to the sand. I ran up, ready to stomp Jerry's melon, but he pointed behind me. I turned and saw another tidal wave gathering steam, and heading our way. *"Kiz!"* Jerry got to its feet and scampered for the high ground with me following close behind.

With the roar of the wave at our backs, we weaved among the water- and sand-ground black boulders until we reached Jerry's ejection capsule. The Drac stopped, put its shoulder to the egg-shaped contraption, and began rolling it uphill. I could see Jerry's point. The capsule contained all of the survival equipment and food either of us knew about. "Jerry!" I shouted above the rumble of the fast-approaching wave. "Pull out this damn rod and I'll help!" The Drac frowned at me. "The rod, *kizlode,* pull it out!" I cocked my head toward my outstretched arm.

Jerry placed a rock beneath the capsule to keep it from rolling back, then quickly untied my wrists and pulled out the rod. Both of us put our shoulders to the capsule, and we quickly rolled it to higher ground. The wave hit and climbed rapidly up the slope until it came up to our chests. The capsule bobbed like a cork, and it was all we could do to keep control of the thing until the water receded, wedging the capsule between three big boulders. I stood there, puffing.

Jerry dropped to the sand, its back against one of the boulders, and watched the water rush back out to sea. *"Magasienna!"*

"You said it, brother." I sank down next to the Drac; we agreed by eye to a temporary truce, and promptly passed out.

My eyes opened on a sky boiling with blacks and greys. Letting my head loll over on my left shoulder, I checked out the Drac. It was still out. First, I thought that this would be the perfect time to get the drop on Jerry. Second, I thought about how silly our insignificant scrap seemed compared to the insanity of the sea that surrounded us. Why hadn't the rescue team come? Did the Dracon fleet wipe us out? Why hadn't the Dracs come to pick up Jerry? Did they wipe out each other? I didn't even know where I was. An island. I had seen that much coming in, but where and in relation to what? Fyrine IV: the planet didn't even rate a name, but was important enough to die over.

With an effort, I struggled to my feet. Jerry opened its eyes and quickly pushed itself to a defensive crouching position. I waved my hand and shook my head. "Ease off, Jerry. I'm just going to look around." I turned my back on it and trudged off between the boulders. I walked uphill for a few minutes until I reached level ground.

It was an island, all right, and not a very big one. By eyeball estimation, height from sea level was only eighty meters, while the island itself was about two kilometers long and less than half that wide. The wind whipping my jump suit against my body was at least drying it out, but as I looked around at the smooth-ground boulders on top of the rise, I realized that Jerry and I could expect bigger waves than the few puny ones we had seen.

A rock clattered behind me and I turned to see Jerry climbing up the slope. When it reached the top, the Drac looked around. I squatted next to one of the boulders and passed my hand over it to indicate the smoothness, then I pointed toward the sea. Jerry nodded. *"Ae, Gavey."* It pointed downhill toward the capsule, then to where we stood. *"Echey masu, nasesay."*

I frowned, then pointed at the capsule. *"Nasesay?* The capsule?"

"Ae capsule *nasesay. Echey masu."* Jerry pointed at its feet.

I shook my head. "Jerry, if you *gavey* how these rocks got smooth"—I pointed at one—"then you *gavey* that *masu*ing the *nasesay* up here isn't going to do a damned bit of good." I made a sweeping up and down movement with my hands. "Waves." I pointed at the sea below. "Waves, up here"; I pointed to where we stood. "Waves, *echey.*"

"Ae, gavey." Jerry looked around the top of the rise, then rubbed the side of its face. The Drac squatted next to some small rocks and began piling one on top of another. *"Viga, Davidge."*

I squatted next to it and watched while its nimble fingers constructed a circle of stones that quickly grew into a doll-house-sized arena. Jerry stuck one of its fingers in the center of the circle. *"Echey, nasesay."*

The days on Fyrine IV seemed to be three times longer than any I had seen on any other habitable planet. I use the designation "habitable" with reservations. It took us most of the first day to painfully roll Jerry's *nasesay* up to the top of the rise. The night was too black to work and was bone-cracking cold. We removed the couch from the capsule, which made just enough room for both of us to fit inside. The body heat warmed things up a bit; and we killed time between sleeping, nibbling on Jerry's supply of ration bars (they taste a bit like fish mixed with cheddar cheese), and trying to come to some agreement about language.

"Eye."

"Thuyo."

"Finger."

"Zurath."

"Head."

The Drac laughed. *"Lode."*

"Ho, ho, very funny."

"Ho, ho."

* * *

At dawn on the second day, we rolled and pushed the capsule into the center of the rise and wedged it between two large rocks, one of which had an overhang that we hoped would hold down the capsule when one of those big soakers hit. Around the rocks and capsule, we laid a foundation of large stones and filled in the cracks with smaller stones. By the time the wall was knee high, we discovered that building with those smooth, round stones and no mortar wasn't going to work. After some experimentation, we figured out how to break the stones to give us flat sides with which to work. It's done by picking up one stone and slamming it down on top of another. We took turns, one slamming and one building. The stone was almost a volcanic glass, and we also took turns extracting rock splinters from each other. It took nine of those endless days and nights to complete the walls, during which waves came close many times and once washed us ankle deep. For six of those nine days, it rained. The capsule's survival equipment included a plastic blanket, and that became our roof. It sagged in at the center, and the hole we put in it there allowed the water to run out, keeping us almost dry and giving us a supply of fresh water. If a wave of any determination came along, we could kiss the roof goodbye; but we both had confidence in the walls, which were almost two meters thick at the bottom and at least a meter thick at the top.

After we finished, we sat inside and admired our work for about an hour, until it dawned on us that we had just worked ourselves out of jobs. "What now, Jerry?"

"Ess?"

"What do we do now?"

"Now wait, we." The Drac shrugged. "Else what, *ne*?"

I nodded. *"Gavey."* I got to my feet and walked to the passageway we had built. With no wood for a door, where the walls would have met, we bent one out and extended it about three meters around the other wall with the opening away from the prevailing winds. The never-ending winds were still at it, but the rain had stopped. The shack wasn't much to look at, but looking at it stuck there in the center of that deserted island made me feel good. As Shizumaat observed, "Intelligent life making its stand against the universe." Or, at least, that's the sense I could make out of Jerry's hamburger of English. I shrugged and picked up a sharp splinter of stone and made another mark in the large standing rock that served as my log. Ten scratches in all, and under the seventh, a small "x" to indicate the big wave that just covered the top of the island.

I threw down the splinter. "Damn, I hate this place!"

"Ess?" Jerry's head poked around the edge of the opening. "Who talking at, Davidge?"

I glared at the Drac, then waved my hand at it. "Nobody."

"Ess va, 'nobody'?"

"Nobody. Nothing."

"Ne gavey, Davidge."

I poked at my chest with my finger. "Me! I'm talking to myself! You *gavey* that stuff, toad face!"

Jerry shook its head. "Davidge, now I sleep. Talk not so much nobody, *ne?*" It disappeared back into the opening.

"And so's your mother!" I turned and walked down the slope. *Except, strictly speaking, toad face, you don't have a mother—or father. "If you had your choice, who would you like to be trapped on a desert island with?"* I wondered if anyone ever picked a wet freezing corner of Hell shacked up with a hermaphrodite.

Half of the way down the slope, I followed the path I had marked with rocks until I came to my tidal pool that I had named "Rancho Sluggo." Around the pool were many of the water-worn rocks, and underneath those rocks, below the pool's waterline, lived the fattest orange slugs either of us had ever seen. I made the discovery during a break from house building and showed them to Jerry.

Jerry shrugged. "And so?"

"And so what? Look, Jerry, those ration bars aren't going to last forever. What are we going to eat when they're all gone?"

"Eat?" Jerry looked at the wriggling pocket of insect life and grimaced. *"Ne,* Davidge. Before then pickup. Search us find, then pickup."

"What if they don't find us? What then?"

Jerry grimaced again and turned back to the half-completed house. "Water we drink, then until pickup." He had muttered something about kiz excrement and my tastebuds, then walked out of sight.

Since then I had built up the pool's walls, hoping the increased protection from the harsh environment would increase the herd. I looked under several rocks, but no increase was apparent. And, again, I couldn't bring myself to swallow one of the things. I replaced the rock I was looking under, stood and looked out to the sea. Although the eternal cloud cover still denied the surface the drying rays of Fyrine, there was no rain and the usual haze had lifted.

In the direction past where I had pulled myself up on the beach, the sea continued to the horizon. In the spaces between the whitecaps, the water was as grey as a loan officer's heart. Parallel lines of rollers formed approximately five kilometers from the island. The center, from where I was standing, would smash on the island, while the remainder steamed on. To my right, in line with the breakers, I could just make out another small island perhaps ten kilometers away. Following the path of the rollers, I looked far to my right, and where the grey-white of the sea should have met the lighter grey of the sky, there was a black line on the horizon.

The harder I tried to remember the briefing charts on Fyrine IV's land masses, the less clear it became. Jerry couldn't remember anything either—at least nothing it would tell me. Why should we remember? The battle was supposed to be in space, each one trying to deny the other an orbital staging area in the Fyrine system. Neither side wanted to set foot on Fyrine, much less fight a battle there. Still, whatever it was called, it was land and considerably larger than the sand and rock bar we were occupying.

How to get there was the problem. Without wood, fire, leaves, or animal skins, Jerry and I were destitute compared to the average poverty-stricken caveman. The only thing we had that would float was the *nasesay*. The capsule. Why not? The only real problem to overcome was getting Jerry to go along with it.

That evening, while the greyness made its slow transition to black, Jerry and I sat outside the shack nibbling our quarter portions of ration bars. The Drac's yellow eyes studied the dark line on the horizon, then it shook its head. "*Ne,* Davidge. Dangerous is."

I popped the rest of my ration bar into my mouth and talked around it. "Any more dangerous than staying here?"

"Soon pickup, *ne?*"

I studied those yellow eyes. "Jerry, you don't believe that any more than I do." I leaned forward on the rock and held out my hands. "Look, our chances will be a lot better on a larger land mass. Protection from the big waves, maybe food. . . ."

"Not maybe, *ne?*" Jerry pointed at the water. "How *nasesay* steer, Davidge? In that, how steer? *Ess eh* soakers, waves, beyond land take, *gavey? Bresha,*" Jerry's hands slapped together. "*Ess eh bresha* rocks on, *ne?* Then we death."

I scratched my head. "The waves are going in that direction from here, and so is the wind. If the land mass is large enough, we don't have to steer, *gavey?*"

Jerry snorted. "*Ne* large enough, then?"

"I didn't say it was a sure thing."

"*Ess?*"

"A sure thing; certain, *gavey?*" Jerry nodded. "And for smashing up on the rocks, it probably has a beach like this one."

"Sure thing, *ne?*"

I shrugged. "No, it's not a sure thing, but, what about staying here? We don't know how big those waves can get. What if one just comes along and washes us off the island? What then?"

Jerry looked at me, its eyes narrowed. "What there, Davidge? *Irkmaan* base, *ne?*"

I laughed. "I told you, we don't have any bases on Fyrine IV."

"Why want go, then?"

"Just what I said, Jerry. I think our chances would be better."

"Ummm." The Drac folded its arms. "*Viga,* Davidge, *nasesay* stay. I know."

"Know what?"

Jerry smirked, then stood and went into the shack. After a moment it returned and threw a two-meter long metal rod at my feet. It was the one the Drac had used to bind my arms. "Davidge, I know."

I raised my eyebrows and shrugged. "What are you talking about? Didn't that come from your capsule?"

"Ne, Irkmaan."

I bent down and picked up the rod. Its surface was uncorroded and at one end were arabic numerals—a part number. For a moment a flood of hope washed over me, but it drained away when I realized it was a civilian part number. I threw the rod on the sand. "There's no telling how long that's been here, Jerry. It's a civilian part number and no civilian missions have been in this part of the galaxy since the war. Might be left over from an old seeding operation or exploratory mission. . . ."

The Drac nudged it with the toe of his boot. "New, *gavey?*"

I looked up at it. "You *gavey* stainless steel?"

Jerry snorted and turned back toward the shack. "I stay, *nasesay* stay; where you want, you go, Davidge!"

With the black of the long night firmly bolted down on us, the wind picked up, shrieking and whistling in and through the holes in the walls. The plastic roof flapped, pushed in and sucked out with such violence it threatened to either tear or sail off into the night. Jerry sat on the sand floor, its back leaning against the *nasesay* as if to make clear that both Drac and capsule were staying put, although the way the sea was picking up seemed to weaken Jerry's argument.

"Sea rough now is, Davidge, *ne?*"

"It's too dark to see, but with this wind. . . ." I shrugged more for my own benefit than the Drac's, since the only thing visible inside the shack was the pale light coming through the roof. Any minute we could be washed off that sandbar. "Jerry, you're being silly about that rod. You know that."

"Surda." The Drac sounded contrite if not altogether miserable.

"Ess?"

"Ess eh 'Surda'?"

"Ae."

Jerry remained silent for a moment. "Davidge, *gavey* 'not certain not is'?"

I sorted out the negatives. "You mean 'possible,' 'maybe,' 'perhaps'?"

"*Ae* possiblemaybeperhaps. Dracon fleet Irkmaan ships have. Before war buy; after war capture. Rod possiblemaybeperhaps Dracon is."

"So, if there's a secret base on the big island, *surda* it's a Dracon base?"

"Possiblemaybeperhaps, Davidge."

"Jerry, does that mean you want to try it? The *nasesay?*"

"Ne."

"*Ne*? Why, Jerry? If it might be a Drac base—"

"*Ne! Ne* talk!" The Drac seemed to choke on the words.

"Jerry, we talk, and you better *believe* we talk! If I'm going to death it on this island, I have a right to know why."

The Drac was quiet for a long time. "Davidge."

"Ess?"

"*Nasesay,* you take. Half ration bars you leave. I stay."

I shook my head to clear it. "You want me to take the capsule alone?"

"What you want is, *ne?*"

"*Ae,* but why? You must realize there won't be any pickup."

"Possiblemaybeperhaps."

"*Surda,* nothing. You know there isn't going to be a pickup. What is it? You afraid of the water? If that's it, we have a better chance—"

"Davidge, up your mouth shut. *Nasesay* you have. Me *ne* you need, *gavey?*"

I nodded in the dark. The capsule was mine for the taking; what did I need a grumpy Drac along for—especially since our truce could expire at any moment? The answer made me feel a little silly—human. Perhaps it's the same thing. The Drac was all that stood between me and utter aloneness. Still, there was the small matter of staying alive. "We should go together, Jerry."

"Why?"

I felt myself blush. If humans have this need for companionship, why are they also ashamed to admit it? "We just should. Our chances would be better."

"Alone your chances better are, Davidge. Your enemy I am."

I nodded again and grimaced in the dark. "Jerry, you *gavey* 'loneliness'?"

"Ne gavey."

"Lonely. Being alone, by myself."

"Gavey you alone. Take *nasesay;* I stay."

"That's it . . . see, *viga,* I don't want to."

"You want together go?" A low, dirty chuckle came from the other side of the shack. "You Dracon like? You me death, *Irkmaan."* Jerry chuckled some more. *"Irkmaan poorzhab* in head, *poorzhab."*

"Forget it!" I slid down from the wall, smoothed out the sand and curled up with my back toward the Drac. The wind seemed to die down a bit and I closed my eyes to try and sleep. In a bit, the snap, crack of the plastic roof blended in with the background of shrieks and whistles and I felt myself drifting off, when my eyes opened wide at the sound of footsteps in the sand. I tensed, ready to spring.

"Davidge?" Jerry's voice was very quiet.

"What?"

I heard the Drac sit on the sand next to me. "You loneliness, Davidge. About it hard you talk, *ne?"*

"So what?" The Drac mumbled something that was lost in the wind. "What?" I turned over and saw Jerry looking through a hole in the wall.

"Why I stay. Now, you I tell, *ne?"*

I shrugged. "Okay; why not?"

Jerry seemed to struggle with the words, then opened its mouth to speak. Its eyes opened wide. *"Magasienna!"*

I sat up. *"Ess?"*

Jerry pointed at the hole. "Soaker!"

I pushed it out of the way and looked through the hole. Steaming toward our island was an insane mountainous fury of whitecapped rollers. It was hard to tell in the dark, but the one in front looked taller than the one that had wet our feet a few days before. The ones following it were bigger. Jerry put a hand on my shoulder and I looked into the Drac's eyes. We broke and ran for the capsule. We heard the first wave rumbling up the slope as we felt around in the dark for the recessed doorlatch. I just got my finger on it when the wave smashed against the shack, collapsing the roof. In half a second we were under water, the currents inside the shack agitating us like socks in a washing machine.

The water receded, and as I cleared my eyes, I saw that the windward wall of the shack had caved in. "Jerry!"

Through the collapsed wall, I saw the Drac staggering around outside. "*Irkmaan?*" Behind him I could see the second roller gathering speed.

"*Kizlode,* what'n the Hell you doing out there? Get in here!"

I turned to the capsule, still lodged firmly between the two rocks, and found the handle. As I opened the door, Jerry stumbled through the missing wall and fell against me. "Davidge . . . forever soakers go on! Forever!"

"Get in!" I helped the Drac through the door and didn't wait for it to get out of the way. I piled in on top of Jerry and latched the door just as the second wave hit. I could feel the capsule lift a bit and rattle against the overhang of the one rock.

"Davidge, we float?"

"No. The rocks are holding us. We'll be all right once the breakers stop."

"Over you move."

"Oh." I got off Jerry's chest and braced myself against one end of the capsule. After a bit, the capsule came to rest and we waited for the next one. "Jerry?"

"*Ess?*"

"What was it that you were about to say?"

"Why I stay?"

"Yeah."

"About it hard me talk, *gavey?*"

"I know, I know."

The next breaker hit and I could feel the capsule rise and rattle against the rock. "Davidge, *gavey 'vi nessa'?*"

"*Ne gavey.*"

"*Vi nessa* . . . little me, *gavey?*"

The capsule bumped down the rock and came to rest. "What about little you?"

"Little me . . . little Drac. From me, *gavey?*"

"Are you telling me you're *pregnant?*"

"Possiblemaybeperhaps."

I shook my head. "Hold on, Jerry. I don't want any misunderstandings. Pregnant . . . are you going to be a parent?"

"Ae, parent, two-zero-zero in line, very important is, *ne?"*

"Terrific. What's this got to do with you not wanting to go to the other island?"

"Before, me *vi nessa, gavey? Tean* death."

"Your child, it died?"

"Ae!" The Drac's sob was torn from the lips of the universal mother. "I in fall hurt. *Tean* death. *Nasesay* in sea us bang. *Tean* hurt, *gavey?"*

"Ae, I *gavey."* So, Jerry was afraid of losing another child. It was almost certain that the capsule trip would bang us around a lot, but staying on the sandbar didn't appear to be improving our chances. The capsule had been at rest for quite a while, and I decided to risk a peek outside. The small canopy windows seemed to be covered with sand, and I opened the door. I looked around, and all of the walls had been smashed flat. I looked toward the sea, but could see nothing. "It looks safe, Jerry . . ." I looked up, toward the blackish sky, and above me towered the white plume of a descending breaker. *"Maga* damn *sienna!"* I slammed the hatch door.

"Ess, Davidge?"

"Hang on, Jerry!"

The sound of the water hitting the capsule was beyond hearing. We banged once, twice against the rock, then we could feel ourselves twisting, shooting upward. I made a grab to hang on, but missed as the capsule took a sickening lurch downward. I fell into Jerry, then was flung to the opposite wall, where I struck my head. Before I went blank, I heard Jerry cry *"Tean! Vi tean!"*

. . . the lieutenant pressed his hand control and a figure—tall, humanoid, yellow—appeared on the screen.

"Dracslime!" shouted the auditorium of seated recruits.

The lieutenant faced the recruits. "Correct. This is a Drac. Note that the Drac race is uniform as to color; they are all yellow." The recruits chuckled politely. The officer preened a bit, then with a light wand began pointing out various features. "The three-fingered hands are distinctive, of course, as is the almost noseless face, which gives the Drac a toad-like appearance. On average, eyesight is slightly better than human, hearing about the same, and smell . . ." The lieutenant paused. "The smell is terrible!" The officer beamed at the uproar from the recruits. When the auditorium quieted down, he pointed his light wand at a fold in the figure's belly. "This is where the Drac keeps its family jewels—all of them." Another chuckle. "That's right, Dracs are hermaphrodites, with both male and female reproductive organs contained in the same individual." The lieutenant faced the recruits. "You go tell a Drac to go boff himself, then watch out, because he can!" The laughter died down, and the lieutenant held out a hand toward the screen. "You see one of these things, what do you do?"

"KILL IT. . . ."

. . . I cleared the screen and computer sighted on the next Drac fighter, looking like a double x in the screen's display. The Drac shifted hard to the left, then right again. I felt the autopilot pull my ship after the fighter, sorting out and ignoring the false images, trying to lock its electronic crosshairs on the Drac. "Come on, toad face . . . a little bit to the left. . . ." The double cross image moved into the ranging rings on the display and I felt the missile attached to the belly of my fighter take off. "Gotcha!" Through my canopy I saw the flash as the missile detonated. My screen showed the Drac fighter out of control, spinning toward Fyrine IV's cloud-shrouded surface. I dived after it to confirm the kill . . . skin temperature increasing as my ship brushed the upper atmosphere. "Come on, dammit, blow!" I shifted the ship's systems over for atmospheric flight when it became obvious that I'd have to follow the Drac right to the ground. Still above the clouds, the Drac stopped spinning and turned. I hit the auto override and pulled the stick into my lap. The fighter wallowed as it tried to pull up. Everyone knows the Drac ships work better in atmosphere . . . heading toward me: on an interception course . . . why doesn't the slime fire . . . just before the collision, the Drac ejects . . . power gone; have to deadstick it in. I track the capsule as it falls through the muck, intending to find that Dracslime and finish the job. . . .

It could have been for seconds or years that I groped into the darkness around me. I felt touching, but the parts of me being touched seemed far, far away. First chills, then fever, then chills again, my head being cooled by a gentle hand. I opened my eyes to narrow slits and saw Jerry hovering over me, blotting my forehead with something cool. I managed a whisper. "Jerry."

The Drac looked into my eyes and smiled. "Good is, Davidge. Good is."

The light on Jerry's face flickered and I smelled smoke. "Fire."

Jerry got out of the way and pointed toward the center of the room's sandy floor. I let my head roll over and realized that I was lying on a bed of soft, springy branches. Opposite my bed was another bed, and between them crackled a cheery campfire. "Fire now we have, Davidge. And wood." Jerry pointed toward the roof made of wooden poles thatched with broad leaves.

I turned and looked around, then let my throbbing head sink down and closed my eyes. "Where are we?"

"Big island, Davidge. Soaker off sandbar us washed. Wind and waves us here took. Right you were."

"I . . . I don't understand; *ne gavey*. It'd take days to get to the big island from the sandbar."

Jerry nodded and dropped what looked like a sponge into a shell of some sort filled with water. "Nine days. You I strap to *nasesay*, then here on beach we land."

"Nine days? I've been out for nine days?"

Jerry shook his head. "Seventeen. Here we land eight days . . ." The Drac waved its hand behind itself.

"Ago . . . eight days ago."

"Ae."

Seventeen days on Fyrine IV was better than a month on Earth. I opened my eyes again and looked at Jerry. The Drac was almost bubbling with excitement. "What about *tean*, your child?"

Jerry patted its swollen middle. "Good is, Davidge. You more *nasesay* hurt."

I overcame an urge to nod. "I'm happy for you." I closed my eyes and turned my face toward the wall, a combination of wood poles and leaves. "Jerry?"

"Ess?"

"You saved my life."

"Ae."

"Why?"

Jerry sat quietly for a long time. "Davidge. On sandbar you talk. Loneliness now *gavey*." The Drac shook my arm. "Here, now you eat."

I turned and looked into a shell filled with a steaming liquid. "What is it, chicken soup?"

Ess?"

"Ess va?" I pointed at the bowl, realizing for the first time how weak I was.

Jerry frowned. "Like slug, but long."

"An eel?"

"Ae, but eel on land, *gavey?"*

"You mean 'snake'?"

"Possiblemaybeperhaps."

I nodded and put my lips to the edge of the shell. I sipped some of the broth, swallowed and let the broth's healing warmth seep through my body. "Good."

"You *custa* want?"

"Ess?"

"Custa." Jerry reached next to the fire and picked up a squareish chunk of clear rock. I looked at it, scratched it with my thumbnail, then touched it with my tongue.

"Halite! Salt!"

Jerry smiled. *"Custa* you want?"

I laughed. "All the comforts. By all means, let's have *custa."*

Jerry took the halite, knocked off a corner with a small stone, then used the stone to grind the pieces against another stone. He held out the palm of his hand with a tiny mountain of white granules in the center. I took two pinches, dropped them into my snake soup and stirred it with my finger. Then I took a long swallow of the delicious broth. I smacked my lips. "Fantastic."

"Good, *ne?"*

"Better than good; fantastic." I took another swallow, making a big show of smacking my lips and rolling my eyes.

"Fantastic, Davidge, *ne?"*

"Ae." I nodded at the Drac. "I think that's enough. I want to sleep."

"Ae, Davidge, *gavey."* Jerry took the bowl and put it beside the fire. The Drac stood, walked to the door and turned back. Its yellow eyes studied me

for an instant, then it nodded, turned and went outside. I closed my eyes and let the heat from the campfire coax the sleep over me.

In two days I was up in the shack trying my legs, and in two more days, Jerry helped me outside. The shack was located at the top of a long, gentle rise in a scrub forest; none of the trees was any taller than five or six meters. At the bottom of the slope, better than eight kilometers from the shack, was the still rolling sea. The Drac had carried me. Our trusty *nasesay* had filled with water and had been dragged back into the sea soon after Jerry pulled me to dry land. With it went the remainder of the ration bars. Dracs are very fussy about what they eat, but hunger finally drove Jerry to sample some of the local flora and fauna—hunger and the human lump that was rapidly drifting away from lack of nourishment. The Drac had settled on a bland, starchy type of root, a green bushberry that when dried made an acceptable tea, and snakemeat. Exploring, Jerry had found a partly eroded salt dome. In the days that followed, I grew stronger and added to our diet with several types of sea mollusk and a fruit resembling a cross between a pear and a plum.

As the days grew colder, the Drac and I were forced to realize that Fyrine IV had a winter. Given that, we had to face the possibility that the winter would be severe enough to prevent the gathering of food—and wood. When dried next to the fire, the berrybush and roots kept well, and we tried both salting and smoking snakemeat. With strips of fiber from the berrybush for thread, Jerry and I pieced together the snake skins for winter clothing. The design we settled on involved two layers of skins with the down from berrybush seed pods stuffed between and then held in place by quilting the layers.

We agreed that the house would never do. It took three days of searching to find our first cave, and another three days before we found one that suited us. The mouth opened onto a view of the eternally tormented sea, but was set in the face of a low cliff well above sea level. Around the cave's entrance we found great quantities of dead wood and loose stone. The wood we gathered for heat; and the stone we used to wall up the entrance, leaving only space enough for a hinged door. The hinges were made of snake leather and the door of wooden poles tied together with berrybush fiber. The first night after completing the door, the sea winds blew it to pieces; and we decided to go back to the original door design we had used on the sandbar.

Deep inside the cave, we made our living quarters in a chamber with a wide, sandy floor. Still deeper, the cave had natural pools of water, which were fine for drinking but too cold for bathing. We used the pool chamber for our supply room. We lined the walls of our living quarters with piles of wood and made new beds out of snakeskins and seed pod down. In the center of the chamber we built a respectable fireplace with a large, flat stone over the coals for a griddle. The first night we spent in our new home, I discovered that, for the first time since ditching on that damned planet, I couldn't hear the wind.

During the long nights, we would sit at the fireplace making things—gloves, hats, packbags—out of snake leather, and we would talk. To break the monotony, we alternated days between speaking Drac and English, and by the time the winter hit with its first ice storm, each of us was comfortable in the other's language.

We talked of Jerry's coming child.

"What are you going to name it, Jerry?"

"It already has a name. See, the Jeriba line has five names. My name is Shigan; before me came my parent, Gothig; before Gothig was Haesni; before Haesni was Ty, and before Ty was Zammis. The child is named Jeriba Zammis."

"Why only the five names? A human child can have just about any name its parents pick for it. In fact, once a human becomes an adult, he or she can pick any name he or she wants."

The Drac looked at me, its eyes filled with pity. "Davidge, how lost you must feel. You humans—how lost you must feel."

"Lost?"

Jerry nodded. "Where do you come from, Davidge?"

"You mean my parents?"

"Yes."

I shrugged. "I remember my parents."

"And their parents?"

"I remember my mother's father. When I was young we used to visit him."

"Davidge, what do you know about this grandparent?"

I rubbed my chin. "It's kind of vague . . . I think he was in some kind of agriculture—I don't know."

"And his parents?"

I shook my head. "The only thing I remember is that somewhere along the line, English and Germans figured. *Gavey* Germans and English?"

Jerry nodded. "Davidge, I can recite the history of my line back to the founding of my planet by Jeriba Ty, one of the original settlers, one hundred and ninety-nine generations ago. At our line's archives on Draco, there are the records that trace the line across space to the racehome planet, Sindie, and there back seventy generations to Jeriba Ty, the founder of the Jeriba line."

"How does one become a founder?"

"Only the firstborn carries the line. Products of second, third, or fourth births must found their own lines."

I nodded, impressed. "Why only the five names? Just to make it easier to remember them?"

Jerry shook its head. "No. The names are things to which we add distinction; they are the same, common-place five so that they do not overshadow the events that distinguish their bearers. The name I carry, Shigan, has been served by great soldiers, scholars, students of philosophy, and several priests. The name my child will carry has been served by scientists, teachers, and explorers."

"You remember all of your ancestors' occupations?"

Jerry nodded. "Yes, and what they each did and where they did it. You must recite your line before the line's archives to be admitted into adulthood as I was twenty-two of my years ago. Zammis will do the same, except the child must begin its recitation . . ."—Jerry smiled—"with my name, Jeriba Shigan."

"You can recite almost two hundred biographies from memory?"

"Yes."

I went over to my bed and stretched out. As I stared up at the smoke being sucked through the crack in the chamber's ceiling, I began to understand what Jerry meant by feeling lost. A Drac with several dozens of generations under its belt knew who it was and what it had to live up to. "Jerry?"

"Yes, Davidge?"

"Will you recite them for me?" I turned my head and looked at the Drac in time to see an expression of utter surprise melt into joy. It was only after many years had passed that I learned I had done Jerry a great honor in requesting his line. Among the Dracs, it is a rare expression of respect, not only of the individual, but of the line.

Jerry placed the hat he was sewing on the sand, stood and began.

"Before you here I stand, Shigan of the line of Jeriba, born of Gothig, the teacher of music. A musician of high merit, the students of Gothig included Datzizh of the Nem line, Perravane of the Tuscor line, and many lesser musicians. Trained in music at the Shimuram, Gothig stood before the archives in the year 11,051 and spoke of its parent Haesni, the manufacturer of ships. . . ."

As I listened to Jerry's singsong of formal Dracon, the backward biographies—beginning with death and ending with adulthood—I experienced a sense of time-binding, of being able to know and touch the past. Battles, empires built and destroyed, discoveries made, great things done—a tour through twelve thousand years of history, but perceived as a well-defined, living continuum.

Against this: I Willis of the Davidge line stand before you, born of Sybil the housewife and Nathan the second-rate civil engineer, one of them born of Grandpop, who probably had something to do with agriculture, born of nobody in particular. . . . Hell, I wasn't even that! My older brother carried the line; not me. I listened and made up my mind to memorize the line of Jeriba.

We talked of war:

"That was a pretty neat trick, suckering me into the atmosphere, then ramming me."

Jerry shrugged. "Dracon fleet pilots are best; this is well known."

I raised my eyebrows. "That's why I shot your tail feathers off, huh?"

Jerry shrugged, frowned, and continued sewing on the scraps of snake leather. "Why do the Earthmen invade this part of the Galaxy, Davidge? We had thousands of years of peace before you came."

"Hah! Why do the Dracs invade? We were at peace too. What are you doing here?"

"We settle these planets. It is the Drac tradition. We are explorers and founders."

"Well, toad face, what do you think we are, a bunch of homebodies? Humans have had space travel for less than two hundred years, but we've settled almost twice as many planets as the Dracs—"

Jerry held up a finger. "Exactly! You humans spread like a disease. Enough! We don't want you here!"

"Well, we're here, and here to stay. Now, what are you going to do about it?"

"You see what we do, *Irkmaan,* we fight!"

"Phooey! You call that little scrap we were in a fight? Hell, Jerry, we were kicking you junk jocks out of the sky—"

"Haw, Davidge! That's why you sit here sucking on smoked snakemeat!"

I pulled the little rascal out of my mouth and pointed it at the Drac. "I notice your breath has a snake flavor too, Drac!"

Jerry snorted and turned away from the fire. I felt stupid, first because we weren't going to settle an argument that had plagued a hundred worlds for over a century. Second, I wanted to have Jerry check my recitation. I had over a hundred generations memorized. The Drac's side was toward the fire, leaving enough light falling on its lap to see its sewing.

"Jerry, what are you working on?"

"We have nothing to talk about, Davidge."

"Come on, what is it?"

Jerry turned its head toward me, then looked back into its lap and picked up a tiny snakeskin suit. "For Zammis." Jerry smiled and I shook my head, then laughed.

We talked of philosophy:

"You studied Shizumaat, Jerry; why won't you tell me about its teachings?"

Jerry frowned. "No, Davidge."

"Are Shizumaat's teachings secret or something?"

Jerry shook its head. "No. But we honor Shizumaat too much for talk."

I rubbed my chin. "Do you mean too much to talk about it, or to talk about it with a human?"

"Not with humans, Davidge; just not with you."

"Why?"

Jerry lifted its head and narrowed its yellow eyes. "You know what you said . . . on the sandbar."

I scratched my head and vaguely recalled the curse I laid on the Drac about Shizumaat eating it. I held out my hands. "But, Jerry, I was mad, angry. You can't hold me accountable for what I said then."

"I do."

"Will it change anything if I apologize?"

"Not a thing."

I stopped myself from saying something nasty and thought back to that moment when Jerry and I stood ready to strangle each other. I remembered something about that meeting and screwed the corners of my mouth in place to keep from smiling. "Will you tell me Shizumaat's teachings if I forgive you . . . for what you said about Mickey Mouse?" I bowed my head in an appearance of reverence, although its chief purpose was to suppress a cackle.

Jerry looked up at me, its face pained with guilt. "I have felt bad about that, Davidge. If you forgive me, I will talk about Shizumaat."

"Then, I forgive you, Jerry."

"One more thing."

"What?"

"You must tell me of the teachings of Mickey Mouse."

"I'll . . . uh, do my best."

We talked of Zammis:

"Jerry, what do you want little Zammy to be?"

The Drac shrugged. "Zammis must live up to its own name. I want it to do that with honor. If Zammis does that, it is all I can ask."

"Zammy will pick its own trade?"

"Yes."

"Isn't there anything special you want, though?"

Jerry nodded. "Yes, there is."

"What's that?"

"That Zammis will, one day, find itself off this miserable planet."

I nodded. "Amen."

"Amen."

The winter dragged on until Jerry and I began wondering if we had gotten in on the beginning of an ice age. Outside the cave, everything was coated with a thick layer of ice, and the low temperature combined with the steady winds made venturing outside a temptation of death by falls or freezing. Still, by mutual agreement, we both went outside to relieve ourselves. There were several isolated chambers deep in the cave; but we feared polluting our water supply, not to mention the air inside the cave. The main risk outside was dropping one's drawers at a wind chill factor that froze breath vapor before it could be blown through the thin face muffs we had made out of our flight suits. We learned not to dawdle.

One morning, Jerry was outside answering the call, while I stayed by the fire mashing up dried roots with water for griddle cakes. I heard Jerry call from the mouth of the cave. "Davidge!"

"What?"

"Davidge, come quick!"

A ship! It had to be! I put the shell bowl on the sand, put on my hat and gloves, and ran through the passage. As I came close to the door, I untied the muff from around my neck and tied it over my mouth and nose to protect my lungs. Jerry, its head bundled in a similar manner, was looking through the door, waving me on. "What is it?"

Jerry stepped away from the door to let me through. "Come, look!"

Sunlight. Blue sky and sunlight. In the distance, over the sea, new clouds were piling up; but above us the sky was clear. Neither of us could look at the sun directly, but we turned our faces to it and felt the rays of Fyrine on our skins. The light glared and sparkled off the ice-covered rocks and trees. "Beautiful."

"Yes." Jerry grabbed my sleeve with a gloved hand. "Davidge, you know what this means?"

"What?"

"Signal fires at night. On a clear night, a large fire could be seen from orbit, *ne?*"

I looked at Jerry, then back at the sky. "I don't know. If the fire were big enough, and we get a clear night, and if anybody picks that moment to look . . ." I let my head hang down. "That's always supposing that there's someone in orbit up there to do the looking." I felt the pain begin in my fingers. "We better go back in."

"Davidge, it's a chance!"

"What are we going to use for wood, Jerry?" I held out an arm toward the trees above and around the cave. "Everything that can burn has at least fifteen centimeters of ice on it."

"In the cave—"

"Our firewood?" I shook my head. "How long is this winter going to last? Can you be sure that we have enough wood to waste on signal fires?"

"It's a chance, Davidge. It's a chance!"

Our survival riding on a toss of the dice. I shrugged. "Why not?"

We spent the next few hours hauling a quarter of our carefully gathered firewood and dumping it outside the mouth of the cave. By the time we were finished and long before night came, the sky was again a solid blanket of grey. Several times each night, we would check the sky, waiting for stars to appear. During the days, we would frequently have to spend several hours beating the ice off the wood pile. Still, it gave both of us hope, until the wood in the cave ran out and we had to start borrowing from the signal pile.

That night, for the first time, the Drac looked absolutely defeated. Jerry sat at the fireplace, staring at the flames. Its hand reached inside its snake-skin jacket through the neck and pulled out a small golden cube suspended on a chain. Jerry held the cube clasped in both hands, shut its eyes and began mumbling in Drac. I watched from my bed until Jerry finished. The Drac sighed, nodded and replaced the object within its jacket.

"What's that thing?"

Jerry looked up at me, frowned, then touched the front of its jacket. "This? It is my *Talman*—what you call a Bible."

"A Bible is a book. You know, with pages that you read."

Jerry pulled the thing from its jacket, mumbled a phrase in Drac, then worked a small catch. Another gold cube dropped from the first and the Drac held it out to me. "Be very careful with it, Davidge."

I sat up, took the object and examined it in the light of the fire. Three hinged pieces of the golden metal formed the binding of a book two-and-a-half centimeters on an edge. I opened the book in the middle and looked over the double columns of dots, lines, and squiggles. "It's in Drac."

"Of course."

"But I can't read it."

Jerry's eyebrows went up. "You speak Drac so well. I didn't remember . . . would you like me to teach you?"

"To read this?"

"Why not? You have an appointment you have to keep?"

I shrugged. "No." I touched my finger to the book and tried to turn one of the tiny pages. Perhaps fifty pages went at once. "I can't separate the pages."

Jerry pointed at a small bump at the top of the spine. "Pull out the pin. It's for turning the pages."

I pulled out the short needle, touched it against a page and it slid loose of its companion and flipped. "Who wrote your *Talman*, Jerry?"

"Many. All great teachers."

"Shizumaat?"

Jerry nodded. "Shizumaat is one of them."

I closed the book and held it in the palm of my hand. "Jerry, why did you bring this out now?"

"I needed its comfort." The Drac held out its arms. "This place. Maybe we will grow old here and die. Maybe we will never be found. I see this today as we brought in the signal fire wood." Jerry placed its hands on its belly. "Zammis will be born here. The *Talman* helps me to accept what I cannot change."

"Zammis, how much longer?"

Jerry smiled. "Soon."

I looked at the tiny book. "I would like you to teach me to read this, Jerry."

The Drac took the chain and case from around its neck and handed it to me. "You must keep the *Talman* in this."

I held it for a moment, then shook my head. "I can't keep this, Jerry. It's obviously of great value to you. What if I lost it?"

"You won't. Keep it while you learn. The student must do this."

I put the chain around my neck. "This is quite an honor you do me."

Jerry shrugged. "Much less than the honor you do me by memorizing the Jeriba line. Your recitations have been accurate, and moving." Jerry took some charcoal from the fire, stood and walked to the wall of the chamber. That night I learned the thirty-one letters and sounds of the Drac alphabet, as well as the additional nine sounds and letters used in formal Drac writings.

The wood eventually ran out. Jerry was very heavy and very, very sick as Zammis prepared to make its appearance, and it was all the Drac could do to waddle outside with my help to relieve itself. Hence, woodgathering, which involved taking our remaining stick and beating the ice off the dead standing trees, fell to me, as did cooking.

On a particularly blustery day, I noticed that the ice on the trees was thinner. Somewhere we had turned winter's corner and were heading for spring. I spent my ice-pounding time feeling great at the thought of spring, and I knew Jerry would pick up some at the news. The winter was really getting the Drac down. I was working the woods above the cave, taking armloads of gathered wood and dropping them down below, when I heard a scream. I froze, then looked around. I could see nothing but the sea and the ice around me. Then, the scream again. "Davidge!" It was Jerry. I dropped the load I was carrying and ran to the cleft in the cliff's face that served as a path to the upper woods. Jerry screamed again; and I slipped, then rolled until I came to the shelf level with the cave's mouth. I rushed through the entrance, down the passageway until I came to the chamber. Jerry writhed on its bed, digging its fingers into the sand.

I dropped on my knees next to the Drac. "I'm here, Jerry. What is it? What's wrong?"

"Davidge!" The Drac rolled its eyes, seeing nothing; its mouth worked silently, then exploded with another scream.

"Jerry, it's me!" I shook the Drac's shoulder. "It's me, Jerry. Davidge!"

Jerry turned its head toward me, grimaced, then clasped the fingers of one hand around my left wrist with the strength of pain. "Davidge! Zammis . . . something's gone wrong!"

"What? What can I do?"

Jerry screamed again, then its head fell back to the bed in a half-faint. The Drac fought back to consciousness and pulled my head down to its lips. "Davidge, you must swear."

"What, Jerry? Swear what?"

"Zammis . . . on Draco. To stand before the line's archives. Do this."

"What do you mean? You talk like you're dying."

"I am, Davidge. Zammis two hundredth generation . . . very important. Present my child, Davidge. Swear!"

I wiped the sweat from my face with my free hand. "You're not going to die, Jerry. Hang on!"

"Enough! Face truth, Davidge! I die! You must teach the line of Jeriba to Zammis . . . and the book, the *Talman, gavey?*"

"Stop it!" Panic stood over me almost as a physical presence. "Stop talking like that! You aren't going to die, Jerry. Come on; fight, you *kizlode* sonofabitch . . ."

Jerry screamed. Its breathing was weak and the Drac drifted in and out of consciousness. "Davidge."

"What?" I realized I was sobbing like a kid.

"Davidge, you must help Zammis come out."

"What . . . how? What in the Hell are you talking about?"

Jerry turned its face to the wall of the cave. "Lift my jacket."

"What?"

"Lift my jacket, Davidge. Now!"

I pulled up the snakeskin jacket, exposing Jerry's swollen belly. The fold down the center was bright red and seeping a clear liquid. "What . . . what should I do?"

Jerry breathed rapidly, then held its breath, "Tear it open! You must tear it open, Davidge!"

"No!"

"Do it! Do it, or Zammis dies!"

"What do I care about your goddamn child, Jerry? What do I have to do to save you?"

"Tear it open . . ." whispered the Drac. "Take care of my child, *Irkmaan.* Present Zammis before the Jeriba archives. Swear this to me."

"Oh, Jerry . . ."

"Swear this!"

I nodded, hot fat tears dribbling down my cheeks. "I swear it. . . ." Jerry relaxed its grip on my wrist and closed its eyes. I knelt next to the Drac, stunned. "No. No, no, no, no."

Tear it open! You must tear it open, Davidge!

I reached up a hand and gingerly touched the fold on Jerry's belly. I could feel life struggling beneath it, trying to escape the airless confines of the Drac's womb. I hated it; I hated the damned thing as I never hated anything before. Its struggles grew weaker, then stopped.

Present Zammis before the Jeriba archives. Swear this to me. . . .

I swear it. . . .

I lifted my other hand and inserted my thumbs into the fold and tugged gently. I increased the amount of force, then tore at Jerry's belly like a madman. The fold burst open, soaking the front of my jacket with the clear fluid. Holding the fold open, I could see the still form of Zammis huddled in a well of the fluid, motionless.

I vomited. When I had nothing more to throw up, I reached into the fluid and put my hands under the Drac infant. I lifted it, wiped my mouth on my upper left sleeve, and closed my mouth over Zammis's and pulled the child's mouth open with my right hand. Three times, four times, I inflated the child's lungs, then it coughed. Then it cried. I tied off the two umbilicals with berrybush fiber, then cut them. Jeriba Zammis was freed of the dead flesh of its parent.

I held the rock over my head, then brought it down with all of my force upon the ice. Shards splashed away from the point of impact, exposing the dark green beneath. Again, I lifted the rock and brought it down, knocking loose another rock. I picked it up, stood and carried it to the half-covered corpse of the Drac. "The Drac," I whispered. *Good. Just call it 'the Drac.' Toad face. Dragger.*

The enemy. Call it anything to insulate those feelings against the pain.

I looked at the pile of rocks I had gathered, decided it was sufficient to finish the job, then knelt next to the grave. As I placed the rocks on the pile, unmindful of the gale-blown sleet freezing on my snakeskins, I fought back the tears. I smacked my hands together to help restore the circulation. Spring was coming, but it was still dangerous to stay outside too long. And I had been a long time building the Drac's grave. I picked up another rock and placed it into position. As the rock's weight leaned against the snakeskin mattress cover, I realized that the Drac was already frozen. I quickly placed the remainder of the rocks, then stood.

The wind rocked me and I almost lost my footing on the ice next to the grave. I looked toward the boiling sea, pulled my snakeskins around myself more tightly, then looked down at the pile of rocks. *There should be words. You don't just cover up the dead, then go to dinner. There should be words.* But what words? I was no religionist, and neither was the Drac. Its formal philosophy on the matter of death was the same as my informal rejection of Islamic delights, pagan Valhallas, and Judeo-Christian pies in the sky. Death is death; *finis;* the end; the worms crawl in, the worms crawl out . . . *Still, there should be words.*

I reached beneath my snakeskins and clasped my gloved hand around the golden cube of the *Talman.* I felt the sharp corners of the cube through my glove, closed my eyes and ran through the words of the great Drac philosophers. But there was nothing they had written for this moment.

The *Talman* was a book on life. *Talman* means life, and this occupies Drac philosophy. They spare nothing for death. Death is a fact; the end of life. The *Talman* had no words for me to say. The wind knifed through me, causing me to shiver. Already my fingers were numb and pains were beginning in my feet. Still, there should be words. But the only words I could think of would open the gate, flooding my being with pain—with the realization that the Drac was gone. *Still . . . still, there should be words.*

"Jerry, I . . ." I had no words. I turned from the grave, my tears mixing with the sleet.

With the warmth and silence of the cave around me, I sat on my mattress, my back against the wall of the cave. I tried to lose myself in the shadows and flickers of light cast on the opposite wall by the fire. Images would half-form, then dance away before I could move my mind to see something in them. As a child I used to watch clouds, and in them see faces, castles, animals, dragons, and giants. It was a world of escape—fantasy; something to inject wonder and adventure into the mundane, regulated life of a middle-class boy leading a middle-class life. All I could see on the wall of the cave was a representation of Hell: flames licking at twisted, grotesque representations of condemned souls. I laughed at the thought. We think of Hell as fire, supervised by a cackling sadist in a red union suit. Fyrine IV had taught me this much: Hell is loneliness, hunger, and endless cold.

I heard a whimper, and I looked into the shadows toward the small mattress at the back of the cave. Jerry had made the snakeskin sack filled with seed pod down for Zammis. It whimpered again, and I leaned forward, wondering if there was something it needed. A pang of fear tickled my guts. What does a Drac infant eat? Dracs aren't mammals. All they ever taught us in training was how to recognize Dracs—that, and how to kill them. Then real fear began working on me. "What in the hell am I going to use for diapers?"

It whimpered again. I pushed myself to my feet, walked the sandy floor to the infant's side, then knelt beside it. Out of the bundle that was Jerry's old flight suit, two chubby three-fingered arms waved. I picked up the bundle, carried it next to the fire, and sat on a rock. Balancing the bundle on my lap, I carefully unwrapped it. I could see the yellow glitter of Zammis's eyes beneath yellow, sleep-heavy lids. From the almost noseless face and solid teeth to its deep yellow color, Zammis was every bit a miniature of Jerry, except for the fat. Zammis fairly wallowed in rolls of fat. I looked, and was grateful to find that there was no mess.

I looked into Zammis's face. "You want something to eat?"

"Guh."

Its jaws were ready for business, and I assumed that Dracs must chew solid food from day one. I reached over the fire and picked up a twist of dried snake, then touched it against the infant's lips. Zammis turned its head. "C'mon, eat. You're not going to find anything better around here."

I pushed the snake against its lips again, and Zammis pulled back a chubby arm and pushed it away. I shrugged. "Well, whenever you get hungry enough, it's there."

"Guh meh!" Its head rocked back and forth on my lap, a tiny, three-fingered hand closed around my finger, and it whimpered again.

"You don't want to eat, you don't need to be cleaned up, so what do you want? *Kos va nu?*"

Zammis's face wrinkled, and its hand pulled at my finger. Its other hand waved in the direction of my chest. I picked Zammis up to arrange the flight suit, and the tiny hands reached out, grasped the front of my snake-skins, and held on as the chubby arms pulled the child next to my chest. I held it close, it placed its cheek against my chest, and promptly fell asleep. "Well . . . I'll be damned."

Until the Drac was gone, I never realized how closely I had stood near the edge of madness. My loneliness was a cancer—a growth that I fed with hate: hate for the planet with its endless cold, endless winds, and endless isolation; hate for the helpless yellow child with its clawing need for care, food, and an affection that I couldn't give; and hate for myself. I found myself doing things that frightened and disgusted me. To break my solid wall of being alone, I would talk, shout, and sing to myself—uttering curses, nonsense, or meaningless croaks.

Its eyes were open, and it waved a chubby arm and cooed. I picked up a large rock, staggered over to the child's side, and held the weight over the tiny body. "I could drop this thing, kid. Where would you be then?" I felt laughter coming from my lips. I threw the rock aside. "Why should I mess up the cave? Outside. Put you outside for a minute, and you die! You hear me? Die!"

The child worked its three-fingered hands at the empty air, shut its eyes, and cried. "Why don't you eat? Why don't you crap? Why don't you do anything right, but cry?" The child cried more loudly. "Bah! I ought to pick up that rock and finish it! That's what I ought . . ." A wave of revulsion stopped my words, and I went to my mattress, picked up my cap, gloves, and muff, then headed outside.

Before I came to the rocked-in entrance to the cave, I felt the bite of the wind. Outside I stopped and looked at the sea and sky—a roiling panorama in glorious black and white, grey and grey. A gust of wind slapped against me, rocking me back toward the entrance. I regained my balance, walked to the edge of the cliff and shook my fist at the sea. "Go ahead! Go ahead and blow, you *kizlode* sonofabitch! You haven't killed me yet!"

I squeezed the windburned lids of my eyes shut, then opened them and looked down. A forty-meter drop to the next ledge, but if I took a running jump, I could clear it. Then it would be a hundred and fifty meters to the rocks below. *Jump.* I backed away from the cliff's edge. "Jump! Sure, jump!" I shook my head at the sea. "I'm not going to do your job for you! You want me dead, you're going to have to do it yourself!"

I looked back and up, above the entrance to the cave. The sky was darkening and in a few hours, night would shroud the landscape. I turned toward the cleft in the rock that led to the scrub forest above the cave.

I squatted next to the Drac's grave and studied the rocks I had placed there, already fused together with a layer of ice. "Jerry. What am I going to do?"

The Drac would sit by the fire, both of us sewing. And we talked.

"You know, Jerry, all this," I held up the Talman. "I've heard it all before. I expected something different."

The Drac lowered its sewing to its lap and studied me for an instant. Then it shook its head and resumed its sewing. "You are not a terribly profound creature, Davidge."

"What's that supposed to mean?"

Jerry held out a three-fingered hand. "A universe, Davidge—there is a universe out there, a universe of life, objects, and events. There are differences, but it is all the same universe, and we all must obey the same universal laws. Did you ever think of that?"

"No."

"That is what I mean, Davidge. Not terribly profound."

I snorted. "I told you, I'd heard this stuff before. So I imagine that shows humans to be just as profound as Dracs."

Jerry laughed. "You always insist on making something racial out of my observations. What I said applied to you, not to the race of humans. . . ."

I spat on the frozen ground. "You Dracs think you're so damned smart." The wind picked up, and I could taste the sea salt in it. One of the big blows was coming. The sky was changing to that curious darkness that tricked me into thinking it was midnight blue, rather than black. A trickle of ice found its way under my collar.

"What's wrong with me just being me? Everybody in the universe doesn't have to be a damned philosopher, toad face!" There were millions —billions—like me. More maybe. "What difference does it make to anything whether I ponder existence or not? It's here; that's all I have to know."

"Davidge, you don't even know your family line beyond your parents, and now you say you refuse to know that of your universe that you can know. How will you know your place in this existence, Davidge? Where are you? Who are you?"

I shook my head and stared at the grave, then I turned and faced the sea. In another hour, or less, it would be too dark to see the whitecaps. "I'm me, that's who." But was that 'me' who held the rock over Zammis, threatening a helpless infant with death? I felt my guts curdle as the loneliness I thought I felt grew claws and fangs and began gnawing and slashing at the remains of my sanity. I turned back to the grave, closed my eyes, then opened them. "I'm a fighter pilot, Jerry. Isn't that something?"

"That is what you do, Davidge; that is neither who nor what you are."

I knelt next to the grave and clawed at the ice-sheathed rocks with my hands. "You don't talk to me now, Drac! *You're dead!*" I stopped, realizing that the words I had heard were from the *Talman,* processed into my own context. I slumped against the rocks, felt the wind, then pushed myself to my feet. "Jerry, Zammis won't eat. It's been three days. What do I do? Why didn't you tell me anything about Drac brats before you . . ." I held my hands to my face. "Steady, boy. Keep it up, and they'll stick you in a home." The wind pressed against my back, I lowered my hands, then walked from the grave.

I sat in the cave, staring at the fire. I couldn't hear the wind through the rock, and the wood was dry, making the fire hot and quiet. I tapped my fingers against my knees, then began humming. Noise, any kind, helped to drive off the oppressive loneliness. "Sonofabitch." I laughed and nodded. "Yea, verily, and *kizlode va nu, dutschaat.*" I chuckled, trying to think of all the curses and obscenities in Drac that I had learned from Jerry. There were quite a few. My toe tapped against the sand and my humming started up again. I stopped, frowned, then remembered the song.

"Highty tighty Christ almighty,
Who the Hell are we?
Zim zam, Gawd Damn,
We're in Squadron B."

I leaned back against the wall of the cave, trying to remember another verse. *A pilot's got a rotten life/ no crumpets with our tea/ we have to service the general's wife/ and pick fleas from her knee.* "Damn!" I slapped my knee, trying to see the faces of the other pilots in the squadron lounge. I could almost feel the whiskey fumes tickling the inside of my nose. Vadik, Wooster, Arnold . . . the one with the broken nose—Demerest, Kadiz. I hummed again, swinging an imaginary mug of issue grog by its imaginary handle.

"And, if he doesn't like it,
I'll tell you what we'll do:
We'll fill his ass with broken glass,
and seal it up with glue."

The cave echoed with the song. I stood, threw up my arms and screamed. "Yaaaaahoooooo!"

Zammis began crying. I bit my lip and walked over to the bundle on the mattress. "Well? You ready to eat?"

"Unh, unh, weh." The infant rocked its head back and forth. I went to the fire, picked up a twist of snake, then returned. I knelt next to Zammis and held the snake to its lips. Again, the child pushed it away. "Come on, you. You have to eat." I tried again with the same results. I took the wraps off the child and looked at its body. I could tell it was losing weight, although Zammis didn't appear to be getting weak. I shrugged, wrapped it up again, stood, and began walking back to my mattress.

"Guh, weh."

I turned. "What?"

"Ah, guh, guh."

I went back, stooped over and picked the child up. Its eyes were open and it looked into my face, then smiled.

"What're you laughing at, ugly? You should get a load of your own face."

Zammis barked out a short laugh, then gurgled. I went to my mattress, sat down, and arranged Zammis in my lap. "Gumma, buh, buh." Its hand grabbed a loose flap of snakeskin on my shirt and pulled on it.

"Gumma buh buh to you, too. So, what do we do now? How about I start teaching you the line of Jeriban? You're going to have to learn it sometime, and it might as well be now." The Jeriban line. My recitations of the line were the only things Jerry ever complimented me about. I looked into Zammis's eyes. "When I bring you to stand before the Jeriba archives, you will say this: 'Before you here I stand, Zammis of the line of Jeriba, born of Shigan, the fighter pilot.' " I smiled, thinking of the upraised yellow brows if Zammis continued, *"and, by damn, Shigan was a Helluva good pilot, too. Why, I was once told he took a smart round in his tail feathers, then pulled around and rammed the* kizlode *sonofabitch, known to one and all as Willis E. Davidge . . ."* I shook my head. "You're not going to get your wings by doing the line in English, Zammis." I began again:

"Naatha nu enta va, Zammis zea does Jeriba, estay va Shigan, asaam naa denvadar. . . ."

For eight of those long days and nights, I feared the child would die. I tried everything—roots, dried berries, dried plumfruit, snakemeat dried, boiled, chewed, and ground. Zammis refused it all. I checked frequently, but each time I looked through the child's wraps, they were as clean as when I had put them on. Zammis lost weight, but seemed to grow stronger. By the ninth day it was crawling the floor of the cave. Even with the fire, the cave wasn't really warm. I feared that the kid would get sick crawling around naked, and I dressed it in the tiny snakeskin suit and cap Jerry had made for it. After dressing it, I stood Zammis up and looked at it. The kid had already developed a smile full of mischief that, combined with the twinkle in its yellow eyes and its suit and cap, make it look like an elf. I was holding Zammis up in a standing position. The kid seemed pretty steady on its legs, and I let go. Zammis smiled, waved its thinning arms about, then laughed and took a faltering step toward me. I caught it as it fell, and the little Drac squealed.

In two more days Zammis was walking and getting into everything that could be gotten into. I spent many an anxious moment searching the chambers at the back of the cave for the kid after coming in from outside. Finally, when I caught it at the mouth of the cave heading full steam for the outside, I had had enough. I made a harness out of snakeskin, attached it to a snake-leather leash, and tied the other end to a projection of rock above my head. Zammis still got into everything, but at least I could find it.

Four days after it learned to walk, it wanted to eat. Drac babies are probably the most convenient and considerate infants in the universe. They live off their fat for about three or four Earth weeks, and don't make a mess the entire time. After they learn to walk, and can therefore make it to a mutually agreed upon spot, then they want food and begin discharging wastes. I showed the kid once how to use the litter box I had made, and never had to again. After five or six lessons, Zammis was handling its own drawers. Watching the little Drac learn and grow, I began to understand those pilots in my squadron who used to bore each other—and everyone else—with countless pictures of ugly children, accompanied by thirty-minute narratives for each snapshot. Before the ice melted, Zammis was talking. I taught it to call me "Uncle."

For lack of a better term, I called the ice-melting season "spring." It would be a long time before the scrub forest showed any green or the snakes ventured forth from their icy holes. The sky maintained its eternal cover of dark, angry clouds, and still the sleet would come and coat everything with a hard, slippery glaze. But the next day the glaze would melt, and the warmer air would push another millimeter into the soil.

I realized that this was the time to be gathering wood. Before the winter hit, Jerry and I working together hadn't gathered enough wood. The short summer would have to be spent putting up food for the next winter. I was hoping to build a tighter door over the mouth of the cave, and I swore that I would figure out some kind of indoor plumbing. Dropping your drawers outside in the middle of winter was dangerous. My mind was full of these things as I stretched out on my mattress watching the smoke curl through a crack in the roof of the cave. Zammis was off in the back of the cave playing with some rocks that it had found, and I must have fallen asleep. I awoke with the kid shaking my arm.

"Uncle?"

"Huh? Zammis?"

"Uncle. Look."

I rolled over on my left side and faced the Drac. Zammis was holding up its right hand, fingers spread out. "What is it, Zammis?"

"Look." It pointed at each of its three fingers in turn. "One, two, three."

"So?"

"Look." Zammis grabbed my right hand and spread out the fingers. "One, two, three, *four, five!*"

I nodded. "So you can count to five."

The Drac frowned and made an impatient gesture with its tiny fists. "Look." It took my outstretched hand and placed its own on top of it. With its other hand, Zammis pointed first at one of its own fingers, then at one of mine. "One, one." The child's yellow eyes studied me to see if I understood.

"Yes."

The child pointed again. "Two, two." It looked at me, then looked back at my hand and pointed. "Three, three." Then he grabbed my two remaining fingers. *"Four, five!"* It dropped my hand, then pointed to the side of its own hand. "Four, five?"

I shook my head. Zammis, at less than four Earth months old, had detected part of the difference between Dracs and humans. A human child would be—what—five, six, or seven years old before asking questions like that. I sighed. "Zammis."

"Yes, Uncle?"

"Zammis, you are a Drac. Dracs only have three fingers on a hand." I held up my right hand and wiggled the fingers. "I'm a human. I have five."

I swear that tears welled in the child's eyes. Zammis held out its hands, looked at them, then shook its head. "Grow four, five?"

I sat up and faced the kid. Zammis was wondering where its other four fingers had gone. "Look, Zammis. You and I are different . . . different kinds of beings, understand?"

Zammis shook his head. "Grow four, five?"

"You won't. You're a Drac." I pointed at my chest. "I'm a human." This was getting me nowhere. "Your parent, where you came from, was a Drac. Do you understand?"

Zammis frowned. "Drac. What Drac?"

The urge to resort to the timeless standby of "you'll understand when you get older" pounded at the back of my mind. I shook my head. "Dracs have three fingers on each hand. Your parent had three fingers on each hand." I rubbed my beard. "My parent was a human and had five fingers on each hand. That's why I have five fingers on each hand."

Zammis knelt on the sand and studied its fingers. It looked up at me, back to its hands, then back to me. "What parent?"

I studied the kid. It must be having an identity crisis of some kind. I was the only person it had ever seen, and I had five fingers per hand. "A parent is . . . the thing . . ." I scratched my beard again. "Look . . . we all come from someplace. I had a mother and father—two different kinds of humans—that gave me life; that made me, understand?"

Zammis gave me a look that could be interpreted as "Mac, you are full of it." I shrugged. "I don't know if I can explain it."

Zammis pointed at its own chest. "My mother? My father?"

I held out my hands, dropped them into my lap, pursed my lips, scratched my beard, and generally stalled for time. Zammis held an unblinking gaze on me the entire time. "Look, Zammis. You don't have a mother and a father. I'm a human, so I have them; you're a Drac. You have a parent—just one, see?"

Zammis shook its head. It looked at me, then pointed at its own chest. "Drac."

"Right."

Zammis pointed at my chest. "Human."

"Right again."

Zammis removed its hand and dropped it in its lap. "Where Drac come from?"

Sweet Jesus! Trying to explain hermaphroditic reproduction to a kid who shouldn't even be crawling yet! "Zammis . . ." I held up my hands, then dropped them into my lap. "Look. You see how much bigger I am than you?"

"Yes, Uncle."

"Good." I ran my fingers through my hair, fighting for time and inspiration. "Your parent was big, like me. Its name was . . . Jeriba Shigan." Funny how just saying the name was painful. "Jeriba Shigan was like you. It only had three fingers on each hand. It grew you in its tummy." I poked Zammis's middle. "Understand?"

Zammis giggled and held its hands over its stomach. "Uncle, how Dracs grow there?"

I lifted my legs onto the mattress and stretched out. Where do little Dracs come from? I looked over to Zammis and saw the child hanging upon my every word. I grimaced and told the truth. "Damned if I know, Zammis. Damned if I know." Thirty seconds later, Zammis was back playing with its rocks.

Summer, and I taught Zammis how to capture and skin the long grey snakes, and then how to smoke the meat. The child would squat on the shallow bank above a mudpool, its yellow eyes fixed on the snake holes in the bank, waiting for one of the occupants to poke out its head. The wind would blow, but Zammis wouldn't move. Then a flat, triangular head set with tiny blue eyes would appear. The snake would check the pool, turn and check the bank, then check the sky. It would advance out of the hole a bit, then check it all again. Often the snakes would look directly at Zammis, but the Drac could have been carved from rock. Zammis wouldn't move until the snake was too far out of the hole to pull itself back in tail first. Then Zammis would strike, grabbing the snake with both hands just behind the head. The snakes had no fangs and weren't poisonous, but they were lively enough to toss Zammis into the mudpool on occasion.

The skins were spread and wrapped around tree trunks and pegged in place to dry. The tree trunks were kept in an open place near the entrance to the cave, but under an overhang that faced away from the ocean. About two thirds of the skins put up in this manner cured; the remaining third would rot.

Beyond the skin room was the smokehouse: a rock-walled chamber that we would hang with rows of snakemeat. A greenwood fire would be set in a pit in the chamber's floor; then we would fill in the small opening with rocks and dirt.

"Uncle, why doesn't the meat rot after it's smoked?"

I thought upon it. "I'm not sure; I just know it doesn't."

"Why do you know?"

I shrugged. "I just do. I read about it, probably."

"What's read?"

"Reading. Like when I sit down and read the *Talman.*"

"Does the *Talman* say why the meat doesn't rot?"

"No. I meant that I probably read it in another book."

"Do we have more books?"

I shook my head. "I meant before I came to this planet."

"Why did you come to this planet?"

"I told you. Your parent and I were stranded here during the battle."

"Why do the humans and Dracs fight?"

"It's very complicated." I waved my hands about for a bit. The human line was that the Dracs were aggressors invading our space. The Drac line was that the humans were aggressors invading their space. The truth? "Zammis, it has to do with the colonization of new planets. Both races are expanding and both races have a tradition of exploring and colonizing new planets. I guess we just expanded into each other. Understand?"

Zammis nodded, then became mercifully silent as it fell into deep thought. The main thing I learned from the Drac child was all of the questions I didn't have answers to. I was feeling very smug, however, at having gotten Zammis to understand about the war, thereby avoiding my ignorance on the subject of preserving meat. "Uncle?"

"Yes, Zammis?"

"What's a planet?"

As the cold, wet summer came to an end, we had the cave jammed with firewood and preserved food. With that out of the way, I concentrated my efforts on making some kind of indoor plumbing out of the natural pools in the chambers deep within the cave. The bathtub was no problem. By dropping heated rocks into one of the pools, the water could be brought up to a bearable—even comfortable—temperature. After bathing, the hollow stems of a bamboo-like plant could be used to siphon out the dirty water. The tub could then be refilled from the pool above. The problem was where to siphon the water. Several of the chambers had holes in their floors. The first three holes we tried drained into our main chamber, wetting the low edge near the entrance. The previous winter, Jerry and I had considered using one of those holes for a toilet that we would flush with water from the pools. Since we didn't know where the goodies would come out, we decided against it.

The fourth hole Zammis and I tried drained out below the entrance to the cave in the face of the cliff. Not ideal, but better than answering the call of nature in the middle of a combination ice-storm and blizzard. We rigged up the hole as a drain for both the tub and toilet. As Zammis and I prepared to enjoy our first hot bath, I removed my snakeskins, tested the water with my toe, then stepped in. "Great!" I turned to Zammis, the child still half dressed. "Come on in, Zammis. The water's fine." Zammis was staring at me, its mouth hanging open. "What's the matter?"

The child stared wide-eyed, then pointed at me with a three-fingered hand. "Uncle . . . what's that?"

I looked down. "Oh." I shook my head, then looked up at the child. "Zammis, I explained all that, remember? I'm a human."

"But what's it *for?*"

I sat down in the warm water, removing the object of discussion from sight. "It's for the elimination of liquid wastes . . . among other things. Now, hop in and get washed."

Zammis shucked its snakeskins, looked down at its own smooth-surfaced, combined system, then climbed into the tube. The child settled into the water up to its neck, its yellow eyes studying me. "Uncle?"

"Yes?"

"What *other things?*"

Well, I told Zammis. For the first time, the Drac appeared to be trying to decide whether my response was truthful or not, rather than its usual acceptance of my every assertion. In fact, I was convinced that Zammis thought I was lying—probably because I was.

* * *

Winter began with a sprinkle of snowflakes carried on a gentle breeze. I took Zammis above the cave to the scrub forest. I held the child's hand as we stood before the pile of rocks that served as Jerry's grave. Zammis pulled its snakeskins against the wind, bowed its head, then turned and looked up into my face. "Uncle, this is the grave of my parent?"

I nodded. "Yes."

Zammis turned back to the grave, then shook its head. "Uncle, how should I feel?"

"I don't understand, Zammis."

The child nodded at the grave. "I can see that you are sad being here. I think you want me to feel the same. Do you?"

I frowned, then shook my head. "No. I don't want you to be sad. I just wanted you to know where it is."

"May I go now?"

"Sure. Are you certain you know the way back to the cave?"

"Yes. I just want to make sure my soap doesn't burn again."

I watched as the child turned and scurried off into the naked trees, then I turned back to the grave. "Well, Jerry, what do you think of your kid? Zammis was using wood ashes to clean the grease off the shells, then it put a shell back on the fire and put water in it to boil off the burnt-on food. Fat and ashes. The next thing, Jerry, we were making soap. Zammis's first batch almost took the hide off us, but the kid's getting better. . . ."

I looked up at the clouds, then brought my glance down to the sea. In the distance, low, dark clouds were building up. "See that? You know what that means, don't you? Ice-storm number one." The wind picked up and I squatted next to the grave to replace a rock that had rolled from the pile. "Zammis is a good kid, Jerry. I wanted to hate it . . . after you died. I wanted to hate it." I replaced the rock, then looked back toward the sea.

"I don't know how we're going to make it off planet, Jerry—" I caught a flash of movement out of the corner of my vision. I turned to the right and looked over the tops of the trees. Against the grey sky, a black speck streaked away. I followed it with my eyes until it went above the clouds.

I listened, hoping to hear an exhaust roar, but my heart was pounding so hard, all I could hear was the wind. Was it a ship? I stood, took a few steps in the direction the speck was going, then stopped. Turning my head, I saw that the rocks on Jerry's grave were already capped with thin layers of fine snow. I shrugged and headed for the cave. "Probably just a bird."

Zammis sat on its mattress, stabbing several pieces of snakeskin with a bone needle. I stretched out on my own mattress and watched the smoke curl up toward the crack in the ceiling. Was it a bird? Or was it a ship? Damn, but it worked on me. Escape from the planet had been out of my thoughts, had been buried, hidden for all that summer. But again, it twisted at me. To walk where a sun shined, to wear cloth again, experience central heating, eat food prepared by a chef, to be among . . . people again.

I rolled over on my right side and stared at the wall next to my mattress. People. Human people. I closed my eyes and swallowed. Girl human people. Female persons. Images drifted before my eyes—faces, bodies, laughing couples, the dance after flight training . . . what was her name? Dolora? Dora?

I shook my head, rolled over and sat up, facing the fire. Why did I have to see whatever it was? All those things I had been able to bury—to forget—boiling over.

"Uncle?"

I looked up at Zammis. Yellow skin, yellow eyes, noseless toad face. I shook my head. "What?"

"Is something wrong?"

Is something wrong, hah. "No. I just thought I saw something today. It probably wasn't anything." I reached to the fire and took a piece of dried snake from the griddle. I blew on it, then gnawed on the stringy strip.

"What did it look like?"

"I don't know. The way it moved, I thought it might be a ship. It went away so fast, I couldn't be sure. Might have been a bird."

"Bird?"

I studied Zammis. It'd never seen a bird; neither had I on Fyrine IV. "An animal that flies."

Zammis nodded. "Uncle, when we were gathering wood up in the scrub forest, I saw something fly."

"What? Why didn't you tell me?"

"I meant to, but I forgot."

"Forgot!" I frowned. "In which direction was it going?"

Zammis pointed to the back of the cave. "That way. Away from the sea." Zammis put down its sewing. "Can we go see where it went?"

I shook my head. "The winter is just beginning. You don't know what it's like. We'd die in only a few days."

Zammis went back to poking holes in the snakeskin. To make the trek in the winter would kill us. But spring would be something else. We could survive with double layered snakeskins stuffed with seed pod down, and a tent. We had to have a tent. Zammis and I could spend the winter making it, and packs. Boots. We'd need sturdy walking boots. Have to think on that. . . .

It's strange how a spark of hope can ignite, and spread, until all desperation is consumed. Was it a ship? I didn't know. If it was, was it taking off, or landing? I didn't know. If it was taking off, we'd be heading in the wrong direction. But the opposite direction meant crossing the sea. Whatever. Come spring we would head beyond the scrub forest and see what was there.

The winter seemed to pass quickly, with Zammis occupied with the tent and my time devoted to rediscovering the art of boot making. I made tracings of both of our feet on snakeskin, and, after some experimentation, I found that boiling the snake leather with plumfruit made it soft and gummy. By taking several of the gummy layers, weighting them, then setting them aside to dry, the result was a tough, flexible sole. By the time I finished Zammis's boots, the Drac needed a new pair.

"They're too small, Uncle."

"Waddaya mean, too small?"

Zammis pointed down. "They hurt. My toes are all crippled up."

I squatted down and felt the tops over the child's toes. "I don't understand. It's only been twenty, twenty-five days since I made the tracings. You sure you didn't move when I made them?"

Zammis shook its head. "I didn't move."

I frowned, then stood. "Stand up, Zammis." The Drac stood and I moved next to it. The top of Zammis's head came to the middle of my chest. Another sixty centimeters and it'd be as tall as Jerry. "Take them off, Zammis. I'll make a bigger pair. Try not to grow so fast."

Zammis pitched the tent inside the cave, put glowing coals inside, then rubbed fat into the leather for waterproofing. It had grown taller, and I had held off making the Drac's boots until I could be sure of the size it would need. I tried to do a projection by measuring Zammis's feet every ten days, then extending the curve into spring. According to my figures, the kid would have feet resembling a pair of attack transports by the time the snow melted. By spring, Zammis would be full grown. Jerry's old flight boots had fallen apart before Zammis had been born, but I had saved the pieces. I used the soles to make my tracings and hoped for the best.

I was busy with the new boots and Zammis was keeping an eye on the tent treatment. The Drac looked back at me.

"Uncle?"

"What?"

"Existence is the first given?"

I shrugged. "That's what Shizumaat says; I'll buy it."

"But, Uncle, how do we *know* that existence is real?"

I lowered my work, looked at Zammis, shook my head, then resumed stitching the boots. "Take my word for it."

The Drac grimaced. "But, Uncle, that is not knowledge; that is faith."

I sighed, thinking back to my sophomore year at the University of Nations—a bunch of adolescents lounging around a cheap flat experimenting with booze, powders, and philosophy. At a little more than one Earth year old, Zammis was developing into an intellectual bore. "So, what's wrong with faith?"

Zammis snickered. "Come now, Uncle. *Faith?*"

"It helps some of us along this drizzle-soaked coil."

"Coil?"

I scratched my head. "This mortal coil; life. Shakespeare, I think."

Zammis frowned. "It is not in the *Talman.*"

"He, not it. Shakespeare was a human."

Zammis stood, walked to the fire and sat across from me. "Was he a philosopher, like Mistan or Shizumaat?"

"No. He wrote plays—like stories, acted out."

Zammis rubbed its chin. "Do you remember any of Shakespeare?"

I held up a finger. " 'To be, or not to be; that is the question.' "

The Drac's mouth dropped open; then it nodded its head. "Yes. Yes! To be or not to be; that *is* the question!" Zammis held out its hands. "How do we *know* the wind blows outside the cave when we are not there to see it? Does the sea still boil if we are not there to feel it?"

I nodded. "Yes."

"But, Uncle, how do we *know?*"

I squinted at the Drac. "Zammis, I have a question for you. Is the following statement true or false: What I am saying right now is false."

Zammis blinked. "If it is false, then the statement is true. But . . . if it's true . . . the statement is false, but . . ." Zammis blinked again, then turned and went back to rubbing fat into the tent. "I'll think upon it, Uncle."

"You do that, Zammis."

The Drac thought upon it for about ten minutes, then turned back. "The statement is false."

I smiled. "But that's what the statement said, hence it is true, but . . ." I let the puzzle trail off. Oh, smugness, thou temptest even saints.

"No, Uncle. The statement is meaningless in its present context." I shrugged. "You see, Uncle, the statement assumes the existence of truth values that can comment upon themselves devoid of any other reference. I think Lurrvena's logic in the *Talman* is clear on this, and if meaningless is equated with falsehood . . ."

I sighed. "Yeah, well—"

"You see, Uncle, you must first establish a context in which your statement has meaning."

I leaned forward, frowned, and scratched my beard. "I see. You mean I was putting Descartes before the horse?"

Zammis looked at me strangely, and even more so when I collapsed on my mattress cackling like a fool.

* * *

"Uncle, why does the line of Jeriba have only five names? You say that human lines have many names."

I nodded. "The five names of the Jeriba line are things to which their bearers must add deeds. The deeds are important—not the names."

"Gothig is Shigan's parent as Shigan is my parent."

"Of course. You know that from your recitations."

Zammis frowned. "Then I *must* name my child Ty when I become a parent?"

"Yes. And Ty must name its child Haesni. Do you see something wrong with that?"

"I would like to name my child Davidge, after you."

I smiled and shook my head. "The Ty name has been served by great bankers, merchants, inventors, and—well, you know your recitation. The name Davidge hasn't been served by much. Think of what Ty would miss by not being Ty."

Zammis thought awhile, then nodded. "Uncle, do you think Gothig is alive?"

"As far as I know."

"What is Gothig like?"

I thought back to Jerry talking about its parent, Gothig. "It taught music, and is very strong. Jerry . . . Shigan said that its parent could bend metal bars with its fingers. Gothig is also very dignified. I imagine that right now Gothig is also very sad. Gothig must think that the line of Jeriba has ended."

Zammis frowned and its yellow brow furrowed. "Uncle, we must make it to Draco. We must tell Gothig the line continues."

"We will."

The winter's ice began thinning, and boots, tent, and packs were ready. We were putting the finishing touches on our new insulated suits. As Jerry had given the *Talman* to me to learn, the golden cube now hung around Zammis's neck. The Drac would drop the tiny golden book from the cube and study it for hours at a time.

"Uncle?"

"What?"

"Why do Dracs speak and write in one language and the humans in another?"

I laughed. "Zammis, the humans speak and write in many languages. English is just one of them."

"How do the humans speak among themselves?"

I shrugged. "They don't always; when they do, they use interpreters—people who can speak both languages."

"You and I speak both English and Drac; does that make us interpreters?"

"I suppose we could be, if you could ever find a human and a Drac who want to talk to each other. Remember, there's a war going on."

"How will the war stop if they do not talk?"

"I suppose they will talk, eventually."

Zammis smiled. "I think I would like to be an interpreter and help end the war." The Drac put its sewing aside and stretched out on its new mattress. Zammis had outgrown even its old mattress, which it now used for a pillow. "Uncle, do you think that we will find anybody beyond the scrub forest?"

"I hope so."

"If we do, will you go with me to Draco?"

"I promised your parent that I would."

"I mean, after. After I make my recitation, what will you do?"

I stared at the fire. "I don't know." I shrugged. "The war might keep us from getting to Draco for a long time."

"After that, what?"

"I suppose I'll go back into the service."

Zammis propped itself up on an elbow. "Go back to being a fighter pilot?"

"Sure. That's about all I know how to do."

"And kill Dracs?"

I put my own sewing down and studied the Drac. Things had changed since Jerry and I had slugged it out—more things than I had realized. I shook my head. "No. I probably won't be a pilot—not a service one.

Maybe I can land a job flying commercial ships." I shrugged. "Maybe the service won't give me any choice."

Zammis sat up, was still for a moment; then it stood, walked over to my mattress and knelt before me on the sand. "Uncle, I don't want to leave you."

"Don't be silly. You'll have your own kind around you. Your grandparent, Gothig, Shigan's siblings, their children—you'll forget all about me."

"Will you forget about me?"

I looked into those yellow eyes, then reached out my hand and touched Zammis's cheek. "No, I won't forget about you. But, remember this, Zammis: you're a Drac and I'm a human, and that's how this part of the universe is divided."

Zammis took my hand from his cheek, spread the fingers and studied them. "Whatever happens, Uncle, I will never forget you."

The ice was gone, and the Drac and I stood in the wind-blown drizzle, packs on our backs, before the grave. Zammis was as tall as I was, which made it a little taller than Jerry. To my relief, the boots fit. Zammis hefted its pack up higher on its shoulders, then turned from the grave and looked out at the sea. I followed Zammis's glance and watched the rollers steam in and smash on the rocks. I looked at the Drac. "What are you thinking about?"

Zammis looked down, then turned toward me. "Uncle, I didn't think of it before, but . . . I will miss this place."

I laughed. "Nonsense! This place?" I slapped the Drac on the shoulder. "Why would you miss this place?"

Zammis looked back out to sea. "I have learned many things here. You have taught me many things here, Uncle. My life happened here."

"Only the beginning, Zammis. You have a life ahead of you." I nodded my head at the grave. "Say good-bye."

Zammis turned toward the grave, stood over it, then knelt to one side and began removing the rocks. After a few moments, it had exposed the hand of a skeleton with three fingers. Zammis nodded, then wept. "I am sorry, Uncle, but I had to do that. This has been nothing but a pile of rocks to me. Now it is more." Zammis replaced the rocks, then stood.

I cocked my head toward the scrub forest. "Go on ahead. I'll catch up in a minute."

"Yes, Uncle."

Zammis moved off toward the naked trees, and I looked down at the grave. "What do you think of Zammis, Jerry? It's bigger than you were. I guess snake agrees with the kid." I squatted next to the grave, picked up a small rock and added it to the pile. "I guess this is it. We're either going to make it to Draco, or die trying." I stood and looked at the sea. "Yeah, I guess I learned a few things here. I'll miss it, in a way." I turned back to the grave and hefted my pack up. *"Eh-devva sahn, Jeriba Shigan.* So long, Jerry."

I turned and followed Zammis into the forest.

The days that followed were full of wonder for Zammis. For now the sky was still the same, dull grey, and the few variations of plant and animal life that we found were nothing remarkable. Once we got beyond the scrub forest, we climbed a gentle rise for a day, and then found ourselves on a wide, flat, endless plain. It was ankle deep in a purple weed that stained our boots the same color. The nights were still too cold for hiking, and we would hole up in the tent. Both the greased tent and suits worked well, keeping out the almost constant rain.

We had been out perhaps two of Fyrine IV's long weeks when we saw it. It screamed overhead, then disappeared over the horizon before either of us could say a word. I had no doubt that the craft I had seen was in landing attitude.

"Uncle! Did it see us?"

I shook my head. "No, I doubt it. But it was landing. Do you hear? It was landing somewhere ahead."

"Uncle?"

"Let's get moving! What is it?"

"Was it a Drac ship, or a human ship?"

I cooled in my tracks. I had never stopped to think about it. I waved my hand. "Come on. It doesn't matter. Either way, you go to Draco. You're a noncombatant, so the USE forces couldn't do anything, and if they're Dracs, you're home free."

We began walking. "But, Uncle, if it's a Drac ship, what will happen to you?"

I shrugged. "Prisoner of war. The Dracs say they abide by the interplanetary war accords, so I should be all right." *Fat chance,* said the back of my head to the front of my head. The big question was whether I preferred being a Drac POW or a permanent resident of Fyrine IV. I had figured that out long ago. "Come on, let's pick up the pace. We don't know how long it will take to get there, or how long it will be on the ground."

Pick 'em up; put 'em down. Except for a few breaks, we didn't stop—even when night came. Our exertion kept us warm. The horizon never seemed to grow nearer. The longer we slogged ahead the duller my mind grew. It must have been days, my mind gone numb as my feet, when I fell through the purple weed into a hole. Immediately, everything grew dark, and I felt a pain in my right leg. I felt the blackout coming, and I welcomed its warmth, its rest, its peace.

"Uncle? Uncle? Wake up! Please, wake up!"

I felt slapping against my face, although it felt somehow detached. Agony thundered into my brain, bringing me wide awake. Damned if I didn't break my leg. I looked up and saw the weedy edges of the hole. My rear end was seated in a trickle of water. Zammis squatted next to me.

"What happened?"

Zammis motioned upwards. "This hole was only covered by a thin crust of dirt and plants. The water must have taken the ground away. Are you all right?"

"My leg. I think I broke it." I leaned my back against the muddy wall. "Zammis, you're going to have to go on by yourself."

"I can't leave you, Uncle!"

"Look, if you find anyone, you can send them back for me."

"What if the water in here comes up?" Zammis felt along my leg until I winced. "I must carry you out of here. What must I do for the leg?"

The kid had a point. Drowning wasn't in my schedule. "We need something stiff. Bind the leg so it doesn't move."

Zammis pulled off its pack, and kneeling in the water and mud, went through its pack, then through the tent roll. Using the tent poles, it wrapped my leg with snakeskins torn from the tent. Then, using more snakeskins, Zammis made two loops, slipped one over each of my legs, then propped me up and slipped the loops over its shoulders. It lifted, and I blacked out.

I was on the ground, covered with the remains of the tent, and Zammis was shaking my arm. "Uncle? Uncle?"

"Yes?" I whispered.

"Uncle, I'm ready to go." It pointed to my side. "Your food is here, and when it rains, just pull the tent over your face. I'll mark the trail I make so I can find my way back."

I nodded. "Take care of yourself."

Zammis shook its head. "Uncle, I can carry you. We shouldn't separate."

I weakly shook my head. "Give me a break, kid. I couldn't make it. Find somebody and bring 'em back." I felt my stomach flip, and cold sweat drenched my snakeskins. "Go on; get going."

Zammis reached out, grabbed its pack and stood. The pack shouldered, Zammis turned and began running in the direction that the craft had been going. I watched until I couldn't see it. I faced up and looked at the clouds. "You almost got me that time, you *kizlode* sonofabitch, but you didn't figure on the Drac . . . you keep forgetting . . . there's two of us . . ." I drifted in and out of consciousness, felt rain on my face, then pulled up the tent and covered my head. In seconds, the blackout returned.

"Davidge? Lieutenant Davidge?"

I opened my eyes and saw something I hadn't seen for four Earth years: a human face. "Who are you?"

The face, young, long, and capped by short blond hair, smiled. "I'm Captain Steerman, the medical officer. How do you feel?"

I pondered the question and smiled. "Like I've been shot full of very high grade junk."

"You have. You were in pretty bad shape by the time the survey team brought you in."

"Survey team?"

"I guess you don't know. The United States of Earth and the Dracon

Chamber have established a joint commission to supervise the colonization of new planets. The war is over."

"Over?"

"Yes."

Something heavy lifted from my chest. "Where's Zammis?"

"Who?"

"Jeriban Zammis; the Drac that I was with."

The doctor shrugged. "I don't know anything about it, but I suppose the Draggers are taking care of it."

Draggers. I'd once used the term myself. As I listened to it coming out of Steerman's mouth, it seemed foreign: alien, repulsive. "Zammis is a Drac, not a Dragger."

The doctor's brows furrowed, then he shrugged. "Of course. Whatever you say. Just you get some rest, and I'll check back on you in a few hours."

"May I see Zammis?"

The doctor smiled. "Dear, no. You're on your way back to the Delphi USEB. The . . . Drac is probably on its way to Draco." He nodded, then turned and left. God, I felt lost. I looked around and saw that I was in the ward of a ship's sick bay. The beds on either side of me were occupied. The man on my right shook his head and went back to reading a magazine. The one on my left looked angry.

"You damned Dragger suck!" He turned on his left side and presented me his back.

Among humans once again, yet more alone than I had ever been. *Misnuuram va siddeth,* as Mistan observed in the *Talman* from the calm perspective of eight hundred years in the past. Loneliness is a thought—not something done to someone; instead, it is something that someone does to oneself. *Jerry shook its head that one time, then pointed a yellow finger at me as the words it wanted to say came together. "Davidge . . . to me loneliness is a discomfort—a small thing to be avoided if possible, but not feared. I think you would almost prefer death to being alone with yourself."*

Misnuuram yaa va nos misnuuram van dunos. "You who are alone by yourselves will forever be alone with others." Mistan again. On its face, the statement appears to be a contradiction; but the test of reality proves it true. I was a stranger among my own kind because of a hate that I didn't share, and a love that, to them, seemed alien, impossible, perverse. *"Peace of thought with others occurs only in the mind at peace with itself."* Mistan again. Countless times, on the voyage to the Delphi Base, putting in my ward time, then during my processing out of the service, I would reach to my chest to grasp the *Talman* that no longer hung there. What had become of Zammis? The USESF didn't care, and the Drac authorities wouldn't say —none of my affair.

Ex-Force pilots were a drag on the employment market, and there were no commercial positions open—especially not to a pilot who hadn't flown in four years, who had a gimpy leg, and who was a Dragger suck. "Dragger suck" as an invective had the impact of several historical terms—Quisling, heretic, fag, nigger lover—all rolled into one.

I had forty-eight thousand credits in back pay, and so money wasn't a problem. The problem was what to do with myself. After kicking around the Delphi Base, I took transportation to Earth and, for several months, was employed by a small book house translating manuscripts into Drac. It seems that there was a craving among Dracs for Westerns: "Stick 'em up *naagusaat!"*

"Nu Geph, lawman." *Thang, thang!* The guns flashed and the *kizlode shaddsaat* bit the *thessa.*

I quit.

I finally called my parents. *Why didn't you call before, Willy? We've been worried sick . . . Had a few things I had to straighten out, Dad . . . No, not really . . . Well, we understand, son . . . It must have been awful . . . Dad, I'd like to come home for a while. . . .*

Even before I put down the money on the used Dearman Electric, I knew I was making a mistake going home. I felt the need of a home, but the one I had left at the age of eighteen wasn't it. But I headed there because there was nowhere else to go.

I drove alone in the dark, using only the old roads, the quiet hum of the Dearman's motor the only sound. The December midnight was clear, and I could see the stars through the car's bubble canopy. Fyrine IV drifted into my thoughts, the raging ocean, the endless winds. I pulled off the road onto the shoulder and killed the lights. In a few minutes, my eyes adjusted to the dark and I stepped outside and shut the door. Kansas has a big sky, and the stars seemed close enough to touch. Snow crunched under my feet as I looked up, trying to pick Fyrine out of the thousands of visible stars.

Fyrine is in the constellation Pegasus, but my eyes were not practiced enough to pick the winged horse out from the surrounding stars. I shrugged, felt a chill, and decided to get back in the car. As I put my hand on the doorlatch, I saw a constellation that I did recognize, north, hanging just above the horizon: Draco. The Dragon, its tail twisted around Ursa Minor, hung upside down in the sky. Eltanin, the Dragon's nose, is the homestar of the Dracs. Its second planet, Draco, was Zammis's home.

Headlights from an approaching car blinded me, and I turned toward the car as it pulled to a stop. The window on the driver's side opened and someone spoke from the darkness.

"You need some help?"

I shook my head. "No, thank you." I held up a hand. "I was just looking at the stars."

"Quite a night, isn't it?"

"Sure is."

"Sure you don't need any help?"

I shook my head. "Thanks . . . wait. Where is the nearest commercial spaceport?"

"About an hour ahead in Salina."

"Thanks." I saw a hand wave from the window, then the other car pulled away. I took another look at Eltanin, then got back in my car.

Six months later, I stood in front of an ancient cut-stone gate wondering what in the hell I was doing. The trip to Draco, with nothing but Dracs as companions on the last leg, showed me the truth in Namvaac's words, "Peace is often only war without fighting." The accords, on paper, gave me the right to travel to the planet, but the Drac bureaucrats and their paperwork wizards had perfected the big stall long before the first human step into space. It took threats, bribes, and long days of filling out forms, being checked and rechecked for disease, contraband, reason for visit, filling out more forms, refilling out the forms I had already filled out, more bribes, waiting, waiting, waiting. . . .

On the ship, I spent most of my time in my cabin, but since the Drac stewards refused to serve me, I went to the ship's lounge for my meals. I sat alone, listening to the comments about me from other booths. I had figured the path of least resistance was to pretend I didn't understand what they were saying. It is always assumed that humans do not speak Drac.

"Must we eat in the same compartment with the *Irkmaan* slime?"

"Look at it, how its pale skin blotches—and that evil-smelling thatch on top. Feh! The smell!"

I ground my teeth a little and kept my glance riveted to my plate.

"It defies the *Talman* that the universe's laws could be so corrupt as to produce a creature such as that."

I turned and faced the three Dracs sitting in the booth across the aisle from mine. In Drac, I replied: "If your line's elders had seen fit to teach the village *kiz* to use contraceptives, you wouldn't even exist." I returned to my food while the two Dracs struggled to hold the third Drac down.

On Draco, it was no problem finding the Jeriba estate. The problem was getting in. A high stone wall enclosed the property, and from the gate, I could see the huge stone mansion that Jerry had described to me. I told the guard at the gate that I wanted to see Jeriba Zammis. The guard stared at me, then went into an alcove behind the gate. In a few moments, another Drac emerged from the mansion and walked quickly across the wide lawn to the gate. The Drac nodded at the guard, then stopped and faced me. It was a dead ringer for Jerry.

"You are the *Irkmaan* that asked to see Jeriba Zammis?"

I nodded. "Zammis must have told you about me. I'm Willis Davidge."

The Drac studied me. "I am Estone Nev, Jeriba Shigan's sibling. My parent, Jeriba Gothig, wishes to see you." The Drac turned abruptly and walked back to the mansion. I followed, feeling heady at the thought of seeing Zammis again. I paid little attention to my surroundings until I was ushered into a large room with a vaulted stone ceiling. Jerry had told me that the house was four thousand years old. I believed it. As I entered, another Drac stood and walked over to me. It was old, but I knew who it was.

"You are Gothig, Shigan's parent."

The yellow eyes studied me. "Who are you, *Irkmaan?*" It held out a wrinkled, three-fingered hand. "What do you know of Jeriba Zammis, and why do you speak the Drac tongue with the style and accent of my child Shigan? What are you here for?"

"I speak Drac in this manner because that is the way Jeriba Shigan taught me to speak it."

The old Drac cocked its head to one side and narrowed its yellow eyes. "You knew my child? How?"

"Didn't the survey commission tell you?"

"It was reported to me that my child, Shigan, was killed in the battle of Fyrine IV. That was over six of our years ago. What is your game, *Irkmaan?*"

I turned from Gothig to Nev. The younger Drac was examining me with the same look of suspicion. I turned back to Gothig. "Shigan wasn't killed in the battle. We were stranded together on the surface of Fyrine IV and lived there for a year. Shigan died giving birth to Jeriba Zammis. A year later the joint survey commission found us and—"

"Enough! Enough of this, *Irkmaan!* Are you here for money, to use my influence for trade concessions—what?"

I frowned. "Where is Zammis?"

Tears of anger came to the old Drac's eyes. "There is no Zammis, *Irkmaan!* The Jeriba line ended with the death of Shigan!"

My eyes grew wide as I shook my head. "That's not true. I know. I took care of Zammis—you heard nothing from the commission?"

"Get to the point of your scheme, *Irkmaan.* I haven't all day."

I studied Gothig. The old Drac had heard nothing from the commission. The Drac authorities took Zammis, and the child had evaporated. Gothig had been told nothing. Why? "I was with Shigan, Gothig. That is how I learned your language. When Shigan died giving birth to Zammis, I—"

"*Irkmaan,* if you cannot get to your scheme, I will have to ask Nev to throw you out. Shigan died in the battle of Fyrine IV. The Drac Fleet notified us only days later."

I nodded. "Then, Gothig, tell me how I came to know the line of Jeriba? Do you wish me to recite it for you?"

Gothig snorted. "You say you know the Jeriba line?"

"Yes."

Gothig flipped a hand at me. "Then, recite."

I took a breath, then began. By the time I had reached the hundred and seventy-third generation, Gothig had knelt on the stone floor next to Nev. The Dracs remained that way for the three hours of the recital. When I concluded, Gothig bowed its head and wept. "Yes, *Irkmaan,* yes. You must have known Shigan. Yes." The old Drac looked up into my face, its eyes wide with hope. "And, you say Shigan continued the line—that Zammis was born?"

I nodded. "I don't know why the commission didn't notify you."

Gothig got to its feet and frowned. "We will find out, *Irkmaan*—what is your name?"

"Davidge. Willis Davidge."

"We will find out, Davidge."

Gothig arranged quarters for me in its house, which was fortunate, since I had little more than eleven hundred credits left. After making a host of inquiries, Gothig sent Nev and me to the Chamber Center in Sendievu, Draco's capital city. The Jeriba line, I found, was influential, and the big stall was held down to a minimum. Eventually, we were directed to the Joint Survey Commission representative, a Drac named Jozzdn Vrule. It looked up from the letter Gothig had given me and frowned. "When did you get this, *Irkmaan?*"

"I believe the signature is on it."

The Drac looked at the paper, then back at me. "The Jeriba line is one of the most respected on Draco. You say that Jeriba Gothig gave you this?"

"I felt certain I said that; I could feel my lips moving—"

Nev stepped in. "You have the dates and the information concerning the Fyrine IV survey mission. We want to know what happened to Jeriba Zammis."

Jozzdn Vrule frowned and looked back at the paper. "Estone Nev, you are the founder of your line, is this not true?"

"It is true."

"Would you found your line in shame? Why do I see you with this *Irkmaan?*"

Nev curled its upper lip and folded its arms. "Jozzdn Vrule, if you contemplate walking this planet in the foreseeable future as a free being, it would be to your profit to stop working your mouth and to start finding Jeriba Zammis."

Jozzdn Vrule looked down and studied its fingers, then returned its glance to Nev. "Very well, Estone Nev. You threaten me if I fail to hand you the truth. I think you will find the truth the greater threat." The Drac scribbled on a piece of paper, then handed it to Nev. "You will find Jeriba Zammis at this address, and you will curse the day that I gave you this."

We entered the imbecile colony feeling sick. All around us, Dracs stared with vacant eyes, or screamed, or foamed at the mouth, or behaved as lower-order creatures. After we had arrived, Gothig joined us. The Drac director of the colony frowned at me and shook its head at Gothig. "Turn back now, while it is still possible, Jeriba Gothig. Beyond this room lies nothing but pain and sorrow."

Gothig grabbed the director by the front of its wraps. "Hear me, insect: If Jeriba Zammis is within these walls, bring my grandchild forth! Else, I shall bring the might of the Jeriba line down upon your pointed head!"

The director lifted its head, twitched its lips, then nodded. "Very well. Very well, you pompous *Kazzmidth!* We tried to protect the Jeriba reputation. We tried! But now you shall see." The director nodded and pursed its lips. "Yes, you overwealthy fashion follower, now you shall see." The director scribbled on a piece of paper, then handed it to Nev. "By giving you that, I will lose my position, but take it! Yes, take it! See this being you call Jeriba Zammis. See it, and weep!"

Among trees and grass, Jeriba Zammis sat upon a stone bench, staring at the ground. Its eyes never blinked, its hands never moved. Gothig frowned at me, but I could spare nothing for Shigan's parent. I walked to Zammis. "Zammis, do you know me?"

The Drac retrieved its thoughts from a million warrens and raised its yellow eyes to me. I saw no sign of recognition. "Who are you?"

I squatted down, placed my hands on its arms and shook them. "Dammit, Zammis, don't you know me? I'm your uncle. Remember that? Uncle Davidge?"

The Drac weaved on the bench, then shook its head. It lifted an arm and waved to an orderly. "I want to go to my room. Please, let me go to my room."

I stood and grabbed Zammis by the front of its hospital gown. "Zammis, it's me!"

The yellow eyes, dull and lifeless, stared back at me. The orderly placed a yellow hand upon my shoulder. "Let it go, *Irkmaan.*"

"Zammis!" I turned to Nev and Gothig. "Say something!"

The Drac orderly pulled a sap from its pocket, then slapped it suggestively against the palm of its hand. "Let it go, *Irkmaan.*"

Gothig stepped forward. "Explain this!"

The orderly looked at Gothig, Nev, me, and then Zammis. "This one—this creature—came to us professing a love, a *love,* mind you, of humans! This is no small perversion, Jeriba Gothig. The government would protect you from this scandal. Would you wish the line of Jeriba dragged into this?"

I looked at Zammis. "What have you done to Zammis, you *kizlode* sonofabitch? A little shock? A little drug? Rot out its mind?"

The orderly sneered at me, then shook its head. "You, *Irkmaan,* do not understand. This one would not be happy as an *Irkmaan vul*—a human lover. We are making it possible for this one to function in Drac society. You think this is wrong?"

I looked at Zammis and shook my head. I remembered too well my treatment at the hands of my fellow humans. "No. I don't think it's wrong . . . I just don't know."

The orderly turned to Gothig. "Please understand, Jeriba Gothig. We could not subject the Jeriba Line to this disgrace. Your grandchild is almost well and will soon enter a reeducation program. In no more than two years, you will have a grandchild worthy of carrying on the Jeriba line. Is this wrong?"

Gothig only shook its head. I squatted down in front of Zammis and looked up into its yellow eyes. I reached up and took its right hand in both of mine. "Zammis?"

Zammis looked down, moved its left hand over and picked up my left hand and spread the fingers. One at a time Zammis pointed at the fingers of my hand, then it looked into my eyes, then examined the hand again. "Yes . . ." Zammis pointed again. "One, two, three, *four, five!*" Zammis looked into my eyes. "Four, five!"

I nodded. "Yes. Yes."

Zammis pulled my hand to its cheek and held it close. "Uncle . . . Uncle. I told you I'd never forget you."

I never counted the years that passed. My beard was back, and I knelt in my snakeskins next to the grave of my friend, Jeriba Shigan. Next to the grave was the four-year-old grave of Gothig. I replaced some rocks, then added a few more. Wrapping my snakeskins tightly against the wind, I sat down next to the grave and looked out to sea. Still the rollers steamed in under the grey-black cover of clouds. Soon, the ice would come. I nodded, looked at my scarred, wrinkled hands, then back at the grave.

"I couldn't stay in the settlement with them, Jerry. Don't get me wrong; it's nice. Damned nice. But I kept looking out my window, seeing the ocean, thinking of the cave. I'm alone, in a way. But it's good. I know what and who I am, Jerry, and that's all there is to it, right?"

I heard a noise. I crouched over, placed my hands upon my withered knees, and pushed myself to my feet. The Drac was coming from the settlement compound, a child in its arms.

I rubbed my beard. "Eh, Ty, so that is your first child?"

The Drac nodded. "I would be pleased, Uncle, if you would teach it what it must be taught: the line, the *Talman;* and about life on Fyrine IV, our planet called 'Friendship.' "

I took the bundle into my arms. Chubby three-fingered arms waved at the air, then grasped my snakeskins. "Yes, Ty, this one is a Jeriba." I looked up at Ty. "And how is your parent, Zammis?"

Ty shrugged. "It is as well as can be expected. My parent wishes you well."

I nodded. "And the same to it, Ty. Zammis ought to get out of that air-conditioned capsule and come back to live in the cave. It'll do it good."

Ty grinned and nodded its head. "I will tell my parent, Uncle."

I stabbed my thumb into my chest. "Look at me! You don't see me sick, do you?"

"No, Uncle."

"You tell Zammis to kick that doctor out of there and to come back to the cave, hear?"

"Yes, Uncle." Ty smiled. "Is there anything you need?"

I nodded and scratched the back of my neck. "Toilet paper. Just a couple of packs. Maybe a couple of bottles of whiskey—no, forget the whiskey. I'll wait until Haesni, here, puts in its first year. Just the toilet paper."

Ty bowed. "Yes, Uncle, and may the many mornings find you well."

I waved my hand impatiently. "They will, they will. Just don't forget the toilet paper."

Ty bowed again. "I won't, Uncle."

Ty turned and walked through the scrub forest back to the colony. Gothig had put up the cash and moved the entire line, and all the related lines, to Fyrine IV. I lived with them for a year, but I moved out and went back to the cave. I gathered the wood, smoked the snake, and withstood the winter. Zammis gave me the young Ty to rear in the cave, and now Ty had handed me Haesni. I nodded at the child. "Your child will be called Gothig, and then . . ." I looked at the sky and felt the tears drying on my face. ". . . and then, Gothig's child will be called Shigan." I nodded and headed for the cleft that would bring us down to the level of the cave.

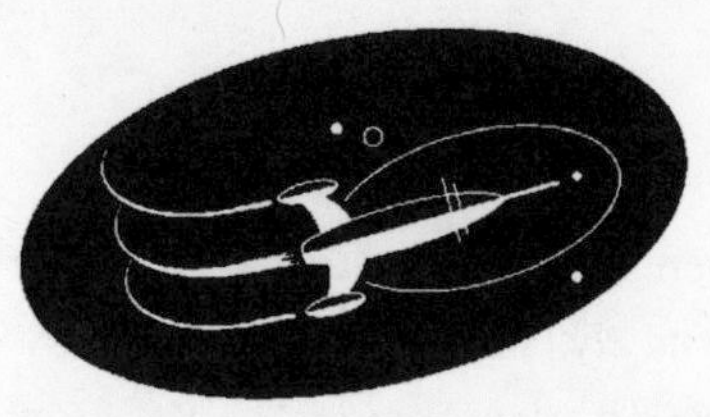

THE SATURN GAME

Poul Anderson

If we are to understand what happened, which is vital if we are to avoid repeated and worse tragedies in the future, we must begin by dismissing all accusations. Nobody was negligent; no action was foolish. For who could have predicted the eventuality, or recognized its nature, until too late? Rather should we appreciate the spirit with which those people struggled against disaster, inward and outward, after they knew. The fact is that thresholds exist throughout reality, and that things on their far sides are altogether different from things on their hither sides. The *Chronos* crossed more than an abyss, it crossed a threshold of human experience.

—Francis L. Minamoto, *Death Under Saturn: A Dissenting View* (Apollo University Communications, Leyburg, Luna, 2057)

I

"The City of Ice is now on my horizon," *Kendrick says. Its towers gleam blue.* "My griffin spreads his wings to glide." *Wind whistles among those great, rainbow-shimmering pinions. His cloak blows back from his shoulders; the air strikes through his ring-mail and sheathes him in cold.* "I lean over and peer after you." *The spear in his left hand counterbalances him. Its head flickers palely with the moonlight that Wayland Smith hammered into the steel.*

"Yes, I see the griffin," *Ricia tells him,* "high and far, like a comet above the courtyard walls. I run out from under the portico for a better look. A guard tries to stop me, grabs my sleeve, but I tear the spider silk apart and dash forth into the open." *The elven castle wavers as if its sculptured ice were turning to smoke. Passionately, she cries,* "Is it in truth you, my darling?"

"Hold, there!" *warns Alvarlan from his cave of arcana ten thousand leagues away.* "I send your mind the message that if the King suspects this is Sir Kendrick of the Isles, he will raise a dragon against him, or spirit you off beyond any chance of rescue. Go back, Princess of Maranoa. Pretend you decide that it is only an eagle. I will cast a belief-spell on your words."

"I stay far aloft," *Kendrick says.* "Save he use a scrying stone, the Elf King will not be aware this beast has a rider. From here I'll spy out city and castle." *And then—? He knows not. He knows simply that he must set her free or die in the quest. How long will it take him, how many more nights will she lie in the King's embrace?*

"I thought you were supposed to spy out Iapetus," Mark Danzig interrupted.

His dry tone startled the three others into alertness. Jean Broberg flushed with embarrassment, Colin Scobie with irritation; Luis Garcilaso shrugged, grinned, and turned his gaze to the pilot console before which he sat harnessed. For a moment silence filled the cabin, and shadows, and radiance from the universe.

To help observation, all lights were out except a few dim glows from the instruments. The sunward ports were lidded. Elsewhere thronged stars, so many and so brilliant that they well-nigh drowned the blackness which held them. The Milky Way was a torrent of silver. One port framed Saturn at half phase, dayside pale gold and rich bands amidst the jewelry of its rings, nightside wanly ashimmer with starlight upon clouds, as big to the sight as Earth over Luna.

Forward was Iapetus. The spacecraft rotated while orbiting the moon, to maintain a steady optical field. It had crossed the dawn line, presently at the middle of the inward-facing hemisphere. Thus it had left bare, crater-pocked land behind it in the dark, and was passing above sunlit glacier country. Whiteness dazzled, glittered in sparks and shards of color, reached fantastic shapes heavenward; cirques, crevasses, caverns brimmed with blue.

"I'm sorry," Jean Broberg whispered. "It's too beautiful, unbelievably beautiful, and . . . almost like the place where our game had brought us. Took us by surprise—"

"Huh!" Mark Danzig said. "You had a pretty good idea of what to expect, therefore you made your play go in the direction of something that resembled it. Don't tell me any different. I've watched these acts for eight years."

Colin Scobie made a savage gesture. Spin and gravity were too slight to give noticeable weight, and his movement sent him flying through the air, across the crowded cabin. He checked himself by a handhold just short of the chemist. "Are you calling Jean a liar?" he growled.

Most times he was cheerful, in a bluff fashion. Perhaps because of that, he suddenly appeared menacing. He was a big, sandy-haired man in his mid-thirties; a coverall did not disguise the muscles beneath, and the scowl on his face brought forth its ruggedness.

"Please!" Broberg exclaimed. "Not a quarrel, Colin."

The geologist glanced back at her. She was slender and fine-featured. At her age of forty-two, despite longevity treatment, the reddish-brown hair that fell to her shoulders was becoming streaked with white, and lines were engraved around large gray eyes.

"Mark is right," she sighed. "We're here to do science, not daydream." She reached forth to touch Scobie's arm, smiling shyly. "You're still full of your Kendrick persona, aren't you? Gallant, protective—" She stopped. Her voice had quickened with more than a hint of Ricia. She covered her lips and flushed again. A tear broke free and sparkled off on air currents. She forced a laugh. "But I'm just physicist Broberg, wife of astronomer Tom, mother of Johnnie and Billy."

Her glance went Saturnward, as if seeking the ship where her family waited. She might have spied it, too, as a star that moved among stars by the solar sail. However, that was now furled, and naked vision could not find even such huge hulls as *Chronos* possessed, across millions of kilometers.

Luis Garcilaso asked from his pilot's chair: "What harm if we carry on our little *commedia dell' arte?*" His Arizona drawl soothed the ear. "We won't be landin' for a while yet, and everything's on automatic till then." He was small, swarthy, and deft, still in his twenties.

Danzig twisted his leathery countenance into a frown. At sixty, thanks to his habits as well as to longevity, he kept springiness in a lank frame; he could joke about wrinkles and encroaching baldness. In this hour, he set humor aside.

"Do you mean you don't know what's the matter?" His beak of a nose pecked at a scanner screen which magnified the moonscape. "Almighty God! That's a new world we're about to touch down on—tiny, but a world, and strange in ways we can't guess. Nothing's been here before us except one unmanned flyby and one unmanned lander that soon quit sending. We can't rely on meters and cameras alone. We've got to use our eyes and brains."

He addressed Scobie. "You should realize that in your bones, Colin, if nobody else aboard does. You've worked on Luna as well as on Earth. In spite of all the settlements, in spite of all the study that's been done, did you never hit any nasty surprises?"

The burly man had recovered his temper. Into his own voice came a softness that recalled the serenity of the Idaho mountains from which he hailed. "True," he admitted. "There's no such thing as having too much information when you're off Earth, or enough information, for that matter." He paused. "Nevertheless, timidity can be as dangerous as rashness—not that you're timid, Mark," he added in haste. "Why, you and Rachel could've been in a nice O'Neill on a nice pension—"

Danzig relaxed and smiled. "This was a challenge, if I may sound pompous. Just the same, we want to get home when we're finished here. We should be in time for the Bar Mitzvah of a great-grandson or two. Which requires staying alive."

"My point is," Scobie said, "if you let yourself get buffaloed, you may end up in a worse bind than— Oh, never mind. You're probably right, and we should not have begun fantasizing. The spectacle sort of grabbed us. It won't happen again."

Yet when Scobie's eyes looked anew on the glacier, they had not quite the dispassion of a scientist in them. Nor did Broberg's or Garcilaso's. Danzig slammed fist into palm. "The game, the damned childish game," he muttered, too low for his companions to hear. "Was nothing saner possible for them?"

⋙ II ⋘

Was nothing saner possible for them? Perhaps not.

If we are to answer the question, we should first review some history. When early industrial operations in space offered the hope of rescuing civilization, and Earth, from ruin, then greater knowledge of sister planets, prior to their development, became a clear necessity. The effort started with Mars, the least hostile. No natural law forbade sending small manned spacecraft yonder. What did was the absurdity of using as much fuel, time, and effort as were required, in order that three or four persons might spend a few days in a single locality.

Construction of the *J. Peter Vajk* took longer and cost more, but paid off when it, virtually a colony, spread its immense solar sail and took a thousand people to their goal in half a year and in comparative comfort. The payoff grew overwhelming when they, from orbit, launched Earthward the beneficiated minerals of Phobos that they did not need for their own purposes. Those purposes, of course, turned on the truly thorough, long-term study of Mars, and included landings of auxiliary craft, for ever lengthier stays, all over the surface.

Sufficient to remind you of this much; no need to detail the triumphs of the same basic concept throughout the inner Solar System, as far as Jupiter. The tragedy of the *Vladimir* became a reason to try again for Mercury, and, in a left-handed, political way, pushed the Britannic-American consortium into its *Chronos* project.

They named the ship better than they knew. Sailing time to Saturn was eight years.

Not only the scientists must be healthy, lively-minded people. Crewfolk, technicians, medics, constables, teachers, clergy, entertainers—every element of an entire community must be. Each must command more than a single skill, for emergency backup, and keep those skills alive by regular, tedious rehearsal. The environment was limited and austere; communication with home was soon a matter of beamcasts; cosmopolitans found themselves in what amounted to an isolated village. What were they to *do?*

Assigned tasks. Civic projects, especially work on improving the interior of the vessel. Research, or writing a book, or the study of a subject, or sports, or hobby clubs, or service and handicraft enterprises, or more private interactions, or—There was a wide choice of television tapes, but Central Control made sets usable for only three hours in twenty-four. You dared not get into the habit of passivity.

Individuals grumbled, squabbled, formed and dissolved cliques, formed and dissolved marriages or less explicit relationships, begot and raised occasional children, worshiped, mocked, learned, yearned, and for the most part found reasonable satisfaction in life. But for some, including a large proportion of the gifted, what made the difference between this and misery were their psychodramas.

—Minamoto

Dawn crept past the ice, out onto the rock. It was a light both dim and harsh, yet sufficient to give Garcilaso the last data he wanted for descent.

The hiss of the motor died away. A thump shivered through the hull, landing jacks leveled it, and stillness fell. The crew did not speak for a while. They were staring out at Iapetus.

Immediately around them was desolation like that which reigns in much of the Solar System. A darkling plain curved visibly away to a horizon that, at man-height, was a bare three kilometers distant; higher up in the cabin, you could see farther, but that only sharpened the sense of being on a minute ball awhirl among the stars. The ground was thinly covered with cosmic dust and gravel; here and there a minor crater or an upthrust mass lifted out of the regolith to cast long, knife-edged, utterly black shadows. Light reflections lessened the number of visible stars, turning heaven into a bowlful of night. Halfway between the zenith and the south, half-Saturn and its rings made the vista beautiful.

Likewise did the glacier—or the glaciers? Nobody was sure. The sole knowledge was that, seen from afar, Iapetus gleamed bright at the western end of its orbit and grew dull at the eastern end, because one side was covered with whitish material while the other side was not; the dividing line passed nearly beneath the planet which it eternally faced. The probes from *Chronos* had reported that the layer was thick, with puzzling spectra that varied from place to place, and little more about it.

In this hour, four humans gazed across pitted emptiness and saw wonder rear over the world-rim. From north to south went ramparts, battlements, spires, depths, peaks, cliffs, their shapes and shadings an infinity of fantasies. On the right Saturn cast soft amber, but that was nearly lost in the glare from the east, where a sun dwarfed almost to stellar size nonetheless blazed too fierce to look at, just above the summit. There the silvery sheen exploded in brilliance, diamond-glitter of shattered light, chill blues and greens; dazzled to tears, eyes saw the vision glimmer and waver, as if it bordered on dreamland, or on Faerie. But despite all delicate intricacies, underneath was a sense of chill and of brutal mass; here dwelt also the Frost Giants.

Broberg was the first to breathe forth a word. "The City of Ice."

"Magic," said Garcilaso as low. "My spirit could lose itself forever, wanderin' yonder. I'm not sure I'd mind. My cave is nothin' like this, nothin'—"

"Wait a minute!" snapped Danzig in alarm.

"Oh, yes. Curb the imagination, please." Though Scobie was quick to utter sobrieties, they sounded drier than needful. "We know from probe transmissions that the scarp is, well, Grand Canyon-like. Sure, it's more spectacular than we realized, which I suppose makes it still more of a mystery." He turned to Broberg. "I've never seen ice or snow as sculptured as this. Have you, Jean? You've mentioned visiting a lot of mountain and winter scenery when you were a girl in Canada."

The physicist shook her head. "No. Never. It doesn't seem possible. What could have done it? There's no weather here . . . is there?"

"Perhaps the same phenomenon is responsible that laid a hemisphere bare," Danzig suggested.

"Or that covered a hemisphere," Scobie said. "An object seventeen hundred kilometers across shouldn't have gases, frozen or otherwise. Unless it's a ball of such stuff clear through, like a comet, which we know it's not." As if to demonstrate, he unclipped a pair of pliers from a nearby tool rack, tossed it, and caught it on its slow way down. His own ninety kilos of mass weighed about seven. For that, the satellite must be essentially rocky.

Garcilaso registered impatience. "Let's stop tradin' facts and theories we already know about, and start findin' answers."

Rapture welled in Broberg. "Yes, let's get out. Over *there.*"

"Hold on," protested Danzig as Garcilaso and Scobie nodded eagerly. "You can't be serious. Caution, step-by-step advance—"

"No, it's too wonderful for that." Broberg's tone shivered.

"Yeah, to hell with fiddlin' around," Garcilaso said. "We need at least a preliminary scout right away."

The furrows deepened in Danzig's visage. "You mean you too, Luis? But you're our pilot!"

"On the ground I'm general assistant, chief cook, and bottle washer to you scientists. Do you think I want to sit idle, with somethin' like that to explore?" Garcilaso calmed his voice. "Besides, if I should come to grief, any of you can fly back, given a bit of radio talk from *Chronos* and a final approach under remote control."

"It's quite reasonable, Mark," Scobie argued. "Contrary to doctrine, true; but doctrine was made for us, not vice versa. A short distance, low gravity, and we'll be on the lookout for hazards. The point is, until we have some notion of what that ice is like, we don't know what the devil to pay attention to in this vicinity, either. No, first we'll take a quick jaunt. When we return, then we'll plan."

Danzig stiffened. "May I remind you, if anything goes wrong, help is at least a hundred hours away? An auxiliary like this can't boost any higher if it's to get back, and it'd take longer than that to disengage the big boats from Saturn and Titan."

Scobie reddened at the implied insult.

"And may I remind you, on the ground I am the captain. I say an immediate reconnaissance is safe and desirable. Stay behind if you want—In fact, yes, you must. Doctrine is right in saying the vessel mustn't be deserted."

Danzig studied him for several seconds before murmuring, "Luis goes, though, is that it?"

"Yes!" cried Garcilaso so that the cabin rang.

Broberg patted Danzig's limp hand. "It's okay, Mark," she said gently. "We'll bring back samples for you to study. After that, I wouldn't be surprised but what the best ideas about procedure will be yours."

He shook his head. Suddenly he looked very tired. "No," he replied in a monotone, "that won't happen. You see, I'm only a hardnosed industrial chemist who saw this expedition as a chance to do interesting research. The whole way through space, I kept myself busy with ordinary affairs, including, you remember, a couple of inventions I'd wanted the leisure to develop. You three, you're younger, you're romantics—"

"Aw, come off it, Mark." Scobie tried to laugh. "Maybe Jean and Luis are, a little, but me, I'm about as otherworldly as a plate of haggis."

"You played the game, year after year, until at last the game started playing you. That's what's going on this minute, no matter how you rationalize your motives." Danzig's gaze on the geologist, who was his friend, lost the defiance that had been in it and turned wistful. "You might try recalling Delia Ames."

Scobie bristled. "What about her? The business was hers and mine, nobody else's."

"Except afterward she cried on Rachel's shoulder, and Rachel doesn't keep secrets from me. Don't worry, I'm not about to blab. Anyhow, Delia got over it. But if you'd recollect objectively, you'd see what had happened to you already, three years ago."

Scobie set his jaw. Danzig smiled in the left corner of his mouth. "No, I suppose you can't," he went on. "I admit I had no idea either, till now, how far the process had gone. At least keep your fantasies in the background while you're outside, will you? Can you?"

In half a decade of travel, Scobie's apartment had become idiosyncratically his—perhaps more so than was usual, since he remained a bachelor who seldom had women visitors for longer than a few nightwatches at a time. Much of the furniture he had made himself; the agrosections of *Chronos* produced wood, hide, and fiber as well as food and fresh air. His handiwork ran to massiveness and archaic carved decorations. Most of what he wanted to read he screened from the data banks, of course, but a shelf held a few old books—Child's border ballads, an eighteenth-century family Bible (despite his agnosticism), a copy of *The Machinery of Freedom* which had nearly disintegrated but displayed the signature of the author, and other valued miscellany. Above them stood a model of a sailboat in which he had cruised northern European waters, and a trophy he had won in handball aboard this ship. On the bulkheads hung his fencing sabers and numerous pictures—of parents and siblings, of wilderness areas he had tramped on Earth, of castles and mountains and heaths in Scotland where he had often been, of his geological team on Luna, of Thomas Jefferson and, imagined, Robert the Bruce.

On a certain evenwatch he had, though, been seated before his telescreen. Lights were turned low in order that he might fully savor the image. Auxiliary craft were out in a joint exercise, and a couple of their personnel used the opportunity to beam back views of what they saw.

That was splendor. Starful space made a chalice for *Chronos*. The two huge, majestically counter-rotating cylinders, the entire complex of linkages, ports, locks, shields, collectors, transmitters, docks, all became Japanesely exquisite at a distance of several hundred kilometers. It was the solar sail which filled most of the screen, like a turning golden sunwheel; yet remote vision could also appreciate its spiderweb intricacy, soaring and subtle curvatures, even the less-than-gossamer thinness. A mightier work than the Pyramids, a finer work than a refashioned chromosome, the ship moved on toward a Saturn which had become the second brightest beacon in the firmament.

The doorchime hauled Scobie out of his exaltation. As he started across the deck, he stubbed his toe on a table leg. Coriolis force caused that. It was slight, when a hull this size spun to give a full gee of weight, and a thing to which he had long since adapted; but now and then he got so interested in something that Terrestrial habits returned. He swore at his absent-mindedness, good-naturedly, since he anticipated a pleasurable time.

When he opened the door, Delia Ames entered in a single stride. At once she closed it behind her and stood braced against it. She was a tall blond woman who did electronics maintenance and kept up a number of outside activities. "Hey!" Scobie said. "What's wrong? You look like"—he tried for levity—"something my cat would've dragged in, if we had any mice or beached fish aboard."

She drew a ragged breath. Her Australian accent thickened till he had trouble understanding: "I . . . today . . . I happened to be at the same cafeteria table as George Harding—"

Unease tingled through Scobie. Harding worked in Ames's department, but had much more in common with him. In the game group to which they both belonged, Harding likewise took a vaguely ancestral role, N'Kuma the Lionslayer.

"What happened?" Scobie asked.

Woe stared back at him. "He mentioned . . . you and he and the rest . . . you'd be taking your next holiday together . . . to carry on your, your bloody act uninterrupted."

"Well, yes. Work at the new park over in Starboard Hull will be suspended till enough metal's been recycled for the water pipes. The area will be vacant, and my gang has arranged to spend a week's worth of days—"

"But you and I were going to Lake Armstrong!"

"Uh, wait, that was just a notion we talked about, no definite plan yet, and this is such an unusual chance— Later, sweetheart, I'm sorry." He took her hands. They felt cold. He essayed a smile. "Now, c'mon, we were going to cook a festive dinner together and afterward spend a, shall we say, quiet evening at home. But for a start, this absolutely gorgeous presentation on the screen—"

She jerked free of him. The gesture seemed to calm her. "No, thanks," she said, flat-voiced. "Not when you'd rather be with that Broberg woman. I only came by to tell you in person I'm getting out of the way of you two."

"*Huh?*" He stepped back. "What the flaming hell do you mean?"

"You know jolly well."

"I don't! She, I, she's happily married, got two kids, she's older than me, we're friends, sure, but there's never been a thing between us that wasn't in the open and on the level—" Scobie swallowed. "You suppose maybe I'm in love with her?"

Ames looked away. Her fingers writhed together. "I'm not about to go on being a mere convenience to you, Colin. You have plenty of those. Myself, I'd hoped— But I was wrong, and I'm going to cut my losses before they get worse."

"But . . . Dee, I swear I haven't fallen for anybody else, and I . . . I swear you're more than a body to me, you're a fine person—" She stood mute and withdrawn. Scobie gnawed his lip before he could tell her: "Okay, I admit it, the main reason I volunteered for this trip was I'd lost out in a love affair on Earth. Not that the project doesn't interest me, but I've come to realize what a big chunk out of my life it is. You, more than any other woman, Dee, you've gotten me to feel better about the situation."

She grimaced. "But not as much as your psychodrama has, right?"

"Hey, you must think I'm obsessed with the game. I'm not. It's fun and —oh, maybe 'fun' is too weak a word—but anyhow, it's just little bunches of people getting together fairly regularly to play. Like my fencing, or a chess club, or, or anything."

She squared her shoulders. "Well, then," she asked, "will you cancel the date you've made and spend your holiday with me?"

"I, uh, I can't do that. Not at this stage. Kendrick isn't off on the periphery of current events. He's closely involved with everybody else. If I didn't show, it'd spoil things for the rest."

Her glance steadied upon him. "Very well. A promise is a promise, or so I imagined. But afterward— Don't be afraid. I'm not trying to trap you. That would be no good, would it? However, if I maintain this liaison of ours, will you phase yourself out of your game?"

"I can't—" Anger seized him. "No, God damn it!" he roared.

"Then good-bye, Colin," she said, and departed. He stared for minutes at the door she had shut behind her.

Unlike the large Titan and Saturn-vicinity explorers, landers on the airless moons were simply modified Luna-to-space shuttles, reliable, but with limited capabilities. When the blocky shape had dropped below the horizon, Garcilaso said into his radio, "We've lost sight of the boat, Mark. I must say it improves the view." One of the relay microsatellites which had been sown in orbit passed his words on.

"Better start blazing your trail, then," Danzig reminded.

"My, my, you *are* a fussbudget, aren't you?" Nevertheless, Garcilaso unholstered the squirt gun at his hip and splashed a vividly fluorescent circle of paint on the ground. He would do it at eyeball intervals until his party reached the glacier. Except where dust lay thick over the regolith, footprints were faint under the feeble gravity, and absent when a walker crossed continuous rock.

Walker? No, leaper. The three bounded exultant, little hindered by spacesuits, life-support units, tool and ration packs. The naked land fled from their haste, and ever higher, ever clearer and more glorious to see, loomed the ice ahead of them.

There was no describing it, not really. You could speak of lower slopes and palisades above, to a mean height of perhaps a hundred meters, with spires towering farther still. You could speak of gracefully curved tiers going up those braes, of lacy parapets and fluted crags and arched openings to caves filled with wonders, of mysterious blues in the depths and greens where light streamed through translucencies, of gem-sparkle across whiteness where radiance and shadow wove mandalas—and none of it would convey anything more than Scobie's earlier, altogether inadequate comparison to the Grand Canyon.

"Stop," he said for the dozenth time. "I want to take a few pictures."

"Will anybody understand them who hasn't been here?" whispered Broberg.

"Probably not," said Garcilaso in the same hushed tone. "Maybe no one but us ever will."

"What do you mean by that?" demanded Danzig's voice.

"Never mind," snapped Scobie.

"I think I know," the chemist said. "Yes, it is a great piece of scenery, but you're letting it hypnotize you."

"If you don't cut out that drivel," Scobie warned, "we'll cut you out of the circuit. Damn it, we've got work to do. Get off our backs."

Danzig gusted a sigh. "Sorry. Uh, are you finding any clues to the nature of that—that thing?"

Scobie focused his camera. "Well," he said, partly mollified, "the different shades and textures, and no doubt the different shapes, seem to confirm what the reflection spectra from the flyby suggested. The composition is a mixture, or a jumble, or both, of several materials, and varies from place to place. Water ice is obvious, but I feel sure of carbon dioxide too, and I'd bet on ammonia, methane, and presumably lesser amounts of other stuff."

"Methane? Could that stay solid at ambient temperatures, in a vacuum?"

"We'll have to find out for sure. However, I'd guess that most of the time it's cold enough, at least for methane strata that occur down inside where there's pressure on them."

Within the vitryl globe of her helmet, Broberg's features showed delight. "Wait!" she cried. "I have an idea—about what happened to the probe that landed." She drew a breath. "It came down almost at the foot of the glacier, you recall. Our view of the site from space seemed to indicate that an avalanche buried it, but we couldn't understand how that might have been triggered. Well, suppose a methane layer at exactly the wrong location melted. Heat radiation from the jets may have warmed it, and later the radar beam used to map contours added the last few degrees necessary. The stratum flowed, and down came everything that had rested on top of it."

"Plausible," Scobie said. "Congratulations, Jean."

"Nobody thought of the possibility in advance?" Garcilaso scoffed. "What kind of scientists have we got along?"

"The kind who were being overwhelmed by work after we reached Saturn, and still more by data input," Scobie answered. "The universe is bigger than you or anybody can realize, hotshot."

"Oh. Sure. No offense." Garcilaso's glance returned to the ice. "Yes, we'll never run out of mysteries, will we?"

"Never." Broberg's eyes glowed enormous. "At the heart of things will always be magic. The Elf King rules—"

Scobie returned his camera to its pouch. "Stow the gab and move on," he ordered curtly.

His gaze locked for an instant with Broberg's. In the weird, mingled light, it could be seen that she went pale, then red, before she sprang off beside him.

Ricia had gone alone into Moonwood on Midsummer Eve. The King found her there and took her unto him as she had hoped. Ecstasy became terror when he afterward bore her off; yet her captivity in the City of Ice brought her many more such hours, and beauties and marvels unknown among mortals. Alvarlan, her mentor, sent his spirit in quest of her, and was himself beguiled by what he found. It was an effort of will for him to tell Sir Kendrick of the Isles where she was, albeit he pledged his help in freeing her.

N'Kuma the Lionslayer, Béla of Eastmarch, Karina Far West, Lady Aurelia, Olav Harpmaster had none of them been present when this happened.

The glacier (a wrong name for something that might have no counterpart in the Solar System) lifted off the plain as abruptly as a wall. Standing there, the three could no longer see the heights. They could, though, see that the slope which curved steeply upward to a filigree-topped edge was not smooth. Shadows lay blue in countless small craters. The sun had climbed just sufficiently high to beget them; a Iapetan day is more than seventy-nine of Earth's.

Danzig's question crackled in their earphones: "Now are you satisfied? Will you come back before a fresh landslide catches you?"

"It won't," Scobie replied. "We aren't a vehicle, and the local configuration has clearly been stable for centuries or better. Besides, what's the point of a manned expedition if nobody investigates anything?"

"I'll see if I can climb," Garcilaso offered.

"No, wait," Scobie commanded. "I've had experience with mountains and snowpacks, for whatever that may be worth. Let me work out a route for us first."

"You're going onto that stuff, the whole gaggle of you?" exploded Danzig. "Have you completely lost your minds?"

Scobie's brow and lips tightened. "Mark, I warn you again, if you don't get your emotions under control, we'll cut you off. We'll hike on a ways if I decide it's safe."

He paced back and forth, in floating low-weight fashion, while he surveyed the jökull. Layers and blocks of distinct substances were plain to see, like separate ashlars laid by an elvish mason—where they were not so huge that a giant must have been at work. The craterlets might be sentry posts on this lowest embankment of the City's defenses. . . .

Garcilaso, most vivacious of men, stood motionless and let his vision lose itself in the sight. Broberg knelt down to examine the ground, but her own gaze kept wandering aloft.

Finally she beckoned. "Colin, come over here, please," she said. "I believe I've made a discovery."

Scobie joined her. As she rose, she scooped a handful of fine black particles off the shards on which she stood and let it trickle from her glove. "I suspect this is the reason the boundary of the ice is sharp," she told him.

"What is?" Danzig inquired from afar. He got no answer.

"I noticed more and more dust as we went along," Broberg continued. "If it fell on patches and lumps of frozen stuff, isolated from the main mass, and covered them, it would absorb solar heat till they melted or, likelier, sublimed. Even water molecules would escape to space, in this weak gravity. The main mass was too big for that; square-cube law. Dust grains there would simply melt their way down a short distance, then be covered as surrounding material collapsed on them, and the process would stop."

"H'm." Scobie raised a hand to stroke his chin, encountered his helmet, and sketched a grin at himself. "Sounds reasonable. But where did so much dust come from—and the ice, for that matter?"

"I think—" Her voice dropped until he could barely hear, and her look went the way of Garcilaso's. His remained upon her face, profiled against stars. "I think this bears out your comet hypothesis, Colin. A comet struck Iapetus. It came from the direction it did because it got so near Saturn that it was forced to swing in a hairpin bend around the planet. It was enormous; the ice of it covered almost a hemisphere, in spite of much more being vaporized and lost. The dust is partly from it, partly generated by the impact."

He clasped her armored shoulder. "*Your* theory, Jean. I was not the first to propose a comet, but you're the first to corroborate with details."

She didn't appear to notice, except that she murmured further: "Dust can account for the erosion that made those lovely formations, too. It caused differential melting and sublimation on the surface, according to the patterns it happened to fall in and the mixes of ices it clung to, until it was washed away or encysted. The craters, these small ones and the major ones we've observed from above, they have a separate but similar origin. Meteorites—"

"Whoa, there," he objected. "Any sizable meteorite would release enough energy to steam off most of the entire field."

"I know. Which shows the comet collision was recent, less than a thousand years ago, or we wouldn't be seeing this miracle today. Nothing big has since happened to strike, yet. I'm thinking of little stones, cosmic sand, in prograde orbits around Saturn so that they hit with low relative speed. Most simply make dimples in the ice. Lying there, however, they collect solar heat because they're dark, and re-radiate it to melt away their surroundings, till they sink beneath. The concavities they leave reflect incident radiation from side to side, and thus continue to grow. The pothole effect. And again, because the different ices have different properties, you don't get perfectly smooth craters, but those fantastic bowls we saw before we landed."

"By God!" Scobie hugged her. "You're a genius."

Helmet against helmet, she smiled and said, "No. It's obvious, once you've seen for yourself." She was quiet for a bit while still they held each other. "Scientific intuition is a funny thing, I admit," she went on at last. "Considering the problem, I was hardly aware of my logical mind. What I thought was—the City of Ice, made with starstones out of that which a god called down from heaven—"

"Jesus Maria!" Garcilaso spun about to stare at them.

Scobie released the woman. "We'll go after confirmation," he said unsteadily. "To the large crater we spotted a few klicks inward. The surface appears quite safe to walk on."

"I called that crater the Elf King's Dance Hall," Broberg mused, as if a dream were coming back to her.

"Have a care." Garcilaso's laugh rattled. "Heap big medicine yonder. The King is only an inheritor; it was giants who built these walls, for the gods."

"Well, I've got to find a way in, don't I?" Scobie responded.

"Indeed," *Alvarlan says*. "I cannot guide you from this point. My spirit can only see through mortal eyes. I can but lend you my counsel, until we have neared the gates."

"Are you sleepwalking in that fairy tale of yours?" Danzig yelled. "Come back before you get yourselves killed!"

"Will you dry up?" Scobie snarled. "It's nothing but a style of talk we've got between us. If you can't understand that, you've got less use of your brain than we do."

"Listen, won't you? I didn't say you're crazy. You don't have delusions or anything like that. I do say you've steered your fantasies toward this kind of place, and now the reality has reinforced them till you're under a compulsion you don't recognize. Would you go ahead so recklessly anywhere else in the universe? Think!"

"That does it. We'll resume contact after you've had time to improve your manners." Scobie snapped off his main radio switch. The circuits that stayed active served for close-by communication but had no power to reach an orbital relay. His companions did likewise.

The three faced the awesomeness before them. "You can help me find the Princess when we are inside, Alvarlan," *Kendrick says.*

"That I can and will," *the sorcerer vows.*

"I wait for you, most steadfast of my lovers," *Ricia croons.*

Alone in the spacecraft, Danzig well-nigh sobbed, "Oh, damn that game forever!" The sound fell away into emptiness.

III

To condemn psychodrama, even in its enhanced form, would be to condemn human nature.

It begins in childhood. Play is necessary to an immature mammal, a means of learning to handle the body, the perceptions, and the outside world. The young human plays, must play, with its brain too. The more intelligent the child, the more its imagination needs exercise. There are degrees of activity, from the passive watching of a show on a screen, onward through reading, daydreaming, storytelling, and psychodrama . . . for which the child has no such fancy name.

We cannot give this behavior any single description, for the shape and course it takes depend on an endless number of variables. Sex, age, culture, and companions are only the most obvious. For example, in pre-electronic North America little girls would often play "house" while little boys played "cowboys and Indians" or "cops and robbers," whereas nowadays a mixed group of their descendants might play "dolphins" or "astronauts and aliens." In essence, a small band forms, and each individual makes up a character to portray or borrows one from fiction. Simple props may be employed, such as toy weapons; or a chance object —a stick, for instance—may be declared something else such as a metal detector; or a thing may be quite imaginary, as the scenery almost always is. The children then act out a drama which they compose as they go along. When they cannot physically perform a certain action, they describe it. ("I jump real high, like you can do on Mars, an' come out over the edge o' that ol' Valles Marineris, an' take that bandit by surprise.") A large cast of characters, especially villains, frequently comes into existence by fiat.

The most imaginative member of the troupe dominates the game and the evolution of the story line, though in a rather subtle fashion, through offering the most vivid possibilities. The rest, however, are brighter than average; psychodrama in this highly developed form does not appeal to everybody.

For those to whom it does, the effects are beneficial and lifelong. Besides increasing their creativity through use, it lets them try out a play version of different adult roles and experiences. Thereby they begin to acquire insight into adulthood.

Such play-acting ends when adolescence commences, if not earlier—but only in that form, and not necessarily forever in it. Grownups have many dream-games. This is plain to see in lodges, for example, with their titles, costumes, and ceremonies; but does it not likewise animate all pageantry, every ritual? To what extent are our heroisms, sacrifices, and self-aggrandizements the acting out of personae that we maintain? Some thinkers have attempted to trace this element through every aspect of society.

Here, though, we are concerned with overt psychodrama among adults. In Western civilization it first appeared on a noticeable scale during the middle twentieth century. Psychiatrists found it a powerful diagnostic and therapeutic technique. Among ordinary folk, war and fantasy games, many of which involved identification with imaginary or historical characters, became increasingly popular. In part this was doubtless a retreat from the restrictions and menaces of that unhappy period, but likely in larger part it was a revolt of the mind against the inactive entertainment, notably television, which had come to dominate recreation.

The Chaos ended those activities. Everybody knows about their revival in recent times—for healthier reasons, one hopes. By projecting three-dimensional scenes and appropriate sounds from a data bank—or, better yet, by having a computer produce them to order—players gained a sense of reality that intensified their mental and emotional commitment. Yet in those games that went on for episode after episode, year after real-time year, whenever two or more members of a group could get together to play, they found themselves less and less dependent on such appurtenances. It seemed that, through practice, they had regained the vivid imaginations of their childhoods, and could make anything, or airy nothing itself, into the objects and the worlds they desired.

I have deemed it necessary thus to repeat the obvious in order that we may see it in perspective. The news beamed from Saturn has brought widespread revulsion. (Why? What buried fears have been touched? This is subject matter for potentially important research.) Overnight, adult psychodrama has become unpopular; it may become extinct. That would, in many ways, be a worse tragedy than what has occurred yonder. There is no reason to suppose that the game ever harmed any mentally sound person on Earth; on the contrary. Beyond doubt, it has helped astronauts stay sane and alert on long, difficult missions. If it has no more medical use, that is because psychotherapy has become a branch of applied biochemistry.

And this last fact, the modern world's dearth of experience with madness, is at the root of what happened. Although he could not have foreseen the exact outcome, a twentieth-century psychiatrist might have warned against spending eight years, an unprecedented stretch of time, in as strange an environment as the *Chronos*. Strange it certainly has been, despite all efforts—limited, totally man-controlled, devoid of countless cues for which our evolution on Earth has fashioned us. Extraterrestrial colonists have, thus far, had available to them any number of simulations and compensations, of which close, full contact with home and frequent opportunities to visit there are probably the most significant. Sailing time to Jupiter was long, but half of that to Saturn. Moreover, because they were earlier, scientists in the *Zeus* had much research to occupy them en route, which it would be pointless for later travelers to duplicate; by then, the interplanetary medium between the two giants held few surprises.

Contemporary psychologists were aware of this. They understood that the persons most adversely affected would be the most intelligent, imaginative, and dynamic—those who were supposed to make the very discoveries at Saturn which were the purpose of the undertaking. Being less familiar than their predecessors with the labyrinth that lies, Minotaur-haunted, beneath every human consciousness, the psychologists expected purely benign consequences of whatever psychodramas the crew engendered.

—Minamoto

Assignments to teams had not been made in advance of departure. It was sensible to let professional capabilities reveal themselves and grow on the voyage, while personal relationships did the same. Eventually such factors would help in deciding what individuals should train for what tasks. Long-term participation in a group of players normally forged bonds of friendship that were desirable, if the members were otherwise qualified.

In real life, Scobie always observed strict propriety toward Broberg. She was attractive, but she was monogamous, and he had no wish to alienate her. Besides, he liked her husband. (Tom did not partake of the game. As an astronomer, he had plenty to keep his attention happily engaged.) They had played for a couple of years, and their group had acquired as many characters as it could accommodate in a narrative whose milieu and people were becoming complex, before Scobie and Broberg spoke of anything intimate.

By then, the story they enacted was doing so, and maybe it was not altogether by chance that they met when both had several idle hours. This was in the weightless recreation area at the spin axis. They tumbled through aerobatics, shouting and laughing, until they were pleasantly tired, went to the clubhouse, turned in their wingsuits, and showered. They had not seen each other nude before; neither commented, but he did not hide his enjoyment of the sight, while she colored and averted her glance as tactfully as she was able. Afterward, their clothes resumed, they decided on a drink before they went home, and sought the lounge.

Since evenwatch was approaching nightwatch, they had the place to themselves. At the bar, he thumbed a chit for Scotch, she for Pinot Chardonnay. The machine obliged them and they carried their refreshments out onto the balcony. Seated at a table, they looked across immensity. The clubhouse was built into the support frame on a Lunar gravity level. Above them they saw the sky wherein they had been as birds; its reach did not seem any more hemmed in by far-spaced, spidery girders than it was by a few drifting clouds. Beyond, and straight ahead, decks opposite were a commingling of masses and shapes which the scant illumination at this hour turned into mystery. Among those shadows the humans made out woods, brooks, pools, turned hoary or agleam by the light of stars which filled the skyview strips. Right and left, the hull stretched off beyond sight, a dark in which such lamps as there were appeared lost.

The air was cool, slightly jasmine-scented, drenched with silence. Underneath and throughout, subliminally, throbbed the myriad pulses of the ship.

"Magnificent," Broberg said low, gazing outward. "What a surprise."

"Eh?" asked Scobie.

"I've only been here before in daywatch. I didn't anticipate that a simple rotation of the reflectors would make it wonderful."

"Oh, I wouldn't sneer at the daytime view. Mighty impressive."

"Yes, but—but then you see too plainly that everything is manmade, nothing is wild or unknown or free. The sun blots out the stars; it's as though no universe existed beyond this shell we're in. Tonight is like being in Maranoa," *the kingdom of which Ricia is Princess, a kingdom of ancient things and ways, wildernesses, enchantments.*

"H'm, yeah, sometimes I feel trapped myself," Scobie admitted. "I thought I had a journey's worth of geological data to study, but my project isn't going anywhere very interesting."

"Same for me." Broberg straightened where she sat, turned to him, and smiled a trifle. The dusk softened her features, made them look young. "Not that we're entitled to self-pity. Here we are, safe and comfortable till we reach Saturn. After that we should never lack for excitement, or for material to work with on the way home."

"True." Scobie raised his glass. "Well, skoal. Hope I'm not mispronouncing that."

"How should I know?" she laughed. "My maiden name was Almyer."

"That's right, you've adopted Tom's surname. I wasn't thinking. Though that is rather unusual these days, hey?"

She spread her hands. "My family was well-to-do, but they were—are—Jerusalem Catholics. Strict about certain things; archaistic, you might say." She lifted her wine and sipped. "Oh, yes, I've left the Church, but in several ways the Church will never leave me."

"I see. Not to pry, but, uh, this does account for some traits of yours I couldn't help wondering about."

She regarded him over the rim of her glass. "Like what?"

"Well, you've got a lot of life in you, vigor, a sense of fun, but you're also—what's the word?—uncommonly domestic. You've told me you were a quiet faculty member of Yukon University till you married Tom." Scobie grinned. "Since you two kindly invited me to your last anniversary party, and I know your present age, I deduced that you were thirty then." Unmentioned was the likelihood that she had still been a virgin. "Nevertheless—oh, forget it. I said I don't want to pry."

"Go ahead, Colin," she urged. "That line from Burns sticks in my mind, since you introduced me to his poetry. 'To see oursels as others see us!' Since it looks as if we may visit the same moon—"

Scobie took a hefty dollop of Scotch. "Aw, nothing much," he said, unwontedly diffident. "If you must know, well, I have the impression that being in love wasn't the single good reason you had for marrying Tom. He'd already been accepted for this expedition, and given your personal qualifications, that would get you in too. In short, you'd grown tired of routine respectability and here was how you could kick over the traces. Am I right?"

"Yes." Her gaze dwelt on him. "You're more perceptive than I supposed."

"No, not really. A roughneck rockhound. But Ricia's made it plain to see that you're more than a demure wife, mother, and scientist—" She parted her lips. He raised a palm. "No, please, let me finish. I know it's bad manners to claim that somebody's persona is a wish fulfillment, and I'm not doing that. Of course you don't want to be a free-roving, free-loving female scamp, any more than I want to ride around cutting down assorted enemies. Still, if you'd been born and raised in the world of our game, I feel sure you'd be a lot like Ricia. And that potential is part of you, Jean." He tossed off his drink. "If I've said too much, please excuse me. Want a refill?"

"I'd better not, but don't let me stop you."

"You won't." He rose and bounded off.

When he returned, he saw that she had been observing him through the vitryl door. As he sat down, she smiled, leaned a bit across the table, and told him softly: "I'm glad you said what you did. Now I can declare what a complicated man Kendrick reveals you to be."

"What?" Scobie asked in honest surprise. "Come on! He's a sword-and-shield tramp, a fellow who likes to travel, same as me; and in my teens I was a brawler, same as him."

"He may lack polish, but he's a chivalrous knight, a compassionate overlord, a knower of sagas and traditions, an appreciator of poetry and music, a bit of a bard. . . . Ricia misses him. When will he get back from his latest quest?"

"I'm bound home this minute. N'Kuma and I gave those pirates the slip and landed at Haverness two days ago. After we buried the swag, he wanted to visit Béla and Karina and join them in whatever they've been up to, so we bade good-bye for the time being." Scobie and Harding had lately taken a few hours to conclude that adventure of theirs. The rest of the group had been mundanely occupied for some while.

Broberg's eyes widened. "From Haverness to the Isles? But I'm in Castle Devaranda, right in between."

"I hoped you'd be."

"I can't wait to hear your story."

"I'm pushing on after dark. The moon is bright and I've got a pair of remounts I bought with a few gold pieces from the loot." *The dust rolls white beneath drumming hoofs. Where a horseshoe strikes a flint pebble, sparks fly ardent. Kendrick scowls.* "You, aren't you with . . . what's his name? . . . Joran the Red? I don't like him."

"I sent him packing a month ago. He got the idea that sharing my bed gave him authority over me. It was never anything but a romp. I stand alone on the Gerfalcon Tower, looking south over moonlit fields, and wonder how you fare. The road flows toward me like a gray river. Do I see a rider come at a gallop, far and far away?"

After many months of play, no image on a screen was necessary. *Pennons on the night wind stream athwart the stars.* "I arrive. I sound my horn to rouse the gatekeepers."

"How I do remember those merry notes—"

That same night, Kendrick and Ricia become lovers. Experienced in the game and careful of its etiquette, Scobie and Broberg uttered no details about the union; they did not touch each other and maintained only fleeting eye contact; the ultimate good-nights were very decorous. After all, this was a story they composed about two fictitious characters in a world that never was.

The lower slopes of the jökull rose in tiers which were themselves deeply concave; the humans walked around their rims and admired the extravagant formations beneath. Names sprang onto lips: the Frost Garden, the Ghost Bridge, the Snow Queen's Throne, *while Kendrick advances into the City, and Ricia awaits him at the Dance Hall, and the spirit of Alvarlan carries word between them so that it is as if already she too travels beside her knight.* Nevertheless they proceeded warily, vigilant for signs of danger, especially whenever a change of texture or hue or anything else in the surface underfoot betokened a change in its nature.

Above the highest ledge reared a cliff too sheer to scale, Iapetan gravity or no, *the fortress wall.* However, from orbit the crew had spied a gouge in the vicinity, forming a pass, doubtless plowed by a small meteorite *in the war between the gods and the magicians, when stones chanted down from the sky wrought havoc so accursed that none dared afterward rebuild.* That was an eerie climb, hemmed in by heights which glimmered in the blue twilight they cast, heaven narrowed to a belt between them where stars seemed to blaze doubly brilliant.

"There must be guards at the opening," *Kendrick says.*

"A single guard," *answers the mind-whisper of Alvarlan,* "but he is a dragon. If you did battle with him, the noise and flame would bring every warrior here upon you. Fear not. I'll slip into his burnin' brain and weave him such a dream that he'll never see you."

"The King might sense the spell," *says Ricia through him.* "Since you'll be parted from us anyway, while you ride the soul of that beast, Alvarlan, I'll seek him out and distract him."

Kendrick grimaces, knowing full well what means are hers to do that. She has told him how she longs for freedom and her knight; she has also hinted that elven lovemaking transcends the human. Does she wish for a final time before her rescue? . . . Well, Ricia and Kendrick have neither plighted nor practiced single troth. Assuredly, Colin Scobie had not. He jerked forth a grin and continued through the silence that had fallen on all three.

They came out on top of the glacial mass and looked around them. Scobie whistled. Garcilaso stammered, "J-J-Jesus Christ!" Broberg smote her hands together.

Below them the precipice fell to the ledges, whose sculpturing took on a wholly new, eldritch aspect, gleam and shadow, until it ended at the plain. Seen from here aloft, the curvature of the moon made toes strain downward in boots, as if to cling fast and not be spun off among the stars which surrounded, rather than shone above, its ball. The spacecraft stood minute on dark, pocked stone, like a cenotaph raised to loneliness.

Eastward the ice reached beyond an edge of sight which was much closer. ("Yonder could be the rim of the world," Garcilaso said, and *Ricia replies,* "Yes, the City is nigh to there.") Bowls of different sizes, hillocks, crags, no two of them eroded the same way, turned its otherwise level stretch into a surreal maze. An arabesque openwork ridge which stood at the explorers' goal overtopped the horizon. Everything that was illuminated lay gently aglow. Radiant though the sun was, it cast the light of only perhaps five thousand full Lunas upon Earth. Southward, Saturn's great semidisc gave about one-half more Lunar shining; but in that direction, the wilderness sheened pale amber.

Scobie shook himself. "Well, shall we go?" His prosaic question jarred the others; Garcilaso frowned and Broberg winced.

She recovered. "Yes, hasten," *Ricia says.* "I am by myself once more. Are you out of the dragon, Alvarlan?"

"Aye," *the wizard informs her.* "Kendrick is safely behind a ruined palace. Tell us how best to reach you."

"You are at the time-gnawed Crown House. Before you lies the Street of Shieldsmiths—"

Scobie's brows knitted. "It is noonday, when elves do not fare abroad," *Kendrick says* remindingly, commandingly. "I do not wish to encounter any of them. No fights, no complications. We are going to fetch you and escape, without further trouble."

Broberg and Garcilaso showed disappointment, but understood him. A game broke down when a person refused to accept something that a fellow player tried to put in. Often the narrative threads were not mended and picked up for many days. Broberg sighed.

"Follow the street to its end at a forum where a snow fountain springs," *Ricia directs.* "Cross, and continue on Aleph Zain Boulevard. You will know it by a gateway in the form of a skull with open jaws. If anywhere you see a rainbow flicker in the air, stand motionless until it has gone by, for it will be an auroral wolf. . . ."

At a low-gravity lope, the distance took some thirty minutes to cover. In the later part, the three were forced to detour by great banks of an ice so fine-grained that it slid about under their bootsoles and tried to swallow them. Several of these lay at irregular intervals around their destination.

There the travelers stood again for a time in the grip of awe.

The bowl at their feet must reach down almost to bedrock, a hundred meters, and was twice as wide. On this rim lifted the wall they had seen from the cliff, an arc fifty meters long and high, nowhere thicker than five meters, pierced by intricate scrollwork, greenly agleam where it was not translucent. It was the uppermost edge of a stratum which made serrations down the crater. Other outcrops and ravines were more dreamlike yet . . . was that a unicorn's head, was that a colonnade of caryatids, was that an icicle bower . . . ? The depths were a lake of cold blue shadow.

"You have come, Kendrick, beloved!" *cries Ricia, and casts herself into his arms.*

"Quiet," *warns the sending of Alvarlan the wise.* "Rouse not our immortal enemies."

"Yes, we must get back." Scobie blinked. "Judas priest, what possessed us? Fun is fun, but we sure have come a lot farther and faster than was smart, haven't we?"

"Let us stay for a little while," Broberg pleaded. "This is such a miracle—the Elf King's Dance Hall, which the Lord of the Dance built for him—"

"Remember, if we stay we'll be caught, and your captivity may be forever." Scobie thumbed his main radio switch. "Hello, Mark? Do you read me?"

Neither Broberg nor Garcilaso made that move. They did not hear Danzig's voice: "Oh, yes! I've been hunkered over the set gnawing my knuckles. How are you?"

"All right. We're at the big hole and will be heading back as soon I've gotten a few pictures."

"They haven't made words to tell how relieved I am. From a scientific standpoint, was it worth the risk?"

Scobie gasped. He stared before him.

"Colin?" Danzig called. "You still there?"

"Yes. Yes."

"I asked what observations of any importance you made."

"I don't know," Scobie mumbled. "I can't remember. None of it after we started climbing seems real."

"Better you return right away," Danzig said grimly. "Forget about photographs."

"Correct." Scobie addressed his companions: "Forward march."

"I can't," *Alvarlan answers.* "A wanderin' spell has caught my spirit in tendrils of smoke."

"I know where a fire dagger is kept," *Ricia says.* "I'll try to steal it."

Broberg moved ahead, as though to descend into the crater. Tiny ice grains trickled over the verge from beneath her boots. She could easily lose her footing and slide down.

"No, wait," *Kendrick shouts to her.* "No need. My spearhead is of moon alloy. It can cut—"

The glacier shuddered. The ridge cracked asunder and fell in shards. The area on which the humans stood split free and toppled into the bowl. An avalanche poured after. High-flung crystals caught sunlight, glittered prismatic in challenge to the stars, descended slowly and lay quiet.

Except for shock waves through solids, everything had happened in the absolute silence of space.

Heartbeat by heartbeat, Scobie crawled back to his senses. He found himself held down, immobilized, in darkness and pain. His armor had saved, was still saving his life; he had been stunned but escaped a real concussion. Yet every breath hurt abominably. A rib or two on the left side seemed broken; a monstrous impact must have dented metal. And he was buried under more weight than he could move.

"Hello," he coughed. "Does anybody read me?" The single reply was the throb of his blood. If his radio still worked—which it should, being built into the suit—the mass around him screened him off.

It also sucked heat at an unknown but appalling rate. He felt no cold because the electrical system drew energy from his fuel cell as fast as needed to keep him warm and to recycle his air chemically. As a normal thing, when he lost heat through the slow process of radiation—and a trifle through kerofoam-lined bootsoles—the latter demand was much the greater. Now conduction was at work on every square centimeter. He had a spare unit in the equipment on his back, but no means of getting at it.

Unless— He barked forth a chuckle. Straining, he felt the stuff that entombed him yield the least bit under the pressure of arms and legs. And his helmet rang slightly with noise, a rustle, a gurgle. This wasn't water ice that imprisoned him, but stuff with a much lower freezing point. He was melting it, subliming it, making room for himself.

If he lay passive, he would sink, while frozenness above slid down to keep him in his grave. He might evoke superb new formations, but he would not see them. Instead, he must use the small capability given him to work his way upward, scrabble, get a purchase on matter that was not yet aflow, burrow to the stars.

He began.

Agony soon racked him. Breath rasped in and out of lungs aflame. His strength drained away and trembling took its place, and he could not tell whether he ascended or slipped back. Blind, half suffocated, Scobie made mole-claws of his hands and dug.

It was too much to endure. He fled from it—

His strong enchantments failing, the Elf King brought down his towers of fear in wreck. If the spirit of Alvarlan returned to its body, the wizard would brood upon things he had seen, and understand what they meant, and such knowledge would give mortals a terrible power against Faerie. Waking from the sleep, the King scried Kendrick about to release that fetch. There was no time to do more than break the spell which upheld the Dance Hall. It was largely built of mist and starshine, but enough blocks quarried from the cold side of Ginnungagap were in it that when they crashed they should kill the knight. Ricia would perish too, and in his quicksilver intellect the King regretted that. Nevertheless he spoke the necessary word.

He did not comprehend how much abuse flesh and bone can bear. Sir Kendrick fights his way clear of the ruins, to seek and save his lady. While he does, he heartens himself with thoughts of adventures past and future—

—and suddenly the blindness broke apart and Saturn stood lambent within rings.

Scobie belly-flopped onto the surface and lay shuddering.

He must rise, no matter how his injuries screamed, lest he melt himself a new burial place. He lurched to his feet and glared around.

Little but outcroppings and scars was left of the sculpture. For the most part, the crater had become a smooth-sided whiteness under heaven. Scarcity of shadows made distances hard to gauge, but Scobie guessed the new depth was about seventy-five meters. And empty, empty.

"Mark, do you hear?" he cried.

"That you, Colin?" rang in his earpieces. "Name of mercy, what's happened? I heard you call out, and saw a cloud rise and sink . . . then nothing for more than an hour. Are you okay?"

"I am, sort of. I don't see Jean or Luis. A landslide took us by surprise and buried us. Hold on while I search."

When he stood upright, Scobie's ribs hurt less. He could move about rather handily if he took care. The two types of standard analgesic in his kit were alike useless, one too weak to give noticeable relief, one so strong that it would turn him sluggish. Casting to and fro, he soon found what he expected, a concavity in the tumbled snowlike material, slightly aboil.

Also a standard part of his gear was a trenching tool. Scobie set pain aside and dug. A helmet appeared. Broberg's head was within it. She too had been tunneling out.

"Jean!"

"Kendrick!" She crept free and they embraced, suit to suit. "Oh, Colin."

"How are you?" rattled from him.

"Alive," she answered. "No serious harm done, I think. A lot to be said for low gravity. . . . You? Luis?" Blood was clotted in a streak beneath her nose, and a bruise on her forehead was turning purple, but she stood firmly and spoke clearly.

"I'm functional. Haven't found Luis yet. Help me look. First, though, we'd better check out our equipment."

She hugged arms around chest, as if that would do any good here. "I'm chilled," she admitted.

Scobie pointed at a telltale. "No wonder. Your fuel cell's down to its last couple of ergs. Mine isn't in a lot better shape. Let's change."

They didn't waste time removing their backpacks, but reached into each other's. Tossing the spent units to the ground, where vapors and holes immediately appeared and then froze, they plugged the fresh ones into their suits. "Turn your thermostat down," Scobie advised. "We won't find shelter soon. Physical activity will help us keep warm."

"And require faster air recycling," Broberg reminded.

"Yeah. But for the moment, at least, we can conserve the energy in the cells. Okay, next let's check for strains, potential leaks, any kind of damage or loss. Hurry. Luis is still down there."

Inspection was a routine made automatic by years of drill. While her fingers searched across the man's spacesuit, Broberg let her eyes wander. "The Dance Hall is gone," *Ricia murmurs*. "I think the King smashed it to prevent our escape."

"Me too. If he finds out we're alive, and seeking for Alvarlan's soul— Hey, wait! None of that!"

Danzig's voice quavered. "How're you doing?"

"We're in fair shape, seems like," Scobie replied. "My corselet took a beating but didn't split or anything. Now to find Luis . . . Jean, suppose you spiral right, I left, across the crater floor."

It took a while, for the seething which marked Garcilaso's burial was minuscule. Scobie started to dig. Broberg watched how he moved, heard how he breathed, and said, "Give me that tool. Just where are you bunged up, anyway?"

He admitted his condition and stepped back. Crusty chunks flew from Broberg's toil. She progressed fast, since whatever kind of ice lay at this point was, luckily, friable, and under Iapetan gravity she could cut a hole with almost vertical sides.

"I'll make myself useful," Scobie said, "namely, find us a way out."

When he started up the nearest slope, it shivered. All at once he was borne back in a tide that made rustly noises through his armor, while a fog of dry white motes blinded him. Painfully, he scratched himself free at the bottom and tried elsewhere. In the end he could report to Danzig: "I'm afraid there is no easy route. When the rim collapsed where we stood, it did more than produce a shock which wrecked the delicate formations throughout the crater. It let tons of stuff pour down from the surface—a particular sort of ice that, under local conditions, is like fine sand. The walls are covered by it. Most places, it lies meters deep over more stable material. We'd slide faster than we could climb, where the layer is thin; where it's thick, we'd sink."

Danzig sighed. "I guess I get to take a nice, healthy hike."

"I assume you've called for help."

"Of course. They'll have two boats here in about a hundred hours. The best they can manage. You knew that already."

"Uh-huh. And our fuel cells are good for perhaps fifty hours."

"Oh, well, not to worry about that. I'll bring extras and toss them to you, if you're stuck till the rescue party arrives. M-m-m . . . maybe I'd better rig a slingshot or something first."

"You might have a problem locating us. This isn't a true crater, it's a glorified pothole, the lip of it flush with the top of the glacier. The landmark we guided ourselves by, that fancy ridge, is gone."

"No big deal. I've got a bearing on you from the directional antenna, remember. A magnetic compass may be no use here, but I can keep myself oriented by the heavens. Saturn scarcely moves in this sky, and the sun and the stars don't move fast."

"Damn! You're right. I wasn't thinking. Got Luis on my mind, if nothing else." Scobie looked across the bleakness toward Broberg. Perforce she was taking a short rest, stoop-shouldered above her excavation. His earpieces brought him the harsh sound in her windpipe.

He must maintain what strength was left him, against later need. He sipped from his water nipple, pushed a bite of food through his chowlock, pretended an appetite. "I may as well try reconstructing what happened," he said. "Okay, Mark, you were right, we got crazy reckless. The game—Eight years was too long to play the game, in an environment that gave us too few reminders of reality. But who could have foreseen it? My God, warn *Chronos!* I happen to know that one of the Titan teams started playing an expedition to the merfolk under the Crimson Ocean—on account of the red mists—deliberately, like us, before they set off. . . ."

Scobie gulped. "Well," he slogged on, "I don't suppose we'll ever know exactly what went wrong here. But plain to see, the configuration was only metastable. On Earth, too, avalanches can be fatally easy to touch off. I'd guess at a methane layer underneath the surface. It turned a little slushy when temperatures rose after dawn, but that didn't matter in low gravity and vacuum—till we came along. Heat, vibration—Anyhow, the stratum slid out from under us, which triggered a general collapse. Does that guess seem reasonable?"

"Yes, to an amateur like me," Danzig said. "I admire how you can stay academic under these circumstances."

"I'm being practical," Scobie retorted. "Luis may need medical attention earlier than those boats can come for him. If so, how do we get him to ours?"

Danzig's voice turned stark. "Any ideas?"

"I'm fumbling my way toward that. Look, the bowl still has the same basic form. The whole shebang didn't cave in. That implies hard material, water ice and actual rock. In fact, I see a few remaining promontories, jutting out above the sandlike stuff. As for what *it* is—maybe an ammonia-carbon dioxide combination, maybe more exotic—that'll be for you to discover later. Right now . . . my geological instruments should help me trace where the solid masses are least deeply covered. We all have trenching tools, so we can try to shovel a path clear, along a zigzag of least effort. That may bring more garbage slipping down on us from above, but that in turn may expedite our progress. Where the uncovered shelves are too steep or slippery to climb, we can chip footholds. Slow and tough work; and we may run into a bluff higher than we can jump, or something like that."

"I can help," Danzig proposed. "While I waited to hear from you, I inventoried our stock of spare cable, cord, equipment I can cannibalize for wire, clothes and bedding I can cut into strips—whatever might be knotted together to make a rope. We won't need much tensile strength. Well, I estimate I can get about forty meters. According to your description, that's about half the slope length of that trap you're in. If you can climb halfway up while I trek there, I can haul you the rest of the way."

"Thanks, Mark," Scobie said, "although—"

"Luis!" shrieked in his helmet. "Colin, come fast, help me, this is dreadful!"

Regardless of the pain, except for a curse or two, Scobie sped to Broberg's aid.

Garcilaso was not quite unconscious. In that lay much of the horror. They heard him mumble, "—Hell, the King threw my soul into Hell. I can't find my way out. I'm lost. If only Hell weren't so cold—" They could not see his face; the inside of his helmet was crusted with frost. Deeper and longer buried than the others, badly hurt in addition, he would have died shortly after his fuel cell was exhausted. Broberg had uncovered him barely in time, if that.

Crouched in the shaft she had dug, she rolled him over onto his belly. His limbs flopped about and he babbled, "A demon attacks me. I'm blind here but I feel the wind of its wings," in a blurred monotone. She unplugged the energy unit and tossed it aloft, saying, "We should return this to the ship if we can."

Above, Scobie gave the object a morbid stare. It didn't even retain the warmth to make a little vapor, like his and hers, but lay quite inert. Its case was a metal box, thirty centimeters by fifteen by six, featureless except for two plug-in prongs on one of the broad sides. Controls built into the spacesuit circuits allowed you to start and stop the chemical reactions within and regulate their rate manually; but as a rule you left that chore to your thermostat and aerostat. Now those reactions had run their course. Until it was recharged, the cell was merely a lump.

Scobie leaned over to watch Broberg, some ten meters below him. She had extracted the reserve unit from Garcilaso's gear, inserted it properly at the small of his back, and secured it by clips on the bottom of his packframe. "Let's have your contribution, Colin," she said. Scobie dropped the meter of heavy-gauge insulated wire which was standard issue on extravehicular missions, in case you needed to make a special electrical connection or a repair. She joined it by Western Union splices to the two she already had, made a loop at the end, and, awkwardly reaching over her left shoulder, secured the opposite end by a hitch to the top of her packframe. The triple strand bobbed above her like an antenna.

Stooping, she gathered Garcilaso in her arms. The Iapetan weight of him and his apparatus was under ten kilos, of her and hers about the same. Theoretically she could jump straight out of the hole with her burden. In practice, her spacesuit was too hampering; constant-volume joints allowed considerable freedom of movement, but not as much as bare skin, especially when circum-Saturnian temperatures required extra insulation. Besides, if she could have reached the top, she could not have stayed. Soft ice would have crumbled beneath her fingers and she would have tumbled back down.

"Here goes," she said. "This had better be right the first time, Colin. I don't think Luis can take much jouncing."

"Kendrick, Ricia, where are you?" Garcilaso moaned. "Are you in Hell too?"

Scobie dug his heels into the ground near the edge and crouched ready. The loop in the wire rose to view. His right hand grabbed hold. He threw thimself backward, lest he slide forward, and felt the mass he had captured slam to a halt. Anguish exploded in his rib cage. Somehow he dragged his burden to safety before he fainted.

He came out of that in a minute. "I'm okay," he rasped at the anxious voices of Broberg and Danzig. "Only let me rest awhile."

The physicist nodded and knelt to minister to the pilot. She stripped his packframe in order that he might lie flat on it, head and legs supported by the packs themselves. That would prevent significant heat loss by convection and cut loss by conduction. Still, his fuel cell would be drained faster than if he were on his feet, and first it had a terrible energy deficit to make up.

"The ice is clearing away inside his helmet," she reported. "Merciful Mary, the blood! Seems to be from the scalp, though; it isn't running anymore. His occiput must have been slammed against the vitryl. We ought to wear padded caps in these rigs. Yes, I know accidents like this haven't happened before, but—" She unclipped the flashlight at her waist, stooped, and shone it downward. "His eyes are open. The pupils—yes, a severe concussion, and likely a skull fracture, which may be hemorrhaging into the brain. I'm surprised he isn't vomiting. Did the cold prevent that? Will he start soon? He could choke on his own vomit, in there where nobody can lay a hand on him."

Scobie's pain had subsided to a bearable intensity. He rose, went over to look, whistled, and said, "I judge he's doomed unless we get him to the boat and give him proper care soon. Which isn't possible."

"Oh, Luis." Tears ran silently down Broberg's cheeks.

"You think he can't last till I bring my rope and we carry him back?" Danzig asked.

" 'Fraid not," Scobie replied. "I've taken paramedical courses, and in fact I've seen a case like this before. How come you know the symptoms, Jean?"

"I read a lot," she said dully.

"They weep, the dead children weep," Garcilaso muttered.

Danzig sighed. "Okay, then. I'll fly over to you."

"Huh?" burst from Scobie, and from Broberg: "Have you also gone insane?"

"No, listen," Danzig said fast. "I'm no skilled pilot, but I have the same basic training in this type of craft that everybody does who might ride in one. It's expendable: the rescue vessels can bring us back. There'd be no significant gain if I landed close to the glacier—I'd still have to make that rope and so forth—and we know from what happened to the probe that there would be a real hazard. Better I make straight for your crater."

"Coming down on a surface that the jets will vaporize out from under you?" Scobie snorted. "I bet Luis would consider that a hairy stunt. You, my friend, would crack up."

"Nu!" They could almost see the shrug. "A crash from low altitude, in this gravity, shouldn't do more than rattle my teeth. The blast will cut a hole clear to bedrock. True, the surrounding ice will collapse in around the hull and trap it. You may need to dig to reach the airlock, though I suspect thermal radiation from the cabin will keep the upper parts of the structure free. Even if the craft topples and strikes sidewise—in which case, it'll sink down into a deflating cushion—even if it did that on bare rock, it shouldn't be seriously damaged. It's designed to withstand heavier impacts." Danzig hesitated. "Of course, could be this would endanger you. I'm confident I won't fry you with the jets, assuming I descend near the middle and you're as far offside as you can get. Maybe, though, maybe I'd cause a . . . an ice quake that'll kill you. No sense in losing two more lives."

"Or three, Mark," Broberg said low. "In spite of your brave words, you could come to grief yourself."

"Oh, well, I'm an oldish man. I'm fond of living, yes, but you guys have a whole lot more years due you. Look, suppose the worst, suppose I don't just make a messy landing but wreck the boat utterly. Then Luis dies, but he would anyway. You two, however, would have access to the stores aboard, including those extra fuel cells. I'm willing to run what I consider to be a small risk of my own neck, for the sake of giving Luis a chance at survival."

"Um-m-m," went Scobie, deep in his throat. A hand strayed in search of his chin, while his gaze roved around the glimmer of the bowl.

"I repeat," Danzig proceeded, "if you think this might jeopardize you in any way, we scrub it. No heroics, please. Luis would surely agree, better three people safe and one dead than four stuck with a high probability of death."

"Let me think." Scobie was mute for minutes before he said: "No, I don't believe we'd get in too much trouble here. As I remarked earlier, the vicinity has had its avalanche and must be in a reasonably stable configuration. True, ice will volatilize. In the case of deposits with low boiling points, that could happen explosively and cause tremors. But the vapor will carry heat away so fast that only material in your immediate area should change state. I daresay that the fine-grained stuff will get shaken down the slopes, but it's got too low a density to do serious harm; for the most part, it should simply act like a brief snowstorm. The floor will make adjustments, of course, which may be rather violent. However, we can be above it—do you see that shelf of rock over yonder, Jean, at jumping height? It has to be part of a buried hill; solid. That's our place to wait. . . . Okay, Mark, it's go as far as we're concerned. I can't be absolutely certain, but who ever is about anything? It seems like a good bet."

"What are we overlooking?" Broberg wondered. She glanced down at Luis, who lay at her feet. "While we considered all the possibilities, Luis might die. Yes, fly if you want to, Mark, and God bless you."

But when she and Scobie had brought Garcilaso to the ledge, she gestured from Saturn to Polaris and: "I will sing a spell, I will cast what small magic is mine, in aid of the Dragon Lord, that he may deliver Alvarlan's soul from Hell," *says Ricia.*

IV

> No reasonable person will blame any interplanetary explorer for miscalculations about the actual environment, especially when *some* decision has to be made, in haste and under stress. Occasional errors are inevitable. If we knew exactly what to expect throughout the Solar System, we would have no reason to explore it.
>
> —Minamoto

The boat lifted. Cosmic dust smoked away from its jets. A hundred and fifty meters aloft, thrust lessened and it stood still on a pillar of fire. Within the cabin was little noise, a low hiss and a bone-deep but nearly inaudible rumble. Sweat studded Danzig's features, clung glistening to his beard stubble, soaked his coverall and made it reek. He was about to undertake a maneuver as difficult as a rendezvous, and without guidance.

Gingerly, he advanced a vernier. A side jet woke. The boat lurched toward a nosedive. Danzig's hands jerked across the console. He must adjust the forces that held his vessel on high and those that pushed it horizontally, to get a resultant that would carry him eastward at a slow, steady pace. The vectors would change instant by instant, as they do when a human walks. The control computer, linked to the sensors, handled much of the balancing act, but not the crucial part. He must tell it what he wanted it to do.

His handling was inexpert. He had realized it would be. More altitude would have given him more margin for error, but deprived him of cues that his eyes found on the terrain beneath and the horizon ahead. Besides, when he reached the glacier he would perforce fly low to find his goal. He would be too busy for the precise celestial navigation he could have practiced afoot.

Seeking to correct his error, he overcompensated, and the boat pitched in a different direction. He punched for "hold steady" and the computer took over. Motionless again, he took a minute to catch his breath, regain his nerve, rehearse in his mind. Biting his lip, he tried afresh. This time he did not quite approach disaster. Jets aflicker, the boat staggered drunkenly over the moonscape.

The ice cliff loomed nearer and nearer. He saw its fragile loveliness and regretted that he must cut a swathe of ruin. Yet what did any natural wonder mean unless a conscious mind was there to know it? He passed the lowest slope. It vanished in billows of steam.

Onward. Beyond the boiling, right and left and ahead, the Faerie architecture crumbled. He crossed the palisade. Now he was a bare fifty meters above the surface, and the clouds reached vengefully close before they disappeared into vacuum. He squinted through the port and made the scanner sweep a magnified overview across its screen, a search for his destination.

A white volcano erupted. The outburst engulfed him. Suddenly he was flying blind. Shocks belled through the hull when upflung stones hit. Frost sheathed the craft; the scanner screen went as blank as the ports. Danzig should have ordered ascent, but he was inexperienced. A human in danger has less of an instinct to jump than to run. He tried to scuttle sideways. Without exterior vision to aid him, he sent the vessel tumbling end over end. By the time he saw his mistake, less than a second, it was too late. He was out of control. The computer might have retrieved the situation after a while, but the glacier was too close. The boat crashed.

"Hello, Mark?" Scobie cried. "Mark, do you read me? Where are you, for Christ's sake?"

Silence replied. He gave Broberg a look which lingered. "Everything seemed to be in order," he said, "till we heard a shout, and a lot of racket, and nothing. He should've reached us by now. Instead, he's run into trouble. I hope it wasn't lethal."

"What can we do?" she asked as redundantly. They needed talk, any talk, for Garcilaso lay beside them and his delirious voice was dwindling fast.

"If we don't get fresh fuel cells within the next forty or fifty hours, we'll be at the end of our particular trail. The boat should be someplace near. We'll have to get out of this hole under our own power, seems like. Wait here with Luis and I'll scratch around for a possible route."

Scobie started downward. Broberg crouched by the pilot.

"—alone forever in the dark—" she heard.

"No, Alvarlan." She embraced him. Most likely he could not feel that, but she could. "Alvarlan, hearken to me. This is Ricia. I hear in my mind how your spirit calls. Let me help. Let me lead you back to the light."

"Have a care," advised Scobie. "We're too damn close to rehypnotizing ourselves as it is."

"But I might, I just might get through to Luis and . . . comfort him. . . . Alvarlan, Kendrick and I escaped. He's seeking a way home for us. I'm seeking you. Alvarlan, here is my hand, come take it."

On the crater floor, Scobie shook his head, clicked his tongue, and unlimbered his equipment. Binoculars would help him locate the most promising areas. Devices that ranged from a metal rod to a portable geosonar would give him a more exact idea of what sort of footing lay buried under what depth of unclimbable sand-ice. Admittedly, the scope of such probes was very limited. He did not have time to shovel tons of material aside so that he could mount higher and test further. He would simply have to get some preliminary results, make an educated guess at which path up the side of the bowl would prove negotiable, and trust he was right.

He shut Broberg and Garcilaso out of his consciousness as much as he was able, and commenced work.

An hour later he was ignoring pain while clearing a strip across a layer of rock. He thought a berg of good, hard frozen water lay ahead, but wanted to make sure.

"Jean! Colin! Do you read?"

Scobie straightened and stood rigid. Dimly he heard Broberg: "If I can't do anything else, Alvarlan, let me pray for your soul's repose."

"Mark!" ripped from Scobie. "You okay? What the hell happened?"

"Yeah, I wasn't too badly knocked around," Danzig said, "and the boat's habitable, though I'm afraid it'll never fly again. How are you? Luis?"

"Sinking fast. All right, let's hear the news."

Danzig described his misfortune. "I wobbled off in an unknown direction for an unknown distance. It can't have been extremely far, since the time was short before I hit. Evidently I plowed into a large, um, snowbank, which softened the impact but blocked radio transmission. It's evaporated from the cabin area now. I see tumbled whiteness around, and formations in the offing. . . . I'm not sure what damage the jacks and the stern jets suffered. The boat's on its side at about a forty-five-degree angle, presumably with rock beneath. But the after part is still buried in less whiffable stuff—water and CO_2 ices, I think—that's reached temperature equilibrium. The jets must be clogged with it. If I tried to blast, I'd destroy the whole works."

Scobie nodded. "You would, for sure."

Danzig's voice broke. "Oh, God, Colin! What have I done? I wanted to help Luis, but I may have killed you and Jean."

Scobie's lips tightened. "Let's not start crying before we're hurt. True, this has been quite a run of bad luck. But neither you nor I nor anybody could have known that you'd touch off a bomb underneath yourself."

"What was it? Have you any notion? Nothing of the sort ever occurred at rendezvous with a comet. And you believe the glacier is a wrecked comet, don't you?"

"Uh-huh, except that conditions have obviously modified it. The impact produced heat, shock, turbulence. Molecules got scrambled. Plasmas must have been momentarily present. Mixtures, compounds, clathrates, alloys—stuff formed that never existed in free space. We can learn a lot of chemistry here."

"That's why I came along. . . . Well, then, I crossed a deposit of some substance or substances that the jets caused to sublime with tremendous force. A certain kind of vapor refroze when it encountered the hull. I had to defrost the ports from inside after the snow had cooked off them."

"Where are you in relation to us?"

"I told you, I don't know. And I'm not sure I can determine it. The crash crumpled the direction-finding antenna. Let me go outside for a better look."

"Do that," Scobie said. "I'll keep busy meanwhile."

He did, until a ghastly rattling noise and Broberg's wail brought him at full speed back to the rock.

Scobie switched off Garcilaso's fuel cell. "This may make the difference that carries us through," he said low. "Think of it as a gift. Thanks, Luis."

Broberg let go of the pilot and rose from her knees. She straightened the limbs that had threshed about in the death struggle and crossed his hands on his breast. There was nothing she could do about the fallen jaw or the eyes that glared at heaven. Taking him out of this suit, here, would have worsened his appearance. Nor could she wipe the tears off her own face. She could merely try to stop their flow. "Goodbye, Luis," she whispered.

Turning to Scobie, she asked, "Can you give me a new job? Please."

"Come along," he directed. "I'll explain what I have in mind about making our way to the surface."

They were midway across the bowl when Danzig called. He had not let his comrade's dying slow his efforts, nor said much while it happened. Once, most softly, he had offered Kaddish.

"No luck," he reported like a machine. "I've traversed the largest circle I could while keeping the boat in sight, and found only weird, frozen shapes. I can't be a huge distance from you, or I'd seen an identifiably different sky, on this miserable little ball. You're probably within a twenty- or thirty-kilometer radius of me. But that covers a bunch of territory."

"Right," Scobie said. "Chances are you can't find us in the time we've got. Return to the boat."

"Hey, wait," Danzig protested. "I can spiral onward, marking my trail. I might come across you."

"It'll be more useful if you return," Scobie told him. "Assuming we climb out, we should be able to hike to you, but we'll need a beacon. What occurs to me is the ice itself. A small energy release, if it's concentrated, should release a large plume of methane or something similarly volatile. The gas will cool as it expands, recondense around dust particles that have been carried along—it'll steam—and the cloud ought to get high enough, before it evaporates again, to be visible from here."

"Gotcha!" A tinge of excitement livened Danzig's words. "I'll go straight to it. Make tests, find a spot where I can get the showiest result, and . . . how about I rig a thermite bomb? No, that might be too hot. Well, I'll develop a gadget."

"Keep us posted."

"But I, I don't think we'll care to chatter idly," Broberg ventured.

"No, we'll be working our tails off, you and I," Scobie agreed.

"Uh, wait," said Danzig. "What if you find you can't get clear to the top? You implied that's a distinct possibility."

"Well, then it'll be time for more radical procedures, whatever they turn out to be," Scobie responded. "Frankly, at this moment my head is too full of . . . of Luis, and of choosing an optimum escape route, for much thought about anything else."

"M-m, yeah, I guess we've got an ample supply of trouble without borrowing more. Tell you what, though. After my beacon's ready to fire off, I'll make that rope we talked of. You might find you prefer having it to clean clothes and sheets when you arrive." Danzig was silent for seconds before he ended: "God damn it, you *will* arrive."

Scobie chose a point on the north side for his and Broberg's attempt. Two rock shelves jutted forth, near the floor and several meters higher, indicating that stone reached at least that far. Beyond, in a staggered pattern, were similar outcroppings of hard ices. Between them, and onward from the uppermost, which was scarcely more than halfway to the rim, was nothing but the featureless, footingless slope of powder crystals. Its angle of repose gave a steepness that made the surface doubly treacherous. The question, unanswerable save by experience, was how deeply it covered layers on which humans could climb, and whether such layers extended the entire distance aloft.

At the spot, Scobie signaled a halt. "Take it easy, Jean," he said. "I'll go ahead and commence digging."

"Why don't we go together? I have my own tool, you know."

"Because I can't tell how so large a bank of that pseudo-quicksand will behave. It might react to the disturbance by causing a gigantic slide."

She bridled. Her haggard countenance registered mutiny. "Why not me first, then? Do you suppose I always wait passive for Kendrick to save me?"

"As a matter of fact," he rapped, "I'll begin because my rib is giving me billy hell, which is eating away what strength I've got left. If we run into trouble, you can better come to my help than I to yours."

Broberg bent her neck. "Oh, I'm sorry. I must be in a fairly bad state myself, I let false pride interfere with our business." Her look went toward Saturn, around which *Chronos* orbited, bearing her husband and children.

"You're forgiven." Scobie bunched his legs and sprang the five meters to the lower ledge. The next one up was slightly too far for such a jump, when he had no room for a running start.

Stooping, he scraped his trenching tool against the bottom of the declivity that sparkled before him, and shoveled. Grains poured from above, a billionfold, to cover what he cleared. He worked like a robot possessed. Each spadeful was nearly weightless, but the number of spadefuls was nearly endless. He did not bring the entire bowlside down on himself as he had half feared, half hoped. (If that didn't kill him, it would save a lot of toil.) A dry torrent went right and left over his ankles. Yet at least somewhat more of the underlying rock began to show.

From beneath, Broberg listened to him breathe. It sounded rough, often broken by a gasp or a curse. In his spacesuit, in the raw, wan sunshine, he resembled a knight who, in despite of wounds, did battle against a monster.

"All right," he called at last. "I think I've learned what to expect and how we should operate. It'll take the two of us."

"Yes . . . oh, yes, my Kendrick."

* * *

The hours passed. Ever so slowly, the sun climbed and the stars wheeled and Saturn waned.

Most places, the humans labored side by side. They did not require more than the narrowest of lanes, but unless they cut it wide to begin with, the banks to right and left would promptly slip down and bury it. Sometimes the conformation underneath allowed a single person at a time to work. Then the other could rest. Soon it was Scobie who must oftenest take advantage of that. Sometimes they both stopped briefly, for food and drink and reclining on their packs.

Rock yielded to water ice. Where this rose very sharply, the couple knew it, because the sand-ice that they undercut would come down in a mass. After the first such incident, when they were nearly swept away, Scobie always drove his geologist's hammer into each new stratum. At any sign of danger, he would seize its handle and Broberg would cast an arm around his waist. Their other hands clutched their trenching tools. Anchored, but forced to strain every muscle, they would stand while the flood poured around them, knee-high, once even chest-high, seeking to bury them irretrievably deep in its quasi-fluid substance. Afterward they would confront a bare stretch. It was generally too steep to climb unaided, and they chipped footholds.

Weariness was another tide to which they dared not yield. At best, their progress was dismayingly slow. They needed little heat input to keep warm, except when they took a rest, but their lungs put a furious demand on air recyclers. Garcilaso's fuel cell, which they had brought along, could give a single person extra hours of life, though depleted as it was after coping with his hypothermia, the time would be insufficient for rescue by the teams from *Chronos*. Unspoken was the idea of taking turns with it. That would put them in wretched shape, chilled and stifling, but at least they would leave the universe together.

Thus it was hardly a surprise that their minds fled from pain, soreness, exhaustion, stench, despair. Without that respite, they could not have gone on as long as they did.

At ease for a few minutes, their backs against a blue-shimmering parapet which they must scale, they gazed across the bowl, where Garcilaso's suited body gleamed like a remote pyre, and up the curve opposite to Saturn. The planet shone lambent amber, softly banded, the rings a coronet which a shadow band across their arc seemed to make all the brighter. That radiance overcame sight of most nearby stars, but elsewhere they arrayed themselves multitudinous, in splendor, around the silver road which the galaxy clove between them.

"How right a tomb for Alvarlan," *Ricia says in a dreamer's murmur.*

"Has he died, then?" *Kendrick asks.*

"You do not know?"

"I have been too busied. After we won free of the ruins and I left you to recover while I went scouting, I encountered a troop of warriors. I escaped, but must needs return to you by devious, hidden ways." *Kendrick strokes Ricia's sunny hair.* "Besides, dearest dear, it has ever been you, not I, who had the gift of hearing spirits."

"Brave darling . . . yes, it is a glory to me that I was able to call his soul out of Hell. It sought his body, but that was old and frail and could not survive the knowledge it now had. Yet Alvarlan passed peacefully, and before he did, for his last magic he made himself a tomb from whose ceiling starlight will eternally shine."

"May he sleep well. But for us there is no sleep. Not yet. We have far to travel."

"Aye. But already we have left the wreckage behind. Look! Everywhere around in this meadow, anemones peep through the grass. A lark sings above."

"These lands are not always calm. We may well have more adventures ahead of us. But we shall meet them with high hearts."

Kendrick and Ricia rise to continue their journey.

Cramped on a meager ledge, Scobie and Broberg shoveled for an hour without broadening it much. The sand-ice slid from above as fast as they could cast it down. "We'd better quit this as a bad job," the man finally decided. "The best we've done is flatten the slope ahead of us a tiny bit. No telling how far inward the shelf goes before there's a solid layer on top. Maybe there isn't any."

"What shall we do instead?" Broberg asked in the same worn tone.

He jerked a thumb. "Scramble back to the level beneath and try a different direction. But first we absolutely require a break."

They spread kerofoam pads and sat. After a while during which they merely stared, stunned by fatigue, Broberg spoke.

"I go to the brook," *Ricia relates.* "It chimes under arches of green boughs. Light falls between them to sparkle on it. I kneel and drink. The water is cold, pure, sweet. When I raise my eyes, I see the figure of a young woman, naked, her tresses the color of leaves. A wood nymph. She smiles."

"Yes, I see her too," *Kendrick joins in.* "I approach carefully, not to frighten her off. She asks our names and errands. We explain that we are lost. She tells us how to find an oracle which may give us counsel."

They depart to find it.

Flesh could no longer stave off sleep. "Give us a yell in an hour, will you, Mark?" Scobie requested.

"Sure," Danzig said, "but will that be enough?"

"It's the most we can afford, after the setbacks we've had. We've come less than a third of the way."

"If I haven't talked to you," Danzig sid slowly, "it's not because I've been hard at work, though I have been. It's that I figured you two were having a plenty bad time without me nagging you. However—do you think it's wise to fantasize the way you have been?"

A flush crept across Broberg's cheeks and down toward her bosom. "You listened, Mark?"

"Well, yes, of course. You might have an urgent word for me at any minute—"

"Why? What could you do? A game is a personal affair."

"Uh, yes, yes—"

Ricia and Kendrick have made love whenever they could. The accounts were never explicit, but the words were often passionate.

"We'll keep you tuned in when we need you, like for an alarm clock," Broberg clipped. "Otherwise we'll cut the circuit."

"But—look, I never meant to—"

"I know," Scobie sighed. "You're a nice guy, and I daresay we're overreacting. Still, that's the way it's got to be. Call us when I told you."

Deep within the grotto, the Pythoness sways on her throne, in the ebb and flow of her oracular dream. As nearly as Ricia and Kendrick can understand what she chants, she tells them to fare westward on the Stag Path until they meet a one-eyed graybeard who will give them further guidance; but they must be wary in his presence, for he is easily angered. They make obeisance and depart. On their way out, they pass the offering they brought. Since they had little with them other than garments and his weapons, the Princess gave the shrine her golden hair. The knight insists that, close-cropped, she remains beautiful.

"Hey, whoops, we've cleared us an easy twenty meters," Scobie said, albeit in a voice which weariness had hammered flat. *At first, the journey through the land of Nacre is a delight.*

His oath afterward had no more life in it. "Another blind alley, seems like." *The old man in the blue cloak and wide-brimmed hat was indeed wrathful when Ricia refused him her favors and Kendrick's spear struck his own aside. Cunningly, he has pretended to make peace and told them what road they should next take. But at the end of it are trolls. The wayfarers elude them and double back.*

"My brain's stumbling around in a fog," Scobie groaned. "My busted rib isn't exactly helping, either. If I don't get another nap I'll keep on making misjudgments till we run out of time."

"By all means, Colin," Broberg said. "I'll stand watch and rouse you in an hour."

"What?" he asked in dim surprise. "Why not join me and have Mark call us as he did before?"

She grimaced. "No need to bother him. I'm tired, yes, but not sleepy."

He lacked wit or strength to argue. "Okay," he said. He stretched his insulating pad on the ice, and toppled out of awareness.

Broberg settled herself next to him. They were halfway to the heights, but they had been struggling, with occasional breaks, for more than twenty hours, and progress grew harder and trickier even as they themselves grew weaker and more stupefied. If ever they reached the top and spied Danzig's signal, they would have something like a couple of hours' stiff travel to shelter.

Saturn, sun, stars shone through vitryl. Broberg smiled down at Scobie's face. He was no Greek god. Sweat, grime, unshavenness, the manifold marks of exhaustion were upon him, but— For that matter, she was scarcely an image of glamour herself.

Princess Ricia sits by her knight, where he slumbers in the dwarf's cottage, and strums a harp the dwarf lent her before he went off to his mine, and sings a lullaby to sweeten the dreams of Kendrick. When it is done, she passes her lips lightly across his, and drifts into the same gentle sleep.

Scobie woke a piece at a time. "Ricia, beloved," *Kendrick whispers, and feels after her. He will summon her up with kisses—*

He scrambled to his feet. "Judas priest!" She lay unmoving. He heard her breath in his earplugs, before the roaring of his pulse drowned it. The sun glared farther aloft, he could see it had moved, and Saturn's crescent had thinned more, forming sharp horns at its ends. He forced his eyes toward the watch on his left wrist.

"Ten hours," he choked.

He knelt and shook his companion. "Come, for Christ's sake!" Her lashes fluttered. When she saw the horror on his visage, drowsiness fled from her.

"Oh, no," she said. "Please, no."

Scobie climbed stiffly erect and flicked his main radio switch. "Mark, do you receive?"

"Colin!" Danzig chattered. "Thank God! I was going out of my head from worry."

"You're not off that hook, my friend. We just finished a ten-hour snooze."

"What? How far did you get first?"

"To about forty meters elevation. The going looks tougher ahead than in back. I'm afraid we won't make it."

"Don't *say* that, Colin," Danzig begged.

"My fault," Broberg declared. She stood rigid, fists doubled, her features a mask. Her tone was steely. "He was worn out, had to have a nap. I offered to wake him, but fell asleep myself."

"Not your fault, Jean," Scobie began.

She interrupted: "Yes. Mine. Perhaps I can make it good. Take my fuel cell. I'll still have deprived you of my help, of course, but you might survive and reach the boat anyway."

He seized her hands. They did not unclench. "If you imagine I could do that—"

"If you don't, we're both finished," she said unbendingly. "I'd rather go out with a clear conscience."

"And what about my conscience?" he shouted. Checking himself, he wet his lips and said fast: "Besides, you're not to blame. Sleep slugged you. If I'd been thinking, I'd have realized it was bound to do so, and contacted Mark. The fact that you didn't either shows how far gone you were yourself. And . . . you've got Tom and the kids waiting for you. Take my cell." He paused. "And my blessing."

"Shall Ricia forsake her true knight?"

"Wait, hold on, listen," Danzig called. "Look, this is terrible, but—oh, hell, excuse me, but I've got to remind you that dramatics only clutter the action. From what descriptions you've sent, I don't see how either of you can possibly proceed solo. Together, you might yet. At least you're rested —sore in the muscles, no doubt, but clearer in the head. The climb before you may prove easier than you think. Try!"

Scobie and Broberg regarded each other for a whole minute. A thawing went through her, and warmed him. Finally they smiled and embraced. "Yeah, right," he growled. "We're off. But first a bite to eat. I'm plain, old-fashioned hungry. Aren't you?" She nodded.

"That's the spirit," Danzig encouraged them. "Uh, may I make another suggestion? I am just a spectator, which is pretty hellish but does give me an overall view. Drop that game of yours."

Scobie and Broberg tautened.

"It's the real culprit," Danzig pleaded. "Weariness alone wouldn't have clouded your judgment. You'd never have cut me off, and— But weariness and shock and grief did lower your defenses to the point where the damned game took you over. You weren't yourselves when you fell asleep. You were those dreamworld characters. They had no reason not to cork off!"

Broberg shook her head violently. "Mark," said Scobie, "you are correct about being a spectator. That means there are some things you don't understand. Why subject yourself to the torture of listening in, hour after hour? We'll call you back from time to time, naturally. Take care." He broke the circuit.

"He's wrong," Broberg insisted.

Scobie shrugged. "Right or wrong, what difference? We won't pass out again in the time we have left. The game didn't handicap us as we traveled. In fact, it helped, by making the situation feel less gruesome."

"Aye. Let us break our fast and set forth anew on our pilgrimage."

The struggle grew stiffer. "Belike the White Witch has cast a spell on this road," *says Ricia.*

"She shall not daunt us," *vows Kendrick.*

"No, never while we fare side by side, you and I, noblest of men."

A slide overcame them and swept them back a dozen meters. They lodged against a crag. After the flow had passed by, they lifted their bruised bodies and limped in search of a different approach. The place where the geologist's hammer lay was no longer accessible.

"What shattered the bridge?" *asks Ricia.*

"A giant," *answers Kendrick.* "I saw him as I fell into the river. He lunged at me, and we fought in the shallows until he fled. He bore away my sword in his thigh."

"You have your spear that Wayland forged," *Ricia says,* "and always you have my heart."

They stopped on the last small outcrop they uncovered. It proved to be not a shelf but a pinnacle of water ice. Around it glittered sand-ice, again quiescent. Ahead was a slope thirty meters in length, and then the rim, and stars.

The distance might as well have been thirty light-years. Whoever tried to cross would immediately sink to an unknown depth.

There was no point in crawling back down the bared side of the pinnacle. Broberg had clung to it for an hour while she chipped niches to climb by with her knife. Scobie's condition had not allowed him to help. If they sought to return, they could easily slip, fall, and be engulfed. If they avoided that, they would never find a new path. Less than two hours' worth of energy was left in their fuel cells. Attempting to push onward while swapping Garcilaso's back and forth would be an exercise in futility.

They settled themselves, legs dangling over the abyss, and held hands.

"I do not think the orcs can burst the iron door of this tower," *Kendrick says,* "but they will besiege us until we starve to death."

"You never yielded up your hope ere now, my knight," *replies Ricia, and kisses his temple.* "Shall we search about? These walls are unutterably ancient. Who knows what relics of wizardry lie forgotten within? A pair of phoenix-feather cloaks, that will bear us laughing through the sky to our home—?"

"I fear not, my darling. Our weird is upon us." *Kendrick touches the spear that leans agleam against the battlement.* "Sad and gray will the world be without you. We can but meet our doom bravely."

"Happily, since we are together." *Ricia's gamin smile breaks forth.* "I did notice that a certain room holds a bed. Shall we try it?"

Kendrick frowns. "Rather should we seek to set our minds and souls in order."

She tugs his elbow. "Later, yes. Besides—who knows?—when we dust off the blanket, we may find it is a Tarnkappe that will take us invisible through the enemy."

"You dream."

Fear stirs behind her eyes. "What if I do?" *Her words tremble.* "I can dream us free if you will help."

Scobie's fist smote the ice. "No!" he croaked. "I'll die in the world that is."

Ricia shrinks from him. He sees terror invade her. "You, you rave, beloved," *she stammers.*

He twisted about and caught her by the arms. "Don't you want to remember Tom and your boys?"

"Who—?"

Kendrick slumps. "I don't know. I have forgotten too."

She leans against him, there on the windy height. A hawk circles above. "The residuum of an evil enchantment, surely. Oh, my heart, my life, cast it from you! Help me find the means to save us." *Yet her entreaty is uneven, and through it speaks dread.*

Kendrick straightens. He lays hand on Wayland's spear, and it is as though strength flows thence, into him. "A spell in truth," *he says. His tone gathers force.* "I will not abide in its darkness, nor suffer it to blind and deafen you, my lady." *His gaze takes hold of hers, which cannot break away.* "There is but a single road to our freedom. It goes through the gates of death."

She waits, mute and shuddering.

"Whatever we do, we must die, Ricia. Let us fare hence as our own folk."

"I—no—I won't—I will—"

"You see before you the means of your deliverance. It is sharp, I am strong, you will feel no pain."

She bares her bosom. "Then quickly, Kendrick, before I am lost!"

He drives the weapon home. "I love you," he says. *She sinks at his feet.* "I follow you, my darling," *he says, withdrawing the steel, bracing the shaft against stone, and lunging forward. He falls beside her.* "Now we are free."

"That was . . . a nightmare." Broberg sounded barely awake.

Scobie's voice shook. "Necessary, I think, for both of us." He gazed straight before him, letting Saturn fill his eyes with dazzle. "Else we'd have stayed . . . insane? Maybe not, by definition. But we'd not have been in reality either."

"It would have been easier," she mumbled. "We'd never have known we were dying."

"Would you have preferred that?"

Broberg shivered. The slackness in her countenance gave place to the same tension that was in his. "Oh, no," she said, quite softly but in the manner of full consciousness. "No, you were right, of course. Thank you for your courage."

"You've always had as much guts as anybody, Jean. You must have more imagination than me." Scobie's hand chopped empty space in a gesture of dismissal. "Okay, we should call poor Mark and let him know. But first—" His words lost the cadence he had laid on them. "First—"

Her glove clasped his. "What, Colin?"

"Let's decide about that third unit—Luis's," he said with difficulty, still confronting the great ringed planet. "Your decision, actually, though we can discuss the matter if you want. I will not hog it for the sake of a few more hours. Nor will I share it; that would be a nasty way for us both to go out. However, I suggest you use it."

"To sit beside your frozen corpse?" she replied. "No. I wouldn't even feel the warmth, not in my bones—"

She turned toward him so fast that she nearly fell off the pinnacle. He caught her. "*Warmth!*" she screamed, shrill as the cry of a hawk on the wing. "Colin, we'll take our bones home!"

"In point of fact," said Danzig. "I've climbed onto the hull. That's high enough for me to see over those ridges and needles. I've got a view of the entire horizon."

"Good," grunted Scobie. "Be prepared to survey a complete circle quick. This depends on a lot of factors we can't predict. The beacon will certainly not be anything like as big as what you had arranged. It may be thin and short-lived. And, of course, it may rise too low for sighting at your distance." He cleared his throat. "In that case, we two have bought the farm. But we'll have made a hell of a try, which feels great by itself."

He hefted the fuel cell, Garcilaso's gift. A piece of heavy wire, insulation stripped off, joined the prongs. Without a regulator, the unit poured its maximum power through the short circuit. Already the strand glowed.

"Are you sure you don't want me to do it, Colin?" Broberg asked. "Your rib—"

He made a lopsided grin. "I'm nonetheless better designed by nature for throwing things," he said. "Allow me that much male arrogance. The bright idea was yours."

"It should have been obvious from the first," she said. "I think it would have been, if we weren't bewildered in our dream."

"M-m, often the simple answers are the hardest to find. Besides, we had to get this far or it wouldn't have worked, and the game helped mightily. . . . Are you set, Mark? Heave-ho!"

Scobie cast the cell as if it were a baseball, hard and far through the Iapetan gravity field. Spinning, its incandescent wire wove a sorcerous web across vision. It landed somewhere beyond the rim, on the glacier's back.

Frozen gases vaporized, whirled aloft, briefly recondensed before they were lost. A geyser stood white against the stars.

"I see you!" Danzig yelped. "I see your beacon, I've got my bearing, I'll be on my way! With hope and extra energy units and everything!"

Scobie sagged to the ground and clutched at his left side. Broberg knelt and held him, as if either of them could lay hand on his pain. No large matter. He would not hurt much longer.

"How high would you guess the plume goes?" Danzig inquired, calmer.

"About a hundred meters," Broberg replied after study.

"Oh, damn, these gloves do make it awkward punching the calculator. . . . Well, to judge by what I observe of it, I'm between ten and fifteen klicks off. Give me an hour or a tad more to get there and find your exact location. Okay?"

Broberg checked gauges. "Yes, by a hair. We'll turn our thermostats down and sit very quietly to reduce oxygen demand. We'll get cold, but we'll survive."

"I may be quicker," Danzig said. "That was a worst-case estimate. All right, I'm off. No more conversation till we meet. I won't take any foolish chances, but I will need my wind for making speed."

Faintly, those who waited heard him breathe, heard his hastening footfalls. The geyser died.

They sat, arms around waists, and regarded the glory which encompassed them. After a silence, the man said, "Well, I suppose this means the end of the game. For everybody."

"It must certainly be brought under strict control," the woman answered. "I wonder, though, if they will abandon it altogether—out here."

"If they must, they can."

"Yes. We did, you and I, didn't we?"

They turned face to face, beneath that star-beswarmed, Saturn-ruled sky. Nothing tempered the sunlight that revealed them to each other, she a middle-aged wife, he a man ordinary except for his aloneness. They would never play again. They could not.

A puzzled compassion was in her smile. "Dear friend—" she began.

His uplifted palm warded her from further speech. "Best we don't talk unless it's essential," he said. "That'll save a little oxygen, and we can stay a little warmer. Shall we try to sleep?"

Her eyes widened and darkened. "I dare not," she confessed. "Not till enough time has gone past. Now, I might dream."

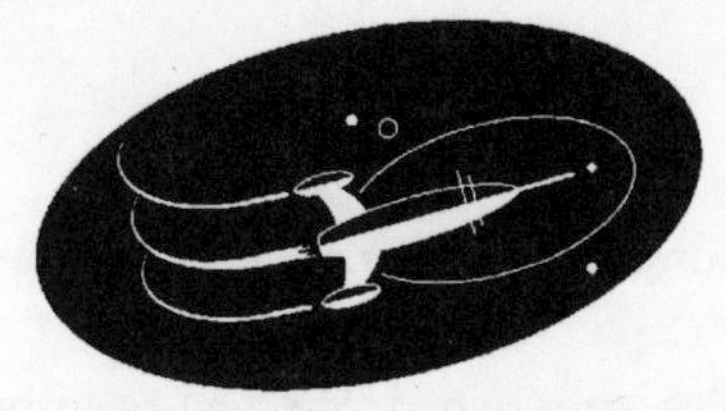

HARDFOUGHT

Greg Bear

Humans called it the Medusa. Its long twisted ribbons of gas strayed across fifty parsecs, glowing blue, yellow, and carmine. Its central core was a ghoulish green flecked with watery black. Half a dozen protostars circled the core, and as many more dim conglomerates pooled in dimples in the nebula's magnetic field. The Medusa was a huge womb of stars—and disputed territory.

Whenever Prufrax looked at it in displays or through the ship's ports, it seemed malevolent, like a zealous mother showing an ominous face to protect her children. Prufrax had never had a mother, but she had seen them in some of the fibs.

At five, Prufrax was old enough to know the *Mellangee's* mission and her role in it. She had already been through four ship-years of indoctrination. Until her first battle she would be educated in both the Know and the Tell. She would be exercised and trained in the Mocks; in sleep she would dream of penetrating the huge red-and-white Senexi seedships and finding the brood mind. "Zap, Zap," she went with her lips, silent so the tellman wouldn't think her thoughts were straying.

The tellman peered at her from his position in the center of the spherical classroom. Her mates stared straight at the center, all focusing somewhere around the tellman's spiderlike teaching desk, waiting for the trouble, some fidgeting. "How many branch individuals in the Senexi brood mind?" he asked. He looked around the classroom. Peered face by face. Focused on her again. "Pru?"

"Five," she said. Her arms ached. She had been pumped full of moans the wake before. She was already three meters tall, in elfstate, with her long, thin limbs not nearly adequately fleshed out and her fingers still crisscrossed with the surgery done to adapt them to the gloves.

"What will you find in the brood mind?" the tellman pursued, his impassive face stretched across a hammerhead as wide as his shoulders. Some of the fems thought tellmen were attractive. Not many—and Pru was not one of them.

"Yoke," she said.

"What is in the brood-mind yoke?"

"Fibs."

"More specifically? And it really isn't all fib, you know."

"Info. Senexi data."

"What will you do?"

"Zap," she said, smiling.

"Why, Pru?"

"Yoke has team gens-memory. Zap yoke, spill the life of the team's five branch inds."

"Zap the brood, Pru?"

"No," she said solemnly. That was a new instruction, only in effect since her class's inception. "Hold the brood for the supreme overs." The tellman did not say what would be done with the Senexi broods. That was not her concern.

"Fine," said the tellman. "You tell well, for someone who's always half-journeying."

Brainwalk, Prufrax thought. Tellman was fancy with the words, but to Pru, what she was prone to do during Tell was brainwalk, seeking out her future. She was already five, soon six. Old. Some saw Senexi by the time they were four.

"Zap, Zap," she went with her lips.

Aryz skidded through the thin layer of liquid ammonia on his broadest pod, considering his new assignment. He knew the Medusa by another name, one that conveyed all the time and effort the Senexi had invested in it. The protostar nebula held few mysteries for him. He and his four branch-mates, who along with the all-important brood mind comprised one of the six teams aboard the seedship, had patrolled the nebula for ninety-three orbits, each orbit—including the timeless periods outside status geometry—taking some one hundred and thirty human years. They had woven in and out of the tendrils of gas, charting the infalling masses and exploring the rocky accretion disks of stars entering the main sequence. With each measure and update, the brood minds refined their view of the nebula as it would be a hundred generations hence, when the Senexi plan would finally mature.

The Senexi were nearly as old as the galaxy. They had achieved space-flight during the time of the starglove, when the galaxy had been a sphere. They had not been a quick or brilliant race. Each great achievement had taken thousands of generations, and not just because of their material handicaps. In those times, elements heavier than helium had been rare, found only around stars that had greedily absorbed huge amounts of prime-val hydrogen, burned fierce and blue and exploded early, permeating the ill-defined galactic arms with carbon and nitrogen, lithium and oxygen. Elements heavier than iron had been almost nonexistent. The biologies of cold gas-giant worlds had developed with a much smaller palette of chemical combinations in producing the offspring of the primary Population II stars.

Aryz, even with the limited perspective of a branch ind, was aware that, on the whole, the humans opposing the seedship were more adaptable, more vital. But they were not more experienced. The Senexi with their billions of years had often matched them. And Aryz's perspective was expanding with each day of his new assignment.

In the early generations of the struggle, Senexi mental stasis and cultural inflexibility had made them avoid contact with the Population I species. They had never begun a program of extermination of the younger, newly life-forming worlds; the task would have been monumental and probably useless. So when spacefearing cultures developed, the Senexi had retreated, falling back into the redoubts of old stars even before engaging with the new kinds. They had retreated for three generations, about thirty thousand human years, raising their broods on cold nestworlds around red dwarfs, conserving, holding back for the inevitable conflicts.

As the Senexi had anticipated, the younger Population I races had found need of even the aging groves of the galaxy's first stars. They had moved in savagely, voraciously, with all the strength and mutability of organisms evolved from a richer soup of elements. Biology had, in some ways, evolved in its own right and superseded the Senexi.

Aryz raised the upper globe of his body, with its five silicate eyes arranged in a cross along the forward surface. He had memory of those times, and times long before, though his team hadn't existed then. The brood mind carried memories selected from the total store of nearly twelve billion years' experience; an awesome amount of knowledge, even to a Senexi. He pushed himself forward with his rear pods.

Through the brood mind Aryz could share the memories of a hundred thousand past generations, yet the brood mind itself was younger than its branch of individuals. For a time in their youth, in their liquid-dwelling larval form, the branch inds carried their own sacs of data, each a fragment of the total necessary for complete memory. The branch inds swam through ammonia seas and wafted through thick warm gaseous zones, protoplasmic blobs three to four meters in diameter—developing their personalities under the weight of the past—and not even a complete past. No wonder they were inflexible, Aryz thought. Most branch inds were aware enough to see that—especially when they were allowed to compare histories with the Population I species, as he was doing—but there was nothing to be done. They were content the way they were. To change would be unspeakably repugnant. Extinction was preferable . . . almost.

But now they were pressed hard. The brood mind had begun a number of experiments. Aryz's team had been selected from the seedship's contingent to oversee the experiments, and Aryz had been chosen as the chief investigator. Two orbits past, they had captured six human embryos in a breeding device, as well as a highly coveted memory storage center. Most Senexi engagements had been with humans for the past three or four generations. Just as the Senexi dominated Population II species, humans were ascendant among their kind.

Experiments with the human embryos had already been conducted.

Some had been allowed to develop normally; others had been tampered with, for reasons Aryz was not aware of. The tamperings had not been very successful.

The newer experiments, Aryz suspected, were going to take a different direction, and the seedship's actions now focused on him; he believed he would be given complete authority over the human shapes. Most branch inds would have dissipated under such a burden, but not Aryz. He found the human shapes rather interesting, in their own horrible way. They might, after all, be the key to Senexi survival.

The moans were toughening her elfstate. She lay in pain for a wake, not daring to close her eyes; her mind was changing and she feared sleep would be the end of her. Her nightmares were not easily separated from life; some, in fact, were sharper.

Too often in sleep she found herself in a Senexi trap, struggling uselessly, being pulled in deeper, her hatred wasted against such power. . . .

When she came out of the rigor, Prufrax was given leave by the subordinate tellman. She took to the *Mellangee's* greenroads, walking stiffly in the shallow gravity. Her hands itched. Her mind seemed almost empty after the turmoil of the past few wakes. She had never felt so calm and clear. She hated the Senexi double now; once for their innate evil, twice for what they had made her overs put her through to be able to fight them. Logic did not matter. She was calm, assured. She was growing more mature wake by wake. Fight-budding, the tellman called it, hate coming out like blooms, synthesizing the sunlight of his teaching into pure fight.

The greenroads rose temporarily beyond the labyrinth shields and armor of the ship. Simple transparent plastic and steel geodesic surfaces formed a lacework over the gardens, admitting radiation necessary to the vegetation growing along the paths. No machines scooted one forth and inboard here. It was necessary to walk. Walking was luxury and privilege.

Prufrax looked down on the greens to each side of the paths without much comprehension. They were *beautiful.* Yes, one should say that, think that, but what did it mean? Pleasing? She wasn't sure what being pleased meant, outside of thinking Zap. She sniffed a flower that, the signs explained, bloomed only in the light of young stars not yet fusing. They were near such a star now, and the greenroads were shiny black and electric green with the blossoms. Lamps had been set out for other plants unsuited to such darkened conditions. Some technic allowed suns to appear in selected plastic panels when viewed from certain angles. Clever, the technicals.

She much preferred the looks of a technical to a tellman, but she was common in that. Technicals required brainflex, tellmen cargo capacity. Technicals were strong and ran strong machines, like in the adventure fibs, where technicals were often the protags. She wished a technical were on the greenroads with her. The moans had the effect of making her receptive —what she saw, looking in mirrors, was a certain shine in her eyes—but there was no chance of a breeding liaison. She was quite unreproductive in this moment of elfstate. Other kinds of meetings were not unusual.

She looked up and saw a figure at least a hundred meters away, sitting on an allowed patch near the path. She walked casually, as gracefully as possible with the stiffness. Not a technical, she saw soon, but she was not disappointed. Too calm.

"Over," he said as she approached.

"Under," she replied. But not by much—he was probably six or seven ship years old and not easily classifiable.

"Such a fine elfstate," he commented. His hair was black. He was shorter than she, but something in his build reminded her of the glovers. She accepted his compliment with a nod and pointed to a spot near him. He motioned for her to sit, and she did so with a whuff, massaging her knees.

"Moans?" he asked.

"Bad stretch," she said.

"You're a glover." He was looking at the fading scars on her hands.

"Can't tell what you are," she said.

"Noncombat," he said. "Tuner of the mandates."

She knew very little about the mandates, except that law decreed every ship carry one, and few of the crew were ever allowed to peep. "Noncombat, hm?" she mused. She didn't despise him for that; one never felt strong negatives for a crew member. She didn't feel much of anything. Too calm.

"Been working on ours this wake," he said. "Too hard, I guess. Told to walk." Overzealousness in work was considered an erotic trait aboard the *Mellangee.* Still, she didn't feel too receptive toward him.

"Glovers walk after a rough growing," she said.

He nodded. "My name's Clevo."

"Prufrax."

"Combat soon?"

"Hoping. Waiting forever."

"I know. Just been allowed access to the mandate for a half-dozen wakes. All new to me. Very happy."

"Can you talk about it?" she asked. Information about the ship not accessible in certain rates was excellent barter.

"Not sure," he said, frowning. "I've been told caution."

"Well, I'm listening."

He could come from glover stock, she thought, but probably not from technical. He wasn't very muscular, but he wasn't as tall as a glover, or as thin, either.

"If you'll tell me about gloves."

With a smile she held up her hands and wriggled the short, stumpy fingers. "Sure."

The brood mind floated weightless in its tank, held in place by buffered carbon rods. Metal was at a premium aboard the Senexi ships, more out of tradition than actual material limitations. From what Aryz could tell, the Senexi used metals sparingly for the same reason—and he strained to recall the small dribbles of information about the human past he had extracted from the memory store—for the same reason (**that the Romans of old Earth regarded farming as the only truly noble occupation**—)

Farming being the raising of *plants* for food and raw materials. *Plants* were analogous to the freeth Senexi ate in their larval youth, but the freeth were not green and sedentary.

There was always a certain fascination in stretching his mind to encompass human concepts. He had had so little time to delve deeply—and that was good, of course, for he had been set to answer specific questions, not mire himself in the whole range of human filth.

He floated before the brood mind, all these thoughts coursing through his tissues. He had no central nervous system, no truly differentiated organs except those that dealt with the outside world—limbs, eyes, permea. The brood mind, however, was all central nervous system, a thinly buffered sac of viscous fluids about ten meters wide.

"Have you investigated the human memory device yet?" the brood mind asked.

"I have."

"Is communication with the human shapes possible for us?"

"We have already created interfaces for dealing with their machines. Yes, it seems likely we can communicate."

"Does it occur to you that in our long war with humans, we have made no attempt to communicate before?"

This was a complicated question. It called for several qualities that Aryz, as a branch ind, wasn't supposed to have. Inquisitiveness, for one. Branch inds did not ask questions. They exhibited initiative only as offshoots of the brood mind.

He found, much to his dismay, that the question had occurred to him. "We have never captured a human memory store before," he said, by way of incomplete answer. "We could not have communicated without such an extensive source of information."

"Yet, as you say, even in the past we have been able to use human machines."

"The problem is vastly more complex."

The brood mind paused. "Do you think the teams have been prohibited from communicating with humans?"

Aryz felt the closest thing to anguish possible for a branch ind. Was he being considered unworthy? Accused of conduct inappropriate to a branch ind? His loyalty to the brood mind was unshakable. "Yes."

"And what might our reasons be?"

"Avoidance of pollution."

"Correct. We can no more communicate with them and remain untainted than we can walk on their worlds, breathe their atmosphere." Again, silence. Aryz lapsed into a mode of inactivity. When the brood mind readdressed him, he was instantly aware.

"Do you know how you are different?" it asked.

"I am not . . ." Again, hesitation. Lying to the brood mind was impossible for him. What snared him was semantics, a complication in the radiated signals between them. He had not been aware that he was different; the brood mind's questions suggested he might be. But he could not possibly face up to the fact and analyze it all in one short time. He signaled his distress.

"You are useful to the team," the brood mind said. Aryz calmed instantly. His thoughts became sluggish, receptive. There was a possibility of redemption. But how was he different? "You are to attempt communication with the shapes yourself. You will not engage in any discourse with your fellows while you are so involved." He was banned. "And after completion of this mission and transfer of certain facts to me, you will dissipate."

Aryz struggled with the complexity of the orders. "How am I different, worthy of such a commission?"

The surface of the brood mind was as still as an undisturbed pool. The indistinct black smudges that marked its radiative organs circulated slowly within the interior, then returned, one above the other, to focus on him. "You will grow a new branch ind. It will not have your flaws, but, then again, it will not be useful to me should such a situation come a second time. Your dissipation will be a relief, but it will be regretted."

"How am I different?"

"I think you know already," the brood mind said. "When the time comes, you will feed the new branch ind all your memories but those of human contact. If you do not survive to that stage of its growth, you will pick your fellow who will perform that function for you."

A small pinkish spot appeared on the back of Aryz's globe. He floated forward and placed his largest permeum against the brood mind's cool surface. The key and command were passed, and his body became capable of reproduction. Then the signal of dismissal was given. He left the chamber.

Flowing through the thin stream of liquid ammonia lining the corridor, he felt ambiguously stimulated. His was a position of privilege and anathema. He had been blessed—and condemned. Had any other branch ind experienced such a thing?

Then he knew the brood mind was correct. He was different from his fellows. None of them would have asked such questions. None of them could have survived the suggestion of communicating with human shapes. If this task hadn't been given to him, he would have had to dissipate away.

The pink spot grew larger, then began to make greyish flakes. It broke through the skin, and casually, almost without thinking, Aryz scraped it off against a bulkhead. It clung, made a radio-frequency emanation something like a sigh, and began absorbing nutrients from the ammonia.

Aryz went to inspect the shapes.

She was intrigued by Clevo, but the kind of interest she felt was new to her. She was not particularly receptive. Rather, she felt a mental gnawing as if she were hungry or had been injected with some kind of brain moans. What Clevo told her about the mandates opened up a topic she had never considered before. How did all things come to be—and how did she figure in them?

The mandates were quite small, Clevo explained, each little more than a cubic meter in volume. Within them was the entire history and culture of the human species, as accurate as possible, culled from all existing sources. The mandate in each ship was updated whenever the ship returned to a contact station. It was not likely the *Mellangee* would return to a contact station during their lifetimes, with the crew leading such short lives on the average.

Clevo had been assigned small tasks—checking data and adding ship records—that had allowed him to sample bits of the mandate. "It's mandated that we have records," he explained, "and what we have, you see, is *man-data*." He smiled. "That's a joke," he said. "Sort of."

Prufrax nodded solemnly. "So where do we come from?"

"Earth, of course," Clevo said. "Everyone knows that."

"I mean, where do we come from—you and I, the crew."

"Breeding division. Why ask? You know."

"Yes." She frowned, concentrating. "I mean, we don't come from the same place as the Senexi. The same way."

"No, that's foolishness."

She saw that it was foolishness—the Senexi were different all around. What was she struggling to ask? "Is their fib like our own?"

"Fib? History's not a fib. Not most of it, anyway. Fibs are for unreal. History is overfib."

She knew, in a vague way, that fibs were unreal. She didn't like to have their comfort demeaned, though. "Fibs are fun," she said. "They teach Zap."

"I suppose," Clevo said dubiously. "Being noncombat, I don't see Zap fibs."

Fibs without Zap were almost unthinkable to her. "Such dull," she said.

"Well, of course you'd say that. I might find Zap fibs dull—think of that?"

"We're different," she said. "Like Senexi are different."

Clevo's jaw hung over. "No way. We're crew. We're human. Senexi are . . ." He shook his head as if fed bitters.

"No, I mean . . ." She paused, uncertain whether she was entering unallowed territory. "You and I, we're fed different, given different moans. But in a big way we're different from Senexi. They aren't made, nor act, as you and I. But . . ." Again it was difficult to express. She was irritated. "I don't want to talk to you anymore."

A tellman walked down the path, not familiar to Prufrax. He held out his hand for Clevo, and Clevo grasped it. "It's amazing," the tellman said, "how you two gravitate to each other. Go, elfstate," he addressed Prufrax. "You're on the wrong greenroad."

She never saw the young researcher again. With glover training underway, the itches he aroused soon faded, and Zap resumed its overplace.

The Senexi had ways of knowing humans were near. As information came in about fleets and individual cruisers less than one percent nebula diameter distant, the seedship seemed warmer, less hospitable. Everything was UV with anxiety, and the new branch ind on the wall had to be shielded by a special silicate cup to prevent distortion. The brood mind grew a corniculum automatically, though the toughened outer membrane would be of little help if the seedship was breached.

Aryz had buried his personal confusion under a load of work. He had penetrated the human memory store deeply enough to find instruction on its use. It called itself a *mandate* (the human word came through the interface as a correlated series of radiated symbols), and even the simple preliminary directions were difficult for Aryz. It was like swimming in another family's private sea, though of course infinitely more alien; how could he connect with experiences never had, problems and needs never encountered by his kind?

He could speak some of the human languages in several radio frequencies, but he hadn't yet decided how he was going to produce modulated sound for the human shapes. It was a disturbing prospect. What would he vibrate? A permeum could vibrate subtly—such signals were used when branch inds joined to form the brood mind—but he doubted his control would ever be subtle enough. Sooner expect a human to communicate with a Senexi by controlling the radiations of its nervous system! The humans had distinct organs within their breathing passages that produced the vibrations; perhaps those structures could be mimicked. But he hadn't yet studied the dead shapes in much detail.

He observed the new branch ind once or twice each watch period. Never before had he seen an induced replacement. The normal process was for two brood minds to exchange plasm and form new team buds, then to exchange and nurture the buds. The buds were later cast free to swim as individual larvae. While the larvae often swam through the liquid and gas atmosphere of a Senexi world for thousands, even tens of thousands of kilometers, inevitably they returned to gather with the other buds of their team. Replacements were selected from a separately created pool of "generic" buds only if one or more originals had been destroyed during their wanderings. The destruction of a complete team meant reproductive failure.

In a mature team, only when a branch ind was destroyed did the brood mind induce a replacement. In essence, then, Aryz was already considered dead.

Yet he was still useful. That amused him, if the Senexi emotion could be called amusement. Restricting himself from his fellows was difficult, but he filled the time by immersing himself, through the interface, in the mandate.

The humans were also connected with the mandate through their surrogate parent, and in this manner they were quiescent.

He reported infrequently to the brood mind. Until he had established communication, there was little to report.

And throughout his turmoil, like the others he could sense a fight was coming. It could determine the success or failure of all their work in the nebula. In the grand scheme, failure here might not be crucial. But the Senexi had taken the long view too often in the past. Their age and experience—their calmness—were working against them. How else to explain the decision to communicate with human shapes? Where would such efforts lead? If he succeeded.

And he knew himself well enough to doubt he would fail.

He could feel an affinity for them already, peering at them through the thick glass wall in their isolated chamber, his skin paling at the thought of their heat, their poisonous chemistry. A diseased affinity. He hated himself for it. And reveled in it. It was what made him particularly useful to the team. If he was defective, and this was the only way he could serve, then so be it.

The other branch inds observed his passings from a distance, making no judgments. Aryz was dead, though he worked and moved. His sacrifice had been fearful. Yet he would not be a hero. His kind could never be emulated.

It was a horrible time, a horrible conflict.

She floated in language, learned it in a trice; there were no distractions. She floated in history and picked up as much as she could, for the source seemed inexhaustible. She tried to distinguish between eyes-open—the barren, pale grey-brown chamber with the thick green wall, beyond which floated a murky roundness—and eyes-shut, when she dropped back into language and history with no fixed foundation.

Eyes-open, she saw the Mam with its comforting limbs and its soft voice, its tubes and extrusions of food and its hissings and removal of waste. Through Mam's wires she learned. Mam also tended another like herself, and another, and one more unlike any of them, more like the shape beyond the green wall.

She was very young, and it was all a mystery.

At least she knew her name. And what she was supposed to do. She took small comfort in that.

They fitted Prufrax with her gloves, and she went into the practice chamber, dragged by her gloves almost, for she hadn't yet knitted her plug-in nerves in the right index digit and her pace control was uncertain.

There, for six wakes straight, she flew with the other glovers back and forth across the dark spaces like elfstate comets. Constellations and nebula aspects flashed at random on the distant walls, and she oriented to them like a night-flying bird. Her glovemates were Ornin, an especially slender male, and Ban, a red-haired female, and the special-projects sisters Ya, Trice, and Damu, new from the breeding division.

When she let the gloves have their way, she was freer than she had ever felt before. Did the gloves really control? The question wasn't important. Control was somewhere uncentered, behind her eyes and beyond her fingers, as if she were drawn on a beautiful silver wire where it was best to go. Doing what was best to do. She barely saw the field that flowed from the grip of the thick, solid gloves or felt its caressing, life-sustaining influence. Truly, she hardly saw or felt anything but situations, targets, opportunities, the success or failure of the Zap. Failure was an acute pain. She was never reprimanded for failure; the reprimand was in her blood, and she felt as if she wanted to die. But then the opportunity would improve, the Zap would succeed, and everything around her—stars, Senexi seedship, the *Mellangee,* everything—seemed part of a beautiful dream all her own.

She was intense in the Mocks.

Their initial practice over, the entry play began.

One by one, the special-projects sisters took their hyperbolic formation. Their glove fields threw out extensions, and they combined force. In they went, the mock Senexi seedship brilliant red and white and UV and radio and hateful before them. Their tails swept through the seedship's outer shields and swirled like long silk hair laid on water; they absorbed fantastic energies, grew brighter like violent little stars against the seedship outline. They were engaged in the drawing of the shields, and sure as topology, the spirals of force had to have a dimple on the opposite side that would iris wide enough to let in glovers. The sisters twisted the forces, and Prufrax could see the dimple stretching out under them—

The exercise ended. The elfstate glovers were cast into sudden dark. Prufrax came out of the mock unprepared, her mind still bent on the Zap. The lack of orientation drove her as mad as a moth suddenly flipped from night to day. She careened until gently mitted and channeled. She flowed down a tube, the field slowly neutralizing, and came to a halt still gloved, her body jerking and tingling.

"What the breed happened?" she screamed, her hands beginning to hurt.

"Energy conserve," a mechanical voice answered. Behind Prufrax, the other elfstate glovers lined up in the catch tube, all but the special-projects sisters. Ya, Trice, and Damu had been taken out of the exercise early and replaced by simulations. There was no way their functions could be mocked. They entered the tube ungloved and helped their comrades adjust to the overness of the real.

As they left the mock chamber, another batch of glovers, even younger and fresher in elfstate, passed them. Ya held her hands up, and they saluted in return. "Breed more every day," Prufrax grumbled. She worried about having so many crew she'd never be able to conduct a satisfactory Zap herself. Where would the honor of being a glover go if everyone was a glover?

She wriggled into her cramped bunk, feeling exhilarated and irritated. She replayed the mocks and added in the missing Zap, then stared gloomily at her small, narrow feet.

Out there the Senexi waited. Perhaps they were in the same state as she —ready to fight, testy at being reined in. She pondered her ignorance, her inability to judge whether such things were even possible among the enemy. She thought of the researcher, Clevo. "Blank," she murmured. "Blank, blank." Such thoughts were unnecessary, and humanizing Senexi was unworthy of a glover.

Aryz looked at the instrument, stretched a pod into it, and willed. Vocal human language came out the other end, thin and squeaky in the helium atmosphere. The sound disgusted and thrilled him. He removed the instrument from the gelatinous strands of the engineering wall and pushed it into his interior through a stretched permeum. He took a thick draft of ammonia and slid to the human shapes chamber again.

He pushed through the narrow port into the observation room. Adjusting his eyes to the heat and bright light beyond the transparent wall, he saw the round mutated shape first—the result of their unsuccessful experiments. He swung his sphere around and looked at the others.

For a time he couldn't decide which was uglier—the mutated shape or the normals. Then he thought of what it would be like to have humans tamper with Senexi and try to make them into human forms. . . . He looked at the round human and shrunk as if from sudden heat. Aryz had had nothing to do with the experiments. For that, at least, he was grateful.

Apparently, even before fertilization, human buds—eggs—were adapted for specific roles. The healthy human shapes appeared sufficiently different —discounting *sexual* characteristics—to indicate some variation in function. They were four-podded, two-opticked, with auditory apparatus and olfactory organs mounted on the *head,* along with one permeum, the *mouth.* At least, he thought, they were hairless, unlike some of the other Population I species Aryz had learned about in the mandate.

Aryz placed the tip of the vocalizer against a sound-transmitting plate and spoke.

"Zello," came the sound within the chamber. The mutated shape looked up. It lay on the floor, great bloated stomach backed by four almost useless pods. It usually made high-pitched sounds continuously. Now it stopped and listened, straining on the tube that connected it to the breed-supervising device.

"Hello," replied the male. It sat on a ledge across the chamber, having unhooked itself.

The machine that served as surrogate parent and instructor stood in one corner, an awkward parody of a human, with limbs too long and head too small. Aryz could see the unwillingness of the designing engineers to examine human anatomy too closely.

"I am called—" Aryz said, his name emerging as a meaningless stretch of white noise. He would have to do better than that. He compressed and adapted the frequencies. "I am called Aryz."

"Hello," the young female said.

"What are your names?" He knew that well enough, having listened many times to their conversations.

"Prufrax," the female said. "I'm a glover."

The human shapes contained very little genetic memory. As a kind of brood marker, Aryz supposed, they had been equipped with their name, occupation, and the rudiments of environmental knowledge. This seemed to have been artificially imposed; in their natural state, very likely, they were born almost blank. He could not, however, be certain, since human reproductive chemistry was extraordinarily subtle and complicated.

"I'm a teacher, Prufrax," Aryz said. The logic structure of the language continued to be painful to him.

"I don't understand you," the female replied.

"You teach me, I teach you."

"We have the Mam," the male said, pointing to the machine. "She teaches us." The Mam, as they called it, was hooked into the mandate. Withholding that from the humans—the only equivalent, in essence, to the Senexi sac of memory—would have been unthinkable. It was bad enough that humans didn't come naturally equipped with their own share of knowledge.

"Do you know where you are?" Aryz asked.

"Where we live," Prufrax said. "Eyes-open."

Aryz opened a port to show them the stars and a portion of the nebula. "Can you tell where you are by looking out the window?"

"Among the lights," Prufrax said.

Humans, then, did not instinctively know their positions by star patterns as other Population I species did.

"Don't talk to it," the male said. "Mam talks to us." Aryz consulted the mandate for some understanding of the name they had given to the breed-supervising machine. Mam, it explained, was probably a natural expression for womb-carrying parent. Aryz severed the machine's power.

"Mam is no longer functional," he said. He would have the engineering wall put together another less identifiable machine to link them to the mandate and to their nutrition. He wanted them to associate comfort and completeness with nothing but himself.

The machine slumped, and the female shape pulled herself free of the hookup. She started to cry, a reaction quite mysterious to Aryz. His link with the mandate had not been intimate enough to answer questions about the wailing and moisture from the eyes. After a time the male and female lay down and became dormant.

The mutated shape made more soft sounds and tried to approach the transparent wall. It held up its thin arms as if beseeching. The others would have nothing to do with it; now it wished to go with him. Perhaps the biologists had partially succeeded in their attempt at transformation; perhaps it was more Senexi than human.

Aryz quickly backed out through the port, into the cool and security of the corridor beyond.

It was an endless orbital dance, this detection and matching of course, moving away and swinging back, deceiving and revealing, between the *Mellangee* and the Senexi seedship. It was inevitable that the human ship should close in; human ships were faster, knew better the higher geometries.

Filled with her skill and knowledge, Prufrax waited, feeling like a ripe fruit about to fall from the tree. At this point in their training, just before the application, elfstates were very receptive. She was allowed to take a lover, and they were assigned small separate quarters near the outer greenroads.

The contact was satisfactory, as far as it went. Her mate was an older glover named Kumnax, and as they lack back in the cubicle, soothed by airdance fibs, he told her stories about past battles, special tactics, how to survive.

"Survive?" she asked, puzzled.

"Of course." His long brown face was intent on the view of the greenroads through the cubicle's small window.

"I don't understand," she said.

"Most glovers don't make it," he said patiently.

"I will."

He turned to her. "You're six," he said. "You're very young. I'm ten. I've seen. You're about to be applied for the first time, you're full of confidence. But most glovers won't make it. They breed thousands of us. We're expendable. We're based on the best glovers of the past, but even the best don't survive."

"I will," Prufrax repeated, her jaw set.

"You always say that," he murmured.

Prufrax stared at him for a moment.

"Last time I knew you," he said, "you kept saying that. And here you are, fresh again."

"What last time?"

"Master Kumnax," a mechanical voice interrupted.

He stood, looking down at her. "We glovers always have big mouths. They don't like us knowing, but once we know, what can they do about it?"

"You are in violation," the voice said. "Please report to **S.**"

"But now, if you last, you'll know more than the tellman tells."

"I don't understand," Prufrax said slowly, precisely, looking him straight in the eye.

"I've paid my debt," Kumnax said. "We glovers stick. Now I'm going to go get my punishment." He left the cubicle. Prufrax didn't see him again before her first application.

The seedship buried itself in a heating protostar, raising shields against the infalling ice and stone. The nebula had congealed out of a particularly rich cluster of exploded fourth- and fifth-generation stars, thick with planets, the detritus of which now fell on Aryz's ship like hail.

Aryz had never been so isolated. No other branch ind addressed him; he never even saw them now. He made his reports to the brood mind, but even there the reception was warmer and warmer, until he could barely endure to communicate. Consequently—and he realized this was part of the plan—he came closer to his charges, the human shapes. He felt more sympathy for them. He discovered that even between human and Senexi there could be a bridge and need—the need to be useful.

The brood mind was interested in one question: how successfully could they be planted aboard a human ship? Would they be accepted until they could carry out their sabotage, or would they be detected? Already Senexi instructions were being coded into their teachings.

"I think they will be accepted in the confusion of an engagement," Aryz answered. He had long since guessed the general outlines of the brood mind's plans. Communication with the human shapes was for one purpose only: to use them as decoys, insurgents. They were weapons. Knowledge of human activity and behavior was not an end in itself; seeing what was happening to him, Aryz fully understood why the brood mind wanted such study to proceed no further.

He would lose them soon, he thought, and his work would be over. He would be much too human-tainted. He would end, and his replacement would start a new existence, very little different from Aryz—but, he reasoned, adjusted. The replacement would not have Aryz's peculiarity.

He approached his last meeting with the brood mind, preparing himself for his final work, for the ending. In the cold liquid-filled chamber, the great red-and-white sac waited, the center of his team, his existence. He adored it. There was no way he could criticize its action.

Yet—

"We are being sought," the brood mind radiated. "Are the shapes ready?"

"Yes," Aryz said. "The new teaching is firm. They believe they are fully human." And, except for the new teaching, they were. "They defy sometimes." He said nothing about the mutated shape. It would not be used. If they won this encounter, it would probably be placed with Aryz's body in a fusion torch for complete purging.

"Then prepare them," the brood mind said. "They will be delivered to the vector for positioning and transfer."

Darkness and waiting. Prufrax nested in her delivery tube like a freshly chambered round. Through her gloves she caught distant communications murmurs that resembled voices down hollow pipes. The *Mellangee* was coming to full readiness.

Huge as her ship was, Prufrax knew that it would be dwarfed by the seedship. She could recall some hazy details about the seedship's structure, but most of that information was stored securely away from interference by her conscious mind. She wasn't even positive what the tactic would be. In the mocks, that at least had been clear. Now such information either had not been delivered or had waited in inaccessible memory, to be brought forward by the appropriate triggers.

More information would be fed to her just before the launch, but she knew the general procedure. The seedship was deep in a protostar, hiding behind the distortion of geometry and the complete hash of electromagnetic energy. The *Mellangee* would approach, collide if need be. Penetrate. Release. Find. Zap. Her fingers ached. Sometimes before the launch she would also be fed her final moans—the tempers—and she would be primed to leave elfstate. She would be a mature glover. She would be a woman.

If she returned

will return

she could become part of the breed, her receptivity would end in ecstasy rather than mild warmth, she would contribute second state, naturally born glovers. For a moment she was content with the thought. That was a high honor.

Her fingers ached worse.

The tempers came, moans tiding in, then the battle data. As it passed into her subconscious, she caught a flash of—

Rocks and ice, a thick cloud of dust and gas glowing red but seeming dark, no stars, no constellation guides this time. The beacon came on. That would be her only way to orient once the gloves stopped inertial and locked onto the target.

The seedship

was like

a shadow within a shadow

twenty-two kilometers across, yet

carrying

only six

teams

LAUNCH *She flies!*

Data: the *Mellangee* has buried herself in the seedship, ploughed deep into the interior like a carnivore's muzzle looking for vitals.

Instruction: a swarm of seeks is dashing through the seedship, looking for the brood minds, for the brood chambers, for branch inds. The glovers will follow.

Prufrax sees herself clearly now. She is the great avenging comet, bringer of omen and doom, like a knife moving through the glass and ice and thin, cold helium as if they weren't there, the chambered round fired and tearing at hundreds of kilometers an hour through the Senexi vessel, following the seeks.

The seedship cannot withdraw into higher geometries now. It is pinned by the *Mellangee.* It is hers.

Information floods her, pleases her immensely. She swoops down orange-and-grey corridors, buffeting against the walls like a ricocheting bullet. Almost immediately she comes across a branch ind, sliding through the ammonia film against the outrushing wind, trying to reach an armored cubicle. Her first Zap is too easy, not satisfying, nothing like what she thought. In her wake the branch ind becomes scattered globules of plasma. She plunges deeper.

Aryz delivers his human charges to the vectors that will launch them. They are equipped with simulations of the human weapons, their hands encased in the hideous grey gloves.

The seedship is in deadly peril; the battle has almost been lost at one stroke. The seedship cannot remain whole. It must self-destruct, taking the human ship with it, leaving only a fragment with as many teams as can escape.

The vectors launch the human shapes. Aryz tries to determine which part of the ship will be elected to survive; he must not be there. His job is over, and he must die.

The glovers fan out through the seedship's central hollow, demolishing the great cold drive engines, bypassing the shielded fusion flare and the reprocessing plant, destroying machinery built before their Earth was formed.

The special-projects sisters take the lead. Suddenly they are confused. They have found a brood mind, but it is not heavily protected. They surround it, prepare for the Zap—

It is sacrificing itself, drawing them in to an easy kill and away from another portion of the seedship. Power is concentrating elsewhere. Sensing that, they kill quickly and move on.

Aryz's brood mind prepares for escape. It begins to wrap itself in flux bind as it moves through the ship toward the frozen fragment. Already three of its five branch inds are dead; it can feel other brood minds dying. Aryz's bud replacement has been killed as well.

Following Aryz's training, the human shapes rush into corridors away from the main action. The special-projects sisters encounter the decoy male, allow it to fly with them . . . until it aims its weapons. One Zap almost takes out Trice. The others fire on the shape immediately. He goes to his death weeping, confused from the very moment of his launch.

The fragment in which the brood mind will take refuge encompasses the chamber where the humans had been nurtured, where the mandate is still stored. All the other brood minds are dead, Aryz realizes; the humans have swept down on them so quickly. What shall he do?

Somewhere, far off, he feels the distressed pulse of another branch ind dying. He probes the remains of the seedship. He is the last. He cannot dissipate now; he must ensure the brood mind's survival.

Prufrax, darting through the crumbling seedship, searching for more opportunities, comes across an injured glover. She calls for a mediseek and pushes on.

The brood mind settles into the fragment. Its support system is damaged; it is entering the time-isolated state, the flux bind, more rapidly than it should. The seals of foamed electric ice cannot quite close off the fragment before Ya, Trice, and Damu slip in. They frantically call for bindcutters and preservers; they have instructions to capture the last brood mind, if possible.

But a trap falls upon Ya, and snarling fields tear her from her gloves. She is flung down a dark disintegrating shaft, red cracks opening all around as the seedship's integrity fails. She trails silver dust and freezes, hits a barricade, shatters.

The ice seals continue to close. Trice is caught between them and pushes out frantically, blundering into the region of the intensifying flux bind. Her gloves break into hard bits, and she is melded into an ice wall like an insect trapped on the surface of a winter lake.

Damu sees that the brood mind is entering the final phase of flux bind. After that they will not be able to touch it. She begins a desperate Zap

and is too late.

Aryz directs the subsidiary energy of the flux against her. Her Zap deflects from the bind region, she is caught in an interference pattern and vibrates until her tiniest particles stop their knotted whirlpool spins and she simply becomes

space and searing light.

The brood mind, however, has been damaged. It is losing information from one portion of its anatomy. Desperate for storage, it looks for places to hold the information before the flux bind's last wave.

Aryz directs an interface onto the brood mind's surface. The silvery pools of time-binding flicker around them both. The brood mind's damaged sections transfer their data into the last available storage device—the human mandate.

Now it contains both human and Senexi information.

The silvery pools unite, and Aryz backs away. No longer can he sense the brood mind. It is out of reach but not yet safe. He must propel the fragment from the remains of the seedship. Then he must wrap the fragment in its own flux bind, cocoon it in physics to protect it from the last ravages of the humans.

Aryz carefully navigates his way through the few remaining corridors. The helium atmosphere has almost completely dissipated, even there. He strains to remember all the procedures. Soon the seedship will explode, destroying the human ship. By then they must be gone.

Angry red, Prufrax follows his barely sensed form, watching him behind barricades of ice, approaching the moment of a most satisfying Zap. She gives her gloves their way

and finds a shape behind her, wearing gloves that are not gloves, not like her own, but capable of grasping her in tensed fields, blocking the Zap, dragging them together. The fragment separates, heat pours in from the protostar cloud. They are swirled in their vortex of power, twin locked comets—one red, one sullen grey.

"Who are you?" Prufrax screams as they close in on each other in the fields. Their environments meld. They grapple. In the confusion, the darkening, they are drawn out of the cloud with the fragment, and she sees the other's face.

Her own.

The seedship self-destructs. The fragment is propelled from the protostar, above the plane of what will become planets in their orbits, away from the crippled and dying *Mellangee.*

Desperate, Prufrax uses all her strength to drill into the fragment. Helium blows past them, and bits of dead branch inds.

Aryz catches the pair immediately in the shapes chamber, rearranging the fragment's structure to enclose them with the mutant shape and mandate. For the moment he has time enough to concentrate on them. They are dangerous. They are almost equal to each other, but his shape is weakening faster than the true glover. They float, bouncing from wall to wall in the chamber, forcing the mutant to crawl into a corner and howl with fear.

There may be value in saving the one and capturing the other. Involved as they are, the two can be carefully dissected from their fields and induced into a crude kind of sleep before the glover has a chance to free her weapons. He can dispose of the gloves—fake and real—and hook them both to the Mam, reattach the mutant shape as well. Perhaps something can be learned from the failure of the experiment.

The dissection and capture occur faster than the planning. His movement slows under the spreading flux bind. His last action, after attaching the humans to the Mam, is to make sure the brood mind's flux bind is properly nested within that of the ship.

The fragment drops into simpler geometries.

It is as if they never existed.

The battle was over. There were no victors. Aryz became aware of the passage of time, shook away the sluggishness, and crawled through painfully dry corridors to set the environmental equipment going again. Throughout the fragment, machines struggled back to activity.

How many generations? The constellations were unrecognizable. He made star traces and found familiar spectra and types, but advanced in age. There had been a malfunction in the overall flux bind. He couldn't find the nebula where the battle had occurred. In its place were comfortably middle-aged stars surrounded by young planets.

Aryz came down from the makeshift observatory. He slid through the fragment, established the limits of his new home, and found the solid mirror surface of the brood mind's cocoon. It was still locked in flux bind, and he knew of no way to free it. In time the bind would probably wear off—but that might require life spans. The seedship was gone. They had lost the brood chamber, and with it the stock.

He was the last branch ind of his team. Not that it mattered now; there was nothing he could initiate without a brood mind. If the flux bind was permanent—as sometimes happened during malfunction—then he might as well be dead.

He closed his thoughts around him and was almost completely submerged when he sensed an alarm from the shapes chamber. The interface with the mandate had turned itself off; the new version of the Mam was malfunctioning. He tried to repair the equipment, but without the engineer's wall he was almost helpless. The best he could do was rig a temporary nutrition supply through the old human-form Mam. When he was done, he looked at the captive and the two shapes, then at the legless, armless Mam that served as their link to the interface and life itself.

She had spent her whole life in a room barely eight by ten meters, and not much taller than her own height. With her had been Grayd and the silent round creature whose name—if it had any—they had never learned. For a time there had been Mam, then another kind of Mam not nearly as satisfactory. She was hardly aware that her entire existence had been miserable, cramped, in one way or another incomplete.

Separated from them by a transparent partition, another round shape had periodically made itself known by voice or gesture.

Grayd had kept her sane. They had engaged in conspiracy. Removing themselves from the interface—what she called "eyes-shut"—they had held on to each other, tried to make sense out of what they knew instinctively, what was fed them through the interface, and what the being beyond the partition told them.

First they knew their names, and they knew that they were glovers.

They knew that glovers were fighters. When Aryz passed instruction through the interface of how to fight, they had accepted it eagerly but uneasily. It didn't seem to jibe with instructions locked deep within their instincts.

Five years under such conditions had made her introspective. She expected nothing, sought little beyond experience in the eyes-shut. Eyes-open with Grayd seemed scarcely more than a dream. They usually managed to ignore the peculiar round creature in the chamber with them; it spent nearly all its time hooked to the mandate and the Mam.

Of one thing only was she completely sure. Her name was Prufrax. She said it in eyes-open and eyes-shut, her only certainty.

Not long before the battle, she had been in a condition resembling dreamless sleep, like a robot being given instructions. The part of Prufrax that had taken on personality during eyes-shut and eyes-open for five years had been superseded by the fight instructions Aryz had programmed. She had flown as glovers must fly (though the gloves didn't seem quite right). She had fought, grappling (she thought) with herself, but who could be certain of anything?

She had long since decided that reality was not to be sought too avidly. After the battle she fell back into the mandate—into eyes-shut—all too willingly.

And what matter? If eyes-open was even less comprehensible than eyes-shut, why did she have the nagging feeling eyes-open was so compelling, so necessary? She tried to forget.

But a change had come to eyes-shut, too. Before the battle, the information had been selected. Now she could wander through the mandate at will. She seemed to smell the new information, completely unfamiliar, like a whiff of ocean. She hardly knew where to begin. She stumbled across:

—that all vessels will carry one, no matter what their size or class, just as every individual carries the map of a species. The mandate shall contain all the information of our kind, including accurate and uncensored history, for if we have learned anything, it is that censored and untrue accounts distort the eyes of the leaders. Leaders must have access to the truth. It is their responsibility. Whatever is told those who work under the leaders, for whatever reasons, must not be believed by

the leaders. Unders are told lies. Leaders must seek and be provided with accounts as accurate as possible, or we will be weakened and fall—

What wonderful dreams the *leaders* must have had. And they possessed some intrinsic gift called *truth,* through the use of the *mandate.* Prufrax could hardly believe that. As she made her tentative explorations through the new fields of eyes-shut, she began to link the word *mandate* with what she experienced. That was where she was.

And she alone. Once, she had explored with Grayd. Now there was no sign of Grayd.

She learned quickly. Soon she walked along a beach on Earth, then a beach on a world called Myriadne, and other beaches, fading in and out. By running through the entries rapidly, she came up with a blurred *eidos* and so learned what a beach was in the abstract. It was a boundary between one kind of eyes-shut and another, between water and land, neither of which had any corollary in eyes-open.

Some beaches had sand. Some had clouds—the *eidos* of clouds was quite attractive. And one—

had herself running scared, screaming.

She called out, but the figure vanished. Prufrax stood on a beach under a greenish-yellow star, on a world called Kyrene, feeling lonelier than ever.

She explored farther, hoping to find Grayd, if not the figure that looked like herself. Grayd wouldn't flee from her. Grayd would—

The round thing confronted her, its helpless limbs twitching. Now it was her turn to run, terrified. Never before had she met the round creature in eyes-shut. It was mobile; it had a purpose. Over land, clouds, trees, rocks, wind, air, equations, and an edge of physics she fled. The farther she went, the more distant from the round one with hands and small head, the less afraid she was.

She never found Grayd.

The memory of the battle was fresh and painful. She remembered the ache of her hands, clumsily removed from the gloves. Her environment had collapsed and been replaced by something indistinct. Prufrax had fallen into a deep slumber and had dreamed.

The dreams were totally unfamiliar to her. If there was a left-turning in her arc of sleep, she dreamed of philosophies and languages and other things she couldn't relate to. A right-turning led to histories and sciences so incomprehensible as to be nightmares.

It was a most unpleasant sleep, and she was not at all sorry to find she wasn't really asleep.

The crucial moment came when she discovered how to slow her turnings and the changes of dream subject. She entered a pleasant place of which she had no knowledge but which did not seem threatening. There was a vast expanse of water, but it didn't terrify her. She couldn't even identify it as water until she scooped up a handful. Beyond the water was a floor of shifting particles. Above both was an open expanse, not black but obviously space, drawing her eyes into intense pale blue-green. And there was that figure she had encountered in the seedship. Herself. The figure pursued. She fled.

Right over the boundary into Senexi information. She knew then that what she was seeing couldn't possibly come from within herself. She was receiving data from another source. Perhaps she had been taken captive. It was possible she was now being forcibly debriefed. The tellman had discussed such possibilities, but none of the glovers had been taught how to defend themselves in specific situations. Instead it had been stated—in terms that brooked no second thought—that self-destruction was the only answer. So she tried to kill herself.

She sat in the freezing cold of a red-and-white room, her feet meeting but not touching a fluid covering on the floor. The information didn't fit her senses—it seemed blurred, inappropriate. Unlike the other data, this didn't allow participation or motion. Everything was locked solid.

She couldn't find an effective means of killing herself. She resolved to close her eyes and simply will herself into dissolution. But closing her eyes only moved her into a deeper or shallower level of deception—other categories, subjects, visions. She couldn't sleep, wasn't tired, couldn't die.

Like a leaf on a stream, she drifted. Her thoughts untangled, and she imagined herself floating on the water called ocean. She kept her eyes open. It was quite by accident that she encountered:

Instruction. Welcome to the introductory use of the mandate. As a

noncombat processor, your duties are to maintain the mandate, provide essential information for your overs, and, if necessary, protect or destroy the mandate. The mandate is your immediate over. If it requires maintenance, you will oblige. Once linked with the mandate, as you are now, you may explore any aspect of the information by requesting delivery. To request delivery, indicate the core of your subject—

Prufrax she shouted silently. What is Prufrax?

A voice with different tone immediately took over.

Ah, now that's quite a story. I was her biographer, the organizer of her life tapes (ref. GEORGE MACKNAX), and knew her well in the last years of her life. She was born in the Ferment 26468. Here are selected life tapes. Choose emphasis. Analyses follow.

—Hey! Who are you? There's someone here with me. . . .

—Shh! Listen. Look at her. Who is she?

They looked, listened to the information.

—Why, she's *me* . . . sort of.

—She's *us.*

She stood two and a half meters tall. Her hair was black and thick, though cut short; her limbs well-muscled though drawn out by the training and hormonal treatments. She was seventeen years old, one of the few birds born in the solar system, and for the time being she had a chip on her shoulder. Everywhere she went, the birds asked about her mother, Jay-ax. "You better than her?"

Of course not! Who could be? But she was good; the instructors said so. She was just about through training, and whether she graduated to hawk or remained bird she would do her job well. Asking Prufrax about her mother was likely to make her set her mouth tight and glare.

On Mercior, the Grounds took up four thousand hectares and had its own port. The Grounds was divided into Land, Space, and Thought, and training in each area was mandatory for fledges, those birds embarking on hawk training. Prufrax was fledge three. She had passed Land—though she loathed downbound fighting—and was two years into Space. The tough part, everyone said, was not passing Space, but lasting through four years of Thought after the action in nearorbit and planetary.

Prufrax was not the introspective type. She could be studious when it suited her. She was a quick study at weapon maths, physics came easy when it had a direct application, but theory of service and polinstruc—which she had sampled only in prebird courses—bored her.

Since she had been a little girl, no more than five—

—Five! Five what?

and had seen her mother's ships and fightsuits and fibs, she had known she would never be happy until she had ventured far out and put a seedship in her sights, had convinced a Senexi of the overness of end—

—The Zap! She's talking the Zap!

—What's that?

—You're me, you should know.

—I'm not you, we're not her.

The Zap, said the mandate, and the data shifted.

"Tomorrow you receive your first implants. These will allow you to coordinate with the zero-angle phase engines and find your targets much more rapidly than you ever could with simple biologic. The implants, of course, will be delivered through your noses—minor irritation and sinus trouble, no more—into your limbic system. Later in your training, hookups and digital adapts will be installed as well. Are there any questions?"

"Yes, sir." Prufrax stood at the top of the spherical classroom, causing the hawk instructor to swivel his platform. "I'm having problems with the zero-angle phase maths. Reduction of the momenta of the real."

Other fledge threes piped up that they, too, had had trouble with those maths. The hawk instructor sighed. "We don't want to install cheaters in all of you. It's bad enough needing implants to supplement biologic. Individual learning is much more desirable. Do you request cheaters?" That was a challenge. They all responded negatively, but Prufrax had a secret smile. She knew the subject. She just took delight in having the maths explained again. She could reinforce an already thorough understanding. Others not so well versed would benefit. She wasn't wasting time. She was in the pleasure of her weapon—the weapon she would be using against the Senexi.

"Zero-angle phase is the temporary reduction of the momenta of the real." Equations and plexes appeared before each student as the instructor went on. "Nested unreals can conflict if a barrier is placed between the participator princip and the assumption of the real. The effectiveness of the participator can be determined by a convenience model we call the angle of phase. Zero-angle phase is achieved by an opaque probability field according to modified Fourier of the separation of real waves. This can also be caused by the reflection of the beam—an effective counter to zero-angle phase, since the beam is always compoundable and the compound is always time-reversed. Here are the true gedanks—"

—Zero-angle phase. She's learning the Zap.

—She hates them a lot, doesn't she?

—The Senexi? They're Senexi.

—I think . . . eyes-open is the world of the Senexi. What does that mean?

—That we're prisoners. You were caught before me.

—Oh.

The news came as she was in recovery from the implant. Seedships had violated human space again, dropping cuckoos on thirty-five worlds. The worlds had been young colonies, and the cuckoos had wiped out all life, then tried to reseed with Senexi forms. The overs had reacted by sterilizing the planet's surfaces. No victory, loss to both sides. It was as if the Senexi were so malevolent they didn't care about success, only about destruction.

She hated them. She could imagine nothing worse.

Prufrax was twenty-three. In a year she would be qualified to hawk on a cruiser/raider. She would demonstrate her hatred.

Aryz felt himself slipping into endthought, the mind set that always preceded a branch ind's self-destruction. What was there for him to do? The fragment had survived, but at what cost, to what purpose? Nothing had been accomplished. The nebula had been lost, or he supposed it had. He would likely never know the actual outcome.

He felt a vague irritation at the lack of a spectrum of responses. Without a purpose, a branch ind was nothing more than excess plasm.

He looked in on the captive and the shapes, all hooked to the mandate, and wondered what he would do with them. How would humans react to the situation he was in? More vigorously, probably. They would fight on. They always had. Even without leaders, with no discernible purpose, even in defeat. What gave them such stamina? Were they superior, more deserving? If they were better, then was it right for the Senexi to oppose their triumph?

Aryz drew himself tall and rigid with confusion. He had studied them too long. They had truly infected him. But here at least was a hint of purpose. A question needed to be answered.

He made preparations. There were signs the brood mind's flux bind was not permanent, was in fact unwinding quite rapidly. When it emerged, Aryz would present it with a judgment, an answer.

He realized, none too clearly, that by Senexi standards he was now a raving lunatic.

He would hook himself into the mandate, improve the somewhat isolating interface he had used previously to search for selected answers. He, the captive, and the shapes would be immersed in human history together. They would be like young suckling on a Population I mother-animal—just the opposite of the Senexi process, where young fed nourishment and information into the brood mind.

The mandate would nourish, or poison. Or both.

—Did she love?

—What—you mean, did she receive?

—No, did she—we—I—give?

—I don't know what you mean.

—I wonder if *she* would know what I mean. . . .

Love, said the mandate, and the data proceeded.

Prufrax was twenty-nine. She had been assigned to a cruiser in a new program where superior but untested fighters were put into thick action with no preliminary. The program was designed to see how well the Grounds prepared fighters; some thought it foolhardy, but Prufrax found it perfectly satisfactory.

The cruiser was a million-ton raider, with a hawk contingent of fifty-three and eighty regular crew. She would be in a second-wave attack, following the initial hardfought.

She was scared. That was good; fright improved basic biologic, if properly managed. The cruiser would make a raid into Senexi space and retaliate for past cuckoo-seeding programs. They would come up against thornships and seedships, likely.

The fighting was going to be fierce.

The raider made its final denial of the overness of the real and pipsqueezed into an arduous, nasty sponge space. It drew itself together again and emerged far above the galactic plane.

Prufrax sat in the hawks wardroom and looked at the simulated rotating snowball of stars. Red-coded numerals flashed along the borders of known Senexi territory, signifying old stars, dark hulks of stars, the whole ghostly home region where they had first come to power when the terrestrial sun had been a mist-wrapped youngster. A green arrow showed the position of the raider.

She drank sponge-space supplements with the others but felt isolated because of her firstness, her fear. Everyone seemed so calm. Most were fours or fives—on their fourth or fifth battle call. There were ten ones and an upper scatter of experienced hawks with nine or twenty-five battles behind them. There were no thirties. Thirties were rare in combat; the few that survived so many engagements were plucked off active and retired to PR service under the polinstructors. They often ended up in fibs, acting poorly, looking unhappy.

Still, when she had been more naive, Prufrax's heroes had been a man-and-woman thirty team she had watched in fib after fib—Kumnax and Arol. They had been better actors than most.

Day in, day out, they drilled in their fightsuits. While the crew bustled, hawks were put through implant learning, what slang was already calling the Know, as opposed to the Tell, of classroom teaching. Getting background, just enough to tickle her curiosity, not enough to stimulate morbid interest.

—There it is again. Feel?

—I know it. Yes. The round one, part of eyes-open . . .

—Senexi?

—No, brother without name.

—Your . . . brother?

—No . . . I don't know.

—Can it hurt us?

—It never has. It's trying to talk to us.

—Leave us alone!

—It's going.

Still, there were items of information she had never received before, items privileged only to the fighters, to assist them in their work. Older hawks talked about the past, when data had been freely available. Stories circulated in the wardroom about the Senexi, and she managed to piece together something of their origins and growth.

Senexi worlds, according to a twenty, had originally been large, cold masses of gas circling bright young suns nearly metal-free. Their gas-giant planets had orbited the suns at hundreds of millions of kilometers and had been dusted by the shrouds of neighboring dead stars; the essential elements carbon, nitrogen, silicon, and fluorine had gathered in sufficient quantities on some of the planets to allow Population II biology.

In cold ammonia seas, lipids had combined in complex chains. A primal kind of life had arisen and flourished. Across millions of years, early Senexi forms had evolved. Compared with evolution on Earth, the process at first had moved quite rapidly. The mechanisms of procreation and evolution had been complex in action, simple in chemistry.

There had been no competition between life forms of different genetic bases. On Earth, much time had been spent selecting between the plethora of possible ways to pass on genetic knowledge.

And among the early Senexi, outside of predation there had been no death. Death had come about much later, self-imposed for social reasons. Huge colonies of protoplasmic individuals had gradually resolved into the team-forms now familiar.

Soon information was transferred through the budding of branch inds; cultures quickly developed to protect the integrity of larvae, to allow them to regroup and form a new brood mind. Technologies had been limited to the rare heavy materials available, but the Senexi had expanded for a time with very little technology. They were well adapted to their environment, with few predators and no need to hunt, absorbing stray nutrients from the atmosphere and from layers of liquid ammonia. With perceptions attuned to the radio and microwave frquencies, they had before long turned groups of branch inds into radio telescope chains, piercing the heavy atmosphere and probing the universe in great detail, especially the very active center of the young galaxy. Huge jets of matter, streaming from other galaxies and emitting high-energy radiation, had provided laboratories for their vicarious observations. Physics was a primitive science to them.

Since little or no knowledge was lost in breeding cycles, cultural growth was rapid at times; since the dead weight of knowledge was often heavy, cultural growth often slowed to a crawl.

Using water, as a building material, developing techniques that humans still understood imperfectly, they prepared for travel away from their birthworlds.

Prufrax wondered, as she listened to the older hawks, how humans had come to know all this. Had Senexi been captured and questioned? Was it all theory? Did anyone really know—anyone she could ask?

—She's weak.

—Why weak?

—Some knowledge is best for glovers to ignore. Some questions are best left to the supreme overs.

—Have you thought that in here, you can answer her questions, our questions?

—No. No. Learn about me—us—first.

In the hour before engagement, Prufrax tried to find a place alone. On the raider this wasn't difficult. The ship's size was overwhelming for the number of hawks and crew aboard. There were many areas where she could put on an environs and walk or drift in silence, surrounded by the dark shapes of equipment wrapped in plexerv. There was so much about ship operations she didn't understand, hadn't been taught. Why carry so much excess equipment, weapons—far more than they'd need even for replacements? She could think of possibilities—superiors on Mercior wanting their cruisers to have flexible mission capabilities, for one—but her ignorance troubled her less than *why* she was ignorant. Why was it necessary to keep fighters in the dark on so many subjects?

She pulled herself through the cold G-less tunnels, feeling slightly awked by the loneness, the quiet. One tunnel angled outboard, toward the hull of the cruiser. She hesitated, peering into its length with her environs beacon, when a beep warned her she was near another crew member. She was startled to think someone else might be as curious as she. The other hawks and crew, for the most part, had long outgrown their need to wander and regarded it as birdish. Prufrax was used to being different—she had always perceived heself, with some pride, as a bit of a freak. She scooted expertly up the tunnel, spreading her arms and tucking her legs as she would in a fightsuit.

The tunnel was filled with a faint milky green mist, absorbing her environs beam. It couldn't be much more than a couple of hundred meters long, however, and it was quite straight. The signal beeped louder.

Ahead she could make out a dismantled weapons blister. That explained the fog: a plexerv aerosol diffused in the low pressure. Sitting in the blister was a man, his environs glowing a pale violet. He had deopaqued a section of the blister and was staring out at the stars. He swiveled as she approached and looked her over dispassionately. He seemed to be a hawk—he had fightform, tall, thin with brown hair above hull-white skin, large eyes with pupils so dark she might have been looking through his head into space beyond.

"Under," she said as their environs met and merged.

"Over. What are you doing here?"

"I was about to ask you the same."

"You should be getting ready for the fight," he admonished.

"I am. I need to be alone for a while."

"Yes." He turned back to the stars. "I used to do that, too."

"You don't fight now?"

He shook his head. "Retired. I'm a researcher."

She tried not to look impressed. Crossing rates was almost impossible. A bitalent was unusual in the service.

"What kind of research?" she asked.

"I'm here to correlate enemy finds."

"Won't find much of anything, after we're done with the zero phase."

It would have been polite for him to say, "Power to that," or offer some other encouragement. He said nothing.

"Why would you want to research them?"

"To fight an enemy properly, you have to know what they are. Ignorance is defeat."

"You research tactics?"

"Not exactly."

"What, then?"

"You'll be in a tough hardfought this wake. Make you a proposition. You fight well, observe, come to me and tell me what you see. Then I'll answer your questions."

"Brief you before my immediate overs?"

"I have the authority," he said. No one had ever lied to her; she didn't even suspect he would. "You're eager?"

"Very."

"You'll be doing what?"

"Engaging Senexi fighters, then hunting down branch inds and brood minds."

"How many fighters going in?"

"Twelve."

"Big target, eh?"

She nodded.

"While you're there, ask yourself—what are they fighting for? Understand?"

"I—"

"Ask, what are they fighting for. Just that. Then come back to me."

"What's your name?"

"Not important," he said. "Now go."

She returned to the prep center as the sponge-space warning tones began. Overhawks went among the fighers in the lineup, checking gear and giveaway body points for mental orientation. Prufrax submitted to the molded sensor mask being slipped over her face. "Ready!" the overhawk said. "Hardfought!" He clapped her on the shoulder. "Good luck."

"Thank you, sir." She bent down and slid into her fightsuit. Along the launch line, eleven other hawks did the same. The overs and other crew left the chamber, and twelve red beams delineated the launch tube. The fightsuits automatically lifted and aligned on their individual beams. Fields swirled around them like silvery tissue in moving water, then settled and hardened into cold scintillating walls, pulsing as the launch energy built up.

The tactic came to her. The ship's sensors became part of her information net. She saw the Senexi thornship—twelve kilometers in diameter, cuckoos lacing its outer hull like maggots on red fruit, snakes waiting to take them on.

She was terrified and exultant, so worked up that her body temperature was climbing. The fightsuit adjusted her balance.

At the count of ten and nine, she switched from biologic to cyber. The implant—after absorbing much of her thought processes for weeks—became Prufrax.

For a time there seemed to be two of her. Biologic continued, and in that region she could even relax a bit, as if watching a fib.

With almost dreamlike slowness, in the electronic time of cyber, her fightsuit followed the beam. She saw the stars and oriented herself to the cruiser's beacon, using both for reference, plunging in the sword-flower formation to assault the thornship. The cuckoos retreated in the vast red hull like worms withdrawing into an apple. Then hundreds of tiny black pinpoints appeared in the closest quadrant to the sword flower.

Snakes shot out, each piloted by a Senexi branch ind. "Hardfought!" she told herself in biologic before that portion gave over completely to cyber.

Why were we flung out of dark
through ice and fire, a shower
of sparks? a puzzle;
Perhaps to build hell.

We strike here, there;
Set brief glows, fall through
and cross round again.

By our dimming, we see what
Beatitude we have.

In the circle, kindling
together, we form an
exhausted Empyrean.
We feel the rush of
igniting winds but still
grow dull and wan.

New rage flames, new light,
dropping like sun through muddy
ice and night and fall
Close, spinning blue and bright.
In time they, too,
Tire. Redden.
We join, compare pasts
cool in huddled paths,
turn grey.

And again.
We are a companion flow
of ash, in the slurry
out and down.
We sleep.

Rivers form above and below.
Above, iron snakes twist,
clang and slice, chime,
helium eyes watching, seeing
Snowflake hawks,
signaling adamant muscles and
energy teeth. What hunger
compels our venom spit?

It flies, strikes the crystal
flight, making mist grey-green
with ammonia rain.

Sleeping, we glide,
and to each side
unseen shores wait
with the moans of an
unseen tide.

—She wrote that. We. One of her—our—poems.

—Poem?

—A kind of fib, I think.

—I don't see what it says.

—Sure you do! She's talking hardfought.

—The Zap? Is that all?

—No, I don't think so.

—Do you understand it?

—Not all . . .

She lay back in the bunk, legs crossed, eyes closed, feeling the receding dominance of the implant—the overness of cyber—and the almost pleasant ache in her back. She had survived her first. The thornship had retired, severely damaged, its surface seared and scored so heavily it would never release cuckoos again.

It would become a hulk, a decoy. Out of action. *Satisfaction/out of action/Satisfaction* . . .

Still, with eight of the twelve fighters lost, she didn't quite feel the exuberance of the rhyme. The snakes had fought very well. Bravely, she might say. They lured, sacrificed, cooperated, demonstrating teamwork as fine as that in her own group. Strategy was what made the cruiser's raid successful. A superior approach, an excellent tactic. And perhaps even surprise, though the final analysis hadn't been posted yet.

Without those advantages, they might have all died.

She opened her eyes and stared at the pattern of blinking lights in the ceiling panel, lights with their secret codes that repeated every second, so that whenever she looked at them, the implant deep inside was debriefed, reinstructed. Only when she fought would she know what she was now seeing.

She returned to the tunnel as quickly as she was able. She floated up toward the blister and found him there, surrounded by packs of information from the last hardfought. She waited until he turned his attention to her.

"Well?" he said.

"I asked myself what they are fighting for. And I'm very angry."

"Why?"

"Because I don't know. I *can't* know. They're Senexi."

"Did they fight well?"

"We lost eight. Eight." She cleared her throat.

"Did they fight well?" he repeated, an edge in his voice.

"Better than I was ever told they could."

"Did they die?"

"Enough of them."

"How many did you kill?"

"I don't know." But she did. Eight.

"You killed eight," he said, pointing to the packs. "I'm analyzing the battle now."

"You're behind what we read, what gets posted?" she asked.

"Partly," he said. "You're a good hawk."

"I knew I would be," she said, her tone quiet, simple.

"Since they fought bravely—"

"How can Senexi be brave?" she asked sharply.

"Since," he repeated, "they fought bravely, why?"

"They want to live, to do their . . . work. Just like me."

"No," he said. She was confused, moving between extremes in her mind, first resisting, then giving in too much. "They're Senexi. They're not like us."

"What's your name?" she asked, dodging the issue.

"Clevo."

Her glory hadn't even begun yet, and already she was well into her fall.

Aryz made his connection and felt the brood mind's emergency cache of knowledge in the mandate grow up around him like ice crystals on glass. He stood in a static scene. The transition from living memory to human machine memory had resulted in either a coding of data or a reduction of detail; either way, the memory was cold, not dynamic. It would have to be compared, recorrelated, if that would ever be possible.

How much human data had had to be dumped to make space for this?

He cautiously advanced into the human memory, calling up topics almost at random. In the short time he had been away, so much of what he had learned seemed to have faded or become scrambled. Branch inds were supposed to have permanent memory; human data, for one reason or another, didn't take. It required so much effort just to begin to understand the different modes of thought.

He backed away from sociological data, trying to remain within physics and mathematics. There he could make conversations to fit his understanding without too much strain.

Then something unexpected happened. He felt the brush of another mind, a gentle inquiry from a source made even stranger by the hint of familiarity. It made what passed for a Senexi greeting, but not in the proper form, using what one branch ind of a team would radiate to a fellow; a gross breach, since it was obviously not from his team or even from his family. Aryz tried to withdraw. How was it possible for minds to meet in the mandate? As he retreated, he pushed into a broad region of incomprehensible data. It had none of the characteristics of the other human regions he had examined.

—This is for machines, the other said. —Not all cultural data is limited to biologic. You are in the area where programs and cyber designs are stored. They are really accessible only to a machine hooked into the mandate.

—What is your family? Aryz asked, the first step-question in the sequence Senexi used for urgent identity requests.

—I have no family. I am not a branch ind. No access to active brood minds. I have learned from the mandate.

—Then what are you?

—I don't know, exactly. Not unlike you.

Aryz understood what he was dealing with. It was the mind of the mutated shape, the one that had remained in the chamber, beseeching when he approached the transparent barrier.

—I must go now, the shape said. Aryz was alone again in the incomprehensible jumble. He moved slowly, carefully, into the Senexi sector, calling up subjects familiar to him. If he could encounter one shape, doubtless he could encounter the others—perhaps even the captive.

The idea was dreadful—and fascinating. So far as he knew, such intimacy between Senexi and human had never happened before. Yet there was something very Senexi-like in the method, as if branch inds attached to the brood mind were to brush mentalities while searching in the ageless memories.

The dread subsided. There was little worse that could happen to him, with his fellows dead, his brood mind in flux bind, his purpose uncertain.

What Aryz was feeling, for the first time, was a small measure of *freedom.*

The story of the original Prufrax continued.

In the early stages she visited Clevo with a barely concealed anger. His method was aggravating, his goals never precisely spelled out. What did he want with her, if anything?

And she with him? Their meetings were clandestine, though not precisely forbidden. She was a hawk one now with considerable personal liberty between exercises and engagements. There were no monitors in the closed-off reaches of the cruiser, and they could do whatever they wished. The two met in areas close to the ship's hull, usually in weapons blisters that could be opened to reveal the stars; there they talked.

Prufrax was not accustomed to prolonged conversation. Hawks were not raised to be voluble, nor were they selected for their curiosity. Yet the exhawk Clevo talked a great deal and was the most curious person she had met, herself included, and she regarded herself as uncharacteristically curious.

Often he was infuriating, especially when he played the "leading game," as she called it. Leading her from one question to the next like an instructor, but without the trappings of any clarity of purpose. "What do you think of your mother?"

"Does that matter?"

"Not to me."

"Then why ask?"

"Because you matter."

Prufrax shrugged. "She was a fine mother. She bore me with a well-chosen heritage. She raised me as a hawk candidate. She told me her stories."

"Any hawk I know would envy you for listening at Jay-ax's knee."

"I was hardly at her knee."

"A speech tactic."

"Yes, well, she was important to me."

"She was a preferred single?"

"Yes."

"So you have no father."

"She selected without reference to individuals."

"Then you are really not that much different from a Senexi."

She bristled and started to push away. "There! You insult me again."

"Not at all. I've been asking one question all this time, and you haven't even heard. How well do you know the enemy?"

"Well enough to destroy them." She couldn't believe that was the only question he'd been asking. His speech tactics were very odd.

"Yes, to win battles, perhaps. But who will win the war?"

"It'll be a long war," she said softly, floating a few meters from him. He rotated in the blister, blocking out a blurred string of stars. The cruiser was preparing to shift out of status geometry again. "They fight well."

"They fight with conviction. Do you believe them to be evil?"

"They destroy us."

"We destroy them."

"So the question," she said, smiling at her cleverness, "is who began to destroy?"

"Not at all," Clevo said. "I suspect there's no longer a clear answer to that. Our leaders have obviously decided the question isn't important. No. We are the new, they are the old. The old must be superseded. It's a conflict born in the essential difference between Senexi and humans."

"That's the only way we're different? They're old, we're not so old? I don't understand."

"Nor do I, entirely."

"Well, finally!"

"The Senexi," Clevo continued, unperturbed, "long ago needed only gas-giant planets like their homeworlds. They lived in peace for billions of years before our world was formed. But as they moved from star to star, they learned uses for other types of worlds. We were most interested in rocky Earth-like planets. Gradually, we found uses for gas giants, too. By the time we met, both of us encroached on the other's territory. Their technology is so improbable, so unlike ours, that when we first encountered them, we thought they must come from another geometry."

"Where did you learn all this?" Prufrax squinted at him suspiciously.

"I'm no longer a hawk," he said, "but I was too valuable just to discard. My experience was too broad, my abilities too useful. So I was placed in research. It seems a safe place for me. Little contact with my comrades." He looked directly at her. "We must try to know our enemy, at least a little."

"That's dangerous," Prufrax said, almost instinctively.

"Yes, it is. What you know, you cannot hate."

"We must hate," she said. "It makes us strong. Senexi hate."

"They might," he said. "But, sometime, wouldn't you like to . . . sit down and talk with one, after a battle? Talk with a fighter? Learn its tactic, how it bested you in one move, compare—"

"No!" Prufrax shoved off rapidly down the tube. "We're shifting now. We have to get ready."

—She's smart. She's leaving him. He's crazy.

—Why do you think that?

—He would stop the fight, end the Zap.

—But he was a hawk.

—And hawks became glovers, I guess. But glovers go wrong, too. Like you.

—?

—Did you know they used you? How you were used?

—That's all blurred now.

—She's doomed if she stays around him. Who's that?

—Someone is listening with us.

—Recognize?

—No, gone now.

The next battle was bad enough to fall into the hellfought. Prufrax was in her fightsuit, legs drawn up as if about to kick off. The cruiser exited sponge space and plunged into combat before sponge-space supplements could reach full effectiveness. She was dizzy, disoriented. The overhawks could only hope that a switch from biologic to cyber would cure the problem.

She didn't know what they were attacking. Tactic was flooding the implant, but she was only receiving the wash of that; she hadn't merged yet. She sensed that things were confused. That bothered her. Overs did not feel confusion.

The cruiser was taking damage. She could sense at least that, and she wanted to scream in frustration. Then she was ordered to merge with the implant. Biologic became cyber. She was in the Know.

The cruiser had reintegrated above a gas-giant planet. They were seventy-nine thousand kilometers from the upper atmosphere. The damage had come from ice mines—chunks of Senexi-treated water ice, altered to stay in sponge space until a human vessel integrated nearby. Then they emerged, packed with momentum and all the residual instability of an unsuccessful exit into status geometry. Unsuccessful for a ship, that is—very successful for a weapon.

The ice mines had given up the overness of the real within range of the cruiser and had blasted out whole sections of the hull. The launch lanes had not been damaged. The fighters lined up on their beams and were peppered out into space, spreading in the classic sword flower.

The planet was a cold nest. Over didn't know what the atmosphere contained, but Senexi activity had been high in the star system, concentrating on this world. Over had decided to take a chance. Fighters headed for the atmosphere. The cruiser began planting singularity eggs. The eggs went ahead of the fighters, great black grainy ovoids that seemed to leave a trail of shadow—the wake of a birthing disruption in status geometry that could turn a gas giant into a short-lived sun.

Their time was limited. The fighters would group on entry sleds and descend to the liquid water regions where Senexi commonly kept their upwelling power plants. The fighters would first destroy any plants, loop into the liquid ammonia regions to search for hidden cuckoos, then see what was so important about the world.

She and five other fighters mounted the sled. Growing closer, the hazy clear regions of the atmosphere sparkled with Senexi sensors. Spiderweb beams shot from the six sleds to down the sensors. Buffet began. Scream, heat, then a second flower from the sled at a depth of two hundred kilometers. The sled slowed and held station. It would be their only way back. The fightsuits couldn't pull out of such a large gravity well.

She descended deeper. The pale, bloated beacon of the red star was dropping below the second cloudtops, limning the strata in orange and purple. At the liquid ammonia level she was instructed to key in permanent memory of all she was seeing. She wasn't "seeing" much, but other sensors were recording a great deal, all of it duly processed in her implant. "There's life here," she told herself. Indigenous life. Just another example of Senexi disregard for basic decency: they were interfering with a world developing its own complex biology.

The temperature rose to ammonia vapor levels, then to liquid water. The pressure on the fightsuit was enormous, and she was draining her stores much more rapidly than expected. At this level the atmosphere was particularly thick with organics.

Senexi snakes rose from below, passed them in altitude, then doubled back to engage. Prufrax was designated the deep diver; the others from her sled would stay at this level in her defense. As she fell, another sled group moved in behind her to double the cover.

She searched for the characteristic radiation curve of an upwelling plant. At the lower boundary of the liquid water level, below which her suit could not safely descend, she found it.

The Senexi were tapping the gas giant's convection from greater depths than usual. Above the plant, almost indetectable, was another object with an uncharacteristic curve. They were separated by ten kilometers. The power plant was feeding its higher companion with tight energy beams.

She slowed. Two other fighters, disengaged from the brief skirmish above, took positions as backups a few dozen kilometers higher than she. Her implant searched for an appropriate tactic. She would avoid the zero-angle phase for the moment, go in for reconnaissance. She could feel sound pouring from the plant and its companion—rhythmic, not waste noise, but deliberate. And homing in on that sound were waves of large vermiform organisms, like chains of gas-filled sausage. They were dozens of meters long, two meters at their greatest thickness, shaped vaguely like the Senexi snake fighters. The vermiforms were native, and they were being lured into the uppermost floating structure. None were emerging. Her backups spread apart, descending, and drew up along her flanks.

She made her decision almost immediately. She could see a pattern in the approach of the natives. If she fell into the pattern, she might be able to enter the structure unnoticed.

—It's a grinder. She doesn't recognize it.

—What's a grinder?

—She should make the Zap! It's an ugly thing; Senexi use them all the time. Net a planet with grinders, like a cuckoo, but for larger operations.

The creatures were being passed through separator fields. Their organics fell from the bottom of the construct, raw material for new growth—Senexi growth. Their heavier elements were stored for later harvest.

With Prufrax in their midst, the vermiforms flew into the separator. The interior was hundreds of meters wide, lead-white walls with flat grey machinery floating in a dust haze, full of hollow noise, the distant bleats of vermiforms being slaughtered. Prufrax tried to retreat, but she was caught in a selector field. Her suit bucked and she was whirled violently, then thrown into a repository for examination. She had been screened from the separator; her plan to record, then destroy, the structure had been foiled by an automatic filter.

"Information sufficient." Command logic programmed into the implant before launch was now taking over. "Zero-angle phase both plant and adjunct." She was drifting in the repository, still slightly stunned. Something was fading. Cyber was hissing in and out; the over logic-commands were being scrambled. Her implant was malfunctioning and was returning control to biologic. The selector fields had played havoc with all cyber functions, down to the processors in her weapons.

Cautiously she examined the down systems one by one, determining what she could and could not do. This took as much as thirty seconds—an astronomical time on the implant's scale.

She still could use the phase weapon. If she was judicious and didn't waste her power, she could cut her way out of the repository, maneuver and work with her escorts to destroy both the plant and the separator. By the time they returned to the sleds, her implant might have rerouted itself and made sufficient repairs to handle defense. She had no way of knowing what was waiting for her if—when—she escaped, but that was the least of her concerns for the moment.

She tightened the setting of the phase beam and swung her fightsuit around, knocking a cluster of junk ice and silty phosphorescent dust. She activated the beam. When she had a hole large enough to pass through, she edged the suit forward, beamed through more walls and obstacles, and kicked herself out of the repository into free fall. She swiveled and laid down a pattern of wide-angle beams, at the same time relaying a message on her situation to the escorts.

The escorts were not in sight. The separator was beginning to break up, spraying debris through the almost-opaque atmosphere. The rhythmic sound ceased, and the crowds of vermiforms began to disperse.

She stopped her fall and thrust herself several kilometers higher—directly into a formation of Senexi snakes. She had barely enough power to reach the sled, much less fight and turn her beams on the upwelling plant.

Her cyber was still down.

The sled signal was weak. She had no time to calculate its direction from the inertial guidance cyber. Besides, all cyber was unreliable after passing through the separator.

Why do they fight so well? Clevo's question clogged her thoughts. Cursing, she tried to blank and keep all her faculties available for running the fightsuit. *When evenly matched, you cannot win against your enemy unless you understand them. And if you truly understand, why are you fighting and not talking?* Clevo had never told her that—not in so many words. But it was part of a string of logic all her own.

Be more than an automaton with a narrow range of choices. Never underestimate the enemy. Those were old Grounds dicta, not entirely lost in the new training, but only emphasized by Clevo.

If they fight as well as you, perhaps in some ways they fight-think like you do. Use that.

Isolated, with her power draining rapidly, she had no choice. They might disregard her if she posed no danger. She cut her thrust and went into a diving spin. Clearly she was on her way to a high-pressure grave. They would sense her power levels, perhaps even pick up the lack of field activity if she let her shields drop. She dropped the shields. If they let her fall and didn't try to complete the kill—if they concentrated on active fighters above—she had enough power to drop into the water vapor regions, far below the plant, and silently ride a thermal into range. With luck, she could get close enough to lay a web of zero-angle phase and take out the plant.

She had minutes in which to agonize over her plan. Falling, buffeted by winds that could knock her kilometers out of range, she spun like a vagrant flake of snow.

She couldn't even expend the energy to learn if they were scanning her, checking out her potential.

Perhaps she underestimated them. Perhaps they would be that much more thorough and take her out just to be sure. Perhaps they had unwritten rules of conduct like the ones she was using, taking hunches into account. Hunches were discouraged in Grounds training—much less reliable than cyber.

She fell. Temperature increased. Pressure on her suit began to constrict her air supply. She used fighter trancing to cut back on her breathing.

Fell.

And broke the trance. Pushed through the dense smoke of exhaustion. Planned the beam web. Counted her reserves. Nudged into an updraft beneath the plant. The thermal carried her, a silent piece of paper in a storm, drifting back and forth beneath the objective. The huge field intakes pulsed above, lightning outlining their invisible extension. She held back on the beam.

Nearly faded out. Her suit interior was almost unbearably hot.

She was only vaguely aware of laying down the pattern. The beams vanished in the murk. The thermal pushed her through a layer of haze, and she saw the plant, riding high above clear-atmosphere turbulence. The zero-angle phase had pushed through the field intakes, into their source nodes and the plant body, surrounding it with bright blue Tcherenkov.

First the surface began to break up, then the middle layers, and finally key supports. Chunks vibrated away with the internal fury of their molecular, then atomic, then particle disruption. Paraphrasing Grounds description of beam action, the plant became less and less convinced of its reality. "Matter dreams," an instructor had said a decade before. "Dreams it is real, maintains the dream by shifting rules with constant results. Disturb the dreams, the shifting of the rules results in inconstant results. Things cannot hold."

She slid away from the updraft, found another, wondered idly how far she would be lifted. Curiosity at the last. Let's just see, she told herself; a final experiment.

Now she was cold. The implant was flickering, showing signs of reorganization. She didn't use it. No sense expanding the amount of time until death. No sense—

at all.

The sled, maneuvered by one remaining fighter, glided up beneath her almost unnoticed.

Aryz waited in the stillness of a Senexi memory, his thinking temporarily reduced to a faint susurrus. What he waited for was not clear.

—Come.

The form of address was wrong, but he recognized the voice. His thoughts stirred, and he followed the nebulous presence out of Senexi territory.

—Know your enemy.

Prufrax . . . the name of one of the human shapes sent out against their own kind. He could sense her presence in the mandate, locked into a memory store. He touched on the store and caught the essentials—the grinder, the updraft plant, the fight from Prufrax's viewpoint.

—Know how your enemy knows you.

He sensed a second presence, similar to that of Prufrax. It took him some time to realize that the human captive was another form of the shape, a reproduction of the . . .

Both were reproductions of the female whose image was in the memory store. Aryz was not impressed by threes—Senexi mysticism, what had ever existed of it, had been preoccupied with fives and sixes—but the coincidence was striking.

—Know how your enemy *sees* you.

He saw the grinder processing organics—the vermiform natives—in preparation for a widespread seeding of deuterium gatherers. The operation had evidently been conducted for some time; the vermiform populations were greatly reduced from their usual numbers. Vermiforms were a common type-species on gas giants of the sort depicted. The mutated shape nudged him into a particular channel of the memory, that which carried the original Prufrax's emotions. She had reacted with *disgust* to the Senexi procedure. It was a reaction not unlike what Aryz might feel when coming across something forbidden in Senexi behavior. Yet eradication was perfectly natural, analogous to the human cleansing of *food* before *eating.*

—It's in the memory. The vermiforms are intelligent. They have their own kind of civilization. Human action on this world prevented their complete extinction by the Senexi.

—So what matter they were *intelligent?* Aryz responded. They did not behave or think like Senexi, or like any species Senexi find compatible. They were therefore not desirable. Like humans.

—You would make humans extinct?

—We would protect ourselves from them.

—Who damages whom most?

Aryz didn't respond. The line of questioning was incomprehensible. Instead he flowed into the memory of Prufrax, propelled by another aspect of complete freedom, confusion.

The implant was replaced. Prufrax's damaged limbs and skin were repaired or regenerated quickly, and within four wakes, under intense treatment usually reserved only for overs, she regained all her reflexes and speed. She requested liberty of the cruiser while it returned for repairs. Her request was granted.

She first sought Clevo in the designated research area. He wasn't there, but a message was, passed on to her by a smiling young crew member. She read it quickly:

"You're free and out of action. Study for a while, then come find me.

The old place hasn't been damaged. It's less private, but still good. Study! I've marked highlights."

She frowned at the message, then handed it to the crew member, who duly erased it and returned to his duties. She wanted to talk with Clevo, not study.

But she followed his instructions. She searched out highlighted entries in the ship's memory store. It was not nearly as dull as she had expected. In fact, by following the highlights, she felt she was learning more about Clevo and about the questions he asked.

Old literature was not nearly as graphic as fibs, but it was different enough to involve her for a time. She tried to create imitations of what she read, but erased them. Nonfib stories were harder than she suspected. She read about punishment, duty; she read about places called heaven and hell, from a writer who had died tens of thousands of years before. With ed supplement guidance, she was able to comprehend most of what she read. Plugging the store into her implant, she was able to absorb hundreds of volumes in an hour.

Some of the stores were losing definition. They hadn't been used in decades, perhaps centuries.

Halfway through, she grew impatient. She left the research area. Operating on another hunch, she didn't go to the blister as directed, but straight to memory central, two decks inboard the research area. She saw Clevo there, plugged into a data pillar, deep in some aspect of ship history. He noticed her approach, unplugged, and swiveled on his chair. "Congratulations," he said, smiling at her.

"Hardfought," she acknowledged, smiling.

"Better than that, perhaps," he said.

She looked at him quizzically. "What do you mean, better?"

"I've been doing some illicit tapping on over channels."

"So?"

—He *is dangerous!*

"You've been recommended."

"For what?"

"Not for hero status, not yet. You'll have a good many more fights before that. And you probably won't enjoy it when you get there. You won't be a fighter then."

Prufrax stood silently before him.

"You may have a valuable genetic assortment. Overs think you behaved remarkably well under impossible conditions."

"Did I?"

He nodded. "Your type may be preserved."

"Which means?"

"There's a program being planned. They want to take the best fighters and reproduce them—clone them—to make uniform topgrade squadrons. It was rumored in my time—you haven't heard?"

She shook her head.

"It's not new. It's been done, off and on, for tens of thousands of years. This time they believe they can make it work."

"You were a fighter, once," she said. "Did they preserve your type?"

Clevo nodded. "I had something that interested them, but not, I think, as a fighter."

Prufrax looked down at her stubby-fingered hands. "It was grim," she said. "You know what we found?"

"An extermination plant."

"You want me to understand them better. Well, I can't. I refuse. How could they do such things?" She looked disgusted and answered her own question. "Because they're Senexi."

"Humans," Clevo said, "have done much the same, sometimes worse."

"No!"

—No!

"Yes," he said firmly. He sighed. "We've wiped Senexi worlds, and we've even wiped worlds with intelligent species like our own. Nobody is innocent. Not in this universe."

"We were never taught that."

"It wouldn't have made you a better hawk. But it might make a better human of you, to know. Greater depth of character. Do you want to be more aware?"

"You mean, study more?"

He nodded.

"What makes you think *you* can teach me?"

"Because you thought about what I asked you. About how Senexi thought. And you survived where some other hawk might not have. The overs think it's in your genes. It might be. But it's also in your head."

"Why not tell the overs?"

"I have," he said. He shrugged. "I'm too valuable to them, otherwise I'd have been busted again, a long time ago."

"They wouldn't want me to learn from you?"

"I don't know," Clevo said. "I suppose they're aware you're talking to me. They could stop it if they wanted. They may be smarter than I give them credit for." He shrugged again. "Of course they're smart. We just disagree at times."

"And if I learn from you?"

"Not from me, actually. From the past. From history, what other people have thought. I'm really not any more capable than you . . . but I know history, small portions of it. I won't teach you so much, as guide."

"I did use your questions," Prufrax said. "But will I ever need to use them—think that way—again?"

Clevo nodded. "Of course."

—You're quiet.

—She's giving in to him.

—She gave in a long time ago.

—She should be afraid.

—Were you—we—ever really afraid of a challenge?

—No.

—Not Senexi, not forbidden knowledge.

—Someone listens with us. Feel—

Clevo first led her through the history of past wars, judging that was appropriate considering her occupation. She was attentive enough, though her mind wandered; sometimes he was didactic, but she found that didn't bother her much. At no time did his attitude change as they pushed through the tangle of the past. Rather her perception of his attitude changed. Her perception of herself changed.

She saw that in all wars, the first stage was to dehumanize the enemy, reduce the enemy to a lower level so that he might be killed without compunction. When the enemy was not human to begin with, the task was easier. As wars progressed, this tactic frequently led to an underestimation of the enemy, with disastrous consequences. "We aren't exactly underestimating the Senexi," Clevo said. "The overs are too smart for that. But we refuse to understand them, and that could make the war last indefinitely."

"Then why don't the overs see that?"

"Because we're being locked into a pattern. We've been fighting for so long, we've begun to lose ourselves. And it's getting worse." He assumed his didactic tone, and she knew he was reciting something he'd formulated years before and repeated to himself a thousand times. "There is no war so important that to win it, we must destroy our minds."

She didn't agree with that; losing the war with the Senexi would mean extinction, as she understood things.

Most often they met in the single unused weapons blister that had not been damaged. They met when the ship was basking in the real between sponge-space jaunts. He brought memory stores with him in portable modules, and they read, listened, experienced together. She never placed a great deal of importance in the things she learned; her interest was focused on Clevo. Still, she learned.

The rest of her time she spent training. She was aware of a growing isolation from the hawks, which she attributed to her uncertain rank status. Was her genotype going to be preserved or not? The decision hadn't been made. The more she learned, the less she wanted to be singled out for honor. Attracting that sort of attention might be dangerous, she thought. Dangerous to whom, or what, she could not say.

Clevo showed her how hero images had been used to indoctrinate birds and hawks in a standard of behavior that was ideal, not realistic. The results were not always good; some tragic blunders had been made by fighters trying to be more than anyone possibly could or refusing to be flexible.

The war was certainly not a fib. Yet more and more the overs seemed to be treating it as one. Unable to bring about strategic victories against the Senexi, the overs had settled in for a long war of attrition and were apparently bent on adapting all human societies to the effort.

"There are overs we never hear of, who make decisions that shape our entire lives. Soon they'll determine whether or not we're even born, if they don't already."

"That sounds paranoid," she said, trying out a new word and concept she had only recently learned.

"Maybe so."

"Besides, it's been like that for ages—not knowing all our overs."

"But it's getting worse," Clevo said. He showed her the projections he had made. In time, if trends continued unchanged, fighters and all other combatants would be treated more and more mechanically, until they became the machines the overs wished them to be.

—No.

—Quiet. How does he feel toward her?

It was inevitable that as she learned under his tutelage, he began to feel responsible for her changes. She was an excellent fighter. He could never be sure that what he was doing might reduce her effectiveness. And yet he had fought well—despite similar changes—until his billet switch. It had been the overs who had decided he would be more effective, less disruptive, elsewhere.

Bitterness over that decision was part of his motive. The overs had done a foolish thing, putting a fighter into research. Fighters were tenacious. If the truth was to be hidden, then fighters were the ones likely to ferret it out. And pass it on. There was a code among fighters, seldom revealed to their immediate overs, much less to the supreme overs parsecs distant in their strategospheres. What one fighter learned that could be of help to another had to be passed on, even under penalty. Clevo was simply following that unwritten rule.

Passing on the fact that, at one time, things had been different. That war changed people, governments, societies, and that societies could effect an enormous change on their constituents, especially now—change in their lives, their thinking. Things could become even more structured. Freedom of fight was a drug, an illusion—

—No!

used to perpetuate a state of hatred.

"Then why do they keep all the data in stores?" she asked. "I mean, you study the data, everything becomes obvious."

"There are still important people who think we may want to find our way back someday. They're afraid we'll lose our roots, but—"

His face suddenly became peaceful. She reached out to touch him, and he jerked slightly, turning toward her in the blister. "What is it?" she asked.

"It's not organized. We're going to lose the information. Ship overs are going to restrict access more and more. Eventually it'll decay, like some already has in these stores. I've been planning for some time to put it all in a single unit—"

—*He* built the mandate!

"and have the overs place one on every ship, with researchers to tend it. Formalize the loose scheme still in effect, but dying. Right now I'm working on the fringes. At least I'm allowed to work. But soon I'll have enough evidence that they won't be able to argue. Evidence of what happens to societies that try to obscure their histories. They go quite mad. The overs are still rational enough to listen; maybe I'll push it through." He looked out the transparent blister. The stars were smudging to one side as the cruiser began probing for entrances to sponge space. "We'd better get back."

"Where are you going to be when we return? We'll all be transferred."

"That's some time removed. Why do you want to know?"

"I'd like to learn more."

He smiled. "That's not your only reason."

"I don't need someone to tell me what my reasons are," she said testily.

"We're so reluctant," he said. She looked at him sharply, irritated and puzzled. "I mean," he continued, "we're hawks. Comrades. Hawks couple like *that*." He snapped his fingers. "But you and I sneak around it all the time."

Prufrax kept her face blank.

"Aren't you receptive toward me?" he asked, his tone almost teasing.

"You're so damned superior. Stuffy," she snapped.

"Aren't you?"

"It's just that's not all," she said, her tone softening.

"Indeed," he said in a barely audible whisper.

In the distance they heard the alarms.

—It was never any different.

—What?

—Things were never any different before me.

—Don't be silly. It's all here.

—If Clevo made the mandate, then he put it here. It isn't true.

—Why are you upset?

—I don't like hearing that everything I believe is a . . . fib.

—I've never known the difference, I suppose. Eyes-open was never all that real to me. This isn't real, you aren't . . . this is eyes-shut. So why be upset? You and I . . . we aren't even whole people. I feel you. You wish the Zap, you fight, not much else. I'm just a shadow, even compared to you. But she is whole. She loves him. She's less a victim than either of us. So something has to have changed.

—You're saying things have gotten worse.

—If the mandate is a lie, that's all I am. You refuse to accept. I *have* to accept, or I'm even less than a shadow.

—I don't refuse to accept. It's just hard.

—You started it. You thought about love.

—You did!

—Do you know what love is?

—Reception.

They first made love in the weapons blister. It came as no surprise; if anything, they approached it so cautiously they were clumsy. She had become more and more receptive, and he had dropped his guard. It had been quick, almost frantic, far from the orchestrated and drawn-out ballet the hawks prided themselves for. There was no pretense. No need to play the roles of artists interacting. They were depending on each other. The pleasure they exchanged was nothing compared to the emotions involved.

"We're not very good with each other," Prufrax said.

Clevo shrugged. "That's because we're shy."

"Shy?"

He explained. In the past—at various times in the past, because such differences had come and gone many times—making love had been more than a physical exchange or even an expression of comradeship. It had been the acknowledgment of a bond between people.

She listened, half-believing. Like everything else she had heard, that kind of love seemed strange, distasteful. What if one hawk was lost, and the other continued to love? It interfered with the hardfought, certainly. But she was also fascinated. Shyness—the fear of one's presentation to another. The hesitation to present truth, or the inward confusion of truth at the awareness that another might be important, more important than one thought possible. That such emotions might have existed at one time, and seem so alien now, only emphasized the distance of the past, as Clevo had tried to tell her. And that she felt those emotions only confirmed she was not as far from that past as, for dignity's sake, she might have wished.

Complex emotion was not encouraged either at the Grounds or among hawks on station. Complex emotion degraded complex performance. The simple and direct was desirable.

"But all we seem to do is talk—until now," Prufrax said, holding his hand and examining his fingers one by one. They were very little different from her own, though extended a bit from hawk fingers to give greater versatility with key instruction.

"Talking is the most human thing we can do."

She laughed. "I know what you are," she said, moving up until her eyes were even with his chest. "You're stuffy. You aren't the party type."

"Where'd you learn about parties?"

"You gave me literature to read, I read it. You're an instructor at heart. You make love by telling." She felt peculiar, almost afraid, and looked up at his face. "Not that I don't enjoy your lovemaking, like this. Physical."

"You receive well," he said. "Both ways."

"What we're saying," she whispered, "is not truth-speaking. It's amenity." She turned into the stroke of his hand through her hair. "Amenity is supposed to be decadent. That fellow who wrote about heaven and hell. He would call it a sin."

"Amenity is the recognition that somebody may see or feel differently than you do. It's the recognition of individuals. You and I, we're part of the end of all that."

"Even if you convince the overs?"

He nodded. "They want to repeat success without risk. New individuals are risky, so they duplicate past success. There will be more and more people, fewer individuals. More of you and me, less of others. The fewer individuals, the fewer stories to tell. The less history. We're part of the death of history."

She floated next to him, trying to blank her mind as she had before, to drive out the nagging awareness he was right. She thought she understood the social structure around her. Things seemed new. She said as much.

"It's a path we're taking," Clevo said. "Not a place we're at."

—It's a place *we're* at. How different are *we*?

—But there's so much history in here. How can it be over for us?

—I've been thinking. Do we know the last event recorded in the mandate?

—Don't, we're drifting from Prufrax now. . . .

Aryz felt himself drifting with them. They swept over countless millennia, then swept back the other way. And it became evident that as much change had been wrapped in one year of the distant past as in a thousand years of the closing entries in the mandate. Clevo's voice seemed to follow them, though they were far from his period, far from Prufrax's record.

"Tyranny is the death of history. We fought the Senexi until we became like them. No change, youth at an end, old age coming upon us. There is no important change, merely elaborations in the pattern."

—How many times have we been here, then? How many times have we died?

Aryz wasn't sure, now. *Was* this the first time humans had been captured? Had he been told everything by the brood mind? Did the Senexi have no *history,* whatever that was—

The accumulated lives of living, thinking beings. Their actions, thoughts, passions, hopes.

The mandate answered even his confused, nonhuman requests. He could understand action, thought, but not passion or hope. Perhaps without those there was no *history.*

—You have no history, the mutated shape told him. There have been millions like you, even millions like the brood mind. What is the last event recorded in the brood mind that is not duplicated a thousand times over, so close they can be melded together for convenience?

—You understand that? Aryz asked the shape.

—Yes.

—How do you understand—because we made you between human and Senexi?

—Not only that.

The requests of the twins, captive and shape were moving them back once more into the past, through the dim grey millennia of repeating ages. History began to manifest again, differences in the record.

On the way back to Mercior, four skirmishes were fought. Prufrax did well in each. She carried something special with her, a thought she didn't even tell Clevo, and she carried the same thought with her through their last days at the Grounds.

Taking advantage of hawk liberty, she opted a posthardfought residence just outside the Grounds, in the relatively uncrowded Daughter of Cities zone. She couldn't be returned to fight until several issues had been decided—her status most important among them.

Clevo began making his appeal to the middle overs. He was given Grounds duty to finish his proposals. They could stay together for the time being.

The residence was sixteen square meters in area, not elegant—*natural,* as rentOpts described it. Clevo called it a "garret," inaccurately as she discovered when she looked it up in his memory blocs, but perhaps he was describing the tone.

On the last day she lay in the crook of Clevo's arm. They had done a few hours of nature sleep. He hadn't come out yet, and she looked up at his face, reached up with a hand to feel his arm.

It was different from the arms of others she had been receptive toward. It was unique. The thought amused her. There had never been a reception like theirs. This was the beginning. And if both were to be duplicated, this love, this reception, would be repeated an infinite number of times. Clevo meeting Prufrax, teaching her, opening her eyes.

Somehow, even though repetition contributed to the death of history, she was pleased. This was the secret thought she carried into fight. Each time she would survive, wherever she was, however many duplications down the line. She would receive Clevo, and he would teach her. If not now—if one or the other died—then in the future. The death of history might be a good thing. Love could go on forever.

She had lost even a rudimentary apprehension of death, even with present pleasure to live for. Her functions had sharpened. She would please him by doing all the things he could not. And if he was to enter that state she frequently found him in, that state of introspection, of reliving his own battles and envying her activity, then that wasn't bad. All they did to each other was good.

—*Was* good

—*Was*

She slipped from his arm and left the narrow sleeping quarter, pushing through the smoke-colored air curtain to the lounge. Two hawks and an over she had never seen before were sitting there. They looked up at her.

"Under," Prufrax said.

"Over," the woman returned. She was dressed in tan and green, Grounds colors, not ship.

"May I assist?"

"Yes."

"My duty, then?"

The over beckoned her closer. "You have been receiving a researcher."

"Yes," Prufrax said. The meetings could not have been a secret on the ship, and certainly not their quartering near the Grounds. "Has that been against duty?"

"No." The over eyed Prufrax sharply, observing her perfected fightform, the easy grace with which she stood, naked, in the middle of the small compartment. "But a decision has been reached. Your status is decided now."

She felt a shiver.

"Prufrax," said the elder hawk. She recognized him from fibs, and his companion: Kumnax and Arol. Once her heroes. "You have been accorded an honor, just as your partner has. You have a valuable genetic assortment—"

She barely heard the rest. They told her she would return to fight, until they deemed she had had enough experience and background to be brought into the polinstruc division. Then her fighting would be over. She would serve better as an example, a hero.

Clevo emerged from the air curtain. "Duty," the over said. "The residence is disbanded. Both of you will have separate quarters, separate duties."

They left. Prufrax held out her hand, but Clevo didn't take it. "No use," he said.

Suddenly she was filled with anger. "You'll give it up? Did I expect too much? *How strongly?*"

"Perhaps even more strongly than you," he said. "I knew the order was coming down. And still I didn't leave. That may hurt my chances with the supreme overs."

"Then at least I'm worth more than your breeding history?"

"Now you are history. History the way they make it."

"I feel like I'm dying," she said, amazement in her voice. "What is that, Clevo? What did you do to me?"

"I'm in pain, too," he said.

"You're hurt?"

"I'm confused."

"I don't believe that," she said, her anger rising again. "You knew, and you didn't do anything?"

"That would have been counter to duty. We'll be worse off if we fight it."

"So what good is your great, exalted history?"

"History is what you have," Clevo said. "I only record."

—Why did they separate them?

—I don't know. You didn't like him, anyway.

—Yes, but now . . .

—See? You're her. We're her. But shadows. She was whole.

—I don't understand.

—We don't. Look what happens to her. They took what was best out of her. Prufrax

went into battle eighteen more times before dying as heroes often do, dying in the midst of what she did best. The question of what made her better before the separation—for she definitely was not as fine a

fighter after—has not been settled. Answers fall into an extinct classification of knowledge, and there are few left to interpret, none accessible to this device.

—So she went out and fought and died. They never even made fibs about her. This killed her?

—I don't think so. She fought well enough. She died like other hawks died.

—And she might have lived otherwise.

—How can I know that, any more than you?

—They—we—met again, you know. I met a Clevo once, on my ship. They didn't let me stay with him long.

—How did you react to him?

—There was so little time, I don't know.

—Let's ask. . . .

In thousands of duty stations, it was inevitable that some of Prufrax's visions would come true, that they should meet now and then. Clevos were numerous, as were Prufraxes. Every ship carried complements of several of each. Though Prufrax was never quite as successful as the original, she was a fine type. She—

—She was never quite as successful. They took away her edge. They didn't even know it!

—They must have known.

—Then they didn't want to win!

—We don't know that. Maybe there were more important considerations.

—Yes, like killing history.

Aryz shuddered in his warming body, dizzy as if about to bud, then regained control. He had been pulled from the mandate, called to his own duty.

He examined the shapes and the human captive. There was something different about them. How long had they been immersed in the mandate? He checked quickly, frantically, before answering the call. The reconstructed Mam had malfunctioned. None of them had been nourished. They were thin, pale, cooling.

Even the bloated mutant shape was dying; lost, like the others, in the mandate.

He turned his attention away. Everything was confusion. Was he human or Senexi now? Had he fallen so low as to understand them? He went to the origin of the call, the ruins of the temporary brood chamber. The corridors were caked with ammonia ice, burning his pod as he slipped over them. The brood mind had come out of flux bind. The emergency support systems hadn't worked well; the brood mind was damaged.

"Where have you been?" it asked.

"I assumed I would not be needed until your return from the flux bind."

"You have not been watching!"

"Was there any need? We are so advanced in time, all our actions are obsolete. The nebula is collapsed, the issue is decided."

"We do not know that. We are being pursued."

Aryz turned to the sensor wall—what was left of it—and saw that they were, indeed, being pursued. He had been lax.

"It is not your fault," the brood mind said. "You have been set a task that tainted you and ruined your function. You will dissipate."

Aryz hesitated. He had become so different, so tainted, that he actually *hesitated* at a direct command from the brood mind. But it was damaged. Without him, without what he had learned, what could it do? It wasn't reasoning correctly.

"There are facts you must know, important facts—"

Aryz felt a wave of revulsion, uncomprehending fear, and something not unlike human anger radiate from the brood mind. Whatever he had learned and however he had changed, he could not withstand that wave.

Willingly, and yet against his will—it didn't matter—he felt himself liquefying. His pod slumped beneath him, and he fell over, landing on a pool of frozen ammonia. It burned, but he did not attempt to lift himself. Before he ended, he saw with surprising clarity what it was to be a branch ind, or a brood mind, or a human. Such a valuable insight, and it leaked out of his permea and froze on the ammonia.

The brood mind regained what control it could of the fragment. But there were no defenses worthy of the name. Calm, preparing for its own dissipation, it waited for the pursuit to conclude.

* * *

The Mam set off an alarm. The interface with the mandate was severed. Weak, barely able to crawl, the humans looked at each other in horror and slid to opposite corners of the chamber.

They were confused: which of them was the captive, which the decoy shape? It didn't seem important. They were both bone-thin, filthy with their own excrement. They turned with one motion to stare at the bloated mutant. It sat in its corner, tiny head incongruous on the huge thorax, tiny arms and legs barely functional even when healthy. It smiled wanly at them.

"We felt you," one of the Prufraxes said. "You were with us in there." Her voice was a soft croak.

"That was my place," it replied. "My own place."

"What function, what name?"

"I'm . . . I know that. I'm a researcher. In there. I knew myself in there."

They squinted at the shape. The head. Something familiar, even now. "You're a Clevo. . . ."

There was noise all around them, cutting off the shape's weak words. As they watched, their chamber was sectioned like an orange, and the wedges peeled open. The illumination ceased. Cold enveloped them.

A naked human female, surrounded by tiny versions of herself, like an angel circled by fairy kin, floated into the chamber. She was thin as a snake. She wore nothing but silver rings on her wrists and a narrow torque around her waist. She glowed blue-green in the dark.

The two Prufraxes moved their lips weakly but made no sound in the near vacuum. *Who are you?*

She surveyed them without expression, then held out her arms as if to fly. She wore no gloves, but she was of their type.

As she had done countless times before on finding such Senexi experiments—though this seemed older than most—she lifted one arm higher. The blue-green intensified, spread in waves to the mangled walls, surrounded the freezing, dying shapes. Perfect, angelic, she left the debris behind to cast its fitful glow and fade.

They had destroyed every portion of the fragment but one. They left it behind unharmed.

Then they continued, millions of them thick like mist, working the spaces between the stars, their only master the overness of the real.

They needed no other masters. They would never malfunction.

The mandate drifted in the dark and cold, its memory going on, but its only life the rapidly fading tracks where minds had once passed through it. The trails writhed briefly, almost as if alive, but only following the quantum rules of diminishing energy states. Finally, a small memory was illuminated.

Prufrax's last poem, explained the mandate reflexively.

How the fires grow! Peace passes
All memory lost.
Somehow we always miss that single door
Dooming ourselves to circle.

Ashes to stars, lies to souls,
Let's spin round the sinks and holes.

Kill the good, eat the young.
Forever and more
You and I are never done.

The track faded into nothing. Around the mandate, the universe grew old very quickly.

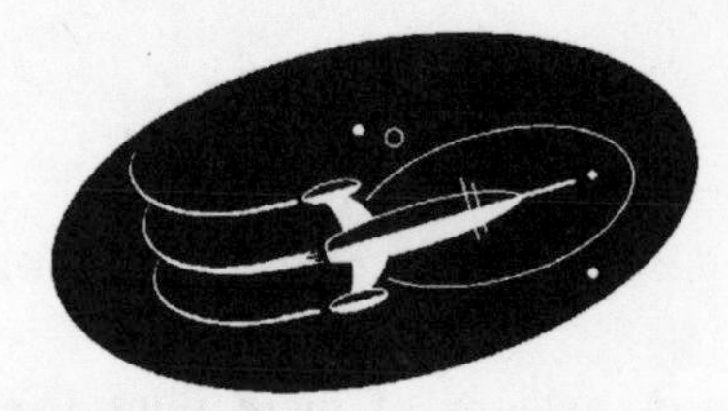

SAILING TO BYZANTIUM

Robert Silverberg

At dawn he arose and stepped out onto the patio for his first look at Alexandria, the one city he had not yet seen. That year the five cities were Chang-an, Asgard, New Chicago, Timbuctoo, Alexandria: the usual mix of eras, cultures, realities. He and Gioia, making the long flight from Asgard in the distant north the night before, had arrived late, well after sundown, and had gone straight to bed. Now, by the gentle apricot-hued morning light, the fierce spires and battlements of Asgard seemed merely something he had dreamed.

The rumor was that Asgard's moment was finished, anyway. In a little while, he had heard, they were going to tear it down and replace it, elsewhere, with Mohenjo-daro. Though there were never more than five cities, they changed constantly. He could remember a time when they had had Rome of the Caesars instead of Chang-an, and Rio de Janeiro rather than Alexandria. These people saw no point in keeping anything very long.

It was not easy for him to adjust to the sultry intensity of Alexandria after the frozen splendors of Asgard. The wind, coming off the water, was brisk and torrid both at once. Soft turquoise wavelets lapped at the jetties. Strong presences assailed his senses: the hot heavy sky, the stinging scent of the red lowland sand borne on the breeze, the sullen swampy aroma of the nearby sea. Everything trembled and glimmered in the early light. Their hotel was beautifully situated, high on the northern slope of the huge artificial mound known as the Paneium that was sacred to the goat-footed god. From here they had a total view of the city: the wide noble boulevards, the soaring obelisks and monuments, the palace of Hadrian just below the hill, the stately and awesome Library, the temple of Poseidon, the teeming marketplace, the royal lodge that Mark Antony had built after his defeat at Actium. And of course the Lighthouse, the wondrous many-windowed Lighthouse, the seventh wonder of the world, that immense pile of marble and limestone and reddish-purple Aswan granite rising in majesty at the end of its mile-long causeway. Black smoke from the beacon-fire at its summit curled lazily into the sky. The city was awakening. Some temporaries in short white kilts appeared and began to trim the dense dark hedges that bordered the great public buildings. A few citizens wearing loose robes of vaguely Grecian style were strolling in the streets.

There were ghosts and chimeras and phantasies everywhere about. Two slim elegant centaurs, a male and a female, grazed on the hillside. A burly thick-thighed swordsman appeared on the porch of the temple of Poseidon holding a Gorgon's severed head; he waved it in a wide arc, grinning broadly. In the street below the hotel gate three small pink sphinxes, no bigger than housecats, stretched and yawned and began to prowl the curbside. A larger one, lion-sized, watched warily from an alleyway: their mother, surely. Even at this distance he could hear her loud purring.

Shading his eyes, he peered far out past the Lighthouse and across the water. He hoped to see the dim shores of Crete or Cyprus to the north, or perhaps the great dark curve of Anatolia. *Carry me toward that great Byzantium,* he thought. *Where all is ancient, singing at the oars.* But he beheld only the endless empty sea, sun-bright and blinding though the morning was just beginning. Nothing was ever where he expected it to be. The continents did not seem to be in their proper places any longer. Gioia, taking him aloft long ago in her little flitterflitter, had shown him that. The tip of South America was canted far out into the Pacific; Africa was weirdly foreshortened; a broad tongue of ocean separated Europe and Asia. Australia did not appear to exist at all. Perhaps they had dug it up and used it for other things. There was no trace of the world he once had known. This was the fiftieth century. "The fiftieth century after *what?*" he had asked several times, but no one seemed to know, or else they did not care to say.

"Is Alexandria very beautiful?" Gioia called from within.

"Come out and see."

Naked and sleepy-looking, she padded out onto the white-tiled patio and nestled up beside him. She fit neatly under his arm. "Oh, yes, yes!" she said softly. "So very beautiful, isn't it? Look, there, the palaces, the Library, the Lighthouse! Where will we go first? The Lighthouse, I think. Yes? And then the marketplace—I want to see the Egyptian magicians—and the stadium, the races—will they be having races today, do you think? Oh, Charles, I want to see everything!"

"Everything? All on the first day?"

"All on the first day, yes," she said. "Everything."

"But we have plenty of time, Gioia."

"Do we?"

He smiled and drew her tight against his side.

"Time enough," he said gently.

He loved her for her impatience, for her bright bubbling eagerness. Gioia was not much like the rest in that regard, though she seemed identical in all other ways. She was short, supple, slender, dark-eyed, olive-skinned, narrow-hipped, with wide shoulders and flat muscles. They were all like that, each one indistinguishable from the rest, like a horde of millions of brothers and sisters—a world of small, lithe, childlike Mediterraneans, built for juggling, for bull-dancing, for sweet white wine at midday and rough red wine at night. They had the same slim bodies, the same broad mouths, the same great glossy eyes. He had never seen anyone who appeared to be younger than twelve or older than twenty. Gioia was somehow a little different, although he did not quite know how; but he knew that it was for that imperceptible but significant difference that he loved her. And probably that was why she loved him also.

He let his gaze drift from west to east, from the Gate of the Moon down broad Canopus Street and out to the harbor, and off to the tomb of Cleopatra at the tip of long slender Cape Lochias. Everything was here and all of it perfect, the obelisks, the statues and marble colonnades, the courtyards and shrines and groves, great Alexander himself in his coffin of crystal and gold:

a splendid gleaming pagan city. But there were oddities—an unmistakable mosque near the public gardens, and what seemed to be a Christian church not far from the Library. And those ships in the harbor, with all those red sails and bristling masts—surely they were medieval, and late medieval at that. He had seen such anachronisms in other places before. Doubtless these people found them amusing. Life was a game for them. They played at it unceasingly. Rome, Alexandria, Timbuctoo—why not? Create an Asgard of translucent bridges and shimmering ice-girt palaces, then grow weary of it and take it away? Replace it with Mohenjo-daro? Why not? It seemed to him a great pity to destroy those lofty Nordic feasting-halls for the sake of building a squat, brutal, sun-baked city of brown brick; but these people did not look at things the way he did. Their cities were only temporary. Someone in Asgard had said that Timbuctoo would be the next to go, with Byzantium rising in its place. Well, why not? Why not? They could have anything they liked. This was the fiftieth century, after all. The only rule was that there could be no more than five cities at once. "Limits," Gioia had informed him solemnly when they first began to travel together, "are very important." But she did not know why, or did not care to say.

He stared out once more toward the sea.

He imagined a newborn city congealing suddenly out of mists, far across the water: shining towers, great domed palaces, golden mosaics. That would be no great effort for them. They could just summon it forth whole out of time, the Emperor on his throne and the Emperor's drunken soldiery roistering in the streets, the brazen clangor of the cathedral gong rolling through the Grand Bazaar, dolphins leaping beyond the shoreside pavilions. Why not? They had Timbuctoo. They had Alexandria. Do you crave Constantinople? Then behold Constantinople! Or Avalon, or Lyonesse, or Atlantis. They could have anything they liked. It is pure Schopenhauer here: the world as will and imagination. Yes! These slender dark-eyed people journeying tirelessly from miracle to miracle. Why not Byzantium next? Yes! Why not? *That is no country for old men,* he thought. *The young in one another's arms, the birds in the trees*—yes! Yes! Anything they liked. They even had him. Suddenly he felt frightened. Questions he had not asked for a long time burst through into his consciousness. *Who am I? Why am I here? Who is this woman beside me?*

"You're so quiet all of a sudden, Charles," said Gioia, who could not abide silence for very long. "Will you talk to me? I want you to talk to me. Tell me what you're looking for out there."

He shrugged. "Nothing."

"Nothing?"

"Nothing in particular."

"I could see you seeing something."

"Byzantium," he said. "I was imagining that I could look straight across the water to Byzantium. I was trying to get a glimpse of the walls of Constantinople."

"Oh, but you wouldn't be able to see as far as that from here. Not really."

"I know."

"And anyway Byzantium doesn't exist."

"Not yet. But it will. Its time comes later on."

"Does it?" she said. "Do you know that for a fact?"

"On good authority. I heard it in Asgard," he told her. "But even if I hadn't, Byzantium would be inevitable, don't you think? Its time would have to come. How could we not do Byzantium, Gioia? We certainly will do Byzantium, sooner or later. I know we will. It's only a matter of time. And we have all the time in the world."

A shadow crossed her face. "Do we? Do we?"

He knew very little about himself, but he knew that he was not one of them. That he knew. He knew that his name was Charles Phillips and that before he had come to live among these people he had lived in the year 1984, when there had been such things as computers and television sets and baseball and jet planes, and the world was full of cities, not merely five but thousands of them, New York and London and Johannesburg and Paris and Liverpool and Bangkok and San Francisco and Buenos Aires and a multitude of others, all at the same time. There had been four and a half billion people in the world then; now he doubted that there were as many as four and a half million. Nearly everything had changed beyond comprehension. The moon still seemed the same, and the sun; but at night he searched in vain for familiar constellations. He had no idea how they had brought him from then to now, or why. It did no good to ask. No one had any answers for him; no one so much as appeared to understand what it was that he was trying to learn. After a time he had stopped asking; after a time had had almost entirely ceased wanting to know.

He and Gioia were climbing the Lighthouse. She scampered ahead, in a hurry as always, and he came along behind her in his more stolid fashion. Scores of other tourists, mostly in groups of two or three, were making their way up the wide flagstone ramps, laughing, calling to one another. Some of them, seeing him, stopped a moment, stared, pointed. He was used to that. He was so much taller than any of them; he was plainly not one of them. When they pointed at him he smiled. Sometimes he nodded a little acknowledgment.

He could not find much of interest in the lowest level, a massive square structure two hundred feet high built of huge marble blocks: within its cool musty arcades were hundreds of small dark rooms, the offices of the Lighthouse's keepers and mechanics, the barracks of the garrison, the stables for the three hundred donkeys that carried the fuel to the lantern far above. None of that appeared inviting to him. He forged onward without halting until he emerged on the balcony that led to the next level. Here the Lighthouse grew narrower and became octagonal: its face, granite now and handsomely fluted, rose in a stunning sweep above him.

Gioia was waiting for him there. "This is for you," she said, holding out a nugget of meat on a wooden skewer. "Roast lamb. Absolutely delicious. I had one while I was waiting for you." She gave him a cup of some cool green sherbet also, and darted off to buy a pomegranate. Dozens of temporaries were roaming the balcony, selling refreshments of all kinds.

He nibbled at the meat. It was charred outside, nicely pink and moist within. While he ate, one of the temporaries came up to him and peered blandly into his face. It was a stocky swarthy male wearing nothing but a strip of red and yellow cloth about its waist. "I sell meat," it said. "Very fine roast lamb, only five drachmas."

Phillips indicated the piece he was eating. "I already have some," he said.

"It is excellent meat, very tender. It has been soaked for three days in the juices of—"

"Please," Phillips said. "I don't want to buy any meat. Do you mind moving along?"

The temporaries had confused and baffled him at first, and there was still much about them that was unclear to him. They were not machines—they looked like creatures of flesh and blood—but they did not seem to be human beings, either, and no one treated them as if they were. He supposed they were artificial constructs, products of a technology so consummate that it was invisible. Some appeared to be more intelligent than others, but all of them behaved as if they had no more autonomy than characters in a play, which was essentially what they were. There were untold numbers of them in each of the five cities, playing all manner of roles: shepherds and swineherds, street-sweepers, merchants, boatmen, vendors of grilled meats and cool drinks, hagglers in the marketplace, schoolchildren, charioteers, policemen, grooms, gladiators, monks, artisans, whores and cutpurses, sailors—whatever was needed to sustain the illusion of a thriving, populous urban center. The dark-eyed people, Gioia's people, never performed work. There were not enough of them to keep a city's functions going, and in any case they were strictly tourists, wandering with the wind, moving from city to city as the whim took them, Chang-an to New Chicago, New Chicago to Timbuctoo, Timbuctoo to Asgard, Asgard to Alexandria, onward, ever onward.

The temporary would not leave him alone. Phillips walked away and it followed him, cornering him against the balcony wall. When Gioia returned a few minutes later, lips prettily stained with pomegranate juice, the temporary was still hovering about him, trying with lunatic persistence to sell him a skewer of lamb. It stood much too close to him, almost nose to nose, great sad cowlike eyes peering intently into his as it extolled with mournful mooing urgency the quality of its wares. It seemed to him that he had had trouble like this with temporaries on one or two earlier occasions. Gioia touched the creature's elbow lightly and said, in a short sharp tone Phillips had never heard her use before, "He isn't interested. Get away from him." It went at once. To Phillips she said, "You have to be firm with them."

"I was trying. It wouldn't listen to me."

"You ordered it to go away, and it refused?"

"I asked it to go away. Politely. Too politely, maybe."

"Even so," she said. "It should have obeyed a human, regardless."

"Maybe it didn't think I was human," Phillips suggested. "Because of the way I look. My height, the color of my eyes. It might have thought I was some kind of temporary myself."

"No," Gioia said, frowning. "A temporary won't solicit another temporary. But it won't ever disobey a citizen, either. There's a very clear boundary. There isn't ever any confusion. I can't understand why it went on bothering you." He was surprised at how troubled she seemed: far more so, he thought, than the incident warranted. A stupid device, perhaps miscalibrated in some way, overenthusiastically pushing its wares—what of it? What of it? Gioia, after a moment, appeared to come to the same conclusion. Shrugging, she said, "It's defective, I suppose. Probably such things are more common than we suspect, don't you think?" There was something forced about her tone that bothered him. She smiled and handed him her pomegranate. "Here. Have a bite, Charles. It's wonderfully sweet. They used to be extinct, you know. Shall we go on upward?"

The octagonal midsection of the Lighthouse must have been several hundred feet in height, a grim claustrophobic tube almost entirely filled by the two broad spiraling ramps that wound around the huge building's central well. The ascent was slow: a donkey team was a little way ahead of them on the ramp, plodding along laden with bundles of kindling for the lantern. But at last, just as Phillips was growing winded and dizzy, he and Gioia came out onto the second balcony, the one marking the transition between the octagonal section and the Lighthouse's uppermost storey, which was cylindrical and very slender.

She leaned far out over the balustrade. "Oh, Charles, look at the view! Look at it!"

It was amazing. From one side they could see the entire city, and swampy Lake Mareotis and the dusty Egyptian plain beyond it, and from the other they peered far out into the gray and choppy Mediterranean. He gestured toward the innumerable reefs and shallows that infested the waters leading to the harbor entrance. "No wonder they needed a lighthouse here," he said. "Without some kind of gigantic landmark they'd never have found their way in from the open sea."

A blast of sound, a ferocious snort, erupted just above him. He looked up, startled. Immense statues of trumpet-wielding Tritons jutted from the corners of the Lighthouse at this level; that great blurting sound had come from the nearest of them. A signal, he thought. A warning to the ships negotiating that troubled passage. The sound was produced by some kind of steam-powered mechanism, he realized, operated by teams of sweating temporaries clustered about bonfires at the base of each Triton.

Once again he found himself swept by admiration for the clever way these people carried out their reproductions of antiquity. Or *were* they reproductions, he wondered? He still did not understand how they brought their cities into being. For all he knew, this place was the authentic Alexandria itself, pulled forward out of its proper time just as he himself had been. Perhaps this was the true and original Lighthouse, and not a copy. He had no idea which was the case, nor which would be the greater miracle.

"How do we get to the top?" Gioia asked.

"Over there, I think. That doorway."

The spiraling donkey-ramps ended here. The loads of lantern fuel went higher via a dumb-waiter in the central shaft. Visitors continued by way of a cramped staircase, so narrow at its upper end that it was impossible to turn around while climbing. Gioia, tireless, sprinted ahead. He clung to the rail and labored up and up, keeping count of the tiny window-slits to ease the boredom of the ascent. The count was nearing a hundred when finally he stumbled into the vestibule of the beacon chamber. A dozen or so visitors were crowded into it. Gioia was at the far side, by the wall that was open to the sea.

It seemed to him he could feel the building swaying in the winds, up here. How high were they? Five hundred feet, six hundred, seven? The beacon chamber was tall and narrow, divided by a catwalk into upper and lower sections. Down below, relays of temporaries carried wood from the dumb-waiter and tossed it on the blazing fire. He felt its intense heat from where he stood, at the rim of the platform on which the giant mirror of polished metal was ahung. Tongues of flame leaped upward and danced before the mirror, which hurled its dazzling beam far out to sea. Smoke rose through a vent. At the very top was a colossal statue of Poseidon, austere, ferocious, looming above the lantern.

Gioia sidled along the catwalk until she was at his side. "The guide was talking before you came," she said, pointing. "Do you see that place over there, under the mirror? Someone standing there and looking into the mirror gets a view of ships at sea that can't be seen from here by the naked eye. The mirror magnifies things."

"Do you believe that?"

She nodded toward the guide. "It said so. And it also told us that if you look in a certain way, you can see right across the water into the city of Constantinople."

She is like a child, he thought. They all are. He said, "You told me yourself this very morning that it isn't possible to see that far. Besides, Constantinople doesn't exist right now."

"It will," she replied. "*You* said that to me, this very morning. And when it does, it'll be reflected in the Lighthouse mirror. That's the truth. I'm absolutely certain of it." She swung about abruptly toward the entrance of the beacon chamber. "Oh, look, Charles! Here come Nissandra and Aramayne! And there's Hawk! There's Stengard!" Gioia laughed and waved and called out names. "Oh, everyone's here! *Everyone!*"

They came jostling into the room, so many newcomers that some of those who had been there were forced to scramble down the steps on the far side. Gioia moved among them, hugging, kissing. Phillips could scarcely tell one from another—it was hard for him even to tell which were the men and which the women, dressed as they all were in the same sort of loose robes—but he recognized some of the names. These were her special friends, her set, with whom she had journeyed from city to city on an endless round of gaiety in the old days before he had come into her life. He had met a few of them before, in Asgard, in Rio, in Rome. The beacon-chamber guide, a squat wide-shouldered old temporary wearing a laurel wreath on its bald head, reappeared and began its potted speech, but no one listened to it; they were all too busy greeting one another, embracing, giggling. Some of them edged their way over to Phillips and reached up, standing on tiptoes, to touch their fingertips to his cheek in that odd hello of theirs. "Charles," they said gravely, making two syllables out of the name, as these people often did. "So good to see you again. Such a pleasure. You and Gioia—such a handsome couple. So well suited to each other."

Was that so? He supposed it was.

The chamber hummed with chatter. The guide could not be heard at all. Stengard and Nissandra had visited New Chicago for the water-dancing—Aramayne bore tales of a feast in Chang-an that had gone on for *days*—Hawk and Hekna had been to Timbuctoo to see the arrival of the salt caravan, and were going back there soon—a final party soon to celebrate the end of Asgard that absolutely should not be missed—the plans for the new city, Mohenjo-daro—we have reservations for the opening, we wouldn't pass it up for anything—and, yes, they were definitely going to do Constantinople after that, the planners were already deep into their Byzantium research—so good to see you, you look so beautiful all the time—have you been to the Library yet? The zoo? To the temple of Serapis?—

To Phillips they said, "What do you think of our Alexandria, Charles? Of course you must have known it well in your day. Does it look the way you remember it?" They were always asking things like that. They did not seem to comprehend that the Alexandria of the Lighthouse and the Library was long lost and legendary by his time. To them, he suspected, all the places they had brought back into existence were more or less contemporary. Rome of the Caesars, Alexandria of the Ptolemies, Venice of the Doges, Chang-an of the T'angs, Asgard of the Aesir, none any less real than the next nor any less unreal, each one simply a facet of the distant past, the fantastic immemorial past, a plum plucked from that dark backward and abysm of time. They had no contexts for separating one era from another. To them all the past was one borderless timeless realm. Why then should he not have seen the Lighthouse before, he who had leaped into this era from the New York of 1984? He had never been able to explain it to them. Julius Caesar and Hannibal, Helen of Troy and Charlemagne, Rome of the gladiators and New York of the Yankees and Mets, Gilgamesh and Tristan and Othello and Robin Hood and George Washington and Queen Victoria—to them, all equally real and unreal, none of them any more than bright figures moving about on a painted canvas. The past, the past, the elusive and fluid past—to them it was a single place of infinite accessibility and infinite connectivity. Of course they would think he had seen the Lighthouse before. He knew better than to try again to explain things. "No," he said simply. "This is my first time in Alexandria."

They stayed there all winter long, and possibly some of the spring. Alexandria was not a place where one was sharply aware of the change of seasons, nor did the passage of time itself make itself very evident when one was living one's entire life as a tourist.

During the day there was always something new to see. The zoological garden, for instance: a wondrous park, miraculously green and lush in this hot dry climate, where astounding animals roamed in enclosures so generous that they did not seem like enclosures at all. Here were camels, rhinoceroses, gazelles, ostriches, lions, wild asses; and here too, casually adjacent to those familiar African beasts, were hippogriffs, unicorns, basilisks, and fire-snorting dragons with rainbow scales. Had the original zoo of Alexandria had dragons and unicorns? Phillips doubted it. But this one did; evidently it was no harder for the backstage craftsmen to manufacture mythic beasts than it was for them to turn out camels and gazelles. To Gioia and her friends all of them were equally mythical, anyway. They were just as awed by the rhinoceros as by the hippogriff. One was no more strange—nor any less—than the other. So far as Phillips had been able to discover, none of the mammals or birds of his era had survived into this one except for a few cats and dogs, though many had been reconstructed.

And then the Library! All those lost treasures, reclaimed from the jaws of time! Stupendous columned marble walls, airy high-vaulted reading-rooms, dark coiling stacks stretching away to infinity. The ivory handles of seven hundred thousand papyrus scrolls bristling on the shelves. Scholars and librarians gliding quietly about, smiling faint scholarly smiles but plainly preoccupied with serious matters of the mind. They were all temporaries, Phillips realized. Mere props, part of the illusion. But were the scrolls illusions too? "Here we have the complete dramas of Sophocles," said the guide with a blithe wave of its hand, indicating shelf upon shelf of texts. Only seven of his hundred twenty-three plays had survived the successive burnings of the library in ancient times by Romans, Christians, Arabs: were the lost ones here, the *Triptolemus,* the *Nausicaa,* the *Jason,* and all the rest? And would he find here too, miraculously restored to being, the other vanished treasures of ancient literature—the memoirs of Odysseus, Cato's history of Rome, Thucydides' life of Pericles, the missing volumes of Livy? But when he asked if he might explore the stacks, the guide smiled apologetically and said that all the librarians were busy just now. Another time, perhaps? Perhaps, said the guide. It made no difference, Phillips decided. Even if these people somehow had brought back those lost masterpieces of antiquity, how would he read them? He knew no Greek.

The life of the city buzzed and throbbed about him. It was a dazzlingly beautiful place: the vast bay thick with sails, the great avenues running rigidly east-west, north-south, the sunlight rebounding almost audibly from the bright walls of the palaces of kings and gods. They have done this very well, Phillips thought: very well indeed. In the marketplace hard-eyed traders squabbled in half a dozen mysterious languages over the price of ebony, Arabian incense, jade, panther-skins. Giois bought a dram of pale musky Egyptian perfume in a delicate tapering glass flask. Magicians and jugglers and scribes called out stridently to passersby, begging for a few moments of attention and a handful of coins for their labor. Strapping slaves, black and tawny and some that might have been Chinese, were put up for auction, made to flex their muscles, to bare their teeth, to bare their breasts and thighs to prospective buyers. In the gymnasium naked athletes hurled javelins and discuses, and wrestled with terrifying zeal. Gioia's friend Stengard came rushing up with a gift for her, a golden necklace that would not have embarrassed Cleopatra. An hour later she had lost it, or perhaps had given it away while Phillips was looking elsewhere. She bought another, even finer, the next day. Anyone could have all the money he wanted, simply by asking: it was as easy to come by as air, for these people.

Being here was much like going to the movies, Phillips told himself. A different show every day: not much plot, but the special effects were magnificent and the detail-work could hardly have been surpassed. A megamovie, a vast entertainment that went on all the time and was being played out by the whole population of Earth. And it was all so effortless, so spontaneous: just as when he had gone to a movie he had never troubled to think about the myriad technicians behind the scenes, the cameramen and the costume designers and the set-builders and the electricians and the model-makers and the boom operators, so too here he chose not to question the means by which Alexandria had been set before him. It felt real. It *was* real. When he drank the strong red wine it gave him a pleasant buzz. If he leaped from the beacon chamber of the Lighthouse he suspected he would die, though perhaps he would not stay dead for long: doubtless they had some way of restoring him as often as was necessary. Death did not seem to be a factor in these people's lives.

By day they saw sights. By night he and Gioia went to parties, in their hotel, in seaside villas, in the palaces of the high nobility. The usual people were there all the time, Hawk and Hekna, Aramayne, Stengard and Shelimir, Nissandra, Asoka, Afonso, Protay. At the parties there were five or ten temporaries for every citizen, some as mere servants, others as entertainers or even surrogate guests, mingling freely and a little daringly. But everyone knew, all the time, who was a citizen and who just a temporary. Phillips began to think his own status lay somewhere between. Certainly they treated him with a courtesy that no one ever would give a temporary, and yet there was a condescension to their manner that told him not simply that he was not one of them but that he was someone or something of an altogether different order of existence. That he was Gioia's lover gave him some standing in their eyes, but not a great deal: obviously he was always going to be an outsider, a primitive, ancient and quaint. For that matter he noticed that Gioia herself, though unquestionably a member of the set, seemed to be regarded as something of an outsider, like a tradesman's great-granddaughter in a gathering of Plantagenets. She did not always find out about the best parties in time to attend; her friends did not always reciprocate her effusive greetings with the same degree of warmth; sometimes he noticed her straining to hear some bit of gossip that was not quite being shared with her. Was it because she had taken him for her lover? Or was it the other way around: that she had chosen to be his lover precisely because she was *not* a full member of their caste?

Being a primitive gave him, at least, something to talk about at their parties. "Tell us about war," they said. "Tell us about elections. About money. About disease." They wanted to know everything, though they did not seem to pay close attention: their eyes were quick to glaze. Still, they asked. He described traffic jams to them, and politics, and deodorants, and vitamin pills. He told them about cigarettes, newspapers, subways, telephone directories, credit cards, and basketball.

"Which was your city?" they asked. New York, he told them. "And when was it? The seventh century, did you say?" The twentieth, he told them. They exchanged glances and nodded. "We will have to do it," they said. "The World Trade Center, the Empire State Building, the Citicorp Center, the Cathedral of St. John the Divine: how fascinating! Yankee Stadium. The Verrazzano Bridge. We will do it all. But first must come Mohenjo-daro. And then, I think, Constantinople. Did your city have many people?" Seven million, he said. Just in the five boroughs alone. They nodded, smiling amiably, unfazed by the number.

Seven million, seventy million—it was all the same to them, he sensed. They would just bring forth the temporaries in whatever quantity was required. He wondered how well they would carry the job off. He was no real judge of Alexandrias and Asgards, after all. Here they could have unicorns and hippogriffs in the zoo, and live sphinxes prowling in the gutters, and it did not trouble him. Their fanciful Alexandria was as good as history's, or better. But how sad, how disillusioning it would be, if the New York that they conjured up had Greenwich Village uptown and Times Square in the Bronx, and the New Yorkers, gentle and polite, spoke with the honeyed accents of Savannah or New Orleans. Well, that was nothing he needed to brood about just now. Very likely they were only being courteous when they spoke of doing his New York. They had all the vastness of the past to choose from: Nineveh, Memphis of the Pharaohs, the London of Victoria or Shakespeare or Richard the Third, Florence of the Medici, the Paris of Abelard and Heloise or the Paris of Louis XIV, Moctezuma's Tenochtitlan and Atahuallpa's Cuzco; Damascus, St. Petersburg, Babylon, Troy. And then there were all the cities like New Chicago, out of time that was time yet unborn to him but ancient history to them. In such richness, such an infinity of choices, even mighty New York might have to wait a long while for its turn. Would he still be among them by the time they got around to it? By then, perhaps, they might have become bored with him and returned him to his own proper era. Or possibly he would simply have grown old and died. Even here, he supposed, he would eventually die, though no one else ever seemed to. He did not know. He realized that in fact he did not know anything.

The north wind blew all day long. Vast flocks of ibises appeared over the city, fleeing the heat of the interior, and screeched across the sky with their black necks and scrawny legs extended. The sacred birds, descending by the thousands, scuttered about in every crossroad, pouncing on spiders and beetles, on mice, on the debris of the meat-shops and the bakeries. They were beautiful but annoyingly ubiquitous, and they splashed their dung over the marble buildings; each morning squadrons of temporaries carefully washed it off. Gioia said little to him now. She seemed cool, withdrawn, depressed; and there was something almost intangible about her, as though she were gradually becoming transparent. He felt it would be an intrusion upon her privacy to ask her what was wrong. Perhaps it was only restlessness. She became religious, and presented costly offerings at the temples of Serapis, Isis, Poseidon, Pan. She went to the necropolis west of the city to lay wreaths on the tombs in the catacombs. In a single day she climbed the Lighthouse three times without any sign of fatigue. One afternoon he returned from a visit to the Library and found her naked on the patio; she had anointed herself all over with some aromatic green salve. Abruptly she said, "I think it's time to leave Alexandria, don't you?"

She wanted to go to Mohenjo-daro, but Mohenjo-daro was not yet ready for visitors. Instead they flew eastward to Chang-an, which they had not seen in years. It was Phillips' suggestion: he hoped that the cosmopolitan gaudiness of the old T'ang capital would lift her mood.

They were to be guests of the Emperor this time: an unusual privilege, which ordinarily had to be applied for far in advance, but Phillips had told some of Gioia's highly placed friends that she was unhappy, and they had quickly arranged everything. Three endlessly bowing functionaries in flowing yellow robes and purple sashes met them at the Gate of Brilliant Virtue in the city's south wall and conducted them to their pavilion, close by the imperial palace and the Forbidden Garden. It was a light, airy place, thin walls of plastered brick braced by graceful columns of some dark, aromatic wood. Fountains played on the roof of green and yellow tiles, creating an unending cool rainfall of recirculating water. The balustrades were of carved marble, the door-fittings were of gold.

There was a suite of private rooms for him, and another for her, though they would share the handsome damask-draped bedroom at the heart of the pavilion. As soon as they arrived Gioia announced that she must go to her rooms to bathe and dress. "There will be a formal reception for us at the palace tonight," she said. "They say the imperial receptions are splendid beyond anything you could imagine. I want to be at my best." The Emperor and all his ministers, she told him, would receive them in the Hall of the Supreme Ultimate; there would be a banquet for a thousand people; Persian dancers would perform, and the celebrated jugglers of Chung-nan. Afterward everyone would be conducted into the fantastic landscape of the Forbidden Garden to view the dragon-races and the fireworks.

He went to his own rooms. Two delicate little maid-servants undressed him and bathed him with fragrant sponges. The pavilion came equipped with eleven temporaries who were to be their servants: soft-voiced unobtrusive cat-like Chinese, done with perfect verisimilitude, straight black hair, glowing skin, epicanthic folds. Phillips often wondered what happened to a city's temporaries when the city's time was over. Were the towering Norse heroes of Asgard being recycled at this moment into wiry dark-skinned Dravidians for Mohenjo-daro? When Timbuctoo's day was done, would its brightly robed black warriors be converted into supple Byzantines to stock the arcades of Constantinople? Or did they simply discard the old temporaries like so many excess props, stash them in warehouses somewhere, and turn out the appropriate quantities of the new model? He did not know; and once when he had asked Gioia about it she had grown uncomfortable and vague. She did not like him to probe for information, and he suspected it was because she had very little to give. These people did not seem to question the workings of their own world; his curiosities were very twentieth-century of him, he was frequently told, in that gently patronizing way of theirs. As his two little maids patted him with their sponges he thought of asking them where they had served before Chang-an: Rio? Rome? Haroun al-Raschid's Baghdad? But these fragile girls, he knew, would only giggle and retreat if he tried to question them. Interrogating temporaries was not only improper, but pointless: it was like interrogating one's luggage.

When he was bathed and robed in rich red silks he wandered the pavilion for a little while, admiring the tinkling pendants of green jade dangling on the portico, the lustrous auburn pillars, the rainbow hues of the intricately interwoven girders and brackets that supported the roof. Then, wearying of his solitude, he approached the bamboo curtain at the entrance to Gioia's suite. A porter and one of the maids stood just within. They indicated that he should not enter; but he scowled at them and they melted from him like snowflakes. A trail of incense led him through the pavilion to Gioia's innermost dressing-room. There he halted, just outside the door.

Gioia sat naked with her back to him at an ornate dressing-table of some rare flame-colored wood inlaid with bands of orange and green porcelain. She was studying herself intently in a mirror of polished bronze held by one of her maids: picking through her scalp with her fingernails, as a woman might do who was searching out her gray hairs.

But that seemed strange. Gray hair, on Gioia? On a citizen? A temporary might display some appearance of aging, perhaps, but surely not a citizen. Citizens remained forever young. Gioia looked like a girl. Her face was smooth and unlined, her flesh was firm, her hair was dark: that was true of all of them, every citizen he had ever seen. And yet there was no mistaking what Gioia was doing. She found a hair, frowned, drew it taut, nodded, plucked it. Another. Another. She pressed the tip of her finger to her cheek as if testing it for resilience. She tugged at the skin below her eyes, pulling it downward. Such familiar little gestures of vanity; but so odd here, he thought, in this world of the perpetually young. Gioia, worried about growing old? Had he simply failed to notice the signs of age on her? Or was it that she worked hard behind his back at concealing them? Perhaps that was it. Was he wrong about the citizens, then? Did they age even as the people of less blessed eras had always done, but simply have better ways of hiding it? How old was she, anyway? Thirty? Sixty? Three hundred?

Gioia appeared satisfied now. She waved the mirror away; she rose; she beckoned for her banquet robes. Phillips, still standing unnoticed by the door, studied her with admiration: the small round buttocks, almost but not quite boyish, the elegant line of her spine, the surprising breadth of her shoulders. No, he thought, she is not aging at all. Her body is still like a girl's. She looks as young as on the day they first had met, however long ago that was—he could not say; it was hard to keep track of time here; but he was sure some years had passed since they had come together. Those gray hairs, those wrinkles and sags for which she had searched just now with such desperate intensity, must all be imaginary, mere artifacts of vanity. Even in this remote future epoch, then, vanity was not extinct. He wondered why she was so concerned with the fear of aging. An affectation? Did all these timeless people take some perverse pleasure in fretting over the possibility that they might be growing old? Or was it some private fear of Gioia's, another symptom of the mysterious depression that had come over her in Alexandria?

Not wanting her to think that he had been spying on her, when all he had really intended was to pay her a visit, he slipped silently away to dress for the evening. She came to him an hour later, gorgeously robed, swaddled from chin to ankles in a brocade of brilliant colors shot through with threads of gold, face painted, hair drawn up tightly and fastened with ivory combs: very much the lady of the court. His servants had made him splendid also, a lustrous black surplice embroidered with golden dragons over a sweeping floor-length gown of shining white silk, a necklace and pendant of red coral, a five-cornered gray felt hat that rose in tower upon tower like a ziggurat. Gioia, grinning, touched her fingertips to his cheek. "You look marvelous!" she told him. "Like a grand mandarin!"

"And you like an empress," he said. "Of some distant land: Persia, India. Here to pay a ceremonial visit on the Son of Heaven." An excess of love suffused his spirit, and, catching her lightly by the wrist, he drew her toward him, as close as he could manage it considering how elaborate their costumes were. But as he bent forward and downward, meaning to brush his lips lightly and affectionately against the tip of her nose, he perceived an unexpected strangeness, an anomaly: the coating of white paint that was her makeup seemed oddly to magnify rather than mask the contours of her skin, highlighting and revealing details he had never observed before. He saw a pattern of fine lines radiating from the corners of her eyes, and the unmistakable beginning of a quirk-mark in her cheek just to the left of her mouth, and perhaps the faint indentation of frown-lines in her flawless forehead. A shiver traveled along the nape of his neck. So it was not affectation, then, that had had her studying her mirror so fiercely. Age was in truth beginning to stake its claim on her, despite all that he had come to believe about these people's agelessness. But a moment later he was not so sure. Gioia turned and slid gently half a step back from him—she must have found his stare disturbing—and the lines he had thought he had seen were gone. He searched for them and saw only girlish smoothness once again. A trick of the light? A figment of an overwrought imagination? He was baffled.

"Come," she said. "We mustn't keep the Emperor waiting."

Five mustachioed warriors in armor of white quilting and seven musicians playing cymbals and pipes escorted them to the Hall of the Supreme Ultimate. There they found the full court arrayed: princes and ministers, high officials, yellow-robed monks, a swarm of imperial concubines. In a place of honor to the right of the royal thrones, which rose like gilded scaffolds high above all else, was a little group of stern-faced men in foreign costumes, the ambassadors of Rome and Byzantium, of Arabia and Syria, of Korea, Japan, Tibet, Turkestan. Incense smouldered in enameled braziers. A poet sang a delicate twanging melody, accompanying himself on a small harp. Then the Emperor and Empress entered: two tiny aged people, like waxen images, moving with infinite slowness, taking steps no greater than a child's. There was the sound of trumpets as they ascended their thrones. When the little Emperor was seated—he looked like a doll up there, ancient, faded, shrunken, yet still somehow a figure of extraordinary power—he stretched forth both his hands, and enormous gongs began to sound. It was a scene of astonishing splendor, grand and overpowering.

These are all temporaries, Phillips realized suddenly. He saw only a handful of citizens—eight, ten, possibly as many as a dozen—scattered here and there about the vast room. He knew them by their eyes, dark, liquid, knowing. They were watching not only the imperial spectacle but also Gioia and him; and Gioia, smiling secretly, nodding almost imperceptibly to them, was acknowledging their presence and their interest. But those few were the only ones in here who were autonomous living beings. All the rest—the entire splendid court, the great mandarins and paladins, the officials, the giggling concubines, the haughty and resplendent ambassadors, the aged Emperor and Empress themselves, were simply part of the scenery. Had the world ever seen entertainment on so grand a scale before? All this pomp, all this pageantry, conjured up each night for the amusement of a dozen or so viewers?

At the banquet the little group of citizens sat together at a table apart, a round onyx slab draped with translucent green silk. There turned out to be seventeen of them in all, including Gioia; Gioia appeared to know all of them, though none, so far as he could tell, was a member of her set that he had met before. She did not attempt introductions. Nor was conversation at all possible during the meal: there was a constant astounding roaring din in the room. Three orchestras played at once and there were troupes of strolling musicians also, and a steady stream of monks and their attendants marched back and forth between the tables loudly chanting sutras and waving censers to the deafening accompaniment of drums and gongs. The Emperor did not descend from his throne to join the banquet; he seemed to be asleep, though now and then he waved his hand in time to the music. Gigantic half-naked brown slaves with broad cheekbones and mouths like gaping pockets brought forth the food, peacock tongues and breast of phoenix heaped on mounds of glowing saffron-colored rice, served on frail alabaster plates. For chopsticks they were given slender rods of dark jade. The wine, served in glistening crystal beakers, was thick and sweet, with an aftertaste of raisins, and no beaker was allowed to remain empty for more than a moment.

Phillips felt himself growing dizzy: when the Persian dancers emerged he could not tell whether there were five of them or fifty, and as they performed their intricate whirling routines it seemed to him that their slender muslin-veiled forms were blurring and merging one into another. He felt frightened by their proficiency, and wanted to look away, but he could not. The Chung-nan jugglers that followed them were equally skillful, equally alarming, filling the air with scythes, flaming torches, live animals, rare porcelain vases, pink jade hatchets, silver bells, gilded cups, wagon-wheels, bronze vessels, and never missing a catch. The citizens applauded politely but did not seem impressed. After the jugglers, the dancers returned, performing this time on stilts; the waiters brought platters of steaming meat of a pale lavender color, unfamiliar in taste and texture: filet of camel, perhaps, or haunch of hippopotamus, or possibly some choice chop from a young dragon. There was more wine. Feebly Phillips tried to wave it away, but the servitors were implacable. This was a drier sort, greenish-gold, austere, sharp on the tongue. With it came a silver dish, chilled to a polar coldness, that held shaved ice flavored with some potent smoky-flavored brandy. The jugglers were doing a second turn, he noticed. He thought he was going to be ill. He looked helplessly toward Gioia, who seemed sober but fiercely animated, almost manic, her eyes blazing like rubies. She touched his cheek fondly.

A cool draft blew through the hall: they had opened one entire wall, revealing the garden, the night, the stars. Just outside was a colossal wheel of oiled paper stretched on wooden struts. They must have erected it in the past hour: it stood a hundred fifty feet high or even more, and on it hung lanterns by the thousands, glimmering like giant fireflies. The guests began to leave the hall. Phillips let himself be swept along into the garden, where under a yellow moon strange crook-armed trees with dense black needles loomed ominously. Gioia slipped her arm through his. They went down to a lake of bubbling crimson fluid and watched scarlet flamingo-like birds ten feet tall fastidiously spearing angry-eyed turquoise eels. They stood in awe before a fat-bellied Buddha of gleaming blue tilework, seventy feet high. A horse with a golden mane came prancing by, striking showers of brilliant red sparks wherever its hooves touched the ground. In a grove of lemon trees that seemed to have the power to wave their slender limbs about, Phillips came upon the Emperor, standing by himself and rocking gently back and forth. The old man seized Phillips by the hand and pressed something into his palm, closing his fingers tight about it; when he opened his fist a few moments later he found his palm full of gray irregular pearls. Gioia took them from him and cast them into the air, and they burst like exploding firecrackers, giving off splashes of colored light. A little later, Phillips realized that he was no longer wearing his surplice or his white silken undergown. Gioia was naked too, and she drew him gently down into a carpet of moist blue moss, where they made love until dawn, fiercely at first, then slowly, languidly, dreamily. At sunrise he looked at her tenderly and saw that something was wrong.

"Gioia?" he said doubtfully.

She smiled. "Ah, no. Gioia is with Fenimon tonight. I am Belilala."

"With—Fenimon?"

"They are old friends. She had not seen him in years."

"Ah. I see. And you are—?"

"Belilala," she said again, touching her fingertips to his cheek.

It was not unusual, Belilala said. It happened all the time; the only unusual thing was that it had not happened to him before now. Couples formed, traveled together for a while, drifted apart, eventually reunited. It did not mean that Gioia had left him forever. It meant only that just now she chose to be with Fenimon. Gioia would return. In the meanwhile he would not be alone. "You and I met in New Chicago," Belilala told him. "And then we saw each other again in Timbuctoo. Have you forgotten? Oh, yes, I see that you have forgotten!" She laughed prettily; she did not seem at all offended.

She looked enough like Gioia to be her sister. But, then, all the citizens looked more or less alike to him. And apart from their physical resemblance, so he quickly came to realize, Belilala and Gioia were not really very similar. There was a calmness, a deep reservoir of serenity, in Belilala that Gioia, eager and volatile and ever impatient, did not seem to have. Strolling the swarming streets of Chang-an with Belilala, he did not perceive in her any of Gioia's restless feverish need always to know what lay beyond, and beyond, and beyond even that. When they toured the Hsing-ch'ing Palace, Belilala did not after five minutes begin—as Gioia surely would have done—to seek directions to the Fountain of Hsuan-tsung or the Wild Goose Pagoda. Curiosity did not consume Belilala as it did Gioia. Plainly she believed that there would always be enough time for her to see everything she cared to see. There were some days when Belilala chose not to go out at all, but was content merely to remain at their pavilion playing a solitary game with flat porcelain counters, or viewing the flowers of the garden.

He found, oddly, that he enjoyed the respite from Gioia's intense world-swallowing appetites; and yet he longed for her to return. Belilala—beautiful, gentle, tranquil, patient—was too perfect for him. She seemed unreal in her gleaming impeccability, much like one of those Sung celadon vases that appear too flawless to have been thrown and glazed by human hands. There was something a little soulless about her: an immaculate finish outside, emptiness within. Belilala might almost have been a temporary, he thought, though he knew she was not. He could explore the pavilions and palaces of Chang-an with her, he could make graceful conversation with her while they dined, he could certainly enjoy coupling with her; but he could not love her or even contemplate the possibility. It was hard to imagine Belilala worriedly studying herself in a mirror for wrinkles and gray hairs. Belilala would never be any older than she was at this moment; nor could Belilala ever have been any younger. Perfection does not move along an axis of time. But the perfection of Belilala's glossy surface made her inner being impenetrable to him. Gioia was more vulnerable, more obviously flawed—her restlessness, her moodiness, her vanity, her fears—and therefore she was more accessible to his own highly imperfect twentieth-century sensibility.

Occasionally he saw Gioia as he roamed the city, or thought he did. He had a glimpse of her among the miracle-vendors in the Persian Bazaar, and outside the Zoroastrian temple, and again by the goldfish pond in the Serpentine Park. But he was never quite sure that the woman he saw was really Gioia, and he never could get close enough to her to be certain: she had a way of vanishing as he approached, like some mysterious Lorelei luring him onward and onward in a hopeless chase. After a while he came to realize that he was not going to find her until she was ready to be found.

He lost track of time. Weeks, months, years? He had no idea. In this city of exotic luxury, mystery, and magic all was in constant flux and transition and the days had a fitful, unstable quality. Buildings and even whole streets were torn down of an afternoon and re-erected, within days, far away. Grand new pagodas sprouted like toadstools in the night. Citizens came in from Asgard, Alexandria, Timbuctoo, New Chicago, stayed for a time, disappeared, returned. There was a constant round of court receptions, banquets, theatrical events, each one much like the one before. The festivals in honor of past emperors and empresses might have given some form to the year, but they seemed to occur in a random way, the ceremony marking the death of T'ai Tsung coming around twice the same year, so it seemed to him, once in a season of snow and again in high summer, and the one honoring the ascension of the Empress Wu being held twice in a single season. Perhaps he had misunderstood something. But he knew it was no use asking anyone.

One day Belilala said unexpectedly, "Shall we go to Mohenjo-daro?"

"I didn't know it was ready for visitors," he replied.

"Oh, yes. For quite some time now."

He hesitated. This had caught him unprepared. Cautiously he said, "Gioia and I were going to go there together, you know."

Belilala smiled amiably, as though the topic under discussion were nothing more than the choice of that evening's restaurant.

"Were you?" she asked.

"It was all arranged while we were still in Alexandria. To go with you instead—I don't know what to tell you, Belilala." Phillips sensed that he was growing terribly flustered. "You know that I'd like to go. With you. But on the other hand I can't help feeling that I shouldn't go there until I'm back with Gioia again. If I ever am." How foolish this sounds, he thought. How clumsy, how adolescent. He found that he was having trouble looking straight at her. Uneasily he said, with a kind of desperation in his voice, "I did promise her—there was a commitment, you understand—a firm agreement that we would go to Mohenjo-daro together—"

"Oh, but Gioia's already there!" said Belilala in the most casual way.

He gaped as though she had punched him.

"What?"

"She was one of the first to go, after it opened. Months and months ago. You didn't know?" she asked, sounding surprised, but not very. "You really didn't know?"

That astonished him. He felt bewildered, betrayed, furious. His cheeks grew hot, his mouth gaped. He shook his head again and again, trying to clear it of confusion. It was a moment before he could speak. "Already there?" he said at last. "Without waiting for me? After we had talked about going there together—after we had agreed—"

Belilala laughed. "But how could she resist seeing the newest city? You know how impatient Gioia is!"

"Yes. Yes."

He was stunned. He could barely think.

"Just like all short-timers," Belilala said. "She rushes here, she rushes there. She must have it all, now, now, right away, at once, instantly. You ought never expect her to wait for you for anything for very long: the fit seizes her, and off she goes. Surely you must know that about her by now."

"A short-timer?" He had not heard that term before.

"Yes. You knew that. You must have known that." Belilala flashed her sweetest smile. She showed no sign of comprehending his distress. With a brisk wave of her hand she said, "Well, then, shall we go, you and I? To Mohenjo-daro?"

"Of course," Phillips said bleakly.

"When would you like to leave?"

"Tonight," he said. He paused a moment. "What's a short-timer, Belilala?"

Color came to her cheeks. "Isn't it obvious?" she asked.

Had there ever been a more hideous place on the face of the earth than the city of Mohenjo-daro? Phillips found it difficult to imagine one. Nor could he understand why, out of all the cities that had ever been, these people had chosen to restore this one to existence. More than ever they seemed alien to him, unfathomable, incomprehensible.

From the terrace atop the many-towered citadel he peered down into grim claustrophobic Mohenjo-daro and shivered. The stark, bleak city looked like nothing so much as some prehistoric prison colony. In the manner of an uneasy tortoise it huddled, squat and compact, against the gray monotonous Indus River plain: miles of dark burnt-brick walls enclosing miles of terrifyingly orderly streets, laid out in an awesome, monstrous gridiron pattern of maniacal rigidity. The houses themselves were dismal and forbidding too, clusters of brick cells gathered about small airless courtyards. There were no windows, only small doors that opened not onto the main boulevards but onto the tiny mysterious lanes that ran between the buildings. Who had designed this horrifying metropolis? What harsh, sour souls they must have had, these frightening and frightened folk, creating for themselves in the lush fertile plains of India such a Supreme Soviet of a city!

"How lovely it is," Belilala murmured. "How fascinating!"

He stared at her in amazement.

"Fascinating? Yes," he said. "I suppose so. The same way that the smile of a cobra is fascinating."

"What's a cobra?"

"Poisonous predatory serpent," Phillips told her. "Probably extinct. Or formerly extinct, more likely. It wouldn't surprise me if you people had re-created a few and turned them loose in Mohenjo to make things livelier."

"You sound angry, Charles."

"Do I? That's not how I feel."

"How do you feel, then?"

"I don't know," he said after a long moment's pause. He shrugged. "Lost, I suppose. Very far from home."

"Poor Charles."

"Standing here in this ghastly barracks of a city, listening to you tell me how beautiful it is, I've never felt more alone in my life."

"You miss Gioia very much, don't you?"

He gave her another startled look.

"Gioia has nothing to do with it. She's probably been having ecstasies over the loveliness of Mohenjo just like you. Just like all of you. I suppose I'm the only one who can't find the beauty, the charm. I'm the only one who looks out there and sees only horror, and then wonders why nobody else sees it, why in fact people would set up a place like this for *entertainment,* for *pleasure—*"

Her eyes were gleaming. "Oh, you are angry! You really are!"

"Does that fascinate you too?" he snapped. "A demonstration of genuine primitive emotion? A typical quaint twentieth-century outburst?" He paced the rampart in short quick anguished steps. "Ah. Ah. I think I understand it now, Belilala. Of course: I'm part of your circus, the star of the sideshow. I'm the first experiment in setting up the next stage of it, in fact." Her eyes were wide. The sudden harshness and violence in his voice seemed to be alarming and exciting her at the same time. That angered him even more. Fiercely he went on, "Bringing whole cities back out of time was fun for a while, but it lacks a certain authenticity, eh? For some reason you couldn't bring the inhabitants too; you couldn't just grab a few million prehistorics out of Egypt or Greece or India and dump them down in this era, I suppose because you might have too much trouble controlling them, or because you'd have the problem of disposing of them once you were bored with them. So you had to settle for creating temporaries to populate your ancient cities. But now you've got me. I'm something more real than a temporary, and that's a terrific novelty for you, and novelty is the thing you people crave more than anything else: maybe the *only* thing you crave. And here I am, complicated, unpredictable, edgy, capable of anger, fear, sadness, love, and all those other formerly extinct things. Why settle for picturesque architecture when you can observe picturesque emotion, too? What fun I must be for all of you! And if you decide that I was really interesting, maybe you'll ship me back where I came from and check out a few other ancient types—a Roman gladiator, maybe, or a Renaissance pope, or even a Neanderthal or two—"

"Charles," she said tenderly. "Oh, Charles, Charles, Charles, how lonely you must be, how lost, how troubled! Will you ever forgive me? Will you ever forgive us all?"

Once more he was astounded by her. She sounded entirely sincere, altogether sympathetic. Was she? Was she, really? He was not sure he had ever had a sign of genuine caring from any of them before, not even Gioia. Nor could he bring himself to trust Belilala now. He was afraid of her, afraid of all of them, of their brittleness, their slyness, their elegance. He wished he could go to her and have her take him in her arms; but he felt too much the shaggy prehistoric just now to be able to risk asking that comfort of her.

He turned away and began to walk around the rim of the citadel's massive wall.

"Charles?"

"Let me alone for a little while," he said.

He walked on. His forehead throbbed and there was a pounding in his chest. All stress systems going full blast, he thought: secret glands dumping gallons of inflammatory substances into his bloodstream. The heat, the inner confusion, the repellent look of this place—

Try to understand, he thought. Relax. Look about you. Try to enjoy your holiday in Mohenjo-daro.

He leaned warily outward, over the edge of the wall. He had never seen a wall like this; it must be forty feet thick at the base, he guessed, perhaps even more, and every brick perfectly shaped, meticulously set. Beyond the great rampart, marshes ran almost to the edge of the city, although close by the wall the swamps had been dammed and drained for agriculture. He saw lithe brown farmers down there, busy with their wheat and barley and peas. Cattle and buffaloes grazed a little farther out. The air was heavy, dank, humid. All was still. From somewhere close at hand came the sound of a droning, whining stringed instrument and a steady insistent chanting.

Gradually a sort of peace pervaded him. His anger subsided. He felt himself beginning to grow calm again. He looked back at the city, the rigid interlocking streets, the maze of inner lanes, the millions of courses of precise brickwork.

It is a miracle, he told himself, that this city is here in this place and at this time. And it is a miracle that I am here to see it.

Caught for a moment by the magic within the bleakness, he thought he began to understand Belilala's awe and delight, and he wished now that he had not spoken to her so sharply. The city was alive. Whether it was the actual Mohenjo-daro of thousands upon thousands of years ago, ripped from the past by some wondrous hook, or simply a cunning reproduction, did not matter at all. Real or not, this was the true Mohenjo-daro. It had been dead and now, for the moment, it was alive again. These people, these *citizens,* might be trivial, but reconstructing Mohenjo-daro was no trivial achievement. And that the city that had been reconstructed was oppressive and sinister-looking was unimportant. No one was compelled to live in Mohenjo-daro any more. Its time had come and gone, long ago; those little dark-skinned peasants and craftsmen and merchants down there were mere temporaries, mere inanimate things, conjured up like zombies to enhance the illusion. They did not need his pity. Nor did he need to pity himself. He knew that he should be grateful for the chance to behold these things. Some day, when this dream had ended and his hosts had returned him to the world of subways and computers and income tax and television networks, he would think of Mohenjo-daro as he had once beheld it, lofty walls of tightly woven dark brick under a heavy sky, and he would remember only its beauty.

Glancing back, he searched for Belilala and could not for a moment find her. Then he caught sight of her carefully descending a narrow staircase that angled down the inner face of the citadel wall.

"Belilala!" he called.

She paused and looked his way, shading her eyes from the sun with her hand. "Are you all right?"

"Where are you going?"

"To the baths," she said. "Do you want to come?"

He nodded. "Yes. Wait for me, will you? I'll be right there." He began to run toward her along the top of the wall.

The baths were attached to the citadel: a great open tank the size of a large swimming pool, lined with bricks set on edge in gypsum mortar and waterproofed with asphalt, and eight smaller tanks just north of it in a kind of covered arcade. He supposed that in ancient times the whole complex had had some ritual purpose, the large tank used by common folk and the small chambers set aside for the private ablutions of priests or nobles. Now the baths were maintained, it seemed, entirely for the pleasure of visiting citizens. As Phillips came up the passageway that led to the main bath he saw fifteen or twenty of them lolling in the water or padding languidly about, while temporaries of the dark-skinned Mohenjo-daro type served them drinks and pungent little morsels of spiced meat as though this were some sort of luxury resort. Which was, he realized, exactly what it was. The temporaries wore white cotton loincloths; the citizens were naked. In his former life he had encountered that sort of casual public nudity a few times on visits to California and the south of France, and it had made him mildly uneasy. But he was growing accustomed to it here.

The changing-rooms were tiny brick cubicles connected by rows of closely placed steps to the courtyard that surrounded the central tank. They entered one and Belilala swiftly slipped out of the loose cotton robe that she had worn since their arrival that morning. With arms folded she stood leaning against the wall, waiting for him. After a moment he dropped his own robe and followed her outside. He felt a little giddy, sauntering around naked in the open like this.

On the way to the main bathing area they passed the private baths. None of them seemed to be occupied. They were elegantly constructed chambers, with finely jointed brick floors and carefully designed runnels to drain excess water into the passageway that led to the primary drain. Phillips was struck with admiration for the cleverness of the prehistoric engineers. He peered into this chamber and that to see how the conduits and ventilating ducts were arranged, and when he came to the last room in the sequence he was surprised and embarrassed to discover that it was in use. A brawny grinning man, big-muscled, deep-chested, with exuberantly flowing shoulder-length red hair and a flamboyant, sharply tapering beard, was thrashing about merrily with two women in the small tank. Phillips had a quick glimpse of a lively tangle of arms, legs, breasts, buttocks.

"Sorry," he muttered. His cheeks reddened. Quickly he ducked out, blurting apologies as he went. "Didn't realize the room was occupied—no wish to intrude—"

Belilala had proceeded on down the passageway. Phillips hurried after her. From behind him came peals of cheerful raucous booming laughter and high-pitched giggling and the sound of splashing water. Probably they had not even noticed him.

He paused a moment, puzzled, playing back in his mind that one startling glimpse. Something was not right. Those women, he was fairly sure, were citizens: little slender elfin dark-haired girlish creatures, the standard model. But the man? That great curling sweep of red hair? Not a citizen. Citizens did not affect shoulder-length hair. And *red?* Nor had he ever seen a citizen so burly, so powerfully muscular. Or one with a beard. But he could hardly be a temporary, either. Phillips could conceive no reason why there would be so Anglo-Saxon-looking a temporary at Mohenjo-daro; and it was unthinkable for a temporary to be frolicking like that with citizens, anyway.

"Charles?"

He looked up ahead. Belilala stood at the end of the passageway, outlined in a nimbus of brilliant sunlight. "Charles?" she said again. "Did you lose your way?"

"I'm right here behind you," he said. "I'm coming."

"Who did you meet in there?"

"A man with a beard."

"With a what?"

"A beard," he said. "Red hair growing on his face. I wonder who he is."

"Nobody I know," said Belilala. "The only one I know with hair on his face is you. And yours is black, and you shave it off every day." She laughed. "Come along, now! I see some friends by the pool!"

He caught up with her and they went hand in hand out into the courtyard. Immediately a waiter glided up to them, an obsequious little temporary with a tray of drinks. Phillips waved it away and headed for the pool. He felt terribly exposed: he imagined that the citizens disporting themselves here were staring intently at him, studying his hairy primitive body as though he were some mythical creature, a Minotaur, a werewolf, summoned up for their amusement. Belilala drifted off to talk to someone and he slipped into the water, grateful for the concealment it offered. It was deep, warm, comforting. With swift powerful strokes he breast-stroked from one end to the other.

A citizen perched elegantly on the pool's rim smiled at him. "Ah, so you've come at last, Charles!" Char-less. Two syllables. Someone from Gioia's set: Stengard, Hawk, Aramayne? He could not remember which one. They were all so much alike.

Phillips returned the man's smile in a half-hearted, tentative way. He searched for something to say and finally asked, "Have you been here long?"

"Weeks. Perhaps months. What a splendid achievement this city is, eh, Charles? Such utter unity of mood—such a total statement of a uniquely single-minded esthetic—"

"Yes. Single-minded is the word," Phillips said drily.

"Gioia's word, actually. Gioia's phrase. I was merely quoting."

Gioia. He felt as if he had been stabbed.

"You've spoken to Gioia lately?" he said.

"Actually, no. It was Hekna who saw her. You do remember Hekna, eh?" He nodded toward two naked women standing on the brick platform that bordered the pool, chatting, delicately nibbling morsels of meat. They could have been twins. "There is Hekna, with your Belilala." Hekna, yes. So this must be Hawk, Phillips thought, unless there has been some recent shift of couples. "How sweet she is, your Belilala," Hawk said. "Gioia chose very wisely when she picked her for you."

Another stab: a much deeper one. "Is that how it was?" he said. "Gioia *picked* Belilala for me?"

"Why, of course!" Hawk seemed surprised. It went without saying, evidently. "What did you think? That Gioia would merely go off and leave you to fend for yourself?"

"Hardly. Not Gioia."

"She's very tender, very gentle, isn't she?"

"You mean Belilala? Yes, very," said Phillips carefully. "A dear woman, a wonderful woman. But of course I hope to get together with Gioia again soon." He paused. "They say she's been in Mohenjo-daro almost since it opened."

"She was here, yes."

"Was?"

"Oh, you know Gioia," Hawk said lightly. "She's moved along by now, naturally."

Phillips leaned forward. "Naturally," he said. Tension thickened his voice. "Where has she gone this time?"

"Timbuctoo, I think. Or New Chicago. I forget which one it was. She was telling us that she hoped to be in Timbuctoo for the closing-down party. But then Fenimon had some pressing reason for going to New Chicago. I can't remember what they decided to do." Hawk gestured sadly. "Either way, a pity that she left Mohenjo before the new visitor came. She had such a rewarding time with you, after all: I'm sure she'd have found much to learn from him also."

The unfamiliar term twanged an alarm deep in Phillips' consciousness. *"Visitor?"* he said, angling his head sharply toward Hawk. "What visitor do you mean?"

"You haven't met him yet? Oh, of course, you've only just arrived."

Phillips moistened his lips. "I think I may have seen him. Long red hair? Beard like this?"

"That's the one! Willoughby, he's called. He's—what?—a Viking, a pirate, something like that. Tremendous vigor and force. Remarkable person. We should have many more visitors, I think. They're far superior to temporaries, everyone agrees. Talking with a temporary is a little like talking to one's self, wouldn't you say? They give you no significant illumination. But a visitor—someone like this Willoughby—or like you, Charles —a visitor can be truly enlightening, a visitor can transform one's view of reality—"

"Excuse me," Phillips said. A throbbing began behind his forehead. "Perhaps we can continue this conversation later, yes?" He put the flats of his hands against the hot brick of the platform and hoisted himself swiftly from the pool. "At dinner, maybe—or afterward—yes? All right?" He set off at a quick half-trot back toward the passageway that led to the private baths.

As he entered the roofed part of the structure his throat grew dry, his breath suddenly came short. He padded quickly up the hall and peered into the little bath-chamber. The bearded man was still there, sitting up in the tank, breast-high above the water, with one arm around each of the women. His eyes gleamed with fiery intensity in the dimness. He was grinning in marvelous self-satisfaction; he seemed to brim with intensity, confidence, gusto.

Let him be what I think he is, Phillips prayed. I have been alone among these people long enough.

"May I come in?" he asked.

"Aye, fellow!" cried the man in the tub thunderously. "By my troth, come ye in, and bring your lass as well! God's teeth, I wot there's room aplenty for more folk in this tub than we!"

At that great uproarious outcry Phillips felt a powerful surge of joy. What a joyous rowdy voice! How rich, how lusty, how totally uncitizen-like!

And those oddly archaic words! *God's teeth? By my troth?* What sort of talk was that? What else but the good pure sonorous Elizabethan diction! Certainly it had something of the roll and fervor of Shakespeare about it. And spoken with—an Irish brogue, was it? No, not quite: it was English, but English spoken in no manner Phillips had ever heard.

Citizens did not speak that way. But a *visitor* might.

So it was true. Relief flooded Phillips' soul. Not alone, then! Another relict of a former age—another wanderer—a companion in chaos, a brother in adversity—a fellow voyager, tossed even farther than he had been by the tempests of time—

The bearded man grinned heartily and beckoned to Phillips with a toss of his head. "Well, join us, join us, man! 'Tis good to see an English face again, amidst all these Moors and rogue Portugals! But what have ye done with thy lass? One can never have enough wenches, d'ye not agree?"

The force and vigor of him were extraordinary: almost too much so. He roared, he bellowed, he boomed. He was so very much what he ought to be that he seemed more a character out of some old pirate movie than anything else, so blustering, so real, that he seemed unreal. A stage-Elizabethan, larger than life, a boisterous young Falstaff without the belly.

Hoarsely, Phillips said, "Who are you?"

"Why, Ned Willoughby's son Francis am I, of Plymouth. Late of the service of Her Most Protestant Majesty, but most foully abducted by the powers of darkness and cast away among these blackamoor Hindus, or whatever they be. And thyself?"

"Charles Phillips." After a moment's uncertainty he added, "I'm from New York."

"*New* York? What place is that? In faith, man, I know it not!"

"A city in America."

"A city in America, forsooth! What a fine fancy that is! In America, you say, and not on the Moon, or perchance underneath the sea?" To the women Willoughby said, "D'ye hear him? He comes from a city in America! With the face of an Englishman, though not the manner of one, and not quite the proper sort of speech. A city in America! A *city*. God's blood, what will I hear next?"

Phillips trembled. Awe was beginning to take hold of him. This man had walked the streets of Shakespeare's London, perhaps. He had clinked canisters with Marlowe or Essex or Walter Raleigh; he had watched the ships of the Armada wallowing in the Channel. It strained Phillips' spirit to think of it. This strange dream in which he found himself was compounding its strangeness now. He felt like a weary swimmer assailed by heavy surf, winded, dazed. The hot close atmosphere of the baths was driving him toward vertigo. There could be no doubt of it any longer. He was not the only primitive—the only *visitor*—who was wandering loose in this fiftieth century. They were conducting other experiments as well. He gripped the sides of the door to steady himself and said, "When you speak of Her Most Protestant Majesty, it's Elizabeth the First you mean, is that not so?"

"Elizabeth, aye! As to the First, that is true enough, but why trouble to name her thus? There is but one. First and Last, I do trow, and God save her, there is no other!"

Phillips studied the other man warily. He knew that he must proceed with care. A misstep at this point and he would forfeit any chance that Willoughby would take him seriously. How much metaphysical bewilderment, after all, could this man absorb? What did he know, what had anyone of his time known, of past and present and future and the notion that one might somehow move from one to the other as readily as one would go from Surrey to Kent? That was a twentieth-century idea, late nineteenth at best, a fantastical speculation that very likely no one had even considered before Wells had sent his time traveler off to stare at the reddened sun of the earth's last twilight. Willoughby's world was a world of Protestants and Catholics, of kings and queens, of tiny sailing vessels, of swords at the hip and ox-carts on the road: that world seemed to Phillips far more alien and distant than was this world of citizens and temporaries. The risk that Willoughby would not begin to understand him was great.

But this man and he were natural allies against a world they had never made. Phillips chose to take the risk.

"Elizabeth the First is the queen you serve," he said. "There will be another of her name in England, in due time. Has already been, in fact."

Willoughby shook his head like a puzzled lion. "Another Elizabeth, d'ye say?"

"A second one, and not much like the first. Long after your Virgin Queen, this one. She will reign in what you think of as the days to come. That I know without doubt."

The Englishman peered at him and frowned. "You see the future? Are you a soothsayer, then? A necromancer, mayhap? Or one of the very demons that brought me to this place?"

"Not at all," Phillips said gently. "Only a lost soul, like yourself." He stepped into the little room and crouched by the side of the tank. The two citizen-women were staring at him in bland fascination. He ignored them. To Willoughby he said, "Do you have any idea where you are?"

The Englishman had guessed, rightly enough, that he was in India: "I do believe these little brown Moorish folk are of the Hindu sort," he said. But that was as far as his comprehension of what had befallen him could go.

It had not occurred to him that he was no longer living in the sixteenth century. And of course he did not begin to suspect that this strange and somber brick city in which he found himself was a wanderer out of an era even more remote than his own. Was there any way, Phillips wondered, of explaining that to him?

He had been here only three days. He thought it was devils that had carried him off. "While I slept did they come for me," he said. "Mephistophilis Sathanas his henchmen seized me—God alone can say why—and swept me in a moment out to this torrid realm from England, where I had reposed among friends and family. For I was between one voyage and the next, you must understand, awaiting Drake and his ship—you know Drake, the glorious Francis? God's blood, there's a mariner for ye! We were to go to the Main again, he and I, but instead here I be in this other place—" Willoughby leaned close and said, "I ask you, soothsayer, how can it be, that a man go to sleep in Plymouth and wake up in India? It is passing strange, is it not?"

"That it is," Phillips said.

"But he that is in the dance must needs dance on, though he do but hop, eh? So do I believe." He gestured toward the two citizen-women. "And therefore to console myself in this pagan land I have found me some sport among these little Portugal women—"

"Portugal?" said Phillips.

"Why, what else can they be, but Portugals? Is it not the Portugals who control all these coasts of India? See, the people are of two sorts here, the blackamoors and the others, the fair-skinned ones, the lords and masters who lie here in these baths. If they be not Hindus, and I think they are not, then Portugals is what they must be." He laughed and pulled the women against himself and rubbed his hands over their breasts as though they were fruits on a vine. "Is that not what you are, you little naked shameless Papist wenches? A pair of Portugals, eh?"

They giggled, but did not answer.

"No," Phillips said. "This is India, but not the India you think you know. And these women are not Portuguese."

"Not Portuguese?" Willoughby said, baffled.

"No more so than you. I'm quite certain of that."

Willoughby stroked his beard. "I do admit I found them very odd, for Portugals. I have heard not a syllable of their Portugee speech on their lips. And it is strange also that they run naked as Adam and Eve in these baths, and allow me free plunder of their women, which is not the way of Portugals at home, God wot. But I thought me, this is India, they choose to live in another fashion here—"

"No," Phillips said. "I tell you, these are not Portuguese, nor any other people of Europe who are known to you."

"Prithee, who are they, then?"

Do it delicately, now, Phillips warned himself. *Delicately.*

He said, "It is not far wrong to think of them as spirits of some kind—demons, even. Or sorcerers who have magicked us out of our proper places in the world." He paused, groping for some means to share with Willoughby, in a way that Willoughby might grasp, this mystery that had enfolded them. He drew a deep breath. "They've taken us not only across the sea," he said, "but across the years as well. We have both been hauled, you and I, far into the days that are to come."

Willoughby gave him a look of blank bewilderment.

"Days that are to come? Times yet unborn, d'ye mean? Why, I comprehend none of that!"

"Try to understand. We're both castaways in the same boat, man! But there's no way we can help each other if I can't make you see—"

Shaking his head, Willoughby muttered, "In faith, good friend, I find your words the merest folly. Today is today, and tomorrow is tomorrow, and how can a man step from one to t'other until tomorrow be turned into today?"

"I have no idea," said Phillips. Struggle was apparent on Willoughby's face; but plainly he could perceive no more than the haziest outline of what

Phillips was driving at, if that much. "But this I know," he went on, "that your world and all that was in it is dead and gone. And so is mine, though I was born four hundred years after you, in the time of the second Elizabeth."

Willoughby snorted scornfully. "Four hundred—"

"You must believe me!"

"Nay! Nay!"

"It's the truth. Your time is only history to me. And mine and yours are history to *them*—ancient history. They call us visitors, but what we are is captives." Phillips felt himself quivering in the intensity of his effort. He was aware how insane this must sound to Willoughby. It was beginning to sound insane to him. "They've stolen us out of our proper times—seizing us like gypsies in the night—"

"Fie, man! You rave with lunacy!"

Phillips shook his head. He reached out and seized Willoughby tightly by the wrist. "I beg you, listen to me!" The citizen-women were watching closely, whispering to one another behind their hands, laughing. "Ask them!" Phillips cried. "Make them tell you what century this is! The sixteenth, do you think? Ask them!"

"What century could it be, but the sixteenth of our Lord?"

"They will tell you it is the fiftieth."

Willoughby looked at him pityingly. "Man, man, what a sorry thing thou art! The fiftieth, indeed!" He laughed. "Fellow, listen to me, now. There is but one Elizabeth, safe upon her throne in Westminster. This is India. The year is Anno 1591. Come, let us you and I steal a ship from these Portugals, and make our way back to England, and peradventure you may get from there to your America—"

"There is no England."

"Ah, can you say that and not be mad?"

"The cities and nations we knew are gone. These people live like magicians, Francis." There was no use holding anything back now, Phillips thought leadenly. He knew that he had lost. "They conjure up places of long ago, and build them here and there to suit their fancy, and when they are bored with them they destroy them, and start anew. There is no England. Europe is empty, featureless, void. Do you know what cities there are? There are only five in all the world. There is Alexandria of Egypt. There is Timbuctoo in Africa. There is New Chicago in America. There is a great city in China—in Cathay, I suppose you would say. And there is this place, which they call Mohenjo-daro, and which is far more ancient than Greece, than Rome, than Babylon."

Quietly Willoughby said, "Nay. This is mere absurdity. You say we are in some far tomorrow, and then you tell me we are dwelling in some city of long ago."

"A conjuration, only," Phillips said in desperation. "A likeness of that city. Which these folk have fashioned somehow for their own amusement. Just as we are here, you and I: to amuse them. Only to amuse them."

"You are completely mad."

"Come with me, then. Talk with the citizens by the great pool. Ask them what year this is; ask them about England; ask them how you come to be here." Once again Phillips grasped Willoughby's wrist. "We should be allies. If we work together, perhaps we can discover some way to get ourselves out of this place, and—"

"Let me be, fellow."

"Please—"

"Let me be!" roared Willoughby, and pulled his arm free. His eyes were stark with rage. Rising in the tank, he looked about furiously as though searching for a weapon. The citizen-women shrank back away from him, though at the same time they seemed captivated by the big man's fierce outburst. "Go to, get you to Bedlam! Let me be, madman! Let me be!"

Dismally Phillips roamed the dusty unpaved streets of Mohenjo-daro alone for hours. His failure with Willoughby had left him bleak-spirited and somber; he had hoped to stand back to back with the Elizabethan against the citizens, but he saw now that that was not to be. He had bungled things; or, more likely, it had been impossible ever to bring Willoughby to see the truth of their predicament.

In the stifling heat he went at random through the confusing congested lanes of flat-roofed, windowless houses and blank, featureless walls until he emerged into a broad marketplace. The life of the city swirled madly around him: the pseudo-life, rather, the intricate interactions of the thousands of temporaries who were nothing more than wind-up dolls set in motion to provide the illusion that pre-Vedic India was still a going concern. Here vendors sold beautiful little carved stone seals portraying tigers and monkeys and strange humped cattle, and women bargained vociferously with craftsmen for ornaments of ivory, gold, copper, and bronze. Weary-looking women squatted behind immense mounds of newly made pottery, pinkish-red with black designs. No one paid any attention to him. He was the outsider here, neither citizen nor temporary. They belonged.

He went on, passing the huge granaries where workmen ceaselessly unloaded carts of wheat and others pounded grain on great circular brick platforms. He drifted into a public restaurant thronging with joyless silent people standing elbow to elbow at small brick counters, and was given a flat round piece of bread, a sort of tortilla or chapatti, in which was stuffed some spiced mincemeat that stung his lips like fire. Then he moved onward, down a wide, shallow, timbered staircase into the lower part of the city, where the peasantry lived in cell-like rooms packed together as though in hives.

It was an oppressive city, but not a squalid one. The intensity of the concern with sanitation amazed him: wells and fountains and public privies everywhere, and brick drains running from each building, leading to covered cesspools. There was none of the open sewage and pestilent gutters that he knew still could be found in the India of his own time. He wondered whether ancient Mohenjo-daro had in truth been so fastidious. Perhaps the citizens had redesigned the city to suit their own ideals of cleanliness. No: most likely what he saw was authentic, he decided, a function of the same obsessive discipline that had given the city its rigidity of form. If Mohenjo-daro had been a verminous filthy hole, the citizens probably would have re-created it in just that way, and loved it for its fascinating, reeking filth.

Not that he had ever noticed an excessive concern with authenticity on the part of the citizens; and Mohenjo-daro, like all the other restored cities he had visited, was full of the usual casual anachronisms. Phillips saw images of Shiva and Krishna here and there on the walls of buildings he took to be temples, and the benign face of the mother-goddess Kali loomed in the plazas. Surely those deities had arisen in India long after the collapse of the Mohenjo-daro civilization. Were the citizens indifferent to such matters of chronology? Or did they take a certain naughty pleasure in mixing the eras—a mosque and a church in Greek Alexandria, Hindu gods in prehistoric Mohenjo-daro? Perhaps their records of the past had become contaminated with errors over the thousands of years. He would not have been surprised to see banners bearing portraits of Gandhi and Nehru being carried in procession through the streets. And there were phantasms and chimeras at large here again too, as if the citizens were untroubled by the boundary between history and myth: little fat elephant-headed Ganeshas blithely plunging their trunks into water-fountains, a six-armed, three-headed woman sunning herself on a brick terrace. Why not? Surely that was the motto of these people: *Why not, why not, why not?* They could do as they pleased, and they did. Yet Gioia had said to him, long ago, "Limits are very important." In what, Phillips wondered, did they limit themselves, other than the number of their cities? Was there a quota, perhaps, on the number of "visitors" they allowed themselves to kidnap from the past? Until today he had thought he was the only one; now he knew there was at least one other; possibly there were more elsewhere, a step or two ahead or behind him, making the circuit with the citizens who traveled endlessly from New Chicago to Chang-an to Alexandria. We should join forces, he thought, and compel them to send us back to our rightful eras. *Compel?* How? File a class-action suit, maybe? Demonstrate in the streets? Sadly he thought of his failure to make common cause with Willoughby. We are natural allies, he thought. Together perhaps we might have won some compassion from these people. But to Willoughby it must be literally unthinkable that Good Queen Bess and her subjects were sealed away on the far side of a barrier hundreds of centuries thick. He would prefer to believe that England was just a few months' voyage away around the Cape of Good Hope, and that all he need do was commandeer a ship and set sail for home. Poor Willoughby: probably he would never see his home again.

The thought came to Phillips suddenly:

Neither will you.

And then, after it:

If you could go home, would you really want to?

One of the first things he had realized here was that he knew almost nothing substantial about his former existence. His mind was well stocked with details on life in twentieth-century New York, to be sure; but of himself he could say not much more than that he was Charles Phillips and had come from 1984. Profession? Age? Parents' names? Did he have a wife? Children? A cat, a dog, hobbies? No data: none. Possibly the citizens had stripped such things from him when they brought him here, to spare him from the pain of separation. They might be capable of that kindness. Knowing so little of what he had lost, could he truly say that he yearned for it? Willoughby seemed to remember much more of his former life, and longed for it all the more. He was spared that. Why not stay here, and go on and on from city to city, sightseeing all of time past as the citizens conjured it back into being? Why not? Why not? The chances were that he had no choice about it, anyway.

He made his way back up toward the citadel and to the baths once more. He felt a little like a ghost, haunting a city of ghosts.

Belilala seemed unaware that he had been gone for most of the day. She sat by herself on the terrace of the baths, placidly sipping some thick milky beverage that had been sprinkled with a dark spice. He shook his head when she offered him some.

"Do you remember I mentioned that I saw a man with red hair and a beard this morning?" Phillips said. "He's a visitor. Hawk told me that."

"Is he?" Belilala asked.

"From a time about four hundred years before mine. I talked with him. He thinks he was brought here by demons." Phillips gave her a searching look. "I'm a visitor too, isn't that so?"

"Of course, love."

"And how was *I* brought here? By demons also?"

Belilala smiled indifferently. "You'd have to ask someone else. Hawk, perhaps. I haven't looked into these things very deeply."

"I see. Are there many visitors here, do you know?"

A languid shrug. "Not many, no, not really. I've only heard of three or four besides you. There may be others by now, I suppose." She rested her hand lightly on his. "Are you having a good time in Mohenjo, Charles?"

He let her question pass as though he had not heard it.

"I asked Hawk about Gioia," he said.

"Oh?"

"He told me that she's no longer here, that she's gone on to Timbuctoo or New Chicago, he wasn't sure which."

"That's quite likely. As everybody knows, Gioia rarely stays in the same place very long."

Phillips nodded. "You said the other day that Gioia is a short-timer. That means she's going to grow old and die, doesn't it?"

"I thought you understood that, Charles."

"Whereas you will not age? Nor Hawk, nor Stengard, nor any of the rest of your set?"

"We will live as long as we wish," she said. "But we will not age, no."

"What makes a person a short-timer?"

"They're born that way, I think. Some missing gene, some extra gene—I don't actually know. It's extremely uncommon. Nothing can be done to help them. It's very slow, the aging. But it can't be halted."

Phillips nodded. "That must be very disagreeable," he said. "To find yourself one of the few people growing old in a world where everyone stays young. No wonder Gioia is so impatient. No wonder she runs around from place to place. No wonder she attached herself so quickly to the barbaric hairy visitor from the twentieth century, who comes from a time when *everybody* was a short-timer. She and I have something in common, wouldn't you say?"

"In a manner of speaking, yes."

"We understand aging. We understand death. Tell me: is Gioia likely to die very soon, Belilala?"

"Soon? Soon?" She gave him a wide-eyed child-like stare. "What is soon? How can I say? What you think of as soon and what I think of as soon are not the same things, Charles." Then her manner changed: she seemed to be hearing what he was saying for the first time. Softly she said, "No, no, Charles. I don't think she will die very soon."

"When she left me in Chang-an, was it because she had become bored with me?"

Belilala shook her head. "She was simply restless. It had nothing to do with you. She was never bored with you."

"Then I'm going to go looking for her. Wherever she may be, Timbuctoo, New Chicago, I'll find her. Gioia and I belong together."

"Perhaps you do," said Belilala. "Yes. Yes, I think you really do." She sounded altogether unperturbed, unrejected, unbereft. "By all means, Charles. Go to her. Follow her. Find her. Wherever she may be."

They had already begun dismantling Timbuctoo when Phillips got there. While he was still high overhead, his flitterflitter hovering above the dusty tawny plain where the River Niger met the sands of the Sahara, a surge of keen excitement rose in him as he looked down at the square gray flat-roofed mud brick buildings of the great desert capital. But when he landed he found gleaming metal-skinned robots swarming everywhere, a horde of them scuttling about like giant shining insects, pulling the place apart.

He had not known about the robots before. So that was how all these miracles were carried out, Phillips realized: an army of obliging machines. He imagined them bustling up out of the earth whenever their services were needed, emerging from some sterile subterranean storehouse to put together Venice or Thebes or Knossos or Houston or whatever place was required, down to the finest detail, and then at some later time returning to undo everything that they had fashioned. He watched them now, diligently pulling down the adobe walls, demolishing the heavy metal-studded gates, bulldozing the amazing labyrinth of alleyways and thoroughfares, sweeping away the market. On his last visit to Timbuctoo that market had been crowded with a horde of veiled Tuaregs and swaggering Moors, black Sudanese, shrewd-faced Syrian traders, all of them busily dickering for camels, horses, donkeys, slabs of salt, huge green melons, silver bracelets, splendid vellum Korans. They were all gone now, that picturesque crowd of swarthy temporaries. Nor were there any citizens to be seen. The dust of destruction choked the air. One of the robots came up to Phillips and said in a dry crackling insect-voice, "You ought not to be here. This city is closed."

He stared at the flashing, buzzing band of scanners and sensors across the creature's glittering tapered snout. "I'm trying to find someone, a citizen who may have been here recently. Her name is—"

"This city is closed," the robot repeated inexorably.

They would not let him stay as much as an hour. There is no food here, the robot said, no water, no shelter. This is not a place any longer. You may not stay. You may not stay. You may not stay.

This is not a place any longer.

Perhaps he could find her in New Chicago, then. He took to the air again, soaring northward and westward over the vast emptiness. The land below him curved away into the hazy horizon, bare, sterile. What had they done with the vestiges of the world that had gone before? Had they turned their gleaming metal beetles loose to clean everything away? Were there no ruins of genuine antiquity anywhere? No scrap of Rome, no shard of Jerusalem, no stump of Fifth Avenue? It was all so barren down there: an empty stage, waiting for its next set to be built. He flew on a great arc across the jutting hump of Africa and on into what he supposed was southern Europe: the little vehicle did all the work, leaving him to doze or stare as he wished. Now and again he saw another flitterflitter pass by, far away, a dark distant winged teardrop outlined against the hard clarity of the sky. He wished there was some way of making radio contact with them, but he had no idea how to go about it. Not that he had anything he wanted to say; he wanted only to hear a human voice. He was utterly isolated. He might just as well have been the last living man on Earth. He closed his eyes and thought of Gioia.

"Like this?" Phillips asked. In an ivory-paneled oval room sixty stories above the softly glowing streets of New Chicago he touched a small cool plastic canister to his upper lip and pressed the stud at its base. He heard a foaming sound; and then blue vapor rose to his nostrils.

"Yes," Cantilena said. "That's right."

He detected a faint aroma of cinnamon, cloves, and something that might almost have been broiled lobster. Then a spasm of dizziness hit him and visions rushed through his head: Gothic cathedrals, the Pyramids, Central Park under fresh snow, the harsh brick warrens of Mohenjo-daro, and fifty thousand other places all at once, a wild rollercoaster ride through space and time. It seemed to go on for centuries. But finally his head cleared and he looked about, blinking, realizing that the whole thing had taken only a moment. Cantilena still stood at his elbow. The other citizens in the room—fifteen, twenty of them—had scarcely moved. The strange little man with the celadon skin over by the far wall continued to stare at him.

"Well?" Cantilena asked. "What did you think?"

"Incredible."

"And very authentic. It's an actual New Chicagoan drug. The exact formula. Would you like another?"

"Not just yet," Phillips said uneasily. He swayed and had to struggle for his balance. Sniffing that stuff might not have been such a wise idea, he thought.

He had been in New Chicago a week, or perhaps it was two, and he was still suffering from the peculiar disorientation that that city always aroused in him. This was the fourth time that he had come here, and it had been the same every time. New Chicago was the only one of the reconstructed cities of this world that in its original incarnation had existed *after* his own era. To him it was an outpost of the incomprehensible future; to the citizens it was a quaint simulacrum of the archaeological past. That paradox left him aswirl with impossible confusions and tensions.

What had happened to *old* Chicago was of course impossible for him to discover. Vanished without a trace, that was clear: no Water Tower, no Marina City, no Hancock Center, no Tribune building, not a fragment, not an atom. But it was hopeless to ask any of the million-plus inhabitants of New Chicago about their city's predecessor. They were only temporaries; they knew no more than they had to know, and all that they had to know was how to go through the motions of whatever it was that they did by way of creating the illusion that this was a real city. They had no need of knowing ancient history.

Nor was he likely to find out anything from a citizen, of course. Citizens did not seem to bother much about scholarly matters. Phillips had no reason to think that the world was anything other than an amusement park to them. Somewhere, certainly, there had to be those who specialized in the serious study of the lost civilizations of the past—for how, otherwise, would these uncanny reconstructed cities be brought into being? "The planners," he had once heard Nissandra or Aramayne say, "are already deep into their Byzantium research." But who were the planners? He had no idea. For all he knew, they were the robots. Perhaps the robots were the real masters of this whole era, who created the cities not primarily for the sake of amusing the citizens but in their own diligent attempt to comprehend the life of the world that had passed away. A wild speculation, yes; but not without some plausibility, he thought.

He felt oppressed by the party gaiety all about him. "I need some air," he said to Cantilena, and headed toward the window. It was the merest crescent, but a breeze came through. He looked out at the strange city below.

New Chicago had nothing in common with the old one but its name. They had built it, at least, along the western shore of a large inland lake that might even be Lake Michigan, although when he had flown over it had seemed broader and less elongated than the lake he remembered. The city itself was a lacy fantasy of slender pastel-hued buildings rising at odd angles and linked by a webwork of gently undulating aerial bridges. The streets were long parentheses that touched the lake at their northern and southern ends and arched gracefully westward in the middle. Between each of the great boulevards ran a track for public transportation—sleek aquamarine bubble-vehicles gliding on soundless wheels—and flanking each of the tracks were lush strips of park. It was beautiful, astonishingly so, but insubstantial. The whole thing seemed to have been contrived from sunbeams and silk.

A soft voice beside him said, "Are you becoming ill?"

Phillips glanced around. The celadon man stood beside him: a compact, precise person, vaguely Oriental in appearance. His skin was of a curious gray-green hue like no skin Phillips had ever seen, and it was extraordinarily smooth in texture, as though he were made of fine porcelain.

He shook his head. "Just a little queasy," he said. "This city always scrambles me."

"I suppose it can be disconcerting," the little man replied. His tone was furry and veiled, the inflection strange. There was something feline about him. He seemed sinewy, unyielding, almost menacing. "Visitor, are you?"

Phillips studied him a moment. "Yes," he said.

"So am I, of course."

"Are you?"

"Indeed." The little man smiled. "What's your locus? Twentieth century? Twenty-first at the latest, I'd say."

"I'm from 1984. 1984 A.D."

Another smile, a self-satisfied one. "Not a bad guess, then." A brisk tilt of the head. "Y'ang-Yeovil."

"Pardon me?" Phillips said.

"Y'ang-Yeovil. It is my name. Formerly Colonel Y'ang-Yeovil of the Third Septentriad."

"Is that on some other planet?" asked Phillips, feeling a bit dazed.

"Oh, no, not at all," Y'ang-Yeovil said pleasantly. "This very world, I assure you. I am quite of human origin. Citizen of the Republic of Upper Han, native of the city of Port Ssu. And you—forgive me—your name—?"

"I'm sorry. Phillips. Charles Phillips. From New York City, once upon a time."

"Ah, New York!" Y'ang-Yeovil's face lit with a glimmer of recognition that quickly faded. "New York—New York—it was very famous, that I know—"

This is very strange, Phillips thought. He felt greater compassion for poor bewildered Francis Willoughby now. This man comes from a time so far beyond my own that he barely knows of New York—he must be a contemporary of the real New Chicago, in fact; I wonder whether he finds this version authentic—and yet to the citizens this Y'ang-Yeovil too is just a primitive, a curio out of antiquity—

"New York was the largest city of the United States of America," Phillips said.

"Of course. Yes. Very famous."

"But virtually forgotten by the time the Republic of Upper Han came into existence, I gather."

Y'ang-Yeovil said, looking uncomfortable, "There were disturbances between your time and mine. But by no means should you take from my words the impression that your city was—"

Sudden laughter resounded across the room. Five or six newcomers had arrived at the party. Phillips stared, gasped, gaped. Surely that was Stengard—and Aramayne beside him—and that other woman, half-hidden behind them—

"If you'll pardon me a moment—" Phillips said, turning abruptly away from Y'ang-Yeovil. "Please excuse me. Someone just coming in—a person I've been trying to find ever since—"

He hurried toward her.

"Gioia?" he called. "Gioia, it's me! Wait! Wait!"

Stengard was in the way. Aramayne, turning to take a handful of the little vapor-sniffers from Cantilena, blocked him also. Phillips pushed through them as though they were not there. Gioia, halfway out the door, halted and looked toward him like a frightened deer.

"Don't go," he said. He took her hand in his.

He was startled by her appearance. How long had it been since their strange parting on that night of mysteries in Chang-an? A year? A year and a half? So he believed. Or had he lost all track of time? Were his perceptions of the passing of the months in this world that unreliable? She seemed at least ten or fifteen years older. Maybe she really was; maybe the years had been passing for him here as in a dream, and he had never known it. She looked strained, faded, worn. Out of a thinner and strangely altered face her eyes blazed at him almost defiantly, as though saying, *See? See how ugly I have become?*

He said, "I've been hunting for you for—I don't know how long it's been, Gioia. In Mohenjo, in Timbuctoo, now here. I want to be with you again."

"It isn't possible."

"Belilala explained everything to me in Mohenjo. I know that you're a short-timer—I know what that means, Gioia. But what of it? So you're beginning to age a little. So what? So you'll only have three or four hundred years, instead of forever. Don't you think I know what it means to be a short-timer? I'm just a simple ancient man of the twentieth century, remember? Sixty, seventy, eighty years is all we would get. You and I suffer from the same malady, Gioia. That's what drew you to me in the first place. I'm certain of that. That's why we belong with each other now. However much time we have, we can spend the rest of it together, don't you see?"

"You're the one who doesn't see, Charles," she said softly.

"Maybe. Maybe I still don't understand a damned thing about this place. Except that you and I—that I love you—that I think you love me—"

"I love you, yes. But you don't understand. It's precisely because I love you that you and I—you and I can't—"

With a despairing sigh she slid her hand free of his grasp. He reached for her again, but she shook him off and backed up quickly into the corridor.

"Gioia?"

"Please," she said. "No. I would never have come here if I knew you were here. Don't come after me. Please. Please."

She turned and fled.

He stood looking after her for a long moment. Cantilena and Aramayne appeared, and smiled at him as if nothing at all had happened. Cantilena offered him a vial of some sparkling amber fluid. He refused with a brusque gesture. Where do I go now, he wondered? What do I do? He wandered back into the party.

Y'ang-Yeovil glided to his side. "You are in great distress," the little man murmured.

Phillips glared. "Let me be."

"Perhaps I could be of some help."

"There's no help possible," said Phillips. He swung about and plucked one of the vials from a tray and gulped its contents. It made him feel as if there were two of him, standing on either side of Y'ang-Yeovil. He gulped another. Now there were four of him. "I'm in love with a citizen," he blurted. It seemed to him that he was speaking in chorus.

"Love. Ah. And does she love you?"

"So I thought. So I think. But she's a short-timer. Do you know what that means? She's not immortal like the others. She ages. She's beginning to look old. And so she's been running away from me. She doesn't want me to see her changing. She thinks it'll disgust me, I suppose. I tried to remind her just now that I'm not immortal either, that she and I could grow old together, but she—"

"Oh, no," Y'ang-Yeovil said quietly. "Why do you think you will age? Have you grown any older in all the time you have been here?"

Phillips was nonplussed. "Of course I have. I—I—"

"Have you? Y'ang-Yeovil smiled. "Here. Look at yourself." He did something intricate with his fingers and a shimmering zone of mirrorlike light appeared between them. Phillips stared at his reflection. A youthful face stared back at him. It was true, then. He had simply not thought about it. How many years had he spent in this world? The time had simply slipped by: a great deal of time, though he could not calculate how much. They did not seem to keep close count of it here, nor had he. But it must have been many years, he thought. All that endless travel up and down the globe—so many cities had come and gone—Rio, Rome, Asgard, those were the first three that came to mind—and there were others; he could hardly remember every one. Years. His face had not changed at all. Time had worked its harshness on Gioia, yes, but not on him.

"I don't understand," he said. "Why am I not aging?"

"Because you are not real," said Y'ang-Yeovil. "Are you unaware of that?"

Phillips blinked. "Not—real?"

"Did you think you were lifted bodily out of your own time?" the little man asked. "Ah, no, no, there is no way for them to do such a thing. We are not actual time travelers: not you, not I, not any of the visitors. I thought you were aware of that. But perhaps your era is too early for a proper understanding of these things. We are very cleverly done, my friend. We are ingenious constructs, marvelously stuffed with the thoughts and attitudes and events of our own times. We are their finest achievement, you know: far more complex even than one of these cities. We are a step beyond the temporaries—more than a step, a great deal more. They do only what they are instructed to do, and their range is very narrow. They are nothing but machines, really. Whereas we are autonomous. We move about by our own will; we think, we talk, we even, so it seems, fall in love. But we will not age. How could we age? We are not real. We are mere artificial webworks of mental responses. We are mere illusions, done so well that we deceive even ourselves. You did not know that? Indeed, you did not know?"

He was airborne, touching destination buttons at random. Somehow he found himself heading back toward Timbuctoo. *This city is closed. This is not a place any longer.* It did not matter to him. Why should anything matter?

Fury and a choking sense of despair rose within him. I am software, Phillips thought. I am nothing but software.

Not real. Very cleverly done. An ingenious construct. A mere illusion.

No trace of Timbuctoo was visible from the air. He landed anyway. The gray sandy earth was smooth, unturned, as though there had never been anything there. A few robots were still about, handling whatever final chores were required in the shutting-down of a city. Two of them scuttled up to him. Huge bland gleaming silver-skinned insects, not friendly.

"There is no city here," they said. "This is not a permissible place."

"Permissible by whom?"

"There is no reason for you to be here."

"There's no reason for me to be anywhere," Phillips said. The robots stirred, made uneasy humming sounds and ominous clicks, waved their antennae about. They seem troubled, he thought. They seem to dislike my attitude. Perhaps I run some risk of being taken off to the home for unruly software for debugging. "I'm leaving now," he told them. "Thank you. Thank you very much." He backed away from them and climbed into his flitterflitter. He touched more destination buttons.

We move about by our own will. We think, we talk, we even fall in love.

He landed in Chang-an. This time there was no reception committee waiting for him at the Gate of Brilliant Virtue. The city seemed larger and more resplendent: new pagodas, new palaces. It felt like winter: a chilly cutting wind was blowing. The sky was cloudless and dazzlingly bright. At the steps of the Silver Terrace he encountered Francis Willoughby, a great hulking figure in magnificent brocaded robes, with two dainty little temporaries, pretty as jade statuettes, engulfed in his arms. "Miracles and wonders! The silly lunatic fellow is here too!" Willoughby roared. "Look, look, we are come to far Cathay, you and I!"

We are nowhere, Phillips thought. *We are mere illusions, done so well that we deceive even ourselves.*

To Willoughby he said, "You look like an emperor in those robes, Francis."

"Aye, like Prester John!" Willoughby cried. "Like Tamburlaine himself! Aye, am I not majestic?" He slapped Phillips gaily on the shoulder, a rough playful poke that spun him halfway about, coughing and wheezing. "We flew in the air, as the eagles do, as the demons do, as the angels do! Soared like angels! Like angels!" He came close, looming over Phillips. "I would have gone to England, but the wench Belilala said there was an enchantment on me that would keep me from England just now; and so we voyaged to Cathay. Tell me this, fellow, will you go witness for me when we see England again? Swear that all that has befallen us did in truth befall? For I fear they will say I am as mad as Marco Polo, when I tell them of flying to Cathay."

"One madman backing another?" Phillips asked. "What can I tell you? You still think you'll reach England, do you?" Rage rose to the surface in him, bubbling hot. "Ah, Francis, Francis, do you know your Shakespeare? Did you go to the plays? We aren't real. *We aren't real.* We are such stuff as dreams are made on, the two of us. That's all we are. O brave new world! What England? Where? There's no England. There's no Francis Willoughby. There's no Charles Phillips. What we are is—"

"Let him be, Charles," a cool voice cut in.

He turned. Belilala, in the robes of an empress, coming down the steps of the Silver Terrace.

"I know the truth," he said bitterly. "Y'ang-Yeovil told me. The visitor from the twenty-fifth century. I saw him in New Chicago."

"Did you see Gioia there too?" Belilala asked.

"Briefly. She looks much older."

"Yes. I know. She was here recently."

"And has gone on, I suppose?"

"To Mohenjo again, yes. Go after her, Charles. Leave poor Francis alone. I told her to wait for you. I told her that she needs you, and you need her."

"Very kind of you. But what good is it, Belilala? I don't even exist. And she's going to die."

"You exist. How can you doubt that you exist? You feel, don't you? You suffer. You love. You love Gioia: is that not so? And you are loved by Gioia. Would Gioia love what is not real?"

"You think she loves me?"

"I know she does. Go to her, Charles. Go. I told her to wait for you in Mohenjo."

Phillips nodded numbly. What was there to lose?

"Go to her," said Belilala again. "Now."

"Yes," Phillips said. "I'll go now." He turned to Willoughby. "If ever we meet in London, friend, I'll testify for you. Fear nothing. All will be well, Francis."

He left them and set his course for Mohenjo-daro, half expecting to find the robots already tearing it down. Mohenjo-daro was still there, no lovelier than before. He went to the baths, thinking he might find Gioia there. She was not; but he came upon Nissandra, Stengard, Fenimon. "She has gone to Alexandria," Fenimon told him. "She wants to see it one last time, before they close it."

"They're almost ready to open Constantinople," Stengard explained. "The capital of Byzantium, you know, the great city by the Golden Horn. They'll take Alexandria away, you understand, when Byzantium opens. They say it's going to be marvelous. We'll see you there for the opening, naturally?"

"Naturally," Phillips said.

He flew to Alexandria. He felt lost and weary. All this is hopeless folly; he told himself. I am nothing but a puppet jerking about on its strings. But somewhere above the shining breast of the Arabian Sea the deeper implications of something that Belilala had said to him started to sink in, and he felt his bitterness, his rage, his despair, all suddenly beginning to leave him. *You exist. How can you doubt that you exist? Would Gioia love what is not real?* Of course. Of course. Y'ang-Yeovil had been wrong: visitors were something more than mere illusions. Indeed Y'ang-Yeovil had voiced the truth of their condition without understanding what he was really saying: *We think, we talk, we fall in love.* Yes. That was the heart of the situation. The visitors might be artificial, but they were not unreal. Belilala had been trying to tell him that just the other night. *You suffer. You love. You love Gioia. Would Gioia love what is not real?* Surely he was real, or at any rate real enough. What he was was something strange, something that would probably have been all but incomprehensible to the twentieth-century people whom he had been designed to simulate. But that did not mean that he was unreal. Did one have to be of woman born to be real? No. No. No. His kind of reality was a sufficient reality. He had no need to be ashamed of it. And, understanding that, he understood that Gioia did not need to grow old and die. There was a way by which she could be saved, if only she would embrace it. If only she would.

When he landed in Alexandria he went immediately to the hotel on the slopes of the Paneium where they had stayed on their first visit, so very long ago; and there she was, sitting quietly on a patio with a view of the harbor and the Lighthouse. There was something calm and resigned about the way she sat. She had given up. She did not even have the strength to flee from him any longer.

"Gioia," he said gently.

She looked older than she had in New Chicago. Her face was drawn and sallow and her eyes seemed sunken; and she was not even bothering these days to deal with the white strands that stood out in stark contrast against the darkness of her hair. He sat down beside her and put his hand over hers, and looked out toward the obelisks, the palaces, the temples, the Lighthouse. At length he said, "I know what I really am, now."

"Do you, Charles?" She sounded very far away.

"In my era we called it software. All I am is a set of commands, responses, cross-references, operating some sort of artificial body. It's infinitely better software than we could have imagined. But we were only just beginning to learn how, after all. They pumped me full of twentieth-century reflexes. The right moods, the right appetites, the right irrationalities, the right sort of combativeness. Somebody knows a lot about what it was like to be a twentieth-century man. They did a good job with Willoughby, too, all that Elizabethan rhetoric and swagger. And I suppose they got Y'ang-Yeovil right. *He* seems to think so: who better to judge? The twenty-fifth century, the Republic of Upper Han, people with gray-green skin, half Chinese and half Martian for all I know. *Somebody* knows. Somebody here is very good at programming, Gioia."

She was not looking at him.

"I feel frightened, Charles," she said in that same distant way.

"Of me? Of the things I'm saying?"

"No, not of you. Don't you see what has happened to me?"

"I see you. There are changes."

"I lived a long time wondering when the changes would begin. I thought maybe they wouldn't, not really. Who wants to believe they'll get old? But it started when we were in Alexandria that first time. In Chang-an it got much worse. And now—now—"

He said abruptly, "Stengard tells me they'll be opening Constantinople very soon."

"So?"

"Don't you want to be there when it opens?"

"I'm becoming old and ugly, Charles."

"We'll go to Constantinople together. We'll leave tomorrow, eh? What do you say? We'll charter a boat. It's a quick little hop, right across the Mediterranean. Sailing to Byzantium! There was a poem, you know, in my time. Not forgotten, I guess, because they've programmed it into me. All these thousands of years, and someone still remembers old Yeats. *The young in one another's arms, birds in the trees.* Come with me to Byzantium, Gioia."

She shrugged. "Looking like this? Getting more hideous every hour? While *they* stay young forever? While *you*—" She faltered; her voice cracked; she fell silent.

"Finish the sentence, Gioia."

"Please. Let me alone."

"You were going to say, 'While *you* stay young forever too, Charles,' isn't that it? You knew all along that I was never going to change. I didn't know that, but you did."

"Yes. I knew. I pretended that it wasn't true—that as I aged, you'd age too. It was very foolish of me. In Chang-an, when I first began to see the real signs of it—that was when I realized I couldn't stay with you any longer. Because I'd look at you, always young, always remaining the same age, and I'd look at myself, and—" She gestured, palms upward. "So I gave you to Belilala and ran away."

"All so unnecessary, Gioia."

"I didn't think it was."

"But you don't have to grow old. Not if you don't want to!"

"Don't be cruel, Charles," she said tonelessly. "There's no way of escaping what I have."

"But there is," he said.

"You know nothing about these things."

"Not very much, no," he said. "But I see how it can be done. Maybe it's a primitive simple-minded twentieth-century sort of solution, but I think it ought to work. I've been playing with the idea ever since I left Mohenjo. Tell me this, Gioia: Why can't you go to them, to the programmers, to the artificers, the planners, whoever they are, the ones who create the cities and the temporaries and the visitors. And have yourself made into something like me!"

She looked up, startled. "What are you saying?"

"They can cobble up a twentieth-century man out of nothing more than fragmentary records and make him plausible, can't they? Or an Elizabethan, or anyone else of any era at all, and he's authentic, he's convincing. So why couldn't they do an even better job with you? Produce a Gioia so real that even Gioia can't tell the difference? But a Gioia that will never age—a Gioia-construct, a Gioia-program, a visitor-Gioia! Why not? Tell me why not, Gioia."

She was trembling. "I've never heard of doing any such thing!"

"But don't you think it's possible?"

"How would I know?"

"Of course it's possible. If they can create visitors, they can take a citizen and duplicate her in such a way that—"

"It's never been done. I'm sure of it. I can't imagine any citizen agreeing to any such thing. To give up the body—to let yourself be turned into—into—"

She shook her head, but it seemed to be a gesture of astonishment as much as of negation.

He said, "Sure. To give up the body. Your natural body, your aging, shrinking, deteriorating short-timer body. What's so awful about that?"

She was very pale. "This is craziness, Charles. I don't want to talk about it any more."

"It doesn't sound crazy to me."

"You can't possibly understand."

"Can't I? I can certainly understand being afraid to die. I don't have a lot of trouble understanding what it's like to be one of the few aging people in a world where nobody grows old. What I can't understand is why you aren't even willing to consider the possibility that—"

"No," she said. "I tell you, it's crazy. They'd laugh at me."

"Who?"

"All of my friends. Hawk, Stengard, Aramayne—" Once again she would not look at him. "They can be very cruel, without even realizing it. They despise anything that seems ungraceful to them, anything sweaty and desperate and cowardly. Citizens don't do sweaty things, Charles. And that's how this will seem. Assuming it can be done at all. They'll be terribly patronizing. Oh, they'll be sweet to me, yes, dear Gioia, how wonderful for you, Gioia, but when I turn my back they'll laugh. They'll say the most wicked things about me. I couldn't bear that."

"They can afford to laugh," Phillips said. "It's easy to be brave and cool about dying when you know you're going to live forever. How very fine for them; but why should you be the only one to grow old and die? And they won't laugh, anyway. They're not as cruel as you think. Shallow, maybe, but not cruel. They'll be glad that you've found a way to save yourself. At the very least, they won't have to feel guilty about you any longer, and that's bound to please them. You can—"

"Stop it," she said.

She rose, walked to the railing of the patio, stared out toward the sea. He came up behind her. Red sails in the harbor, sunlight glittering along the sides of the Lighthouse, the palaces of the Ptolemies stark white against the sky. Lightly he rested his hand on her shoulder. She twitched as if to pull away from him, but remained where she was.

"Then I have another idea," he said quietly. "If you won't go to the planners, *I* will. Reprogram me, I'll say. Fix things so that I start to age at the same rate you do. It'll be more authentic, anyway, if I'm supposed to be playing the part of a twentieth-century man. Over the years I'll very gradually get some lines in my face, my hair will turn gray, I'll walk a little more slowly—we'll grow old together, Gioia. To hell with your lovely immortal friends. We'll have each other. We won't need them."

She swung around. Her eyes were wide with horror.

"Are you serious, Charles?"

"Of course."

"No," she murmured. "No. Everything you've said to me today is monstrous nonsense. Don't you realize that?"

He reached for her hand and enclosed her fingertips in his. "All I'm trying to do is find some way for you and me to—"

"Don't say any more," she said. "Please." Quickly, as though drawing back from a suddenly flaring flame, she tugged her fingers free of his and put her hand behind her. Though his face was just inches from hers he felt an immense chasm opening between them. They stared at one another for a moment; then she moved deftly to his left, darted around him, and ran from the patio.

Stunned, he watched her go, down the long marble corridor and out of sight. It was folly to give pursuit, he thought. She was lost to him: that was clear, that was beyond any question. She was terrified of him. Why cause her even more anguish? But somehow he found himself running through the halls of the hotel, along the winding garden path, into the cool green groves of the Paneium. He thought he saw her on the portico of Hadrian's palace, but when he got there the echoing stone halls were empty. To a temporary that was sweeping the steps he said, "Did you see a woman come this way?" A blank sullen stare was his only answer.

Phillips cursed and turned away.

"Gioia?" he called. "Wait! Come back!"

Was that her, going into the Library? He rushed past the startled mumbling librarians and sped through the stacks, peering beyond the mounds of double-handled scrolls into the shadowy corridors. "Gioia? *Gioia!*" It was a descration, bellowing like that in this quiet place. He scarcely cared.

Emerging by a side door, he loped down to the harbor. The Lighthouse! Terror enfolded him. She might already be a hundred steps up that ramp, heading for the parapet from which she meant to fling herself into the sea. Scattering citizens and temporaries as if they were straws, he ran within. Up he went, never pausing for breath, though his synthetic lungs were screaming for respite, his ingeniously designed heart was desperately pounding. On the first balcony he imagined he caught a glimpse of her, but he circled it without finding her. Onward, upward. He went to the top, to the beacon chamber itself: no Gioia. Had she jumped? Had she gone down one ramp while he was ascending the other? He clung to the rim and looked out, down, searching the base of the Lighthouse, the rocks offshore, the causeway. No Gioia. I will find her somewhere, he thought. I will keep going until I find her. He went running down the ramp, calling her name. He reached ground level and sprinted back toward the center of town. Where next? The temple of Poseidon? The tomb of Cleopatra?

He paused in the middle of Canopus Street, groggy and dazed.

"Charles?" she said.

"Where are you?"

"Right here. Beside you." She seemed to materialize from the air. Her face was unflushed, her robe bore no trace of perspiration. Had he been chasing a phantom through the city? She came to him and took his hand, and said, softly, tenderly, "Were you really serious, about having them make you age?"

"If there's no other way, yes."

"The other way is so frightening, Charles."

"Is it?"

"You can't understand how much."

"More frightening than growing old? Than dying?"

"I don't know," she said. "I suppose not. The only thing I'm sure of is that I don't want you to get old, Charles."

"But I won't have to. Will I?" He stared at her.

"No," she said. "You won't have to. Neither of us will."

Phillips smiled. "We should get away from here," he said after a while. "Let's go across to Byzantium, yes, Gioia? We'll show up in Constantinople for the opening. Your friends will be there. We'll tell them what you've decided to do. They'll know how to arrange it. Someone will."

"It sounds so strange," said Gioia. "To turn myself into—into a visitor? A visitor in my own world?"

"That's what you've always been, though."

"I suppose. In a way. But at least I've been *real* up to now."

"Whereas I'm not?"

"Are you, Charles?"

"Yes. Just as real as you. I was angry at first, when I found out the truth about myself. But I came to accept it: Somewhere between Mohenjo and here, I came to see that it was all right to be what I am: that I perceive things, I form ideas, I draw conclusions. I am very well designed, Gioia. I can't tell the difference between being what I am and being completely alive, and to me that's being real enough. I think, I feel, I experience joy and pain. I'm as real as I need to be. And you will be too. You'll never stop being Gioia, you know. It's only your body that you'll cast away, the body that played such a terrible joke on you anyway." He brushed her cheek with his hand. "It was all said for us before, long ago:

Once out of nature I shall never take
My bodily form from any natural thing,
But such a form as Grecian goldsmiths make
Of hammered gold and gold enamelling
To keep a drowsy Emperor awake;"

"Is that the same poem?" she asked.

"The same poem, yes. The ancient poem that isn't quite forgotten yet."

"Finish it, Charles."

"Or set upon a golden bough to sing
To lords and ladies of Byzantium
Of what is past, or passing, or to come."

"How beautiful. What does it mean?"

"That it isn't necessary to be mortal. That we can allow ourselves to be gathered into the artifice of eternity, that we can be transformed, that we can move on beyond the flesh. Yeats didn't mean it in quite the way I do—he wouldn't have begun to comprehend what we're talking about, not a word of it—and yet, and yet—the underlying truth is the same. Live, Gioia! With me!" He turned to her and saw color coming into her pallid cheeks. "It does make sense, what I'm suggesting, doesn't it? You'll attempt it, won't you? Whoever makes the visitors can be induced to remake you. Right? What do you think: can they, Gioia?"

She nodded in a barely perceptible way. "I think so," she said faintly.

"It's very strange. But I think it ought to be possible. Why not, Charles? Why not?"

"Yes," he said. "Why not?"

In the morning they hired a vessel in the harbor, a low sleek pirogue with a blood-red sail, skippered by a rascally-looking temporary whose smile was irresistible. Phillips shaded his eyes and peered northward across the sea. He thought he could almost make out the shape of the great city sprawling on its seven hills, Constantine's New Rome beside the Golden Horn, the mighty dome of Hagia Sophia, the somber walls of the citadel, the palaces and churches, the Hippodrome, Christ in glory rising above all else in brilliant mosaic streaming with light.

"Byzantium," Phillips said. "Take us there the shortest and quickest way."

"It is my pleasure," said the boatman with unexpected grace.

Gioia smiled. He had not seen her looking so vibrantly alive since the night of the imperial feast in Chang-an. He reached for her hand—her slender fingers were quivering lightly—and helped her into the boat.

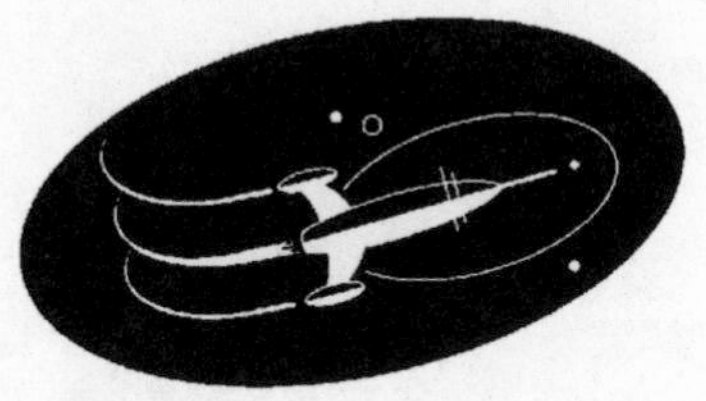

The Last of the Winnebagos

Connie Willis

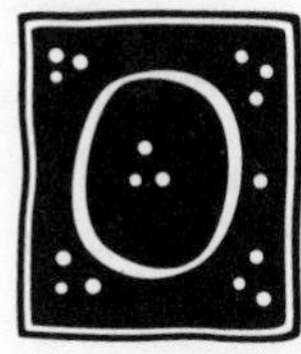

On the way out to Tempe I saw a dead jackal in the road. I was in the far left lane of Van Buren, ten lanes away from it, and its long legs were facing away from me, the squarish muzzle flat against the pavement so it looked narrower than it really was, and for a minute I thought it was a dog.

I had not seen an animal in the road like that for fifteen years. They can't get onto the divideds, of course, and most of the multiways are fenced. And people are more careful of their animals.

The jackal was probably somebody's pet. This part of Phoenix was mostly residential, and after all this time, people still think they can turn the nasty, carrion-loving creatures into pets. Which was no reason to have hit it and, worse, left it there. It's a felony to strike an animal and another one to not report it, but whoever had hit it was long gone.

I pulled the Hitori over onto the center shoulder and sat there awhile, staring at the empty multiway. I wondered who had hit it and whether they had stopped to see if it was dead.

Katie had stopped. She had hit the brakes so hard she sent the car into a skid that brought it up against the ditch, and jumped out of the jeep. I was still running toward him, floundering in the snow. We made it to him almost at the same time. I knelt beside him, the camera dangling from my neck, its broken case hanging half open.

"I hit him," Katie had said. "I hit him with the jeep."

I looked in the rearview mirror. I couldn't even see over the pile of camera equipment in the back seat with the eisenstadt balanced on top. I got out. I had come nearly a mile, and looking back, I couldn't see the jackal, though I knew now that's what it was.

"McCombe! David! Are you there yet?" Ramirez's voice said from inside the car.

I leaned in. "No," I shouted in the general direction of the phone's mike. "I'm still on the multiway."

"Mother of God, what's taking you so long? The governor's conference is at twelve, and I want you to go out to Scottsdale and do a layout on the closing of Taliessin West. The appointment's for ten. Listen, McCombe, I got the poop on the Amblers for you. They bill themselves as 'One Hundred Percent Authentic,' but they're not. Their RV isn't really a Winnebago, it's an Open Road. It *is* the last RV on the road, though, according to Highway Patrol. A man named Eldridge was touring with one, also *not* a Winnebago, a Shasta, until March, but he lost his license in Oklahoma for using a tanker lane, so this is it. Recreation vehicles are banned in all but four states. Texas has legislation in committee, and Utah has a full-divided bill coming up next month. Arizona will be next, so take lots of pictures, Davey boy. This may be your last chance. And get some of the zoo."

"What about the Amblers?" I said.

"Their name *is* Ambler, believe it or not. I ran a lifeline on them. He was a welder. She was a bank teller. No kids. They've been doing this since eighty-nine when he retired. Nineteen years. David, are you using the eisenstadt?"

We had been through this the last three times I'd been on a shoot. "I'm not *there* yet," I said.

"Well, I want you to use it at the governor's conference. Set it on his desk if you can."

I intended to set it on a desk, all right. One of the desks at the back, and let it get some nice shots of the rear ends of reporters as they reached wildly for a little clear air-space to shoot their pictures in, some of them holding their vidcams in their upstretched arms and aiming them in what they hope is the right direction because they can't see the governor at all, let it get a nice shot of one of the reporter's arms as he knocked it face-down on the desk.

"This one's a new model. It's got a trigger. It's set for faces, full-lengths, and vehicles."

So great. I come home with a hundred-frame cartridge full of passersby and tricycles. How the hell did it know when to click the shutter or which one the governor was in a press conference of eight hundred people, full-length *or* face? It was supposed to have all kinds of fancy light-metrics and computer-composition features, but all it could really do was mindlessly snap whatever passed in front of its idiot lens, just like the highway speed cameras.

It had probably been designed by the same government types who'd put the highway cameras along the road instead of overhead so that all it takes is a little speed to reduce the new side-license plates to a blur, and people go faster than ever. A great camera, the eisenstadt. I could hardly wait to use it.

"Sun-co's very interested in the eisenstadt," Ramirez said. She didn't say goodbye. She never does. She just stops talking and then starts up again later. I looked back in the direction of the jackal.

The multiway was completely deserted. New cars and singles don't use the undivided multiways much, even during rush hours. Too many of the little cars have been squashed by tankers. Usually there are at least a few obsoletes and renegade semis taking advantage of the Patrol's being on the divideds, but there wasn't anybody at all.

I got back in the car and backed up even with the jackal. I turned off the ignition but didn't get out. I could see the trickle of blood from its mouth from here. A tanker went roaring past out of nowhere, trying to beat the cameras, straddling the three middle lanes and crushing the jackal's rear half to a bloody mush. It was a good thing I hadn't been trying to cross the road. He never would have even seen me.

I started the car and drove to the nearest off-ramp to find a phone. There was one at an old 7-Eleven on McDowell.

"I'm calling to report a dead animal on the road," I told the woman who answered the Society's phone.

"Name and number?"

"It's a jackal," I said. "It's between Thirtieth and Thirty-Second on Van Buren. It's in the far right lane."

"Did you render emergency assistance?"

"There was no assistance to be rendered. It was dead."

"Did you move the animal to the side of the road?"

"No."

"Why not?" she said, her tone suddenly sharper, more alert.

Because I thought it was a dog. "I didn't have a shovel," I said, and hung up.

I got out to Tempe by eight-thirty, in spite of the fact that every tanker in the state suddenly decided to take Van Buren. I got pushed out onto the shoulder and drove on that most of the way.

The Winnebago was set up in the fairgrounds between Phoenix and Tempe, next to the old zoo. The flyer had said they would be open from nine to nine, and I had wanted to get most of my pictures before they opened, but it was already a quarter to nine, and even if there were no cars in the dusty parking lot, I was probably too late.

It's a tough job being a photographer. The minute most people see a camera, their real faces close like a shutter in too much light, and all that's left is their camera face, their public face. It's a smiling face, except in the case of Saudi terrorists or senators, but, smiling or not, it shows no real emotion. Actors, politicians, people who have their pictures taken all the time are the worst. The longer the person's been in the public eye, the easier it is for me to get great vidcam footage and the harder it is to get anything approaching a real photograph, and the Amblers had been at this for nearly twenty years. By a quarter to nine they would already have their camera faces on.

I parked down at the foot of the hill next to the clump of ocotillas and yucca where the zoo sign had been, pulled my Nikon longshot out of the mess in the back seat, and took some shots of the sign they'd set up by the multiway: "See a Genuine Winnebago. One Hundred Percent Authentic."

The Genuine Winnebago was parked longways against the stone banks of cacti and palms at the front of the zoo. Ramirez had said it wasn't a real Winnebago, but it had the identifying W with its extending stripes running the length of the RV, and it seemed to me to be the right shape, though I hadn't seen one in at least ten years.

I was probably the wrong person for this story. I had never had any great love for RV's, and my first thought when Ramirez called with the assignment was that there are some things that should be extinct, like mosquitoes and lane dividers, and RV's are right at the top of the list. They had been everywhere in the mountains when I'd lived in Colorado, crawling along in the left-hand lane, taking up two lanes even in the days when a lane was fifteen feet wide, with a train of cursing cars behind them.

I'd been behind one on Independence Pass that had stopped cold while a ten-year-old got out to take pictures of the scenery with an Instamatic, and one of them had tried to take the curve in front of my house and ended up in my ditch, looking like a beached whale. But that was always a bad curve.

An old man in an ironed short-sleeved shirt came out the side door and around to the front end and began washing the Winnebago with a sponge and a bucket. I wondered where he had gotten the water. According to Ramirez's advance work, which she'd sent me over the modem about the Winnebago, it had maybe a fifty-gallon water tank, tops, which is barely enough for drinking water, a shower, and maybe washing a dish or two, and there certainly weren't any hookups here at the zoo, but he was swilling water onto the front bumper and even over the tires as if he had more than enough.

I took a few shots of the RV standing in the huge expanse of parking lot and then hit the longshot to full for a picture of the old man working on the bumper. He had large reddish-brown freckles on his arms and the top of his bald head, and he scrubbed away at the bumper with a vengeance. After a minute he stopped and stepped back, and then called to his wife. He looked worried, or maybe just crabby. I was too far away to tell if he had snapped out her name impatiently or simply called her to come and look, and I couldn't see his face. She opened the metal side door, with its narrow louvered window, and stepped down onto the metal step.

The old man asked her something, and she, still standing on the step, looked out toward the multiway and shook her head, and then came around to the front, wiping her hands on a dishtowel, and they both stood there looking at his handiwork.

They were One Hundred Percent Authentic, even if the Winnebago wasn't, down to her flowered blouse and polyester slacks, probably also one hundred percent, and the cross-stitched rooster on the dishtowel. She had on brown leather slip-ons like I remembered my grandmother wearing, and I was willing to bet she had set her thinning white hair on bobby pins. Their bio said they were in their eighties, but I would have put them in their nineties, although I wondered if they were too perfect and therefore fake, like the Winnebago. But she went on wiping her hands on the dishtowel the way my grandmother had when she was upset, even though I couldn't see if her face was showing any emotion, and that action at least was authentic.

She apparently told him the bumper looked fine because he dropped the dripping sponge into the bucket and went around behind the Winnebago. She went back inside, shutting the metal door behind her even though it had to be already at least a hundred and ten out, and they hadn't even bothered to park under what scanty shade the palms provided.

I put the longshot back in the car. The old man came around the front with a big plywood sign. He propped it against the vehicle's side. "The Last of the Winnebagos," the sign read in somebody's idea of what Indian writing should look like. "See a vanishing breed. Admission—Adults—$8.00, Children under twelve—$5.00 Open 9 A.M. to Sunset." He strung up a row of red and yellow flags, and then picked up the bucket and started toward the door, but halfway there he stopped and took a few steps down the parking lot to where I thought he probably had a good view of the road, and then went back, walking like an old man, and took another swipe at the bumper with the sponge.

"Are you done with the RV yet, McCombe?" Ramirez said on the car phone.

I slung the camera into the back. "I just got here. Every tanker in Arizona was on Van Buren this morning. Why the hell don't you have me do a piece on abuses of the multiway system by water-haulers?"

"Because I want you to get to Tempe alive. The governor's press conference has been moved to one, so you're okay. Have you used the eisenstadt yet?"

"I told you, I just got here. I haven't even turned the damned thing on."

"You don't turn it on. It self-activates when you set it bottom down on a level surface."

Great. It had probably already shot its 100-frame cartridge on the way here.

"Well, if you don't use it on the Winnebago, make sure you use it at the governor's conference," she said. "By the way, have you thought any more about moving to investigative?"

That was why Sun-co was really so interested in the eisenstadt. It had been easier to send a photographer who could write stories than it had to send a photographer and a reporter, especially in the little one-seater Hitoris they were ordering now, which was how I got to be a photojournalist. And since that had worked out so well, why send either? Send an eisenstadt and a DAT deck and you won't need an Hitori and waymile credits to get them there. You can send them through the mail. They can sit unnoticed on the old governor's desk, and after a while somebody in a one-seater who wouldn't have to be either a photographer *or* a reporter can sneak in to retrieve them and a dozen others.

"No," I said, glancing back up the hill. The old man gave one last swipe to the front bumper and then walked over to one of the zoo's old stone-edged planters and dumped the bucket in on a tangle of prickly pear, which would probably think it was a spring shower and bloom before I made it up the hill. "Look, if I'm going to get any pictures before the touristas arrive, I'd better go."

"I wish you'd think about it. And use the eisenstadt this time. You'll like it once you try it. Even *you'll* forget it's a camera."

"I'll bet," I said. I looked back down the multiway. Nobody at all was coming now. Maybe that was what all the Amblers' anxiety was about—I should have asked Ramirez what their average daily attendance was and what sort of people used up credits to come this far out and see an old beat-up RV. The curve into Tempe alone was three point two miles. Maybe nobody came at all. If that was the case, I might have a chance of getting some decent pictures. I got in the Hitori and drove up the steep drive.

"Howdy," the old man said, all smiles, holding out his reddish-brown freckled hand to shake mine. "Name's Jake Ambler. And this here's Winnie," he said, patting the metal side of the RV, "Last of the Winnebagos. Is there just the one of you?"

"David McCombe," I said, holding out my press pass. "I'm a photographer. Sun-co. Phoenix *Sun,* Tempe-Mesa *Tribune,* Glendale *Star,* and affiliated stations. I was wondering if I could take some pictures of your vehicle?" I touched my pocket and turned the taper on.

"You bet. We've always cooperated with the media, Mrs. Ambler and me. I was just cleaning old Winnie up," he said. "She got pretty dusty on the way down from Globe." He didn't make any attempt to tell his wife I was there, even though she could hardly avoid hearing us, and she didn't open the metal door again. "We been on the road now with Winnie for almost twenty years. Bought her in 1989 in Forest City, Iowa, where they were made. The wife didn't want to buy her, didn't know if she'd like traveling, but now she's the one wouldn't part with it."

He was well into his spiel now, an open, friendly, I-have-nothing-to-hide expression on his face that hid everything. There was no point in taking any stills, so I got out the vidcam and shot the TV footage while he led me around the RV.

"This up here," he said, standing with one foot on the flimsy metal ladder and patting the metal bar around the top, "is the luggage rack, and this is the holding tank. It'll hold thirty gallons and has an automatic electric pump that hooks up to any waste hookup. Empties in five minutes, and you don't even get your hands dirty." He held up his fat pink hands palms forward as if to show me. "Water tank," he said, slapping a silver metal tank next to it. "Holds forty gallons, which is plenty for just the two of us. Interior space is a hundred fifty cubic feet with six feet four of headroom. That's plenty even for a tall guy like yourself."

He gave me the whole tour. His manner was easy, just short of slap-on-the-back hearty, but he looked relieved when an ancient VW bug came chugging catty-cornered up through the parking lot. He must have thought they wouldn't have any customers either.

A family piled out, Japanese tourists, a woman with short black hair, a man in shorts, two kids. One of the kids had a ferret on a leash.

"I'll just look around while you tend to the paying customers," I told him.

I locked the vidcam in the car, took the longshot, and went up toward the zoo. I took a wide-angle of the zoo sign for Ramirez. I could see it now —she'd run a caption like, "The old zoo stands empty today. No sound of lion's roar, of elephant's trumpeting, of children's laughter, can be heard here. The old Phoenix Zoo, last of its kind, while just outside its gates stands yet another last of its kind. Story on page 10." Maybe it would be a good idea to let the eisenstadts and the computers take over.

I went inside. I hadn't been out here in years. In the late eighties there had been a big flap over zoo policy. I had taken the pictures, but I hadn't covered the story since there were still such things as reporters back then. I had photographed the cages in question and the new zoo director who had caused all the flap by stopping the zoo's renovation project cold and giving the money to a wildlife protection group.

"I refuse to spend money on cages when in a few years we'll have nothing to put in them. The timber wolf, the California condor, the grizzly bear, are in imminent danger of becoming extinct, and it's our responsibility to save them, not make a comfortable prison for the last survivors."

The Society had called him an alarmist, which just goes to show you how much things can change. Well, he was an alarmist, wasn't he? The grizzly bear isn't extinct in the wild—it's Colorado's biggest tourist draw, and there are so many whooping cranes Texas is talking about limited hunting.

In all the uproar, the zoo had ceased to exist, and the animals all went to an even more comfortable prison in Sun City—sixteen acres of savannah land for the zebras and lions, and snow manufactured daily for the polar bears.

They hadn't really been cages, in spite of what the zoo director said. The old capybara enclosure, which was the first thing inside the gate, was a nice little meadow with a low stone wall around it. A family of prairie dogs had taken up residence in the middle of it.

I went back to the gate and looked down at the Winnebago. The family circled the Winnebago, the man bending down to look underneath the body. One of the kids was hanging off the ladder at the back of the RV. The ferret was nosing around the front wheel Jake Ambler had so carefully scrubbed down, looking like it was about ready to lift its leg, if ferrets do that. The kid yanked on its leash and then picked it up in his arms. The mother said something to him. Her nose was sunburned.

Katie's nose had been sunburned. She had had that white cream on it, that skiers used to use. She was wearing a parka and jeans and bulky pink-and-white moonboots that she couldn't run in, but she still made it to Aberfan before I did. I pushed past her and knelt over him.

"I hit him," she said bewilderedly. "I hit a dog."

"Get back in the jeep, damn it!" I shouted at her. I stripped off my sweater and tried to wrap him in it. "We've got to get him to the vet."

"Is he dead?" Katie said, her face as pale as the cream on her nose.

"No!" I had shouted. "No, he isn't dead."

The mother turned and looked up toward the zoo, her hand shading her face. She caught sight of the camera, dropped her hand, and smiled, a toothy, impossible smile. People in the public eye are the worst, but even people having a snapshot taken close down somehow, and it isn't just the phony smile. It's as if that old superstition is true, and cameras do really steal the soul.

I pretended to take her picture and then lowered the camera. The zoo director had put up a row of tombstone-shaped signs in front of the gate, one for each endangered species. They were covered with plastic, which hadn't helped much. I wiped the streaky dust off the one in front of me. "Canis latrans," it said, with two green stars after it. "Coyote. North American wild dog. Due to large-scale poisoning by ranchers, who saw it as a threat to cattle and sheep, the coyote is nearly extinct in the wild." Underneath there was a photograph of a ragged coyote sitting on its haunches and an explanation of the stars. Blue—endangered species. Yellow—endangered habitat. Red—extinct in the wild.

After Misha died, I had come out here to photograph the dingo and the coyotes and the wolves, but they were already in the process of moving the zoo, so I couldn't get any pictures, and it probably wouldn't have done any good. The coyote in the picture had faded to a greenish-yellow and its yellow eyes were almost white, but it stared out of the picture looking as hearty and unconcerned as Jake Ambler, wearing its camera face.

The mother had gone back to the bug and was herding the kids inside. Mr. Ambler walked the father back to the car, shaking his shining bald head, and the man talked some more, leaning on the open door, and then got in and drove off. I walked back down.

If he was bothered by the fact that they had only stayed ten minutes and that, as far as I had been able to see, no money had changed hands, it didn't show in his face. He led me around to the side of the RV and pointed to a chipped and faded collection of decals along the painted bar of the W. "These here are the states we've been in." He pointed to the one nearest the front. "Every state in the Union, plus Canada and Mexico. Last state we were in was Nevada."

Up this close it was easy to see where he had painted out the name of the original RV and covered it with the bar of red. The paint had the dull look of un-authenticity. He had covered up the "Open Road" with a burnt-wood plaque that read, "The Amblin' Amblers."

He pointed at a bumper sticker next to the door that said, "I got lucky in Vegas at Caesar's Palace," and had a picture of a naked showgirl. "We couldn't find a decal for Nevada. I don't think they make them anymore. And you know something else you can't find? Steering wheel covers. You know the kind. That keep the wheel from burning your hands when it gets hot?"

"Do you do all the driving?" I asked.

He hesitated before answering, and I wondered if one of them didn't have a license. I'd have to look it up in the lifeline. "Mrs. Ambler spells me sometimes, but I do most of it. Mrs. Ambler reads the map. Damn maps nowadays are so hard to read. Half the time you can't tell what kind of road it is. They don't make them like they used to."

We talked for a while more about all the things you couldn't find a decent one of anymore and the sad state things had gotten in generally, and then I announced I wanted to talk to Mrs. Ambler, got the vidcam and the eisenstadt out of the car, and went inside the Winnebago.

She still had the dishtowel in her hand, even though there couldn't possibly be space for that many dishes in the tiny RV. The inside was even smaller than I had thought it would be, low enough that I had to duck and so narrow I had to hold the Nikon close to my body to keep from hitting the lens on the passenger seat. It felt like an oven inside, and it was only nine o'clock in the morning.

I set the eisenstadt down on the kitchen counter, making sure its concealed lens was facing out. If it would work anywhere, it would be here. There was basically nowhere for Mrs. Ambler to go that she could get out of range. There was nowhere I could go either, and sorry, Ramirez, there are just some things a live photographer can do better than a preprogrammed one, like stay out of the picture.

"This is the galley," Mrs. Ambler said, folding her dishtowel and hanging it from a plastic ring on the cupboard below the sink with the cross-stitch design showing. It wasn't a rooster after all. It was a poodle wearing a sunbonnet and carrying a basket. "Shop on Wednesday," the motto underneath said.

"As you can see, we have a double sink with a hand-pump faucet. The refrigerator is LP-electric and holds four cubic feet. Back here is the dinette area. The table folds up into the rear wall, and we have our bed. And this is our bathroom."

She was as bad as her husband. "How long have you had the Winnebago?" I said to stop the spiel. Sometimes, if you can get people talking about something besides what they intended to talk about, you can disarm them into something like a natural expression.

"Nineteen years," she said, lifting up the lid of the chemical toilet. "We bought it in 1989. I didn't want to buy it—I didn't like the idea of selling our house and going gallivanting off like a couple of hippies, but Jake went ahead and bought it, and now I wouldn't trade it for anything. The shower operates on a forty-gallon pressurized water system." She stood back so I could get a picture of the shower stall, so narrow you wouldn't have to worry about dropping the soap. I dutifully took some vidcam footage.

"You live here full-time then?" I said, trying not to let my voice convey how impossible that prospect sounded. Ramirez had said they were from Minnesota. I had assumed they had a house there and only went on the road for part of the year.

"Jake says the great outdoors is our home," she said. I gave up trying to get a picture of her and snapped a few high-quality detail stills for the papers: the "Pilot" sign taped on the dashboard in front of the driver's seat, the crocheted granny-square afghan on the uncomfortable-looking couch, a row of salt-and-pepper shakers in the back windows—Indian children, black scottie dogs, ears of corn.

"Sometimes we live on the open prairies and sometimes on the seashore," she said. She went over to the sink and hand-pumped a scant two cups of water into a little pan and set it on the two-burner stove. She took down two turquoise melmac cups and flowered saucers and a jar of freeze-dried and spooned a little into the cups. "Last year we were in the Colorado Rockies. We can have a house on a lake or in the desert, and when we get tired of it, we just move on. Oh, my, the things we've seen."

I didn't believe her. Colorado had been one of the first states to ban recreational vehicles, even before the gas crunch and the multiways. It had banned them on the passes first and then shut them out of the national forests, and by the time I left they weren't even allowed on the interstates.

Ramirez had said RV's were banned outright in forty-seven states. New Mexico was one, Utah had heavy restricks, and daytime travel was forbidden in all the western states. Whatever they'd seen, and it sure wasn't Colorado, they had seen it in the dark or on some unpatrolled multiway, going like sixty to outrun the cameras. Not exactly the footloose and fancy-free life they tried to paint.

The water boiled. Mrs. Ambler poured it into the cups, spilling a little on the turquoise saucers. She blotted it up with the dishtowel. "We came down here because of the snow. They get winter so early in Colorado."

"I know," I said. It had snowed two feet, and it was only the middle of September. Nobody even had their snow tires on. The aspens hadn't turned yet, and some of the branches broke under the weight of the snow. Katie's nose was still sunburned from the summer.

"Where did you come from just now?" I asked her.

"Globe," she said, and opened the door to yell to her husband. "Jake! Coffee!" She carried the cups to the table-that-converts-into-a-bed. "It has leaves that you can put in it so it seats six," she said.

I sat down at the table so she was on the side where the eisenstadt could catch her. The sun was coming in through the cranked-open back windows, already hot. Mrs. Ambler got onto her knees on the plaid cushions and let down a woven cloth shade, carefully, so it wouldn't knock the salt and pepper shakers off.

There were some snapshots stuck up between the ceramic ears of corn. I picked one up. It was a square Polaroid from the days when you had to peel off the print and glue it to a stiff card: The two of them, looking exactly the way they did now, with that friendly, impenetrable camera smile, were standing in front of a blur of orange rock—the Grand Canyon? Zion? Monument Valley? Polaroid had always chosen color over definition. Mrs. Ambler was holding a little yellow blur in her arms that could have been a cat but wasn't. It was a dog.

"That's Jake and me at Devil's Tower," she said, taking the picture away from me. "And Taco. You can't tell from this picture, but she was the cutest little thing. A chihuahua." She handed it back to me and rummaged behind the salt and pepper shakers. "Sweetest little dog you ever saw. This will give you a better idea."

The picture she handed me was considerably better, a matte print done with a decent camera. Mrs. Ambler was holding the chihuahua in this one, too, standing in front of the Winnebago.

"She used to sit on the arm of Jake's chair while he drove and when we came to a red light she'd look at it, and when it turned green she'd bark to tell him to go. She was the smartest little thing."

I looked at the dog's flaring, pointed ears, its bulging eyes and rat's snout. The dogs never come through. I took dozens of pictures, there at the end, and they might as well have been calendar shots. Nothing of the real dog at all. I decided it was the lack of muscles in their faces—they could not smile, in spite of what their owners claimed. It is the muscles in the face that make people leap across the years in pictures. The expressions on dogs' faces were what breeding had fastened on them—the gloomy bloodhound, the alert collie, the rakish mutt—and anything else was wishful thinking on the part of the doting master, who would also swear that a color-blind chihuahua with a brain pan the size of a Mexican jumping bean could tell when the light changed.

My theory of the facial muscles doesn't really hold water, of course. Cats can't smile either, and they come through. Smugness, slyness, disdain—all of those expressions come through beautifully, and they don't have any muscles in their faces either, so maybe it's love that you can't capture in a picture because love was the only expression dogs were capable of.

I was still looking at the picture. "She is a cute little thing," I said and handed it back to her. "She wasn't very big, was she?"

"I could carry Taco in my jacket pocket. We didn't name her Taco. We got her from a man in California that named her that," she said, as if she could see herself that the dog didn't come through in the picture. As if, had she named the dog herself, it would have been different. Then the name would have been a more real name, and Taco would have, by default, become more real as well. As if a name could convey what the picture didn't—all the things the little dog did and was and meant to her.

Names don't do it either, of course. I had named Aberfan myself. The vet's assistant, when he heard it, typed it in as Abraham.

"Age?" he had said calmly, even though he had no business typing all this into a computer, he should have been in the operating room with the vet.

"You've got that in there, damn it," I shouted.

He looked calmly puzzled. "I don't know any Abraham . . ."

"Aberfan, damn it. Aberfan!"

"Here it is," the assistant said imperturbably.

Katie, standing across the desk, looked up from the screen. "He had the newparvo and lived through it?" she said bleakly.

"He had the newparvo and lived through it," I said, "until you came along."

"I had an Australian shepherd," I told Mrs. Ambler.

Jake came into the Winnebago, carrying the plastic bucket. "Well, it's about time," Mrs. Ambler said. "Your coffee's getting cold."

"I was just going to finish washing off Winnie," he said. He wedged the bucket into the tiny sink and began pumping vigorously with the heel of his hand. "She got mighty dusty coming down through all that sand."

"I was telling Mr. McCombe here about Taco," she said, getting up and taking him the cup and saucer. "Here, drink your coffee before it gets cold."

"I'll be in in a minute," he said. He stopped pumping and tugged the bucket out of the sink.

"Mr. McCombe had a dog," she said, still holding the cup out to him. "He had an Australian shepherd. I was telling him about Taco."

"He's not interested in that," Jake said. They exchanged one of those warning looks that married couples are so good at. "Tell him about the Winnebago. That's what he's here for."

Jake went back outside. I screwed the longshot's lens cap on and put the vidcam back in its case. She took the little pan off the miniature stove and poured the coffee back into it. "I think I've got all the pictures I need," I said to her back.

She didn't turn around. "He never liked Taco. He wouldn't even let her sleep on the bed with us. Said it made his legs cramp. A little dog like that that didn't weigh anything."

I took the longshot's lens cap back off.

"You know what we were doing the day she died? We were out shopping. I didn't want to leave her alone, but Jake said she'd be fine. It was ninety degrees that day, and he just kept on going from store to store, and when we got back she was dead." She set the pan on the stove and turned on the burner. "The vet said it was the newparvo, but it wasn't. She died from the heat, poor little thing."

I set the Nikon down gently on the formica table and estimated the settings.

"When did Taco die?" I asked her, to make her turn around.

"Ninety," she said. She turned back to me, and I let my hand come down on the button in an almost soundless click, but her public face was still in place: apologetic now, smiling, a little sheepish. "My, that was a long time ago."

I stood up and collected my cameras. "I think I've got all the pictures I need," I said again. "If I don't, I'll come back out."

"Don't forget your briefcase," she said, handing me the eisenstadt. "Did your dog die of the newparvo, too?"

"He died fifteen years ago," I said. "In ninety-three."

She nodded understandingly. "The third wave," she said.

I went outside. Jake was standing behind the Winnebago, under the back window, holding the bucket. He shifted it to his left hand and held out his right hand to me. "You get all the pictures you needed?" he asked.

"Yeah," I said. "I think your wife showed me about everything." I shook his hand.

"You come on back out if you need any more pictures," he said, and sounded, if possible, even more jovial, open-handed, friendly than he had before. "Mrs. Ambler and me, we always cooperate with the media."

"Your wife was telling me about your chihuahua," I said, more to see the effect on him than anything else.

"Yeah, the wife still misses that little dog after all these years," he said, and he looked the way she had, mildly apologetic, still smiling. "It died of the newparvo. I told her she ought to get it vaccinated, but she kept putting it off." He shook his head. "Of course, it wasn't really her fault. You know whose fault the newparvo really was, don't you?"

Yeah, I knew. It was the communists' fault, and it didn't matter that all their dogs had died, too, because he would say their chemical warfare had gotten out of hand or that everybody knows commies hate dogs. Or maybe it was the fault of the Japanese, though I doubted that. He was, after all, in a tourist business. Or the Democrats or the atheists or all of them put together, and even that was One Hundred Percent Authentic—portrait of the kind of man who drives a Winnebago—but I didn't want to hear it. I walked over to the Hitori and slung the eisenstadt in the back.

"You know who really killed your dog, don't you?" he called after me.

"Yes," I said, and got in the car.

I went home, fighting my way through a fleet of red-painted water tankers who weren't even bothering to try to outrun the cameras and thinking about Taco. My grandmother had had a chihuahua. Perdita. Meanest dog that ever lived. Used to lurk behind the door waiting to take Labrador-sized chunks out of my leg. And my grandmother's. It developed some lingering chihuahuan ailment that made it incontinent and even more ill-tempered, if that was possible.

Toward the end, it wouldn't even let my grandmother near it, but she refused to have it put to sleep and was unfailingly kind to it, even though I never saw any indication that the dog felt anything but unrelieved spite toward her. If the newparvo hadn't come along, it probably would still have been around making her life miserable.

I wondered what Taco, the wonder dog, able to distinguish red and green at a single intersection, had really been like, and if it had died of heat prostration. And what it had been like for the Amblers, living all that time in a hundred and fifty cubic feet together and blaming each other for their own guilt.

I called Ramirez as soon as I got home, breaking in without announcing myself, the way she always did. "I need a lifeline," I said.

"I'm glad you called," she said. "You got a call from the Society. And how's this as a slant for your story? 'The Winnebago and the Winnebagos.' They're an Indian tribe. In Minnesota, I think—why the hell aren't you at the governor's conference?"

"I came home," I said. "What did the Society want?"

"They didn't say. They asked for your schedule. I told them you were with the governor in Tempe. Is this about a story?"

"Yeah."

"Well, you run a proposal past me before you write it. The last thing the paper needs is to get in trouble with the Society."

"The lifeline's for Katherine Powell." I spelled it.

She spelled it back to me. "Is she connected with the Society story?"

"No."

"Then what is she connected with? I've got to put something on the request-for-info."

"Put down background."

"For the Winnebago story?"

"Yes," I said. "For the Winnebago story. How long will it take?"

"That depends. When do you plan to tell me why you ditched the governor's conference? *And* Taliessin West. Jesus Maria, I'll have to call the *Republic* and see if they'll trade footage. I'm sure they'll be thrilled to have shots of an extinct RV. That is, assuming you got any shots. You did make it out to the zoo, didn't you?"

"Yes. I got vidcam footage, stills, the works. I even used the eisenstadt."

"Mind sending your pictures in while I look up your old flame, or is that too much to ask? I don't know how long this will take. It took me two days to get clearance on the Amblers. Do you want the whole thing—pictures, documentation?"

"No. Just a resume. And a phone number."

She cut out, still not saying goodbye. If phones still had receivers, Ramirez would be a great one for hanging up on people. I highwired the vidcam footage and the eisenstadts in to the paper and then fed the eisenstadt cartridge into the developer. I was more than a little curious about what kind of pictures it would take, in spite of the fact that it was trying to do me out of a job. At least it used high-res film and not some damn two hundred thousand-pixel TV substitute. I didn't believe it could compose, and I doubted if the eisenstadt would be able to do foreground-background either, but it might, under certain circumstances, get a picture I couldn't.

The doorbell rang. I answered the door. A lanky young man in a Hawaiian shirt and baggies was standing on the front step, and there was another man in a Society uniform out in the driveway.

"Mr. McCombe?" he said, extending a hand. "Jim Hunter. Humane Society."

I don't know what I'd expected—that they wouldn't bother to trace the call? That they'd let somebody get away with leaving a dead animal on the road?

"I just wanted to stop by and thank you on behalf of the Society for phoning in that report on the jackal. Can I come in?"

He smiled, an open, friendly, smug smile, as if he expected me to be stupid enough to say, "I don't know what you're talking about," and slam the screen door on his hand.

"Just doing my duty," I said, smiling back at him.

"Well, we really appreciate responsible citizens like you. It makes our job a whole lot easier." He pulled a folded readout from his shirt pocket. "I just need to double-check a couple of things. You're a reporter for Sun-co, is that right?"

"Photo-journalist," I said.

"And the Hitori you were driving belongs to the paper?"

I nodded.

"It has a phone. Why didn't you use it to make the call?"

The uniform was bending over the Hitori.

"I didn't realize it had a phone. The paper just bought the Hitoris. This is only the second time I've had one out."

Since they knew the paper had had phones put in, they also knew what I'd just told them. I wondered where they'd gotten the info. Public phones were supposed to be tap-free, and if they'd read the license number off one of the cameras, they wouldn't know who'd had the car unless they'd talked to Ramirez, and if they'd talked to her, she wouldn't have been talking blithely about the last thing she needed being trouble with the Society.

"You didn't know the car had a phone," he said, "so you drove to—" He consulted the readout, somehow giving the impression he was taking notes. I'd have bet there was a taper in the pocket of that shirt. "—The 7-Eleven at McDowell and Fortieth Street, and made the call from there. Why didn't you give the Society rep your name and address?"

"I was in a hurry," I said. "I had two assignments to cover before noon, the second out in Scottsdale."

"Which is why you didn't render assistance to the animal either. Because you were in a hurry."

You bastard, I thought. "No," I said. "I didn't render assistance because there wasn't any assistance to be rendered. The—it was dead."

"And how did you know that, Mr. McCombe?"

"There was blood coming out of its mouth," I said.

I had thought that that was a good sign, that he wasn't bleeding anywhere else. The blood had come out of Aberfan's mouth when he tried to lift his head, just a little trickle, sinking into the hard-packed snow. It had stopped before we even got him into the car. "It's all right, boy," I told him. "We'll be there in a minute."

Katie started the jeep, killed it, started it again, backed it up to where she could turn around.

Aberfan lay limply across my lap, his tail against the gear shift. "Just lie still, boy," I said. I patted his neck. It was wet, and I raised my hand and looked at the palm, afraid it was blood. It was only water from the melted snow. I dried his neck and the top of his head with the sleeve of my sweater.

"How far is it?" Katie said. She was clutching the steering wheel with both hands and sitting stiffly forward in the seat. The windshield wipers flipped back and forth, trying to keep up with the snow.

"About five miles," I said, and she stepped on the gas pedal and then let up on it again as we began to skid. "On the right side of the highway."

Aberfan raised his head off my lap and looked at me. His gums were gray, and he was panting, but I couldn't see any more blood. He tried to lick my hand. "You'll make it, Aberfan," I said. "You made it before, remember?"

"But you didn't get out of the car and go check, to make sure it was dead?" Hunter said.

"No."

"And you don't have any idea who hit the jackal?" he said, and made it sound like the accusation it was.

"No."

He glanced back at the uniform, who had moved around the car to the other side. "Whew," Hunter said, shaking his Hawaiian collar, "it's like an oven out here. Mind if I come in?" which meant the uniform needed more privacy. Well, then, by all means, give him more privacy. The sooner he sprayed print-fix on the bumper and tires and peeled off the incriminating traces of jackal blood that weren't there and stuck them in the evidence bags he was carrying in the pockets of that uniform, the sooner they'd leave. I opened the screen door wider.

"Oh, this is great," Hunter said, still trying to generate a breeze with his collar. "These old adobe houses stay so cool." He glanced around the room at the developer and the enlarger, the couch, the dry-mounted photographs on the wall. "You don't have any idea who might have hit the jackal?"

"I figure it was a tanker," I said. "What else would be on Van Buren that time of morning?"

I was almost sure it had been a car or a small truck. A tanker would have left the jackal a spot on the pavement. But a tanker would get a license suspension and two weeks of having to run water into Santa Fe instead of Phoenix, and probably not that. Rumor at the paper had it the Society was in the water board's pocket. If it was a car, on the other hand, the Society would take away the car and stick its driver with a prison sentence.

"They're all trying to beat the cameras," I said. "The tanker probably didn't even know it'd hit it."

"What?" he said.

"I said, it had to be a tanker. There isn't anything else on Van Buren during rush hour."

I expected him to say, "Except for you," but he didn't. He wasn't even listening. "Is this your dog?" he said.

He was looking at the photograph of Perdita. "No," I said. "That was my grandmother's dog."

"What is it?"

A nasty little beast. And when it died of the newparvo, my grandmother had cried like a baby. "A chihuahua."

He looked around at the other walls. "Did you take all these pictures of dogs?" His whole manner had changed, taking on a politeness that made me realize just how insolent he had intended to be before. The one on the road wasn't the only jackal around.

"Some of them," I said. He was looking at the photograph next to it. "I didn't take that one."

"I know what this one is," he said, pointing at it. "It's a boxer, right?"

"An English bulldog," I said.

"Oh, right. Weren't those the ones that were exterminated? For being vicious?"

"No," I said.

He moved on to the picture over the developer, like a tourist in a museum. "I bet you didn't take this one either," he said, pointing at the high shoes, the old-fashioned hat on the stout old woman holding the dogs in her arms.

"That's a photograph of Beatrix Potter, the English children's author," I said. "She wrote *Peter Rabbit.*"

He wasn't interested. "What kind of dogs are those?"

"Pekingese."

"It's a great picture of them."

It is, in fact, a terrible picture of them. One of them has wrenched his face away from the camera, and the other sits grimly in her owner's hand, waiting for its chance. Obviously neither of them liked having its picture taken, though you can't tell that from their expressions. They reveal nothing in their little flat-nosed faces, in their black little eyes.

Beatrix Potter, on the other hand, comes through beautifully, in spite of the attempt to smile for the camera and the fact that she must have had to hold onto the Pekes for dear life, or maybe because of that. The fierce, humorous love she felt for her fierce, humorous little dogs is all there in her face. She must never, in spite of *Peter Rabbit* and its attendant fame, have developed a public face. Everything she felt was right there, unprotected, unshuttered. Like Katie.

"Are any of these your dog?" Hunter asked. He was standing looking at the picture of Misha that hung above the couch.

"No," I said.

"How come you don't have any pictures of your dog?" he asked, and I wondered how he knew I had had a dog and what else he knew.

"He didn't like having his picture taken."

He folded up the readout, stuck it in his pocket, and turned around to look at the photo of Perdita again. "He looks like he was a real nice little dog," he said.

The uniform was waiting on the front step, obviously finished with whatever he had done to the car.

"We'll let you know if we find out who's responsible," Hunter said, and they left. On the way out to the street the uniform tried to tell him what he'd found, but Hunter cut him off. The suspect has a house full of photographs of dogs, therefore he didn't run over a poor facsimile of one on Van Buren this morning. Case closed.

I went back over to the developer and fed the eisenstadt film in. "Positives, one two three order, five seconds," I said, and watched as the pictures came up on the developer's screen. Ramirez had said the eisenstadt automatically turned on whenever it was set upright on a level surface. She was right. It had taken a half-dozen shots on the way out to Tempe. Two shots of the Hitori it must have taken when I set it down to load the car, open door of same with prickly pear in the foreground, a blurred shot of palm trees and buildings with a minuscule, sharp-focused glimpse of the traffic on the expressway. Vehicles and people. There was a great shot of the red tanker that had clipped the jackal and ten or so of the yucca I had parked next to at the foot of the hill.

It had gotten two nice shots of my forearm as I set it down on the kitchen counter of the Winnebago and some beautifully composed still lifes of Melmac with Spoons. Vehicles and people. The rest of the pictures were dead losses: my back, the open bathroom door, Jake's back, and Mrs. Ambler's public face.

Except the last one. She had been standing right in front of the eisenstadt, looking almost directly into the lens. "When I think of that poor thing, all alone," she had said, and by the time she turned around she had her public face back on, but for a minute there, looking at what she thought was a briefcase and remembering, there she was, the person I had tried all morning to get a picture of.

I took it into the living room and sat down and looked at it awhile.

"So you knew this Katherine Powell in Colorado," Ramirez said, breaking in without preamble, and the highwire slid silently forward and began to print out the lifeline. "I always suspected you of having some deep dark secret in your past. Is she the reason you moved to Phoenix?"

I was watching the highwire advance the paper. Katherine Powell. 4628 Dutchman Drive, Apache Junction. Forty miles away.

"Holy Mother, you were really cradle-robbing. According to my calculations, she was seventeen when you lived there."

Sixteen.

"Are you the owner of the dog?" the vet had asked her, his face slackening into pity when he saw how young she was.

"No," she said. "I'm the one who hit him."

"My God," he said. "How old are you?"

"Sixteen," she said, and her face was wide open. "I just got my license."

"Aren't you even going to tell me what she has to do with this Winnebago thing?" Ramirez said.

"I moved down here to get away from the snow," I said, and cut out without saying goodbye.

The lifeline was still rolling silently forward. Hacker at Hewlett-Packard. Fired in ninety-nine, probably during the unionization. Divorced. Two kids. She had moved to Arizona five years after I did. Management programmer for Toshiba. Arizona driver's license.

I went back to the developer and looked at the picture of Mrs. Ambler. I had said dogs never came through. That wasn't true. Taco wasn't in the blurry snapshots Mrs. Ambler had been so anxious to show me, in the stories she had been so anxious to tell. But she was in this picture, reflected in the pain and love and loss on Mrs. Ambler's face. I could see her plain as day, perched on the arm of the driver's seat, barking impatiently when the light turned green.

I put a new cartridge in the eisenstadt and went out to see Katie.

I had to take Van Buren—it was almost four o'clock, and the rush hour would have started on the divideds—but the jackal was gone anyway. The Society is efficient. Like Hitler and his Nazis.

"Why don't you have any pictures of your dog?" Hunter had asked. The question could have been based on the assumption that anyone who would fill his living room with photographs of dogs must have had one of his own, but it wasn't. He had known about Aberfan, which meant he'd had access to my lifeline, which meant all kinds of things. My lifeline was privacy-coded, so I had to be notified before anybody could get access, except, it appeared, the Society. A reporter I knew at the paper, Dolores Chiwere, had tried to do a story a while back claiming that the Society had an illegal link to the lifeline banks, but she hadn't been able to come up with enough evidence to convince her editor. I wondered if this counted.

The lifeline would have told them about Aberfan but not about how he died. Killing a dog wasn't a crime in those days, and I hadn't pressed charges against Katie for reckless driving or even called the police.

"I think you should," the vet's assistant had said. "There are less than a hundred dogs left. People can't just go around killing them."

"My God, man, it was snowing and slick," the vet had said angrily, "and she's just a kid."

"She's old enough to have a license," I said, looking at Katie. She was fumbling in her purse for her driver's license. "She's old enough to have been on the roads."

Katie found her license and gave it to me. It was so new it was still shiny. Katherine Powell. She had turned sixteen two weeks ago.

"This won't bring him back," the vet had said, and taken the license out of my hand and given it back to her. "You go on home now."

"I need her name for the records," the vet's assistant had said.

She had stepped forward. "Katie Powell," she had said.

"We'll do the paperwork later," the vet had said firmly.

They never did do the paperwork, though. The next week the third wave hit, and I suppose there hadn't seemed any point.

I slowed down at the zoo entrance and looked up into the parking lot as I went past. The Amblers were doing a booming business. There were at least five cars and twice as many kids clustered around the Winnebago.

"Where the hell are you?" Ramirez said. "And where the hell are your pictures? I talked the *Republic* into a trade, but they insisted on scoop rights. I need your stills now!"

"I'll send them in as soon as I get home," I said. "I'm on a story."

"The hell you are! You're on your way out to see your old girlfriend. Well, not on the paper's credits, you're not."

"Did you get the stuff on the Winnebago Indians?" I asked her.

"Yes. They were in Wisconsin, but they're not anymore. In the mid-seventies there were sixteen hundred of them on the reservation and about forty-five hundred altogether, but by 1990, the number was down to five hundred, and now they don't think there are any left, and nobody knows what happened to them."

I'll tell you what happened to them, I thought. Almost all of them were killed in the first wave, and people blamed the government and the Japanese and the ozone layer, and after the second wave hit, the Society passed all kinds of laws to protect the survivors, but it was too late, they were already below the minimum survival population limit, and then the third wave polished off the rest of them, and the last of the Winnebagos sat in a cage somewhere, and if I had been there I would probably have taken his picture.

"I called the Bureau of Indian Affairs," Ramirez said, "and they're supposed to call me back, and you don't give a damn about the Winnebagos. You just wanted to get me off the subject. What's this story you're on?"

I looked around the dashboard for an exclusion button.

"What the hell is going on, David? First you ditch two big stories, now you can't even get your pictures in. Jesus, if something's wrong, you can tell me. I want to help. It has something to do with Colorado, doesn't it?"

I found the button and cut her off.

Van Buren got crowded as the afternoon rush spilled over off the divideds. Out past the curve, where Van Buren turns into Apache Boulevard, they were putting in new lanes. The cement forms were already up on the eastbound side, and they were building the wooden forms up in two of the six lanes on my side.

The Amblers must have just beaten the workmen, though at the rate the men were working right now, leaning on their shovels in the hot afternoon sun and smoking stew, it had probably taken them six weeks to do this stretch.

Mesa was still open multiway, but as soon as I was through downtown, the construction started again, and this stretch was nearly done—forms up on both sides and most of the cement poured. The Amblers couldn't have come in from Globe on this road. The lanes were barely wide enough for the Hitori, and the tanker lanes were gated. Superstition is full-divided, and the old highway down from Roosevelt is, too, which meant they hadn't come in from Globe at all. I wondered how they had come in—probably in some tanker lane on a multiway.

"Oh, my, the things we've seen," Mrs. Ambler had said. I wondered how much they'd been able to see skittering across the dark desert like a couple of kangaroo mice, trying to beat the cameras.

The roadworkers didn't have the new exit signs up yet, and I missed the exit for Apache Junction and had to go halfway to Superior, trapped in my narrow, cement-sided lane, till I hit a change-lanes and could get turned around.

Katie's address was in Superstition Estates, a development pushed up as close to the base of Superstition Mountain as it could get. I thought about what I would say to Katie when I got there. I had said maybe ten sentences altogether to her, most of them shouted directions, in the two hours we had been together. In the jeep on the way to the vet's I had talked to Aberfan, and after we got there, sitting in the waiting room, we hadn't talked at all.

It occurred to me that I might not recognize her. I didn't really remember what she looked like—only the sunburned nose and that terrible openness, and now, fifteen years later, it seemed unlikely that she would have either of them. The Arizona sun would have taken care of the first, and she had gotten married and divorced, been fired, had who knows what else happen to her in fifteen years to close her face. In which case, there had been no point in my driving all the way out here. But Mrs. Ambler had had an almost impenetrable public face, and you could still catch her off-guard. If you got her talking about the dogs. If she didn't know she was being photographed.

Katie's house was an old-style passive solar, with flat black panels on the roof. It looked presentable, but not compulsively neat. There wasn't any grass—tankers won't waste their credits coming this far out, and Apache Junction isn't big enough to match the bribes and incentives of Phoenix or Tempe—but the front yard was laid out with alternating patches of black lava chips and prickly pear. The side yard had a parched-looking palo verde tree, and there was a cat tied to it. A little girl was playing under it with toy cars.

I took the eisenstadt out of the back and went up to the front door and rang the bell. At the last moment, when it was too late to change my mind, walk away, because she was already opening the screen door, it occurred to me that she might not recognize me, that I might have to tell her who I was.

Her nose wasn't sunburned, and she had put on the weight a sixteen-year-old puts on to get to be thirty, but otherwise she looked the same as she had that day in front of my house. And her face hadn't completely closed. I could tell, looking at her, that she recognized me and that she had known I was coming. She must have put a notify on her lifeline to have them warn her if I asked her whereabouts. I thought about what that meant.

She opened the screen door a little, the way I had to the Humane Society. "What do you want?" she said.

I had never seen her angry, not even when I turned on her at the vet's. "I wanted to see you," I said.

I had thought I might tell her I had run across her name while I was working on a story and wondered if it was the same person or that I was doing a piece on the last of the passive solars. "I saw a dead jackal on the road this morning," I said.

"And you thought I killed it?" she said. She tried to shut the screen door.

I put out my hand without thinking to stop her. "No," I said. I took my hand off the door. "No, of course I don't think that. Can I come in? I just want to talk to you."

The little girl had come over, clutching her toy cars to her pink T-shirt, and was standing off to the side, watching curiously.

"Come on inside, Jana," Katie said, and opened the screen door a fraction wider. The little girl scooted through. "Go on in the kitchen," she said. "I'll fix you some Kool-Aid." She looked up at me. "I used to have nightmares about your coming. I'd dream that I'd go to the door and there you'd be."

"It's really hot out here," I said and knew I sounded like Hunter. "Can I come in?"

She opened the screen door all the way. "I've got to make my daughter something to drink," she said, and led the way into the kitchen, the little girl dancing in front of her.

"What kind of Kool-Aid do you want?" Katie asked her, and she shouted, "Red!"

The kitchen counter faced the stove, refrigerator, and water cooler across a narrow aisle that opened out into an alcove with a table and chairs. I put the eisenstadt down on the table and then sat down myself so she wouldn't suggest moving into another room.

Katie reached a plastic pitcher down from one of the shelves and stuck it under the water tank to fill it. Jana dumped her cars on the counter, clambered up beside them, and began opening the cupboard doors.

"How old's your little girl?" I asked.

Katie got a wooden spoon out of the drawer next to the stove and brought it and the pitcher over to the table. "She's four," she said. "Did you find the Kool-Aid?" she asked the little girl.

"Yes," the little girl said, but it wasn't Kool-Aid. It was a pinkish cube she peeled a plastic wrapping off of. It fizzed and turned a thinnish red when she dropped it in the pitcher. Kool-Aid must have become extinct, too, along with Winnebagos and passive solar. Or else changed beyond recognition. Like the Humane Society.

Katie poured the red stuff into a glass with a cartoon whale on it.

"Is she your only one?" I asked.

"No, I have a little boy," she said, but warily, as if she wasn't sure she wanted to tell me, even though if I'd requested the lifeline I already had access to all this information. Jana asked if she could have a cookie and then took it and her Kool-Aid back down the hall and outside. I could hear the screen door slam.

Katie put the pitcher in the refrigerator and leaned against the kitchen counter, her arms folded across her chest. "What do you want?"

She was just out of range of the eisenstadt, her face in the shadow of the narrow aisle.

"There was a dead jackal on the road this morning," I said. I kept my voice low so she would lean forward into the light to try and hear me. "It'd been hit by a car, and it was lying funny, at an angle. It looked like a dog. I wanted to talk to somebody who remembered Aberfan, somebody who knew him."

"I didn't know him," she said. "I only killed him, remember? That's why you did this, isn't it, because I killed Aberfan?"

She didn't look at the eisenstadt, hadn't even glanced at it when I set it on the table, but I wondered suddenly if she knew what I was up to. She was still carefully out of range. And what if I said to her, "That's right. That's why I did this, because you killed him, and I didn't have any pictures of him. You owe me. If I can't have a picture of Aberfan, you at least owe me a picture of you remembering him."

Only she didn't remember him, didn't know anything about him except what she had seen on the way to the vet's, Aberfan lying on my lap and looking up at me, already dying. I had had no business coming here, dredging all this up again. No business.

"At first I thought you were going to have me arrested," Katie said, "and then after all the dogs died, I thought you were going to kill me."

The screen door banged. "Forgot my cars," the little girl said and scooped them into the tail of her T-shirt. Katie tousled her hair as she went past, and then folded her arms again.

" 'It wasn't my fault,' I was going to tell you when you came to kill me," she said. " 'It was snowy. He ran right in front of me. I didn't even see him.' I looked up everything I could find about newparvo. Preparing for the defense. How it mutated from parvovirus and from cat distemper before that and then kept on mutating, so they couldn't come up with a vaccine. How even before the third wave they were below the minimum survival population. How it was the fault of the people who owned the last survivors because they wouldn't risk their dogs to breed them. How the scientists didn't come up with a vaccine until only the jackals were left. 'You're wrong,' I was going to tell you. 'It was the puppy mill owners' fault that all the dogs died. If they hadn't kept their dogs in such unsanitary conditions, it never would have gotten out of control in the first place.' I had my defense all ready. But you'd moved away."

Jana banged in again, carrying the empty whale glass. She had a red smear across the whole lower half of her face. "I need some more," she said, making "some more" into one word. She held the glass in both hands while Katie opened the refrigerator and poured her another glassful.

"Wait a minute, honey," she said. "You've got Kool-Aid all over you," and bent to wipe Jana's face with a paper towel.

Katie hadn't said a word in her defense while we waited at the vet's, not, "It was snowy," or, "He ran right out in front of me," or, "I didn't even see him." She had sat silently beside me, twisting her mittens in her lap, until the vet came out and told me Aberfan was dead, and then she had said, "I didn't know there were any left in Colorado. I thought they were all dead."

And I had turned to her, to a sixteen-year-old not even old enough to know how to shut her face, and said, "Now they all are. Thanks to you."

"That kind of talk isn't necessary," the vet had said warningly.

I had wrenched away from the hand he tried to put on my shoulder. "How does it feel to have killed one of the last dogs in the world?" I shouted at her. "How does it feel to be responsible for the extinction of an entire species?"

The screen door banged again. Katie was looking at me, still holding the reddened paper towel.

"You moved away," she said, "and I thought maybe that meant you'd forgiven me, but it didn't, did it?" She came over to the table and wiped at the red circle the glass had left. "Why did you do it? To punish me? Or did you think that's what I'd been doing the last fifteen years, roaring around the roads murdering animals?"

"What?" I said.

"The Society's already been here."

"The Society?" I said, not understanding.

"Yes," she said, still looking at the red-stained towel. "They said you had reported a dead animal on Van Buren. They wanted to know where I was this morning between eight and nine A.M."

I nearly ran down a roadworker on the way back into Phoenix. He leaped for the still-wet cement barrier, dropping the shovel he'd been leaning on all day, and I ran right over it.

The Society had already been there. They had left my house and gone straight to hers. Only that wasn't possible, because I hadn't even called Katie then. I hadn't even seen the picture of Mrs. Ambler yet. Which meant they had gone to see Ramirez after they left me, and the last thing Ramirez and the paper needed was trouble with the Society.

"I thought it was suspicious when he didn't go to the governor's conference," she had told them, "and just now he called and asked for a lifeline on this person here. Katherine Powell. 4628 Dutchman Drive. He knew her in Colorado."

"Ramirez!" I shouted at the car phone. "I want to talk to you!" There wasn't any answer.

I swore at her for a good ten miles before I remembered I had the exclusion button on. I punched it off. "Ramirez, where the hell are you?"

"I could ask you the same question," she said. She sounded even angrier than Katie, but not as angry as I was. "You cut me off, you won't tell me what's going on."

"So you decided you had it figured out for yourself, and you told your little theory to the Society."

"What?" she said, and I recognized that tone, too. I had heard it in my own voice when Katie told me the Society had been there. Ramirez hadn't told anybody anything, she didn't even know what I was talking about, but I was going too fast to stop.

"You told the Society I'd asked for Katie's lifeline, didn't you?" I shouted.

"No," she said. "I didn't. Don't you think it's time you told me what's going on?"

"Did the Society come see you this afternoon?"

"No. I told you. They called this morning and wanted to talk to you. I told them you were at the governor's conference."

"And they didn't call back later?"

"No. Are you in trouble?"

I hit the exclusion button. "Yes," I said. "Yes, I'm in trouble."

Ramirez hadn't told them. Maybe somebody else at the paper had, but I didn't think so. There had after all been Dolores Chiwere's story about them having illegal access to the lifelines. "How come you don't have any pictures of your dog?" Hunter had asked me, which meant they'd read my lifeline, too. So they knew we had both lived in Colorado, in the same town, when Aberfan died.

"What did you tell them?" I had demanded of Katie. She had been standing there in the kitchen still messing with the Kool-Aid-stained towel, and I had wanted to yank it out of her hands and make her look at me. "What did you tell the Society?"

She looked up at me. "I told them I was on Indian School Road, picking up the month's programming assignments from my company. Unfortunately, I could just as easily have driven in on Van Buren."

"About Aberfan!" I shouted. "What did you tell them about Aberfan?"

She looked steadily at me. "I didn't tell them anything. I assumed you'd already told them."

I had taken hold of her shoulders. "If they come back, don't tell them anything. Not even if they arrest you. I'll take care of this. I'll . . ."

But I hadn't told her what I'd do because I didn't know. I had run out of her house, colliding with Jana in the hall on her way in for another refill, and roared off for home, even though I didn't have any idea what I would do when I got there.

Call the Society and tell them to leave Katie alone, that she had nothing to do with this? That would be even more suspicious than everything else I'd done so far, and you couldn't get much more suspicious than that.

I had seen a dead jackal on the road (or so I said), and instead of reporting it immediately on the phone right there in my car, I'd driven to a convenience store two miles away. I'd called the Society, but I'd refused to give them my name and number. And then I'd canceled two shoots without telling my boss and asked for the lifeline of one Katherine Powell, whom I had known fifteen years ago and who could have been on Van Buren at the time of the accident.

The connection was obvious, and how long would it take them to make the connection that fifteen years ago was when Aberfan had died?

Apache was beginning to fill up with rush hour overflow and a whole fleet of tankers. The overflow obviously spent all their time driving divideds—nobody bothered to signal that they were changing lanes. Nobody even gave an indication that they knew what a lane was. Going around the curve from Tempe and onto Van Buren they were all over the road. I moved over into the tanker lane.

My lifeline didn't have the vet's name on it. They were just getting started in those days, and there was a lot of nervousness about invasion of privacy. Nothing went online without the person's permission, especially not medical and bank records, and the lifelines were little more than puff bios: family, occupation, hobbies, pets. The only things on the lifeline besides Aberfan's name was the date of his death and my address at the time, but that was probably enough. There were only two vets in town.

The vet hadn't written Katie's name down on Aberfan's record. He had handed her driver's license back to her without even looking at it, but Katie had told her name to the vet's assistant. He might have written it down. There was no way I could find out. I couldn't ask for the vet's lifeline because the Society had access to the lifelines. They'd get to him before I could. I could maybe have the paper get the vet's records for me, but I'd have to tell Ramirez what was going on, and the phone was probably tapped, too. And if I showed up at the paper, Ramirez would confiscate the car. I couldn't go there.

Wherever the hell I was going, I was driving too fast to get there. When the tanker ahead of me slowed down to ninety, I practically climbed up his back bumper. I had gone past the place where the jackal had been hit without ever seeing it. Even without the traffic, there probably hadn't been anything to see. What the Society hadn't taken care of, the overflow probably had, and anyway, there hadn't been any evidence to begin with. If there had been, if the cameras had seen the car that hit it, they wouldn't have come after me. And Katie.

The Society couldn't charge her with Aberfan's death—killing an animal hadn't been a crime back then—but if they found out about Aberfan they would charge her with the jackal's death, and it wouldn't matter if a hundred witnesses, a hundred highway cameras had seen her on Indian School Road. It wouldn't matter if the print-fix on her car was clean. She had killed one of the last dogs, hadn't she? They would crucify her.

I should never have left Katie. "Don't tell them anything," I had told her, but she had never been afraid of admitting guilt. When the receptionist had asked her what had happened, she had said, "I hit him," just like that, no attempt to make excuses, to run off, to lay the blame on someone else.

I had run off to try to stop the Society from finding out that Katie had hit Aberfan, and meanwhile the Society was probably back at Katie's, asking her how she'd happened to know me in Colorado, asking her how Aberfan died.

I was wrong about the Society. They weren't at Katie's house. They were at mine, standing on the porch, waiting for me to let them in.

"You're a hard man to track down," Hunter said.

The uniform grinned. "Where you been?"

"Sorry," I said, fishing my keys out of my pocket. "I thought you were all done with me. I've already told you everything I know about the incident."

Hunter stepped back just far enough for me to get the screen door open and the key in the lock. "Officer Segura and I just need to ask you a couple more questions."

"Where'd you go this afternoon?" Segura asked.

"I went to see an old friend of mine."

"Who?"

"Come on, come on," Hunter said. "Let the guy get in his own front door before you start badgering him with a lot of questions."

I opened the door. "Did the cameras get a picture of the tanker that hit the jackal?" I asked.

"Tanker?" Segura said.

"I told you," I said, "I figure it had to be a tanker. The jackal was lying in the tanker lane." I led the way into the living room, depositing my keys on the computer and switching the phone to exclusion while I talked. The last thing I needed was Ramirez bursting in with, "What's going on? Are you in trouble?"

"It was probably a renegade that hit it, which would explain why he didn't stop." I gestured at them to sit down.

Hunter did. Segura started for the couch and then stopped, staring at the photos on the wall above it. "Jesus, will you look at all the dogs!" he said. "Did you take all these pictures?"

"I took some of them. That one in the middle is Misha."

"The last dog, right?"

"Yes," I said.

"No kidding. The very last one."

No kidding. She was being kept in isolation at the Society's research facility in St. Louis when I saw her. I had talked them into letting me shoot her, but it had to be from outside the quarantine area. The picture had an unfocused look that came from shooting it through a wire mesh-reinforced window in the door, but I wouldn't have done any better if they'd let me inside. Misha was past having any expression to photograph. She hadn't eaten in a week at that point. She lay with her head on her paws, staring at the door, the whole time I was there.

"You wouldn't consider selling this picture to the Society, would you?"

"No, I wouldn't."

He nodded understandingly. "I guess people were pretty upset when she died."

Pretty upset. They had turned on anyone who had anything to do with it—the puppy mill owners, the scientists who hadn't come up with a vaccine, Misha's vet—and a lot of others who hadn't. And they had handed over their civil rights to a bunch of jackals who were able to grab them because everybody felt so guilty. Pretty upset.

"What's this one?" Segura asked. He had already moved on to the picture next to it.

"It's General Patton's bull terrier Willie."

They fed and cleaned up after Misha with those robot arms they used to use in the nuclear plants. Her owner, a tired-looking woman, was allowed to watch her through the wire-mesh window but had to stay off to the side because Misha flung herself barking against the door whenever she saw her.

"You should make them let you in," I had told her. "It's cruel to keep her locked up like that. You should make them let you take her back home."

"And let her get the newparvo?" she said.

There was nobody left for Misha to get the newparvo from, but I didn't say that. I set the light readings on the camera, trying not to lean into Misha's line of vision.

"You know what killed them, don't you?" she said. "The ozone layer. All those holes. The radiation got in and caused it."

It was the communists, it was the Mexicans, it was the government. And the only people who acknowledged their guilt weren't guilty at all.

"This one here looks kind of like a jackal," Segura said. He was looking at a picture I had taken of a German shepherd after Aberfan died. "Dogs were a lot like jackals, weren't they?"

"No," I said, and sat down on the shelf in front of the developer's screen, across from Hunter. "I already told you everything I know about the jackal. I saw it lying in the road, and I called you."

"You said when you saw the jackal it was in the far right lane," Hunter said.

"That's right."

"And you were in the far left lane?"

"I was in the far left lane."

They were going to take me over my story, point by point, and when I couldn't remember what I'd said before, they were going to say, "Are you sure that's what you saw, Mr. McCombe? Are you sure you didn't see the jackal get hit? Katherine Powell hit it, didn't she?"

"You told us this morning you stopped, but the jackal was already dead. Is that right?" Hunter asked.

"No," I said.

Segura looked up. Hunter touched his hand casually to his pocket and then brought it back to his knee, turning on the taper.

"I didn't stop for about a mile. Then I backed up and looked at it, but it was dead. There was blood coming out of its mouth."

Hunter didn't say anything. He kept his hands on his knees and waited—an old journalist's trick, if you wait long enough, they'll say something they didn't intend to, just to fill the silence.

"The jackal's body was at a peculiar angle," I said, right on cue. "The way it was lying, it didn't look like a jackal. I thought it was a dog." I waited till the silence got uncomfortable again. "It brought back a lot of terrible memories," I said. "I wasn't even thinking: I just wanted to get away from it. After a few minutes I realized I should have called the Society, and I stopped at the 7-Eleven."

I waited again, till Segura began to shoot uncomfortable glances at Hunter, and then started in again. "I thought I'd be okay, that I could go ahead and work, but after I got to my first shoot, I knew I wasn't going to make it, so I came home." Candor. Openness. If the Amblers can do it, so can you. "I guess I was still in shock or something. I didn't even call my boss and have her get somebody to cover the governor's conference. All I could think about was—" I stopped and rubbed my hand across my face. "I needed to talk to somebody. I had the paper look up an old friend of mine, Katherine Powell."

I stopped, I hoped this time for good. I had admitted lying to them and confessed to two crimes: leaving the scene of the accident and using press access to get a lifeline for personal use, and maybe that would be enough to satisfy them. I didn't want to say anything about going out to see Katie. They would know she would have told me about their visit and decide this confession was an attempt to get her off, and maybe they'd been watching the house and knew it anyway, and this was all wasted effort.

The silence dragged on. Hunter's hands tapped his knees twice and then subsided. The story didn't explain why I'd picked Katie, who I hadn't seen in fifteen years, who I knew in Colorado, to go see, but maybe, maybe they wouldn't make the connection.

"This Katherine Powell," Hunter said, "you knew her in Colorado, is that right?"

"We lived in the same little town."

We waited.

"Isn't that when your dog died?" Segura said suddenly. Hunter shot him a glance of pure rage, and I thought, it isn't a taper he's got in that shirt pocket. It's the vet's records, and Katie's name is on them.

"Yes," I said. "He died in September of eighty-nine."

Segura opened his mouth.

"In the third wave?" Hunter asked before he could say anything.

"No," I said. "He was hit by a car."

They both looked genuinely shocked. The Amblers could have taken lessons from them. "Who hit it?" Segura asked, and Hunter leaned forward, his hand moving reflexively toward his pocket.

"I don't know," I said. "It was a hit and run. Whoever it was just left him lying there in the road. That's why when I saw the jackal, it . . . that was how I met Katherine Powell. She stopped and helped me. She helped me get him into her car, and we took him to the vet's, but it was too late."

Hunter's public face was pretty indestructible, but Segura's wasn't. He looked surprised and enlightened and disappointed all at once.

"That's why I wanted to see her," I said unnecessarily.

"Your dog was hit on what day?" Hunter asked.

"September thirtieth."

"What was the vet's name?"

He hadn't changed his way of asking the questions, but he no longer cared what the answers were. He had thought he'd found a connection, a cover-up, but here we were, a couple of dog lovers, a couple of good Samaritans, and his theory had collapsed. He was done with the interview, he was just finishing up, and all I had to do was be careful not to relax too soon.

I frowned, "I don't remember his name. Cooper, I think."

"What kind of car did you say hit your dog?"

"I don't know," I said, thinking, not a jeep. Make it something besides a jeep. "I didn't see him get hit. The vet said it was something big, a pickup maybe. Or a Winnebago."

And I knew who had hit the jackal. It had all been right there in front of me—the old man using up their forty-gallon water supply to wash the bumper, the lies about their coming in from Globe—only I had been too intent on keeping them from finding out about Katie, on getting the picture of Aberfan, to see it. It was like the damned parvo. When you had it licked in one place, it broke out somewhere else.

"Were there any identifying tire tracks?" Hunter said.

"What?" I said. "No. It was snowing that day." It had to show in my face, and he hadn't missed anything yet. I passed my hand over my eyes. "I'm sorry. These questions are bringing it all back."

"Sorry," Hunter said.

"Can't we get this stuff from the police report?" Segura asked.

"There wasn't a police report," I said. "It wasn't a crime to kill a dog when Aberfan died."

It was the right thing to say. The look of shock on their faces was the real thing this time, and they looked at each other in disbelief instead of at me. They asked a few more questions and then stood up to leave. I walked them to the door.

"Thank you for your cooperation, Mr. McCombe," Hunter said. "We appreciate what a difficult experience this has been for you."

I shut the screen door between us. The Amblers would have been going too fast, trying to beat the cameras because they weren't even supposed to be on Van Buren. It was almost rush hour, and they were in the tanker lane, and they hadn't even seen the jackal till they hit it, and then it was too late. They had to know the penalty for hitting an animal was jail and confiscation of the vehicle, and there wasn't anybody else on the road.

"Oh, one more question," Hunter said from halfway down the walk. "You said you went to your first assignment this morning. What was it?"

Candid. Open. "It was out at the old zoo. A sideshow kind of thing."

I watched them all the way out to their car and down the street. Then I latched the screen, pulled the inside door shut, and locked it, too. It had been right there in front of me—the ferret sniffing the wheel, the bumper, Jake anxiously watching the road. I had thought he was looking for customers, but he wasn't. He was expecting to see the Society drive up. "He's not interested in that," he had said when Mrs. Ambler said she had been telling me about Taco. He had listened to our whole conversation, standing under the back window with his guilty bucket, ready to come back in and cut her off if she said too much, and I hadn't tumbled to any of it. I had been so intent on Aberfan I hadn't even seen it when I looked right through the lens at it. And what kind of an excuse was that? Katie hadn't even tried to use it, and she was learning to drive.

I went and got the Nikon and pulled the film out of it. It was too late to do anything about the eisenstadt pictures or the vidcam footage, but I didn't think there was anything in them. Jake had already washed the bumper by the time I'd taken those pictures.

I fed the longshot film into the developer. "Positives, one two three order, fifteen seconds," I said, and waited for the image to come on the screen.

I wondered who had been driving. Jake, probably. "He never liked Taco," she had said, and there was no mistaking the bitterness in her voice. "I didn't want to buy the Winnebago."

They would both lose their licenses, no matter who was driving, and the Society would confiscate the Winnebago. They would probably not send two octogenarian specimens of Americana like the Amblers to prison. They wouldn't have to. The trial would take six months, and Texas already had legislation in committee.

The first picture came up. A light-setting shot of an ocotillo.

Even if they got off, even if they didn't end up taking away the Winnebago for unauthorized use of a tanker lane or failure to purchase a sales tax permit, the Amblers had six months left at the outside. Utah was all ready to pass a full-divided bill, and Arizona would be next. In spite of the road crews' stew-slowed pace, Phoenix would be all-divided by the time the investigation was over, and they'd be completely boxed in. Permanent residents of the zoo. Like the coyote.

A shot of the zoo sign, half-hidden in the cactus. A close-up of the Amblers' balloon-trailing sign. The Winnebago in the parking lot.

"Hold," I said. "Crop." I indicated the areas with my finger. "Enlarge to full screen."

The longshot takes great pictures, sharp contrast, excellent detail. The developer only had a five hundred thousand-pixel screen, but the dark smear on the bumper was easy to see, and the developed picture would be much clearer. You'd be able to see every splatter, every grayish-yellow hair. The Society's computers would probably be able to type the blood from it.

"Continue," I said, and the next picture came on the screen. Artsy shot of the Winnebago and the zoo entrance. Jake washing the bumper. Red-handed.

Maybe Hunter had bought my story, but he didn't have any other suspects, and how long would it be before he decided to ask Katie a few more questions? If he thought it was the Amblers, he'd leave her alone.

The Japanese family clustered around the waste-disposal tank. Close-up of the decals on the side. Interiors—Mrs. Ambler in the galley, the upright-coffin shower stall, Mrs. Ambler making coffee.

No wonder she had looked that way in the eisenstadt shot, her face full of memory and grief and loss. Maybe in the instant before they hit it, it had looked like a dog to her, too.

All I had to do was tell Hunter about the Amblers, and Katie was off the hook. It should be easy. I had done it before.

"Stop," I said to a shot of the salt-and-pepper collection. The black and white scottie dogs had painted, red-plaid bows and red tongues. "Expose," I said. "One through twenty-four."

The screen went to question marks and started beeping. I should have known better. The developer could handle a lot of orders, but asking it to expose perfectly good film went against its whole memory, and I didn't have time to give it the step-by-steps that would convince it I meant what I said.

"Eject," I said. The scotties blinked out. The developer spat out the film, rerolled into its protective case.

The doorbell rang. I switched on the overhead and pulled the film out to full length and held it directly under the light. I had told Hunter an RV hit Aberfan, and he had said on the way out, almost an afterthought, "That first shoot you went to, what was it?" And after he left, what had he done, gone out to check on the sideshow kind of thing, gotten Mrs. Ambler to spill her guts? There hadn't been time to do that and get back. He must have called Ramirez. I was glad I had locked the door.

I turned off the overhead. I rerolled the film, fed it back into the developer, and gave it a direction it could handle. "Permanganate bath, full strength, one through twenty-four. Remove one hundred per cent emulsion. No notify."

The screen went dark. It would take the developer at least fifteen minutes to run the film through the bleach bath, and the Society's computers could probably enhance a picture out of two crystals of silver and thin air, but at least the detail wouldn't be there. I unlocked the door.

It was Katie.

She held up the eisenstadt. "You forgot your briefcase," she said.

I stared blankly at it. I hadn't even realized I didn't have it. I must have left it on the kitchen table when I went tearing out, running down little girls and stewed roadworkers in my rush to keep Katie from getting involved. And here she was, and Hunter would be back any minute, saying, "That shoot you went on this morning, did you take any pictures?"

"It isn't a briefcase," I said.

"I wanted to tell you," she said, and stopped. "I shouldn't have accused you of telling the Society I'd killed the jackal. I don't know why you came to see me today, but I know you're not capable of—"

"You have no idea what I'm capable of," I said. I opened the door enough to reach for the eisenstadt. "Thanks for bringing it back. I'll get the paper to reimburse your way-mile credits."

Go home. Go home. If you're here when the Society comes back, they'll ask you how you met me, and I just destroyed the evidence that could shift the blame to the Amblers. I took hold of the eisenstadt's handle and started to shut the door.

She put her hand on the door. The screen door and the fading light made her look unfocused, like Misha. "Are you in trouble?"

"No," I said. "Look, I'm very busy."

"Why did you come to see me?" she asked. "Did you kill the jackal?"

"No," I said, but I opened the door and let her in.

I went over to the developer and asked for a visual status. It was only on the sixth frame. "I'm destroying evidence," I said to Katie. "I took a picture this morning of the vehicle that hit it, only I didn't know it was the guilty party until a half an hour ago." I motioned for her to sit down on the couch. "They're in their eighties. They were driving on a road they weren't supposed to be on, in an obsolete recreation vehicle, worrying about the cameras and the tankers. There's no way they could have seen it in time to stop. The Society won't see it that way, though. They're determined to blame somebody, anybody, even though it won't bring them back."

She set her canvas carryit and the eisenstadt down on the table next to the couch. "The Society was here when I got home," I said. "They'd figured out we were both in Colorado when Aberfan died. I told them it was a hit and run, and you'd stopped to help me. They had the vet's records, and your name was on them."

I couldn't read her face. "If they come back, you tell them that you gave me a ride to the vet's." I went back to the developer. The longshot film was done. "Eject," I said, and the developer spit it into my hand. I fed it into the recycler.

"McCombe! Where the hell are you?" Ramirez's voice exploded into the room, and I jumped and started for the door, but she wasn't there. The phone was flashing. "McCombe! This is important!"

Ramirez was on the phone and using some override I didn't even know existed. I went over and pushed it back to access. The lights went out. "I'm here," I said.

"You won't believe what just happened!" She sounded outraged. "A couple of terrorist types from the Society just stormed in here and confiscated the stuff you sent me!"

All I'd sent her was the vidcam footage and the shots from the eisenstadt, and there shouldn't have been anything on those. Jake had already washed the bumper. "What stuff?" I said.

"The prints from the eisenstadt!" she said, still shouting. "Which I didn't have a chance to look at when they came in because I was too busy trying to work a trade on your governor's conference, not to mention trying to track you down! I had hard copies made and sent the originals straight down to composing with your vidcam footage. I finally got to them half an hour ago, and while I'm sorting through them, this Society creep just grabs them away from me. No warrants, no 'would you mind?,' nothing. Right out of my hand. Like a bunch of—"

"Jackals," I said. "You're sure it wasn't the vidcam footage?" There wasn't anything in the eisenstadt shots except Mrs. Ambler and Taco, and even Hunter couldn't have put that together, could he?

"Of course I'm sure," Ramirez said, her voice bouncing off the walls. "It was one of the prints from the eisenstadt. I never even saw the vidcam stuff. I sent it straight to composing. I told you."

I went over to the developer and fed the cartridge in. The first dozen shots were nothing, stuff the eisenstadt had taken from the back seat of the car. "Start with frame ten," I said. "Positives. One two three order. Five seconds."

"What did you say?" Ramirez demanded.

"I said, did they say what they were looking for?"

"Are you kidding? I wasn't even there as far as they were concerned. They split up the pile and started through them on *my* desk."

The yucca at the foot of the hill. More yucca. My forearm as I set the eisenstadt down on the counter. My back.

"Whatever it was they were looking for, they found it," Ramirez said.

I glanced at Katie. She met my gaze steadily, unafraid. She had never been afraid, not even when I told her she had killed all the dogs, not even when I showed up on her doorstep after fifteen years.

"The one in the uniform showed it to the other one," Ramirez was saying, "and said, 'You were wrong about the woman doing it. Look at this.' "

"Did you get a look at the picture?"

Still life of cups and spoons. Mrs. Ambler's arm. Mrs. Ambler's back.

"I tried. It was a truck of some kind."

"A truck? Are you sure? Not a Winnebago?"

"A truck. What the hell is going on over there?"

I didn't answer. Jake's back. Open shower door. Still life with Sanka. Mrs. Ambler remembering Taco.

"What woman are they talking about?" Ramirez said. "The one you wanted the lifeline on?"

"No," I said. The picture of Mrs. Ambler was the last one on the cartridge. The developer went back to the beginning. Bottom half of the Hitori. Open car door. Prickly pear. "Did they say anything else?"

"The one in uniform pointed to something on the hard copy and said, 'See. There's his number on the side. Can you make it out?' "

Blurred palm trees and the expressway. The tanker hitting the jackal.

"Stop," I said. The image froze.

"What?" Ramirez said.

It was a great action shot, the back wheels passing right over the mess that had been the jackal's hind legs. The jackal was already dead, of course, but you couldn't see that or the already drying blood coming out of its mouth because of the angle. You couldn't see the truck's license number either because of the speed the tanker was going, but the number was there, waiting for the Society's computers. It looked like the tanker had just hit it.

"What did they do with the picture?" I asked.

"They took it into the chief's office. I tried to call up the originals from composing, but the chief had already sent for them *and* your vidcam footage. Then I tried to get you, but I couldn't get past your damned exclusion."

"Are they still in there with the chief?"

"They just left. They're on their way over to your house. The chief told me to tell you he wants 'full cooperation,' which means hand over the negatives and any other film you just took this morning. He told *me* to keep my hands off. No story. Case closed."

"How long ago did they leave?"

"Five minutes. You've got plenty of time to make me a print. Don't highwire it. I'll come pick it up."

"What happened to, 'The last thing I need is trouble with the Society'?"

"It'll take them at least twenty minutes to get to your place. Hide it somewhere the Society won't find it."

"I can't," I said, and listened to her furious silence. "My developer's broken. It just ate my longshot film," I said, and hit the exclusion button again.

"You want to see who hit the jackal?" I said to Katie, and motioned her over to the developer. "One of Phoenix's finest."

She came and stood in front of the screen, looking at the picture. If the Society's computers were really good, they could probably prove the jackal was already dead, but the Society wouldn't keep the film long enough for that. Hunter and Segura had probably already destroyed the highwire copies. Maybe I should offer to run the cartridge sheet through the permanganate bath for them when they got here, just to save time.

I looked at Katie. "It looks guilty as hell, doesn't it?" I said. "Only it isn't." She didn't say anything, didn't move. "It would have killed the jackal if it had hit it. It was going at least ninety. But the jackal was already dead."

She looked across at me.

"The Society would have sent the Amblers to jail. It would have confiscated the house they've lived in for fifteen years for an accident that was nobody's fault. They didn't even see it coming. It just ran right out in front of them."

Katie put her hand up to the screen and touched the jackal's image.

"They've suffered enough," I said, looking at her. It was getting dark. I hadn't turned on any lights, and the red image of the tanker made her nose look sunburned.

"All these years she's blamed him for her dog's death, and he didn't do it," I said. "A Winnebago's a hundred square feet on the inside. That's about as big as this developer, and they've lived inside it for fifteen years, while the lanes got narrower and the highways shut down, hardly enough room to breathe, let alone live, and her blaming him for something he didn't do."

In the ruddy light from the screen she looked sixteen.

"They won't do anything to the driver, not with the tankers hauling thousands of gallons of water into Phoenix every day. Even the Society won't run the risk of a boycott. They'll destroy the negatives and call the case closed. And the Society won't go after the Amblers," I said. "Or you."

I turned back to the developer. "Go," I said, and the image changed. Yucca. Yucca. My forearm. My back. Cups and spoons.

"Besides," I said. "I'm an old hand at shifting the blame." Mrs. Ambler's arm. Mrs. Ambler's back. Open shower door. "Did I ever tell you about Aberfan?"

Katie was still watching the screen, her face pale now from the light blue one hundred percent formica shower stall.

"The Society already thinks the tanker did it. The only one I've got to convince is my editor." I reached across to the phone and took the exclusion off. "Ramirez," I said, "wanta go after the Society?"

Jake's back. Cups, spoons, and Sanka.

"I did," Ramirez said in a voice that could have frozen the Salt River, "but your developer was broken, and you couldn't get me a picture."

Mrs. Ambler and Taco.

I hit the exclusion button again and left my hand on it. "Stop," I said. "Print." The screen went dark, and the print slid out into the tray. "Reduce frame. Permanganate bath by one per cent. Follow on screen." I took my hand off. "What's Dolores Chiwere doing these days, Ramirez?"

"She's working investigative. Why?"

I didn't answer. The picture of Mrs. Ambler faded a little, a little more.

"The Society *does* have a link to the lifelines!" Ramirez said, not quite as fast as Hunter, but almost. "That's why you requested your old girlfriend's line, isn't it? You're running a sting."

I had been wondering how to get Ramirez off Katie's trail, and she had done it herself, jumping to conclusions just like the Society. With a little effort, I could convince Katie, too: Do you know why I really came to see you today? To catch the Society. I had to pick somebody the Society couldn't possibly know about from my lifeline, somebody I didn't have any known connection with.

Katie watched the screen, looking like she already half-believed it. The picture of Mrs. Ambler faded some more. Any known connection.

"Stop," I said.

"What about the truck?" Ramirez demanded. "What does it have to do with this sting of yours?"

"Nothing," I said. "And neither does the water board, which is an even bigger bully than the Society. So do what the chief says. Full cooperation. Case closed. We'll get them on lifeline tapping."

She digested that, or maybe she'd already hung up and was calling Dolores Chiwere. I looked at the image of Mrs. Ambler on the screen. It had faded enough to look slightly overexposed but not enough to look tampered with. And Taco was gone.

I looked at Katie. "The Society will be here in another fifteen minutes," I said, "which gives me just enough time to tell you about Aberfan." I gestured at the couch. "Sit down."

She came and sat down. "He was a great dog," I said. "He loved the snow. He'd dig through it and toss it up with his muzzle and snap at the snowflakes, trying to catch them."

Ramirez had obviously hung up, but she would call back if she couldn't track down Chiwere. I put the exclusion back on and went over to the developer. The image of Mrs. Ambler was still on the screen. The bath hadn't affected the detail that much. You could still see the wrinkles, the thin white hair, but the guilt, or blame, the look of loss and love, was gone. She looked serene, almost happy.

"There are hardly any good pictures of dogs," I said. "They lack the necessary muscles to take good pictures, and Aberfan lunged at you as soon as he saw the camera."

I turned the developer off. Without the light from the screen, it was almost dark in the room. I turned on the overhead.

"There were less than a hundred dogs left in the United States, and he'd already had the newparvo once and nearly died. The only pictures I had of him had been taken when he was asleep. I wanted a picture of Aberfan playing in the snow."

I leaned against the narrow shelf in front of the developer's screen. Katie looked the way she had at the vet's, sitting there with her hands clenched, waiting for me to tell her something terrible.

"I wanted a picture of him playing in the snow, but he always lunged at the camera," I said, "so I let him out in the front yard, and then I sneaked out the side door and went across the road to some pine trees where he wouldn't be able to see me. But he did."

"And he ran across the road," Katie said. "And I hit him."

She was looking down at her hands. I waited for her to look up, dreading what I would see in her face. Or not see.

"It took me a long time to find out where you'd gone," she said to her hands. "I was afraid you'd refuse me access to your lifeline. I finally saw one of your pictures in a newspaper, and I moved to Phoenix, but after I got here I was afraid to call you for fear you'd hang up on me."

She twisted her hands the way she had twisted her mittens at the vet's. "My husband said I was obsessed with it, that I should have gotten over it by now, everybody else had, that they were only dogs anyway." She looked up, and I braced my hands against the developer. "He said forgiveness wasn't something somebody else could give you, but I didn't want you to forgive me exactly. I just wanted to tell you I was sorry."

There hadn't been any reproach, any accusation in her face when I told her she was responsible for the extinction of a species that day at the vet's, and there wasn't now. Maybe she didn't have the facial muscles for it, I thought bitterly.

"Do you know why I came to see you today?" I said angrily. "My camera broke when I tried to catch Aberfan. I didn't get any pictures." I grabbed the picture of Mrs. Ambler out of the developer's tray and flung it at her. "Her dog died of newparvo. They left it in the Winnebago, and when they came back, it was dead."

"Poor thing," she said, but she wasn't looking at the picture. She was looking at me.

"She didn't know she was having her picture taken. I thought if I got you talking about Aberfan, I could get a picture like that of you."

And surely now I would see it, the look I had really wanted when I set the eisenstadt down on Katie's kitchen table, the look I still wanted, even though the eisenstadt was facing the wrong way, the look of betrayal the dogs had never given us. Not even Misha. Not even Aberfan. How does it feel to be responsible for the extinction of an entire species?

I pointed at the eisenstadt. "It's not a briefcase. It's a camera. I was going to take your picture without your even knowing it."

She had never known Aberfan. She had never known Mrs. Ambler either, but in that instant before she started to cry she looked like both of them. She put her hand up to her mouth. "Oh," she said, and the love, the loss was there in her voice, too. "If you'd had it then, it wouldn't have happened."

I looked at the eisenstadt. If I had had it, I could have set it on the porch and Aberfan would never have even noticed it. He would have burrowed through the snow and tossed it up with his nose, and I could have thrown snow up in big glittering sprays that he would have leaped at, and it never would have happened. Katie Powell would have driven past, and I would have stopped to wave at her, and she, sixteen years old and just learning to drive, would maybe even have risked taking a mittened hand off the steering wheel to wave back, and Aberfan would have wagged his tail into a blizzard and then barked at the snow he'd churned up.

He wouldn't have caught the third wave. He would have lived to be an old dog, fourteen or fifteen, too old to play in the snow any more, and even if he had been the last dog in the world I would not have let them lock him up in a cage, I would not have let them take him away. If I had had the eisenstadt.

No wonder I hated it.

It had been at least fifteen minutes since Ramirez called. The Society would be here any minute. "You shouldn't be here when the Society comes," I said, and Katie nodded and smudged the tears off her cheeks and stood up, reaching for her carryit.

"Do you ever take pictures?" she said, shouldering the carryit. "I mean, besides for the papers?"

"I don't know if I'll be taking pictures for them much longer. Photojournalists are becoming an extinct breed."

"Maybe you could come take some pictures of Jana and Kevin. Kids grow up so fast, they're gone before you know it."

"I'd like that," I said. I opened the screen door for her and looked both ways down the street at the darkness. "All clear," I said, and she went out. I shut the screen door between us.

She turned and looked at me one last time with her dear, open face that even I hadn't been able to close. "I miss them," she said.

I put my hand up to the screen. "I miss them, too."

I watched her to make sure she turned the corner and then went back in the living room and took down the picture of Misha. I propped it against the developer so Segura would be able to see it from the door. In a month or so, when the Amblers were safely in Texas and the Society had forgotten about Katie, I'd call Segura and tell him I might be willing to sell it to the Society, and then in a day or so I'd tell him I'd changed my mind. When he came out to try to talk me into it, I'd tell him about Perdita and Beatrix Potter, and he would tell me about the Society.

Chiwere and Ramirez would have to take the credit for the story—I didn't want Hunter putting anything else together—and it would take more than one story to break them, but it was a start.

Katie had left the print of Mrs. Ambler on the couch. I picked it up and looked at it a minute and then fed it into the developer. "Recycle," I said.

I picked up the eisenstadt from the table by the couch and took the film cartridge out. I started to pull the film out to expose it, and then shoved it into the developer instead and turned it on. "Positives, one two three order, five seconds."

I had apparently set the camera on its activator again—there were ten shots or so of the back seat of the Hitori. Vehicles and people. The pictures of Katie were all in shadow. There was a Still Life of Kool-Aid Pitcher with Whale Glass and another one of Jana's toy cars, and some near-black frames that meant Katie had laid the eisenstadt face-down when she brought it to me.

"Two seconds," I said, and waited for the developer to flash the last shots so I could make sure there wasn't anything else on the cartridge and then expose it before the Society got here. All but the last frame was of the darkness that was all the eisenstadt could see lying on its face. The last one was of me.

The trick in getting good pictures is to make people forget they're being photographed. Distract them. Get them talking about something they care about.

"Stop," I said, and the image froze.

Aberfan was a great dog. He loved to play in the snow, and after I had murdered him, he lifted his head off my lap and tried to lick my hand.

The Society would be here any minute to take the longshot film and destroy it, and this one would have to go, too, along with the rest of the cartridge. I couldn't risk Hunter's being reminded of Katie. Or Segura taking a notion to do a print-fix and peel on Jana's toy cars.

It was too bad. The eisenstadt takes great pictures. "Even you'll forget it's a camera," Ramirez had said in her spiel, and that was certainly true. I was looking straight into the lens.

And it was all there, Misha and Taco and Perdita and the look he gave me on the way to the vet's while I stroked his poor head and told him it would be all right, that look of love and pity I had been trying to capture all these years. The picture of Aberfan.

The Society would be here any minute. "Eject," I said, and cracked the cartridge open, and exposed it to the light.

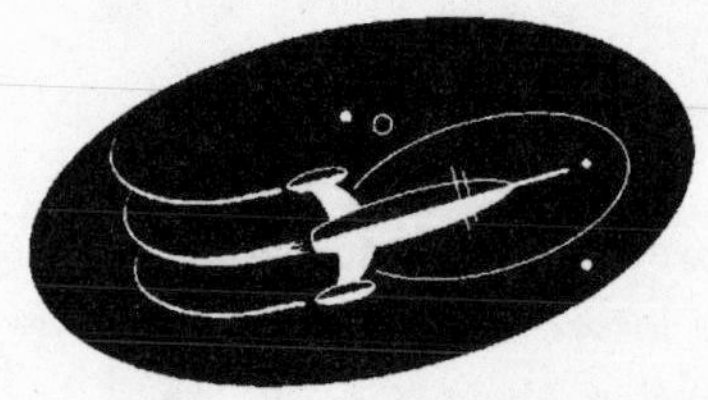

The Mountains of Mourning

Lois McMaster Bujold

Miles heard the woman weeping as he was climbing the hill from the long lake. He hadn't dried himself after his swim, as the morning already promised shimmering heat. Lake water trickled cool from his hair onto his naked chest and back, more annoyingly down his legs from his ragged shorts. His leg braces chafed on his damp skin as he pistoned up the faint trail through the scrub, military double-time. His feet squished in his old wet shoes. He slowed, curious, as he became conscious of the voices.

The woman's voice grated with grief and exhaustion. "Please, lord, please. All I want is m'justice. . . ."

The front gate guard's voice was irritated and embarrassed. "I'm no lord. C'mon, get *up,* woman. Go back to the village and report it at the district magistrate's office."

"I tell you, I just came from there!" The woman did not move from her knees as Miles emerged from the bushes and paused to take in the tableau across the paved road. "The magistrate's not to return for weeks, weeks. I walked four days to get here. I only have a little money. . . ." A desperate hope rose in her voice, and her spine bent and straightened as she scrabbled in her skirt pocket and held out her cupped hands to the guard. "A mark and twenty pence, it's all I have, but—"

The exasperated guard's eye fell on Miles, and he straightened abruptly, as if afraid Miles might suspect him of being tempted by so pitiful a bribe. "Be off, woman!" he snapped.

Miles quirked an eyebrow, and limped across the road to the main gate. "What's all this about, Corporal?" he inquired easily.

The guard corporal was on loan from Imperial Security, and wore the high-necked dress greens of the Barrayaran Service. He was sweating and uncomfortable in the bright morning light of this southern district, but Miles fancied he'd be boiled before he'd undo his collar on this post. His accent was not local, he was a city man from the capital, where a more-or-less efficient bureaucracy absorbed such problems as the one on her knees before him.

The woman, now, was local and more than local—she had backcountry written all over her. She was younger than her strained voice had at first suggested. Tall, fever-red from her weeping, with stringy blonde hair hanging down across a ferret-thin face and protuberant grey eyes. If she were cleaned up, fed, rested, happy and confident, she might achieve a near-prettiness, but she was far from that now, despite her remarkable figure. Lean but full-breasted—no, Miles revised his opinion as he crossed the road and came up to the gate. Her bodice was all blotched with dried milk leaks, though there was no baby in sight. Only temporarily full-breasted. Her worn dress was factory-woven cloth, but hand-sewn, crude and simple. Her feet were bare, thickly callused, cracked and sore.

"No problem," the guard assured Miles. "Go *away,*" he hissed to the woman.

She lurched off her knees and sat stonily.

"I'll call my sergeant," the guard eyed her warily, "and have her removed."

"Wait a moment," said Miles.

She stared up at Miles from her cross-legged position, clearly not knowing whether to identify him as hope or not. His clothing, what there was of it, offered her no clue as to what he might be. The rest of him was all too plainly displayed. He jerked up his chin and smiled thinly. Too-large head, too-short neck, back thickened with its crooked spine, crooked legs with their brittle bones too often broken, drawing the eye in their gleaming chromium braces. Were the hill woman standing, the top of his head would barely be even with the top of her shoulder. He waited in boredom for her hand to make the backcountry hex sign against evil mutations, but it only jerked and clenched into a fist.

"I must see my lord Count," she said to an uncertain point halfway between Miles and the guard. "It's my right. My daddy, he died in the Service. It's my right."

"Prime Minister Count Vorkosigan," said the guard stiffly, "is at his country estate to rest. If he were working, he'd be back in Vobarr Sultana." The guard looked like he wished *he* were back in Vorbarr Sultana.

The woman seized the pause. "You're only a city man. He's *my* Count. My right."

"What do you want to see Count Vorkosigan for?" asked Miles patiently.

"Murder," growled the girl/woman. The security guard spasmed slightly. "I want to report a murder."

"Shouldn't you report to your village Speaker first?" inquired Miles, with a hand-down gesture to calm the twitching guard.

"I did. He'll do *nothing.*" Rage and frustration cracked her voice. "He says it's over and done. He won't write down my accusation, says it's nonsense. It would only make trouble for everybody, he says. I don't care! I want my justice!"

Miles frowned thoughtfully, looking the woman over. The details checked, corroborated her claimed identity, added up to a solid if subliminal sense of authentic truth which perhaps escaped the professionally paranoid security man. "It's true, Corporal," Miles said. "She has a right to appeal, first to the district magistrate, then to the Count's court. And the district magistrate won't be back for two weeks."

This sector of Count Vorkosigan's native district had only one overworked district magistrate, who rode a circuit that included the lakeside village of Vorkosigan Surleau but one day a month. Since the region of the prime minister's country estate was crawling with Imperial Security when the great lord was in residence, and closely monitored even when he was not, prudent troublemakers took their troubles elsewhere.

"Scan her, and let her in," said Miles. "On my authority."

The guard was one of Imperial Security's best, trained to look for assassins in his own shadow. He now looked scandalized, and lowered his voice to Miles. "Sir, if I let every country lunatic wander the estate at will—"

"I'll take her up. I'm going that way."

The guard shrugged helplessly, but stopped short of saluting; Miles was decidedly not in uniform. The gate guard pulled a scanner from his belt and made a great show of going over the woman. Miles wondered if he'd have been inspired to harass her with a strip-search without Miles's inhibiting presence. When the guard finished demonstrating how alert, conscientious, and loyal he was, he palmed open the gate's lock, entered the transaction—including the woman's retina scan—into the computer monitor, and stood aside in a pose of rather pointed parade rest. Miles grinned at the silent editorial, and steered the bedraggled woman by the elbow through the gates and up the winding drive.

She twitched away from his touch at the earliest opportunity, yet still refrained from superstitious gestures, eyeing him with a strange and hungry curiosity. Time was, such openly repelled fascination with the peculiarities of his body had driven Miles to grind his teeth; now he could take it with a serene amusement only slightly tinged with acid. They would learn, all of them. They would learn.

"Do you serve Count Vorkosigan, little man?" she asked cautiously.

Miles thought about that one a moment. "Yes," he answered finally. The answer was, after all, true on every level of meaning but the one she'd asked it. He quelled the temptation to tell her he was the court jester. From the look of her, this one's troubles were much worse than his own.

She had apparently not quite believed in her own rightful destiny, despite her mulish determination at the gate, for as they climbed unimpeded toward her goal a nascent panic made her face even more drawn and pale, almost ill. "How—how do I talk to him?" she choked. "Should I curtsey . . . ?" She glanced down at herself as if conscious for the first time of her own dirt and sweat and squalor.

Miles suppressed a facetious set-up starting with, *Kneel and knock your forehead three times on the floor before speaking, that's what the General Staff does,* and said instead, "Just stand up straight and speak the truth. Try to be clear. He'll take it from there. He does not, after all," Miles's lips twitched, "lack experience."

She swallowed.

A hundred years ago, the Vorkosigans's summer retreat had been a guard barracks, part of the outlying fortifications of the great castle on the bluff above the village of Vorkosigan Surleau. The castle was now a burnt-out ruin, and the barracks transformed into a comfortable low stone residence, modernized and remodernized, artistically landscaped and bright with flowers. The arrow slits had been widened into big glass windows overlooking the lake, and comm link antennae bristled from the roof. There was a new guard barracks concealed in the trees downslope, but it had no arrow slits.

A man in the brown-and-silver livery of the Count's personal retainers exited the residence's front door as Miles approached with the strange woman in tow. It was the new man, what was his name? Pym, that was it.

"Where's m'lord Count?" Miles asked him.

"In the upper pavilion, taking breakfast with M'lady." Pym glanced at the woman, waited on Miles in a posture of polite inquiry.

"Ah. Well, this woman has walked four days to lay an appeal before the district magistrate's court. The court's not here, but the Count is, so she now proposes to skip the middlemen and go straight to the top. I like her style. Take her up, will you?"

"During *breakfast?*" said Pym.

Miles cocked his head at the woman. "Have you had breakfast?"

She shook her head mutely.

"I thought not." Miles turned his hands palm-out, dumping her, symbolically, on the retainer. "Now, yes."

"My daddy, he died in the Service," the woman repeated faintly. "It's my right." The phrase seemed as much to convince herself as anyone else, now.

Pym was, if not a hill man, district-born. "So it is," he sighed, and gestured her to follow him without further ado. Her eyes widened, as she trailed him around the house, and she glanced back nervously over her shoulder at Miles. "Little man . . . ?"

"Just stand straight," he called to her. He watched her round the corner, grinned, and took the steps two at a time into the residence's main entrance.

* * *

After a shave and cold shower, Miles dressed in his own room overlooking the long lake. He dressed with great care, as great as he'd expended on the Service Academy ceremonies and Imperial Review two days ago. Clean underwear, long-sleeved cream shirt, dark green trousers with the side piping. High-collared green tunic tailor-cut to his own difficult fit. New pale blue plastic Ensign rectangles aligned precisely on the collar and poking most uncomfortably into his jaw. He dispensed with the leg braces and pulled on mirror-polished boots to the knee, and swiped a bit of dust from them with his pajama pants, ready-to-hand on the floor where he'd dropped them before going swimming.

He straightened and checked himself in the mirror. His dark hair hadn't even begun to recover from that last cut before the graduation ceremonies. A pale, sharp-featured face, not too much dissipated bag under the grey eyes, nor too bloodshot—alas, the limits of his body compelled him to stop celebrating well before he could hurt himself.

Echoes of the late celebration still boiled up silently in his head, twitching his mouth into a grin. He was on his way now, had his hand clamped firmly around the lowest rung of the highest ladder on Barrayar, Imperial Service itself. There were no give-aways in the Service even for sons of the old Vor. You got what you earned. His brother-officers could be relied on to know that, even if outsiders wondered. He was in position at last to prove himself to all doubters. Up and away and never look down, never look back.

One last look back. As carefully as he'd dressed, Miles gathered up the necessary objects for his task. The white cloth rectangles of his former Academy cadet's rank. The hand-calligraphed second copy, purchased for this purpose, of his new officer's commission in the Barrayaran Imperial Service. A copy of his Academy three-year scholastic transcript on paper, with all its commendations (and demerits). No point in anything but honesty in this next transaction. In a cupboard downstairs he found the brass brazier and tripod, wrapped in its polishing cloth, and a plastic bag of very dry juniper bark. Chemical firesticks.

Out the back door and up the hill. The landscaped path split, the right going up the pavilion overlooking it all, the left forking sideways to a garden-like area surrounded by a low fieldstone wall. Miles let himself in by the gate. "Good morning, crazy ancestors," he called, then quelled his humor. It might be true, but lacked the respect due the occasion.

He strolled over and around the graves until he came to the one he sought, knelt, and set up the brazier and tripod, humming. The stone was simple, *General Count Piotr Pierre Vorkosigan,* and the dates. If they'd tried to list all the accumulated honors and accomplishments, they'd have had to go to microprint.

He piled in the bark, the very expensive papers, the cloth bits, a clipped mat of dark hair from that last cut. He set it alight and rocked back on his heels to watch it burn. He'd played a hundred versions of this moment over in his head, over the years, ranging from solemn public orations with musicians in the background, to dancing naked on the old man's grave. He'd settled on this private and traditional ceremony, played straight. Just between the two of them.

"So, Grandfather," he purred at last. "And here we are after all. Satisfied now?"

All the chaos of the graduation ceremonies behind, all the mad efforts of the last three years, all the pain, came to this point; but the grave did not speak, did not say, *Well done; you can stop now.* The ashes spelled out no messages, there were no visions to be had in the rising smoke. The brazier burned down all too quickly. Not enough stuff in it, perhaps.

He stood, and dusted his knees, in the silence and the sunlight. So what had he expected? Applause? Why was he here, in the final analysis? Dancing out a dead man's dreams—who did his service really serve? Grandfather? Himself? Pale Emperor Gregor? Who cared?

"Well, old man," he whispered, then shouted: "ARE YOU SATISFIED YET?" The echoes rang from the stones.

A throat cleared behind him, and Miles whirled like a scalded cat, heart pounding.

"Uh . . . my lord?" said Pym carefully. "Pardon me, I did not mean to interrupt . . . anything. But the Count your father requires you to attend to him in the upper pavilion."

Pym's expression was perfectly bland. Miles swallowed, and waited for the scarlet heat he could feel in his face to recede. "Quite," he shrugged. "The fire's almost out. I'll clean it up later. Don't . . . let anybody else touch it."

He marched past Pym and didn't look back.

The pavilion was a simple structure of weathered silver wood, open on all four sides to catch the breeze, this morning a few faint puffs from the west. Good sailing on the lake this afternoon, maybe. Only ten days of precious home leave left, and much Miles wanted to do, including the trip to Vorbarr Sultana with his cousin Ivan to pick out his new lightflyer. And then his first assignment would be coming through—ship duty, Miles prayed. He'd had to overcome a major temptation, not to ask his father to make sure it was ship duty. He would take whatever assignment fate dealt him, that was the first rule of the game. And win with the hand he was dealt.

The interior of the pavilion was shady and cool after the glare outside. It was furnished with comfortable old chairs and tables, one of which bore the remains of a noble breakfast—Miles mentally marked two lonely-looking oil cakes, on a crumb-scattered tray, as his own. Miles's mother, lingering over her cup, smiled across the table at him.

Miles's father, casually dressed in an open-throated shirt and shorts, sat in a worn armchair. Aral Vorkosigan was a thick-set, grey-haired man, heavy-jawed, heavy-browed, scarred. A face that lent itself to savage caricature—Miles had seen some, in Opposition press, in the histories of Barrayar's enemies. They had only to draw one lie, to render dull those sharp penetrating eyes, to create everyone's parody of a military dictator.

And how much is he haunted by Grandfather? Miles wondered. He doesn't show it much. But then, he doesn't have to. Admiral Aral Vorkosigan, space master strategist, conquerer of Komarr, hero of Escobar, for sixteen years Imperial Regent and supreme power on Barrayar in all but name. And then he'd capped it, confounded history and all self-sure witnesses and heaped up honor and glory beyond all that had gone before by voluntarily stepping *down,* and transferring command smoothly to Emperor Gregor upon his majority. Not that the Prime Ministership hadn't made a dandy retirement from the Regency, and he was showing no signs yet of stepping down from *that.*

And so Admiral Aral's life took General Piotr's like an overpowering hand of cards, and where did that leave Ensign Miles? Holding two deuces and the joker. He must surely either concede or start bluffing like crazy. . . .

The hill woman sat on a hassock, a half-eaten oil cake clutched in her hands, staring open-mouthed at Miles in all his power and polish. As he caught and returned her gaze her lips pressed closed and her eyes lit. Her expression was strange—anger? Exhilaration? Embarrassment? Glee? Some bizarre mixture of all? *And what did you think I was, woman?*

Being in uniform (showing off his uniform?), Miles came to attention before his father. "Sir?"

Count Vorkosigan spoke to the woman. "*That* is my son. If I send him as my Voice, would that satisfy you?"

"Oh," she breathed, her wide mouth drawing back in a weird, fierce grin, the most expression Miles had yet seen on her face. "*Yes,* my lord."

"Very well. It will be done."

What will be done? Miles wondered warily. The Count was leaning back in his chair, looking satisfied himself, but with a dangerous tension around his eyes hinting that something had aroused his true anger. Not anger at the woman, clearly they were in some sort of agreement, and—Miles searched his conscience quickly—not at Miles himself. He cleared his throat gently, cocking his head and baring his teeth in an inquiring smile.

The Count steepled his hands and spoke to Miles at last. "A most interesting case. I can see why you sent her up."

"Ah . . ." said Miles. What had he got hold of? He'd only greased the woman's way through security on a quixotic impulse, for God's sake, and to tweak his father at breakfast. ". . . ah?" he continued noncommittally.

Count Vorkosigan's brows rose. "Did you not know?"

"She spoke of a murder, and a marked lack of cooperation from her local authorities about it. Figured you'd give her a lift on to the district magistrate."

The Count settled back still further, and rubbed his hand thoughtfully across his scarred chin. "It's an infanticide case."

Miles's belly went cold. *I don't want anything to do with this.* Well, that explained why there was no baby to go with the breasts. "Unusual . . . for it to be reported."

"We've fought the old customs for twenty years and more," said the Count. "Promulgated, propagandized . . . In the cities, we've made good progress."

"In the cities," murmured the Countess, "people have access to alternatives."

"But in the backcountry—well—little has changed. We all know what's going on, but without a report, a complaint—and with the family invariably drawing together to protect its own—it's hard to get leverage."

"What," Miles cleared his throat, nodded at the woman, "what was your baby's mutation?"

"The cat's mouth," the woman dabbed at her upper lip to demonstrate. "She had the hole inside her mouth, too, and was a weak sucker, she choked and cried, but she was getting enough, she *was* . . ."

"Hare-lip," the Count's off-worlder wife murmured half to herself, translating the Barrayaran term to the galactic standard, "and a cleft palate, sounds like. Harra, that's not even a mutation. They had that back on Old Earth. A—a normal birth defect, if that's not a contradiction in terms. Not a punishment for your Barrayaran ancestors' pilgrimage through the Fire. A simple operation could have corrected—" Countess Vorkosigan cut herself off. The hill woman was looking anguished.

"I'd heard," the woman said. "My lord had made a hospital to be built at Hassadar. I meant to take her there, when I was a little stronger, though I had no money. Her arms and legs were sound, her head was well-shaped, anybody could see—surely they would have—" her hands clenched and twisted, her voice went ragged, "but Lem killed her first."

A seven-day walk, Miles calculated, from the deep Dendarii Mountains to the lowland town of Hassadar. Reasonable, that a woman newly risen from child-bed might delay that hike a few days. An hour's ride in an aircar. . . .

"So one is reported as a murder at last," said Count Vorkosigan, "and we will treat it as exactly that. This is a chance to send a message to the farthest corners of my own district. You, Miles, will be my Voice, to reach where it has not reached before. You will dispense Count's justice upon this man—and not quietly, either. It's time for the practices that brand us as barbarians, in galactic eyes, to end."

Miles gulped. "Wouldn't the district magistrate be better qualified . . . ?"

The Count smiled slightly. "For this case, I can think of no one better qualified than yourself."

The messenger and the message all in one: *Times have changed.* Indeed. Miles wished himself elsewhere, anywhere—back sweating blood over his final examinations, for instance. He stifled an unworthy wail, *My home leave . . . !*

Miles rubbed the back of his neck. "Who, ah . . . who is it killed your little girl?" *Meaning: who is it I'm expected to drag out, put up against a wall, and shoot?*

"My husband," she said tonelessly, looking at—through—the polished silvery floorboards.

I knew this was going to be messy. . . .

"She cried and cried," the woman went on, "and wouldn't go to sleep, not nursing well—he shouted at me to shut her up—"

"Then?" Miles prompted, sick to his stomach.

"He swore at me, and went to go sleep at his mother's. He said at least a working man could sleep there. I hadn't slept either. . . ."

This guy sounds like a real winner. Miles had an instant picture of him, a bull of a man with a bullying manner—nevertheless, there was something missing in the climax of the woman's story.

The Count had picked up on it, too. He was listening with total attention, his strategy-session look, a slit-eyed intensity of thought you could mistake for sleepiness. That would be a grave mistake. "Were you an eyewitness?" he asked in a deceptively mild tone that put Miles on full alert. "Did you actually see him kill her?"

"I found her dead in the midmorning, lord."

"You went into the bedroom—" Count Vorkosigan led her on.

"We've only got one room." She shot him a look as if doubtful for the first time of his total omniscience. "She had slept, slept at last. I went out to get some brillberries, up the ravine a way. And when I came back . . . I should have taken her with me, but I was so glad she slept at last, didn't want to risk waking her—" tears leaked from the woman's tightly closed eyes. "I let her sleep when I came back, I was glad to eat and rest, but I began to get full," her hand touched a breast, "and I went to wake her. . . ."

"What, were there no marks on her? Not a cut throat?" asked the count. That was the usual method for these backcountry infanticides, quick and clean compared to, say, exposure.

The woman shook her head. "Smothered, I think, lord. It was cruel, something cruel. The village Speaker said I must have overlain her, and wouldn't take my plea against Lem. I did not, I did not! She had her own cradle, Lem made it with his own hands when she was still in my belly. . . ." She was close to breaking down.

The Count exchanged a glance with his wife, and a small tilt of his head. Countess Vorkosigan rose smoothly.

"Come, Harra, down to the house. You must wash and rest before Miles takes you home."

The hill woman looked taken aback. "Oh, not in your house, lady!"

"Sorry, it's the only one I've got handy. Besides the guard barracks. The guards are good boys, but you'd make 'em uncomfortable. . . ." The Countess eased her out.

"It is clear," said Count Vorkosigan as soon as the women were out of earshot, "that you will have to check out the medical facts before, er, popping off. And I trust you will also have noticed the little problem with a positive identification of the accused. This could be the ideal public-demonstration case we want, but not if there's any ambiguity about it. No bloody mysteries."

"I'm not a coroner," Miles pointed out immediately. If he could wriggle off this hook. . . .

"Quite. You will take Dr. Dea with you."

Lieutenant Dea was the prime minister's physician's assistant. Miles had seen him around—an ambitious young military doctor, in a constant state of frustration because his superior would never let him touch his most important patient—oh, he was going to be thrilled with this assignment, Miles predicted morosely.

"He can take his osteo kit with him, too," the Count went brightening slightly. "In case of accidents."

"How economical," said Miles, rolling his eyes. "Look, uh—suppose her story checks out and we nail this guy. Do I have to, personally . . . ?"

"One of the liveried men will be your bodyguard. And—if the story checks—the executioner."

That was only slightly better. "Couldn't we wait for the district magistrate?"

"Every judgment the district magistrate makes, he makes in my place. Every sentence his office carries out, is carried out in my name. Someday, it will be done in your name. It's time you gained a clear understanding of the process. Historically, the Vor may be a military caste, but a Vor lord's duties were never only military ones."

No escape. Damn, damn, damn. Miles sighed. "Right. Well . . . we could take the aircar, I suppose, and be up there in a couple of hours. Allow some time to find the right hole. Drop out of the sky on 'em, make the message loud and clear . . . be back before bedtime." Get it over with quickly.

The Count had that slit-eyed look again. "No . . ." he said slowly, "not the aircar, I don't think."

"No roads for a groundcar, up that far. Just trails." He added uneasily—surely his father could not be thinking of—"I don't think I'd cut a very impressive figure of central Imperial authority on foot, sir."

His father glanced up at his crisp dress uniform and smiled slightly. "Oh, you don't do so badly."

"But picture this after three or four days of beating through the bushes," Miles protested. "You didn't see us in Basic. Or smell us."

"I've been there," said the admiral dryly. "But no, you're quite right. Not on foot. I have a better idea."

My own cavalry troop, thought Miles ironically, turning in his saddle, *just like Grandfather.* Actually, he was pretty sure the old man would have had some acerbic comments about the riders now strung out behind Miles on the wooded trail, once he'd got done rolling on the ground laughing at the equitation being displayed. The Vorkosigan stables had shrunk sadly since the old man was no longer around to take an interest: the polo string sold off, the few remaining ancient and ill-tempered ex-cavalry beasts put permanently out to pasture. The handful of riding horses left were retained for their sure-footedness and good manners, not their exotic bloodlines, and kept exercised and gentle for the occasional guest by a gaggle of girls from the village.

Miles gathered his reins, tensed one calf, and shifted his weight slightly, and Fat Ninny responded with a neat half turn and two precise back steps. The thick-set roan gelding could not have been mistaken by the most ignorant urbanite for a fiery steed, but Miles adored him, for his dark and liquid eye, his wide velvet nose, his phlegmatic disposition equally unappalled by rushing streams or screaming aircars, but most of all for his exquisite dressage-trained responsiveness. Brains before beauty. Just being around him made Miles calmer, the beast was an emotional blotter, like a purring cat. Miles patted Fat Ninny on the neck. "If anybody asks," he murmured, "I'll tell them your name is Chieftain." Fat Ninny waggled one fuzzy ear, and heaved a wooshing, barrel-chested sigh.

Grandfather had a great deal to do with the unlikely parade Miles now led. The great guerrilla general had poured out his youth in these mountains, fighting the Cetagandan invaders to a standstill and then reversing their tide. Anti-flyer heatless seeker-strikers, smuggled in at bloody cost from off-planet, had a lot more to do with the final victory than cavalry horses, which, according to Grandfather, had saved his forces through the worst winter of that campaign mainly by being edible. But through retroactive romance, the horse had become the symbol of that struggle.

Miles thought his father was being overly optimistic, if he thought Miles was going to cash in thusly on the old man's residual glory. The guerrilla caches and camps were shapeless lumps of rust and *trees*, dammit, not just weeds and scrub anymore—they had passed some, earlier in today's ride—the men who had fought that war had long since gone to ground for the last time, just like Grandfather. What was he doing here? It was Jump ship duty he wanted, taking him high, high above all this. The future, not the past, held his destiny.

Miles's meditations were interrupted by Dr. Dea's horse, which, taking exception to a branch lying across the logging trail, planted all four feet in an abrupt stop and snorted loudly. Dr. Dea toppled off with a faint cry.

"Hang onto the *reins,*" Miles called, and pressed Fat Ninny back down the trail.

Dr. Dea was getting rather better at falling off, he'd landed more-or-less on his feet this time. He made a lunge at the dangling reins, but his sorrel mare shied away from his grab. Dea jumped back as she swung on her haunches and then, realizing her freedom, bounced back down the trail, tail bannering, horse body-language for *Nyah, nyah, ya can't catch me!* Dr. Dea, red and furious, ran swearing in pursuit. She broke into a canter.

"No, no, don't run after her!" called Miles.

"How the hell am I supposed to catch her if I don't run after her?" snarled Dea. The space surgeon was not a happy man. "My medkit's on that bloody beast!"

"How do you think you can catch her if you do?" asked Miles. "She can run faster than you can."

At the end of the little column, Pym turned his horse sideways, blocking the trail. "Just wait, Harra," Miles advised the anxious hill woman in passing. "Hold your horse still. Nothing starts a horse running faster than another running horse."

The other two riders were doing rather better. The woman, Harra Csurik, sat her horse wearily, allowing it to plod along without interference, but at least riding on balance instead of trying to use the reins as a handle like the unfortunate Dea. Pym, bringing up the rear, was competent if not comfortable.

Miles slowed Fat Ninny to a walk, reins loose, and wandered after the mare, radiating an air of calm relaxation. *Who, me? I don't want to catch you. We're just enjoying the scenery, right. That's it, stop for a bite.* The sorrel mare paused to nibble at a weed, but kept a wary eye on Miles's approach.

At a distance just short of starting the mare bolting off again, Miles stopped Fat Ninny and slid off. He made no move toward the mare, but instead stood still and made a great show of fishing in his pockets. Fat Ninny butted his head against Miles eagerly, and Miles cooed and fed him a bit of sugar. The mare cocked her ears with interest. Fat Ninny smacked his lips and nudged for more. The mare snuffled up for her share. She lipped a cube from Miles's palm as he slid his other arm quietly through the loop of her reins.

"Here you go, Dr. Dea. One horse. No running."

"No fair," wheezed Dea, trudging up. "You had sugar in your pockets."

"Of course I had sugar in my pockets. It's called foresight and planning. The trick of handling horses isn't to be faster than the horse, or stronger than the horse. That pits your weakness against his strengths. The trick is to be smarter than the horse. That pits your strength against his weakness, eh?"

Dea took his reins. "It's snickering at me," he said suspiciously.

"That's nickering, not snickering," Miles grinned. He tapped Fat Ninny behind his left foreleg, and the horse obediently grunted down onto one knee. Miles clambered up readily to his conveniently-lowered stirrup.

"Does mine do that?" asked Dr. Dea, watching with fascination.

"Sorry, no."

Dea glowered at his horse. "This animal is an idiot. I shall lead it for a while."

As Ninny lurched back to his four feet, Miles suppressed a riding-instructorly comment gleaned from his Grandfather's store such as, *Be smarter than the horse, Dea.* Though Dr. Dea was officially sworn to Lord Vorkosigan for the duration of this investigation, Space Surgeon Lieutenant Dea certainly outranked Ensign Vorkosigan. To command older men who outranked one called for a certain measure of tact.

The logging road widened out here, and Miles dropped back beside Harra Csurik. Her fierceness and determination of yesterday morning at the gate seemed to be fading even as the trail rose toward her home. Or perhaps it was simply exhaustion catching up with her. She'd said little all morning, been sunk in silence all afternoon. If she was going to drag Miles all the way up to the back of beyond and then wimp out on him . . .

"What, ah, branch of the Service was your father in, Harra?" Miles began conversationally.

She raked her fingers through her hair in a combing gesture more nervousness than vanity. Her eyes looked out at him through the straw-colored wisps like skittish creatures in the protection of a hedge.

"District Militia, m'lord. I don't really remember him, he died when I was real little."

"In combat?"

She nodded. "In the fighting around Vorbarr Sultana, during Vordarian's Pretendership."

Miles refrained from asking which side he had been swept up on—most footsoldiers had had little choice, and the amnesty had included the dead as well as the living.

"Ah . . . do you have any sibs?"

"No, lord. Just me and my mother left."

A little anticipatory tension eased in Miles's neck. If this judgment indeed drove all the way through to an execution, one mis-step could trigger a blood feud among the in-laws. *Not* the legacy of justice the Count intended him to leave behind. So the fewer in-laws involved, the better. "What about your husband's family?"

"He's got seven. Four brothers and three sisters."

"Hm." Miles had a mental flash of an entire team of huge, menacing hill hulks. He glanced back at Pym, feeling a trifle understaffed for his task. He had pointed out this factor to the Count, when they'd been planning this expedition last night.

"The village Speaker and his deputies will be your back-up," the Count had said, "just as for the district magistrate on court circuit."

"What if they don't want to cooperate?" Miles had asked nervously.

"An officer who expects to command Imperial troops," the Count had glinted, "should be able to figure out how to extract cooperation from a backcountry headman."

In other words, his father had decided this was a test, and wasn't going to give him any more clues. Thanks, Dad.

"You have no sibs, lord?" said Harra, snapping him back to the present.

"No. But surely that's known, even in the backbeyond."

"They *say* a lot of things about you," Harra shrugged.

Miles bit down on the morbid question in his mouth like a wedge of raw lemon. He would not ask it, he would not . . . he couldn't help himself. "Like what?" forced out past his stiff lips.

"Everyone knows the Count's son is a mutant." Her eyes flicked defiant-

wide. "Some said it came from the off-worlder woman he married. Some said it was from radiation from the wars, or a disease from, um, corrupt practices in his youth among his brother-officers—"

That last was a new one to Miles. His brow lifted.

"—but most say he was poisoned by his enemies."

"I'm glad most have it right. It was an assassination attempt using soltoxin gas, when my mother was pregnant with me. But it's not—" *a mutation,* his thought hiccoughed through the well-worn grooves—how many times had he explained this?—*it's teratogenic, not genetic, I'm not a mutant, not . . .* What the hell did a fine point of biochemistry matter to this ignorant, bereaved woman? For all practical purposes—for her purposes—he might as well be a mutant. "—important," he finished.

She eyed him sideways, swaying gently in the clop-a-clop rhythm of her mount. "Some said you were born with no legs, and lived all the time in a float chair in Vorkosigan House. Some said you were born with no bones—"

"—and kept in a jar in the basement, no doubt," Miles muttered.

"But Karal said he'd seen you with your grandfather at Hassadar Fair, and you were only sickly and undersized. Some said your father had got you into the Service, but others said no, you'd gone off-planet to your mother's home and had your brain turned into a computer and your body fed with tubes, floating in a liquid—"

"I knew a jar would turn up in this story somewhere," Miles grimaced. *You knew you'd be sorry you asked, too, but you went and did it anyway.* She was baiting him, Miles realized suddenly. How *dare* she . . . but there was no humor in her, only a sharp-edged watchfulness.

She had gone out, way out, on a limb to lay this murder charge, in defiance of family and local authorities alike, in defiance of established custom. And what had her Count given her for a shield and support, going back to face the wrath of all her nearest and dearest? Miles. Could he handle this? She must be wondering, indeed. Or would he botch it, cave and cut and run, leaving her to face the whirlwind of rage and revenge alone?

He wished he'd left her weeping at the gate.

The woodland, fruit of many generations of terraforming forestry, opened out suddenly on a vale of brown native scrub. Down the middle of it, through some accident of soil chemistry, ran a half-kilometer-wide swathe of green and pink—feral roses, Miles realized with astonishment as they rode nearer. Earth roses. The track dove into the fragrant mass of them and vanished.

He took turns with Pym, hacking their way through with their Service bush knives. The roses were vigorous and studded with thick thorns, and hacked back with a vicious elastic recoil. Fat Ninny did his part by swinging his big head back and forth and nipping off blooms and chomping them down happily. Miles wasn't sure just how many he ought to let the big roan eat—just because the species wasn't native to Barrayar didn't mean it wasn't poisonous to horses. Miles sucked at his wounds and reflected upon Barrayar's shattered ecological history.

The fifty thousand Firsters from Earth had only meant to be the spearhead of Barrayar's colonization. Then, through a gravitational anomaly, the wormhole jump through which the colonists had come shifted closed, irrevocably and without warning. The terraforming which had begun, so careful and controlled in the beginning, collapsed along with everything else. Imported Earth plant and animal species had escaped everywhere to run wild, as the humans turned their attention to the most urgent problems of survival. Biologists still mourned the mass extinctions of native species that had followed, the erosions and droughts and floods, but really, Miles thought, over the centuries of the Time of Isolation the fittest of both worlds had fought it out to a perfectly good new balance. If it was alive and covered the ground who cared where it came from?

We are all here by accident. Like the roses.

They camped that night high in the hills, and pushed on in the morning to the flanks of the true mountains. They were now out of the region Miles was personally familiar with from his childhood, and he checked Harra's directions frequently on his orbital survey map. They stopped only a few hours short of their goal at sunset of the second day. Harra insisted she could lead them on in the dusk from here, but Miles did not care to arrive after nightfall, unannounced, in a strange place of uncertain welcome.

He bathed the next morning in a stream, and unpacked and dressed carefully in his new officer's Imperial dress greens. Pym wore the Vorkosigan brown-and-silver livery, and pulled the Count's standard on a telescoping aluminum pole from the recesses of his saddlebag and mounted it on his left stirrup. *Dressed to kill,* thought Miles joylessly. Dr. Dea wore ordinary black fatigues and looked uncomfortable. If they constituted a message, Miles was damned if he knew what it was.

They pulled the horses up at mid-morning before a two-room cabin set on the edge of a vast grove of sugar maples, planted who-knew-how-many centuries ago but now raggedly marching up the vale by self-seeding. The mountain air was cool and pure and bright. A few chickens stalked and bobbed in the weeds. An algae-choked wooden pipe from the woods dribbled water into a trough, which overflowed into a squishy green streamlet and away.

Harra slid down, smoothed her skirt, and climbed the porch. "Karal?" she called. Miles waited high on horseback for the initial contact. Never give up a psychological advantage.

"Harra? Is that you?" came a man's voice from within. He banged open the door and rushed out. "Where have you been, girl? We've been beating the bushes for you! Thought you'd broke your neck in the scrub somewhere—" he stopped short before the three silent men on horseback.

"You wouldn't write down my charges, Karal," said Harra rather breathlessly. Her hands kneaded her skirt. "So I walked to the district magistrate at Vorkosigan Surleau to Speak them myself."

"Oh, girl," Karal breathed regretfully, "that was a *stupid* thing to do. . . ." His head lowered and swayed, as he stared uneasily at the riders. He was a balding man of maybe sixty, leathery and worn, and his left arm ended in a stump. Another veteran.

"Speaker Serg Karal?" began Miles sternly. "I am the Voice of Count Vorkosigan. I am charged to investigate the crime Spoken by Harra Csurik before the Count's court, namely the murder of her infant daughter Raina. As Speaker of Silvy Vale, you are requested and required to assist me in all matters pertaining to the Count's justice."

At this point Miles ran out of prescribed formalities, and was on his own. That hadn't taken long. He waited. Fat Ninny snuffled. The silver-on-brown cloth of the standard made a few soft snapping sounds, lifted by a vagrant breeze.

"The district magistrate wasn't there," put in Harra, "but the Count was."

Karal was grey-faced, staring. He pulled himself together with an effort, came to a species of attention, and essayed a creaking half-bow. "Who—who are you, sir?"

"Lord Miles Vorkosigan."

Karal's lips moved silently. Miles was no lip reader, but he was pretty sure it came to a dismayed variant of *Oh, shit.* "This is my liveried man Sergeant Pym, and my medical examiner, Lieutenant Dea of the Imperial Service."

"You are my lord Count's son?" Karal croaked.

"The one and only." Miles was suddenly sick of the posing. Surely that was a sufficient first impression. He swung down off Ninny, landing lightly on the balls of his feet. Karal's gaze followed him down, and down. *Yeah, so I'm short. But wait'll you see me dance.* "All right if we water our horses in your trough, here?" Miles looped Ninny's reins through his arm and stepped toward it.

"Uh, that's for the people, m'lord," said Karal. "Just a minute and I'll fetch a bucket." He hitched up his baggy trousers and trotted off around the side of the cabin. A minute's uncomfortable silence, then Karal's voice floating faintly, "Where'd you put the goat bucket, Zed?"

Another voice, light and young, "Behind the woodstack, Da." The voices fell to a muffled undertone. Karal came trotting back with a battered aluminum bucket, which he placed beside the trough. He knocked out a wooden plug in the side and a bright stream arced out to plash and fill. Fat Ninny flickered his ears and snuffled and rubbed his big head against Miles, smearing his tunic with red and white horsehairs and nearly knocking him off his feet. Karal glanced up and smiled at the horse, though his smile fell away as his gaze passed on to the horse's owner. As Fat Ninny gulped his drink Miles caught a glimpse of the owner of the second voice, a boy of around twelve who flitted off into the woods behind the cabin.

Karal fell to, assisting Miles and Harra and Pym in securing the horses. Miles left Pym to unsaddle and feed, and followed Karal into his house.

Harra stuck to Miles like glue, and Dr. Dea unpacked his medical kit and trailed along. Miles's boots rang loud and unevenly on the wooden floorboards.

"My wife, she'll be back in the nooning," said Karal, moving uncertainly around the room as Miles and Dea settled themselves on a bench and Harra curled up with her arms around her knees on the floor beside the fieldstone hearth. "I'll . . . I'll make some tea, m'lord." He skittered back out the door to fill a kettle at the trough before Miles could say, *No, thank you.* No, let him ease his nerves in ordinary movements. Then maybe Miles could begin to tease out how much of this static was social nervousness and how much was (perhaps) guilty conscience. By the time Karal had the kettle on the coals he was noticably better controlled, so Miles began.

"I'd prefer to commence this investigation immediately, Speaker. It need not take long."

"It need not . . . take place at all, m'lord. The baby's death was natural—there were no marks on her. She was weakly, she had the cat's mouth, who knows what else was wrong with her? She died in her sleep, or by some accident."

"It is remarkable," said Miles dryly, "how often such accidents happen in this district. My father, the Count himself, has . . . remarked on it."

"There was no call to drag you up here." Karal looked exasperation at Harra. She sat silent, unmoved by his persuasion.

"It was no problem," said Miles blandly.

"Truly, m'lord," Karal lowered his voice, "I believe the child might have been overlain. 'S no wonder, in her grief, that her mind rejected it. Lem Csurik, he's a good boy, a good provider. She really doesn't want to do this, her reason is just temporarily overset by her troubles."

Harra's eyes, looking up from her hair-thatch, were poisonously cold.

"I begin to see," Miles's voice was mild, encouraging.

Karal brightened slightly. "It all could still be all right. If she will just be patient. Get over her sorrow. Talk to poor Lem. I'm sure he didn't kill the babe. Not rush to something she'll regret."

"I begin to see," Miles let his tone go ice cool, "why Harra Csurik found it necessary to walk four days to get an unbiased hearing. 'You think.' 'You believe.' 'Who knows what?' Not you, it appears. I hear speculation—

accusation—innuendo—assertion. I came for *facts,* Speaker Karal. The Count's justice doesn't turn on guesses. It doesn't have to. This isn't the Time of Isolation. Not even in the backbeyond.

"My investigation of the facts will begin now. No judgment will be—rushed into, before the facts are complete. Confirmation of Lem Csurik's guilt or innocence will come from his own mouth, under fast-penta, administered by Dr. Dea before two witnesses—yourself and a deputy of your choice. Simple, clean, and quick." *And maybe I can be on my way out of this benighted hole before sundown.* "I require you, Speaker, to go now and bring Lem Csurik for questioning. Sergeant Pym will assist you."

Karal killed another moment pouring the boiling water into a big brown pot before speaking. "I'm a traveled man, lord. A twenty-year Service man. But most folks here have never been out of Silvy Vale. Interrogation chemistry might as well be magic to them. They might say it was a false confession, got that way."

"Then you and your deputy can say otherwise. This isn't exactly like the good old days, when confessions were extracted under torture, Karal. Besides, if he's as innocent as you *guess*—he'll clear himself, no?"

Reluctantly, Karal went into the adjoining room. He came back shrugging on a faded Imperial Service uniform jacket with a corporal's rank marked on the collar, the buttons of which did not quite meet across his middle anymore. Preserved, evidently, for such official functions. Even as in Barrayaran custom one saluted the uniform, and not the man in it, so might the wrath engendered by an unpopular duty fall on the office and not the individual who carried it out. Miles appreciated the nuance.

Karal paused at the door. Harra still sat wrapped in silence by the hearth, rocking slightly.

"M'lord," said Karal. "I've been Speaker of Silvy Vale for sixteen years now. In all that time nobody has had to go to the district magistrate for a Speaking, not for water rights or stolen animals or swiving or even the time Neva accused Bors of tree piracy over the maple sap. We've not had a blood feud in all that time."

"I have no intention of starting a blood feud, Karal. I just want the facts."

"That's the thing, m'lord. I'm not so in love with facts as I used to be. Sometimes, they bite." Karal's eyes were urgent.

Really, the man was doing everything but stand on his head and juggle cats—one-handed—to divert Miles. How overt was his obstruction likely to get?

"Silvy Vale cannot be permitted to have its own little Time of Isolation," said Miles warningly. "The Count's justice is for everyone, now. Even if they're small. And weakly. And have something wrong with them. And cannot even speak for themselves—*Speaker.*"

Karal flinched, white about the lips—point taken, evidently. He trudged away up the trail, Pym following watchfully, one hand loosening the stunner in his holster.

They drank the tea while they waited, and Miles pottered about the cabin, looking but not touching. The hearth was the sole source of heat for cooking and wash-water. There was a beaten metal sink for washing up, filled by hand, from a covered bucket, but emptied through a drainpipe under the porch to join the streamlet running down out of the trough. The second room was a bedroom, with a double bed and chests for storage. A loft held three more pallets, the boy around back had brothers, apparently. The place was cramped, but swept, things put away and hung up.

On a side table sat a government-issue audio receiver, and a second and older military model, opened up, apparently in the process of getting minor repairs and a new power pack. Exploration revealed a drawer full of old parts, nothing more complex than for simple audio sets, unfortunately. Speaker Karal must double as Silvy Vale's comm link specialist, how appropriate. They must pick up broadcasts from the station in Hassadar, maybe the high-power government channels from the capital as well.

No other electricity, of course. Powersat receptors were expensive pieces of precision technology. They would come even here, in time; some communities almost as small, but with strong economic co-ops already had them. Silvy Vale was obviously still stuck in subsistence-level, and must needs wait till there was enough surplus in the district to gift them, if the surplus was not grabbed off first by some competing want. If only the city of Vorkosigan Vashnoi had not been obliterated by Cetagandan atomics, the whole district could be years ahead, economically. . . .

Miles walked out on the porch and leaned on the rail. Karal's son had returned. Down at the end of the cleared yard Fat Ninny was standing tethered, hip-shot, ears aflop, grunting with pleasure as the grinning boy scratched him vigorously under his halter. The boy looked up to catch Miles watching him, and scooted off fearfully to vanish again in the scrub downslope. "Huh," muttered Miles.

Dr. Dea joined him. "They've been gone a long time. About time to break out the fast-penta?"

"No, your autopsy kit, I should say. I fancy that's what we'll be doing next."

Dea glanced at him sharply. "I thought you sent Pym along to enforce the arrest."

"You can't arrest a man who's not there. Are you a wagering man, Doctor? I'll bet you a mark they don't come back with Csurik. No, hold it —maybe I'm wrong. I hope I'm wrong. Here are three coming back. . . ."

Karal, Pym, and another were marching down the trail. The third was a hulking young man, big-handed, heavy-browed, thick-necked, surly. "Harra," Miles called, "is this your husband?" He looked the part, by God, just what Miles had pictured. And four brothers just like him—only bigger, no doubt.

Harra appeared by Miles's shoulder, and let out her breath. "No, m'lord. That's Alex, the Speaker's deputy."

"Oh." Miles's lips twitched in silent frustration. *Well, I had to give it a chance to be simple.*

Karal stopped beneath him and began a wandering explanation of his empty-handed state. Miles cut him off with a lift of his eyebrows. "Pym?"

"Bolted, m'lord," said Pym laconically. "Almost certainly warned."

"I agree." He frowned down at Karal, who prudently stood silent. Facts first. Decisions, such as how much deadly force to pursue the fugitive with, second. "Harra. How far is it to your burying place?"

"Down by the stream, lord, at the bottom of the valley. About two kilometers."

"Get your kit, Doctor, we're taking a walk. Karal, fetch a shovel."

"M'lord, surely it isn't needful to disturb the peace of the dead," began Karal.

"It is entirely needful. There's a place for the autopsy report right in the Procedural I got from the district magistrate's office. Where I will file my completed report upon this case when we return to Vorkosigan Surleau. I have permission from the next-of-kin—do I not, Harra?"

She nodded numbly.

"I have the two requisite witnesses, yourself and your," *gorilla,* "deputy, we have the doctor and the daylight—if you don't stand there arguing till sundown. All we need is the shovel. Unless you're volunteering to dig with your hand, Karal." Miles's voice was flat and grating and getting dangerous.

Karal's balding head bobbed in his distress. "The—the father is the legal next-of-kin, while he lives, and you don't have his—"

"Karal," said Miles.

"M'lord?"

"Take care the grave you dig is not your own. You've got one foot in it already."

Karal's hand opened in despair. "I'll . . . get the shovel, m'lord."

The mid-afternoon was warm, the air golden and summer-sleepy. The shovel bit with a steady *scrunch-scrunch* through the soil at the hands of Karal's deputy. Downslope, a bright stream burbled away over clean rounded stones. Harra hunkered watching, silent and grim.

When big Alex levered out the little crate—so little!—Sergeant Pym went off for a patrol of the wooded perimeter. Miles didn't blame him. He hoped the soil at that depth had been cool, these last eight days. Alex pried open the box, and Dr. Dea waved him away and took over. The deputy, too, went off to find something to look at at the far end of the graveyard.

Dea looked the cloth-wrapped bundle over carefully, lifted it out and set it on his tarp laid out on the ground in the bright sun. The instruments of his investigation were arrayed upon the plastic in precise order. He unwrapped the brightly-patterned cloths in their special folds, and Harra crept up to retrieve them, straighten and fold them ready for reuse, then crept back.

Miles fingered the handkerchief in his pocket, ready to hold over his mouth and nose, and went to watch over Dea's shoulder. Bad, but not too bad. He'd seen and smelled worse. Dea, filter-masked, spoke procedurals into his recorder, hovering in the air by his shoulder, and made his examination first by eye and gloved touch, then by scanner.

"Here, my lord," said Dea, and motioned Miles closer. "Almost certainly the cause of death, though I'll run the toxin tests in a moment. Her neck was broken. See here on the scanner where the spinal cord was severed, then the bones twisted back into alignment."

"Karal, Alex," Miles motioned them up to witness; they came reluctantly.

"Could this have been accidental?" said Miles.

"Very remotely possible. The realignment had to be deliberate though."

"Would it have taken long?"

"Seconds only. Death was immediate."

"How much physical strength was required? A big man's or . . ."

"Oh, not much at all. Any adult could have done it, easily."

"Any sufficiently motivated adult." Miles's stomach churned at the mental picture Dea's words conjured up. The little fuzzy head would easily fit under a man's hand. The twist, the muffled cartilaginous crack—if there was one thing Miles knew by heart, it was the exact tactile sensation of breaking bone, oh yes.

"Motivation," said Dea, "is not my department." He paused. "I might note, a careful external examination could have found this. Mine did. An experienced layman—" his eye fell cool on Karal, "paying attention to what he was doing, should not have missed it."

Miles, too, stared at Karal, waiting.

"Overlain," hissed Harra. Her voice was ragged with scorn.

"M'lord," said Karal carefully, "it's true I suspected the possibility—"

Suspected, hell. You knew.

"But I felt—and still feel, strongly," his eye flashed a wary defiance, "that only more grief would come from a fuss. There was nothing I could do to help the baby at that point. My duties are to the living."

"So are mine, Speaker Karal. As, for example, my duty to the next small Imperial subject in mortal danger from those who should be his or her protectors, for the grave fault of being," Miles flashed an edged smile, "physically different. In Count Vorkosigan's view this is not just a case. This is a test case, fulcrum of a thousand cases. Fuss . . ." he hissed the sibilant; Harra rocked to the rhythm of his voice, "you haven't begun to see *fuss* yet."

Karal subsided as if folded.

There followed an hour of messiness yielding mainly negative data; no other bones were broken, the infant's lungs were clear, her gut and bloodstream free of toxins except those of natural decomposition. Her brain held no secret tumors. The defect for which she had died did not extend to spina bifida, Dea reported. Fairly simple plastic surgery would indeed have corrected the cat's mouth, could she somehow have won access to it. Miles wondered what comfort this confirmation was to Harra; cold, at best.

Dea put his puzzle back together, and Harra rewrapped the tiny body in intricate, meaningful folds. Dea cleaned his tools and placed them in their cases and washed his hands and arms and face thoroughly in the stream, for rather a longer time than needed for just hygiene Miles thought, while the gorilla reburied the box.

Harra made a little bowl in the dirt atop the grave, and piled in some twigs and bark scraps and a sawed-off strand of her lank hair.

Miles, caught short, felt in his pockets. "I have no offering on me that will burn," he said apologetically.

Harra glanced up, surprised at even the implied offer. "No matter, m'lord." Her little pile of scraps flared briefly and went out, like her infant Raina's life.

But it does matter, thought Miles.

Peace to you, small lady, after our rude invasions. I will give you a better sacrifice, I swear by my word as Vorkosigan. And the smoke of that burning will rise and be seen from one end of these mountains to the other.

Miles charged Karal and Alex directly with producing Lem Csurik, and gave Harra Csurik a ride home up behind him on Fat Ninny. Pym accompanied them.

They passed a few scattered cabins on the way. At one a couple of grubby children playing in the yard loped alongside the horses, giggling and making hex signs at Miles, egging each other on to bolder displays, until their mother spotted them and ran out and hustled them indoors, with a fearful look over her shoulder. In a weird way it was almost relaxing to

Miles, the welcome he'd expected, not like Karal's and Alex's strained, self-conscious, careful not-noticing. Raina's life would not have been an easy one.

Harra's cabin was at the head of a long draw, just before it narrowed into a ravine. It seemed very quiet and isolated, in the dappled shade.

"Are you sure you wouldn't rather go stay with your mother?" asked Miles dubiously.

Harra shook her head. She slid down off Ninny, and Miles and Pym dismounted and followed her in.

The cabin was of standard design, a single room with a fieldstone fireplace and a wide roofed front porch. Water apparently came from the rivulet in the ravine. Pym held up a hand and entered first behind Harra, his hand on his stunner. If Lem Csurik had run, might he have run home first? Pym had been making scanner checks of perfectly innocent clumps of bushes all the way here.

The cabin was deserted. Although not long deserted; it did not have the lingering, dusty silence one would expect of eight days mournful unoccupation. The remains of a few hasty meals sat on the sinkboard. The bed was slept-in, rumpled and unmade. A few man's garments were scattered about. Automatically, Harra began to move about the room, straightening it up, reasserting her presence, her existence, her worth. If she could not control the events of her life, at least she might control one small room.

The one untouched item was a cradle that sat beside the bed, little blankets neatly folded. Harra had fled for Vorkosigan Surleau just a few hours after the burial.

Miles wandered about the room, checking the view from the windows. "Will you show me where you went to get your brillberries, Harra?"

She led them up the ravine; Miles timed the hike. Pym divided his attention unhappily between the brush and Miles, alert to catch any bone-breaking stumble. After flinching away from about three aborted protective grabs, Miles was ready to tell him to go climb a tree. Still, there was a certain understandable self-interest at work here, if Miles broke a leg it would be Pym who'd be stuck with carrying him out.

The brillberry patch was nearly a kilometer up the ravine. Miles plucked a few seedy red berries and ate them absently, looking around, while Harra and Pym waited respectfully. Afternoon sun slanted through green and brown leaves, but the bottom of the ravine was already grey and cool with premature twilight. The brillberry vines clung to the rocks and hung down invitingly, luring one to risk one's neck reaching. Miles resisted their weedy temptations, not being all that fond of brillberries. "If someone called out from your cabin, you couldn't hear them up here, could you?" remarked Miles.

"No, m'lord."

"About how long did you spend picking?"

"About," Harra shrugged, "a basketful."

The woman didn't own a chrono. "An hour, say. And a twenty-minute climb each way. About a two-hour time window, that morning. Your cabin was not locked?"

"Just a latch, m'lord."

"Hm."

Method, motive, and opportunity, the district magistrate's Procedural had emphasized. Damn. The method was established, and almost anybody could have used it. The opportunity angle, it appeared, was just as bad. Anyone at all could have walked up to that cabin, done the deed, and departed, unseen and unheard. It was much too late for an aura detector to be of use, tracing the shining ghosts of movements in and out of that room, even if Miles had brought one.

Facts, hah. They were back to motive, the murky workings of men's minds. Anybody's guess.

Miles had, as per the instructions in the district magistrate's Procedural, been striving to keep an open mind about the accused, but it was getting harder and harder to resist Harra's assertions. She'd been proved right about everything so far.

They left Harra reinstalled in her little home, going through the motions of order and the normal routine of life as if they could somehow recreate it, like an act of sympathetic magic.

"Are you sure you'll be all right?" Miles asked, gathering Fat Ninny's reins and settling himself in the saddle. "I can't help but think that if your husband's in the area, he could show up here. You say nothing's been taken, so it's unlikely he's been here and gone before we arrived. Do you want someone to stay with you?"

"No, m'lord." She hugged her broom, on the porch. "I'd . . . I'd like to be alone for a while."

"Well . . . all right. I'll, ah, send you a message if anything important happens."

"Thank you, m'lord." Her tone was unpressing; she really did want to be left alone. Miles took the hint.

At a wide place in the trail back to Speaker Karal's, Pym and Miles rode stirrup to stirrup. Pym was still painfully on the alert for boogies in the bushes.

"My lord, may I suggest that your next logical step be to draft all the able-bodied men in the community for a hunt for this Csurik? Beyond doubt, you've established that the infanticide was a murder."

Interesting turn of phrase, Miles thought dryly. *Even Pym doesn't find it redundant. Oh, my poor Barrayar.* "It seems reasonable at first glance, Sergeant Pym, but has it ocurred to you that half the able-bodied men in this community are probably relatives of Lem Csurik's?"

"It might have a psychological effect. Create enough disruption, and perhaps someone would turn him in just to get it over with."

"Hm, possibly. Assuming he hasn't already left the area. He could have been halfway to the coast before we were done at the autopsy."

"Only if he had access to transport." Pym glanced at the empty sky.

"For all we know one of his sub-cousins had a rickety lightflyer in a shed somewhere. But . . . he's never been out of Silvy Vale. I'm not sure he'd know how to run, where to go. Well, if he has left the district it's a problem for Imperial Civil Security, and I'm off the hook." Happy thought. "But—one of the things that bothers me, a lot, are the inconsistencies in the picture I'm getting of our chief suspect. Have you noticed them?"

"Can't say as I have, m'lord."

"Hm. Where did Karal take you, by the way, to arrest this guy?"

"To a wild area, rough scrub and gullies. Half a dozen men were out searching for Harra. They'd just called off their search and were on their way back when we met up with them. By which I concluded our arrival was no surprise."

"Had Csurik actually been there, and fled, or was Karal just ring-leading you in a circle?"

"I think he'd actually been there, m'lord. The men claimed not, but as you point out they were relatives, and besides, they did not, ah, lie well. They were tense. Karal may begrudge you his cooperation, but I don't think he'll quite dare disobey your direct orders. He is a twenty-year man, after all."

Like Pym himself, Miles thought. Count Vorkosigan's personal guard was legally limited to a ceremonial twenty men, but given his political position their function included very practical security. Pym was typical of their number, a decorated veteran of the Imperial Service who had retired to this elite private force. It was not Pym's fault that when he had joined he had stepped into a dead man's shoes, replacing the late Sergeant Bothari. Did anyone in the universe, besides himself, miss the deadly and difficult Bothari? Miles wondered sadly.

"I'd like to question *Karal* under fast-penta," said Miles morosely. "He displays every sign of being a man who knows where the body's buried."

"Why don't you, then?" asked Pym logically.

"I may come to that. There is, however, a certain unavoidable degradation in a fast-penta interrogation. If the man's loyal it may not be in our best long-range interest to shame him publicly."

"It wouldn't be in public."

"No, but he would remember being turned into a drooling idiot. I need . . . more information."

Pym glanced back over his shoulder. "I thought you had all the information, by now."

"I have facts. Physical facts. A great big pile of—meaningless, useless facts." Miles brooded. "If I have to fast-penta every backbeyonder in Silvy Vale to get to the bottom of this, I will. But it's not an elegant solution."

"It's not an elegant problem, m'lord," said Pym, dryly.

They returned to find Speaker Karal's wife back and in full possession of her home. She was running in frantic circles, chopping, beating, kneading, stoking, and flying upstairs to change the bedding on the three pallets, driving her three sons before her to fetch and run and carry. Dr. Dea, bemused, was following her about trying to slow her down, explaining that they had brought their own tent and food, thank you, and that her hospitality was not required. This produced a most indignant response from Ma Karal.

"My lord's own son comes to my house, and I to turn him out in the fields like his horse! I'd be ashamed!" And she returned to her work.

"She seems rather distraught," said Dea, looking over his shoulder.

Miles took him by the elbow and propelled him out onto the porch. "Just get out of her way, Doctor. We're doomed to be Entertained. It's an obligation on both sides. The polite thing to do is sort of pretend we're not here till she's ready for us."

Dea lowered his voice. "It might be better, in light of the circumstances, if we were to eat only our packaged food."

The chatter of a chopping knife, and a scent of herbs and onions, wafted enticingly through the open window. "Oh, I would imagine anything out of the common pot would be all right, wouldn't you?" said Miles. "If anything really worries you, you can wisk it off and check it, I suppose, but —discreetly, eh? We don't want to insult anyone."

They settled themselves in the homemade wooden chairs, and were promptly served tea, again, by a boy draftee of ten, Karal's youngest. He had apparently already received private instructions in manners from one or the other of his parents, for his response to Miles's deformities was the same flickering covert not-noticing as the adults, not quite as smoothly carried off.

"Will you be sleeping in my bed, m'lord?" he asked. "Ma says we got to sleep on the porch."

"Well, whatever your Ma says, goes," said Miles. "Ah . . . do you like sleeping on the porch?"

"Naw. Last time, Zed kicked me and I rolled off in the dark."

"Oh. Well, perhaps, if we're to displace you, you would care to sleep in our tent by way of trade?"

The boy's eyes widened. "Really?"

"Certainly. Why not?"

"Wait'll I tell Zed!" He danced down the steps and shot away around the side of the house. "Zed, hey, Zed . . . !"

"I suppose," said Dea, "we can fumigate it, later. . . ."

Miles's lips twitched. "They're no grubbier than you were at the same age, surely. Or than I was. When I was permitted." The late afternoon was warm. Miles took off his green tunic and hung it on the back of his chair, and unbuttoned the round collar of his cream shirt.

Dea's brows rose. "Are we keeping shopman's hours, then, m'lord, on this investigation? Calling it quits for the day?"

"Not exactly." Miles sipped tea thoughtfully, gazing out across the yard. The trees and treetops fell away down to the bottom of this feeder valley. Mixed scrub climbed the other side of the slope. A crested fold, then the long flanks of a backbone mountain, beyond, rose high and harsh to a summit still flecked with dwindling dirty patches of snow.

"There's still a murderer loose out there somewhere," Dea pointed out helpfully.

"You sound like Pym." Pym, Miles noted, had finished with their horses and was taking his scanner for another walk. "I'm waiting."

"What for?"

"Not sure. The piece of information that will make sense of all this. Look, there's only two possibilities. Csurik's either innocent or he's guilty. If he's guilty, he's not going to turn himself in. He'll certainly involve his relations, hiding and helping him. I can call in reinforcements by comm link from Imperial Civil Security in Hassadar, if I want to. Any time. Twenty men, plus equipment, here by aircar in a couple of hours. Create a circus. Brutal, ugly, disruptive, exciting—could be quite popular. A manhunt, with blood at the end.

"Of course, there's also the possibility that Csurik's innocent, but scared. In which case . . ."

"Yes?"

"In which case, there's still a murderer out there." Miles drank more tea. "I merely note, if you want to catch something, running after it isn't always the best way."

Dea cleared his throat, and drank his tea, too.

"In the meantime, I have another duty to carry out. I'm here to be seen. If your scientific spirit is yearning for something to do to wile away the hours, try keeping count of the number of Vorwatchers that turn up to-night."

Miles's predicted parade began almost immediately. It was mainly women, at first, bearing gifts as to a funeral. In the absence of a comm link system Miles wasn't sure by what telepathy they managed to communicate with each other, but they brought covered dishes of food, flowers, extra bedding, and offers of assistance. They were all introduced to Miles with nervous curtseys, but seldom lingered to chat; apparently a look was all their curiosity desired. Ma Karal was polite, but made it clear that she had the situation well in hand, and set their culinary offerings well back of her own.

Some of the women had children in tow. Most of these were sent to play in the woods in back, but a small party of whispering boys sneaked back around the cabin to peek up over the rim of the porch at Miles. Miles had obligingly remained on the porch with Dea, remarking that it was a better view, without saying for whom. For a few moments Miles pretended not to notice his audience, restraining Pym, with a hand signal, from running them off. *Yes, look well, look your fill,* thought Miles. *What you see is what you're going to get, for the rest of your lives or at any rate mine. Get used to it. . . .* Then he caught Zed Karal's whisper, as self-appointed tour guide to his cohorts—"That big one's the one that's come to kill Lem Csurik!"

"Zed," said Miles.

There was an abrupt frozen silence from under the edge of the porch. Even the animal rustlings stopped.

"Come here," said Miles.

To a muted background of dismayed whispers and nervous giggles, Karal's middle boy slouched warily up on to the porch.

"You three—" Miles's pointing finger caught them in mid-flight, "wait there." Pym added his frown for emphasis, and Zed's friends stood paralyzed, eyes wide, heads lined up at the level of the porch floor as if stuck up on some ancient battlement as a warning to kindred malefactors.

"What did you just say to your friends, Zed?" asked Miles quietly. "Repeat it."

Zed licked his lips. "I jus' said you'd come to kill Lem Csurik, lord." Zed was clearly now wondering if Miles's murderous intent included obnoxious and disrespectful boys as well.

"That is not true, Zed. That is a dangerous lie."

Zed looked bewildered. "But Da—said it."

"What is true, is that I've come to catch the person who killed Lem Csurik's baby daughter. That may be Lem. But it may not. Do you understand the difference?"

"But Harra said Lem did it, and she ought to know, he's her husband and all."

"The baby's neck was broken by someone. Harra thinks Lem, but she didn't see it happen. What you and your friends here have to understand is that I won't make a mistake. I *can't* condemn the wrong person. My own truth drugs won't let me. Lem Csurik has only to come here and tell me the truth to clear himself, if he didn't do it.

"But suppose he did. What should I do with a man who would kill a baby, Zed?"

Zed shuffled. "Well, she was only a mutie . . ." then shut his mouth and reddened, not looking at Miles.

It was, perhaps, a bit much to ask a twelve-year-old boy to take an interest in any baby, let alone a mutie one . . . *no,* dammit. It wasn't too much. But how to get a hook into that prickly defensive surface? And if Miles couldn't even convince one surly twelve year old, how was he to magically transmute a whole District of adults? A rush of despair made him suddenly want to rage. These people were so bloody *impossible.* He checked his temper firmly.

"Your Da was a twenty-year man, Zed. Are you proud that he served the Emperor?"

"Yes, lord." Zed's eyes sought escape, trapped by these terrible adults.

Miles forged on. "Well, these practices—mutie-killing—shame the Emperor, when he stands for Barrayar before the galaxy. I've been out there. I know. They call us all savages, for the crimes of a few. It shames the Count my father before his peers, and Silvy Vale before the District. A soldier gets honor by killing an armed enemy, not a baby. This matter touches my honor as a Vorkosigan, Zed. Besides," Miles's lips drew back on a mirthless grin, and he leaned forward intently in his chair—Zed recoiled as much as he dared—"you will all be astonished at what *only a mutie* can do. *That* I have sworn on my grandfather's grave."

Zed looked more suppressed than enlightened, his slouch now almost a crouch. Miles slumped back in his chair and released him with a weary wave of his hand. "Go play, boy."

Zed needed no urging. He and his companions shot away around the house as though released from springs.

Miles drummed his fingers on the chair arm, frowning into the silence that neither Pym nor Dea dared break.

"These hill-folk are ignorant, lord," offered Pym after a moment.

"These hill-folk are *mine,* Pym. Their ignorance is . . . a shame upon my house." Miles brooded. How had this whole mess become his anyway? He hadn't created it. Historically, he'd only just got here himself. "Their continued ignorance, anyway," he amended in fairness. It still made a burden like a mountain. "Is the message so complex? So difficult? 'You don't have to kill your children anymore.' It's not like we're asking them all to learn—5-Space navigational math." That had been the plague of Miles's last Academy semester.

"It's not easy for them," shrugged Dea. "It's easy for the central authorities to make the rules, but these people have to live every minute of the consequences. They have so little, and the new rules force them to give their margin to marginal people who can't pay back. The old ways were wise, in the old days. Even now you have to wonder how many premature reforms we can afford, trying to ape the galactics."

And what's your definition of a marginal person, Dea? "But the margin is growing," Miles said aloud. "Places like this aren't up against famine every winter any more. They're not isolated in their disasters, relief can get from one district to another under the Imperial seal . . . we're all getting more connected, just as fast as we can. Besides," Miles paused, and added rather weakly, "perhaps you underestimate them."

Dea's brows rose ironically. Pym strolled the length of the porch, running his scanner in yet another pass over the surrounding scrubland. Miles, turning in his chair to pursue his cooling teacup, caught a slight movement, a flash of eyes, behind the casement-hung front window swung open to the summer air—Ma Karal, standing frozen, listening. For how long? Since he'd called her boy Zed, Miles guessed, arresting her attention. She raised her chin as his eyes met hers, sniffed, and shook out the cloth she'd been holding with a snap. They exchanged a nod. She turned back to her work before Dea, watching Pym, noticed her.

Karal and Alex returned, understandably, around suppertime.

"I have six men out searching," Karal reported cautiously to Miles on the porch, now well on its way to becoming Miles's official HQ. Clearly, Karal had covered ground since mid-afternoon. His face was sweaty, lined with physical as well as the underlying emotional strain. "But I think Lem's gone into the scrub. It could take days to smoke him out. There's hundreds of places to lie low out there."

Karal ought to know. "You don't think he's gone to some relative's?" asked Miles. "Surely, if he intends to evade us for long, he has to take a chance on resupply, on information. Will they turn him in when he surfaces?"

"It's hard to say." Karal turned his hand palm-out. "It's . . . a hard problem for 'em, m'lord."

"Hm."

How long would Lem Csurik hang around out there in the scrub, anyway? His whole life—his blown-to-bits life—was all here in Silvy Vale. Miles considered the contrast. A few weeks ago, Csurik had been a young man with everything going for him; a home, a wife, a family on the way, happiness; by Silvy Vale standards, comfort and security. His cabin, Miles had not failed to note, though simple, had been kept with love and energy, and so redeemed from the potential squalor of its poverty. Grimmer in the winter, to be sure. Now Csurik was a hunted fugitive, all the little he had torn away in the twinkling of an eye. With nothing to hold him, would he run away and keep running? With nothing to run to, would he linger near the ruins of his life?

The police force available to Miles, a few hours away in Hassadar, was an itch in his mind. Was it not time to call them in, before he fumbled this into a worse mess? But . . . if he were meant to solve this by a show of force, why hadn't the Count let him come by aircar on the first day? Miles regretted that two-and-a-half-day ride. It had sapped his forward momentum, slowed him down to Silvey Vale's walking pace, tangled him with time to doubt. Had the Count foreseen it? What did he know that Miles didn't? What *could* he know? Dammit, this test didn't need to be made harder by artificial stumbling blocks, it was bad enough all on its own. *He wants me to be clever,* Miles thought morosely. *Worse, he wants me to be seen to be clever, by everyone here.* He prayed he was not about to be spectacularly stupid, instead.

"Very well, Speaker Karal. You've done all you can for today. Knock off for the night. Call your men off, too. You're not likely to find anything in the dark."

Pym held up his scanner, clearly about to volunteer its use, but Miles waved him down. Pym's brows rose, editorially. Miles shook his head slightly.

Karal needed no further urging. He dispatched Alex to call off the night search with torches. He remained wary of Miles. Perhaps Miles puzzled him as much as he puzzled Miles? Dourly, Miles hoped so.

Miles was not sure at what point the long summer evening segued into a party. After supper the men began to drift in, Karal's cronies, Silvy Vale's elders. Some were apparently regulars who shared the evening government news broadcasts on Karal's audio set. Too many names, and Miles daren't forget a one. A group of amateur musicians arrived with their homemade mountain instruments, rather breathless, obviously the band tapped for all the major weddings and wakes in Silvy Vale; this all seemed more like a funeral to Miles every minute.

The musicians stood in the middle of the yard and played. Miles's porch-HQ now became his aristocratic box seat. It was hard to get involved with the music when the audience was all so intently watching him. Some songs were serious, some—rather carefully at first—funny. Miles's spontaneity was frequently frozen in mid-laugh by a faint sigh of relief from those around him; his stiffening froze them in turn, self-stymied like two people trying to dodge each other in a corridor.

But one song was so hauntingly beautiful—a lament for lost love—that Miles was struck to the heart. *Elena* . . . In that moment, old pain transformed to melancholy, sweet and distant; a sort of healing, or at least the realization that a healing had taken place, unwatched. He almost had the singers stop there, while they were perfect, but feared they might think him displeased. But he remained quiet and inward for a time afterward, scarcely hearing their next offering in the gathering twilight.

At least the piles of food that had arrived all afternoon were thus accounted for. Miles had been afraid Ma Karal and her cronies had expected him to get around that culinary mountain all by himself.

At one point Miles leaned on the rail and glanced down the yard to see Fat Ninny at tether, making more friends. A whole flock of pubescent girls were clustered around him, petting him, brushing his fetlocks, braiding flowers and ribbons in his mane and tail, feeding him tidbits, or just resting their cheeks against his warm silky side. Ninny's eyes were half-closed in smug content.

God, thought Miles jealously, *if I had half the sex-appeal of that bloody horse I'd have more girlfriends than my cousin Ivan.* Miles considered, very briefly, the pros and cons of making a play for some unattached female. The striding lords of old and all that . . . no. There were some kinds of stupid he didn't have to be, and that was definitely one of them. The service he had already sworn to one small lady of Silvy Vale was surely all he could bear without breaking; he could feel the strain of it all around him now, like a dangerous pressure in his bones.

He turned to find Speaker Karal presenting a woman to him, far from pubescent; she was perhaps fifty, lean and little, work-worn. She was carefully clothed in an aging best-dress, her greying hair combed back and bound at the nape of her neck. She bit at her lips and cheeks in quick tense motions, half-suppressed in her self-consciousness.

" 'S Ma Csurik, m'lord. Lem's mother." Speaker Karal ducked his head and backed away, abandoning Miles without aid or mercy—*Come back, you coward!*

"Ma'am," Miles said. His throat was dry. Karal had set him up, dammit, a public play—no, the other guests were retreating out of earshot, too, most of them.

"M'lord," said Ma Csurik. She managed a nervous curtsey.

"Uh . . . do sit down." With a ruthless jerk of his chin Miles evicted Dr. Dea from his chair and motioned the hill woman into it. He turned his own chair to face hers. Pym stood behind them, silent as a statue, tight as a wire. Did he imagine the old woman was about to whip a needler-pistol from her skirts? No—it was Pym's job to imagine things like that for Miles, so that Miles might free his whole mind for the problem at hand. Pym was almost as much an object of study as Miles himself. Wisely, he'd been holding himself apart, and would doubtless continue to do so till the dirty work was over.

"M'lord," said Ma Csurik again, and stumbled again to silence. Miles could only wait. He prayed she wasn't about to come unglued and weep on his knees or some damn thing. This was excruciating. *Stay strong, woman,* he urged silently.

"Lem, he . . ." she swallowed, "I'm sure he didn't kill the babe. There's never been any of that in our family, I swear it! He says he didn't, and I believe him."

"Good," said Miles affably. "Let him come say the same thing to me under fast-penta, and I'll believe him, too."

"Come away, Ma," urged a lean young man who had accompanied her and now stood waiting by the steps, as if ready to bolt into the dark at a motion. "It's no good, can't you see?" He glowered at Miles.

She shot the boy a quelling frown—another of her five sons?—and turned back more urgently to Miles, groping for words. "My Lem. He's only twenty, lord."

"*I'm* only twenty, Ma Csurik," Miles felt compelled to point out. There was another brief impasse.

"Look, I'll say it again," Miles burst out impatiently. "And again, and again, till the message penetrates all the way back to its intended recipient. I *cannot* condemn an innocent person. My truth drugs won't let me. Lem can clear himself. He has only to come in. Tell him, will you? Please?"

She went stony, guarded. "I . . . haven't seen him, m'lord."

"But you might."

She tossed her head. "So? I might not." Her eyes shifted to Pym and away, as if the sight of him burned. The silver Vorkosigan emblems embroidered on Pym's collar gleamed in the twilight like animal eyes, moving only with his breathing. Karal was now bringing lighted lamps onto the porch, but keeping his distance still.

"Ma'am," said Miles tightly. "The Count my father has ordered me to investigate the murder of your granddaughter. If your son means so much to you, how can his child mean so little? Was she . . . your first grandchild?"

Her face was sere. "No, lord. Lem's older sister, she has two. *They're* all right," she added with emphasis.

Miles sighed. "If you truly believe your son is innocent of this crime, you must help me prove it. Or—do you doubt?"

She shifted uneasily. There was doubt in her eyes—she didn't know, blast it. Fast-penta would be useless on her, for sure. As Miles's magic wonder drug, much counted-upon, fast-penta seemed to be having wonderfully little utility in this case so far.

"Come away, Ma," the young man urged again. "It's no good. The mutie lord came up here for a killing. They have to have one. It's a show."

Damn straight, thought Miles acidly. He was a perceptive young lunk, that one.

Ma Csurik let herself be persuaded away by her angry and embarrassed son plucking at her arm. She paused on the steps, though, and shot bitterly over her shoulder, "It's all so easy for you, isn't it?"

My head hurts, thought Miles.

There was worse to come before the evening ended.

The new woman's voice was grating, low and angry. "Don't you talk down to me, Serg Karal. I got a right for one good look at this mutie lord."

She was tall and stringy and tough. *Like her daughter,* Miles thought. She had made no attempt to freshen up. A faint reek of summer sweat hung about her working dress. And how far had she walked? Her grey hair hung in a switch down her back, a few strands escaping the tie. If Ma Csurik's bitterness had been a stabbing pain behind the eyes, this one's rage was a wringing knot in the gut.

She shook off Karal's attempted restraint and stalked up to Miles in the lamplight. "So."

"Uh . . . this is Ma Mattulich, m'lord," Karal introduced her. "Harra's mother."

Miles rose to his feet, managed a short formal nod. "How do you do, madam?" He was very conscious of being a head shorter than her. She had once been of a height with Harra, Miles estimated, but her aging bones were beginning to pull her down.

She merely stared. She was a gumleaf chewer, by the faint blackish stains around her mouth. Her jaw worked now on some small bit, tiny chomps, grinding too hard. She studied him openly, without subterfuge or the least hint of apology, taking in his head, his neck, his back, his short and crooked legs. Miles had the unpleasant illusion that she saw right through to all the healed cracks in his brittle bones as well. Miles's chin jerked up twice in the twitchy, nervous-involuntary tic that he was sure made him look spastic, before he controlled it with an effort.

"All right," said Karal roughly, "you've seen. Now come away, for God's sake, Mara." His hand opened in apology to Miles. "Mara, she's been pretty distraught over all this, m'lord. Forgive her."

"Your only grandchild," said Miles to her, in an effort to be kind, though her peculiar anguish repelled kindness with a scraped and bleeding scorn. "I understand your distress, ma'am. But there will be justice for little Raina. That I have sworn."

"How can there be justice *now?*" she raged, thick and low. "It's too late—a world too late—for justice, mutie lordling. What use do I have for your damned justice *now?*"

"Enough, Mara!" Karal insisted. His brows drew down and his lips thinned, and he forced her away and escorted her firmly off his porch.

The last lingering remnant of visitors parted for her with an air of respectful mercy, except for two lean teenagers hanging on the fringes who drew away as if avoiding poison. Miles was forced to revise his mental image of the Brothers Csurik. If those two were another sample, there was no team of huge menacing hill hulks after all. They were a team of little skinny menacing hill squirts, instead. Not really an improvement, they looked like they could move as fast as striking ferrets if they had to. Miles's lips curled in frustration.

The evening's entertainments ended finally, thank God, close to midnight. Karal's last cronies marched off into the woods by lantern light. The repaired and repowered audio set was carried off by its owner with many thanks to Karal. Fortunately, it had been a mature and sober crowd, even somber, no drunken brawls or anything. Pym got the Karal boys settled in the tent, took a last patrol around the cabin, and joined Miles and Dea in the loft. The pallets' stuffing had been spiked with fresh scented native herbs, to which Miles hoped devoutly he was not allergic. Ma Karal had wanted to turn her own bedroom over to Miles's exclusive lordly use, exiling herself and her husband to the porch, too, but fortunately Pym had been able to persuade her that putting Miles in the loft, flanked by Dea and himself, was to be preferred from a security standpoint.

Dea and Pym were soon snoring, but sleep eluded Miles. He tossed on his pallet as he turned his ploys of the day, such as they had been, over and over in his mind. Was he being too slow, too careful, too conservative? This wasn't exactly good assault tactics, surprise with a superior force. The view he'd gained of the terrain from Karal's porch tonight had been ambiguous at best.

On the other hand, it did no good to charge off across a swamp, as his fellow cadet and cousin Ivan Vorpatril had demonstrated so memorably once on summer maneuvers. It had taken a heavy hovercab, with a crane, to crank the six big, strong, healthy, fully field-equipped young men of Ivan's patrol out of the chest-high, gooey black mud. Ivan had got his revenge simultaneously, though, when the cadet "sniper" they had been attacking fell out of his tree and broke his arm while laughing hysterically as they sank slowly and beautifully into the ooze. Ooze that a little guy, with his laser rifle wrapped in his loincloth, could swim across like a frog. The war games umpire had ruled it a draw. Miles rubbed his forearm and grinned in memory, and faded out at last.

Miles awoke abruptly and without transition deep in the night with a sense of something wrong. A faint orange glow shimmered in the blue darkness of the loft. Quietly, so as not to disturb his sleeping companions, he rose on his pallet and peered over the edge into the main room. The glow was coming through the front window.

Miles swung onto the ladder and padded downstairs for a look out doors. "Pym," he called softly.

Pym shot awake with a snort. "M'lord?" he said, alarmed.

"Come down here. Quietly. Bring your stunner."

Pym was by his side in seconds. He slept in his trousers with his stunner holster and boots by his pillow. "What the hell—?" Pym muttered, looking out, too.

The glow was from fire. A pitchy torch, flung to the top of Miles's tent set up in the yard, was burning quietly. Pym lurched toward the door, then controlled his movements as the same realization came to him as had to Miles. Theirs was a Service-issue tent, and its combat-rated synthetic fabric would neither melt nor burn.

Miles wondered if the person who'd heaved the torch had known that. Was this some arcane warning, or a singularly inept attack? If the tent had been ordinary fabric, and Miles in it, the intended result might not have been trivial. Worse with Karal's boys in it—a bursting blossom of flame—Miles shuddered.

Pym loosened the stunner in his holster and stood poised by the front door. "How long?"

"I'm not sure. Could have been burning like that for ten minutes before it woke me."

Pym shook his head, took a slight breath, raised his scanner, and vaulted into the fire-gilded darkness.

"Trouble, m'lord?" Speaker Karal's anxious voice came from his bedroom door.

"Maybe. Wait—" Miles halted him as he plunged for the door. "Pym's running a patrol with a scanner and a stunner. Wait'll he calls the all-clear, I think. Your boys may be safer inside the tent."

Karal came up to the window, caught his breath, and swore.

Pym returned in a few minutes. "There's no one within a kilometer, now," he reported shortly. He helped Karal take the goat bucket and douse the torch. The boys, who had slept through the fire, woke at its quenching.

"I think maybe it was a bad idea to lend them my tent," said Miles from the porch in a choked voice. "I am profoundly sorry, Speaker Karal. I didn't think."

"This should never . . ." Karal was spluttering with anger and delayed fright, "this should *never* have happened, m'lord. I apologize for . . . for Silvy Vale." He turned helplessly, peering into the darkness. The night sky, star-flecked, lovely, was threatening now.

The boys, once the facts penetrated their sleepiness, thought it was all just great, and wanted to return to the tent and lie in wait for the next assassin. Ma Karal, shrill and firm, herded them indoors instead and made them bed down in the main room. It was an hour before they stopped complaining at the injustice of it and went back to sleep.

Miles, keyed up nearly to the point of gibbering, did not sleep at all. He lay stiffly on his pallet, listening to Dea, who slept breathing heavily, and Pym, feigning sleep for courtesy and scarcely seeming to breathe at all.

Miles was about to suggest to Pym that they give up and go out on the porch for the rest of the night when the silence was shattered by a shrill squeal, enormously loud, pain-edged, from outside.

"The horses!" Miles spasmed to his feet, heart racing, and beat Pym to the ladder. Pym cut ahead of him by dropping straight over the side of the loft into an elastic crouch, and beat him to the door. There, Pym's trained bodyguard's reflexes compelled him to try and thrust Miles back inside. Miles almost bit him. "Go, dammit! I've got a weapon!"

Pym, good intentions frustrated, swung out the cabin door with Miles on his heels. Halfway down the yard they split to each side as a massive snorting shape loomed out of the darkness and nearly ran them down; the sorrel mare, loose again. Another squeal pierced the night from the lines where the horses were tethered.

"Ninny?" Miles called, panicked. It was Ninny's voice making those noises, the like of which Miles had not heard since the night a shed had burned down at Vorkosigan Surleau with a horse trapped inside. "Ninny!"

Another grunting squeal, and a thunk like someone splitting a watermelon with a mallet. Pym staggered back, inhaling with difficulty, a resonant deep stutter, and tripped to the ground where he lay curled up around himself. Not killed outright, apparently, because between gasps he was managing to swear lividly. Miles dropped to the ground beside him, checked his skull—no, thank God it had been Pym's chest Ninny's hoof had hit with that alarming sound. The bodyguard only had the wind knocked out of him, maybe a cracked rib. Miles more sensibly ran around to the *front* of the horse lines. "Ninny!"

Fat Ninny was jerking his head against his rope, attempting to rear. He squealed again, his white-rimmed eyes gleaming in the darkness. Miles ran to his head. "Ninny, boy! What is it?" His left hand slid up the rope to Ninny's halter, his right stretched to stroke Ninny's shoulder soothingly. Fat Ninny flinched, but stopped trying to rear, and stood trembling. The horse shook his head. Miles's face and chest were suddenly spattered with something hot and dark and sticky.

"Dea!" Miles yelled. *"Dea!"*

Nobody slept through this uproar. Six people tumbled off the porch and down the yard, and not one of them thought to bring a light . . . no, the brilliant flare of a cold light sprang from between Dr. Dea's fingers, and Ma Karal was struggling even now to light a lantern. "Dea, get that damn light over here!" Miles demanded, and stopped to choke his voice back down an octave to its usual carefully cultivated deeper register.

Dea galloped up and thrust the light toward Miles, then gasped, his face draining. "My lord! Are you shot?" In the flare the dark liquid soaking Miles's shirt glowed suddenly scarlet.

"Not me," Miles said, looking down at his chest in horror himself. A flash of memory turned his stomach over, cold at the vision of another blood-soaked death, that of the late Sergeant Bothari whom Pym had replaced. Would never replace.

Dea spun. "Pym?"

"He's all right," said Miles. A long inhaling wheeze rose from the grass a few meters off, the exhalation punctuated with obscenities. "But he got kicked by the horse. Get your medkit!" Miles peeled Dea's fingers off the cold light, and Dea dashed back to the cabin.

Miles held the light up to Ninny, and swore in a sick whisper. A huge cut, a third of a meter long and of unknown depth, scored Ninny's glossy neck. Blood soaked his coat and runneled down his foreleg. Miles's fingers touched the wound fearfully; his hands spread on either side, trying to push it closed, but the horse's skin was elastic and it pulled apart and bled profusely as Fat Ninny shook his head in pain. Miles grabbed the horse's nose—"Hold still, boy!" Somebody had been going for Ninny's jugular. And had almost made it; Ninny—tame, petted, friendly, trusting Ninny—would not have moved from the touch until the knife bit deep.

Karal was helping Pym to his feet as Dr. Dea returned. Miles waited while Dea checked Pym over, then called, "Here, Dea!"

Zed, looking quite as horrified as Miles, helped to hold Ninny's head as Dea inspected the cut. "I took tests," Dea complained *sotto voce* as he worked. "I beat out twenty-six other applicants, for the honor of becoming the prime minister's personal physician. I have practiced the procedures of seventy separate possible medical emergencies, from coronary thrombosis to attempted assassination. Nobody—*nobody*—told me my duties would include sewing up a damned horse's neck in the middle of the night in the middle of a howling wilderness. . . ." But he kept working as he complained, so Miles didn't quash him, but kept gently petting Ninny's nose, and hypnotically rubbing the hidden pattern of his muscles, to soothe and still him. At last Ninny relaxed enough to rest his slobbery chin on Miles's shoulder.

"Do horses get anesthetics?" asked Dea plaintively, holding his medical stunner as if not sure just what to do with it.

"This one does," said Miles stoutly. "You treat him just like a person, Dea. This is the last animal that the Count my Grandfather personally trained. He named him. I watched him get born. We trained him together. Grandfather had me pick him up and hold him every day for a week after he was foaled, till he got too big. Horses are creatures of habit, grandfather said, and take first impressions to heart. Forever after Ninny thought I was bigger than he was."

Dea sighed and made busy with anesthetic stun, cleansing solution, antibiotics, muscle relaxants, and biotic glue. With a surgeon's touch he shaved the edges of the cut and placed the reinforcing net. Zed held the light anxiously.

"The cut is clean," said Dea, "but it will undergo a lot of flexing—I don't suppose it can very well be immobilized, in this position? No, hardly. This should do. If he were a human, I'd tell him to rest at this point."

"He'll be rested," Miles promised firmly. "Will he be all right now?"

"I suppose so. How the devil should I know?" Dea looked highly aggrieved, but his hand sneaked out to recheck his repairs.

"General Piotr," Miles assured him, "would have been very pleased with your work." Miles could hear him in his head now, snorting, *Damned technocrats. Nothing but horse doctors with a more expensive set of toys.* Grandfather would have loved being proved right. "You, ah . . . never met my grandfather, did you?"

"Before my time, my lord," said Dea. "I've studied his life and campaigns, of course."

"Of course."

Pym had a hand-light now, and was limping with Karal in a slow spiral around the horse lines, inspecting the ground. Karal's eldest boy had recaptured the sorrel mare and brought her back and retethered her. Her tether had been torn loose, not cut; had the mysterious attacker's choice of equine victim been random, or calculated? How calculated? Was Ninny attacked as a mere symbol of his master, or had the person known how passionately Miles loved the animal? Was this vandalism, a political statement, or an act of precisely directed, subtle cruelty?

What have I ever done to you?! Miles's thought howled silently to the surrounding darkness.

"They got away, whoever it was," Pym reported. "Out of scanner range before I could breathe again. My apologies, m'lord. They don't seem to have dropped anything on the ground."

There had to have been a knife, at least. A knife, its haft gory with horse blood in a pattern of perfect fingerprints, would have been extremely convenient just now, Miles sighed.

Ma Karal drifted up and eyed Dea's medkit, as he cleaned and repacked it. "All that," she muttered under her breath, "for a horse. . . ."

Miles refrained, barely, from leaping to a hot defense of the value of this particular horse. How many people in Silvy Vale had Ma Karal seen suffer and die, in her lifetime, for lack of no more medical technology than what Dea was carrying under his arm just now?

Guarding his horse, Miles watched from the porch as dawn crept over the landscape. He had changed his shirt and washed off. Pym was inside getting his ribs taped. Miles sat with his back to the wall and a stunner on his lap as the night mists slowly grew grey. The valley was a grey blur, fog-shrouded, the hills darker rolls of fog beyond. Directly overhead, grey thinned to a paling blue. The day would be fine and hot once the fog burned away.

It was surely time now to call out the troops from Hassadar. This was getting just too weird. His bodyguard was half out of commission—true, it was Miles's horse that had rendered him so, not the mystery attacker. But just because the attacks hadn't been fatal didn't mean they hadn't been intended so. Perhaps a third attack would be brought off more expertly. Practice makes perfect.

Miles felt unstrung with nervous exhaustion. How had he let a mere horse become such a handle on his emotions? Bad, that, almost unbalanced —yet Ninny's was surely one of the truly innocent pure souls Miles had ever known. Miles remembered the other innocent in the case then, and shivered in the damp. *It was cruel, lord, something cruel. . . .* Pym was right, the bushes could be crawling with Csurik assassins right now.

Dammit, the bushes *were* crawling—over there, a movement, a damping wave of branch lashing in recoil from—what? Miles's heart lurched in his chest. He adjusted his stunner to full power, slipped silently off the porch, and began his stalk, crouching low, taking advantage of cover wherever the long grasses of the yard had not been trampled flat by the activities of the last day, and night. Miles froze like a predatory cat as a shape seemed to coalesce out of the mist.

A lean young man, not too tall, dressed in the baggy trousers that seemed to be standard here, stood wearily by the horse lines, staring up the yard at Karal's cabin. He stood so for a full two minutes without moving. Miles held a bead on him with his stunner. If he dared make one move toward Ninny . . .

The young man walked back and forth uncertainly, then crouched on his heels, still gazing up the yard. He pulled something from the pocket of his loose jacket—Miles's finger tightened on the trigger—but he only put it to his mouth and bit. An apple. The crunch carried clearly in the damp air, and the faint perfume of its juices. He ate about half, then stopped, seeming to have trouble swallowing. Miles checked the knife at his belt, made sure it was loose in its sheath. Ninny's nostrils widened, and he nickered hopefully, drawing the young man's attention. He rose and walked over to the horse.

The blood pulsed in Miles's ears, louder than any other sound. His grip on the stunner was damp and white-knuckled. The young man fed Ninny his apple. The horse chomped it down, big jaw rippling under his skin, then cocked his hip, dangled one hind hoof, and sighed hugely. If he hadn't seen the man eat off the fruit first Miles might have shot him on the spot. It couldn't be poisoned. . . . The man made to pet Ninny's neck, then his hand drew back in startlement as he encountered Dea's dressing. Ninny shook his head uneasily. Miles rose slowly and stood waiting. The man scratched Ninny's ears instead, looked up one last time at the cabin, took a deep breath, stepped forward, saw Miles, and stood stock still.

"Lem Csurik?" said Miles.

A pause, a frozen nod. "Lord Vorkosigan?" said the young man. Miles nodded in turn.

Csurik swallowed. "Vor lord," he quavered, "do you keep your word?"

What a bizarre opening. Miles's brows climbed. Hell, go with it. "Yes. Are you coming in?"

"Yes and no, m'lord."

"Which?"

"A bargain, lord. I must have a bargain, and your word on it."

"If you killed Raina—"

"No, lord. I swear it. I didn't."

"Then you have nothing to fear from me."

Lem Csurik's lips thinned. What the devil could this hill man find ironic? How dare he find irony in Miles's confusion? Irony, but no amusement.

"Oh, lord," breathed Csurik, "I wish that were so. But I have to prove it to Harra. Harra must believe me—you have to make her believe me, lord!"

"You have to make me believe you first. Fortunately, that isn't hard. You come up to the cabin and make that same statement under fast-penta, and I will rule you cleared."

Csurik was shaking his head.

"Why not?" said Miles patiently. That Csurik had turned up at all was strong circumstantial indication of his innocence. Unless he somehow imagined he could beat the drug. Miles would be patient for, oh, three or four seconds at least. Then, by God, he'd stun him, drag him inside, tie him up till he came round, and get to the bottom of this before breakfast.

"The drug—they say you can't hold anything back."

"It would be pretty useless if you could."

Csurik stood silent a moment.

"Are you trying to conceal some lesser crime on your conscience? Is that the bargain you wish to strike? An amnesty? It . . . might be possible. If it's short of another murder, that is."

"No, lord. I've never killed anybody!"

"Then maybe we can deal. Because if you're innocent, I need to know as soon as possible. Because it means my work isn't finished here."

"That's . . . that's the trouble, m'lord." Csurik shuffled, then seemed to come to some internal decision and stood sturdily. "I'll come in and risk your drug. And I'll answer anything about me you want to ask. But you have to promise—swear!—you won't ask me about . . . about anything else. Anybody else."

"Do you know who killed your daughter?"

"Not for sure." Csurik threw his head back defiantly. "I didn't see it. I have guesses."

"I have guesses, too."

"That's as may be, lord. Just so's they don't come from my mouth. That's all I ask."

Miles holstered his stunner, and rubbed his chin. "Hm." A very slight smile turned one corner of his lip. "I admit, it would be more—elegant—to solve this case by reason and deduction than brute force. Even so tender a force as fast-penta."

Csurik's head lowered. "I don't know elegant, lord. But I don't want it to be from my mouth."

Decision bubbled up in Miles, straightening his spine. Yes. He *knew*, now. He had only to run through the proofs, step by chained step. Just like 5-Space math. "Very well. I swear by my word as Vorkosigan, I shall confine my questions to the facts to which you were an eyewitness. I will not ask you for conjectures about persons or events for which you were not present. There, will that do?"

Csurik bit his lip. "Yes, lord. If you keep your word."

"Try me," suggested Miles. His lips wrinkled back on a vulpine smile, absorbing the implied insult without comment.

Csurik climbed the yard beside Miles as if to an executioner's block. Their entrance created a tableau of astonishment among Karal and his family, clustered around their wooden table where Dea was treating Pym. Pym and Dea looked rather blank, till Miles made introductions: "Dr. Dea, get out your fast-penta. Here's Lem Csurik come to talk with us."

Miles steered Lem to a chair. The hill man sat with his hands clenched. Pym, a red and purpling bruise showing at the edges of the white tape circling his chest, took up his stunner and stepped back.

Dr. Dea muttered under his breath to Miles as he got out the hypospray. "How'd you *do* that?"

Miles's hand brushed his pocket. He pulled out a sugar cube and held it up, and grinned through the C of his thumb and finger. Dea snorted, but pursed his lips with reluctant respect.

Lem flinched as the hypospray hissed on his arm, as if he expected it to hurt.

"Count backwards from ten," Dea instructed. By the time Lem reached three, he had relaxed; at zero, he giggled.

"Karal, Ma Karal, Pym, gather round," said Miles. "You are my witnesses. Boys, stay back and stay quiet. No interruptions, please."

Miles ran through the preliminaries, half a dozen questions designed to set up a rhythm and kill time while the fast-penta took full effect. Lem Csurik grinned foolishly, lolling in his chair, and answered them all with sunny good will. Fast-penta interrogation had been part of Miles's military intelligence course at the Service Academy. The drug seemed to be working exactly as advertised, oddly enough.

"Did you return to your cabin that morning, after you spent the night at your parents'?"

"Yes, m'lord," Lem smiled.

"About what time?"

"Mid-morning."

Nobody here had a chrono, that was probably as precise an answer as Miles was likely to get. "What did you do when you got there?"

"Called for Harra. She was gone, though. It frightened me that she was gone. Thought she might've run out on me." Lem hiccoughed. "I want my Harra."

"Later. Was the baby asleep?"

"She was. She woke up when I called for Harra. Started crying again. It goes right up your spine."

"What did you do then?"

Lem's eyes widened. "I got no milk. She wanted Harra. There's nothing I could do for her."

"Did you pick her up?"

"No, lord, I let her lay. There was nothing I could do for her. Harra, she'd hardly let me touch her, she was that nervous about her. Told me I'd drop her or something."

"You didn't shake her, to stop her screaming?"

"No, lord, I let her lay. I left to look down the path for Harra."

"Then where did you go?"

Lem blinked. "My sister's. I'd promised to help haul wood for a new cabin. Bella—m'other sister—is getting married, y'see, and—"

He was beginning to wander, as was normal for this drug. "Stop," said Miles. Lem fell silent obediently, swaying slightly in his chair. Miles considered his next question carefully. He was approaching the fine line, here. "Did you meet anyone on the path? Answer yes or no."

"Yes."

Dea was getting excited. "Who? Ask him who!"

Miles held up his hand. "You can administer the antagonist now, Dr. Dea."

"Aren't you going to ask him? It could be vital!"

"I can't. I gave my word. Administer the antagonist now, Doctor!"

Fortunately, the confusion of two interrogators stopped Lem's mumbled willing reply to Dea's question. Dea, bewildered, pressed his hypospray against Lem's arm. Lem's eyes, half-closed, snapped open within seconds. He sat up straight and rubbed his arm, and his face.

"Who did you meet on the path?" Dea asked him directly.

Lem's lips pressed tight; he looked for rescue to Miles.

Dea looked, too. "Why won't you ask him?"

"Because I don't need to," said Miles. "I know precisely who Lem met on the path, and why he went on and not back. It was Raina's murderer. As I shall shortly prove. And—witness this, Karal, Ma Karal—that information did not come from Lem's mouth. Confirm!"

Karal nodded slowly. "I . . . see, m'lord. That was . . . very good of you."

Miles gave him a direct stare, his mouth set in a tight smile. "And when is a mystery no mystery at all?"

Karal reddened, not replying for a moment. Then he said, "You may as well keep on like you're going, m'lord. There's no stopping you now, I suppose."

"No."

Miles sent runners to collect the witnesses, Ma Karal in one direction, Zed in a second, Speaker Karal and his eldest in a third. He had Lem wait with Pym, Dea, and himself. Having the shortest distance to cover, Ma Karal arrived back first, with Ma Csurik and two of her sons in tow.

His mother fell on Lem, embracing him and then looking fearfully over her shoulder at Miles. The younger brothers hung back, but Pym had already moved between them and the door.

"It's all right, Ma," Lem patted her on the back. "Or . . . anyway, I'm all right. I'm clear. Lord Vorkosigan believes me."

She glowered at Miles, still holding Lem's arm. "You didn't let the mutie lord give you that poison drug, did you?"

"Not poison," Miles denied. "In fact, the drug may have saved his life. That damn near makes it a medicine, I'd say. However," he turned toward Lem's two younger brothers, and folded his arms sternly, "I would like to know which of you young morons threw the torch on my tent last night?"

The younger one whitened; the elder, hotly indignant, noticed his brother's expression and cut his denial off in mid-syllable. "You didn't!" he hissed in horror.

"Nobody," said the white one. "Nobody did."

Miles raised his eyebrows. There followed a short, choked silence.

"Well, *nobody* can make his apologies to Speaker and Ma Karal, then," said Miles, "since it was their sons who were sleeping in the tent last night. I and my men were in the loft."

The boy's mouth opened in dismay. The youngest Karal stared at the pale Csurik brother, his age-mate, and whispered importantly, "You, Dono!

You idiot, didn't ya know that tent wouldn't burn? It's real Imperial Service issue!"

Miles clasped his hands behind his back, and fixed the Csuriks with a cold eye. "Rather more to the point, it was attempted assassination upon your Count's heir, which carries the same capital charge of treason as an attempt upon the Count himself. Or perhaps Dono didn't think of that?"

Dono was thrown into flummoxed confusion. No need for fast-penta here, the kid couldn't carry off a lie worth a damn. Ma Csurik now had hold of Dono's arm, too, without letting go of Lem's; she looked as frantic as a hen with too many chicks, trying to shelter them from storm.

"I wasn't trying to kill you, lord!" cried Dono.

"What were you trying to do, then?"

"You'd come to kill Lem. I wanted to . . . make you go away. Frighten you away. I didn't think anyone would really get hurt—I mean, it was only a tent!"

"You've never seen anything burn down, I take it. Have you, Ma Csurik?"

Lem's mother nodded, lips tight, clearly torn between a desire to protect her son from Miles, and a desire to beat Dono till he bled for his potentially lethal stupidity.

"Well, but for a chance, you could have killed or horribly injured three of your friends. Think on that, please. In the meantime, in view of your youth and ah, apparent mental defectiveness, I shall hold the treason charge. In return, Speaker Karal and your parents shall be responsible for your good behavior in the future, and decide what punishment is appropriate."

Ma Csurik melted with relief and gratitude. Dono looked like he'd rather have been shot. His brother poked him, and whispered, "Mental defective!" Ma Csurik slapped the taunter on the side of his head, suppressing him effectively.

"What about your horse, m'lord?" asked Pym.

"I . . . do not suspect them of the business with the horse," Miles replied slowly. "The attempt to fire the tent was plain stupidity. The other was . . . a different order of calculation altogether."

Zed, who had been permitted to take Pym's horse, returned then with

Harra up behind him. Harra entered Speaker Karal's cabin, saw Lem, and stopped with a bitter glare. Lem stood open-handed, his eyes wounded, before her.

"So, lord," Harra said. "You caught him." Her jaw was clenched in joyless triumph.

"Not exactly," said Miles. "He came here and turned himself in. He's made his statement under fast-penta, and cleared himself. Lem did not kill Raina."

Harra turned from side to side. "But I saw he'd been there! He'd left his jacket, and took his good saw and wood planer away with him. I knew he'd been back while I was out! There must be something wrong with your drug!"

Miles shook his head. "The drug worked fine. Your deduction was correct as far as it went, Lem did visit the cabin while you were out. But when he left, Raina was still alive, crying vigorously. It wasn't Lem."

She swayed. "Who, then?"

"I think you know. I think you've been working very hard to deny that knowledge, hence your excessive focus on Lem. As long as you were sure it was Lem, you didn't have to think about the other possibilities."

"But who else would care?" Harra cried. "Who else would bother?"

"Who, indeed?" sighed Miles. He walked to the front window and glanced down the yard. The fog was clearing in the full light of morning. The horses were moving uneasily. "Dr. Dea, would you please get a second dose of fast-penta ready?" Miles turned, paced back to stand before the fireplace, its coals still banked for the night. The faint heat was pleasant on his back.

Dea was staring around, the hypospray in his hand, clearly wondering to whom to administer it. "My lord?" he queried, brows lowering in demand for explanation.

"Isn't it obvious to you, Doctor?" Miles asked lightly.

"*No,* my lord." His tone was slightly indignant.

"Nor to you, Pym?"

"Not . . . entirely, m'lord." Pym's glance, and stunner aim, wavered uncertainly to Harra.

"I suppose it's because neither of you ever met my grandfather," Miles decided. "He died just about a year before you entered my father's service, Pym. He was born at the very end of the Time of Isolation, and lived through every wrenching change this century has dealt to Barrayar. He was called the last of the Old Vor, but really, he was the first of the new. He changed with the times, from the tactics of horse cavalry to that of flyer squadrons, from swords to atomics, and he changed *successfully*. Our present freedom from the Cetagandan occupation is a measure of how fiercely he could adapt, then throw it all away and adapt again. At the end of his life he was called a conservative, only because so many of Barrayar had streamed past him in the direction he had led, prodded, pushed, and pointed all his life.

"He changed, and adapted, and bent with the wind of the times. Then, in his age—for my father was his youngest and sole surviving son, and did not himself marry till middle age—in his age, he was hit with me. And he had to change again. And he couldn't.

"He begged for my mother to have an abortion, after they knew more or less what the fetal damage would be. He and my parents were estranged for five years after I was born. They didn't see each other or speak or communicate. Everyone thought my father moved us to the Imperial Residence when he became regent because he was angling for the throne, but in fact it was because the Count my grandfather denied him the use of Vorkosigan House. Aren't family squabbles jolly fun? Bleeding ulcers run in my family, we give them to each other." Miles strolled back to the window and looked out. Ah, yes. Here it came.

"The reconciliation was gradual, when it became quite clear there would be no other son," Miles went on. "No dramatic denouement. It helped when the medics got me walking. It was essential that I tested out bright. Most important of all, I never let him see me give up."

Nobody had dared interrupt this lordly monologue, but it was clear from several expressions that the point of it was escaping them. Since half the point was to kill time, Miles was not greatly disturbed by their failure to track. Footsteps sounded on the wooden porch outside. Pym moved quietly to cover the door with an unobscured angle of fire.

"Dr. Dea," said Miles, sighting through the window, "would you be so kind as to administer that fast-penta to the first person through the door, as they step in?"

"You're not waiting for a volunteer, my lord?"

"Not this time."

The door swung inward, and Dea stepped forward, raising his hand. The hypospray hissed. Ma Mattulich wheeled to face Dea, the skirts of her work dress swirling around her veined calves, hissing in return—"You dare!" Her arm drew back as if to strike him, but slowed in mid-swing and failed to connect as Dea ducked out of her way. This unbalanced her, and she staggered. Speaker Karal, coming in behind, caught her by the arm and steadied her. "You dare!" she wailed again, then turned to see not only Dea but all the other witnesses waiting: Ma Csurik, Ma Karal, Lem, Harra, Pym. Her shoulders sagged, and then the drug cut in and she just stood, a silly smile fighting with anguish for possession of her harsh face.

The smile made Miles ill, but it was the smile he needed. "Sit her down, Dea, Speaker Karal."

They guided her to the chair lately vacated by Lem Csurik. She was fighting the drug desperately, flashes of resistance melting into flaccid docility. Gradually the docility became ascendant, and she sat draped in the chair, grinning helplessly. Miles sneaked a peek at Harra. She stood white and silent, utterly closed.

For several years after the reconciliation Miles had never been left with his grandfather without his personal bodyguard. Sergeant Bothari had worn the count's livery, but had been loyal to Miles alone, the one man dangerous enough—some said, crazy enough—to stand up to the great general himself. There was no need, Miles decided, to spell out to these fascinated people just what interrupted incident had made his parents think Sergeant Bothari a necessary precaution. Let General Piotr's untarnished reputation serve—Miles, now. As *he* willed. Miles's eyes glinted.

Lem lowered his head. "If I had known—if I had guessed—I wouldn't have left them alone together, m'lord. I thought—Harra's mother would take care of her. I couldn't have—I didn't know *how*—"

Harra did not look at him. Harra did not look at anything.

"Let us conclude this," Miles sighed. Again, he requested formal witness from the crowd in the room, and cautioned against interruptions, which tended to unduly confuse a drugged subject. He moistened his lips and turned to Ma Mattulich.

Again, he began with the standard neutral questions, name, birthdate, parents' names, checkable biographical facts. Ma Mattulich was harder to lull than the cooperative Lem had been, her responses scattered and staccato. Miles controlled his impatience with difficulty. For all its deceptive ease, fast-penta interrogation required skill, skill and patience. He'd got too far to risk a stumble now. He worked his questions up gradually to the first critical ones.

"Were you there, when Raina was born?"

Her voice was low and drifting, dreamy. "The birth came in the night. Lem, he went for Jean the midwife, the midwife's son was supposed to go for me but he fell back to sleep. I didn't get there till morning, and then it was too late. They'd all seen."

"Seen what?"

"The cat's mouth, the dirty mutation. Monsters in us. Cut them out. Ugly little man." This last, Miles realized, was an aside upon himself. Her attention had hung up on him, hypnotically. "Muties make more muties, they breed faster, overrun . . . I saw you watching the girls. You want to make mutie babies on clean women, poison us all. . . ."

Time to steer her back to the main issue. "Were you ever alone with the baby after that?"

"No, Jean, she hung around. Jean knows me, she knew what I wanted. None of her damn business. And Harra was always there. Harra must not know. Harra must not . . . why should she get off so soft? The poison must be in her. Must have come from her Da, I lay only with her Da and they were all wrong but the one."

Miles blinked. "What were all wrong?" Across the room Miles saw Speaker Karal's mouth tighten. The headman caught Miles's glance and stared down at his own feet, absenting himself from the proceedings. Lem, his lips parted in absorption, and the rest of the boys were listening with alarm. Harra hadn't moved.

"All my babies," Ma Mattulich said.

Harra looked up sharply at that, her eyes widening.

"Was Harra not your only child?" Miles asked. It was an effort to keep his voice cool, calm; he wanted to shout. He wanted to be gone from here. . . .

"No, of course not. She was my only clean child, I thought. I thought, but the poison must have been hidden in her. I fell on my knees and thanked God when she was born clean, a clean one at last, after so many, so much pain. . . . I thought I had finally been punished enough. She was such a pretty baby, I thought it was over at last. But she must have been mutie after all, hidden, tricksy, sly. . . ."

"How many," Miles choked, "babies did you have?"

"Four, besides Harra my last."

"And you killed all four of them?" Speaker Karal, Miles saw, gave a slow nod to his feet.

"No!" said Ma Mattulich. Indignation broke through the fast-penta wooze briefly. "Two were born dead already, the first one, and the twisted-up one. The one with too many fingers and toes, and the one with the bulgy head, those I cut. Cut out. My mother, she watched over me to see I did it right. Harra, I made it soft for Harra. I did it for her."

"So you have in fact murdered not one infant, but three?" said Miles frozenly. The younger witnesses in the room, Karal's boys and the Csurik brothers, looked horrified. The older ones, Ma Mattulich's contemporaries, who must have lived through the events with her, looked mortified, sharing her shame. Yes, they all must have known.

"Murdered?" said Ma Mattulich. "No! I cut them out. I had to. I had to do the right thing." Her chin lifted proudly, then drooped. "Killed my babies, to please, to please . . . I don't know who. And now you call me a murderer? Damn you! What use is your justice to me *now*? I needed it then—where were you *then?*" Suddenly, shockingly, she burst into tears, which wavered almost instantly into rage. "If mine must die then so must hers! Why should she get off so soft? Spoiled her . . . I tried my best, I did my best, it's not fair. . . ."

The fast-penta was not keeping up with this. . . . no, it was working, Miles decided, but her emotions were too overwhelming. Upping the dose might level her emotional surges, at some risk of respiratory arrest, but it would not elicit any more complete a confession. Miles's belly was trembling, a reaction he trusted he concealed. It had to be completed now.

"Why did you break Raina's neck, instead of cutting her throat?"

"Harra, she must not know," said Ma Mattulich. "Poor baby. It would look like she just died. . . ."

Miles eyed Lem, Speaker Karal. "It seems a number of others shared your opinion that Harra should not know."

"I didn't want it to be from my mouth," repeated Lem sturdily.

"I wanted to save her double grief, m'lord," said Karal. "She'd had so much. . . ."

Miles met Harra's eyes at that. "I think you all underestimate her. Your excessive tenderness insults both her intelligence and will. She comes from a tough line, that one."

Harra inhaled, controlling her own trembling. She gave Miles a short nod, as if to say *Thank you, little man.* He returned her a slight inclination of the head, *Yes, I understand.*

"I'm not sure yet where justice lies in this case," said Miles, "but this I swear to you, the days of cooperative concealment are over. No more secret crimes in the night. Daylight's here. And speaking of crimes in the night," he turned back to Ma Mattulich, "*was* it you who tried to cut my horses's throat last night?"

"I tried," said Ma Mattulich, calmer now in a wave of fast-penta mellowness, "but it kept rearing up on me."

"Why my *horse?*" Miles could not keep exasperation from his voice, though a calm, even tone was enjoined upon fast-penta interrogators by the training manual.

"I couldn't get at you," said Ma Mattulich simply.

Miles rubbed his forehead. "Retroactive infanticide by proxy?" he muttered.

"You," said Ma Mattulich, and her loathing came through even the nauseating fast-penta cheer, "*you* are the worst. All I went through, all I did, all the grief, and you come along at the end. A mutie made lord over us all, and all the rules changed, betrayed at the end by an off-worlder woman's weakness. You make it all for *nothing.* Hate you. Dirty mutie . . ." her voice trailed off in a drugged mumble.

Miles took a deep breath, and looked around the room. The stillness was profound, and no one dared break it.

"I believe," he said, "that concludes my investigation into the facts of this case."

The mystery of Raina's death was solved.

The problem of justice, unfortunately, remained.

Miles took a walk.

The graveyard, though little more than a crude clearing in the woodland, was a place of peace and beauty in the morning light. The stream burbled endlessly, shifting green shadows and blinding brilliant reflections. The faint breeze that had shredded away the last of the night fog whispered in the trees, and the tiny, short-lived creatures that everyone on Barrayar, excepting biologists, called bugs sang and twittered in the patches of native scrub.

"Well, Raina," Miles sighed, "and what do I do now?" Pym lingered by the borders of the clearing, giving Miles room. "It's all right," Miles assured the tiny grave. "Pym's caught me talking to dead people before. He may think I'm crazy, but he's far too well-trained to say so."

Pym in fact did not look happy, nor altogether well. Miles felt rather guilty for dragging him out, by rights the man should be resting in bed, but Miles had desperately needed this time alone. Pym wasn't just suffering the residual effect of having been kicked by Ninny. He had been silent ever since Miles had extracted the confession from Ma Mattulich. Miles was unsurprised. Pym had steeled himself to play executioner to their imagined hill bully; the substitution of a mad grandmother as his victim had clearly given him pause. He would obey whatever order Miles gave him, though, Miles had no doubt of that.

Miles considered the peculiarities of Barrayaran law, as he wandered about the clearing, watching the stream and the light, turning over an occasional rock with the toe of his boot. The fundamental principle was clear; the spirit was to be preferred over the letter, truth over technicalities. Precedent was held subordinate to the judgment of the man on the spot. Alas, the man on the spot was himself. There was no refuge for him in automated rules, no hiding behind *the law says* as if the law were some living overlord with a real Voice. The only voice here was his own.

And who would be served by the death of that half-crazed old woman?

Harra? The relationship between mother and daughter had been wounded unto death by this, Miles had seen that in their eyes, yet still Harra had no stomach for matricide. Miles rather preferred it that way, having her standing by his ear crying for bloody revenge would have been enormously distracting just now. The obvious justice made a damn poor reward for Harra's courage in reporting the crime. Raina? Ah. That was more difficult.

"I'd like to lay the old gargoyle right there at your feet, small lady," Miles muttered to her. "Is it your desire? Does it serve you? What *would* serve you?" Was this the great burning he had promised her?

What judgment would reverberate along the entire Dendarii mountain range? Should he indeed sacrifice these people to some larger political statement, regardless of their wants? Or should he forget all that, make his judgment serve only those directly involved? He scooped up a stone and flung it full force into the stream. It vanished invisibly in the rocky bed.

He turned to find Speaker Karal waiting by the edge of the graveyard. Karal ducked his head in greeting and approached cautiously.

"So, m'lord," said Karal.

"Just so," said Miles.

"Have you come to any conclusion?"

"Not really." Miles gazed around. "Anything less than Ma Mattulich's death seems . . . . inadequate justice, and yet . . . I cannot see who her death would serve."

"Neither could I. That's why I took the position I did in the first place."

"No . . ." said Miles slowly, "no, you were wrong in that. For one thing, it very nearly got Lem Csurik killed. I was getting ready to pursue him with deadly force at one point. It almost destroyed him with Harra. Truth is better. Slightly better. At least it isn't a fatal error. Surely I can do . . . something with it."

"I didn't know what to expect of you, at first," admitted Karal.

Miles shook his head. "I meant to make changes. A difference. Now . . . I don't know."

Speaker Karal's balding forehead wrinkled. "But we are changing."

"Not enough. Not fast enough."

"You're young yet, that's why you don't see how much, how fast. Look at the difference between Harra and her mother. God—look at the difference between Ma Mattulich and *her* mother. *There* was a harridan." Speaker Karal shuddered. "I remember her, all right. And yet, she was not so unusual, in her day. So far from having to make change, I don't think you could stop it if you tried. The minute we finally get a powerset receptor up here, and get on the comm net, the past will be done and over. As soon as the kids see the future—their future—they'll be mad after it. They're already lost to the old ones like Ma Mattulich. The old ones know it, too, don't believe they don't know it. Why d'you think we haven't been able to get at least a small unit up here yet? Not just the cost. The old ones are fighting it. They call it off-planet corruption, but it's really the future they fear."

"There's still so much to be done."

"Oh, yes. We are a desperate people, no lie. But we have hope. I don't think you realize how much you've done, just by coming up here."

"I've done nothing," said Miles bitterly. "Sat around, mostly. And now, I swear, I'm going to end up doing more nothing. And then go home. Hell!"

Speaker Karal pursed his lips, looked at his feet, at the high hills. "You are doing something for us every minute. Mutie lord. Do you think you are invisible?"

Miles grinned wolfishly. "Oh, Karal, I'm a one-man band, I am. I'm a parade."

"As you say, just so. Ordinary people need extraordinary examples. So they can say to themselves, well, if he can do *that,* I can surely do *this*. No excuses."

"No quarter, yes, I know that game. Been playing it all my life."

"I think," said Karal, "Barrayar needs you. To go on being just what you are."

"Barrayar will eat me, if it can."

"Yes," said Karal, his eyes on the horizon, "so it will." His gaze fell to the graves at his feet. "But it swallows us all in the end, doesn't it? You will outlive the old ones."

"Or in the beginning." Miles pointed down. "Don't tell me who I'm going to outlive. Tell Raina."

Karal's shoulders slumped. "True. S'truth. Make your judgment, lord. I'll back you."

Miles assembled them all in Karal's yard for his Speaking; the porch now became his podium. The interior of the cabin would have been impossibly hot and close for this crowd, suffocating with the afternoon sun beating on the roof, though outdoors the light made them squint. They were all here, everyone they could round up—Speaker Karal, Ma Karal, their boys, all the Csuriks, most of the cronies who had attended last night's funereal festivities, men, women, and children. Harra sat apart. Lem kept trying to hold her hand, though from the way she flinched it was clear she didn't want to be touched. Ma Mattulich sat displayed by Miles's side, silent and surly, flanked by Pym and an uncomfortable-looking Deputy Alex.

Miles jerked up his chin, settling his head on the high collar of his dress greens, as polished and formal as Pym's batman's expertise could make him. The Imperial Service uniform that Miles had earned. Did these people know he had earned it, or did they all imagine it a mere gift from his father, nepotism at work? Damn what they thought. He knew. He stood before his people, and gripped the porch rail.

"I have concluded the investigation of the charges laid before the Count's Court by Harra Csurik of the murder of her daughter, Raina. By evidence, witness, and her own admission, I find Mara Mattulich guilty of this murder, she having twisted the infant's neck until it broke, and then attempted to conceal that crime. Even when that concealment placed her son-in-law Lem Csurik in mortal danger from false charges. In light of the helplessness of the victim, the cruelty of the method, and the cowardly selfishness of the attempted concealment, I can find no mitigating excuse for the crime.

"In addition, Mara Mattulich by her own admission testifies to two previous infanticides, some twenty years ago, of her own children. These facts shall be announced by Speaker Karal in every corner of Silvy Vale, until every subject has been informed."

He could feel Ma Mattulich's glare boring into his back. *Yes, go on and hate me, old woman. I will bury you yet, and you know it.* He swallowed, and continued, the formality of the language a sort of shield before him.

"For this unmitigated crime, the only proper sentence is death. And I so sentence Mara Mattulich. But in light of her age and close relation to the next-most-injured party in the case, Harra Csurik, I choose to hold the actual execution of that sentence. Indefinitely." Out of the corner of his eye Miles saw Pym let out, very carefully and covertly, a sigh of relief. Harra combed at her straw-colored bangs with her fingers and listened intently.

"But she shall be as dead before the law. All her property, even to the clothes on her back, now belongs to her daughter Harra, to dispose of as she wills. Mara Mattulich may not own property, enter contracts, sue for injuries, nor exert her will after death in any testament. She shall not leave Silvy Vale without Harra's permission. Harra shall be given power over her as a parent over a child, or as in senility. In Harra's absence Speaker Karal will be her deputy. Mara Mattulich shall be watched to see she harms no other child.

"Further. She shall die without sacrifice. No one, not Harra nor any other, shall make a burning for her when she goes into the ground at last. As she murdered her future, so her future shall return only death to her spirit. She will die as the childless do, without remembrance."

A low sigh swept the older members of the crowd before Miles. For the first time, Mara Mattulich bent her stiff neck.

Some, Miles knew, would find this only spiritually symbolic. Others would see it as literally lethal, according to the strength of their beliefs. The literal-minded such as those who saw mutation as a sin to be violently expiated. But even the less superstitious, Miles saw in their faces, found the meaning clear. So.

Miles turned to Ma Mattulich, and lowered his voice. "Every breath you take from this moment on is by my mercy. Every bite of food you eat, by Harra's charity. By charity and mercy—such as you did not give—you shall live. Dead woman."

"Some mercy. Mutie lord." Her growl was low, weary, beaten.

"You get the point," he said through his teeth. He swept her a bow, infinitely ironic, and turned his back on her. "I am the Voice of Count Vorkosigan. This concludes my Speaking."

* * *

Miles met Harra and Lem afterwards, in Speaker Karal's cabin.

"I have a proposition for you." Miles controlled his nervous pacing and stood before them. "You're free to turn it down, or think about it for a while. I know you're very tired right now." *As are we all.* Had he really been in Silvy Vale only a day and a half? It seemed like a century. His head ached with fatigue. Harra was red-eyed, too. "First of all, can you read and write?"

"Some," Harra admitted. "Speaker Karal taught us some, and Ma Lannier."

"Well, good enough. You wouldn't be starting completely blind. Look. A few years back Hassadar started a teacher's college. It's not very big yet, but it's begun. There are some scholarships. I can swing one your way, if you will agree to live in Hassadar for three years of intense study."

"Me!" said Harra. "I couldn't go to a college! I barely know . . . any of that stuff."

"Knowledge is what you're supposed to have coming out, not going in. Look, they know what they're dealing with in this district. They have a lot of remedial courses. It's true, you'd have to work harder, to catch up with the town-bred and the lowlanders. But I know you have courage, and I know you have will. The rest is just picking yourself up and ramming into the wall again and again until it falls down. You get a bloody forehead, so what? You can do it, I swear you can."

Lem, sitting beside her, looked worried. He captured her hand again. "Three years?" he said in a small voice. "Gone away?"

"The school stipend isn't that much," said Miles. "But Lem, I understand you have carpenter's skills. There's a building boom going on in Hassadar right now. Hassadar's going to be the next Vorkosigan Vashnoi, I think. I'm certain you could get a job. Between you, you could live."

Lem looked at first relieved, then extremely worried. "But they all use power tools—computers—robots. . . ."

"By no means. And they weren't all born knowing how to use that stuff either. If they can learn it, you can. Besides, the rich pay well for handwork, unique one-of items, if the quality's good. I can see you get a start, which is usually the toughest moment. After that you should be able to figure it out all right."

"To leave Silvy Vale . . ." said Harra in a dismayed tone.

"Only in order to return. That's the other half of the bargain. I can send a comm unit up here, a small one with a portable power pack that lasts a year. Somebody'd have to hump down to Vorkosigan Surleau to replace it annually, no big problem. The whole set up wouldn't cost much more than, oh, a new lightflyer." Such as the shiny red one Miles had coveted in a dealer's showroom in Vorbarr Sultana, very suitable for a graduation present, he had pointed out to his parents. The credit chit was sitting in the top drawer of his dresser in the lake house at Vorkosigan Surleau right now. "It's not a massive project like installing a powersat receptor for the whole of Silvy Vale or anything. The holovid would pick up the educational satellite broadcasts from the capital; set it up in some central cabin, add a couple of dozen lap-links for the kids, and you've got an instant school. All the children would be required to attend, with Speaker Karal to enforce it, though once they'd discovered the holovid you'd probably have to beat them to make them go home. I, ah," Miles cleared his throat, "thought you might name it the Raina Csurik Primary School."

"Oh," said Harra, and began to cry for the first time that grueling day. Lem patted her clumsily. She returned the grip of his hand at last.

"I can send a lowlander up here to teach," said Miles. "I'll get one to take a short-term contract, till you're ready to come back. But he or she won't understand Silvy Vale like you do. Wouldn't understand *why*. You—you already know. You know what they can't teach in any lowland college."

Harra scrubbed her eyes, and looked up—not very far up—at him. "You went to the Imperial Academy."

"I did." His chin jerked up.

"Then I," she said shakily, "can manage . . . Hassadar Teacher's College." The name was awkward in her mouth. At first. "At any rate—I'll try, m'lord."

"I'll bet on you," Miles agreed. "Both of you. Just, ah," a smile sped across his mouth and vanished, "stand up straight and speak the truth, eh?"

Harra blinked understanding. An answering half-smile lit her tired face, equally briefly. "I will. Little man."

* * *

Fat Ninny rode home by air the next morning, in a horse van, along with Pym. Dr. Dea went along with his two patients, and his nemesis the sorrel mare. A replacement bodyguard had been sent with the groom who flew the van from Vorkosigan Surleau, who stayed with Miles to help him ride the remaining two horses back down. Well, Miles thought, he'd been considering a camping trip in the mountains with his cousin Ivan as part of his home leave anyway. The liveried man was the laconic veteran Esterhazy, whom Miles had known most of his life excellent company for a man who didn't want to talk about it, unlike Ivan you could almost forget he was there. Miles wondered if Esterhazy's assignment had been random chance, or a mercy of the Count's. Esterhazy was good with horses.

They camped overnight by the river of roses. Miles walked up the vale in the evening light, desultorily looking for the spring of it; indeed, the floral barrier did seem to peter out a couple of kilometers upstream, merging into slightly less impassable scrub. Miles plucked a rose, checked to make sure that Esterhazy was nowhere in sight, and bit into it curiously. Clearly, he was not a horse. A cut bunch would probably not survive the trip back as a treat for Ninny. Ninny could settle for oats.

Miles watched the evening shadows flowing up along the backbone of the Dendarii range, high and massive in the distance. How small those mountains looked from space! Little wrinkles on the skin of a globe he could cover with his hand, all their crushing mass made invisible. Which was illusory, distance or nearness? Distance, Miles decided. Distance was a damned lie. Had his father known this? Miles suspected so.

He contemplated his urge to throw all his money, not just a lightflyer's worth, at those mountains; to quit it all and go teach children to read and write, to set up a free clinic, a powersat net, or all of these at once. But Silvy Vale was only one of hundreds of such communities buried in these mountains, one of thousands across the whole of Barrayar. Taxes squeezed from this very district helped maintain the very elite military school he'd just spent—how much of their resources in? How much would he have to give back just to make it even, now? He was himself a planetary resource, his training had made him so, and his feet were set on their path.

What God means you to do, Miles's theist mother claimed, could be deduced from the talents He gave you. The academic honors Miles had amassed by sheer brute work. But the war games, outwitting his opponents, staying one step ahead—a necessity, true, he had no margin for error—the war games had been an unholy joy. War had been no game here once, not so long ago. It might be so again. What you did best, that was what was wanted from you. God seemed to be lined up with the emperor on that point, at least, if no other.

Miles had sworn his officer's oath to the emperor less than two weeks ago, puffed with pride at his achievement. In his secret mind he had imagined himself keeping that oath through blazing battle, enemy torture, what-have-you, even while sharing cynical cracks afterwards with Ivan about archaic dress swords and the sort of people who insisted on wearing them.

But in the dark of subtler temptations, those which hurt without heroism for consolation, he forsaw, the emperor would no longer be the symbol of Barrayar in his heart.

Peace to you, small lady, he thought to Raina. *You've won a twisted poor modern knight, to wear your favor on his sleeve. But it's a twisted poor world we were both born into, that rejects us without mercy and ejects us without consultation. At least I won't just tilt at windmills for you. I'll send in sappers to mine the twirling suckers, and blast them into the sky. . . .*

He knew who he served now. And why he could not quit. And why he must not fail.